COMA &
ABDUCTION

A bestselling author for many years, Dr. Robin Cook has
written twenty-four previous novels. He is currently on leave
from the Massachusetts Eye and Ear Infirmary, and lives and
works in Florida.

ALSO BY ROBIN COOK

ROBIN COOK

COMA
&
ABDUCTION

PAN BOOKS

Coma first published in Great Britain 1977 by Macmillan.
First published in paperback 1978 by Pan Books.
Abduction first published 2000 by Berkley, New York.
First published in Great Britain in paperback 2000 by Pan Books.

This omnibus first published 2008 by Pan Books
an imprint of Pan Macmillan Ltd
Pan Macmillan, 20 New Wharf Road, London N1 9RR
Basingstoke and Oxford
Associated companies throughout the world
www.panmacmillan.com

ISBN 978-0-330-45781-1

1 3 5 7 9 8 6 4 2

A CIP catalogue record for this book is available from
the British Library.

Printed and bound in Great Britain
by Mackays of Chatham, Chatham, Kent

COMA

In memory of my father,
recognition of my mother,
and thanks to Sharron

Prologue
February 14, 1976

Nancy Greenly lay on the operating table on her back, staring up at the large kettledrum-shaped lights in operating room no.8, trying to be calm. She had had several pre-op injections, which she was told would make her sleepy and happy. She was neither. Nancy was more nervous and apprehensive than before the shots. Worst of all, she felt totally, completely, and absolutely defenceless. In all her twenty-three years, she had never before felt so embarrassed and so vulnerable. Covering her was a white linen bed sheet. The edge was frayed, and there was a small tear at the corner. That bothered her, and she didn't know why. Under the sheet, she had on one of those hospital gowns which tie behind the neck and descend only to mid-thigh. The back was open. Other than that, there was only the sanitary napkin, which she knew was already soaked with her own blood. She hated and feared the hospital at that moment and wanted to scream, to run out of the room and down the corridor. But she didn't. She feared the bleeding that she had been experiencing more than the cruel detached environment of the hospital; both made her acutely aware of her mortality, and that was something she rarely liked to face.

At 7:11 on the morning of February 14, 1976, the eastern sky over Boston was a chalky grey, and the bumper-to-bumper cars coming into the city had their headlights on. The temperature was thirty-eight degrees, and the people in the streets walked quickly on their separate tracks. There were no voices, just the sound of the machines and the wind.

Within the Boston Memorial Hospital, things were different. The stark fluorescent lights illuminated every square inch of the OR area. The bustle of activity and excited voices lent credence to the dictum that surgery started at 7:30 sharp. That meant the scalpels actually cut the skin at 7:30; the patient fetching, the prep, the scrub, and the induction under anaesthesia had to be all completed before 7:30.

As a consequence, at 7:11, the activity in the OR area was in full swing, including room number 8. There was nothing special about no.8. It was a typical OR in the Memorial. The walls were a neutral-coloured tile; the floors were a speckled vinyl. At 7:30, February 14, 1976, a D&C – dilation and curettage, a routine gynaecological procedure – was scheduled in room no.8. The patient was Nancy Greenly; the anaesthesiologist was Dr Robert Billing, a second-year anaesthesiology resident; the scrub nurse was Ruth Jenkins; the circulating nurse was Gloria D'Mateo. The surgeon was George Major – the new, young partner of one of the older, established OB-GYN men – and he was in the dressing room donning his surgical scrub suit, while the others were hard at work.

Nancy Greenly had been bleeding for eleven days. At first she passed it off as a normal period, despite the fact that it was several weeks early. There had been no premenstrual discomfort, maybe a vague cramp on the morning the first spotting occurred. But after that it had been a painless affair, waxing and waning. Each night she hoped to·have seen the last of it but had awakened to find the tampon soaked. The telephone conversations, first with Dr Major's nurse, then with the doctor himself, had allayed her fears for progressively shorter and shorter durations. And it was a bother, a gigantic nuisance, and as it was with such things, it had come at a most inopportune time. She thought about Kim Devereau coming up to spend his spring break from Duke Law School with her in Boston. Her roommate had fortuitously made plans to spend that week skiing at Killington. Everything seemed to have been falling into beautiful, romantic place, everything except the bleeding. There was no way Nancy could blithely dismiss it. She was a delicately angular and attractive girl with an aristocratic appearance. About her person she was fastidious. If her hair was the slightest bit dirty she felt uneasy. So the continued bleeding made her feel messy, unattractive, out of control. Eventually it began to frighten her.

Nancy remembered lying on the couch with her feet up on the arm, reading the editorial page of the *Globe* while Kim was in the kitchen making drinks. She had become aware of a strange sensation in her vagina. It was different from anything she had ever felt before. It felt as if she was being inflated by a warm soft mass. There had been absolutely no pain or discomfort. At first she was perplexed as to the origin of the sensation, but then she felt a warmth on her inner thighs and a trickling of fluid run down into the recess of her buttocks. Without undue anxiety, she recognized that she was bleeding, bleeding very fast. Casually, without moving her body, she had turned her head toward the kitchen and called out:

'Kim, would you do me a favour and call an ambulance?'

'What's wrong?' asked Kim, hurrying to her.

'I'm bleeding very fast,' said Nancy calmly, 'but it's nothing to get alarmed about. An extra-heavy period, I guess. I just should go to the hospital right away. So please call the ambulance.'

The ambulance ride had been uneventful, without sirens or drama. She had to wait longer than she thought reasonable in the holding area of the emergency room. Dr Major had appeared and for the first time awakened a feeling of gladness in Nancy. She had always detested the routine vaginal exams to which she had submitted and had associated the face, the bearing, and the smell of Dr Major with them. But when he appeared in the emergency room, she felt glad to see him, to the point of suppressing tears.

The vaginal examination in the emergency room had been, without doubt, the worst she had ever experienced. A flimsy curtain, which was constantly being whisked back and forth, was the sole barrier between the throng in the emergency room and Nancy's flayed self-respect. Blood pressure was taken every few minutes; blood was drawn; she had to change from her clothes into the hospital gown; and each time something was done the curtain flashed aside and Nancy was confronted with an array of faces in white clothes, children with cuts, and old, tired people. And there was the bedpan sitting there right in the open for everyone to gape at. It contained a large, semiformed dark red blood clot. Meanwhile Dr Major was down there between her legs touching her and talking to the nurse about another case. Nancy closed her eyes as tightly as she could and cried silently.

But it was all to be over shortly, or so Dr Major had promised. In great detail he had told Nancy about the lining of her uterus and how it changes during the normal cycle and what happens when it doesn't change. There was something about the blood vessels and the need for an egg to be released from the ovary. The definitive cure was a dilation and curettage. Nancy had agreed without question and asked that her parents not be notified. She could do that herself after the fact. She was sure her mother would think she had had to have an abortion.

Now, as Nancy gazed up at the large overhead operating room light, the only thought that made her the slightest bit happy was the fact that the whole goddamned nightmare was going to be over within the hour, and her life would return to normal. The activity in the operating room was so totally foreign to her that she avoided looking at anyone or anything, save for the light above.

'Are you comfortable?'

Nancy glanced to the right. Deep brown eyes regarded her from between the synthetic fibres of the surgical hood. Gloria D'Mateo was folding the draw sheet around Nancy's right arm, securing it to her side and immobilizing her further.

'Yes,' answered Nancy with a certain detachment. Actually she was as uncomfortable as hell. The operating table was as hard as her cheap Formica kitchen table. But the Phenergan and Demerol she had been given were beginning to exert their effects somewhere within the depths of her cerebrum. Nancy was far more awake than she would have liked; but at the same time she was beginning to feel a detachment and dissociation from her surroundings. The atrophine she had been given was having an effect as well, making her throat and mouth feel dry and her tongue sticky.

Dr Robert Billing was engrossed with his machine. It was a tangle of stainless steel, upright manometers, and a few colourful cylinders of compressed gas. A brown bottle of halothane stood on top of the machine. On the label was written: '2-bromo-2-chloro-1,1,1,-trifluoroethane ($C_2HBrClF_3$).' An almost perfect anaesthetic agent. 'Almost' because every so often it seemed to destroy the patient's liver. But that rarely happened, and halothane's other characteristics far overshadowed the potential for liver damage. Dr Billing was crazy about the stuff. Somewhere in his imagination he pictured himself developing halothane, introducing it to the medical community in the lead article of the *New England Journal of Medicine*, and then walking up to receive his Nobel prize in the same tuxedo he had worn when he was married.

Dr Billing was a damned good anaesthesiology resident, and he knew it. In fact, he thought most everyone knew it. He was convinced he knew as much anaesthesiology as most of the attendings, more than some. And he was careful, very careful. He had had no serious complications as a resident, and that was indeed rare.

Like a 747 pilot, he had made himself a checklist, and religiously he adhered to a policy of checking off each step of the induction procedure. This meant having Xeroxed off a thousand of the checklists and bringing a copy along with the other equipment at the start of each operation. By 7:15, the anaesthesiologist was right on schedule at step number 12: that meant hooking up the rubber scubalike tubing to the machine. One end went into the ventilating bag, whose four-to five-litre capacity afforded him an opportunity to inflate forcibly the patient's lungs at any time during the procedure. The other end went to the soda-lime canister in which the patient's expired carbon dioxide would be absorbed. Step number 13 on his list was to make sure the undirectional check valves in the breathing lines were lined up in the right direction. Step number 14 was to connect the anaesthesia machine to the compressed air, nitrous oxide, and oxygen sources on the wall of the OR room. The anaesthesia machine had emergency oxygen cylinders hanging from the side, and Dr Billing checked the gauge pressures on both cylinders. They were fully charged. Dr Billing felt fine.

'I'm going to place some electrodes on your chest so we can monitor your heart,' said Gloria D'Mateo while pulling down the sheet and pulling up the hospital gown, exposing Nancy's midriff to the sterile air. The gown just barely covered Nancy's nipples. 'This will feel cold for a sec,' added Gloria D'Mateo as she squeezed a bit of colourless jelly onto three locations on Nancy's exposed lower chest.

Nancy wanted to say something, but she couldn't deal rapidly enough with her ambivalent attitudes about what she was experiencing. She was grateful, because it was going to help her, or so she had been assured; she was furious because she felt so exposed, literally and figuratively.

'You're going to feel a little stick now,' said Dr Billing, slapping the back of Nancy's left hand to make the veins stand out. He had placed a piece of rubber tubing tightly around Nancy's wrist, and she could feel her heart beat in the tips of her fingers. It was all happening too fast for Nancy to assimilate.

'Good morning, Miss Greenly,' said an ebullient Dr Major as he whisked through the OR door. 'I hope you had a good night's sleep. We'll get this affair over with in a few minutes and have you back to your bed for a restful sleep.'

Before Nancy could respond, the nerves from the tissues on the back of her hand became alive with urgent messages for her pain centre. After the initial thrust, the intensity of the pain increased to a point and then dissipated. The snug rubber tourniquet disappeared, and blood surged into Nancy's hand. She felt tears well up from within her head.

'I.V.,' said Dr Billing to no one, as he made a black check next to number 16 on his list.

'You'll be going to sleep shortly, Nancy,' continued Dr Major. 'Isn't that right, Dr Billing? Nancy, you're a lucky girl today. Dr Billing is number one.' Dr Major called all his patients girls no matter what age they were. It was one of those condescending mannerisms he had adopted unquestioningly from his older partner.

'That's correct,' said Dr Billing, placing a rubber mask on the anaesthesia tubing. 'Number eight tube, Gloria, please. And you, Dr Major, can scrub; we'll be ready at seven-thirty sharp.'

'OK,' said Dr Major, heading for the door. Pausing, he turned to Ruth Jenkins, who was setting up the Mayo stand with instruments. 'I want my own dilators and curettes, Ruth. Last time you gave me that mediaeval rubbish that belongs to the house.' He was gone before the nurse could answer.

Somewhere behind her, Nancy could hear the sonar-like beep of the cardiac monitor. It was her own heart rhythm resounding in the room.

'All right, Nancy,' said Gloria. 'I want you to slide down the table a bit and put your legs up here in the stirrups.' Gloria grasped Nancy's legs in turn under the knees and lifted them up into the stainless steel stirrups. The sheet slid between Nancy's legs, exposing them from mid-thigh down. The lower part of the table fell away, and the sheet slid to the floor. Nancy closed her eyes and tried not to picture herself spread-eagled on the table. Gloria picked up the sheet and haphazardly put it on Nancy's abdomen so that it draped between her legs, covering her bloodied and recently shaved perineum.

Nancy wanted to be calm, but she was getting more and more anxious. She wanted to be grateful, but the tide was swinging more and more in the direction of undirected anger and emotion.

'I'm not sure I want to go through with this,' said Nancy, looking at Dr Billing.

'Everything is just fine,' said Dr Billing in an artificially concerned tone of voice, while checking off number 18 on his list. 'You'll be asleep in a jiffy,' he added, while holding up a syringe and tapping it so that the bubbles all fled upward to the room air. 'I'm going to give you some Pentothal right away. Don't you feel sleepy now?'

'No,' said Nancy.

'Well, you should have told me,' said Dr Billing.

'I don't know how I'm supposed to feel,' returned Nancy.

'It's all right now,' said Dr Billing, pulling his anaesthesia machine close to Nancy's head. With well-rehearsed adeptness, he attached his Pentothal syringe to the three-way valve on the I.V. line. 'Now I want you to count to fifty for me, Nancy.' He expected that Nancy would never get past fifteen. In fact, it gave Dr Billing a certain sense of satisfaction to watch the patient go to sleep. It represented repetitive proof for him of the validity of the scientific method. Besides, it made him feel powerful; it was as if he had command of the patient's brain. Nancy was a strong-willed individual, however, and although she wanted to go to sleep, her brain involuntarily fought against the drug. She was still audibly counting when Dr Billing gave an additional dose of Pentothal. She said twenty-seven before the two grams of the drug succeeded in inducing sleep. Nancy Greenly fell asleep at 7:24 on February 14, 1976, for the last time.

Dr Billing had no idea this healthy young woman was going to be his first major complication. He was confident that everything was under control. The list was almost complete. He had Nancy breathe a mixture of halothane, nitrous oxide, and oxygen through a mask. Then he injected 2 cc's of a 0.2 per cent succinylcholine chloride solution into Nancy's I.V. to effect a paralysis of all her skeletal muscles. This would make the placement of the endotracheal tube in the trachea easier. It would also allow Dr Major to perform a bimanual exam, to rule out ovarian pathology.

The effect of the succinylcholine was seen almost immediately. At first there were minute fasciculations of the muscles of the face, then the abdomen. As the bloodstream sped the drug throughout the body, the motor and end plates of the muscles became depolarized, and total paralysis of the skeletal muscles occurred. Smooth muscles, like the heart, were unaffected, and the beep from the monitor continued without a waver.

Nancy's tongue was paralysed and it fell back, blocking her airway. But that didn't matter. The muscles of the thorax and abdomen were paralysed as well, and any attempt at breathing ceased. Although chemically different from the curare of the Amazon savages, the drug had the same effect, and Nancy would have died in five minutes. But at this point nothing was wrong. Dr Billing was in total control. The effect was expected and desirable. Outwardly calm, inwardly very tense, Dr Billing put down the breathing mask and reached for the laryngoscope, step number 22 on his list. With the tip of the blade, he pulled the tongue forward and manoeuvred past the white epiglottis, while he visualized the entrance to the trachea. The vocal cords were ajar, paralysed with the rest of the skeletal muscles.

Swiftly Dr Billing squirted some topical anaesthetic into the trachea, followed by the endotracheal tube. The laryngoscope made a characteristic metallic snap as Dr Billing folded the blade onto the handle. With the help of a small syringe, he inflated the cuff on the endotracheal tube, providing a seal. Quickly he attached the tip of the rubber hose, without the face mask, to the open end of the endotracheal tube. As he compressed the ventilating bag, Nancy's chest rose in a symmetrical fashion. Dr Billing listened to Nancy's chest with his stethoscope and was pleased. The entubation had been as characteristically smooth as expected. He was in total control of the patient's respiratory state. He adjusted his flow meters and set the combination of halothane, nitrous oxide, and oxygen he wanted. A few pieces of tape secured the endotracheal tube. A twist of the finger adjusted the I.V. rate. Dr Billing's own heart began to slow down. He never showed it, but he always got very tense during the entubation procedure. With the patient paralysed one has to work fast, and do it right.

With a nod, Dr Billing indicated that Gloria D'Mateo could begin the prep of Nancy's shaved perineum. Meanwhile Dr Billing began to make himself comfortable for the case. His job was now reduced to close observation of the patient's vital signs : heart rate and rhythm, blood pressure, and temperature. As long as the patient was paralysed, he had to compress the ventilating bag, to breathe the patient. The succinylcholine would wear off in eight to ten minutes; then the patient could breathe herself, and the anaesthesiologist could relax. Nancy's blood pressure stayed at 105/70. The pulse had steadily fallen from the anxiety state prior to anaesthesia to a comfortable seventy-two beats per minute. Dr Billing was happy, and he looked forward to a coffee break in about forty minutes.

The case went smoothly. Dr Major did his bimanual examination and asked for some more relaxation. This meant that Nancy's blood had detoxified the succinylcholine given during the entubation. Dr Billing was happy to give another 2 cc. He dutifully recorded this in his anaesthesia record. The result was immediate, and Dr Major thanked Dr Billing and informed the crew that the ovaries felt like little smooth, normal plums. He always said that when he felt normal ovaries. The dilation of the cervix went without a hitch. Nancy had a normally antero-flexed uterus, and the curve on the dilators was a perfect match. A few blood clots were sucked out from the vaginal vault with the suction machine. Dr Major carefully curetted the inside of the uterus, noting the consistency of the endometrial tissue. As Dr Major passed the second curette, Dr Billing noted a slight change in the rhythm of the cardiac monitor. He watched the electronic blip trace across the oscilloscope screen. The pulse fell to about sixty. Instinctively he inflated the blood pressure cuff and listened intently for the familiar far-away deep sound of the blood surging through the collapsed artery. As the air pressure drained off more, he heard the rebound sound indicating the diastolic pressure. The blood pressure was 90/60. This was not terribly low, but it puzzled his analytical brain. Could Nancy be getting some vagal feedback from her uterus, he wondered? He doubted it, but just the same he took the stethoscope from his ears.

'Dr Major, could you hold on for just a minute? The blood pressure has sagged a little. How much blood loss do you estimate?'

'Couldn't be more than 500 cc,' said Dr Major, looking up from between Nancy's legs.

'That's funny,' said Dr Billing, replacing the stethoscope in his ears. He inflated the cuff again. Blood pressure was 90/58. He looked at the monitor: pulse sixty.

'What's the pressure?' asked Dr Major.

'Ninety over sixty, with a pulse of sixty,' said Dr Billing, taking the stethoscope from his ears and rechecking the flow valves on the anaesthesia machine.

'What the hell's wrong with that, for Christ's sake?' snapped Dr Major, showing some early surgical irritation.

'Nothing,' agreed Dr Billing, 'but it's a change. She had been so steady.'

'Well, her colour is fantastic. Down here, she's as red as a cherry,' said Dr Major, laughing at his own joke. No one else laughed.

Dr Billing looked at the clock. It was 7 : 48. 'OK, go ahead. I'll tell you if she changes any more,' said Dr Billing, while giving the breathing bag a healthy squeeze to inflate Nancy's lungs maximally. Something was bothering Dr Billing; something was keying-off his sixth sense, activating his adrenals and pushing up his own heart rate. He watched the breathing bag sag and remain still. He compressed it again, mentally recording the degree of resistance afforded by Nancy's bronchial tubes and lungs. She was very easy to breathe. He watched the bag again. No motion, no respiratory effect on Nancy's part, despite the fact that the second dose of the succinylcholine should have been metabolized by then.

The blood pressure came up slightly, then went down again : 80/58. The monotonous beep of the monitor skipped once. Dr Billing's eyes shot to the oscilloscope screen. The rhythm picked up again.

'I'll be finished here in five minutes,' said Dr Major for Dr Billing's benefit. With a sense of relief, Dr Billing reached over and turned down both the nitrous oxide and the halothane flow, while turning up the oxygen. He wanted to lighten Nancy's level of anaesthesia. The blood pressure came up to 90/60, and Dr Billing felt a little better. He even allowed himself the luxury of running the back of his hand across his forehead to scatter the beads of perspiration that had appeared as evidence of his increasing anxiety. He glanced at the soda-lime CO_2 absorber. It appeared normal. Time was 7 : 56. With his right hand he reached up and lifted Nancy's eyelids. They moved with no resistance and the pupils were maximally dilated. The fear returned to Dr Billing in a rush. Something was wrong ... something was very wrong.

Monday February 23
7:15am

Several small flakes of snow danced down Longwood Avenue in the half-light of February 23, 1976. The temperature was a crisp twenty degrees and the delicate crystalline structures fluttering earthward were intact even after striking the pavement. The sun was obscured by a low cover of thick grey clouds which shrouded the waking city. More and more clouds were swept in by the sea breeze, enveloping the tops of the taller buildings in a mist, making it become paradoxically darker as dawn spread its frail fingers over Boston. It was not supposed to snow, yet a few flakes had crystallized over Cohasset and had blown all the way into the city. The few that reached Longwood Avenue and were blown right on Avenue Louis Pasteur were the survivors until a sudden down-draught slammed them against a third-storey window of the medical school dorm. They would have slid off had it not been for the layer of greasy Boston grime on the pane. Instead they stuck there while the glass slowly transmitted the heat from within, and their delicate bodies dissolved and mingled with the dirt.

Within her room Susan Wheeler was totally unaware of the drama on the window pane. Her mind was preoccupied with extracting itself from the clutches of a meaningless, disturbing dream after a restless, near-sleepless night. February 23 was going to be a difficult day at best and possibly a disaster. Medical school is made up of a thousand minor crises occasionally interrupted by truly epochal upheavals. February 23 was in the latter category for Susan Wheeler. Five days earlier she had completed the first two years of medical school, the basic science part taught in the lecture halls and science labs with books and other inanimate objects. Susan Wheeler had done very well because she could handle the classroom, the lab, and the papers. Her class notes were renowned and people always wanted to borrow them. At first she lent them indiscriminately.

Later, as she began to perceive the realities of the competitive system which she thought she had left behind in Radcliffe, she changed her tactics. She lent her notes only to a small group of people who were her friends, or at least were people from whom she could borrow notes if she had had to miss a class. But she rarely missed a class.

A number of people chided Susan playfully about her marvellous attendance record. She always responded by saying she needed all the help she could get. Of course that was not the reason. Having entered a profession dominated by males, in which essentially all the professors and instructors were males, Susan Wheeler could not skip a class without being missed. Despite the fact that Susan looked on her mentors in a neutral sexless way as her professional superiors, they did not return the view in kind. The fact of the matter was that Susan Wheeler was a very attractive twenty-three-year-old female.

Her hair was the colour of winter wheat and very wispy. Since it was long and fine it drove her batty in the wind unless she had it pulled back and clasped with a barrette at the back of her head. From there it fell in a sheen to the lower edges of her shoulder blades. Her face was broad with high cheekbones, and her eyes, set well back in their sockets, were a mixture of blue and green with flecks of brown so that the chromatic effect changed with different light sources. Her teeth were ultra white and perfectly straight, the result of fifty per cent nature and fifty per cent suburbanite orthodontist.

All in all Susan Wheeler appeared like the girl of the Pepsi-Cola people's dreams. At twenty-three years old she was young, healthy, and sexy with that American, Californian style that made eyes turn and hypothalamuses awaken. And on top of it all, perhaps in spite of it all, Susan Wheeler was very sharp. Her grammer school IQ ratings had hovered around the 140 range and were a source of infinite delight to her socially committed parents. Her school record was a monotonous series of A's with numerous other evidences of achievement. Susan liked school and learning and revelled in using her brain. She read voraciously. Radcliffe had been perfect for her. She did well but she earned her grades. She had majored in chemistry but had taken as much literature as possible. She had no trouble getting into medical school.

But being attractive as Susan was had certain definite drawbacks. One was the difficulty of missing class without being noticed. Whenever questions were asked, she was among those unfortunate few who served to demonstrate the stupidity of the students or the brilliance of the professors. Another drawback was that people formed opinions about Susan, with very little information. She so resembled models glaring out from advertisements that people continuously confused her with those frequently mindless girls.

There were advantages, though, to being bright and beautiful, and Susan was slowly beginning to realize that it was reasonable to exploit them to a degree. If she needed a further explanation regarding some complicated topic, she only had to ask once. Instructors and professors alike would hasten to help Susan understand a fine point of endocrinology or a subtle point of anatomy.

Socially, Susan did not date as much as people imagined she would. The explanation for this paradox was several-fold. First, Susan preferred reading in her room to a boring date, and with her intelligence, Susan found quite a few men boring. Second, few men actually asked Susan out, just because Susan's combination of beauty and brains was a bit intimidating. Susan spent many Saturday nights engrossed in novels, some literary, some otherwise.

Starting February 23, Susan feared her comfortable world was going to be blown up. The familiar lecture routine was over. Susan Wheeler and one hundred and twenty-two of her classmates were being rudely weaned from the security of the inanimate and tossed into the arena of the clinical years. All the confidence in one's abilities formed during the basic science years were hardly proof against the uncertainties of actual patient care.

Susan Wheeler had no illusions concerning the fact that she knew nothing about actually being a doctor, about taking care of real live patients. Inwardly she doubted that she ever would. It wasn't something she could read about and assimilate intellectually. The idea of trial by fire was diametrically opposed to her basic methodology. Yet on February 23 she was going to have to deal with patients some way, somehow. It was this crisis of confidence that made sleep difficult for her and filled the night with bizarre, disturbing dreams in which she found herself wandering through foreign mazes searching for horrible goals. Susan had no idea how closely her dreams would approximate her experience during the next few days.

At 7:15 the mechanical click of the clock radio broke her dream's feedback circuit and Susan's brain awakened to full consciousness. She turned off the radio before the transistors had a chance to fill the room with raucous folk music. Normally she relied on the music to wake her. But on this particular morning she needed little assistance. She was too keyed up.

Susan put her feet onto the floor and sat on the edge of the bed. The floor was cold and uninviting. Her hair descended from her head haphazardly, leaving only a two-to-three-inch gap through which to regard her room. It wasn't much of a room, about twelve by fourteen feet, with two multi-paned windows at the end. The windows gave out onto another brick building and a parking lot so that Susan rarely looked out. The paint was reasonably fresh because she had painted the room herself about two years previously. The colour was a pleasing pastel yellow which accented perfectly the Marimekko Printex fabric she had used to make the curtains. Their colours were several shades of electric green, separated by dark blue. On the walls hung a variety of coloured posters, framed with stainless steel, advertising past cultural events.

The furniture was medical school issue. There was an old-fashioned single bed, which was too soft, and difficult for entertaining. There was a worn, overstuffed easy chair, which Susan never used save for depositing dirty laundry. Susan liked to read on the bed and study at the desk so that the easy chair really wasn't 'critical,' in her words. The desk was oak and ordinary except for the pattern of initials and scratches carved in the top. In its right corner, Susan had even found a few obscene words associated with the word *biochem*. A physical diagnosis book was open on the desk. During the last three days she had totally reread it, but the text had failed to buoy her sagging confidence.

'Shit,' she said out loud, with little inflection. The remark was directed at no one and at nothing. It was a basal response as she comprehended that February 23 had indeed arrived. Susan liked to swear and she did it a lot, but mostly to herself. Since such language contrasted sharply with her wholesome image, the effect was truly remarkable. She had found it a useful and entertaining tool.

Having pulled herself from the warmth of her covers with such dispatch, Susan realized that she had an extra fifteen minutes to spare. That was the usual duration of her ritual of repeatedly turning off her radio alarm before actually making it into the bathroom. Her ambivalence toward starting this day made her squander the time by just sitting and staring ahead, wishing that she had gone to law school or graduate school in literature ... anything besides medical school.

The coldness of the bare waxed floor worked its way into Susan's feet. As she sat there, her circulatory system dissipated her body heat into the cold room, making her nipples rise up from the summits of her shapely breasts. Goose pimples appeared from nowhere along the insides of her naked thighs. She wore only a thin worn-out flannel nightgown she had gotten for Christmas when she was in the fifth grade. She still wore it to bed almost every night, at least when she was sleeping alone. Somehow she loved that nightgown. Amid the furious pace of change in her life, it seemed to afford a sanctuary of consistency. Besides, it had always been her father's favourite.

Susan had enjoyed pleasing her father from a very early age. Her first remembrance of him was his smell: a mixture of the outdoors and deodorant soap covering a distinctive odour she later realized was male. He had always been good to her, and she knew that she was his favourite. That secret she never shared with anyone, especially not with her two younger brothers. It had always been a source of confidence for her as she faced the usual hurdles of childhood and adolescence.

Susan's father was a strong-willed individual, a dominant

but generous and gentle man who ran his family and his insurance business like an enlightened despot. A charming man whose brood acknowledged him as the last word on any subject. It wasn't that Susan's mother was a weak-willed individual. It was just that she had met more than her match in the man she married. For much of her life Susan accepted this situation as the invariable norm. Eventually, however, it began to cause her some inner confusion. Susan was very much like her father, and her father encouraged her development in that direction. Then Susan began to realize she could not be like her father and expect one day to have a home of her own like the one in which she was reared. For a time she wanted desperately to be like her mother, and consciously tried. But it was to no avail. Her personality showed more and more her father's traits, and in high school she was literally forced into a leadership role. Susan was voted president of her graduating class at a time in her life when she thought that she would have preferred to be more in the background.

Susan's father was never particularly demanding, and certainly never pushy. He remained a source of confidence and encouragement for Susan to do whatever she wanted, without considering her sex. After Susan had entered medical school and became familiar with some of her female classmates, she realized that many of them had emerged from a similar paternalistic background. In fact when she met some of their parents, the fathers seemed to be vaguely familiar, as if she had actually known them in the past.

A resonant thumping issued from the radiator beneath the window, heralding the coming of heat. A tiny bit of steam hissed from the overflow valve. The radiator's stirring reminded Susan of the coldness of the room. Stiffly she stood up, stretched, and closed the window. It had been open only about a half-inch. Susan lifted the nightgown over her head and regarded her naked body in the mirror on the bathroom door. Mirrors held a strange attraction for her. It was almost impossible for her to pass a mirror without at least a quick reassuring look.

'Maybe you should be a dancer, Susan Wheeler,' she said

rising up onto her tiptoes and stretching her arms straight up, 'and give up this idea of becoming a fucking doctor.' Like a balloon being deflated, she let herself sag until she was slumped over. She was still looking at herself in the mirror. 'I wish I could do that,' she added more quietly. Susan was proud of her body. It was soft and supple, yet strong and well tuned. She could have been a dancer. She had good balance and she was filled with a sense of rhythm and movement. She envied Carla Curtis, a friend from Radcliffe who had gone into dance after college and was somewhere in the New York world. But Susan knew she could not actually go into dance despite her fantasy about it. She needed a vocation which would constantly exercise her brain. Susan made a horrible grimace and stuck her tongue out at the girl in the mirror, who did the same. Then Susan went into the bathroom.

In the bathroom she turned on the shower. It took four or five minutes to get hot. She looked at her face in the bathroom mirror, after shaking her hair from her line of sight. If only her nose had been made a little more narrow, she thought that she would be quite attractive. Then she started her bathroom routine with one lavender tablet of Ortho-Novum. Among her other characteristics, Susan Wheeler was a practical woman; strong-willed and practical.

Monday February 23
7:30am

The Boston Memorial Hospital is certainly not an architectural landmark, despite the disproportionately large number of architects in the Boston area. The central building is attractive and interesting. It was constructed over a century ago with brownstone blocks carefully fitted together with skill and feeling. But the structure is inconveniently small and only two storeys tall. Besides, it was designed with large, general wards, now outmoded. Hence its present-day practicality is minuscule. Only the ooze of medical history which permeates its halls keeps the wreckers and the planners at bay.

The innumerable larger buildings are studies in American gothic. Extending off at obtuse angles, millions upon millions of bricks join together to hold up dirty windows and flat monotonous roofs. The buildings were added in spurts, responding to the purported need for beds or the availability of funds. There is no doubt that it is an ugly combination of buildings, except perhaps for a few smaller research buildings. Those had architects and money to burn.

But very few people ever notice the appearance of the buildings. The whole is larger than the sum of its parts; perception is too clouded by innumerable layers of emotional response. The buildings are not buildings by themselves. They are the famed Boston Memorial Hospital, containing all the mystery and wizardry of modern medicine. Fear and excitement intermingle in an ambivalent dialogue as lay people approach the structure. And for the professional individual, it is the mecca: the pinnacle of academic medicine.

The setting for the hospital adds very little. On one side a maze of railroad tracks leading to North Station and a bewildering array of elevated highways forms an enormous sculpture of rusting steel. On the other side is a modern housing project for low income families. Somehow that goal got mixed up in the renowned corruptness of the Boston government. The apartment buildings look like housing for the underprivileged because of their lack of outward design. But the rents are out of sight and only the rich and privileged live there. In front of the hospital is a stagnant corner of Boston Harbour with water like black coffee, sweetened with sewer gas. Separating the hospital and the water is a cement playground filled with discarded newspapers.

By seven-thirty this Monday morning all the operating

rooms at the Memorial hummed with activity. Within a five-minute interval, twenty-one scalpels sliced through unresisting human skin as the scheduled operations commenced. The fate of a sizeable number of people depended on what was done or not done, what was found or not found in the twenty-one tiled rooms. A furious pace was set which would not slow down until two or three in the afternoon. By eight or nine o'clock in the evening only two rooms would still be functioning, and they often continued until the seven-thirty rush the following morning.

In sharp contrast to the bustle in the OR area, the surgical lounge presented a luxuriant hush. Only two people were there, because the coffee break pattern did not begin until after nine. By the sink was a sickly-looking man appearing much older than his sixty-two years. He was busy trying to clean the sink without moving the twenty-odd coffee cups left there half-filled with water by their owners. Walters was his name, although few knew if it was his first or last name. His whole name was Chester P. Walters. No one at all knew what the P stood for, not even Walters himself. He'd been an employee of the Memorial OR since he was sixteen, and no one had the temerity to fire him despite the fact that he did almost nothing. He wasn't well, he'd say, and, indeed, he did not look well. His skin was a pasty white and every few minutes he'd cough. His cough rattled with phlegm deep within his bronchial tubes, but he never coughed hard enough to get it up and out. It was as if he was content to merely keep his tubes grossly patent without disturbing the cigarette he had constantly in the right corner of his mouth. Half the time he had to have his head cocked over to the left so that the smoke would not burn his eyes.

The other occupant of the surgical lounge was an intermediate surgical resident, Mark H. Bellows. The H stood for Halpern, his mother's maiden name. Mark Bellows was busy writing on a yellow legal tablet. Walters's coughing as well as Walters's cigarette definitely bugged Bellows, and Bellows would look up each time Walters started yet another coughing sequence. To Bellows it was incomprehensible how an individual could do so much bodily damage to himself and still keep it up. Bellows did not smoke; Bellows had never smoked. It was equally incomprehensible to Bellows how Walters managed to stay around the OR despite his appearance, personality, and the fact that he didn't do a damn thing. Surgery at the Memorial was the apogee, the zenith of the art of modern surgery, and being on its staff offered Nirvana, as far as Bellows was concerned. Bellows had striven hard and long for his appointment as a resident. Yet here, smack in the middle of all this excellence, was, as Bellows put it to his fellow residents, this ghoul. It seemed too ridiculously inconsistent.

Under normal circumstances Mark Bellows would have been inside one of the twenty-one operating rooms contributing to or directing one of the acts of mayhem. But on February 23 he was adding five medical students to his burgeoning list of responsibilities. Bellows was currently assigned to Beard 5, meaning the fifth floor of the Beard Building. It was a good general surgical rotation, maybe the best. As the intermediate resident of Beard 5, Bellows was also in charge of the surgical intensive care unit physically adjacent to the ORs.

Bellows reached for the table next to his chair and grasped a coffee mug without looking up from his work. He sipped the hot coffee loudly before abruptly replacing the cup with a minor clatter. He'd thought of another 'attending' who would be good at lecturing to the students, and he quickly pencilled the name onto the tablet. In front of him on a low table lay a piece of Surgical Department stationery. He picked it up and studied the names of the five students: George Niles, Harvey Goldberg, Susan Wheeler, Geoffrey Fairweather III, and Paul Carpin. Only two of the names made any impression. The Fairweather name made him smile and conjure up the image of a spoiled, slender fellow with glasses, Brooks Brothers shirts, and a long New England genealogy. The other name, Susan Wheeler, caught his eye purely because Bellows liked women in a general way. He also thought that women liked him in return; after all, he was athletic and a doctor. Bellows was not very subtle in his social concepts; he was rather naive, like most of his fellow doctors. Looking at the name Susan Wheeler, he reflected that having one female student might make the next month a little bit less of a pain in the ass. His mind didn't struggle to find a mental image for the name Susan Wheeler. The part of his brain concerned with stereotypes told him it wasn't worth it.

Mark Bellows had been at the Memorial for two and one half years. Things had been going well, and he was reasonably sure of finishing the programme. In fact, it had begun to look as if he might have a fighting chance for the chief resident position if everything went smoothly. Having been selected while he was an intermediate resident to get a group of medical students was certainly auspicious, although a bother. It had been an unexpected turn and was the immediate result of Hugh Casey coming down with hepatitis. Hugh Casey was one of the senior residents whose job included teaching two groups of medical students during the course of the year. The hepatitis came on only three weeks earlier. Right after that Bellows had received the message to come to Dr Howard Stark's office. Bellows had never associated the message with Casey's illness. In fact, with the usual paranoia following a request to come to the Chief of the Department of Surgery's office, Bellows had mentally tried to relive all his latest blunders so as to be prepared for the tirade he expected. But contrary to his usual self, Stark had been very pleasant and had actually commended Bellows on his performance related to a recent Whipple procedure Bellows had done. After the unanticipated honeyed words, Stark had asked if Bellows would be interested in taking the medical students scheduled to be with Casey. Truthfully, Bellows would have preferred to pass up the chance while being on the Beard 5 rotation, except that one did not pass up a request by Stark even if it were carefully couched in the form of an offer. It would have been professional suicide for Bellows to have done so and he knew it. Bellows comprehended the vengeance of the affronted surgical personality, so he had agreed with the proper amount of alacrity.

With a straightedge Bellows filled the front page of his yellow legal tablet with little squares about an inch on a side. He then proceeded to fill in the dates of the subsequent thirty or so days the medical students were scheduled to be under his tutelage. Within each square he blocked off morning and afternoon. Each morning he planned to give a lecture; each afternoon he was going to enlist one of the attendings to give a lecture. Bellows wanted to schedule all the topics in advance to avoid duplication.

Bellows was twenty-nine years old, having just celebrated a birthday the week before. However, it was relatively hard to guess his age. His skin was smooth for a man and he was in excellent physical shape. Almost without fail he jogged two to three miles per day. The only outward evidence of the fact that he was almost thirty was the thinning area on the crown of his head and the slightly receding hairline at the temples. Bellows had blue eyes and an almost imperceptible salting of grey over his ears. He had a friendly face, and he was endowed with the enviable quality of making people feel comfortable. Most everyone liked Mark Bellows.

Two interns were also assigned to the Beard 5 rotation. Under the new terminology they were called first-year residents, but Bellows and most of the other residents still called them interns. They were Daniel Cartwright from Johns Hopkins and Robert Reid from Yale. They had been interns since July and hence had come a long way. But in February they were both experiencing the familiar intern depression. Enough of the year had passed to blunt the uniqueness of their roles as well as the terror of the responsibility, and yet so much remained before the year would be over and they would earn relief from the burden of every other night on call. Hence they demanded a certain amount of attention from Bellows. Cartwright was presently assigned to the intensive care unit, while Reid was on Beard 5. Bellows decided he would also use them for the medical students. Cartwright was a bit more outgoing and would probably be more helpful. Reid was black and had recently begun to attribute being called and harassed so much to his colour and not his role as an intern. That was just another symptom of the February blues, but Bellows decided that Cartwright would be more helpful.

'Terrible weather,' said Walters, presumably to Bellows but

in an offhand undirected way. That was what Walters always said because to him the weather was always terrible. The only conditions which made him feel comfortable were seventy-six degrees and thirty per cent humidity. That temperature and water content apparently agreed with the ailing bronchial tubes in the depths of Walters's lungs. Boston weather rarely fulfilled such narrow limits, so to Walters the weather was always terrible.

'Yeah,' said Bellows in a noncommittal sort of way while he directed his attention outside. Most people would have agreed with Walters at that point. The sky was darkened by racing grey clouds. But Bellows wasn't thinking about the weather. Rather suddenly he was pleased about the pending five medical students. He decided that they probably would help him in his standing in the programme. And if that were the case, then the time investment was more than worthwhile. Bellows was Machiavellianly practical in the final analysis; he had to have been to have got a position at the Memorial. The competition was fierce.

'Actually, Walters, this is my favourite kind of weather,' said Bellows, getting up from the lounge chair, indecently teasing the coughing Walters. Walters's cigarette twitched in the corner of his mouth as he looked up at Bellows. But before he could say anything Bellows was through the door, on his way to meet his five medical students. He was convinced he could turn the burden into an asset.

Monday February 23

9:00am

Susan Wheeler got a ride in Geoffrey Fairweather's Jaguar from the dorm to the hospital. It was an older vintage model, an X150, and only three of them could squeeze into it. Paul Carpin was good friends with Fairweather so he was the other lucky one. George Niles and Harvey Goldberg had to bear the brunt of the rush hour Boston MBTA in order to get to the Memorial for the nine o'clock meeting with Mark Bellows.

Once the Jaguar started, which was a minor ordeal typically associated with English motor cars, it covered the four miles in good time. Wheeler, Fairweather and Carpin walked into the main entrance of the Memorial at 8:45. The two others, having expected a miracle of modern transport to carry them the same distance in thirty minutes, arrived at 8:55. It had taken about one hour. The meeting with Bellows was to take place in the lounge of Beard 5 ward. No one knew where the hell they were going. They all trusted to fate to lead them to the proper place as long as they walked into the Memorial itself. Medical students tend to be rather passive, especially after the first two years of sitting in lecture halls daily from nine until five. The groups met up partly by chance, partly by design, at the main elevators. Wheeler, Fairweather, and Carpin had tried to get to Beard 5 by going up the Thompson Building elevators directly opposite the main entrance. Having been built in haphazard spurts, the Memorial was labyrinthine.

'I'm not sure I'm going to like this place,' said George Niles rather quietly to Susan Wheeler as the group squeezed on to the crowded elevator amid the morning rush. Susan was well aware of the meaning behind Niles's simple statement. When you don't want to go somewhere and then have trouble finding it, it's like adding insult to injury. Besides, all five medical students were in an acute crisis of confidence. They all knew the Memorial was the most renowned teaching hospital and for that reason wanted to be there. But at the same time they felt diametrically opposed to the concept of actually being a doctor, to actually being able to handle some judgmental decision. Their white coats ostensibly associated them with the medical community and yet their ability to handle even the most simple patient-related matter was non-existent. The stethoscopes which dangled conspicuously from their left side pockets had been used only on each other and a few hand-picked patients. Their memory of the complicated biochemical steps in the degradation of glucose within the cell afforded little support and even less practical information.

Yet they were medical students from one of the best medical schools in the country and that should count for something. They all shared this delusion as the elevator lifted them floor by floor to Beard 5. The doors opened for a doctor in a scrub suit to get out on Beard 2. The five medical students caught a glimpse of the OR holding area in full swing.

Emerging on the fifth floor, the medical students spun on their heels, not sure of which direction to take. Susan took the lead by walking down the corridor to the nurses' station. Like the OR area below, the nurses' station on Beard 5 was a bee-hive of activity. The ward clerk had his right ear glued to the telephone getting A.M. stat blood-work reports. The head nurse, Terry Linquivist, was checking the OR schedule to be sure the pre-op meds had been given to those patients who would be called within the next hour or so. The other six nurses and three LPNs were in all stages of endeavour trying either to get those patients to surgery who had been called or to take care of those patients whose surgery was already part of the past.

Susan Wheeler approached this area of directed activity with an outward show of aplomb, carefully concealing her inner uncertainties. The ward clerk seemed the most accessible.

'Excuse me, but could you tell me ... ,' began Susan.

The ward clerk raised his left hand toward Susan. 'Tell me that hematocrit again. There's pandemonium here,' he shouted into the telephone he held between his head and cocked-up shoulder. He wrote on a pad in front of him. 'And the patient had a BUN ordered too!' He looked up at Susan, shaking his head about the person he was talking to on the phone. Before she could say anything, his eyes went back to the patient's chart he had out. 'Of course I'm sure a BUN was ordered.' He frantically looked through the chart to find the order sheet. 'I filled out the lab request myself.' He checked in the order sheet. 'Look, Dr Needem is going to be bananas if there's no BUN ... What? ... Well if you don't have enough serum get your ass up here and get some more. The patient is scheduled for eleven. And what about Berman; you got his lab work now? Of course I want it!'

The clerk looked up at Susan, keeping the phone pressed between his ear and his shoulder. 'What can I do for you?' he asked Susan rapidly.

'We're medical students and I wondered if ...'

'You'd better talk to Miss Linquivist,' said the clerk suddenly as he looked down at his paper and began madly scribbling figures. He paused long enough to extend his pencil toward Terry Linquivist for Susan's benefit.

Susan looked over at Terry Linquivist. She noted that the nurse was probably about four or five years her senior. She was attractive in a wholesome sort of way, but definitely overweight according to Susan's taste. She seemed no less busy than the clerk but Susan was not about to argue. With a quick glance at the rest of her group, who were more than willing to let Susan take the initiative, Susan walked up to Miss Linquivist.

'Excuse me,' said Susan in a polite tone, 'we are medical students assigned to ...'

'Oh no,' interrupted Terry Linquivist, looking up and then rapidly putting the back of her right hand to her forehead as if she were in the throes of a migraine attack. 'Just what I need,' said Linquivist to the wall, carefully emphasizing each word. 'On one of the busiest days of the year, I get a new batch of medical students.' She turned to Susan and eyed her with an obvious air of exasperation. 'Please don't bother me now.'

'I don't intend to bother you at all,' said Susan defensively. 'I was just hoping you could tell me where the Beard 5 lounge is.'

'Through those doors opposite the main desk,' said Terry Linquivist, mellowing slightly.

As Susan turned and moved toward her group, Terry Linquivist called out to one of the other nurses. 'You're not going to believe it, Nance, but today is going to be one of those days. Guess what we just got? ... We got ourselves a new group of green med students.'

Susan's ears, sensitized as they were, could pick out a few sighs and groans from the Beard 5 team.

Susan moved around the clerk's desk. He was still on the phone and still writing. She walked toward the two plain white doors opposite the desk. The others fell in beside her.

'Some welcoming committee,' said Carpin.

'Yeah, real red carpet treatment,' said Fairweather. Despite problems of confidence, medical students still thought of themselves as very important people.

'Ah ... a couple of days and the nurses will be eating out of your hand,' said Goldberg smugly. Susan turned and flashed a disdainful glare at Goldberg, who missed it altogether. Goldberg missed most subtle social interpersonal communications. Even some that weren't very subtle.

Susan pushed through the swinging doors. The room was a jumble of old books, mostly outdated *PDR*'s (*Physician's Desk Reference*), scratch paper, dirty coffee cups, and an assortment of disposable needles and I.V. paraphernalia. There was a counter, desk height, that ran along the length of the wall on the left. A large commercial-type coffee maker was in the middle. At the far end was a curtainless window covered on the outside with Boston grime. Only a meagre amount of February morning light penetrated the glass and fell in a pale patch on the ageing linoleum floor. The illumination in the room depended entirely on an ample bank of fluorescent lights in the ceiling. The right wall had a bulletin board filled with messages, reminders, and announcements. Next was a blackboard, which had a fine covering of chalk dust. In the centre of the room was a group of classroom chairs with a small desk piece on each right arm. One of them was pulled in front of the blackboard for Bellows. He was sitting with his yellow legal tablet in front of him. As the medical students filed in, he lifted his left hand and studied his watch. The manoeuvre was for the benefit of the students, and they recognized the gesture immediately. Especially Goldberg, who was extremely sensitive about nuances which might have an effect on his grade average.

No one said anything for several minutes. Bellows was silent for effect. He'd had no experience with medical students but from his own background he felt obliged to be authoritarian. The medical students were silent because they already felt ill at ease and a bit paranoid.

'It is nine-twenty,' said Bellows eyeing each student in turn. 'This meeting was supposed to take place at nine, not nine-twenty.' No one contracted a single facial muscle lest Bellows's attention be drawn to him. 'I think we'd better start out on the right foot,' continued Bellows with authority. He got up laboriously and picked up a piece of chalk. 'There's one thing about surgery, especially here at the Memorial. Things happen on time. You people better take that to heart, or, believe me, your experience here is going to be ...' Bellows searched for the proper word while he tapped the chalk on the blackboard. He looked at Susan Wheeler, whose appearance added to his momentary confusion. He glanced out of the window, '... a long cold winter.'

Bellows looked back at the students and began a semi-prepared introductory talk. He examined the faces of the students as he talked. He was sure he recognized Fairweather. The very narrow amber-coloured horn-rimmed glasses fitted into Bellows's preconception. And Goldberg: Bellows was reasonably confident he could pick him out. The other two males were nondescript entities at that point to Bellows. He hazarded another glance at Susan and felt the same instantaneous confusion. He had not been prepared for the attractiveness of the girl. She was wearing dark blue slacks which seemed to cling disturbingly snugly about her thighs. Above, she had on a lighter blue Oxford cloth shirt, accented by a darker blue and red silk scarf tied around her neck. Her medical student white coat was casually opened. Her ample breasts defiantly advertised her sex, and Bellows was not at all ready to deal with this concept in light of the plans he had formulated for dealing with the students. With some effort he avoided looking at Susan for the time being.

'You'll be assigned to Beard 5 for only one month of your three month surgical rotation here at the Memorial,' said Bellows, shifting into a familiar monotone associated with medical pedagogy. 'In some ways this is an advantage and in others a disadvantage, like so many things in life.'

Carpin chuckled at this feeble attempt at philosophy, but noticing that he was alone, he shut up quickly.

Bellows fixed his gaze on Carpin and continued, 'Beard 5 rotation includes the surgical intensive care unit. Hence you will be subjected to an intensive teaching experience. That's the good part. The disadvantage is that it occurs so early in your clinical exposure. I understand this is your first clinical rotation. Is that correct?'

Carpin looked from side to side to make sure that this last question was directed at him. 'We ...' His voice faltered, and he cleared his throat. 'That's right,' he managed to say with some difficulty.

'The intensive care unit,' continued Bellows, 'is an area where you all have the most to learn, but it represents the most critical area for patient care. All the orders that you write on any patient must be countersigned by myself or one of the two interns on the service, whom you will meet presently. If you write orders in the ICU they have to be countersigned the moment you write them. Orders for patients on the ward can be countersigned en masse at various times during the day. Is that clear?'

Bellows looked at each student, including Susan, who returned his gaze without altering her neutral expression. Susan's immediate impression of Bellows was not particularly favourable. His manner seemed artificial and his opening mini-lecture on punctuality seemed a little unnecessary so early in the course of events. The monotone of his remarks combined with the pitiful stab at philosophy tended to support the image Susan had begun to construct of the surgical personality from previous conversations and her reading ... unstable, egotistical, sensitive to criticism, and above all, dull. Susan did not notice that Mark Bellows was male. Such a thought did not even register in her mind.

'Now,' said Bellows in his artificial monotone, 'I'll have some schedules Xeroxed for you which will outline the basic calendar we'll follow while you are assigned to Beard 5. The patients on the ward and in the ICU will be divided among you, and you are to work directly with the intern on the case. As for admissions, I want you to set up your own schedule for equitably dividing them. One of you will do a full work-up on each admission. As for night call, I want at least one of you to stay here. That means you'll be on only one in five nights and that's not overburdening you. In fact, that is less than usual. If others want to stay in the evenings, that's fine, but at least one of you stays here all night. Get together some time today and give me a schedule of who will be on when.'

'Rounds will begin each morning in the ICU at six-thirty. Before then I want you to have seen your patients, collated all the necessary information to present during the rounds. Is that clear?'

Fairweather looked at Carpin in dismay. He leaned over and whispered in Carpin's ear, 'Christ, I'll have to get up before I go to bed!'

'Do you have a question, Mr Fairweather?' demanded Bellows.

'No,' answered Fairweather rapidly. He was intimidated by the fact that Bellows knew his name.

'As for the rest of the morning,' said Bellows, eying his watch again. 'First I will take you to the ward and introduce you to the nursing staff, who will be thrilled to meet you all, I'm sure,' said Bellows with a wry smile.

'We have experienced their joy already,' said Susan, speaking for the first time. Her voice brought Bellows's eyes around and held them. 'We didn't expect a brass band for our arrival but at the same time we didn't expect a cold shoulder.'

Susan's appearance had already somewhat unnerved Bellows. With the animation that the sound of her voice provided, Bellows's pulse quickened slightly. There was a certain surge within his body which reminded him of watching cheerleaders in high school and wishing that they were naked. Bellows searched for words.

'Miss Wheeler, you'll have to understand that the nurses here are primarily interested in one thing.'

Niles winked in agreement to Goldberg, who didn't understand what Niles was implying.

'And that is patient care, damn good patient care. And when new medical students and/or new interns arrive that becomes a rather difficult goal. From actual experience they have all learned that new house staff is probably more deadly than bacteria and virus put together. So don't expect to be greeted as saviours here, least of all from the nurses.'

Bellows paused but Susan did not respond. She was thinking about Bellows. At least he was a realist and that was a glimmer of hope in the otherwise poor impression he had made on her.

'At any rate, after showing you the ward, we'll head up to surgery. There's a staff gallbladder at ten-thirty and it will give you all a chance to get into a scrub suit and see the inside of an OR.'

'And the handle of a retractor,' added Fairweather. For the first time the atmosphere lightened and everyone laughed.

Down in the OR area Dr David Cowley was absolutely pissed and he spared no one. The circulating nurse had broken into tears before the case was over and had to be replaced. The anaesthesiology resident had had to weather one of the worst bombardments of foul words and captious epithets that had ever been hurled over an anaesthesia screen. The surgical resident first assisting had a small cut in his right index finger from Cowley's scalpel.

Cowley was one of the more prosperous of the general surgeons at the Memorial with a spacious private office on Beard

10. He had been spawned, trained, and now nurtured by the Memorial. When things went well, he was a most pleasant chap, full of jokes and ribald stories, always eager to offer an opinion, to bet on a game, to laugh. But when things went contrary to his wishes, he was a firebrand of the most vicious nature, a seething cauldron of invective. In short, he was a juvenile in adult clothing.

His only case that day had gone poorly. To start with, the circulating nurse had put out the wrong surgical instruments. She had set up the Mayo stand with the gallbladder instruments used by the residents. Dr Cowley had responded by picking up the whole tray and dashing it to the floor. Next the patient quivered a little as he made the initial incision. It was only with great self-discipline that Cowley had curbed his inclination to hurl the scalpel at the anaesthesiology resident. Then there was X-ray, who failed to show up at exactly the moment he called. Cowley's viciousness had so unnerved the poor technician that the first couple of films were totally black.

Somehow Cowley forgot the real reason the case went poorly. Cowley himself had accidentally pulled off the proximal tie on the artery to the gallbladder, causing the wound to fill up with blood in seconds. It had been a struggle to reisolate the vessel and get a tie around it without disturbing the integrity of the hepatic artery. Even after the bleeding had been controlled, Cowley still was not positive that he had not compromised the blood supply to the liver.

Coming into the deserted doctors' lounge, Cowley was raging. He was mumbling inaudibly as he passed down the row of lockers to his own. With emphasis he flung his scrub hat and mask onto the floor. Then he kicked his locker with jarring force.

'Fucking incompetent assholes. This Goddamned place is going to the dogs.'

The fury of his kick followed by an overhead fist which he brought against the door of the locker did several things. First, it raised a cloud of previously undisturbed dust which had settled on top of the locker over some five years. Second, it dislodged a single scrub shoe, which fell, just missing Cowley's head. Third, it jarred open the locker next to Cowley's, causing some of the contents to spill out onto the floor.

Cowley dealt with the shoe first. He threw it as he hard as he could against the far wall. Then he kicked open the locker next to his in preparation to replace the objects which had fallen out. One glance into the locker, however, made him pause.

Looking closer, Cowley was astonished to see that the locker contained an enormous collection of medications. Many were open, half-used containers and vials, but there were also many unopened. There were ampules, bottles, and pills in a bewildering assortment. Of the drugs that had fallen out, Cowley noted Demerol, succinylcholine, Innovar, Barocca-C, and curare. Within the locker were many more varieties, including an entire carton of unopened morphine bottles, syringes, plastic tubing, and tape.

Quickly Cowley replaced the medicines that had fallen to the floor. Then he locked the locker once again. In his calendar book he wrote the number 338. Cowley was going to check on that locker and see to whom it was assigned. Despite his anger, he had the presence of mind to realize that such a cache was important and had serious implications for the entire hospital. And with things that bothered him, Cowley had the memory of a sage.

Monday February 23

10:15am

Susan Wheeler could not go into the doctors' lounge to change into a scrub suit because the doctors' lounge was synonymous with the men's lounge. Susan had to go into the nurses' locker, which was synonymous with women's lounge. So creeps society from day to day, thought Susan angrily. To her it was just another blatant example of male chauvinism and it gave her a momentary lift to think that she was upsetting this unfair identification. The locker room was at that moment deserted and Susan located an empty locker with ease and began to change by hanging up her white coat. Nearby the shower entrance she found the scrub suits. They were one-piece pale blue dresses made from plain cotton fabric. They were actually for the scrub nurses. She held it up and then against herself. Looking into the mirror, she felt suddenly rebellious despite the intimidating surroundings.

'Screw the dress,' said Susan to the mirror. The scrub dress arched in a tumble into the canvas hamper while Susan retraced her steps into the hall. She paused before the doctors' lounge, and she almost lost her nerve. Impulsively she pushed open the door.

Bellows was at that very instant next to the door that Susan opened. He was reaching into one of the cabinets at the entrance for a scrub suit. He was clothed in his James Bond-style skivvies (that's what he called them) and black socks. He looked as if he belonged in the beginning of a grade C porno movie. Horror spread across his face as he caught sight of Susan. In a flash, he fled into the safety of the depths of the dressing room. As in the nurses' locker room, one could not see into the dressing room from the door. Spurred by her rebelliousness despite the unexpected encounter, Susan advanced to the cabinet and selected a small scrub top and pants; then she left as quickly as she had entered. She could hear a tangle of excited voices in the interior of the doctors' lounge.

Back in the nurses' locker, she completed changing rapidly. The pale green shirt was too large, as were the pants. Because of her narrow waist she had to cinch up the pants to their absolute maximum before tying the cord. Mentally she began to prepare for the inevitable diatribe from Bellows, the mighty surgeon-to-be, by deciding how she would counter. During their brief introductions on the ward, Susan had been very aware of the condescending attitude Bellows had directed toward the nurses. This attitude was ironical coming so soon after the commendable defence of the nurses he had made to explain their lack of enthusiasm toward new medical students. It was pretty obvious to Susan that Bellows was, among other things, a typical chauvinist. Susan decided that she would challenge that aspect of Bellows's personality. Maybe it would make the surgical rotation at the Memorial a bit more bearable. Of course she had not planned to see Bellows in his underwear in the dressing room, but the image and symbolic aspects made Susan laugh out loud before she passed through the door into the OR area.

'Miss Wheeler, I presume,' said Bellows as Susan emerged. Bellows was leaning casually against the wall to the left of the doorway, obviously waiting for Susan to appear. His right elbow was on the wall, with the hand supporting his head. Susan literally jumped at the sound of his voice since she hardly expected him to be waiting there for her.

'I must admit,' continued Bellows, 'you really caught me with my pants down.' A broad smile spread across his face, changing him in Susan's eyes to a rather human individual. 'That was one of the funniest things that has happened to me in a long time.'

Susan smiled in return but it was a half-smile. She was expecting the tirade to commence immediately.

'After I recovered and realized what you were after,' continued Bellows, 'I started to think that it was a pretty ridiculous response on my part to bolt. If I had had any sense I would have stood there and faced you despite my dress ... or the lack of it. At any rate, it made me think that I might have been relying on appearances a bit too much this morning. I'm a second-year resident, that's all. You and your friends are my first group of students. What I really want to do is to make this time here as profitable as possible for you all, and in the process, profitable for me as well. Least of all, we should enjoy ourselves.'

With a final smile and slight nod of the head, Bellows walked away from the stunned Susan to check which room the staff gallbladder was in. It was Susan's turn to feel a sense of confusion as she looked after him. The resolve her feelings of anger and rebelliousness had evoked had been undermined by Bellows's sudden insight into himself. In fact it made her rebelliousness seem a trifle foolish and out of place. The fact that Susan had stimulated the insight fortuitously made it obvious that she couldn't take credit for it and that she would have to revise some of her impressions about Mark Bellows. She watched Bellows walk all the way over to the main OR desk; he was obviously at home in the alien environment. For the first time Susan was a little impressed. In fact, she thought that he really wasn't that bad looking either.

The others were already prepared to go down to the OR. George Niles showed Susan how to put on the paper booties over her shoes and tuck in the conductive tape. Next she put on the hood and finally the mask. Once everyone was so attired, they passed the main OR desk and pushed through the swinging doors into the 'clean' area of the ORs themselves.

Susan had never been in an OR before. She had seen a couple of operations through the gallery windows but such an experience was akin to watching it on TV. The glass partition effectively isolated the drama. One did not feel a part of it. While walking down the long corridor Susan felt a certain excitement mixed with fear of the mortality of people. As they passed OR after OR, Susan could see clusters of figures bent over what she knew were sleeping patients with their fragile insides open to the elements. A hospital gurney approached them with a scrub nurse pulling and an anaesthesiologist pushing. As the group came abreast Susan could see that the anaesthesiologist was matter-of-factly holding the patient's chin back while the patient retched violently. 'I hear there's almost forty inches of packed powder at Waterville Valley,' said the anaesthesiologist to the scrub nurse. 'I'm going Friday right after work,' returned the scrub nurse as the pair passed by Susan toward the recovery room. The image of the tortured face of the patient so recently operated on imprinted itself in Susan's susceptible consciousness and she shuddered involuntarily.

The group pulled up in front of room 18.

'Try to keep the chatter to a minimum,' said Bellows, looking through the window in the door. 'The patient is already asleep. Too bad, I wanted you to see that. Well, no matter. There will be a lot of moving around during the draping procedure, etcetera, so stay back against the right wall. Once they get underway, move around so that you can see something. If you have questions, save them until later, OK?' Bellows looked at each student. He smiled anew when he met Susan's gaze, then pushed open the OR door.

'Ah, Professor Bellows, welcome,' boomed a large, gowned, gloved, and sterile figure hovering in the background near some X-rays. 'Professor Bellows has brought his brood of students to watch the fastest hands in the East,' he said laughing. He held up his arms in an exaggerated Hollywood surgical fashion with the hands up and bent outward as far as they would go. 'I hope you have told the impressionable youths that the spectacle they are about to see is a rare treat.'

'That hulk,' said Bellows to the students while motioning toward the laughing character by the X-rays and loud enough for all in the OR to hear, 'is the result of staying in the programme too long. That's Stuart Johnston, one of the three senior residents. We only have to put up with him for four more months. He had promised me he'd be civil, but I cannot be sure of that.'

'You're just a poor sport, Bellows, because I stole this case from you,' said Johnston, still laughing. Then to his two assistants he said without laughing, 'Let's get the patient draped, you guys. What are you trying to do, make this your life's work?'

44

The draping proceeded rapidly. A small piece of tubular metal arched over the top of the patient's head and separated the anaesthesiologist from the surgical area. By the time the draping was completed, only a small portion of the patient's right upper abdomen was exposed. Johnston moved to the patient's right side; one of the assistants went over to the left side. The scrub nurse moved over the draped Mayo stand, straining with a full complement of surgical instruments. A profusion of haemostats was lined up in a perfect array along the back of the tray. The scalpel had a new razor-sharp blade snapped into its jaws.

'Knife,' said Johnston. The scalpel slapped into his gloved right hand. With his left hand he pulled the abdominal skin away from him to provide countertraction. The medical students all moved forward silently and strained to see with a foreboding curiosity. It was like watching an execution. Their minds tried to prepare themselves for the image that was going to be imminently transmitted to their brains.

Johnston held the scalpel about two inches above the pale skin while he looked over the screen at the anaesthesiologist. The anaesthesiologist was slowly letting the air out of the blood pressure cuff and watching the gauge. 120/80. He looked up at Johnston and gave an imperceptible nod, tripping the poised guillotine. The scalpel dived deep into the tissues, and then with a smooth soundless slice, slid down the skin at an angle of approximately 45 degrees. The wound fell open and little jets of pulsating arterial blood sprayed the area, then ebbed and died.

Meanwhile curious phenomena occurred in George Nile's brain. The image of the knife plunging into the skin of the patient was displayed instantly in his occipital cortex. Association fibres picked up the message and transported the information to his parietal lobe, where it was associated. The association spread so rapidly and so widely that it activated an area of his hypothalamus, causing widespread dilation of his blood vessels in his muscles. The blood literally drained from his brain to fill all the dilated vessels, causing George Niles to lose consciousness. In a dead faint he fell straight backward.

His flaccid neck snapped his head against the vinyl floor with a resonant thump.

Johnston spun around in response to the sound of George's head smashing against the floor. His surprise quickly metamorphosed into typically labile surgical anger.

'For Christ sake, Bellows, get these kids outa here until they can stand the sight of a few red cells.' Shaking his head, he went back to catching bleeders with his hemostats.

The circulating nurse broke a capsule under George's nose and the acrid smell of the ammonia shocked him back to consciousness. Bellows bent down and felt along his neck and the back of his head. As soon as George was fully conscious, he sat up, somewhat confused about his whereabouts. Realizing what happened, he felt immediately embarrassed.

Johnston meanwhile wouldn't let the matter rest.

'Holy shit, Bellows, why didn't you tell me these students were absolute greenhorns? I mean, what would have happened if the kid fell into my wound here?'

Bellows didn't say anything. He helped George to his feet by degrees until he was satisfied George was really OK. Then he motioned for the group to leave OR no.18.

Just before the OR door shut, Johnston could be heard angrily yelling at one of his junior residents, 'Are you here to help me or hinder me ... ?'

Monday February 23

11:15am

George Niles's pride was hurt more than anything else. He developed a rather sizeable lump on the back of his head but there was no laceration. His pupils stayed equal in size and his memory was unimpaired. Consensus had it that he was going to make it. However, the episode dampened the spirits of the whole group. Bellows was nervous that the fainting would reflect on his judgment to bring the students into the OR on the first day. George Niles was concerned lest the incident foreshadowed similar responses every time he tried to watch a surgical case. The others were bothered to a greater or lesser degree simply because within a group, the actions of one individual tend to reflect the whole group's performance. Actually Susan was not concerned with this aspect as were the others. Susan was more distressed about the sudden and unexpected response and change in attitude of Johnston and, to a lesser extent, Bellows. One minute they were jovial and friendly; the next minute they were angry, almost vengeful, simply because of an unexpected turn of events. Susan rekindled her preconceptions regarding the surgical personality. Perhaps such generalizations were appropriate.

After changing back to their street clothes, they all had a cup of coffee in the surgical lounge. It was surprisingly good coffee, thought Susan, trying to overcome the oppressive haze of cigarette smoke which hung like Los Angeles smog from the ceiling to a level about five feet from the floor. Susan was mindless of the people in the lounge until her eyes met the stare of a pasty white-skinned man hovering in the corner near the sink. It was Walters. Susan looked away and then back again, thinking that the man was not really watching her. But he was. His beady eyes burned through the cigarette haze. Walters's omnipresent cigarette hung by some partially dried saliva holding the extreme tip in the corner of his lips. A trail of smoke snaked upward from the ash. For some unknown reason he reminded Susan of the hunchback of Notre Dame, only without a hunchback: a ghoulish figure out of place yet obviously at home in the shadows of the Memorial surgical area. Susan tried to look away but her eyes were involuntarily drawn toward the uncomfortable stare of Walters. Susan was glad when Bellows motioned to leave and they drained their cups. The exit was near to the sink, and as the group left the room, Susan had the feeling she was walking down Walters's line of vision. Walters coughed and the phlegm rattled. 'Terrible day, eh, Miss,' said Walters as Susan passed.

Susan didn't respond. She was glad to be rid of the staring eyes. It had added to her nascent dislike of the surgical environment of the Memorial.

The group moved en masse into the ICU. As the oversized ICU door closed, the outside world faded and disappeared. A surrealistic alien environment emerged out of the gloom as the students' eyes adjusted to the lower level of illumination. The usual sounds like voices and footsteps were muted by the sound-absorbing baffling in the ceiling. Mechanical and electronic noises dominated, particularly the rhythmical beep of the cardiac monitors and the to-and-fro hiss of the respirators. The patients were in separate alcoves, in high beds with the side rails pulled up. There was the usual profusion of intravenous bottles and lines hanging above them, connected to impaled blood vessels by sharp needles. Some of the patients were lost in layer upon layer of mummylike bandages. A few of the patients were awake and their darting eyes betrayed their fear and the fine line that divided them from acute insanity.

Susan surveyed the room. Her eyes caught the flourescent blips racing across the front of the oscilloscope screens. She realized how little information she could garner from the instruments in her present state of ignorance. And the I.V. bottles themselves with their complicated labels signifying the ionic content of the contained fluid. In an instant, Susan and the other students felt the sickening feeling of incompetence; it was as if the entire first two years of medical school had meant nothing.

Feeling a modicum of safety in numbers, the five students moved even closer together and walked in unison to one of the centre desks. They were following Bellows like a group of puppies.

'Mark,' called one of the ICU nurses. Her name was June Shergood. She had thick luxurious blonde hair and intelligent eyes that looked through rather thick glasses. She definitely was attractive and Susan's keen eye could detect a certain change in Bellows's demeanour. 'Wilson has been having a few runs of PVCs, and I told Daniel that we should hang a lidocaine drip.' She walked over to the desk. 'But good old Daniel couldn't seem to make up his mind, or ... something.' She extended an EKG tracing in front of Bellows. 'Just look at these PVCs.'

Bellows looked down at the tracing.

'No, not there, you ninny,' continued Miss Shergood, 'those are his usual PACs. Here, right here.' She pointed for Bellows and then looked up at him expectantly.

'Looks like he needs a lidocaine drip,' said Bellows with a smile.

'You bet your ass,' returned Shergood. 'I mixed it up so I could give about 2 mg per minute in 500 D5W. Actually it's all hooked up and I'll run over and start it. And when you write the order include the fact that I gave him a bolus of 50 mg when I first saw the runs of PVCs. Also maybe you should say something to Cartwright. I mean, this is about the fourth time he couldn't make up his mind about a simple order. I don't want any codes in here we can avoid.'

Miss Shergood bounced over to one of the patients before Bellows could respond to her comments. Deftly and with assurance she sorted out the twisted I.V. lines to determine which line came from which bottle. She started the lidocaine drip, timing the rate of the drops falling into the plastic chamber below the bottle. This rapid exchange between the nurse and Bellows did little to buoy the already nonexistent confidence of the students. The obvious competence of the nurse made them feel even less capable. It also surprised them. The directness and seeming aggressiveness of the nurse was a far cry from their rather traditional concept of the professional nurse-physician relationship under which they all still laboured.

Bellows pulled out a large hospital chart from the rack and placed it on the desk. Then he sat down. Susan noticed the name on the chart. *N. Greenly.* The students crowded around Bellows.

'One of the most important aspects of surgical care, any patient care really, is fluid balance,' said Bellows, opening the chart, 'and this is a good case to prove the point.'

The door to the ICU swung open, allowing a bit of light and hospital sounds to spill into the room. With it came Daniel Cartwright, one of the interns on Beard 5. He was a small man, about five seven. His white outfit was rumpled and blood-spattered. He sported a moustache but his beard was not very thick and each hair was individually discernible from its origin to its tip. On the crown of his head he was going bald rather rapidly. Cartwright was a friendly sort and he came up to the group directly.

'Hi, Mark,' said Cartwright making a gesture of greeting with his left hand. 'We finished early on the gastrectomy so I thought I'd tag along with you if I may.'

Bellows introduced Cartwright to the group and then asked him to give a capsule summary on Nancy Greenly.

'Nancy Greenly,' began Cartwright in a mechanical fashion, 'twenty-three-year-old female, entered the Memorial approximately one week ago for a D&C. Past medical history entirely benign and noncontributory. Routine pre-op workup normal, including negative pregnancy test. During surgery she suffered an anaesthetic complication and she has been comatose and unresponsive since that time. EEG two days ago was essentially flat. Current status is stable: weight holding; urine output good; BP, pulse, electrolytes, etcetera, all OK. There was a slight temperature elevation yesterday afternoon but breath sounds are normal. All in all, she seems to be holding her own.'

'Holding her own with a good deal of help from us,' corrected Bellows.

'Twenty-three?' asked Susan suddenly while glancing around at the alcoves. Her face reflected a tinge of anxiety. The soft light of the ICU hid this from the others. Susan Wheeler was twenty-three years old.

'Twenty-three or twenty-four, that doesn't make much difference,' said Bellows as he tried to think of the best way to present the fluid balance problem.

It made a difference to Susan.

'Where is she?' asked Susan, not sure if she really wanted to be told.

'In the corner on the left,' said Bellows without looking up from the input-output sheet in the chart. 'What we need to check is the exact amount of fluid the patient has put out versus the exact amount that has been given. Of course this is static data and we are more interested in the dynamic state. But we can get a pretty good idea. Now let's see, she put out 1650 cc of urine . . .'

Susan was not listening at this point. Her eyes fought to discern the motionless figure in the bed in the corner. From where she was standing, she could make out only a blotch of dark hair, a pale face, and a tube issuing from the area of the mouth. The tube was connected to a large square machine next to the bed that hissed to and fro, breathing for the patient. The patient's body was covered by a white sheet; the arms were uncovered and positioned at forty-five-degree angles from the torso. An I.V. line ran into the left arm. An I.V. line ran into the right side of her neck. Heightening the sombre effect, a small spotlight directed its concentrated beam down from the ceiling above the patient, splashing over the head and upper body. The rest of the corner was lost in shadow. There was no motion, no sign of life save for the rhythmical hiss of the breathing machine. A plastic line curled down from under the patient and was connected to a calibrated urine container.

'We also have to have an accurate daily weight,' continued Bellows.

But for Susan his voice drifted in and out of her awareness. 'A twenty-three-year-old woman ...' The thought reverberated in Susan's mind. Without the aid of an extensive clinical experience, Susan was instantly lost in the human element. The age and sex similarity struck too close to home for her to avoid the identification. In a naive way she associated such serious medicine with old people who had had their fling at life.

'How long has she been unresponsive?' asked Susan absently, without taking her eyes from the patient in the corner, without even blinking.

Bellows, interrupted by this non sequitur, turned his head up to glance at Susan. He was insensitive to Susan's state of mind. 'Eight days,' said Bellows, slightly vexed at the interruption of his harangue about fluid balance. 'But that has little to do with today's sodium level, Miss Wheeler. Could you kindly keep your mind on the subject at hand.'

Bellows shifted his attention to the others. 'I'm going to be expecting you people to start writing routine fluid orders by the end of the week. Now where the hell was I?' Bellows returned to his input-output calculations, and everyone except Susan leaned over to catch the expanding figures.

Susan continued to stare at the motionless individual in the corner, racing through a mental checklist of her friends who had had D&Cs, wondering what really divided herself or her friends from the plight of Nancy Greenly. Several minutes passed as she bit her lower lip, as was her custom when in deep thought.

'How'd it happen?' asked Susan, again unexpectedly.

Bellows's head popped up for the second time, but more rapidly, as if he expected some imminent catastrophe. 'How'd what happen?' he countered, scanning the room for some telltale activity.

'How'd the patient become comatose?'

Bellows sat up straight, closed his eyes and put his pencil down. As if counting to ten he paused before speaking.

'Miss Wheeler, you've got to try to give me a hand,' said Bellows slowly and condescendingly. 'You've got to stay with us. As for the patient, it was just one of those inexplicable twists of the fickle finger of fate. OK? Perfect health … routine D&C … anaesthesia and induction without a ripple. She just never woke up. Some sort of cerebral hypoxia. The squash didn't get the oxygen it needed. OK? Now let's get back to work. We'll be here all day getting these orders written and we've got Grand Rounds at noon.'

'Does that kind of complication occur often?' persisted Susan.

'No,' said Bellows, 'rare as hell, maybe one in a hundred thousand.'

'One hundred per cent for her, though,' added Susan with an edge on the tips of her words.

Bellows looked up at Susan without any idea of what she was driving at. The human element in Nancy Greenly's case had ceased to be a part of his concern. Bellows was intent on keeping the ions at the right level, keeping the urine output up, and keeping the bacteria at bay. He did not want Nancy Greenly to die while she was on his service because if she did, it would reflect on the kind of care he was capable of providing, and Stark would have some choice comments for him. He remembered all too well what Stark had said to Johnston after a similar case had resulted in death while Johnston was on the service.

It wasn't that Bellows didn't care about the human element, it was just that he didn't have time for it. Besides the sheer number of cases he had been and was involved with provided a cushion or a numbness associated with anything done repeatedly. Bellows did not make the association between Susan's and Nancy Greenly's ages, nor did he remember the emotional susceptibility associated with an individual's initial clinical experiences in the hospital environment.

'Now for the hundredth time, let's get back to work,' said Bellows, pulling his chair in closer to the desk and running his hand nervously through his hair. He looked at his watch before going back to his calculations. 'OK, if we use 1/4 normal saline, let's see how many milliequivalents we'll get in 2500 cc.'

Susan was totally detached from the conversation, almost in a fugue. Following some inner curiosity, she moved around the desk and approached Nancy Greenly. She moved slowly, warily, as if she were approaching something dangerous, and absorbing all the details of the scene as they came available. Nancy Greenly's eyes were only half closed and the lower edges of her blue irises were visible. Her face was a marble white, which contrasted sharply with the sable brown of her hair. Her lips were dried and cracked, her mouth held open with a plastic mouthpiece so she wouldn't bite the endotracheal tube. Brownish material had crusted and hardened on her front teeth; it was old blood.

Feeling slightly giddy, Susan looked away for a moment and then back. The harshness of the image of the previously normal young woman made her tremble with undirected emotion. It wasn't sadness per se. It was another kind of inner pain, a sense of mortality, a sense of the meaningless in life which could be so easily disrupted, a sense of hopelessness, and a sense of helplessness. All those thoughts cascaded into the centre of Susan's mind, bringing unaccustomed moisture to the palms of her hands.

As if reaching for a delicate piece of porcelain, Susan lifted one of Nancy Greenly's hands. It was surprisingly cold and totally limp. Was she alive or dead? The thought crossed Susan's mind. But there directly above was the cardiac monitor with its reassuring electronic blip tracing excitedly its pattern.

'I shall assume you are a whiz at fluid balance, Miss Wheeler,' said Bellows at Susan's side. His voice broke the semitrance Susan had assumed and she replaced carefully Nancy Greenly's hand. To Susan's surprise the whole group had moved over to the bedside.

'This, everybody, is the CVP line, the central venous pressure,' said Bellows holding up the plastic tube whose tip snaked into Nancy Greenly's neck. 'We just keep that open for now. The I.V. goes in the other side, and that's where we'll

54

hang our 1/4 normal saline with the 25 milliequivalents of potassium to run at 125 cc per hour.'

'Now then,' continued Bellows after a slight pause, obviously thinking while looking vacantly at Nancy Greenly, 'Cartwright, be sure to order electrolytes on her urine today but leave the standing order for daily serum electrolytes. Oh yeah, include magnesium levels too, OK.'

Cartwright was madly writing these orders down on the index card he had for Nancy Greenly. Bellows took his reflex hammer and absently tried for deep tendon reflexes on Nancy Greenly's legs. There were none.

'Why didn't you do a tracheostomy?' asked Fairweather.

Bellows looked up at Fairweather and paused. 'That's a very good question, Mr Fairweather.' Bellows turned to Cartwright, 'Why didn't we do a tracheostomy, Daniel?'

Cartwright looked from the patient to Bellows, then back to the patient. He became visibly flustered and consulted his index card despite the fact that he knew the information was not there.

Bellows looked back at Fairweather. 'That's a very good question, Mr Fairweather. And if I remember correctly I did tell Dr Cartwright to get the ENT boys over here to do a trach. Isn't that right, Dr Cartwright?'

'Yeah, that's right,' enjoined Cartwright. 'I put in the call but they never called back.'

'And you never followed up on it,' added Bellows with uncamouflaged irritation.

'No, I got involved . . . ,' began Cartwright.

'Cut the bullshit, Dr Cartwright,' interrupted Bellows. 'Just get the ENT boys up here stat. It doesn't look like this one is going to come to, and for long-term respiratory care we need a trach. You see, Mr Fairweather, the cuffed endotracheal tube will eventually cause necrosis of the walls of the trachea. It is a good point.'

Harvey Goldberg fidgeted, wishing he had asked Fairweather's question.

Susan revived from the depths of her daydream as a result of the verbal exchange between Bellows and Cartwright.

'Does anybody have any idea why this horrible thing has happened to this patient?' asked Susan.

'What horrible thing?' asked Bellows nervously while he mentally checked the I.V., the respirator, and the monitor. 'Oh, you mean the fact that she never woke up. Well ...' Bellows paused. 'That reminds me. Cartwright, while you're calling consults, have neurology get their asses up here and do another EEG on this patient. If it is still flat, maybe we can get the kidneys.'

'Kidneys?' questioned Susan with horror, trying not to think about what such a statement meant for Nancy Greenly.

'Look,' said Bellows putting his hands on the railing with his arms extended. 'If her squash is gone, I mean wiped out, then we might as well get the kidneys for someone else, provided of course, we can talk the family into it.'

'But she might wake up,' protested Susan with colour rising in her cheeks, her eyes flashing.

'Some of them wake up,' shrugged Bellows, 'but most don't when they have a flat EEG. Let's face it; it means the brain is infarcted, dead, and there is no way to bring it back. You can't do a brain transplant although there are some cases where it might be very useful.' Bellows looked teasingly at Cartwright, who caught the innuendo and laughed.

'Doesn't anyone know why this patient's brain didn't get the oxygen it needed during surgery?' asked Susan, going back to her previous question in a desperate attempt to avoid even the thought of taking the kidneys out of Nancy Greenly.

'No,' said Bellows plainly and looking directly at Susan. 'It was a clean case. They've gone over every inch of the anaesthesia procedure. It happened to be one of the most compulsive of all the anaesthesiology residents and he's sucked the case dry. I mean, he's been merciless on himself. But there's been no explanation. It could have been some sort of stroke, I guess. Maybe she had some condition which made her susceptible to having a stroke, I don't know. In any case, oxygen was apparently kept from the brain long enough so that too many of the brain cells died. It so happens that the cells of the cerebrum are very sensitive to low levels of oxygen. So they die first when the oxygen falls below a critical level and the result is what we have here' – Bellows made a gesture with his hand, palm up, over Nancy Greenly – 'a vegetable. The heart beats because it doesn't depend on the brain. But everything else must be done for the patient. We have to breathe her with the respirator there.' Bellows motioned toward the hissing machine to the right of Nancy's head. 'We have to maintain the critical balance of fluids and electrolytes as we were doing a few moments ago. We have to feed her, regulate the temperature . . .' Bellows paused after he said the word *temperature*. The concept keyed off his memory. 'Cartwright, order a portable chest X-ray today. I almost forgot about that temp elevation you mentioned a little while ago.' Bellows looked at Susan. 'That's how most of these brainstem patients depart from this life, pneumonia . . . their only friend. Sometimes I wonder what the shit I'm doing when I treat the pneumonia. But in medicine we don't ask questions like that. We treat the pneumonia because we have the antibiotics.'

At that moment the page system came to life as it had been doing intermittently. This time it paged 'Dr Wheeler, Dr Wheeler, Dr Susan Wheeler, 938 please.' Paul Carpin nudged Susan and informed her about the page. Susan looked up at Bellows quite surprised.

'That was for me?' asked Susan in disbelief. 'It said "Doctor Wheeler." '

'I gave the nurses on the floor a list of your names to put on the charts in order to divide up the patients among you. You'll be paged for all the blood work and other fascinating scut.'

'It's going to be strange getting used to being called Doctor,' said Susan looking around for the nearest phone.

'You'd better get used to it because that's the way you'll be paged. It's not meant to flatter you. The idea is to make it easier on the patients. You shouldn't hide the fact that you're students, but don't advertise it either. Some of the patients wouldn't let you touch them if they thought you were med students; they'd yell and scream they were being used as guinea pigs. Anyway go answer the page, Dr Wheeler, and then catch up with us. After we finish here we'll be up in the conference room on ten.'

Susan walked over to the main desk and dialled 938. Bellows watched her cross the room. He couldn't help but notice that under the white coat lurked a sensuous figure. Bellows was being attracted to Susan Wheeler by quantum leaps.

Monday February 23

11:40am

It gave Susan a feeling of unreality to answer a page for 'Dr Wheeler.' She felt transparent as if she were an actress playing the role of a doctor. She had on the white coat and the scene was melodramatic and appropriate. Yet on the inside she just didn't feel like the part, and there was the thought that she would be exposed at any moment as a charlatan.

At the other end of the phone line, the nurse was matter-of-fact and to the point.

'We need an I.V. started on a pre-op. The case has been delayed and anaesthesia wants some fluid in him.'

'When would you like me to start it?' asked Susan twisting the phone cord.

'NOW!' answered the nurse before hanging up.

The other members of Susan's group had moved on to another patient and were again huddled about the desk, straining to see the chart Bellows had pulled from the rack and had in front of him. No one looked up as Susan traversed the half-light of the ICU. She reached the door and her left hand wrapped around the upturned stainless steel handle. Turning her head slowly to the right she chanced another glance at the

Immobile and lifeless-appearing Nancy Greenly. Once again Susan's mind stumbled through a painful identification. She left the ICU with difficulty but also with a sense of relief.

The sense of relief was short-lived. Hurrying along the crowded corridor, Susan began to prepare herself for the next mini-hurdle. Susan had never started an I.V. before. She had drawn blood from several patients, including her lab partner, but she had never started an I.V. Intellectually she knew what was required and she knew that she could do it. After all, it only involved punching a razor-sharp needle through some thin skin and impaling a vein without going all the way through the vessel. The difficulties arose from the fact that frequently the vein was only the size of thin spaghetti with a corresponding smaller lumen. In addition, sometimes the vein could not be seen from the surface of the skin and had to be attacked blindly with only the help of the sense of touch.

With these difficulties in mind Susan knew that even something as mundane as starting an IV was going to be a challenge of sorts. Her biggest concern was that it was going to be very apparent that she was new at the game, and perhaps the patient might rebel and demand a real doctor. Besides, she was in no frame of mind to have to put up with any exasperated ridicule from any of those bitchy nurses.

When Susan arrived at Beard 5, the scene was unchanged. The bustle of activity was as hectic as ever. Terry Linquivist gave a fleeting look at Susan before disappearing into the treatment room. One of the other nurses, whose cap had a bright orange stripe and whose name tag read 'Sarah Sterns,' responded to Susan's arrival by handing her the I.V. tray and a bottle of I.V. fluid.

'The name's Berman. He's in 503,' said Sarah Sterns. 'Don't worry about the rate. I'll be down there in a few minutes to regulate it.'

Susan nodded and headed for 503. En route she examined the I.V. tray. There were all sorts of needles: scalp needles, long-dwelling catheters, CVP lines, and traditional disposable needles. There were packets of alcohol sponges, a few lengths of flat rubber tubing to be used as the tourniquets, and a flashlight. Eyeing the flashlight, Susan wondered how many times she would repeat the scene of trudging off in the middle of the night to start an I.V.

Susan passed 507, then 505. As 503 loomed she rummaged in the I.V. tray among the scalp needles until she located a no.21 in a bright yellow packet. That was the needle she had seen an I.V. started with in the past. She was tempted to try one of the impressive-looking long-dwells but she decided to keep the experimenting to a minimum, at least on her first I.V.

'Room 503' was stencilled plainly on the door. It stood slightly ajar. Susan didn't know whether she should knock or just walk in. With a self-conscious glance over her shoulder to make sure she was not being watched, she knocked.

'Come in,' said a voice from within.

Susan pushed open the door with her foot, clutching the I.V. tray in her right hand and the D5W bottle in her left. Expecting to see an elderly ill individual, Susan moved into the room. It was a typical private room at the Memorial: small, old, the floor tiled with vinyl squares. The window was curtainless and dirty. An old radiator stood in the corner covered with a dozen layers of paint.

Contrary to Susan's expectations, the patient was neither old nor infirm. Propped up in the hospital bed was a youngish man, seemingly in perfect health. Susan quickly estimated that he was about thirty. He was wearing the usual hospital garb with the sheet pulled up to his waist. His hair was dark and very thick, and it was brushed back on both sides of his temples so that it covered the top part of each ear. His face was narrow, intelligent, and tanned despite the winter season. He had a sharp nose with flared nostrils, making him appear as if he were constantly breathing in. He looked athletic and in good physical condition. His muscular arms encircled his updrawn knees. His hands worked at each other nervously as if they were cold. Susan sensed immediately the man's anxiety through a patina of contrived calmness.

'Don't be bashful, come right in. It's like Grand Central here,' smiled Berman. The smile wavered. It was apparent that the man welcomed an interruption in the tenseness of waiting to be called for surgery.

Susan entered and allowed herself only a short look at Berman while she returned the smile. She then pushed the door to its original position. She put the tray on the foot of the bed and hung the I.V. bottle from the stand at the head of the bed. She consciously avoided Berman's eyes while she wondered why in God's name did Berman have to be so young, healthy, and obviously in charge of all his faculties. Susan certainly would have preferred an unconscious centenarian.

'Not another needle!' said Berman with partially feigned over concern.

'I'm afraid so,' said Susan opening a package of I.V. tubing, which she inserted into the bottle of D5W on the stand, allowing some of the fluid to run through the tube before securing it with a stopcock. With that accomplished, Susan looked up at Berman, to find that he was staring intently at her.

'Are you a doctor?' asked Berman with a tone of disbelief.

Susan didn't respond immediately. She continued to look directly into Berman's deep brown eyes. In her mind she weighed the possibilities of her response. She wasn't a doctor, that was obvious. What did she want to say? She wanted to say that she was a doctor. But Susan was a realist and she wondered if she would ever be able to say she was a doctor and believe it herself.

'No,' said Susan with finality while returning her gaze to the no.21 scalp needle. The reality disappointed her and she thought that it would add to Berman's anxiety. 'I'm just a medical student,' she added.

Berman's hands stopped their nervous activity. 'There's no need to be defensive about that,' he said with sincerity. 'You just don't look like a doctor or a doctor-to-be.'

Berman's innocent comment struck a tender chord in Susan's mind. Her embryonic professionalism made her rather paranoid and she immediately misconstrued Berman's comment, which was meant as a backhanded compliment.

'What is your name?' continued Berman, totally unaware of

the effect of his previous comment. He shielded his eyes from the glare of the overhead fluorescent lights and motioned for Susan to turn slightly to the left so he could see her name tag on her lapel. 'Susan Wheeler ... Dr Susan Wheeler. It has a natural sound to it.'

Susan quickly realized that Berman was not challenging her as a doctor after all. Still she did not respond. Something about Berman was distantly but comfortably familiar to her but she could not characterize it. Her mind tried but it was too subtly hidden in the immediacy of their encounter. It had something to do with Berman's charming authoritarian manner.

Partially as a method to concentrate her own thoughts and partially to control the conversation, Susan plunged into the I.V. affair. In a businesslike manner she placed the tourniquet about Berman's left wrist and pulled it tight. She tore open the packets containing the scalp needle and the alcohol sponge. Berman's eyes followed these preparations with great interest.

'Gotta admit from the start, I'm not crazy about needles,' said Berman, trying to maintain a degree of aplomb. He looked back and forth from his hand to Susan.

Susan sensed Berman's mounting concern and she wondered what he'd say if she told him that it was her first attempt at starting an I.V. She was quite certain that he would simply become unhinged. She felt certain because she realized that if the roles were reversed, that would be how she would react.

The tourniquet combined forces with Berman's ectomorphic body to make the veins on the back of his hand stand out like garden hoses. Susan took a deep breath and held it. Berman did the same. After a swipe with the alcohol pledget, Susan tried to jam the needle into the back of Berman's hand. But the skin advanced, resisting penetration.

'Ahhh,' cried Berman gripping the sheet with his free right hand. He was purposely overdoing the theatrics as a self-preservation manoeuvre. However, its effect was to unnerve Susan, who desisted in her attempt to break the skin.

'If it's any consolation, you feel just like a doctor,' said Berman looking at the back of his left hand. The tourniquet was still in place and the hand had an overall bluish discolouration.

'Mr Berman, you're going to have to be a little more co-operative,' said Susan, mustering her forces for a renewed attempt and wishing to spread the responsibility for any failure.

'Cooperate, she says,' echoed Berman while rolling his eyes up inside of his head. 'I've been as quiet as a sacrificial lamb.'

Susan replaced Berman's left hand flat on the bed. With her own left hand she effected countertraction on Berman's skin. With the same amount of effort the needle entered the scanty tissue.

'I give up,' pleaded Berman with a tinge of humour.

Susan concentrated on the submerged needle point. At first it tended to push the vein in front of itself. She tried the countertraction trick: same problem. She tried countertraction combined with a decisive lunge with the needle. She could feel the pop as the needle burst into the vein. Blood flowed back through the needle, filling the attached plastic tubing. Quickly she hooked up the I.V. line, opened the stopcock, and removed the tourniquet. The I.V. flowed smoothly.

Both parties felt definite relief.

Having actually accomplished something, something medical for a patient, Susan felt a tinge of euphoria. It was a small affair, a mere I.V., but nonetheless a definite service. Maybe there was a future for her overall. The euphoria brought a feeling of expansiveness to Susan which included a heightened sense of warmth with a shade of condescension toward Berman in spite of the hospital environment.

'You said before that I don't look like a doctor,' said Susan, getting the tape out to secure the I.V. line to the back of Berman's hand. 'What does it mean, to look like a doctor?' There was a slight tease to her voice as if she were more interested in hearing Berman speak than in actually listening to what he had to say.

'Maybe it was a silly comment,' said Berman, watching every move Susan made while taping the I.V. line. 'But I do know a few girls who went into medicine from my graduating class in college. Several of them were OK; all of them were bright; there was no doubt about that, but they were hardly feminine.'

'They probably weren't feminine to you because they went into medicine rather than vice versa,' said Susan, slowing the I.V. to a steady drip.

'Possible ... possible ... ,' said Berman thoughtfully. He recognized that Susan's interpretation represented a new perspective. 'But I don't think so. Two of them I happen to know quite well. In fact I knew them all the way through college. They really didn't decide on medicine until the last year. They were just as non-feminine before as after their decision. Whereas you, Dr Wheeler-to-be, have a distinct aura of femininity that envelops you like a cloud.'

Susan, eager to take exception to Berman's comment regarding his friends' femininity, was caught off guard by Berman's reference to her own femininity. On the one hand she was tempted to respond, 'Are you for real, buddy?' while on the other hand she thought that Berman might be serious and actually paying her a compliment. Berman himself decided which way Susan's mind would turn.

'If I had to pick what your vocation was,' continued Berman, 'I'd have to say you were a dancer.'

Having stumbled onto Susan's own fantasy concerning her alter ego, Berman opened the door on Susan's personality. To her, appearing like a dancer was definitely a compliment, and therefore she was more than willing to accept Berman's comment about her femininity as a compliment as well.

'Thank you, Mr Berman,' said Susan with sincerity.

'Please call me Sean,' said Berman.

'Thank you, Sean,' repeated Susan. She stopped her activity of gathering up the debris from the I.V. paraphernalia and looked out the dirty window. She didn't notice the dirt, the brick, the dark clouds, nor the lifeless trees. She looked back at Berman. 'You know, I wouldn't be able to tell you how much I appreciate your compliment. It might sound rather strange to you, but to be quite honest I haven't felt feminine over the last year or so. To hear someone like yourself say so is enormously reassuring. It's not that I have dwelt on it, but just the same I have begun to think of myself as ...' Susan paused, thinking of the right word. 'Neutral, or neuter. Yes that's the right word, neuter. It has happened slowly, in degrees, and I guess I'm really only aware of it by comparison when I get together with some of my former college classmates, especially my former roommate.'

Susan suddenly stopped in the middle of her thought and straightened up. She was slightly embarrassed and surprised at her own unexpected candour. 'What am I talking about? Sometimes I can't believe myself.' She smiled and then laughed at herself. 'I can't even act like a doctor, much less look like one. I'm sure that the last thing you want to hear about is my professional adjustment difficulties!'

Berman looked up at Susan with a broad smile. He was obviously enjoying the interlude.

'The patient is the one who is supposed to do the talking,' continued Susan, 'not the doctor. Why don't you tell me what you do so that I have to shut up?'

'I'm an architect,' said Berman. 'One of the million or so that haunt the Cambridge scene. But that is another story. I'd much prefer to get back to you. You cannot guess how reassuring it is to me to hear you talk like a human being in this place.' Berman's eyes swept around the room. 'I don't mind having a little operation, but this waiting around is driving me up the wall. And everybody is so Goddamn matter-of-fact.' He looked back at Susan. 'Tell me what you were going to say about your former roommate; I'd like to hear.'

'Are you putting me on?' asked Susan with narrowed eyes. 'Honest.'

'Well it's not all that important. It's just that she was smart. She went to law school and has maintained herself as a woman yet has satisfied her urge and capacity to compete and contribute intellectually.'

'I have no idea how you have been doing intellectually but there is no doubt about your being a woman. You couldn't be any less than the absolute antithesis of neuter.'

At first Susan was tempted to get into an argument with Berman over the fact that he equated being a woman with outward appearance. She felt that was only a part, a small part. But she caught herself and refrained. After all, Berman was on his way to surgery and didn't need a debate.

'I can't help the way I feel,' said Susan, 'and "neuter" is the best description. Initially I thought that medicine would be good for a number of reasons, including the fact that it would provide the social insurance I needed; I didn't want to think or worry about any social pressure to get married. Well,' sighed Susan, 'it provided social insurance all right, and a good deal more. Actually, I have begun to feel excommunicated from normal society.'

'In that vein I would love to be of assistance,' said Berman, pleased with his pun. 'Provided, of course, you consider architects normal society. There are some who don't, I can assure you. Anyway ...' Berman scratched the back of his head while he put his words in order. 'I hardly feel capable of carrying on a reasonable conversation in this humiliating nightgown, in this depersonalized milieu, and I would like very much to continue this conversation. I'm sure you get accosted continuously and I hate to add to your burden, but perhaps we could get together for some coffee or a drink or something after I get this Goddamn knee taken care of.' Berman held up his right knee. 'Screwed the thing up years ago playing football. It's been my Achilles heel ever since, so to speak.'

'Is that what you're scheduled for today?' asked Susan while she thought about how to respond to Berman's offer. She knew that it was hardly professional by any stretch of the imagination. At the same time she was attracted to Berman.

'That's right, a minuscule-ectomy, or something like that,' said Berman.

A knock at the door, followed by the rapid entry of Sarah Sterns before Susan could even respond, made Susan jump, and nervously she began to fuss with the stopcock on the I.V. Almost at the same time Susan realized how childish this action was, and it made her angry that the system could affect her to such a degree.

'Not another needle!' voiced Berman, dejected.

'Another needle. It's your pre-op. Roll over, my friend,' said

66

Miss Sterns. She crowded Susan in order to put her tray on the night table.

Berman glanced at Susan in a self-conscious way before rolling over on his right side. Miss Sterns bared Berman's left buttock and grabbed a handful of flesh. The needle flashed into the muscle. It was over almost before it began.

'Don't worry about the I.V. rate,' said Miss Sterns on her way to the door. 'I'll adjust it shortly.' She was gone.

'Well, I must be going,' said Susan quickly.

'Is it a date?' asked Berman, trying not to lean on his left buttock.

'Sean, I don't know. I'm not sure how I feel about it; I mean professionally and all that.'

'Professionally?' Berman was genuinely surprised. 'You must be being brainwashed.'

'Maybe I am,' said Susan. She looked at her watch, the door, and back at Berman. 'All right,' said Susan finally, 'we'll get together. Meanwhile you have to get back to normal. I'll live with being unprofessional but I don't want to be accused of taking advantage of a cripple. I'll stop in here before you go home. Do you have any idea how long you are going to be in the hospital?'

'My doctor said three days.'

'I'll stop back before you go,' said Susan already on her way to the door.

At the door she had to give way to an orderly arriving with a gurney to transport Berman to the OR, to room no.8, for his meniscectomy. Susan glanced back at Berman before turning down the corridor. She gave him the thumbs-up sign, which he returned with a smile. As she moved down toward the nurses' station, Susan pondered over her mixed emotions. There was the warmth of meeting someone with whom she felt a rather immediate chemical attraction; at the same time there was the nagging reality of the unprofessionalism of it all. Susan couldn't help but acknowledge that for her to be a doctor was going to be very difficult in every respect.

Monday February 23
12:10pm

Like a slalom skier Susan wove her way down the hospital corridor crowded with lunch carts filled with an assortment of colourless food. The reasonably pleasant aromas emanating from the evenly stacked trays reminded her that she hadn't eaten that day; two pieces of toast on the run hardly constituted a meal.

The arrival of the lunch carts added to the appearance of utter chaos at the nurses' station on Beard 5. It seemed to Susan that it was a wonder indeed that the right patient got the right drug, therapy, or meal. To Susan's pleasant surprise, Sarah Sterns had a smile and a quick thank-you for Susan before pointing to the resting place for the I.V. tray. No one else even acknowledged Susan's presence and she left. It took her about three seconds to decide to use the stairs rather than wait for the crowded elevator. After all, it was only three floors down to the ICU.

The stairs were made of metal with an embossed surface like beaten silver. The colour had been orange but now had become something approaching a dirty tan except in the centre of each step, which was worn shiny by multitudinous footsteps. The walls of the stairwell were made of cinder block, painted dark grey. But the paint was old and peeling. Some previous plumbing catastrophe or accident had provided a series of longitudinal stains that descended from above along the wall to the right. The stains reappeared each time Susan rounded the platform and started down another flight. The only light in the stairwell came from a bare bulb at each floor landing. On the fourth floor the bulb had blown, and because of the relative darkness Susan had to proceed with caution, advancing her foot to find the first stair on the next flight down to three. The distances between the floors seemed remarkably long to Susan.

By leaning out over the metal banister Susan could see down into the sub-basement and up to where the spiralling stairs became lost in collapsing perspective. Susan felt slightly ill at ease in the stairwell. The decaying darkness of the walls seemed to move in on her, awakening some atavistic fear. Perhaps it reminded her of a recurrent dream she used to have as a child. Although she had not had the dream for a long time, she remembered it well. It did not concern a stairwell but the overall effect was similar. The dream involved moving through a tunnel of twisted shapes which would progressively impede her progress. She never made it to the end of the tunnel in her dream despite the fact that the goal seemed very important.

In spite of the mildly disquieting atmosphere in the stairwell, Susan descended slowly, step by step. Her deliberate footsteps rang out with a dull metallic echo. She was alone. There were no people and it gave her a few uninterrupted moments to think. For a short period of time the immediacy of the hospital receded from Susan's consciousness.

The encounter with Berman became more complicated in her mind. The lack of professionalism was diluted because, in reality, Berman was not Susan's patient. She had been called simply to provide a peripheral service. The fact that Berman was a patient was important only in facilitating their chance meeting. But Susan wasn't sure if she were just rationalizing. Rounding the landing on the third floor, she paused at the head of the next flight.

She had reacted to Berman as a woman. For a constellation of inexplicable reasons, Berman had appealed to her in a basic, natural, even chemical way. To an extent that was encouraging and reassuring. There was no doubt in Susan's mind that she had begun to think of herself in a sexless sort of way over the first two years of medical school. She had used the word *neuter* in talking with Berman but only because she had been forced on the spur of the moment to find a term for it. Obviously she was female; she felt female and her monthly menstrual flow emphasized its reality. But was she a woman?

Susan started down the next flight of stairs. For the first time events had forced her to intellectualize a tendency which had been developing for several years. She wondered if Carpin had been called instead of her and if Berman had been some equally attractive female, would Carpin have responded as a male? Susan stopped again, considering this hypothetical situation.

From her experience she decided that there was a very good possibility that Carpin would have performed in an equivalent fashion.

Susan recommenced descending the stairs, very slowly now. But if it were true that a male would respond in a way similar to hers, why was it so different for her? Why did she dwell on it?

It was more than the debatable question of medical ethics. Berman had made Susan feel like a woman. All at once it came to Susan. The biggest difference between herself and Carpin was that Susan had an extra obstacle. She knew that both of them wanted to become doctors; to act like doctors, think like doctors, to be taken for doctors. But for Susan there was an additional step. Susan wanted also to become a woman; to feel like a woman, to be taken for and respected as a woman. When she had entered medicine, she knew it was a male-dominated career choice. That had been one of the challenges. Susan had never imagined that medicine would make it difficult for her to achieve fulfilment in a social sense. Academically she could compete; she was reasonably sure of that. The next step was going to be harder, an uncharted course. And Carpin? Well, for him the social part was easy. He was a male in a recognized male role. Being in medicine only supported his image of himself as a man. Carpin only had to worry about convincing himself he was a doctor; Susan had to convince herself that she was a doctor and a woman.

Arriving on the second floor, Susan was greeted by a sign which stated in bold letters: 'Operating Room Area: Unauthorized Entry Forbidden.' But the sign wasn't necessary. To Susan's momentary consternation, the door was locked! Her overly active imagination suddenly had all the doors from the stairwell locked, and she thought of herself caught within a vertical prison. It was a fleeting thought, totally irrational.

'Wheeler, you're too much,' she said aloud for her own benefit and encouragement. She quickly descended to the first floor. The door opened easily and Susan joined the surging mob on the main floor.

She took the elevator and returned to the ICU entrance. It took a bit of fortitude to begin to open the door. Once she started, it took strength. The ICU door was massive and very heavy.

Susan stepped once again into the nether world of the ICU interior. One of the nurses looked up from the desk but then went back to an EKG tracing in front of her. As Susan scanned the room, she was again struck by the purely mechanical appearance, the lack of human voices, even the lack of movement save for the fluorescent blips tracing their incessant patterns. And there was Nancy Greenly, as immobile as a statue, a casualty of medicine, a victim of technology. Susan wondered about her life, her loves. Everything was gone, all because of a simple menstrual irregularity, a routine D&C.

Susan forced her eyes away from Nancy Greenly and ascertained that her group had since departed from the ICU, presumably for Grand Rounds. At the same instant Susan acknowledged to herself her acute discomfort about being in the ICU. The psychological and technical complexity of the room caused any residual euphoria from the I.V. episode to vanish. Her imagination forced her to ponder the situation if something suddenly went wrong with one of the patients while she was standing there. What if someone expected her to make some life-death decision to go along with her white coat and her impotent stethoscope in her pocket?

Controlling the urge to succumb to a minor panic, Susan tugged at the inertia of the door and escaped into the corridor. Retracing her steps to the elevator, Susan mused about the difference between fact and fancy, between reality and mythology, between what it really was like being a medical student and what people thought it was like.

Remembering Bellows's comment about Grand Rounds on 10, Susan pushed the tenth-floor button and allowed herself to be compressed toward the rear of the elevator. It was a miserable trip. The car was a potpourri of human beings with every conceivable affliction, and it stopped at every floor. The air was heavy and hot, particularly since one rude passenger was smoking despite the sign plainly forbidding it. The occupants did not look at each other; they stared blankly at the light progressing from number to number, as did Susan, wishing that the doors would open and close more quickly.

Impetuously she pushed her way to the front of the elevator at the ninth floor. At 10, she broke from the crowded cubicle with relief.

The atmosphere changed immediately. The tenth floor was carpeted and the walls shone with an even lustre of newly applied semi-gloss paint. Gilded frames set off portraits of former Memorial greats in their sartorial academic splendour. Chippendale tables topped with a variety of lamps were interspersed between comfortable chairs along the length of the corridor. Neat piles of *New Yorker* magazines were arranged at rational intervals.

A large sign opposite the elevator directed Susan to the conference room. As she walked down the corridor she could see into the offices. These were the private offices for some of the more established doctors at the Memorial. A few patients were scattered along the corridor, reading and waiting. They all looked up as Susan passed. Their faces were uniformly expressionless.

At the end of the corridor Susan passed the office of the Chief of Surgery, Dr H. Stark. The door was ajar, and inside Susan caught a glimpse of two secretaries typing furiously. Just beyond Stark's office and on the other side of the corridor was a second stairwell. At the very end of the corridor, over two swinging mahogany doors an illuminated sign proclaimed: 'Conference in Progress.'

Susan entered the conference room, letting the doors close quietly behind her. It took a few moments for her eyes to adjust to the darkness, since the room lights were out. The focal point of light at the end of the room was the projected image of a Kodachrome of a human lung. Susan could just make out the outline of a man with a pointer describing the details of the photograph.

From the gloom in the foreground Susan began to discern the rows of seats and their occupants. The room was about thirty feet wide and some fifty feet long. There was a gentle downward slope of the floor to the podium, which was raised by two steps. The projection equipment was professionally hidden from view. The projected beam of light, however, was visible throughout its entire path due to the swirls of cigarette and pipe smoke. Even in the darkness Susan could tell that the conference room was new, well designed, and sumptuously appointed.

The next colour slide was a microscopic section, and it provided relatively more light in the room. Susan was able to pick out the back of Niles's head with its prominent lump. He was sitting in an aisle seat. She walked down to the proper row and tapped Niles on the shoulder. Susan could see that they had saved a seat for her. She had to squeeze past Niles and Fairweather before she could sit down. It was next to Bellows.

'Did you do a laparotomy or start an I.V.?' whispered Bellows sarcastically, leaning toward Susan. 'You were gone over a half-hour.'

'It was an interesting patient,' said Susan, bracing for another lecture on punctuality.

'You can think of a better one than that, I hope.'

'To tell the truth, it was a dressing change on Robert Redford's circumcision.' Susan pretended to be absorbed in the projected slide for a few moments. Then she looked over at Bellows, who snickered and shook his head.

'You're too much, I ...'

Bellows was interrupted by becoming aware that the man on the podium was directing a question at him. All he heard was '... you can enlighten us on that point, Dr Bellows, can you not?'

'I'm sorry, Dr Stark, but I did not hear the question,' said Bellows, mildly flustered.

'Has she shown any signs of pneumonia?' repeated Stark.

A large X-ray of a chest with the right side clouded silhouetted Stark's thin figure on the podium. His features could not be seen.

A fellow resident sitting directly behind Bellows leaned forward and whispered for Bellows's benefit, 'He's talking about Greenly, you asshole.'

'Well,' coughed Bellows, rising to his feet. 'She did have a low-grade temperature elevation yesterday. However, her chest is still clear to auscultation. A chest film two days ago was normal, but we have one pending for today. There has been some bacteria in her urine and we believe that cystitis rather than pneumonitis is the cause of the temperature elevation.'

'Is that the pronoun you intended to use, Dr Bellows?' demanded Dr Stark, as he walked over to the lectern, placing his hands on each side. Susan struggled to see the man; this was the infamous and famous Chief of Surgery. But his face was still lost in shadow.

'Pronoun, sir?' intoned Bellows rather meekly and with obvious confusion.

'Pronoun. Yes, pronoun. You do know what a pronoun is, don't you, Dr Bellows?'

There was a bit of scattered laughter.

'Yes, I think I do.'

'That's better,' said Stark.

'What's better?' persisted Bellows. As soon as he said it he wished that he hadn't. More laughter.

'Your pronoun choice is better, Dr Bellows. I'm getting rather tired of hearing *we* or some indeterminate third person singular. Part of your training as surgeons involves being able to deal with information, assimilate it, and then make a decision. When I ask a question of one of you residents, I want *your* opinion, not the group's. It doesn't mean that other people don't contribute to the decision process but once you have made the decision, I want to hear *I*, not *we* or *one*.'

Stark walked a few steps from the lectern and leaned on the pointer. 'Now then, back to the care of the comatose patient. I want to stress again that you must be fully vigilant with these patients, gentlemen. Although it can be frustrating because of the intense chronic care that is required and, perhaps, because of the grim ultimate prognosis, the rewards can be fabulous. The teaching aspect alone is priceless. Homeostasis is indeed extremely difficult to maintain over protracted periods of time when the brain ...'

A red light on the side wall suddenly sprang to life, blinking frantically. All eyes in the conference room turned toward it. Silently a message flashed onto a TV screen below the red light: 'Cardiac Arrest Intensive Care Unit Beard 2.'

'Shit,' muttered Bellows as he jumped up. Cartwright and Reid followed at his heels, and the three pushed their way to the aisle. Susan and the other four med students hesitated for a moment, looking at each other for encouragement. Then they followed en masse.

'As I was saying, homeostasis is difficult to maintain when the brain is damaged beyond repair. Next slide, please,' said Stark consulting his notes on the lectern, hardly paying heed to the group storming from the room.

Monday February 23
12:16pm

There was no doubt that Sean Berman was very nervous about being in the hospital, facing imminent surgery. He knew very little about medicine, and although he wished that he were better informed, he had not bothered to inquire intelligently about his problem and its treatment. He was frightened about medicine and disease. In fact he tended to equate the two rather than think of them as antagonists. Hence the thought of undergoing surgery offended his sensibility; there was no way for him to deal rationally with the idea that someone was going to cut his skin with a knife. The thought made his stomach sink and sweat appear on his forehead. So he tried not to think about it. In psychiatric terms this was called *denial*. He had been reasonably successful until he had come to the hospital the afternoon before his scheduled surgery.

'The name is Berman. Sean Berman.' Berman remembered the admission sequence all too well. What should have been a smooth affair got hopelessly caught in the bureaucratic tangle of the hospital.

'Berman? Are you sure you're to come to the Memorial today?' questioned the well-meaning, overly made-up receptionist, who wore black nail polish.

'Yes, I'm sure,' returned Berman, marvelling at the black nail polish. It made him realize that hospitals were monopolies of sorts. In a competitive business someone would have the sense to keep the receptionist from wearing black nail polish.

'Well, I'm sorry but I don't have a file for you. You'll have to take a seat while I handle these other patients. Then I'll call Admitting and I'll be with you shortly.'

So commenced the first of several snafus which characterized Sean Berman's admission. He sat down and waited. The big hand of the clock worked its way through an entire revolution before he was admitted.

'May I have your X-ray request, please?' asked a young and extremely thin X-ray technician. Berman had waited over forty minutes in X-ray before being called.

'I don't have an X-ray request,' said Berman, glancing through the papers he'd been given.

'You must have one. All admissions have one.'

'But I don't.'

'You must.'

'I tell you I don't.'

Despite the obvious frustration, the ridiculous admission sequence had had one positive effect. It had totally occupied Berman's consciousness, and he did not dwell upon his impending surgery. But once in his room, hearing the random moans through partially closed hospital doors, Sean Berman was forced to confront his imminent experience. Even more difficult to dismiss were the people with bandages or even tubes that issued forth mysteriously from areas of the human body without natural orifices. Once in the hospital environment, *denial* was no longer an effective means of psychological defence.

Berman then tried another tactic; he switched to what the psychiatrists call *reaction formation*. He let himself think about his upcoming operation to the point where he seemingly made light of the idea.

'I'm one of the dieticians and I'd like to discuss your meal selection,' said an overweight woman with a clipboard who entered Berman's room after a sharp knock. 'You are here to have surgery, I presume.'

'Surgery?' Berman smiled. 'Yeah, I have it about once a year. It's a hobby.'

The dietician, the lab technician, anyone who would listen, became a victim of Berman's offhand comment about his scheduled operation.

To an extent this method of defence was successful, at least until the actual morning of the operation. Berman had been awakened at six-thirty by the sound of some jangling cart in the corridor. Try as he might, he had been unable to fall back to sleep. Reading had been impossible. The time had dragged horribly, slowly yet inexorably toward 11, when his surgery was scheduled. His stomach had growled from its emptiness.

At 11:05 the door to his room burst open. Berman's pulse fluttered. It was one of the harried nurses.

'Mr Berman, there's going to be a delay.'

'A delay? How long?' Berman forced himself to be civil. The agony of anticipation was taking its toll.

'Can't say. Thirty minutes, an hour.' The nurse shrugged.

'But why? I'm starved.' Berman really wasn't hungry; he was too nervous.

'The OR's backed up. I'll be back later to give you your pre-op meds. Just relax.' The nurse departed. Berman's mouth was open, ready for another question, a hundred questions. Relax? Fat chance. In fact, until Susan's appearance, Sean

Berman had spent the entire morning in an uninterrupted cold sweat, dreading the passage of each moment, yet at the same time wishing time would hurry by. Several times he had felt a tinge of embarrassment at the depth of his anxiety, and he wondered if his feelings were relative to the seriousness of the anticipated surgery. If that were the case, he felt he could never undergo a truly serious operation. Berman was worried about feeling pain, worried that his leg might not be ninety-eight per cent better, as his doctor had promised, worried about the cast he would have to wear on his leg for several weeks after the operation. He wasn't worried about the anaesthesia. If anything, he worried that they might not put him to sleep. He did not want local anaesthesia; he wanted to be out cold.

Berman did not worry about possible complications, nor did he worry about his mortality. He was too young and healthy for that. If he had, he would have thought twice about having the operation. It had always been one of Berman's faults, to miss the forest for the trees. Once he had designed an architecturally award-winning building only to have it turned down by the local city council just because it did not fit into the surroundings. Fortunately Berman was unaware of the stricken Nancy Greenly in the ICU.

For Berman, Susan Wheeler had been a star on a cloudy night. In his overly sensitized and anxiety-ridden state, she had seemed like an apparition coming to help him pass the time, to ease his mind. But she had done more. For the first few moments of the morning Berman had been able to think of something besides his knee and the knife. He had given every ounce of concentration to Susan's comments and all too brief self-revelation. Whether it was Susan's attractiveness or her obvious wit or just Berman's own emotional vulnerability, he had been charmed and delighted and felt immeasurably more comfortable on his ride in the elevator down to the operating room. He also considered that the shot Ms Sterns had given him might have contributed, because he began to get a little light-headed and images began to be slightly discontinuous.

'Guess you see a lot of people on their way to surgery,' said Berman to the orderly, as the elevator approached floor two.

Berman was on his back, his hands beneath his head.

'Yup,' said the orderly, uninterested, cleaning under his nails.

'Have you ever had surgery here?' asked Berman, enjoying a sensation of calmness and detachment spreading through his limbs.

'Nope. I'd never have an operation here,' said the orderly, looking up at the floor indicator as the car eased to a stop on two.

'Why not?' asked Berman.

'I've seen too much, I guess,' said the orderly, pushing Berman into the hall.

By the time his gurney was parked in the patient holding area, Berman was happily inebriated. The shot he had received on orders from the anaesthesiologist, a Dr Norman Goodman, was 1 cc of Innovar, a relatively new combination of extremely potent agents. Berman tried to talk to the woman next to him in the patient holding area, but his tongue seemed to have become unresponsive, and he laughed at his own ineffectual efforts. He tried to grab a nurse who walked by, but he missed, and he laughed. Time ceased to be a concern and Berman's brain no longer recorded what happened.

Down in the OR things were progressing well. Penny O'Rilley was already scrubbed and gowned and had brought in the steaming tray of instruments to put out on the Mayo stand. Mary Abruzzi, the circulating nurse, had located one of the pneumatic tourniquets and had carried it into the room.

'One more to go, Dr Goodman,' said Mary, activating the foot pedal to raise the operating table to gurney height.

'How right you are,' said Dr Goodman cheerfully. He let I.V. fluid run through the tube onto the floor to remove the bubbles. 'This should be a rapid case. Dr Spallek is one of the fastest surgeons I know and the patient is a healthy young man. I bet we're out of here by one.'

Doctor Norman Goodman had been on the staff at the Memorial for eight years and held a joint appointment at the medical school. He had a lab on the fourth floor of the Hilman Building with a large population of monkeys. His interests involved developing newer concepts of anaesthesia by selectively controlling various brain areas. He felt that eventually drugs were going to be specific enough so that just the reticular formation itself would be altered, thereby reducing the amount of drugs necessary to control anaesthesia. In fact, only a few weeks earlier he and his laboratory assistant, Dr Clark Nelson, had stumbled onto a butyrophenone derivative which had slowed the electrical activity only in the reticular formation of a monkey. With great discipline he had kept himself from becoming overly encouraged at such an early time, especially when the results had been from a single animal. But then the results had become reproducible. So far he had tested eight monkeys and all had responded the same.

Dr Norman Goodman would have preferred to give up all activities and devote twenty-four hours a day to his new discovery. He was eager to advance to more sophisticated experiments with his drug, especially a trial on a human. Dr Nelson, if anything, was even more eager and optimistic. It had been with difficulty that Dr Goodman had talked Dr Nelson out of trying a small subpharmacological dose on himself.

But Dr Goodman knew that true science rested on a foundation of painstaking methodology. One had to proceed slowly, objectively. Premature trials, claims, or disclosure could be disastrous for all concerned. Accordingly Dr Goodman had to rein in his excitement and maintain his normal schedule and commitments unless he was willing to divulge his discovery; and that he was unwilling to do as yet. So on Monday morning he had to 'pass gas,' as they called it in the vernacular ... devote time to clinical anaesthesia.

'Damn,' said Dr Goodman straightening up. 'Mary, I forgot to bring down an endotracheal tube. Would you run back to the anaesthesia room and bring me a number eight.'

'Coming up,' said Mary Abruzzi, disappearing through the OR door. Dr Goodman sorted out the gas line connectors and plugged into the nitrous oxide and oxygen sources on the wall.

Sean Berman was Dr Goodman's fourth and final case for February 23, 1976. Already that day he had smoothly anaesthetized three patients. A two-hundred-and-sixty-seven-pound flatulent female with gallstones had been the only potential problem. Dr Goodman had feared that the enormous bulk of fatty tissue would have absorbed such large quantities of the anaesthetic agent that termination of the anaesthesia would have been very difficult. But that had not proved to be the case. Despite the fact that the case had been prolonged the patient had awakened very quickly and extubation had been carried out almost immediately after the final skin suture had been tied.

The other two cases that morning had been very routine: a vein stripping and a haemorrhoid. The final case for Dr Goodman, Berman, was to be a meniscectomy of the right knee and Dr Goodman expected to be in his lab by 1:15 at the latest. Every Monday morning Dr Goodman thanked his lucky stars that he had had enough foresight to have continued his research proclivities. He found clinical anaesthesia a bore; it was too easy, too routine, and frightfully dull.

The only way he kept his sanity those Monday mornings, he'd tell his neighbour, was to vary his technique to provide food for his brain, to force him to think rather than just sit there and daydream. If there were no contraindications, he liked balanced anaesthesia the best, meaning he did not have to give the patient some gargantuan dose of any one agent, but rather he balanced the needs by a number of different agents. Neurolept anaesthesia was his favourite because in certain respects it was a crude precursor to the types of anaesthetic agents he was looking for.

Mary Abruzzi returned with the endotracheal tube.

'Mary, you're a doll,' said Dr Goodman, checking off his preparations. 'I think we're ready. How about bringing the patient down?'

'My pleasure. I'm not going to get lunch until we finish this case.' Mary Abruzzi left for the second time.

Since Berman did not offer any contraindications, Goodman decided to use neurolept-anaesthesia. He knew Spallek didn't care. Most orthopaedic surgeons didn't care. 'Just get them down enough so I can put on the Goddamn tourniquet, that's all I care about' was the usual orthopaedic response to the query about which anaesthetic agent they might prefer.

Neurolept anaesthesia was a balanced technique. The patient was given a potent neurolept, or tranquillizing agent, and a potent analgesic, or painkiller. Both agents provided easily arousable sleep as a side effect. Dr Goodman liked droperidol and fentanyl best of the agents cleared for use. After they were given, the patient was put to sleep with Pentothal and maintained asleep on nitrous oxide. Curare was used to paralyse the skeletal muscles for entubation and surgical relaxation. During the case aliquots of the neurlept and analgesic agents were used as needed to maintain the proper depth of anaesthesia. The patient had to be watched very closely through all this, and Dr Goodman liked that. For him the time passed more quickly when he was busy.

The OR door was opened by one of the orderlies helping to guide Berman's gurney into room no.8 Mary Abruzzi was pushing.

'Here's your baby, Dr Goodman. He's sound asleep,' said Mary Abruzzi.

They put down the arm rails.

'OK, Mr Berman. Time to move over onto the table.' Mary Abruzzi gently shook Berman's shoulder. He opened his eyelids about halfway. 'You have to help us, Mr Berman.'

With some difficulty they got Berman over onto the table. Smacking his lips, turning on his side, and drawing up the sheet around his neck, Berman gave the impression that he thought he was home in his own bed.

'OK, Rip Van Winkle, on your back.' Mary Abruzzi coaxed Berman onto his back and secured his right arm to his side. Berman slept, apparently unaware of the activity about him. The cuff of the pneumatic tourniquet was placed about his right thigh and tested. The heel of his right foot was placed in a sling and hung from a stainless steel rod at the foot of the operating table, lifting the entire right leg. Ted Colbert, the assisting resident, began the prep by scrubbing the right knee with pHisoHex.

Dr Goodman went right to work. The time was 12:20. Blood pressure was 110/75; pulse was seventy-two and regular. He started an I.V. with deftness which belied the difficulties of handling a large-bore intravenous catheter. The whole process from skin puncture to tape took less than sixty seconds.

Mary Abruzzi attached the cardiac monitor leads, and the room echoed with the high-pitched but low-amplitude beeps.

With the anaesthesia machine rigged and ready, Dr Goodman attached a syringe to the I.V. line.

'OK, Mr Berman, I want you to relax now,' kidded Dr Goodman, smiling at Mary Abruzzi.

'If he relaxes any more, he's going to pour off the table,' laughed Mary.

Dr Goodman injected intravenously a 6 cc bolus of Innovar, the same droperidol and fentanyl combination that had been used as the pre-op medication. Then he tested the lid reflex and noted that Berman had already achieved a deep level of sleep. Consequently Dr Goodman decided that the Pentothal was not needed. Instead he began the nitrous oxide/oxygen mixture by holding the black rubber mask over Berman's face. Blood pressure was 105/75; pulse was sixty-two and regular. Dr Goodman injected 0.40 mg of d-tubocurarine, the drug which represents a debt modern society owes to the Amazon peoples. There were a few muscle twitches in Berman's body, then relaxation followed; breathing stopped. The entubation was rapid and Dr Goodman inflated Berman's lungs with the ventilating bag while he listened to each side of the chest with his stethoscope. Both sides aerated evenly and fully.

Once the pneumatic tourniquet was cajoled into functioning, Dr Spallek breezed into the room, and the case went rapidly. Dr Spallek was into the joint in one dramatic slice.

'Voilà,' he said, holding the scalpel in the air and tilting his head to admire his handiwork. 'And now for the Michelangelo touch.'

Penny O'Rilley's eyes rolled up inside of her head in response to Dr Spallek's theatrics. She handed him the meniscus knife with a trace of a smile on her lips.

'Anoint my blade,' said Dr Spallek holding the knife out

for the resident to squirt irrigation fluid over its tip.

The knife was then inserted into the joint and for a few moments Dr Spallek rooted around blindly, his face upturned toward the ceiling. He was cutting by feel alone. There was a faint grinding sound, then a snap.

'OK,' said Dr Spallek tightening his teeth, 'here comes the culprit.'

Out came the damaged cartilage. 'Now I want everyone to see this. See this little tear on the inside edge. That's what's been causing this chap's problems.'

Dr Colbert looked from the specimen to Penny O'Rilley. They both nodded approval while both secretly wondered if the little tear hadn't been caused by the blind cutting with the meniscus knife.

Dr Spallek stepped back from the table, pleased with himself. He snapped off his gloves. 'Dr Colbert, why don't you close up. 4 - 0 chromatic, 5 - 0 plain, then 6 - 0 silk for the skin. I'll be in the lounge.' Then he was gone.

Dr Colbert dabbed ineffectually at the wound for a few moments.

'How much longer do you estimate?' questioned Dr Goodman over the ether screen.

Dr Colbert looked up. 'Fifteen or twenty minutes, I guess.' He palmed a pair of toothed forceps and took the first suture from Penny O'Rilley. He took a bite with the suture and Berman moved. At the same time Dr Goodman felt a tenseness in the ventilating bag when he tried to breathe Berman. He sensed that Berman was trying to breathe on his own. Concurrently the blood pressure rose to 110/80.

'He must be a little light,' said Dr Colbert, trying to sort out the layers of tissue in the wound.

'I'll give him a bit more of this love potion,' said Dr Goodman. He injected another full cc of Innovar, since the syringe with the Innovar was still connected to the I.V. line. Later he admitted that this could have been a mistake. He should have used only the analgesic, fentanyl. The blood pressure responded rapidly and fell as Berman's anaesthesia deepened again. The blood pressure levelled off at 90/60. The pulse increased to 80 per minute, then fell to a comfortable 72 per minute.

'He's OK now,' said Dr Goodman.

'Good. OK, Penny, feed me those chromic sutures and I'll get this point closed,' said Colbert.

The resident made fine headway, closing the joint capsule and then the subcutaneous tissues. There was no conversation. Mary Abruzzi sat down in the corner and turned on a small transistor radio. Very faint music trickled through the room. Dr Goodman started the final notations on the anaesthesia record.

'Skin sutures,' said Dr Colbert, straightening up from his crouch over the knee.

There was the familiar slapping sound as the needle holder was thrust into his open hand. Mary Abruzzi changed her worn-out gum for a new stick by lifting the lower part of her mask.

At first it was only one premature ventricular contraction followed by a compensatory pause. Dr Goodman's eyes looked up at the monitor. The resident asked for more suture. Dr Goodman increased the oxygen flow to wash out the nitrous oxide. Then there were two more abnormal ectopic heartbeats and the heart rate increased to about 90 per minute. The change in the audible rhythm caught the attention of the scrub nurse, who looked at Dr Goodman. Satisfied that he was aware, she went back to supplying the resident with skin sutures, slapping a loaded needle holder in his hand every time he reached up.

Dr Goodman stopped the oxygen, thinking that maybe the myocardium or heart muscle was particularly sensitive to the high oxygen levels that were obviously in the blood. Later he admitted that this might have been a mistake as well. He began to use compressed air for aerating Berman's lungs. Berman was still not breathing on his own.

In quick succession there were several back-to-back runs of the strange premature-type heartbeats, which made Dr Goodman's own heart jump in his chest from fright. He knew all too well that such runs of premature ventricular contractions often were the immediate harbinger of cardiac arrest. Dr Goodman's hands visibly trembled as he inflated the blood pressure cuff.

Blood pressure was 80/55; it had fallen for no apparent reason. Dr Goodman looked up at the monitor as the premature beats began to increase in frequency. The beeping sound became faster and faster, screaming its urgent information into Dr Goodman's brain. His eyes swept over the anaesthesia machine, the carbon dioxide canister. His mind raced for an answer. He could feel his bowels loosen and he had to clamp down voluntarily with the muscles of his anus. Terror spread through him. Something was wrong. The premature beats were increasing to the point that normal beats were being crowded out as the electronic blip on the monitor began to trace a senseless pattern.

'What the hell's going on?' yelled Dr Colbert, looking up from his suturing job.

Dr Goodman didn't answer. His trembling hands searched for a syringe. 'Lidocaine,' he yelled to the circulating nurse. He tried to pull the plastic cap from the end of the needle but it would not come off. 'Christ,' he yelled and flung the syringe against the wall in utter frustration. He tore the cellophane cover from another syringe and managed to get the cap off the needle. Mary Abruzzi tried to hold the lidocaine bottle for him but his trembling hands made it impossible. He snatched the bottle from her and thrust in the needle.

'Holy shit, this guy's going to arrest,' said Dr Colbert in disbelief. He was staring at the monitor. The needle holder was still in his right hand; a pair of fine-toothed forceps were in his left hand.

Dr Goodman filled the syringe with the lidocaine, dropping the bottle in the process so that it shattered on the tile floor. Struggling with his trembling he tried to insert the needle into the I.V. line and succeeded only in jabbing his own index finger, bringing a drop of blood. Glen Campbell whined in the background from the transistor.

Before Dr Goodman could get the lidocaine into the I.V. line, the monitor abruptly returned to its steady, pre-crisis rhythm. In utter disbelief Dr Goodman looked at the electronic blip moving through its familiar and normal pattern. Then he grasped the ventilating bag and inflated Berman's lungs. Blood pressure read 100/60 and the pulse slowed evenly to about seventy per minute. Perspiration coalesced on Dr Goodman's forehead and dripped off the bridge of his nose onto the anaesthesia record. His own heart rate was over one hundred per minute. Dr Goodman decided that clinical anaesthesia was not always dull.

'What in God's name was all that about?' asked Dr Colbert.

'I haven't the slightest idea,' said Dr Goodman. 'But finish up. I want to wake this guy up.'

'Maybe it's something wrong with the monitor,' said Mary Abruzzi, trying to be optimistic.

The resident finished the skin sutures. For a few minutes Dr Goodman had them hold off deflating the tourniquet. When they did, the heart rate increased slightly but then returned to normal.

The resident started to cast Berman's leg. Dr Goodman continued to aerate the patient while he kept one eye on the monitor. The rate stayed normal. Dr Goodman tried to record the events on the anaesthesia record in between compressions of the ventilating bag. When the cast was completed, Dr Goodman waited to see if Berman would breathe on his own. There was no breathing effort at all, and Dr Goodman took over again. He looked at the clock. It was 12:45. He wondered if he should give an antagonist for the fentanyl to try to curtail the respiratory depressant effect it was apparently causing. At the same time he wanted to keep the medication that he gave to Berman to a minimum. His own clammy skin reminded him vividly that Berman was no routine case.

Dr Goodman wondered if Berman was getting light despite the fact that he was not breathing. He decided to test the lid reflex to find out. There was no response. Instead of stroking the lid, Dr Goodman lifted the lid and he noted something very strange. Usually the fentanyl, like other strong narcotics, produced very small pupils. Berman's pupils were enormous. The black area almost filled the clear cornea. Dr Goodman reached for a penlight and directed the beam into Berman's eye. A ruby red reflex flashed back but the pupil did not budge.

In total disbelief, Dr Goodman did it again, then again. He did it once more before his own eyes looked up at nothing. Dr Goodman said two words out loud ... 'Good God!'

Monday February 23
12:34pm

For Susan Wheeler and the other four medical students, the charge down the hall to the elevator fitted perfectly their pre-conceptions of the excitement of clinical medicine. There was something horribly dramatic about the headlong rush. Startled patients sitting there casually leafing through old *New Yorker* magazines while waiting to see their doctors reacted to the stampeding group by drawing their legs and feet more closely to their chairs. They stared at the running figures who clutched at pens, penlights, stethoscopes, and other paraphernalia to keep them from flying from their pockets.

As the group came abreast of, then passed, each patient, the patient's head swung around to watch the group recede down the corridor. Each assumed that a group of doctors had been called on an emergency, and it was reassuring for the patients to see how earnestly the doctors responded; the Memorial was a great hospital.

At the elevator there was momentary confusion and delay. Bellows repeatedly pushed the 'down' button as if manhandling the plastic object would bring the elevator more quickly. The floor indicator above each elevator door suggested that the elevators were taking their own sweet time, slowly rising from floor to floor, obviously discharging and taking on passengers in the usual slow motion. For such emergencies there was a phone next to the elevators. Bellows snatched it off its cradle and dialled the operator. But the operator didn't answer. It usually took the operators at the Memorial about five minutes to answer a house phone.

'Fucking elevators,' said Bellows striking the button for the tenth time. His eyes darted from the exit sign over the stairwell back to the floor indicator above the elevator. 'The stairs,' said Bellows with decision.

In rapid succession the group entered the stairwell and began the long twisting plunge from the tenth floor to the second floor. The journey seemed interminable. Taking two or three steps at a time, constantly turning to the left, the group began to spread out a bit. They passed the sixth floor, then the fifth. At the fourth floor the whole group slowed to a cautious walk in the dark because of the missing bulb. Then down again at the previous pace.

Fairweather began to slow and Susan passed him on the inside.

'I don't know what the hell we are running for,' panted Fairweather as Susan passed.

Susan managed to brush her hair from her face, hooking it behind her right ear. 'As long as Bellows *et al.* are in the lead, I don't mind running. I want to see what goes on but I don't want to be the first one on the scene.'

Fairweather assumed a comfortable walk and was quickly left behind. Susan was nearing the third floor landing when she heard Bellows pound on the locked door on two. He yelled at the top of his lungs for someone to open the door, and his voice carried up the stairwell, reverberating strangely, taking on a warbling quality. As Susan rounded the final landing, the door on two was opened. Niles kept the door open for her and she entered the hall. The constant turning to the left in the stairwell made Susan feel a bit dizzy, but she did not stop. Following the others, she ran directly into the ICU.

In sharp contrast to the former dimness of the room, it was now brightly illuminated with stark fluorescent light that provided a shimmering aura to objects within the room. The white vinyl floor added to this effect. In the corner the three ICU nurses were engaged in giving closed chest massage to Nancy Greenly. Bellows, Cartwright, Reid, and the medical students crowded around the bed.

'Hold up,' said Bellows watching the cardiac monitor. The nurse giving the closed chest massage straightened up from her efforts. She was kneeling on the edge of the bed on the right side of Nancy Greenly. The monitor pattern was wildly erratic.

'She's been fibrillating for four minutes,' said Shergood watching the monitor. 'We started the massage within ten seconds.'

Bellows moved rapidly over to the right of Nancy Greenly and while watching the monitor, he thumped the patient's sternum with his fist. Susan winced at the dull sound of the blow. The monitor's pattern did not alter. Bellows began closed chest massage.

'Cartwright, feel for a pulse in the groin,' said Bellows without taking his eyes from the monitor. 'Charge the defibrillator to 400 joules.' The last command was directed to anyone. One of the ICU nurses carried it out.

Susan and the other students backed up against the wall, acutely aware that they were mere observers, and although they wanted to, they could not help in the frantic activity occurring before them.

'You've got a good pulse going,' said Cartwright with his hand pressed in Nancy Greenly's groin.

'Was there any warning for this or did it drop out of the blue?' said Bellows with some difficulty between compressions of the chest. He nodded his head toward the monitor.

'Very little warning,' answered Shergood. 'She began to have a suggestion of increased excitability of her heart by having a few premature ventricular beats and a suggestion of a mild atrioventricular conduction defect which we picked up on the recorder.' Shergood held up a strip of EKG paper for Bellows to see. 'Then she had a sudden run of extra systoles, and wham ... fibrillation.'

'What has she got so far?' asked Bellows.

'Nothing,' said Shergood.

'OK,' said Bellows. 'Push an amp of bicarbonate and draw up

10 cc of a 1 : 1000 epinephrine in a syringe with a cardiac needle.'

One of the ICU nurses injected the bicarbonate; another prepared the epinephrine.

'Someone draw blood for stat electrolytes and calcium,' said Bellows, letting Reid take over the massage. Bellows felt the femoral pulse under Cartwright's hand and was satisfied.

'From what Billings said at the complication conference on this case, the same thing is happening here that happened in the OR to cause all her troubles in the first place,' said Bellows thoughtfully. He took the 10 cc syringe with the epinephrine from the nurse, holding it up to let the last traces of air escape.

'Not quite,' said Reid between compressions. 'She never fibrillated in the OR.'

'She didn't fibrillate but she did have premature ventricular contractions. Obviously she had an excitable heart then as now. 'All right, hold up!' Bellows moved along Nancy Greenly's left side, brandishing the syringe with the cardiac needle. Reid straightened up from his resuscitative efforts so that Bellows could feel along Nancy Greenly's sternum for the landmark called the angle of Louis. Using that as a guide, he located the fourth interspace between the ribs.

The needle on Bellows's syringe was three and a half inches long and a sparkle of reflected light danced off its stainless steel shaft. Decisively Bellows pushed it into the girl's chest, all the way to the hilt. When the plunger was pulled back, dark red blood swirled up into the clear epinephrine solution.

'Right on,' said Bellows as he rapidly injected the epinephrine directly into the heart.

Susan's skin crawled with the vivid thought of the long needle tearing its way down into Nancy Greenly's chest and spearing the quivering mass of cardiac muscle. Susan could almost feel the coldness of the needle in her own heart.

'Go to it,' said Bellows to Reid as he stepped back from the bed. Reid immediately recommenced his cardiac massage. Cartwright nodded, indicating that there was a strong femoral pulse. 'Stark is going to be pissed when he hears about this,' continued Bellows, eyeing the monitor, 'especially right after his lecture on vigilance in these cases. Shit, I really don't deserve this kind of headache. If she croaks, my ass is grass.'

Susan had trouble comprehending that Bellows had actually said what he did. Once again she was faced with the fact that Bellows and probably the entire crew were not thinking of Nancy Greenly as a person. The patient seemed more like the part of a complicated game, like the relationship between the football and the teams at play. The football was important only as an object to advance the position and advantage of one of the teams. Nancy Greenly had become a technical challenge, a game to be played. The final, ultimate result had become less important than the day-to-day plays and moves and ripostes.

Susan felt a strong surge of ambivalence toward clinical medicine. Her nascent female sensitivities seemed to be a handicap within the mechanistic and tactically orientated atmosphere. She silently longed for the old familiar lecture hall and its abstractions. Reality was too bitter, too cold, too detached.

And yet there was something fascinating and academically satisfying seeing the application of the basic scientific knowledge she had acquired. From physiology experiments with animal hearts, she comprehended the disorganization that the fibrillating heart within Nancy Greenly represented. If only the whole mass could be depolarized to stop all electrical activity, then the intrinsic rhythm could possibly begin again.

Susan strained to watch as Bellows placed the defibrillating paddles on Nancy Greenly's exposed chest. One of the paddles was held directly over the sternum, the other was placed against the left lateral chest, slightly distorting the left breast with its pale nipple.

'Everyone away from the bed!' ordered Bellows. His right thumb made contact and a powerful electric charge spread through Nancy Greenly's chest, arcing from one paddle to the other. Her body jerked upward; her arms flopped across her chest with her hands twisting inward. The electronic blip disappeared from the screen, then it returned. It traced a relatively normal pattern.

'She's got a good pulse,' said Cartwright.

Reid held up on the external massage. The rate held steady for several minutes. Then a premature ventricular contraction appeared. The rate was again steady for several minutes followed by three premature ventricular contractions in a row.

'V tach,' said Shergood confidently. 'The heart is still very easily excitable. There has to be something very basic wrong here.'

'If you know what it is, don't keep it from us,' said Bellows. 'Meanwhile let's have some lidocaine, 50 cc.'

One of the nurses drew up the lidocaine and handed it to Bellows. Bellows injected it into the I.V. line. Susan moved so that she could see the monitor screen more clearly.

Despite the lidocaine, the rhythm rapidly deteriorated to senseless fibrillation once more. Bellows swore, Reid started massage, and the nurse recharged the defibrillator.

'What the hell is going on here?' queried Bellows, motioning for another amp of bicarbonate to be given. He didn't expect an answer; he was posing a purely rhetorical question.

Another dose of epinephrine given I.V., followed by a second defibrillation attempt, returned the rate to a semblance of normal. But premature contractions returned, despite additional lidocaine.

'This has to be the same problem that they had in the OR,' said Bellows, watching the premature contractions increase in frequency until the rhythm dissolved into fibrillation. 'You're up again, Reid ole boy. Let's go, team.'

By 1:15 Nancy Greenly had been defibrillated twenty-one times. After each shock a relatively normal rhythm would return only to disintegrate into fibrillation after a short duration. At 1:16 the ICU phone rang. It was answered by the ward clerk, who took the information. It was the lab calling with the stat electrolyte values. Everything was normal except the potassium level. It was very low, only 2.8 milliequivalents per litre.

The ward clerk handed the results to one of the nurses, who showed them to Bellows.

'My God! 2.8. How in Christ's name did that happen? At

least we have an answer. OK, let's get some potassium in her. Put 80 milliequivalents into that I.V. bottle and speed it up to 200 cc per hour.'

Nancy Greenly responded to this command by immediately lapsing back into fibrillation for the twenty-second time. Reid started compression while Bellows readied the paddles. The potassium was added to the I.V.

Susan was totally absorbed by the whole resuscitation procedure. In fact, her concentration had been so great that she had almost missed hearing her name crackle out of the page system speaker near the main desk. The page system had been intermittently active throughout the entire cardiac arrest procedure by calling out the names of physicians followed by an extension number. But the sound had blended and merged with the general background noise, and Susan had been oblivious to it. At least until her own name floated out into the room along with the extension 381.

Somewhat reluctantly Susan left her place by the wall and used the phone at the main desk to answer her page.

381 turned out to be the extension of the recovery room and Susan was quite surprised to be paged from there. She gave her name as Susan Wheeler, not Dr Susan Wheeler, and said that she had been paged. The clerk told her to hold the line. He returned immediately.

'There's an arterial blood gas to be drawn on a patient up here.'

'Blood gas?'

'Right. Oxygen, carbon dioxide, and acid levels. And we need it stat.'

'How did you get my name?' asked Susan, twisting the cord on the phone. She hoped it was by some sort of mistake that she had been called.

'I just do as I'm told. Your name is on the chart. Remember it's stat.' The line went dead. The clerk had hung up before Susan could respond again. Actually she had little else to say. She replaced the receiver and walked back to Nancy Greenly's bedside. Bellows was repositioning the paddles again. The shock swept through the patient's body, the arms ineffectually flopping across the chest. It seemed both dramatic and pitiful at the same time. The monitor showed a normal rhythm.

'She's got a good pulse,' said Cartwright at the groin.

'I think she's holding her sinus rhythm better now that some of the potassium has gotten into her system,' said Bellows, his eyes glued to the monitor screen.

'Dr Bellows,' said Susan during the lull in the action. 'I got a call to draw an arterial blood gas on a patient in the recovery room.'

'Enjoy yourself,' said Bellows, distracted. He turned to Shergood. 'Where in heaven's name are those medical residents? God, when you need them they lie low. But just try to take someone to surgery and they hang around like a group of vultures, cancelling your case because of a borderline serum porcelain.'

Cartwright and Reid forced a laugh for political reasons.

'You don't understand, Dr Bellows,' continued Susan. 'I've never drawn an arterial blood gas. I've never seen one drawn.'

Bellows turned from the monitor to Susan. 'Jesus Christ, as if I don't have enough to worry about. It's just like getting venous blood only you get it out of an artery. What the hell did you learn during the first two years of medical school?'

Susan felt a defensive surge; her face reddened.

'Don't answer that,' added Bellows quickly. 'Cartwright, head over with Susan and ...'

'I've got that thyroidectomy you put me on with Dr Jacobs in five minutes,' interrupted Cartwright, looking at his watch.

'Shit,' said Bellows. 'OK, Dr Wheeler, I'll head over with you and show you how to do an arterial stick but not until things are reasonably quiet here. Things are looking a little better; I've got to admit that.' Bellows turned to Reid. 'Send up another blood sample for a repeat potassium. Let's see how we are doing. Maybe we are out of the woods.'

While she was waiting, Susan thought about Bellows's last comment. He had used the pronoun *we* rather than saying that Nancy Greenly was out of the woods. It fitted the pattern and she pondered about depersonalization. It also reminded her of Stark. He didn't seem to care for Bellows's pronouns either.

Monday February 23
1:35pm

'Some days are like this,' said Bellows, holding the door open for Susan as they left the ICU. 'Lunch can be considered a luxury. Even a nice ...' Bellows paused as they walked down the corridor. They were both eyeing the floor. Bellows was searching for a word. Then he changed his incompleted sentence. 'On occasion it is even hard to find time to relieve oneself.'

'You meant to say "a nice shit," didn't you?'

Bellows glanced at Susan. She looked up at him with a slight smile. 'You don't have to act differently on my account,' said Susan.

Bellows continued to study her face, which she carefully kept as neutral as possible. They walked in silence past the holding area for surgery.

'As I mentioned before, an arterial stick is just about the same as a venous stick,' said Bellows, changing the subject. He sensed the unnerving effect Susan had on him and he sought to regain the upper hand. 'You isolate the artery, either the brachial, radial, or femoral, it really doesn't matter which, with your middle and index fingers, like this ...' Bellows held up his left hand and extended his middle and index fingers and pretended to palpate an artery in the air. 'Once you have the artery between the fingers, you can feel the pulse. Then simply guide the needle in by feel. The best method is to let arterial pressure fill the syringe. In that way you can avoid air bubbles, which tend to distort the values.'

Bellows backed into the recovery room door, still gesturing the technique of the arterial stick. 'Two important points: you have to use a heparinized syringe to keep the blood from clotting, and you have to keep pressure over the site for five minutes after the stick. The patient can get a frightful haematoma from an arterial stick if the pressure part is forgotten.'

To Susan the recovery room seemed superficially similar to the ICU except that it was brighter, noisier, and more crowded. There were about fifteen to twenty spaces designated for beds. Each space had a complement of equipment built into the wall, including monitors, gas lines, and suction lines. Most of the spaces were occupied by high beds with the side rails pulled up. In each bed was a patient with fresh bandages over some part of his body. Bottles of intravenous fluid were clustered on the tops of poles, like some hideous fruit on leafless trees.

New patients were arriving, others leaving, causing mini-traffic jams of moving beds. Conversation flowed freely from those who worked there and felt at home in the environment. There was even some occasional laughter. But there were also some groans, and a baby was wailing an unheeded lament in a crib by the nurses' station. Some of the beds had groups of doctors and nurses busily engaged in adjusting the hundreds of lines, valves, and tubes. Some of the doctors were dressed in wrinkled scrub suits, stained with all sorts of secretions, although blood was the most prevalent. Others wore long white coats starched painfully stiff. It was a busy place, a crossroads filled with patients, charts, motion, and talk.

Bellows was anxious to dispense with the task ahead and approached the main desk, which was strategically placed in the centre of the large room. In response to his inquiry he was handed a tray with a heparinized syringe and directed to one of the recovery room beds to the left, opposite the door through which they had entered.

'Why don't I go ahead and do this one, and you do the next one,' said Bellows. Susan nodded in agreement as they approached the bed. They could not see the patient because of the people standing in the way. There were several nurses on the left, two doctors in scrub suits at the foot, and a tall black doctor in a long white coat on the right. As Bellows and Susan drew near, it was obvious that the latter individual had been talking although at that moment he was adjusting the pressure setting on the respirator. Susan sensed the emotional climate instantly. Both of the doctors in scrub suits were obviously intensely concerned. The smaller individual, Dr Goodman, was visibly shaking. The other, Dr Spallek, had his mouth angrily set with clenched teeth, audibly breathing through his nostrils as if he were about to attack the next person in his path.

'There's got to be some sort of an explanation,' snarled the infuriated Spallek. He took hold of his face mask still tied around his neck and yanked it free, snapping the cord. He flung it to the floor. 'That doesn't seem too much to ask,' he hissed before abruptly turning away and leaving. He collided with Bellows, who miraculously managed to juggle the small tray he was carrying without dropping any of its contents. There were no words of apology from Dr Spallek. He crossed the recovery room and blasted open the doors to the hall.

Bellows went directly to the left of the bed and put down the tray. Susan advanced warily, watching the expressions of the remaining people. The black doctor straightened up and his dark eyes followed the exit of the irate Dr Spallek. Susan was immediately taken by the imposing image of the man. His tag gave his name: Dr Robert Harris. He was tall, well over six feet, his dark hair textured into a restrained Afro. His blemishless tawny skin shone, and his face reflected a curious combination of culture and restrained violence. His movements were calm, almost to the point of deliberate slowness. As his eyes returned from watching Spallek's exit they passed over Susan's face before returning to the respirator at the side of the bed. If he had noticed Susan, he gave no hint whatsoever.

'What did you use for the pre-op, Norman?' asked Harris, pronouncing each word carefully. He had a cultured Texan accent – if that were possible.

'Innovar,' said Goodman. The pitch of his voice was abnormally high and cracking under the strain.

Susan moved up to the foot of the bed where Spallek had been standing. She studied the crumpled man next to her, Dr Goodman. He looked pale and his hair was matted with perspiration to his forehead. He had a prominent nose, which Susan saw in perfect profile. His deep-set eyes were riveted to the patient. He did not blink.

Susan looked down at the patient, her eyes wandering to the wrist which Bellows was prepping for the arterial stick. With an exaggerated double-take, her eyes shot back to the face of the patient as recognition occurred. It was Berman!

In contrast to the tanned visage Susan recalled from their meeting in room 503 only ninety minutes ago, Berman's face was a dusky grey colour. The skin was pulled taut over his cheekbones. An endotracheal tube protruded from the left side of his mouth and some dried secretion was crusted along his lower lip. His eyes were closed but not completely. His right leg was in a huge plaster cast.

'Is he all right?' blurted Susan looking from Harris to Goodman. 'What happened?' Susan spoke from emotion, without thinking; she sensed something was wrong and she reacted impulsively. Bellows was surprised at her sudden questions and looked up from his work, holding the syringe in his right hand. Harris straightened up slowly and turned toward Susan. Goodman's eyes did not stray.

'Everything is absolutely perfect,' said Harris with a pronunciation suggesting an Oxford sojourn some time in his past. 'Blood pressure, pulse, temperature all perfectly normal. However, he has apparently enjoyed his anaesthetic slumber so much that he has decided not to wake up.'

'Not another one,' said Bellows, switching his attention to Harris and concerned that he was going to be saddled with another problem like Greenly. 'What does the EEG look like?'

'You'll be the first to know,' said Harris with a trace of sarcasm. 'It's been ordered.'

Comprehension for Susan was delayed by emotion, for hope

was momentarily stronger than reason. But eventually it flooded over her.

'EEG?' asked Susan apprehensively. 'You mean he's like the patient down in the ICU?' Her eyes darted back and forth between Berman and Harris, then to Bellows.

'Which patient is that?' asked Harris, picking up the anaesthesia record.

'The D&C mishap,' said Bellows. 'You remember, about eight days ago, the twenty-three-year-old girl.'

'Well I hope not,' said Harris, 'but it's beginning to look that way.'

'What was the anaesthesia?' asked Bellows lifting Berman's right eyelid and glancing down into the widely dilated pupil.

'Neurolept anaesthesia with nitrous,' said Harris. 'The girl's was halothane. If the problem is the same clinically, it wasn't the anaesthetic agent.' Harris looked up from the anaesthesia record toward Goodman. 'Why did you give this extra cc of Innovar toward the end of the case, Norman?'

Dr Goodman did not respond immediately. Dr Harris called his name again.

'The patient seemed to be getting too light,' said Goodman, suddenly breaking his trance.

'But why Innovar so late in the case? Wouldn't fentanyl alone have been more prudent?'

'Probably. I should have used the fentanyl alone. The Innovar was just handy and I knew that I'd only use an additional cc.'

'Can't something be done?' asked Susan with a hint of desperation. Images of Nancy Greenly streamed back with bits and pieces of the recent conversation with Berman. She could distinctly remember his vitality, which was in sharp contrast to the waxy, lifeless-appearing figure before her.

'It's been done, whatever it was,' said Harris with finality, returning the anaesthesia record to Goodman. 'All we can do now is watch and see what kind of cerebal function returns, if any. The pupils are widely dilated and they do not react to light. That is not a good sign, to say the least. It probably means that there was extensive brain death.'

Susan experienced a sickening feeling rise up within herself. She shuddered and the feeling passed but she felt light-headed. Above all, she felt helplessly desperate.

'This is too much,' said Susan suddenly and with obvious emotion. Her voice quivered. 'A normal healthy man with a minor peripheral problem ends up like a ... like a vegetable. My God, this can't go on. Two young people within just a couple of weeks. I mean, it's an unacceptable risk. Why doesn't the Chief of Anaesthesia close the department? Something's got to be wrong. It's absurd to allow ...'

Robert Harris's eyes began to narrow as Susan began her tirade. Then he interrupted her with an obvious edge to his voice. Bellows's mouth had dropped open in total dismay.

'I happen to be the Chief of Anaesthesia, young lady. And who, may I ask, are you?'

Susan started to speak, but Bellows cut in nervously. 'This is Susan Wheeler, Dr Harris, a third-year medical student who is rotating on surgery, and, ah ... we just wanted to get this blood gas drawn here, then we'll be off.' Bellows recommenced his prep on Berman's right wrist, stroking rapidly with the Betadine sponge.

'Miss Wheeler,' continued Harris in a condescending tone, 'your emotionalism is out of place and frankly will not serve constructive purposes. What one needs in these cases is to establish a causal factor. I've just mentioned to Dr Bellows that the anaesthetic agent was different in these two cases. The anaesthetic care was unimpeachable save for a few minor debatable points. In short, both these cases were obviously unavoidable idiosyncratic reactions to the combination of anaesthesia and surgery. One needs to try to determine from these people if there is a way in order to forecast this kind of disastrous sequelae. To condemn anaesthesia across the board and deprive the populace of needed surgery would be far worse than to accept a certain minimal risk involved in anaesthesia. What ...'

'Two cases in eight days is hardly a minimal risk,' interrupted Susan contentiously.

Bellows tried to catch Susan's eye to get her to break off with

Harris, but Susan was staring directly at Harris, converting her emotionalism to defiance.

'How many such cases have there been in the last year?' asked Susan.

Harris's eyes scanned Susan's face for several seconds before he responded. 'I suddenly find this conversation somewhat akin to being cross-examined, and in that sense intolerable and unnecessary.' Without waiting for a response, Harris walked past Susan toward the recovery room door.

Susan turned to face him. Bellows reached for her right arm to try and shut her up. Susan fended him off. She called after Harris, 'Without wishing to sound impertinent, it does seem to me that some questions need to be asked by someone, and something done.'

Harris stopped abruptly about ten feet from Susan and turned very slowly. Bellows shut his eyes tightly, as if he expected to receive a blow to the head.

'And I suppose that someone should be a medical student! For your information, in case you are planning to be our Socratic gadfly, there have been six cases prior to this present problem in the last few years. Now if I may have your permission, I will get back to work.'

Harris turned again and started for the door.

'I suppose *your* emotionalism serves constructive purposes,' called Susan. Bellows supported himself by leaning onto the bed. Harris stopped for the second time, but he did not turn around. Then he continued, and he too blasted open the door to the hall.

Bellows put his left hand up to his forehead. 'Holy fuck, Susan, what are you trying to do, commit medical suicide?' Bellows reached out and turned Susan around to face him. 'That was Robert Harris, Chief of Anaesthesia. Christ!'

Bellows commenced the prep for the third time, rapidly, nervously. 'You know, just being here with you when you act like that makes me look bad. Shit, Susan, why did you want to get him pissed?' Bellows palpated the radial artery and then jammed the needle of the heparinized syringe into the skin on the thumb side of Berman's wrist. 'I'm going to have to say something to Stark before he hears about it through the grapevine. Susan, I mean, what's the point of getting him mad? You obviously don't have any idea what hospital politics are like.'

Susan watched Bellows performing the arterial stick. She consciously avoided looking at Berman's sickly face. The syringe began to fill with blood spontaneously. The blood was a very bright crimson.

'He got mad because he wanted to get mad. I don't think I was impertinent until that last question, and he deserved that.'

Bellows didn't answer.

'Anyway I really didn't want to make him angry ... well, maybe I did in a way.' Susan thought for a few moments. 'You see, I talked with this patient only an hour or so ago. He was the patient I had to leave the ICU for. It's just so unbelievable; he was a functioning, normal human being. And ... I ... we had a conversation and I felt like I knew something about him. I even took a liking to him in a way. That's what makes me mad or sad or both. And Harris, his attitude made it worse.'

Bellows didn't respond immediately. He searched in the tray for a syringe cap. 'Don't tell me anymore,' he said at length. 'I don't want to hear about it. Here, hold the syringe for me.' Bellows gave Susan the syringe while he prepared the ice bed. 'Susan, I'm afraid you're going to be poison for me around here. You have no idea how miserable someone like Harris can make it. Here, put pressure on the puncture site.'

'Mark?' said Susan pressing on Berman's wrist but looking at Bellows directly. 'You don't mind if I call you Mark, do you?'

Bellows took the syringe and placed it into the ice bath. 'I'm not sure, to be perfectly honest.'

'Well, anyway, Mark, you have to admit that six, and maybe seven, cases, if Berman proves to be like Greenly, represents a lot of cases of brain death, or vegetables, as you call them.'

'But a lot of surgery goes on here, Susan. It's often more than a hundred cases a day, some twenty-five thousand per year. That drops the six cases below two hundredths of one per cent in incidence. That's still within the surgical anaesthesia risk.'

'That may be true, but these six cases represent only one type of possible complication, not surgical anaesthesia risk in general. Mark, it's got to be too high. In fact, down in the ICU this morning you said that the particular complication Nancy Greenly represented occurred only about one in a hundred thousand. Now you're trying to tell me that six in twenty-five thousand is OK. Bullshit. It's too high whether you or Harris or anybody in the hospital accept it. I mean would *you* want to have some minor surgery tomorrow with that kind of risk? You know this whole thing really bothers me, the more I think about it.'

'Well then, don't think about it. Come on, we've got to get moving.'

'Wait a minute. You know what I'm going to do?'

'I can't guess and I'm not sure I want to know.'

'I'm going to look into this particular problem. Six cases. That should be enough for some reasonable conclusions. I do have a third-year paper to do and I think I owe that much to Sean here.'

'Oh for Christ sake, Susan, let's not be melodramatic.'

'I'm not being melodramatic. I think I'm responding to a challenge. Sean challenged me earlier with my image of myself as a doctor. I failed. I wasn't detached or professional. You might even say I acted like a schoolgirl. Now I'm challenged again. But this time intellectually with a problem, a serious problem. Maybe I can respond to this challenge in a more commendable fashion. Maybe these cases represent a new symptom complex or disease process. Maybe they represent a new complication of anaesthesia because of some peculiar susceptibility these people had from some previous insult which they suffered in the past.'

'All the more power to you,' said Bellows getting the remains from the arterial stick together. 'Frankly though, it sounds like a hell of a hard way to work out some emotional or psychological adjustment problem of your own. Besides, I think you'll be wasting your time. I told you before that Dr Billing, the anaesthesiology resident on Greenly's case, went over it with a fine-toothed comb. And believe me, he's bright. He said that there was absolutely no explanation for what happened.'

'Your support is appreciated,' said Susan. 'I'll start with your patient in the ICU.'

'Just a minute, Susan dear. I want to make one point crystal clear.' Bellows held up his index and middle finger like Nixon's victory sign. 'With Harris on the rag, I don't want to be involved, no how. Understood? If you're crazy enough to want to get involved, it's your bag from A to Z.'

'Mark, you sound like an invertebrate.'

'I just happen to be aware of hospital realities and I want to be a surgeon.'

Susan looked Mark directly in the eye. 'That, Mark, in a nutshell, is probably your tragic flaw.'

Monday February 23
1:53pm

The cafeteria at the Memorial could have been in any one of a thousand hospitals. The walls were a drab yellow that tended toward mustard. The ceiling was constructed of a low-grade acoustical tile. The steam table was a long L-shaped affair with brown, stained trays stacked at the beginning.

The excellence of the Memorial's clinical services did not extend into the food service. The first food seen by an unlucky customer coming into the cafeteria was the salad, the lettuce invariably as crisp as wet Kleenex. To heighten the disagreeable effect, the salads were stacked one on top of the other.

The steam table itself presented the hot selections, which posed a baffling mystery. So many things tasted alike that they were indistinguishable. Only carrots and corn stood aside. The carrots had their own disagreeable taste; the corn had absolutely no taste at all.

By quarter to two in the afternoon, the cafeteria was almost empty. The few people who were sitting around were mostly kitchen employees, resting after the mad lunchtime rush. As bad as the food was, the cafeteria was still heavily patronized because it enjoyed a monopoly. Few people in the hospital complex took more than thirty minutes for lunch, and there simply was not enough time to go elsewhere.

Susan took a salad but after one look at the limp lettuce, she replaced it. Bellows went directly to the sandwich area and took one.

'There's not much they can do to a tuna sandwich,' he called back to Susan.

Susan eyed the hot entrees and moved on. Following Bellows's lead, she selected a tuna sandwich.

The woman who was supposed to be at the cash register was nowhere to be seen.

'Come on,' motioned Bellows, 'we ain't got much time.'

Feeling a bit like a shoplifter by not paying, Susan followed Bellows to a table and sat down. The sandwich was repellent. Somehow too much water had gotten into the tunafish and the tasteless white bread was soggy. But it was food and Susan was famished.

'We've got a lecture at two,' garbled Bellows through a huge bite of sandwich. 'So eat hearty.'

'Mark?'

'Yeah?' said Bellows as he gulped half his milk in one swig. It was apparent that Bellows was a speed eater of Olympic calibre.

'Mark, you wouldn't be hurt if I cut your first surgery lecture, would you?' Susan had a twinkle in her eye.

Bellows stopped the second half of his tuna sandwich midway to his mouth and regarded Susan. He had an idea that she was flirting with him, but he dismissed it.

'Hurt? No, why do you ask?' Bellows had a helpless feeling that he was being manipulated.

'Well I just don't think I could sit through a lecture at this moment in time,' said Susan, opening her milk carton. 'I'm a little spaced from this affair with Berman ... *Affair* is not the right word. Anyway I'm really uptight; I couldn't handle a lecture. If I do something active I'll be much better off. I was thinking that I'd go to the library and look up something about anaesthesia complications. It will give me a chance to start my "little" investigation as well as sort out this morning in my mind.'

'Would you like to talk about it?' asked Bellows.

'No, I'll be OK, really.' Susan was surprised and touched by his sudden warmth.

'The lecture isn't critical. It's an introductory kind of thing by one of the emeritus professors. Afterwards I planned for you students to come on the ward to meet your patients.'

'Mark?'

'What?'

'Thanks.'

Susan stood up, smiled at Bellows, and left.

Bellows put the second half of his tuna sandwich into his mouth and chewed it on the right side, then he moved it over to the left cheek. He wasn't even sure what Susan had thanked him for. He watched her cross the cafeteria and deposit her tray in the rack. She rescued her unfinished milk and sandwich before leaving. At the door she turned and waved. Bellows waved in return but by the time he got his hand up, she had already disappeared.

Bellows looked around self-consciously, wondering if anyone had noticed him with his hand in the air. Replacing his hand on the table, he thought about Susan. He had to admit that she attracted him in a refreshing, basic way, reminding him of the way he felt early in his social career: an excitement, an unsettling impatience. His imagination conjured up sudden romantic pursuits with Susan as the object. But as soon as he did so, he reprimanded himself for being juvenile.

Bellows polished off his milk with another gigantic gulp while carrying his tray to the dirty-dish cart. En route he wondered if he dared to ask Susan out. There were two problems. One was the residency and Stark. Bellows had no idea how the chief would react to one of his residents dating a student assigned to him. Bellows was not sure if such a worry was rational or not. He did know that Stark tended to favour married residents. The idea was that the married ones would be more dependable, which, as far as Bellows was concerned, was pure bunk. But there was little hope of keeping a relationship between himself and one of the students a secret. Stark would find out and it could be bad. The second problem was Susan herself. She was sharp; there was no question about that. But could she be warm? Bellows had no idea. Maybe she was just too busy, or too intellectualized, or too ambitious. The last thing that Bellows wanted to do was to squander his limited free time on some cold, castrating bitch.

And what about himself? Could Bellows handle a sharp girl who was in his own field even if she were warm and lovable? He had dated a few nurses, but that was different because nurses were allied with but distinct from doctors. Bellows had never dated another doctor or even doctor-to-be. Somehow the idea was a bit disturbing.

Leaving the cafeteria, Susan enjoyed a greater sense of direction than she had felt all day. Although she had no idea how she was actually going to investigate the problem of prolonged coma after anaesthesia, she felt that it represented an intellectual challenge which could be met by applying scientific methods and reasoning. For the first time all day she had a feeling that the first two years of medical school had meant something. Her sources were to be the literature in the library and the charts of the patients, particularly Greenly's and Berman's.

Near to the cafeteria was the hospital gift shop. It was a pleasant place, populated and run by an assortment of gracefully ageing surburbanite women dressed in cute pink smocks. The windows of the shop faced the main hospital corridor and were mullioned, giving the shop an appearance of a cottage smack dab in the middle of the busy hospital. Susan entered the gift shop and quickly found what she was after: a small black looseleaf notebook. She slipped the purchase into her pocket of her white coat and left for the ICU. Her jumping-off point would be the case of Nancy Greenly.

The ICU was back to its pre-arrest hush. The harsh illu-

mination had been dampened to the level Susan recalled from
her first visit. The instant the heavy door closed behind her,
Susan tasted the same anxiety she had noted before, the same
feeling of incompetence. Again she wanted to leave before
something happened and she was asked the simplest of questions to which she would undoubtedly have to answer a de-
moralizing 'I don't know.' But she did not bolt. Now she at
least had something to do which gave her a modicum of confidence. She wanted the chart of Nancy Greenly.

Looking to the left, Susan noticed that no one was standing
by Nancy Greenly's bed. The potassium level had apparently
been rectified and the heart was beating normally once again.
The crisis over, Nancy Greenly was forgotten and allowed to
return to her own infinity. Willing machines resumed the vigil
over her vegetable-like functions.

Drawn by an irresistible curiosity, Susan walked over to
Nancy Greenly's side. She had to struggle to keep her emotions
in check and to keep the identification transference to a minimum. Looking down at Nancy Greenly, it was difficult for
Susan to comprehend that she was looking at a brainless shell
rather than a sleeping human being. She wanted to reach out
and gently shake Nancy's shoulder so that she would awaken
so that they could talk.

Instead, Susan reached out and picked up Nancy's wrist.
Susan noted the delicate pallor of the hand as it drooped, life-
lessly. Nancy was totally paralysed, completely limp. Susan
began to think about paralysis from destruction of the brain.
The reflex circuits from the periphery would still be intact,
at least to some degree.

Susan grasped Nancy's hand as if she were shaking it and
slowly flexed and extended the wrist. There was no resistance.
Then Susan forced the wrist forcefully to its limit, the fingers
almost touching the forearm. Unmistakenly Susan felt resistance, only for an instant but nonetheless definite. Susan tried it
with the other wrist; it was the same. So Nancy Greenly was
not totally flaccid. Susan felt a certain sense of academic pleasure; the irrational joy of the positive finding.

Susan found a percussion hammer for tendon reflexes. It was

made of hard red rubber with a stainless steel handle. She had had one used on herself and had tried one on fellow students in physical diagnosis classes, but never used one on a patient. Clumsily Susan tried to elicit a reflex by tapping Nancy Greenly's right wrist. Nothing. But Susan was not exactly sure where to tap. Instead she pulled up the sheet on the right side and tapped under the knee. Nothing. She flexed the knee with her left hand and tapped again. Still nothing. From neuro-anatomy class Susan remembered that the reflex she was searching for came from a sudden stretch of the tendon. So she stretched Nancy Greenly's knee more, then tapped. The thigh muscle contracted almost imperceptibly. Susan tried it again, eliciting a reflex that was no more than a slight tightening of the flaccid muscle. Susan tried it on the left leg, with the same result. Nancy Greenly had weak but definite reflexes, and they were symmetrical.

Susan tried to think of other parts of the neuroanatomy examination. She remembered level-of-consciousness testing. In Nancy Greenly's case the only test would be reaction to pain stimulus. Yet when she pinched Nancy Greenly's Achilles tendon, there was no response no matter how hard she squeezed. Without any specific reason other than wondering if the pain sensation would be more potent the closer to the brain, Susan pinched Nancy Greenly's thigh and then recoiled in horror. Susan thought that Nancy Greenly was getting up because her body stiffened, arms straightening from her sides and rotating inward in a painful contraction. There was a side-to-side chewing motion with her jaw almost as if she were awakening. But it passed and Nancy Greenly reverted to her limpness equally suddenly. Eyes widening, Susan had moved back, pressing herself against the wall. She had no idea what she had done or how she had managed to do it. But she knew she was toying in the area well beyond her present abilities and knowledge. Nancy Greenly had had a seizure of some kind, and Susan was immensely thankful that it had passed so quickly.

Guiltily, Susan glanced around the room to see if anyone was watching. She was relieved to note that no one was. She was also relieved that the cardiac monitor above Nancy Greenly continued its steady and normal pace. There were no premature contractions.

Susan had the uncomfortable feeling that she was doing something wrong, that she was trespassing, and that any moment she would be deservedly reprimanded, perhaps by Nancy Greenly's arresting once again. Susan quickly decided that she would withhold further patient examination until after some serious reading.

With great effort at appearing nonchalant, Susan made her way over to the central desk. The charts were kept in a circular stainless steel file built into the counter top. With her left hand she began to turn the chart rack slowly. It squeaked painfully. Susan turned it more slowly. The squeaking persisted.

'Can I help you?' asked June Shergood from behind Susan, causing her to start and to withdraw her hands as if she were a child caught at the cookie jar.

'I'd just like the chart,' said Susan, expecting some sour words from the nurse.

'What chart?' Shergood's voice was pleasant.

'Nancy Greenly's. I'm going to try to get an idea about her case so that I can participate in her care.'

June Shergood rummaged among the charts, coming up with Nancy Greenly's. 'You might find it easier to concentrate in there,' said Shergood with a smile, pointing toward a door.

Susan thanked her, welcoming the opportunity to withdraw. The door that Shergood had indicated opened into a tiny room ringed about with glass-faced, locked medicine cabinets. A counter top ran around three sides of the room, providing desk space. On the right wall was a sink, and in the left corner was the omnipresent coffeepot.

Susan sat down with the chart. Although Nancy Greenly had not been in the hospital for even two weeks, her chart was voluminous. That was usual for a case placed in the ICU. The elaborate, constant care generated reams of paper.

Susan took out the remains of her tuna sandwich and milk and poured herself a cup of coffee. Then she took out her notebook and removed a number of blank pages. She started to work. Unaccustomed to using a patient chart, she spent a few minutes figuring out its organization. The order sheets were first, followed by the graphs of the patient's vital signs. Next was the history and physical examination dictated on the day of admission. The rest of the chart included the progress notes, the operative and anaesthesia notes, the nurses' notes, and the innumerable laboratory values, X-ray reports, and records of sundry tests and procedures.

Since she did not know what she was looking for, Susan decided to make copious notes. At this early stage there was no way of determining what was going to be the important information. She started with Nancy Greenly's name, age, sex, and race. Next she included the meagre medical history attesting to the fact that Nancy Greenly had been a healthy individual. There were bits and pieces of family history, including reference to a grandmother who had had a stroke. The only illness of note in Nancy's past was a case of mononucleosis at age 18, with an apparently uneventful recovery. The review of Nancy's systems, including her cardiovascular and respiratory systems, were normal. Susan wrote down the laboratory values from her routine pre-op screen: the blood and urine were both normal. She also wrote down the results of the pregnancy test, negative; various blood clotting studies, blood type, tissue type, chest X-ray, and EKG. There was also the chemistry profile, which included a wide battery of tests. Nancy Greenly's reports were well within normal limits.

Susan ate the last of the tuna sandwich and washed it down with a slug of milk. Turning the pages of the operative section and locating the anaesthesia record, she noted the pre-op medication: Demerol and Phenergan given at 6:45am by one of the nurses on Beard 5. The endotracheal tube was a number 8. Pentothal 2 grams given I.V. at 7:24am. Halothane, nitrous oxide, and oxygen started at 7:25. The halothane concentration was initially 2 per cent through the Fluotec Temperature Compensated Vapourizer. Within several minutes it was reduced to 1 per cent. The nitrous oxide and oxygen flow rates were 3 litres and 2 litres per minute respectively. For muscle relaxation a 2 cc dose of 0.2 per cent succinylcholine was given at 7:26 and a second dose at 7:4

Susan noted that the blood pressure fell at 7:48 after maintaining a plateau of 105/75. The halothane percentage was reduced to 1/2 per cent at that point, while the nitrous oxide and oxygen flow was changed to 2 and 3 litres. The blood pressure drifted back up to 100/60. Susan made a rough copy of the information which was graphed in the anaesthesia record.

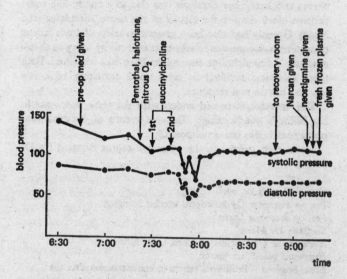

But from that point on the anaesthesia record became hard to decipher. As far as Susan could tell, the blood pressure and the pulse stayed about 100/60 and seventy per minute respectively. Although the heart rate stayed stable, there was some sort of variation in the rhythm, but Dr Billing had not described it.

From the record Susan could see that Nancy Greenly had been moved from the OR into the recovery room at 8:51. A Block Ade square-wave nerve stimulator had been used to test the function of Nancy's peripheral nerves. It had been originally suspected that she had been unable to metabolize the additional dose of succinylcholine. But nerve function had been detected in both ulnar nerves, meaning that the problem was most likely central, in the brain.

Over the following hour Nancy Greenly had been given Narcan 4 mg to rule out an idiosyncratic hypersusceptibility to her pre-op narcotic. There had been no response. At 9:15 she had been given neostigmine 2.5 mg to see if the block on her nerves and hence her paralysis was due to a curare-like competitive block despite the results of the nerve stimulator test. Nancy Greenly had also been given two units of fresh frozen plasma with documented cholinesterase activity to try to eliminate any succinylcholine that might have still remained. Both these measures resulted in some mild twitching of a few muscles but no real response.

The anaesthesia record ended with the terse statement in Dr Billing's handwriting: 'Delayed return of consciousness post anaesthesia; cause unknown.'

Susan next turned to the operative report dictated by Dr Major.

Date February 14, 1976
Pre op diagnosis Dysfunctional uterine bleeding
Post op diagnosis Same
Surgeon Dr Major
Anaesthesia General endotracheal using halothane
Estimated blood loss 500 cc
Complications – Prolonged return to consciousness after the termination of anaesthesia.
Procedure After appropriate pre-op medication (Demerol and Phenergan) the patient was brought to the operating room and attached to the cardiac monitor. She was smoothly inducted under general anaesthesia utilizing an endotracheal tube. The perineum was prepped and draped in the usual fashion. A bimanual examination was carried out revealing normal ovaries, adnexa and an antero-flexed uterus. A no.4 Pederson speculum was inserted into the vagina and secured. Blood clots were sucked from the vaginal vault. The cervix was inspected and appeared normal. The uterus was sounded to 5 cm with a Simpson sound. Cervical dilation was carried out with ease and minimal trauma. Cervical dilators no.1 through no.4 were passed with ease. A no.3 Sime curette was passed and the endometrium was curetted. A specimen was sent

to the laboratory. Bleeding was minimal at the termination of the procedure. The speculum was removed. At that point it became apparent that the patient was making a slow recovery from anaesthesia.

Susan rested her weary right hand by letting it dangle by her side. She had a habit of writing by holding a pencil or pen so tightly that blood flow was restricted. The blood tingled as it returned to her fingertips. Before going back to work, she took several sips of her coffee.

The pathology report described the endometrial scrapings as proliferative in character. The diagnosis was then listed as anovulatory uterine bleeding with a proliferative endometrium. No clue there.

Next Susan turned to the most interesting page: the initial neurology consult, signed by a Dr Carol Harvey. Without knowing the meaning of most of what she wrote, Susan copied the consult note as well as she could. The handwriting was atrocious.

History The patient is a twenty-three-year-old, white female admitted to the hospital with a problem of (illegible phrase). Past medical history of self and family negative for significant neurological disorders. Patient's pre-op work-up (illegible phrase). Surgery itself uneventful and immediate result diagnostic and most likely curative of the presenting complaint. However, during surgery some minor problems with the blood pressure were noted, and after surgery there was noted a prolonged unconsciousness and apparent paralysis. Overdose of succinylcholine and/or halothane ruled out. (Entire sentence totally illegible.)
Examination Patient in deep coma unresponsive to spoken word, light touch or deep pain. Patient appears to be paralysed although trace deep tendon reflexes elicited from both biceps and quadriceps symmetrically. Muscle tone decreased but not totally flaccid. Pendulousness increased. No tremor.
Cranial nerves (illegible phrase) ... pupils dilated and unresponsive. Absent corneal reflex.
Square-Wave Nerve Stimulator: Persistent although decreased function of the peripheral nerves.
Cerebral Spinal Fluid (CSF): Atraumatic puncture, clear fluid, opening pressure 125 mm of water.

EEG: Flat wave in all leads.
Impression (illegible sentence). (illegible phrase) ... with no
localizing signs ... (illegible phrase) ... coma due to diffuse
cerebral edema is the primary diagnosis. The possibility of
a cerebral vascular accident or stroke cannot be ruled out without
cerebral angiography. An idiosyncratic response to any of the
agents used for anaesthesia remains a possibility although I
believe ... (illegible phrase). Pneumoencephalography and/or
a CAT scan may be of help but I believe it would be of academic
interest only and would not provide any additional information
for diagnosis in this difficult case. The EEG with its suppression
of all organized and otherwise activity certainly suggests
extensive brain death or damage. This same picture has been
seen with tranquillizer/alcohol combinations but it is extremely
rare. There are only three cases in the literature. Whatever the
cause, this patient has suffered an acute insult to the brain. There
is no chance that this patient represents any degenerative
neurological syndrome.
Thank you very much for letting me see this very interesting
patient.
Dr Carol Harvey, resident, neurology

Susan cursed the handwriting as she surveyed the many blanks
on her own notebook sheet. She took another sip of coffee and
turned the page in the chart. On the next page was another note
from Dr Harvey.

February 15, 1975. Follow up by Neurology
Patient status = unchanged. Repeat EEG = no electrical activity.
CSF laboratory values were all within normal limits.
Impression I have discussed this case with my attending and with
the other neurology residents who agree on the diagnosis of acute
brain insult leading to brain death. It is also the general consensus
that cerebral edema from acute hypoxia was the immediate cause
of the problem. The cause of the hypoxia was probably some sort
of cerebral vascular accident perhaps due to a transient blood clot,
platelet clot, fibrin clot, or other embolus related to the endometrial
scraping. Some sort of acute idiopathic polyneuritis or vasculitis
may have played a part. Two papers of interest are:
'Acute Idiopathic Polyneuritis; a Report of Three Cases,' *Australian
Journal of Neurology*, volume 13, Sept. 1973, pp 98-101.
'Prolonged Coma and Brain Death Following Ingestion of

Sleeping Pills by Eighteen Year Old Female,' *New England Journal of Neurology*, volume 73, July 1974, pp 301-302.
Cerebral angiography, pneumoencephalography, and a CAT scan can be done, but it is the combined opinion that the results would be normal.
Thank you very much
Dr Carol Harvey

Susan let her aching hand rest for a few moments after copying the lengthy neurology notes. She moved on in the chart, passing the nurses' notes until she reached the laboratory results. There were numerous X-ray reports, including a normal series of skull X-rays. Next came the extensive chemistry and haematology reports, which Susan laboriously copied into her notebook pages. Since all the results were essentially normal, Susan concentrated on finding out if there were any changes between the pre-op values and the post-op values. There was only one value that fell into this category; after the operation Nancy Greenly had exhibited a higher serum sugar as if she had developed a diabetic tendency. The serial EKGs were not very revealing, although they did show some non-specific S and ST wave changes following the D&C. However, there was no pre-op EKG to compare.

Finishing, Susan closed the cover of the chart and leaned back, stretching her hands up toward the ceiling. At the very limit of her stretch, she grunted and exhaled. She leaned forward and glanced over the eight pages of minute handwriting which she had just completed. She felt no further in her investigation but she did not expect to. Much of what she had copied she really did not understand.

Susan believed in the scientific method and she believed in the power of books and knowledge. For her there was no substitute for information. Although she did not know very much about clinical medicine, she had the positive feeling that by combining method with information she could solve the problem at hand – why had Nancy Greenly lapsed into coma. First she had to gather as much observational data as possible; that was the purpose of the charts. Next she had to understand the data; for that she must turn to the literature. Analysis leading to synthesis: pure Cartesian magic. Susan was optimistic at this stage. And it did not faze her that she did not understand much of the material she had taken from Nancy Greenly's chart. She felt confident that within the maze of information were critical points which could lead her to the solution. But to see it Susan needed more information, a lot more.

The hospital medical library was on the second floor of the Harding building. After multiple false starts Susan was directed to a flight of stairs which led up to the personnel office, and past it, to the library itself.

It was called the Nancy Darling Memorial Library, and as Susan entered she passed a small daguerreotype of a matronly woman dressed in black. A copper plaque on the frame was engraved: *In fond memory of Nancy Darling*. Susan thought the name Nancy Darling, with its amorous connotations, hardly fitted the prim scowling figure. But it was New England one hundred per cent.

With the reassuring warmth of the books about her, Susan felt instantly at home in the library, in sharp contrast to her feelings in the ICU and the hospital in general. She put down her notebook and got her bearings. The centre of the room, with its two-storeyed ceiling, had large oak tables with black academic colonial-style chairs. The end of the room was dominated by a large window that reached up to the ceiling, giving out onto the small inner courtyard of the hospital, which contained a patch of anaemic grass, a single leafless tree, and a tennis court. The net on the tennis court sagged sadly from midwinter disuse.

Bookshelves flanked both sides of the tables and were oriented at right angles to the long axis of the room. There was a cast-iron circular staircase which led up to the balcony. On that level the shelves to the right contained books, while bound periodicals were in stacks to the left. Against the wall opposite the window stood the dark mahogany card catalogue.

Consulting the card catalogue, Susan searched out the books on anaesthesiology. Once in the proper area, she went from book to book. She knew next to nothing about anaesthesiology and needed a good introductory text. Specifically she was interested in anaesthetic complications. She picked out five books, the most promising of which was titled *Anaesthetic Complications: Recognition and Management*.

As she was carrying the books over to the table where she had placed her notebook, her name came over the page system, gently subdued, distinctly followed by the number 482.

Susan let the books slide from her hands onto the table. She turned and eyed the phone. Then she turned back to the table and looked down at the books and her notebook. With her hands resting on the back of one of the chairs, Susan vacillated. She felt torn between her strongly reinforced compulsion to do as she was told and her newly discovered challenge, the problem of prolonged coma after anaesthesia. It was not an easy choice. Following the accepted pathways had served her well in the past. She owed her current position to that. And that position was particularly important for Susan because of her sex. All of the females in medicine tended to follow a rather conservative road simply because they were a minority and hence had the feeling that they were constantly on trial.

But then Susan thought about Nancy Greenly in the ICU and Sean Berman in the recovery room. She didn't think about them as patients but rather as people. She thought about their personal tragedies. Then she knew what she had to do. Medicine had already forced her to make many compromises. This time she was going to do what she thought was right, at least for a couple of intensive days.

'Screw 482,' she said half out loud, smiling at the rhyme. She sat down deliberately and cracked the book on anaesthetic complications. The more she thought about Greenly and Berman, the more convinced she was that she was doing the right thing.

Monday February 23

2:45pm

Bellows impatiently tapped the top of the extension telephone No. 482, expecting it to ring any second. He was going to answer it before the first ring was completed. In the background the droning voice of the ageing professor emeritus, Dr Allen Druery, could be heard, extolling the virtues of Halstead. The four students appeared lost within the emptiness of the surgical conference room. Bellows had originally thought that the atmosphere of the conference room would add a positive note to the lectures he had planned for the students. But now he wasn't so sure. The room was too big, too cold for four students, and the lecturer looked a bit ludicrous standing at the podium and facing tier after tier of empty seats.

From where Bellows was sitting, he could see only the backs of the four students. Goldberg was busy taking notes in a furious fashion, getting every word. Dr Druery's lecture was mildly interesting but certainly not worth notetaking. Bellows knew the syndrome, though. He'd seen it in action a thousand times and even suffered from it to an extent himself. As soon as the lights would dim, and someone would start speaking, many medical students would respond in a Pavlovian fashion by taking notes, madly trying to get every word down onto paper without any thought as to the content. The medical student responded in this utterly unintellectual way because, more often than not, he was asked to regurgitate whatever trivia he had been fed.

Bellows was sorry he had not told Susan that he indeed would be hurt if she missed the lecture. In such a small group, her absence was painfully apparent above and beyond the fact that she was so visually distinctive. Bellows was nervous that Stark would decide to pop in and welcome the group. Of course he'd wonder where the fifth student was, and what could Bellows say? He thought about saying that she was scrubbing on a case. But so early in the game, that was unlikely.

The worry about Stark had finally caused Bellows to page Susan so that he could retract his previous silent acquiescence to her cutting the lecture. It was a bad precedent to establish. So he thought he would just inform her that she was sincerely missed and should get herself up to the tenth-floor conference room on the double. Bellows specifically decided to use the word *sincerely* because in the context it was used, it had several implications.

Bellows had made up his mind to ask Susan out on a date. There were several unanswerable questions and aspects involved in such a move, yet the payoff was worth the risk. Susan was bright and spirited, and Bellows was almost positive she had a dynamite figure. Whether she could be feminine and warm according to Bellows's interpretations of those qualities remained to be seen. The trouble was that Bellows had some pretty outdated notions about femininity. For him surgery and his schedule came first; thus an important aspect of Bellows's definition of femininity concerned availability. He expected his female friends to respect his schedule as much as he did and to rearrange their schedules to accord with it. An interesting aspect of Susan's situation, it occurred to Bellows, was that for the next month or so, they would have similar schedules. That was encouraging. And if all else failed, Bellows reasoned that at least Susan would be a damn interesting screw.

But the phone remained silent under Bellows's expectant hand. Impatiently he redialled the page operator and told her to repeat the page for Dr Susan Wheeler for 482. Replacing the receiver, he again waited for the ring as the minutes slid by. Bellows began to think that maybe things would not go so smoothly with Susan. Perhaps she wouldn't even go out with him. She could already be tight with someone else. Under his breath he cursed females in general, and he told himself that he should be sensible and leave well enough alone. At the same time he knew that Susan was triggering off his keen sense of competition. He also visualized that curve of Susan's low back as it spread out over her ass. He decided to page once more.

Gerald Kelley was as Irish as one could be and still live in

Boston and not Dublin. His hair was reddish blond and thick and curly despite the fact that he was fifty-four years old. His face had a ruddy hue, almost as if he wore theatrical makeup, especially over the crests of his cheekbones.

Kelley's most notable feature and by far the dominant aspect of his profile was his enormous paunch. Every night three bottles of stout contributed to its awe-inspiring dimensions. For the last few years it had been pointed out that when Kelley was vertical, his belt buckle was horizontal.

Gerald Kelley had worked for the Memorial since he was fifteen years old. He had started out in the maintenance department, the boiler room to be exact, and now he was in charge. From his long experience and mechanical aptitude he knew the power plant of the hospital inside and out. In fact, he knew almost all the mechanical aspects of the building by heart. It was for this reason that he was in charge and also why he was paid $13,700 a year. The hospital administration knew he was indispensable, and they would have paid more if Gerald Kelley had made an issue of it. The fact was, each party was satisfied.

Gerald Kelley sat at his desk in the machinery spaces of the basement, thumbing through work orders. He had a day crew of eight men, and he tried to distribute the work according to need and capability. Any work on the power plant itself, though, Kelley did himself. The work orders in front of him were all routine, including the drain in the nurses' station on the fourteenth floor. That plugged up on schedule, once per week. Placing the work orders in the sequence he felt they should be done, Kelley began to match them up with his crew.

Although the general din in the machinery spaces was at a relatively high level, especially for people unaccustomed to the area, Kelley's ears were sensitive to the character of the mixed sounds. Thus when the clank of metal on metal reached his ears from the direction of the main electrical panel, he turned his head. Most people would not have heard the sound amid all the other mechanical noises. However, it did not repeat itself and Kelley returned to his administrative job at hand. He did not like the paperwork attached to his position; he would have preferred to fix the sink on the fourteenth floor himself. Yet he also understood that organization was a necessity if he were to keep things running. There was no way he could attend to every repair himself.

The clank recurred, louder than before. Kelley turned again and surveyed the area near the electrical panel, behind the main boilers. He returned to his papers but found himself staring ahead, trying to understand what could have caused the kind of sound he had heard. It had a sharp, brief metallic resonance foreign to the indigenous sounds of the area. Finally curiosity got the best of him and he wandered over to the main boiler. To get near to the electrical panel situated next to the main chase, which contained all the piping rising up in the building, he had to go around the boiler in either direction. He chose to go right, which gave him an opportunity to check the gauges on the boiler. This was an unnecessary manoeuvre because the system had been fully automated with back-up safety devices and automatic cut-off switches. But it was an instinctive move for Kelley, having originated in the days when the boiler had to be watched minute by minute. So as he rounded the boiler his eyes were on the system, his mind appreciating its marvellous compactness compared to the system when he had started at the Memorial. When he looked ahead toward the electrical panel, he froze in his tracks, his right arm lifted involuntarily in self-defence.

'God, you scared the life out of me,' said Kelley, catching his breath and allowing his arm to come back to his side.

'I could say the same,' said a slim man dressed in a khaki uniform. The shirt was open at the neck, and the man wore a white crew neck t-shirt which reminded Kelley of navy chiefs during his wartime duty. The man's left breast pocket bulged with pens, small screwdrivers, and a ruler. Above the pocket was embroidered 'Liquid Oxygen, Inc.'

'I had no idea anyone else was in here,' said Kelley.

'Same with me,' said the man in khaki.

The two men looked at each other for a moment. The man in khaki was carrying a small green cylinder of compressed gas. A flow meter was attached to the cylinder head. 'Oxygen' was stencilled plainly on the side.

'My name is Darell,' said the man in khaki. 'John Darell. Sorry to have scared you. I've been checking the oxygen lines out to the central storage tank. Everything seems fine. In fact, I'm on my way out. Could you tell me the shortest route?'

'Sure. Through those swinging doors, up the stairway to the main hall. Then you have a choice. Nashua Street is to the right, Causeway Street to the left.'

'Thanks a million,' said Darell, heading for the door.

Kelley watched him leave, and then looked around in disbelief. He couldn't figure how Darell had managed to get where he had been without being noticed. Kelley had no idea he could get so absorbed in his Goddamn paperwork.

Kelley walked back to his desk and returned to work. After a few minutes he thought of something else that bothered him. There were no oxygen lines in the boiler room. Kelley made a mental note to ask Peter Barker, assistant administrator, about oxygen line checks. The trouble was that Kelley had a poor memory for anything except mechanical details.

Monday February 23
3:36pm

With the cloud cover Boston had enjoyed little daylight that day, and by 3:30 dusk settled over the city. It took a bit of imagination to comprehend that above the clouds shone the same six-thousand-degree fiery star which in summer turned the macadam on Boylston Street molten. The temperature had responded to the surrounding sun by precipitously falling to nineteen degrees. Another flurry of minute crystalline bodies wafted over the city. The outside lights along the hospital walkways had been on for almost a half-hour.

From within the illuminated library, it already appeared pitch black outside. The two-storey window at the end of the room responded to the dropping temperature by starting an active convection current of cold air across its face. The weighted colder air fell to the floor at the foot of the window and then swept the length of the room under the tables toward the hissing radiators in the back. It was the cold current which first began to nudge Susan from the depths of her intense concentration.

As with so many academic subjects, Susan began to perceive that the more she read about coma, the less she felt she knew. To her surprise, it was an enormous subject, spanning many disciplines of medical specialization. And perhaps the most frustrating of all was Susan's realization that it was not known what determined consciousness, other than saying that the individual was not unconscious. The definition of one consisted of being the opposite of the other. Such a tautologous circle was a travesty of logic until Susan accepted the fact that medical science had not advanced enough to define consciousness precisely. In fact, being fully conscious and being totally unconscious (coma) seemed to represent opposite ends of a continuous spectrum which included partway states like confusion and stupor. Hence the inexact, unscientific terms were more an admission of ignorance than poorly conceived definitions.

Despite the semantics Susan was well aware of the stark difference between normal consciousness and coma. She had observed both states that very day in a patient ... Berman. And despite the lack of precision in definition, there was no lack of information regarding coma. Under the heading of 'acute coma,' Susan began to fill page after page in her notebook with her characteristically small handwriting.

Her particular interest was in causation. Since science had not decided on what particular aspect of brain function had to be disrupted, Susan had to be content with precipitating factors. Being interested in acute coma, or coma of sudden onset, also helped to narrow the field but still the list was impressive and growing. Susan looked back over the list of causes that she had noted so far:

Trauma = concussion, contusion, or any type of stroke
Hypoxia = low oxygen:
  1 mechanical
    strangulation
    blocked airway
    insufficient ventilation
  2 lung abnormality
    alveolar block
  3 vascular block
    blood cannot get to brain
  4 cellular block of oxygen use
High Carbon Dioxide
Hyper (hypo) Glycemia = high (low) blood sugar
Acidosis = high acid in blood
Uremia = kidney failure with high uric acid in the blood
Hyper (hypo) Kalemia = high (low) potassium
Hyper (hypo) Natremia = high (low) sodium
Hepatic Failure   = increase of toxins which would
                           normally be detoxified by the liver
Addison's Disease   = severe endocrine or glandular
                           abnormality
Chemicals or Drugs . . .

Susan took an extra couple of pages for the chemicals and
drugs associated with acute coma and listed them alphabetic-
ally, each with a separate line to make it possible to add information as she got it:

Alcohol	Carbon tetrachloride	Naphazoline
Amphetamines	Chloral hydrate	Naphthaline
Anaesthetics	Cyanide	Opium derivatives
Anticonvulsants	Glutethimide	Pentachlorophenol
Antihistamines	Herbicides	Phenol
Aromatic hydrocarbons	Hydrocarbons	Salicylates
Arsenic	Insulin	Sulphanilamide
Barbiturates	Iodine	Sulphides
Bromides	Mercurial diuretics	Tetrahydrozaline
Cannabis	Metaldehyde	Vitamin D
Carbon disulphide	Methyl bromide	Hypnotic agents
Carbon monoxide	Methyl chloride	

Susan knew that the list was not complete but nonetheless it gave her something to go on, something to keep in mind during her subsequent investigations, and it could be enlarged at any time.

Turning next to the general internal medicine textbooks, Susan opened the ponderous *Principles of Internal Medicine* and read the appropriate sections dealing with coma. The articles in Cecil and Loeb were about the same. Both books provided a rather good overview, although no new concepts were added. Several references were cited which Susan duly copied down in an ever-expanding list of necessary reading.

It felt good to get up and stretch. Susan allowed a deep comforting yawn. She wiggled her toes to try to encourage the blood to go there. The cold draught along the floor had made her stir sooner than she might have otherwise. But once up she turned to the *Index Medicus*, the exhaustive listing of all articles published in all the medical journals.

Starting with the most recent volumes and working backward, Susan searched for and extracted every article concerning acute coma and every article under the heading 'Anaesthetic complications: delayed return to consciousness.' By the time she had worked herself back to 1972, Susan had a list of thirty-seven prospective papers worth reading.

One title especially caught Susan's attention: 'Acute Coma at the Boston City Hospital: A Retrospective Statistical Study of Causes,' *Journal of the American Association of Emergency Room Physicians*, volume 21, August 1974, pp401-3. She found the bound volume containing the article and was soon immersed in it, taking notes as she read.

Bellows had to call her by name before she looked up at him. He had come into the library, located her, and had taken the seat directly across from her. But she did not look up from her reading. Bellows had tried clearing his throat with absolutely no effect. It was as if Susan were in a trance.

'Dr Susan Wheeler, I believe,' said Bellows, leaning over the table, his shadow falling across the journal in front of her.

Susan finally responded and looked up. 'Dr Bellows, I presume.' Susan smiled.

'Dr Bellows is right. God what a relief. I thought for a moment you were in a coma.' Bellows shook his head up and down, as if he were agreeing with himself.

Neither one of them spoke for a few moments. Bellows had prepared a short speech during which he was going to correct any impression he might have given Susan that she was free to cut lectures. He had decided to tell her in plain language that she had to get her ass in gear. But once confronting her, sense of purpose failed, leaving him as directionless as a sailboat becalmed. Susan remained silent because her intuition had informed her that Bellows had something to say. The silence soon became mildly awkward.

Susan broke it.

'Mark, I've been doing a bit of interesting reading here. Look at these figures.'

She stood up and leaned across the table, holding out the journal so that Bellows could see the page. As she did so, her blouse fell away from her chest. Bellows found himself staring down at her splendid breasts, barely contained by a sheer flimsy bra, their skin of a smoothness Bellows imagined to be like velvet. He tried to concentrate on the page Susan was showing him, but his peripheral vision continued to record the insistent image of Susan's lovely torso. Self-consciously Bellows scanned the library, certain that his preoccupation would be transparent to anyone in the room.

Susan was oblivious to the mental havoc she was inadvertently causing.

'This chart here shows the order of incidence of the various types of acute coma appearing at the emergency room at the Boston City Hospital,' said Susan, running her finger along the lines. 'One of the most amazing facts is that only fifty per cent of the cases are ever diagnosed. I find that amazing; wouldn't you agree? That means that fifty per cent of the cases are never diagnosed. They just come in to the ER in coma and die. Just like that.'

'Yeah, it's amazing,' said Bellows, putting his left hand up to his temple to try to keep from seeing what he was seeing.

'And look here, Mark, at the causes of the cases which they do diagnose: sixty per cent are due to alcohol, thirteen per cent due to trauma, ten per cent to strokes, three per cent to drugs or poisons, and the rest divided up among epilepsy, diabetes, meningitis, and pneumonia. Now obviously ... ,' said Susan, sitting back down and relieving the stress on Bellows's hypothalmus.

Bellows glanced around once more to make sure that no one had noticed the episode.

'... we can dismiss alcohol and trauma as far as causing acute coma in the OR is concerned. So ... that leaves us with strokes, then drugs or poisons, and the others in decreasing probability as possible culprits.'

'Wait a second, Susan,' said Bellows pulling himself together. He put his elbows on the table with his forearms up in the air, his hands drooped but engaged. His head was down at first, then he picked it up and looked at Susan. 'That's all very interesting. A little far fetched, but interesting.'

'Far fetched?'

'Yeah. You cannot possibly extrapolate data from the ER to the OR. But anyway, I didn't come in here looking for you to argue about that. I came in here because you haven't been answering your pages. I know, because it was me who was paging you. Look, I'm going to have trouble if you don't show up for conferences. You're going to make trouble for yourself, and the fact of the matter is that, while you're on my service, your trouble is my trouble. I can only make excuses for you for so long. I mean, you can be drawing blood or scrubbing just so often. Stark will be asking questions before you know it. He's phenomenal. He knows everything that's going on around here. Besides, you'll get the reputation of being a phantom among your own section students. Susan, I'm afraid you're going to have to restrict your research proclivities to after-hours.'

'Are you finished?' asked Susan, rising to the defence.

'I'm finished.'

'Well, answer me this one question. Has Berman or Greenly awakened yet?'

'Of course not . . .'

'Then frankly. I believe that my current activities eclipse the importance of a few boring surgical conferences.'

'Oh my aching back! Susan, be reasonable. You're not going to save the world during your first week on surgery. I'm going out on a limb for you as it is.'

'I appreciate it, Mark. Really I do. But listen. My few hours here in the library have already provided some very interesting information. The complication of prolonged coma after anaesthesia is about one hundred times more prevalent here at Memorial than the incidence given for the rest of the country over the past year. Mark, I think I'm onto something. When I started, it was more of an emotional thing which I thought I could work out in a day or two here in the library. But one hundred times! God, I could be on the track of something big, like a new disease, or a lethal combination of normally safe drugs. What if this is some sort of viral encephalitis, or even the result of a previous infection which makes the brain somehow more susceptible to certain drugs or mild lack of oxygen?'

Susan had been part of the medical world for only two years, and yet she was already cognizant of the potential benefits which would accrue to someone who discovered a new disease or syndrome. She thought this one might become known as the Wheeler syndrome, and Susan's success within the medical community would be guaranteed. More often than not, the discoverer of the new disease became far more famous than the discoverer of the cure for the same disease. Eponyms abound in medicine like the tetralogy of Fallot, Cogan's disease, the Tolpin syndrome, or Depperman's degeneration. Whereas names like the Salk vaccine are an anomaly. Penicillin is called penicillin, not Fleming's agent.

'We could call it the Free Wheeler Syndrome,' said Susan, allowing herself to laugh at her own enthusiasm.

'Christ,' said Bellows, cradling his head in his hands. 'What an imagination. But that's OK. Naiveté has a certain license. But, Susan you are in a real world situation with certain specific responsibilities. You are still a medical student, low man – or woman – on the totem pole. You'd better get your tail in gear and honour your surgery rotation obligations or, believe me, your ass will be grass. I'll give you one more day for this project, provided you show up for rounds in the morning. After that you work on it in your free time. Now, if I need you I'll page Dr Wheels instead of Wheeler, so answer it, understood?'

'Understood,' said Susan looking squarely at Bellows. 'I'll do that, if you do something for me.'

'What's that?'

'Pull out these articles and have them Xeroxed. I'll pay you later.' Susan tossed her list of references to Bellows, jumped up from the table and breezed out of the room before Bellows could respond. He found himself looking at a list of thirty-seven journal articles. Since he knew the library like the bones of his hand, he located the volumes with ease, marking each article with a piece of paper. He took the first group over to the desk and told the girl to copy the indicated articles and put it on his library charge. Bellows knew that he had been manipulated again, but he didn't mind. It had taken only ten minutes. He would get them back, with interest.

And he had been right; she had a dynamite figure.

Monday February 23
5:05pm

As she had been telling Bellows that the incidence of coma following anaesthesia at the Memorial was one hundred times the national incidence, Susan had realized that she was basing her calculations on the six cases Harris had mentioned in his outburst. Susan had to check that figure. If it was actually higher, she would have more ammunition to base her commitment to the project. Besides, she needed the names of the coma victims so that she could obtain their charts. What she needed more than anything else, she recognized, was hard data.

Susan knew that she had to get access to the central computer. Harris would be unwilling to supply the names of the patients. Susan was certain of that. Bellows might have been able to get them if he were sufficiently motivated. But that was a big if. Susan felt that the best route was for her to try to get the information herself. So she was thankful she had taken the introductory course in PL 1 computer programming as a junior in college. Already it had paid off in surprising ways, and her need for the information at hand was just another example.

The computer centre in the hospital was located in the Hardy wing, occupying the entire top floor. Many people joked about the symbolic aspects of the computer being above everything else in the hospital, and it had added a new meaning to the phrase 'with a little help from above.'

As the elevator door slid open on the foyer of the eighteenth floor, Susan knew she was going to have to improvise if she were to be successful. Beyond the foyer Susan could see through glass partitions into the main computer reception area. The place had the appearance of a bank. The only difference was that the medium of exchange here was information, not currency.

Susan entered the reception room and walked directly to a counter top that ran the length of the room along the right wall. There were about eight other people in the room, most of them sitting in comfortable-looking blue corduroy chairs. A few were at the counter top bent over computer request forms. All looked up as Susan traversed the room, but they quickly returned to their own affairs. Without the slightest hint of uncertainty Susan took one of the computer request forms. Ostensibly concentrating on the form, Susan had her real attention on the room.

In the back of the room, about twelve feet from Susan, was a large white Formica desk. Above it hung a sign: 'Information.' It was so appropriate that it brought a smile to Susan's face. The man at the desk sat motionlessly, a slight proud smile on his face. He was about sixty, pudgy but neat. Behind him, visible through another glass partition, were the gleaming input-output terminals of the computer itself. While Susan was pretending to be absorbed in the form in front of her, the man at the desk accepted several computer request forms. Each time he went over the form, converting the request to computer language and writing it on the lower portion of the form. He also checked the authorization by calling the department involved, unless he knew the requesting individual personally. Finally he placed the form – or several stapled together – in the 'in' box on the corner of the desk. The requesting individual was told when to expect the information, depending on the priority assigned to the request.

Having assessed the procedure, Susan gave full attention to the form before her. It was certainly simple enough. She filled in the date in the indicated box. She left blank the box for the authorizing department, and she also omitted the name of the requesting party or organization. Susan also left blank the box reserved for method of payment for computer time. She concentrated on the information desired. Susan was not sure how she should word the request for several reasons. One was the concern that the hospital might be uptight about leaking information on cases of coma resulting from anaesthesia. Perhaps they might have programmed a subroutine into the computer so that any requests for such information would be automatically cancelled, or at least alert the computer that the information had been requested. Another point that occurred to Susan was that a disease or disease process might have several modes or degrees of expression. Prolonged coma after an anaesthetic might be one of them, maybe the most severe. Susan wanted to obtain a wide range of information and in that way be able to select what she thought was significant.

But requesting all cases of coma for the past year might yield a printout that was too extensive. Since coma was a symptom and not a disease itself, Susan could end with a list of every heart attack, stroke, and cancer victim who had succumbed to those diseases over the last year. Susan decided to call only for cases of coma occurring in people who had no known chronic or debilitating disease. Then she realized that, she was already making assumptions. If she were on the track of a new disease, there was no reason why it couldn't affect people who had other diseases. In fact, if it were infectious in nature, other disease processes would encourage its expression by lowering defences.

Susan changed her request to all cases of coma occurring to inpatients (in hospital) which were unrelated to the patient's known disease processes. Susan next asked for a correlate between her sample and those having surgery during their stay at the Memorial prior to their coma, with a time correlation between surgery and the onset of the coma. With a certain amount of difficulty Susan translated her request into computer language. She had not used it for almost a year, and it took a few moments to get it right. This portion of the request was below two red lines and the admonishment 'Do not write below this line.'

Susan then waited for the next request to be turned in to the man at the desk. Luckily she did not have to wait long. About four minutes after she finished writing, the elevator arrived. Through the glass she saw a man squeeze past the elevator door before it had fully opened and approach the reception desk at a lope. About forty, slight of build, with flaxen hair parted from a deeply recessed hairline, the man waved a handful of the computer request forms nervously.

'George,' said the man pulling up in front of the reception desk, 'you gotta help me.'

'Ah, my old friend Henry Schwartz,' said the man behind the desk. 'We're always ready to help the accounting department. After all, that's where our checks come from. What can I do for you?'

Susan carefully pencilled in 'Henry Schwartz' onto her own form in the box for the requesting party. In the area for authorizing department, Susan wrote 'Accounting.'

'I need a couple of things, but most of all I need a list of all the Blue Cross/Blue Shield subscribers who have had surgery in the last year,' said Schwartz in a rapid-fire fashion. 'If you asked why I need it, you'd crack up, I swear you would. But I need it and fast. The day shift was supposed to have had it ready for me.'

'We can run it in an hour or so. I'll have it for you by seven,' said George, stapling Schwartz's requests together and tossing them into the box.

'George, you're a lifesaver,' said Schwartz, running his hand through his hair over and over again. He then headed toward the elevator. 'I'll be back at seven sharp.'

Susan watched Schwartz press the 'down' button and then walk back and forth in the elevator foyer. It looked as if he was talking to himself. He hit the 'down' button several more times. After the elevator picked him up, Susan watched the floor indicator above the elevator. It stopped at six, then three, then one. Susan would have to look up which floor the accounting department was located on.

Susan took another blank request form and, carefully placing it over her own, she headed for the desk.

'Excuse me,' said Susan, marshalling a smile she hoped would be convincing. George looked up at her, over the tops of his black-rimmed glasses, which perched midway down his nose. 'I'm a medical student,' continued Susan, making her voice as sweet as possible, 'and I'm very interested in the computer here at the hospital.' She held up the request forms, the blank one hiding the one she had filled out.

'You are, are you?' said George, sitting back with a smile broadening on his own face.

'I am,' repeated Susan shaking her head in the affirmative. 'I think that the potential of the computer in medicine is very great, and since it is obviously not a part of our formal orientation here, I thought I'd just come up and sort of get acquainted.'

George looked at Susan, then over his shoulder through the glass partition at the gleaming IBM hardware. When he turned back to Susan his pride was effervescing.

'It's a marvellous set up, Miss ...'

'Susan Wheeler.'

'It is a fantastic machine, Miss Wheeler,' said George, leaning forward in his seat and lowering his voice and emphasizing his words, suggesting that he was telling Susan a tremendous secret. 'The hospital couldn't do without it.'

'In order to get an idea how it is used, I've been studying the request form here.' Susan held the request forms so that George would see only the blank one, but he had turned again to look into the terminal room.

'I was interested to see a completed form,' continued Susan reaching over and taking the top group of stapled forms from the 'in' box. 'I was curious about how the requests were fed into the computer. Is it all right if I look at one of these?' She placed the forms Schwartz had delivered over her own.

'Sure,' said George turning back to Susan. He stood up and leaned over toward Susan, placing his left hand on the desk. With his other hand he pointed to the space where the request was written in normal English.

'Here the requesting party indicates what it is they want. Then down here . . .' George's finger moved down below the red lines '. . . we have the area where the request is translated into a language that the computer will understand.'

Susan slipped her blank form from under the pile of Schwartz's forms, as if comparing them and she put it down on the desk beside them – leaving her own filled-out form underneath Schwartz's.

'So if someone wants several different kinds of information, they have to fill out separate forms?' asked Susan.

'Exactly, and if . . .'

Susan turned Schwartz's first request form back from the rest of them rapidly, pulling it free of the staple in the upper left corner.

'Oh, I'm terribly sorry,' said Susan putting the top sheet back in position. 'Look what I've done. Let me staple it for you.'

'No matter,' said George, fumbling for the staple machine himself. 'One staple will fix it.' George pressed the staple machine as Susan held the completed forms, together with her own request on the underside.

'Let me put these back before I destroy them completely,'

said Susan contritely, replacing the forms in the 'in' box.

'No harm done,' reassured George.

'Now once the request is in, what happens to it?' asked Susan looking into the terminal room and taking George's attention from the 'in' box.

'Well, I take them inside to the key puncher, who prepares the cards for the card reader. Then ...'

Susan was not listening; she was thinking of how best to terminate her visit. About five minutes later she was down at the directory for the hospital, looking up Henry Schwartz of the accounting department.

With a spare hour and a half, Susan left the Memorial for her dorm. Her stomach growled in opposition to her forgetfulness of basic needs. The tuna sandwich, as bad as it was, had long since disappeared into her metabolic mill, and Susan looked forward to dinner.

Monday February 23
6:55pm

It was a little before seven when Susan alighted from the MBTA at the North Station stop. Crossing the footbridge spanning the street, Susan was exposed to the rush of wind whipping up from the partially frozen harbour water. She bent against its force, clutching her sheepskin ski hat with her left hand and the lapels of her peajacket with her right hand. She tried to keep the cold from her neck by snuggling her chin as far as possible into the recesses of her collar.

When she rounded the edge of the building, the wind increased. An empty beer can tumbled past her into the street. The familiar rush hour sea of red tail lights and wisps of exhaust fumes stretched as far as Susan could see. The windows on the cars were frosted, and they reflected the images about them with a silver sheen, giving the impression of the often white, unseeing pupils of the blind.

Susan began to run at a slow jog with an exaggerated to and fro roll of her body since her arms were pressed against herself. The main entrance to the hospital yawned in front of her, and with relief she pushed through the revolving door.

Susan stuffed her hat into the right sleeve of her coat and left it in the coatroom behind the main information desk. Then she used the hospital telephone directory and rang up the computer centre.

'Hello, this is the accounting department,' said Susan slightly out of breath and struggling to make her voice sound normal. 'Has Mr Schwartz picked up his material yet?'

The answer was affirmative; he had collected it about five minutes earlier. The timing seemed perfect as far as Susan was concerned, and she left for the Hardy building elevator and the third floor accounting offices.

The evening accounting crew was a mere skeleton compared to the day shift. When Susan entered the room only three people were visible at the far end. Two men and one woman looked up in unison as Susan entered.

'Excuse me,' called Susan, approaching the group. 'Can you tell me where I can find Mr Schwartz?'

'Schwartz? Sure. He's in the office in the corner,' said one of the men, pointing down the opposite side of the room.

Susan's eyes followed his finger. 'Thanks,' she said, reversing her direction.

Henry Schwartz was in the middle of the computer printout he had requested. The office was small but extraordinarily neat. The books in the bookcase were arranged so that their heights descended in an orderly fashion. The depth of the book backs in the shelves was one inch, no more, no less.

'Mr Schwartz?' asked Susan smiling and walking up to his desk.

'Yes?' said Schwartz without removing his index finger from his place in the printout.

'It seems that my printout got mixed up with yours, or at least that was the combined opinion upstairs. I was wondering if you had noticed any material you had not requested?'

'No, but I haven't looked through it all yet. What was it you're missing?'

'It's some information on coma we need for a section presentation. Do you mind if I see if it's included with your material?'

'Not at all,' said Schwartz lifting sections of the printout to find the break points.

'If it's there, it would be the last section,' offered Susan. 'They said it was run right after yours.'

Schwartz lifted the bulk of the material from the desk. Remaining was the information Susan needed. Attached to the top was her request form.

'That's it,' said Susan.

'But the form indicates I requested it,' questioned Schwartz glancing at the request form.

'No wonder they got it mixed up with your material,' said Susan, reaching for the material. 'But I assure you, you wouldn't be interested in this stuff. And it's certainly not your fault, by any means.'

'I'd better say something to George ... ,' said Schwartz replacing his own printout in front of him.

'No need,' said Susan, exciting. 'We already discussed it at length. Thanks a million.'

'You're welcome,' said Schwartz, but Susan had already left.

'Susan, you are too much, really too much,' said Bellows between spoonfuls of custard he had taken from the tray of a patient who was too nauseated to eat. 'You skip the lecture, afternoon rounds, and avoid your patients, and now you're hanging around here until eight pm. The only consistency about your performance so far is constant variation.' Bellows laughed as he scraped the bottom of the custard cup.

Susan and Bellows were sitting in the lounge on Beard 5 where the hospital day had begun for Susan. She was sitting in the same seat she had occupied that morning. Spilling over onto the floor was the IBM printout sheet she had obtained. She was running down the list of names and marking appropriate ones with a yellow felt-tip pen.

Bellows took a drink from his coffee.

'Well, that proves it,' said Susan, putting the cap on the pen.

'Proves what?' asked Bellows.

'Proves that there haven't been six cases of unexplained coma, excluding Berman, here at the Memorial this last year.'

'Hurray,' cheered Bellows, toasting with his coffee mug. 'Now I can stop worrying about anaesthesia and have my haemorrhoids fixed.'

'I would recommend that you stick to your suppositories,' said Susan, counting the names she'd marked. 'There haven't been six because there've been eleven. And if Berman continues on his present course, then there will have been twelve.'

'Are you sure?' Bellows's tone changed abruptly and he showed interest in the IBM printout sheet for the first time.

'That's all that came out on this printout,' said Susan. 'I wouldn't be surprised if there were a few more if I had been able to call up the information straight away.'

'You really think so? God, eleven cases!' Bellows leaned over toward Susan, his tongue working at the empty spoon. 'How'd you manage to get this IBM printout?'

'Henry Schwartz was nice enough to help me,' said Susan nonchalantly.

'Who the hell is Henry Schwartz?' asked Bellows.

'Damned if I know.'

'Spare me,' said Bellows covering his eyes with his hand, 'I'm too tired for mental games.'

'Is that a chronic ailment or an acute affliction?'

'Cut the crap. How'd you get this data? Something like this has to be cleared through the department.'

'I went upstairs this afternoon, filled out one of those M804 forms, gave it to the nice man at the desk, and then went back tonight and picked it up.'

'I'm sorry I asked,' said Bellows getting up and waving his

spoon to suggest he would let the issue ride. 'But eleven cases. Did they all happen during surgery?'

'No,' said Susan, going back to the printout. 'Harris was on the level when he said six. The other five were from inpatients on the medical service. Their diagnosis was idiosyncratic reaction. Doesn't that strike you as pretty odd?'

'No.'

'Oh, come on,' said Susan impatiently. 'The word idiosyncratic sounds great but it really means that they had no idea what the diagnosis was.'

'That might be true, but Susan, dear, this happens to be a major hospital, not a country club. It serves as a referral base for the whole New England area. Do you know how many deaths we have here on an average in a single day?'

'Deaths have causes ... these cases of coma do not ... at least not as yet.'

'Well, deaths don't always have apparent causes. That's the purpose of autopsy.'

'There, you hit the nail on the head,' said Susan. 'When someone dies, then you do an autopsy and you find out what was the cause of death so that you can possibly add to your fund of knowledge. Well, in the coma cases you can't do an autopsy because the patients are somewhere hovering between life and death. That makes it even more important that you do another kind of 'opsy,' a live-opsy, if you will. You study all the clues you have available, short of dismembering the victim. The diagnosis is just as important, maybe even more important than the autopsy diagnosis. If we could find out what was wrong with these people, maybe we could bring them out of their comas. Or better still, avoid the coma in the first place.'

'Even the autopsy,' said Bellows, 'doesn't always provide the answers. There are plenty of deaths where the exact cause is never determined whether they do an autopsy or not. I happen to know that two patients threw in the towel today, and I doubt very much if a diagnosis will be made.'

'Why do you think that the diagnosis won't be made?' asked Susan.

'Because both patients expired from respiratory arrest. They apparently just stopped breathing, very calmly with no warning. They were just discovered dead. And in respiratory arrest you don't always find anything to hang the blame on.'

Bellows had captured Susan's interest. She was staring at him without moving, without blinking.

'Are you OK?' asked Bellows, waving his hand in front of her face. Still Susan did not move until she looked down at the IBM printout.

'What the hell do you have, psychomotor epilepsy or something?' asked Bellows.

Susan looked up at him. 'Epilepsy? No, of course not. You said these cases today died of respiratory arrest?'

'Apparently. I mean they stopped breathing. They just gave up.'

'What were they in the hospital for?'

'I'm not positive. I think one of them was in for some problem with his leg. Maybe he had phlebitis and they might find a pulmonary embolus or something. The other one was in for Bell's palsy.'

'Were they both on I.V.s?'

'I don't remember but I wouldn't be surprised if they had been. Why do you ask?'

Susan bit her lower lip, thinking about what Bellows had just told her.

'Mark, do you know something? These deaths you mentioned could be related to the coma victims.' Susan patted the printout with the back of her hand. 'You might have hit on something. What were the names? Can you remember?'

'For Christ's sake, Susan, you've got this thing on the brain. You're working overtime and you're starting to have delusions.' Bellows switched to an artificially concerned tone. 'Don't be concerned, though; it happens to the best of us after we've stayed up for two or three nights in a row.'

'Mark, I'm serious.'

'I know you're serious; that's what worries me. Why don't you give yourself a break and forget about it for a day or so? Then you can pick it up and be more objective. I tell you what. I've got tomorrow night off and with a little luck I can get out of here by seven. How about some dinner? You've only been here a day but you have to get away from the hospital as much as I do.'

Bellows hadn't planned on asking Susan out quite as soon and in such a fashion. But he was pleased because it had come so apparently spontaneously and consequently it would be easy to deal with a refusal if it occurred. It sounded more like an offer to get together than an actual date.

'Dinner's fine, can't pass up an offer for a dinner even with an invertebrate. But really, Mark, what were the names of the two deaths today?'

'Crawford and Ferrer. They were patients on Beard 6.'

Susan pursed her lips as she wrote the names down in her notebook. 'I'll have to look into those in the morning. In fact ...' Susan looked at her watch '... maybe tonight. If they were going to do an autopsy on these cases, when would it be?'

'Probably tonight or first thing in the morning,' shrugged Bellows.

'Well then I'd better check tonight.'

Susan refolded her printout.

'Thanks, Mark, old boy; you've been a help again.'

'Again?'

'Yeah. Thanks for those articles you Xeroxed for me. You'll make a good secretary someday.'

'Up yours.'

'Tut, tut. See you tomorrow night. How about the Ritz? I haven't eaten there for several weeks,' teased Susan, heading for the door.

'Not so fast, Susan. I'll see you at rounds in the morning at six-thirty. Remember our deal. I'll cover for you another day if you come to rounds.'

'Mark, you've been such a dear, really. Let's not louse it up so soon.' Susan smiled and pulled some of her hair across her face with coquettish exaggeration. 'I'll be up till all hours reading all this material you got for me. I need one more full day. We'll discuss it further tomorrow night.'

Then she was gone. Again Bellows felt encouraged about Susan as he sipped his coffee. Then he got up. He had plenty of work to do.

Monday February 23
8:32pm

The pathology lab was in the basement of the main building. Susan descended the stairs and emerged in the middle of a basement corridor which disappeared into utter darkness to the right and twisted out of view to the left. Stark bare light bulbs glowed from the ceiling at intervals of twenty to thirty feet. The light from each bulb met the light from the next in an uneasy penumbra, causing a strange interplay of shadows from the tangle of pipes along the ceiling. In a vain attempt to provide colour to the dim subterranean world, angled stripes of bright orange paint had been painted on the walls.

Directly opposite Susan, partially hidden from view, was an arrow pointing to the left, with the word *Pathology* stencilled above it. Susan turned down the corridor, her shoes making hollow noises on the concrete floor, competing with the hiss of the steam pipes. The atmosphere was oppressive; the location within the bowels of the hospital was sinisterly appropriate. She was not heading for the pathology lab with any favourable anticipation. As far as Susan was concerned pathology represented the black side of medicine, the speciality that seemed to derive its nourishment from medical failure, death. Arguments about the benefits of biopsies which the pathologists analysed or the obvious beneficial spinoffs for the living from the autopsies the pathologists performed were all lost on Susan.

She had only seen one autopsy done during her course in pathology, and that had been one too many. Life had never seemed quite so fragile nor had death seemed quite so final as when Susan had watched the two overweight pathologists disembowel the body of a recently deceased patient.

The memory of that event slowed Susan's steps, but it did not halt them. She was determined. But she had seemingly been walking for a hundred yards as the corridor twisted first in one direction then in another. She cast a nervous glance over her shoulder, wondering if she could have missed the door to the lab. With increased misgivings she continued. At several places, the light bulbs were not functioning and Susan's shadow would appear in front of her and lengthen. Then as she moved into the sphere of influence of the next functioning light her shadow would pale and disappear.

Finally she faced two swinging doors. The upper portion of each contained opaque windows.

'Unauthorized Entry Forbidden' was lettered boldly across the cracked, frosted glass on each door. Stencilled in peeling gold paint below the window on the right door was 'Pathology Laboratory.' Susan hesitated at the door, building up her confidence, wondering what sort of scene to prepare herself for. Cracking the door, she got a glimpse of the interior. A long black stone table dominated the room, running most of its length. Cluttered about on the table were microscopes, slides, slide boxes, chemicals, books, and an array of other equipment. Susan pushed open the door and stepped into the lab. The acrid smell of formaldehyde hung over the room.

The entire wall on the right had shelving from floor to ceiling. With hardly a square inch remaining, the shelves were full of varying sized bottles and jars. Looking more closely, Susan realized that the amorphous colourless mass in the large jar closest to her was an entire human head cut neatly in half, sagitally. Just behind the halved tongue in the wall of the throat was a granular mass. The label on the glass simply said, 'Pharyngeal carcinoma, no.304-A6 1932.' Susan shuddered and tried to keep herself from glancing at other equally gruesome specimens.

At the far end of the room was another set of swinging doors identical to those from the corridor. From the room beyond, Susan could hear a mixture of voices and metallic sounds. She walked toward the doors as silently as possible, feeling herself an intruder in an alien and potentially hostile environment.

Susan tried to peer through the crack between the doors. Although her visual field was limited she knew immediately that she was looking into the autopsy room. Slowly she began to open the left door.

A loud ringing noise echoed around the room causing Susan to spin around, letting the autopsy room door snap shut behind her. At first she thought that she had tripped some alarm system and she felt the urge to bolt for the door into the corridor. But before she could move, a pathology resident appeared out of another side door.

'Well, hello there,' said the resident to Susan as he walked over to the sink and picked up a distilled water irrigator. He smiled at Susan as he squirted water over a tray of slides he was staining. The colour went from a deep violet to clear. 'Welcome to the path lab. You a med student?'

'Yes.' Susan forced a smile.

'We don't see many med students this time of day ... or night. Is there anything special we can do for you?'

'No, not really. I'm just looking around. I'm quite new here,' said Susan putting her hands in the pockets of her white coat, her pulse racing.

'Make yourself at home. There's coffee in the office here if you're interested.'

'No thanks,' said Susan walking back along the desk, aimlessly touching some of the slide boxes.

The resident added another amber stain to the tray of slides and reset the timer.

'Actually, maybe you could help me,' said Susan fingering a few slides on the table. 'Several patients from Beard 6 expired today. I wondered if they've been ... um ...' Susan tried to think of the right word.

'What were the names?' asked the resident wiping his hands. 'There's a post going on right now.'

'Ferrer and Crawford.'

The resident walked over to a clipboard hanging from a nail on the wall.

'Hmmm ... Crawford. That rings a bell. I think that was a medical examiner's case. Here's Ferrer ... that's a medical examiner's case. And I was right, Crawford is too. They're both medical examiner's cases, but hold on.'

The resident walked quickly over to the doors into the autopsy room and banged one open with the palm of his hand. With his right hand holding the edge of the remaining closed door he leaned into the room beyond, his head just out of Susan's view.

'Hey, Hamburger, what's the name of the case you're doing?'

There was a pause and a voice but Susan could not hear it.

'Crawford! I thought that was an examiner's case.' There was another pause.

The resident came back into the room as the timer went off again. The ringing noise made Susan jump once more. The resident squirted more distilled water onto the slides.

'The medical examiner released both cases to the department, as usual. Lazy son of a bitch. Anyway they're doing Crawford right now.'

'Thanks,' said Susan. 'All right if I go in and take a look?'

'By all means, our pleasure,' said the resident, shrugging his shoulders.

Susan paused momentarily at the doors, but she knew the resident was watching her, so she pushed open one of the doors and entered the room.

The room was probably forty feet square, old and dingy. Its walls were surfaced in white tile, which was ancient, cracked, and missing in places. The floor was a type of grey terrazzo. In the centre of the room there were three marble tables built with slanted tops. A stream of water constantly ran down each table toward a drain at the foot, which emitted a constant sucking noise. Over each table hung a hooded light, a scale, and a microphone. Susan found herself standing on a level three to four steps above the level of the main floor. Immediately to her right were several wooden benches on progressively lower tiers.

These benches were a remnant from older days when groups would assemble to observe autopsies.

Only one of the hooded lights was on, that over the table nearest to Susan. It cast its relatively narrow beam down onto the naked corpse on the table immediately below. On each side of the table stood a pathology resident wearing an oilcloth apron and rubber gloves. The focal point of light caused the rest of the room to slide into graded burnt umber shadow like a sinister Rembrandt painting. The table in the centre of the room was in shadow but it was possible for Susan to see that it also held a naked corpse, a manilla tag tied around its right big toe. A large Y-shaped sutured incision crossed the thorax and abdomen. The third table was barely visible in the darkness, but it appeared to be empty.

Susan's entrance stopped all progress in the room. Both residents were staring at her with their heads tilted down to avoid the glare of the overhead light. One of the residents, with a large moustache and sideburns, was in the process of suturing the Y-shaped incision on the male corpse under the light. The other resident, taller by almost a foot, was standing before a basin containing the disembowelled organs.

Having sized up Susan, the taller resident went back to work. He reached into the tangle of organs with his left hand, grasping the liver. His right hand gripped a large, razor-sharp butcher knife. A few strokes freed the liver from the other organs. The liver made a sloshing sound as it oozed into the scale. The resident stepped on a foot pedal on the floor, speaking into the microphone. 'The liver appears reddish brown with a lightly mottled surface, period. The gross weight is ... a ... two point four kilograms, period.' He then reached into the pan and lifted the liver out, dropping it back into the basin.

Susan descended several steps toward the group. The smell was slightly fishy; the air seemed greasy and heavy, like an uncleaned bus depot restroom.

'The liver consistency is more firm than usual but definitely pliant, period.' The knife flashed in the light and the liver surface separated. 'The cut surface demonstrates an enhanced lobar pattern, period.' The knife sliced across the liver in four or five more places, then finally cut a piece out of the centre. The cut specimen demonstrates the usual friable character, period.'

Susan moved up to the foot of the table. The sucking drain was directly in front of her. The tallest resident on the left reached into the basin for another organ but he stopped when the moustached resident spoke.

'Well, hello . . .'

'Greetings,' said Susan; 'sorry to bother you.'

'No bother. Join the party, except we've almost finished.'

'Thanks, but I'm happy to just watch. Is this Crawford or Ferrer?'

'This is Ferrer,' said the resident. Then he pointed at the other body. 'That's Crawford.'

'I was wondering if you've determined a cause of death.'

'No,' said the taller resident. 'But we haven't opened the lungs on this case yet. Crawford was clean grossly. Maybe the microscopic section will shed some light.'

'Do you expect something in the lungs?' asked Susan.

'Well, from the history of apparent respiratory arrest, we were considering pulmonary embolism. But I don't think we're going to find anything, though. Maybe there'll be something in the brain sections.'

'Why don't you think you'll find anything?'

'Well, because I've posted a few cases like this before, and I've never found anything. And the history is exactly the same. Relatively young, somebody comes by and they're not breathing. There's a resuscitation attempt but without luck. Then we get them, or at least after the medical examiner turns them over to us.'

'About how many such cases would you estimate?'

'Over what time span?'

'Whatever . . . a year, two years.'

'Maybe six or seven over the last two years. I'm guessing.'

'And you don't have any ideas about the cause of death?'

'Nope.'

'None?' asked Susan, a bit surprised.

'Well, I think it's something with the brain. Something turns off their breathing. Maybe a stroke, but I did brain sections like you wouldn't believe on two similar cases.'

'And?'

'Nothing. Clean as a whistle.'

Susan began to feel a bit queasy. The atmosphere, the smell, the images, the noises all joined forces to make her feel light-headed and she shuddered with a mild wave of nausea. She swallowed.

'Are the hospital charts for Ferrer and Crawford down here?'

'Sure, they're in the coffee room through the lab.'

'I'd like to look at them for a few minutes. If you find any-thing significant, would you give me a yell? I'd be interested in seeing it.'

The taller resident lifted the heart and placed it on the scale. 'These your patients?'

'Not exactly,' said Susan, starting toward the exit, 'but they might be.'

The taller resident looked quizzically over at the other as Susan left. His companion was watching Susan exit, trying to figure out a smooth way of getting her name and number.

The coffee room could have been anywhere in the hospital. The coffee machine was an ancient device, the paint on one side burned and the wire frayed to the point of being a real hazard. The counter-top desk along both side walls was spread with charts, paper, books, coffee cups, and a welter of ball-point pens.

'That was quick,' said the resident who had been staining the slides. He was sitting at one of the desks, with a half-filled cup of coffee and a half-eaten doughnut. He was busy signing a large stack of typed pathology reports.

'Autopsies are apparently too much for me,' admitted Susan.

'You get used to it, like everything else,' said the resident, stuffing more doughnut into his mouth.

'Possibly. Where would I look for the charts of the patients they are posting?'

The resident washed down the doughnut with coffee, swal-lowing with some effort.

'In that shelf marked "Post." When you finish with them,

put them over there in the shelf marked "Medical Records" because we're finished with them.'

Turning to the rear wall, Susan faced a series of cubic shelves. One of the shelves was marked 'Post.' On it she found Ferrer's and Crawford's charts. Clearing one of the desks of debris, Susan sat down and took out her notebook. At the top of an empty page she wrote, 'Crawford,' on the top of another she wrote, 'Ferrer.' Methodically she began to extract the charts as she had done with Nancy Greenly's.

Tuesday February 24
8:05am

Susan had found it unbelievably difficult to emerge from the warmth and comfort of her bed when the radio alarm went off the following morning. The fact that it was a Linda Ronstadt selection was a big help in that it caused some degree of pleasant association in Susan's mind and instead of turning the radio off, she lay there and let the sounds and rhythm course through her. By the time the song was over Susan was fully awake, her mind beginning to race over the events of the previous day. The night before, at least until three A.M., had been passed in deep concentration with the large pile of journal articles, the books on anaesthesiology, her own internal medicine books, and her clinical neurology text. She had amassed an enormous amount of notes, and her bibliography had increased to some one hundred articles that she planned to drag from the library stacks. The project had become more complex, more demanding, yet at the same time more fascinating, more absorbing. As a consequence Susan had become even more determined, and she realized that she was going to have to accomplish a great deal that day.

Shower, dressing, and breakfast were dispatched with commendable speed. During breakfast, she reread some of her notes, realizing that she would have to reread the last few articles she had read the night before.

The walk to the MBTA stop on Huntington Avenue proved to Susan that the weather had not changed and she cursed the fact that Boston had to be situated so far north. With luck she found a seat on the ageing street car and was able to unfold a portion of her IBM printout. She wanted to check once more the number of cases which it suggested.

'Good to see you, Susan. Don't tell me you're going to go to lecture today?'

Susan looked up into the grinning face of George Niles, who was holding on to the bar above her head.

'I'd never miss lecture, George; you know that.'

'Looks like you missed rounds. It's after nine.'

'I could say the same to you.' Susan's tone hovered between being friendly and combative.

'I was told in no uncertain terms that I had to be seen in Student Health to rule out a comminuted compound skull fracture from yesterday's gala event in the OR.'

'You are OK, aren't you?' asked Susan with genuine sincerity and concern.

'Yeah, I'm fine. It's just hard to patch up my injured ego. That was the only thing that broke. But the clinic doc said that the ego had to heal itself.'

Susan allowed herself to laugh. Niles joined. The car stopped at Northeastern University.

'Missing half of your first day at Surgery at the Memorial, then skipping rounds the next day, that's commendable, Miss Wheeler.' George assumed a serious expression. 'In no time at all you'll be able to run for medical student Phantom of the Year. If you keep it up you'll be able to challenge the record set by Phil Greer during second-year Pathology.'

Susan didn't answer. She went back to her IBM sheets.

'What are you working on, anyway?' asked Niles, twisting

himself in an attempt to view the printout right side up.

Susan looked up at Niles. 'I'm working on my Nobel Prize acceptance speech. I'd tell you about it but you might miss lecture.'

The car plunged down into the tunnel, beginning its transit under the city. Conversation became impossible. Susan resumed her check of the IBM printout sheet. She wanted to be damn sure of the numbers.

With its private offices Beard 8 resembled Beard 10. Susan walked down the corridor, stopping at room 810. The door had crisp black lettering across its aged but polished mahogany surface: 'Department of Medicine, Professor J. P. Nelson, MD, PHD.'

Nelson was Chief of Medicine, Stark's counterpart, but associated with internal medicine and its subspecialities. Nelson was also a powerful figure in the medical centre but not quite as influential as Stark, nor was he as dynamic, and as a fund raiser, he couldn't even compare. Nevertheless, it took a bit of fortitude on Susan's part to get up the nerve to approach this Olympian figure. With some hesitation she pushed open the mahogany door and faced a secretary with wire-rimmed glasses and a comfortable smile.

'My name is Susan Wheeler and I called a few minutes ago to see Dr Nelson.'

'Yes of course. You're one of our medical students?'

'That's right,' said Susan, unsure of what 'our' meant in that context.

'You're lucky, Miss Wheeler, to catch Dr Nelson in. Plus I believe he remembers you from a class or something. Anyway, he'll be with you shortly.'

Susan thanked her and retreated to one of the stiff black waiting-room chairs. She pulled out her notebook to scan more of her notes, but instead found herself viewing the room, the secretary, and the lifestyle it meant for Dr Nelson. As far as the value system in medical school was concerned, such a position represented the final triumph of years of effort and even luck. It was just the kind of luck Susan felt could be behind her present quest. All someone needed was one lucky break and the doors would open.

The reverie was cut short by the door to the inner office being opened. Two doctors in long white coats came from within, continuing their conversation at the door. Susan could get bits and pieces and it seemed to be about an enormous amount of drugs that had been located in a locker in the surgical lounge. The younger of the two men was quite agitated and spoke in a whisper whose sound level was approximately equal to normal speech. The other gentleman had the portly bearing of a mature physician, replete with soft, knowing eyes, luxuriant greying hair, and a consoling smile. Susan knew it had to be Dr Nelson. He seemed to be trying to console the other with reassuring words and a lingering pat on the shoulder. Once the other doctor had left, Dr Nelson turned to Susan and beckoned for her to follow him.

Nelson's office was a tumble of reprinted journal articles, scattered books, and stacks of letters. It appeared as if a tornado had swept through the room several years previously with no subsequent effort at reconstruction. The furniture consisted of a large desk and an old cracked leather chair that squeaked as Dr Nelson lowered his weight into it. There were two other smaller leather chairs facing the desk. Susan was motioned to take one of them as Dr Nelson took one of his briars and opened a tobacco canister on the desk. Before filling the pipe he hit it on the palm of his left hand a few times. The few ashes that appeared were carelessly scattered on the floor.

'Ah yes, Miss Wheeler,' began Dr Nelson, scanning a note card on his desk. 'I remember you well from physical diagnosis class. You were from Wellesley.'

'Radcliffe.'

'Radcliffe, of course.' Dr Nelson corrected his note card. 'What can we do for you?'

'I'm not sure how to start. But I've become very interested in the problem of prolonged coma, and I have begun to look into it.'

Dr Nelson leaned back, the chair squeaking in agony. He placed the tips of his fingers together.

'That's fine, but coma is a big subject, and, more important, it is a symptom rather than a disease in itself. It is the cause of the coma that is important. What is the cause of the coma you have become interested in?'

'I don't know. In short, that's why I'm interested in it. I'm interested in the kind of coma that just seems to happen and no cause is found.'

'Are you concerned with emergency room patients or in-hospital patients?' asked Dr Nelson, whose voice changed slightly.

'Inpatients.'

'Are you referring to the few cases that have occurred during surgery?'

'If you call seven few.'

'Seven,' said Dr Nelson taking several long pulls from his pipe, 'I believe is a rather high estimate.'

'It's not an estimate. Six previous cases occurred during surgery. Presently there is another case upstairs, operated on yesterday, that appears to fit into the same category. In addition, there have been at least five cases on the medical floor occurring in patients admitted for some seemingly unrelated complaint.'

'How did you get this information, Miss Wheeler?' asked Dr Nelson with an altogether different tone of voice. The previous warmth was gone. His eyes regarded Susan without blinking. Susan was unaware of this change in apparent mood.

'I got the information from this computer printout right here.' Susan leaned forward with the printout and handed it across the desk to Dr Nelson. 'The cases I've mentioned have been indicated with yellow ink. You'll see that there is no mistake. Besides, this represents only coma cases for the last year. I don't know what the incidence was before then, and I think it would be essential to get a year-by-year printout. In that way one could have a better idea if this problem is static or on a dynamic upswing. And perhaps even more important, or at least equally important, I have a feeling that a number of sudden deaths here at the Memorial could be ascribed to the same unknown category. I believe the computer could help on that as well. Anyway, it is for these reasons that I wanted to speak with you. I was wondering if you would support me on this endeavour. What I need is full clearance to use the computer and the opportunity to get the hospital charts on these patients. I came to you because I have an intuitive feeling that it represents some sort of unknown medical problem.'

With her case presented, Susan allowed herself to sit back into the chair. She felt she had put the matter fairly and completely; if Dr Nelson was going to be interested, he certainly had enough to go on to make up his mind.

Dr Nelson did not speak right away. Instead he continued to regard Susan; then he studied the printout, taking short, quick puffs on his pipe.

'This is all very interesting information, young lady. Of course I have been aware of the problem. However, there are other implications in these statistics and I can assure you that this apparent high incidence is occurring because ... well, frankly ... we have been lucky over the last five or six years that we haven't had any such cases. Statistics have a way of catching up with you, though ... and indeed that seems to be the case at present. As to your request, I'm afraid I'm not in a position to grant it. You undoubtedly understand one of the major impediments to our establishing our central computer information bank was the creation of adequate safeguards concerning the confidentiality of most of the information stored. It is impossible for me to give blanket authorization. In fact, this type of endeavour is really ... what should I say ... hmm ... beyond ... or above that which a medical student of your level is equipped to deal with. I think it would be in everyone's best interest, yours included, if you would limit your research interests to more scientific projects. I'm certain I could find room for you in our liver lab, if you were interested.'

Susan was so accustomed to academic encouragement that she was totally caught off guard by Dr Nelson's negative response to her investigation. Not only was he not interested, but he was obviously trying to talk Susan out of the project as well.

Susan hesitated, then stood up.

'Thank you very much for the offer. But I've just gotten so

involved with this study that I think I'll follow it up for a while.'

'Suit yourself, Miss Wheeler. But I'm sorry; I cannot help you.'

'Thank you for your time,' said Susan, reaching out for her computer printout.

'I'm afraid this information cannot be made available for you any longer,' said Dr Nelson interposing his hand between Susan's and the IBM sheet.

Susan kept her hand extended for a second of indecision. Once again Dr Nelson had caught her off guard with an unexpected response. It seemed absurd that he would actually have the gall to confiscate material she already had.

Susan did not say another word and she avoided looking at Dr Nelson. She got her things together and left. Dr Nelson instantly picked up the telephone and placed a call.

Tuesday February 24
10:48am

In Dr Harris's office there was an entire bookcase full of the latest books on anaesthesiology, some still in pre-publication bound galleys, sent for his endorsement. For Susan this was a boon, and her eyes scanned the titles for any books specifically on complications. She located one, and she wrote down the title and publisher. Next she looked for any general texts which she had not seen in the library. And her eyes registered another find: *Coma: Pathophysiological Basis of Clinical States*. Excitedly she withdrew the volume and thumbed through it, noticing the chapter headings. She wished she had had the book at the onset of her reading.

The door to the office opened and Susan looked up to face Dr Robert Harris for the second time. Instantly she felt a certain sense of intimidation or scorn as Dr Harris regarded her without the slightest sign of recognition or friendliness. It had not been Susan's idea to wait for him in his office; it had been the direct order of the secretary who had arranged the meeting for Susan. Now Susan felt an uneasiness, as if she were an interloper in Dr Harris's private sanctum. The fact that she was holding one of his books made it that much worse.

'Be sure to put the volume back where you found it,' said Harris as he turned to close the door, his speech slow and deliberate as if addressed to a child. He removed his long white coat and hung it on the hook on the back of the door. Without another word he retreated behind his desk to open a large ledger and make several notations. He acted as if Susan were not even there.

Susan closed the textbook and replaced it on the shelf. Then she returned to the director's chair in which she had started her wait for Dr Harris thirty minutes before.

The only window was directly behind Harris, and its light, combining with the overhead fluorescent light, gave a strange shimmering quality to Harris's appearance. Susan had to squint against the glare coming directly at her.

The smooth tawny colour of Harris's arms was a perfect setting for the gold digital watch on his left wrist. His forearms were massive, tapering to surprisingly narrow shafts. Despite the time of year and the temperature, Dr Harris was dressed in a short-sleeved blue shirt. Several minutes went by before he finished with the ledger. After closing the cover he pressed a buzzer for his secretary to come in and take it. Only then did he turn and acknowledge Susan's existence.

'Miss Wheeler, I am certainly surprised to see you in my office.' Dr Harris slowly leaned back in his chair. He seemed to have some difficulty looking directly at Susan. Because of the background lighting Susan could not see the details of his face. His tone was cold. There was a silence.

'I would like to apologize,' began Susan, 'for my apparent impertinence yesterday in the recovery room. As you probably are aware, this is my first clinical rotation, and I'm unaccustomed to the hospital environment, particularly to the recovery room. On top of that there had been a strange coincidence. About two hours prior to our meeting I had spent some time with the very patient you were attending. I had started his I.V. prior to surgery.'

Susan paused, hoping for some sign of acknowledgment from the faceless figure in front of her. There was none. There was no movement whatsoever. Susan continued.

'The fact of the matter was that my conversation with the patient had not remained on an entirely professional level; in fact, we had tentatively agreed to meet sometime on a social basis.'

Susan paused again but silence continued from Dr Harris.

'I'm offering this information more as an explanation than an excuse for my reaction in the recovery room. Needless to say, when I was confronted with the reality of the patient's condition, I became quite upset.'

'So you reverted to the vestiges of your sex,' said Harris condescendingly.

'Excuse me?' Susan had heard his comment, but by reflex she questioned whether she had heard him correctly.

'I said, so you reverted to the vestiges of your sex.'

Susan felt a flush spread across her cheeks. 'I'm not sure how to take that.'

'Take it at face value.'

There was an awkward pause. Susan fidgeted, then spoke. 'If that is your opinion of being a woman, then I plead guilty; emotionalism under such circumstances is understandable from any human being. I admit the fact that I was not the archetypical professional at the first meeting with the patient, but I think that if the roles had been reversed, I being the patient and the patient being the doctor, it probably would have come out the same. I hardly think that susceptibility to human responses is a frailty reserved for female medical students, especially when I have to put up with the patronizing attitudes of my male counterparts with the female nurses. But I did not come here to discuss such matters. I came here to apologize for impertinence to you and that is all. I'm not apologizing for being a woman.'

Susan paused again, expecting some sort of reply. None was forthcoming. Susan felt a definite feeling of irritation spread through her.

'If my being a woman bothers you, then that's your problem,' said Susan with emphasis.

'You're being impertinent again, my dear,' said Harris.

Susan stood up. Gazing down, she looked at Harris's face, his narrowed eyes, his full cheeks and broad chin. Light played through the edge of his hair, making it appear like silver filigree.

'I can see this is getting us nowhere. I'm sorry I came. Goodbye, Dr Harris.'

Susan turned and opened the door to the corridor.

'Why did you come?' said Harris after her.

With her hand on the door, Susan looked out into the corridor and considered Harris's question. Obviously debating with herself whether to leave or not, she finally turned and faced the Chief of Anaesthesiology again.

'I thought I'd apologize so that we could let bygones be bygones. I had the irrational hope that you might be willing to lend me some assistance.'

'In what regard?' said Harris, his voice relaxing its aloofness by a degree.

Susan hesitated again, debating, then let the door shut. She walked up to the chair she had been sitting in but she did not sit down. She eyed Harris and thought that she had nothing to lose and should say what she had originally come to say despite his coldness.

'Since you said that there have been six cases of prolonged coma following anaesthesia during the last year, I decided to look into the problem as a potential subject for my third-year paper. Well, I found out that you were absolutely correct. There have been six cases following anaesthesia during the last year. But there also have been five cases of sudden unexplained coma occurring in patients on the medical floors during the past year. Yesterday there were two deaths from apparent respiratory arrest. These patients gave no history to suggest that such an event might take place. They were in the hospital for essentially peripheral problems; one had a minor foot operation followed by phlebitis, the other had Bell's palsy. Both were essentially well individuals, except one of them had glaucoma. There was no explanation for their respiratory arrest and I have a feeling that they are possibly related to the other coma cases. In other words, I think I have twelve cases representing gradations of the same problem. And if Berman turns out to be in the same boat as the others, then there are thirteen people suffering from some unexplained phenomenon. Perhaps worst of all, the incidence seems to be on the upswing, especially for the cases occurring during anaesthesia. The interval between cases seems to be getting shorter and shorter. Anyway, I have decided to try to look into the problem. In order for me to continue my investigation I need some help from someone like yourself. I need authorization to search the data bank and see how many cases the computer could find if it's asked directly. Also I need the charts of the previous victims.'

Harris leaned forward and slowly placed his arms on his desk.

'So the Medical Department has had some trouble too,' he murmured. 'Jerry Nelson didn't mention that.'

Looking up at Susan, he spoke louder.

'Miss Wheeler, you are dabbling in troubled waters. It's refreshing to hear someone, fresh from the basic science years of medical school, interested in clinical research. But this is not the proper subject for you. There are many reasons for my saying this. First of all, the problem of coma is far more complex than might be apparent to you. It is a wastepaper-basket term, a mere description. And for someone to immediately assume all cases of coma are related simply because the causative agent is not precisely known is intellectually absurd. Miss Wheeler, I advise you to stick to something more specific, less speculative, for your so-called third year paper. As far as helping you is concerned, I must admit I do not have the time.

And let me admit something else that might be rather apparent to you. I don't try to hide it. I'm not keen on women in medicine.'

Harris pointed his finger at Susan and aimed across it almost as if it were a gun.

'They treat it like a game, something to do for now ... something chic ... later, who knows. It's a fad. And on top of that, they are invariably, impossibly emotional and ...'

'Dr Harris, cut the bullshit,' interrupted Susan, lifting up the back of the chair and letting it fall a few inches. She was furious. 'I didn't come here to listen to this type of nonsense. In fact it's people like you who keep medicine in the old rut, unable to respond to the challenge of relevancy and change.'

Harris pounded the top of the desk with his open hand causing a few papers and pencils to flee for safety. Almost in one step he came from behind his desk with a speed that caught Susan off guard. His movement brought his face only inches from Susan's. She froze before the unexpected fury she had unleashed.

'Miss Wheeler, you do not know your place here,' hissed Harris, holding himself in check with great difficulty. 'You are not to be the Messiah who is going to miraculously deliver us from a problem which has already been under the scrutiny of the best minds in this hospital. In fact, I see you as a very destructive influence and I can promise you this: you'll be out of this hospital in twenty-four hours. Now get out of my office.'

Susan backed up, afraid to expose her unguarded back to this man who seemed about to explode with hatred. She opened the door and ran down the corridor, feeling the tears well up from her mixture of fear and anger.

Behind her, Harris kicked the door shut and snatched the phone off the hook. He told his secretary to get him the director of the hospital without delay.

Tuesday February 24

11:00am

Susan slowed to a deliberate walk, avoiding the questioning expressions of the people using the corridor. Her emotions, she was afraid, could be read from her face like an open book. Usually when she cried or was about to cry, her cheeks and eyelids turned bright crimson. Although she knew she wasn't going to cry now, the proper neutral connections had been made. If someone she knew stopped her and said something innocuous, like 'What's the matter, Susan?' she probably would have cried. So Susan wanted to be alone for a few moments. As it was, she was more angry and frustrated than anything else as the fear generated by her encounter with Harris evaporated. Fear seemed so out of place in the context of a meeting with a professional superior that she wondered if she was becoming delusional. Had she really crossed Harris to the extent that he had had to keep himself in check to avoid some sort of physical encounter? Was he just about to strike her, as she had feared, when he came bounding out from behind his desk? The idea seemed ludicrous and it was difficult for her to believe that the situation had been so precipitous. She knew that she could never make someone else believe what she had felt. It reminded her of the situation with Captain Queeg in *The Caine Mutiny*.

The stairwell was the only haven she could think of, and she pushed through the metal door. It closed behind her rapidly, cutting off the raw fluorescent lights and the voices. The single bare incandescent bulb above her had a warmer glow and the stairway offered a soothing silence.

Susan was still clutching her notebook and a ballpoint pen. Gritting her teeth, and swearing loudly enough to hear an echo, she threw the notebook and the pen down the course of stairs to the landing below. The notebook bounced on the edge of a stair, then fell flat, cover down, on to the floor. It skidded across the landing and struck the wall, coming to a rest unhurt

163

and open. The pen flipped over the edge of the stairs and a few telltale sounds suggested that it had descended to the bowels of the hospital.

Uninviting as it was, Susan sat down on the top stair, her feet on the very next step, bringing her knees up at acute angles. Her elbows rested on the tops of her knees. She closed her eyes tightly. So much of her experience in medicine with relationships had been reemphasized in the short time she had been at the Memorial. Professional superiors, instructors to professors, reacted to her in a manner that unpredictably varied from warm acceptance to overt hostility. Usually the hostility was more passive-aggressive than Harris's had been; Nelson's reaction was more typical. Nelson had been friendly at first, then later had slipped into an obstructive stance. Susan felt an old familiar feeling, a feeling which had developed ever since she had chosen medicine as a career : it was a paradoxical loneliness. Although constantly surrounded by people who reacted to her, she felt apart. The day and a half at the Memorial had not been an auspicious beginning for her clinical years. Even more than during her first days at medical school, she felt that she was entering a male club; she was an outsider forced to adapt, to compromise.

Susan opened her eyes and looked down at her notebook sprawled on the landing below. Throwing the book had given some vent to her frustrations, and she felt a degree more relaxed. Control was returning. At the same time the childish aspect of the gesture surprised her. It was not like her to do such a thing. Perhaps Nelson and Harris were, in the final analysis, right. Perhaps being a medical student so early in training, she was not the right person to investigate such a serious clinical problem. And perhaps her emotionalism was a built-in handicap. Would a male have responded in the same way to Harris's reaction? Was she more emotional than her male counterparts? Susan thought about Bellows and his cool detached manner, how he could concentrate on the sodium ions while confronting a tragedy. Susan had found fault with his behaviour the day before, but now, daydreaming in the stairwell, she was no longer so sure. She wondered if she could achieve that type of detachment if it were necessary.

A door opening somewhere far above brought Susan to her feet. There were some hushed and hurried footsteps on the metal stairs, then the sound of another door, then silence returned. The crude cement walls of the stairwell combined with the curious longitudinal rust-coloured stains enhanced Susan's sense of isolation. In slow motion she descended to where her notebook lay. By chance it had opened to the page copied from Nancy Greenly's chart. Reaching for the book, Susan read her own handwriting. 'Age 23, Caucasian, previous medical history negative except for mononucleosis at age 18.' Quickly Susan's mind conjured up the image of Nancy Greenly, her ghostly pallor, lying in the ICU. 'Age twenty-three,' Susan said aloud. In a rush she re-experienced the intensity of her feelings of transference. Susan felt a rekindling of her commitment to investigating the coma problem to the limit of her abilities despite Harris, despite Nelson. Without questioning why, she felt a strong urge to find Bellows. Within a single day her feeling toward Bellows had taken a one-hundred-and-eighty-degree turn.

'Susan, for Christ's sake, haven't you had enough yet?' With his elbows on the table, Bellows placed his palms against his face so that his fingers could lightly massage his closed eyes. His hands rotated, bringing his fingers below his ears. With his face cradled in his hands, he looked at Susan sitting across from him in the hospital coffee shop. The place had a relatively clean appearance with indeterminate modern furnishings. It was primarily meant for visitors to the hospital, although the staff frequented it on occasion. The prices were higher than the cafeteria's but the quality was equivalently better. At eleven-thirty it was crowded but Susan had found a table in the corner and had paged Bellows. She was pleased when he agreed to see her immediately.

'Susan,' continued Bellows after a pause, 'you've got to give up this self-destructive crusade. I mean it's absolutely sure suicide. Susan, there's one thing about medicine; you've got to flow with the river or you'll drown. I've learned that. God, whatever could have possessed you to go to Harris, especially after that little episode yesterday?'

Susan sipped her coffee in silence, keeping her eyes on Bellows. She wanted him to talk because it sounded good; he seemed to care. But also she wanted him to get involved, if that were at all possible. Bellows shook his head as he took a drink of his coffee.

'Harris is powerful, but he's not omnipotent around here,' added Bellows. 'Stark can reverse anything Harris does if he has reason to do so. Stark has raised most of the money for construction around here, millions. So people listen to what he says. So why not give him a reason; why not pretend to be a normal medical student for a few days? Christ, I need it myself. Guess who was on rounds this morning to welcome you medical students? Stark. And the first thing he wanted to know was why there were only three students out of five. Well I told him that, foolishly enough, I had taken you all in to see a case on the first day, and one of you had fainted and smashed his head on the floor. You can guess how that went over. And then I couldn't think of anything appropriate to say about you. So I said you were doing a literature search on coma following anaesthesia. I decided that since I couldn't think of a good lie I might as well tell the truth. Well he immediately assumed that it had been my idea to put you on the project. I cannot repeat what he said to me in response. It should be enough for me to say that I need you to behave like a normal medical student. I've covered for you to the extent that I'm already overdrawn.'

Susan felt an urge to touch Bellows, kind of a reassuring people-to-people hug. But she didn't; instead she played with her coffee spoon with her head down. Then she looked at Bellows.

'I'm really sorry if I've caused you some difficulties, Mark, really I am. Needless to say, it was unintentional. I'm the first to admit this thing has gotten out of hand so rapidly that it's uncanny. I started because of an emotional crisis of sorts. Nancy Greenly is the same age as I, and I've had some occasional irregularities with my periods, probably just like Nancy

Greenly. I cannot help but feel some ... some kinship with her. And then Berman ... what a Goddamned coincidence. By the way, did Berman have an EEG?'

'Yeah, it was completely flat. The brain is gone.'

Susan searched Bellows's face for some response, some sign of emotion. Bellows lifted the coffee cup to his lips and took a sip.

'The brain is gone?'

'Gone.'

Susan bit her lower lip and looked down into her coffee cup. A small amount of oil opalesced on the surface in colourful swirls. Somehow she had expected the news, but it still cut into her and she fought with her mind, suppressing emotion as best she could.

'Are you OK?' asked Bellows, reaching across and gently lifting her chin with his hands.

'Don't say anything for a second,' said Susan, not daring to look at him. The last thing she wanted to do was cry and if Bellows persisted it would happen. Bellows cooperated and returned to his coffee while keeping his eyes on Susan.

After a few moments Susan looked up; her eyelids were slightly reddened.

'Anyway,' continued Susan, avoiding eye contact with Bellows, 'I started with an emotional sort of commitment, but that quickly mixed with intellectual commitment. I really thought I had stumbled onto something ... a new disease or a new complication of anaesthesia or a new syndrome ... something, I don't know what. But then there was another change. The problem loomed bigger than I had imagined initially. They've had coma cases on the medical floors as well as in surgery. On top of that, there were those deaths you told me about. I know you think it's crazy, but I think they are related, and the pathologist intimated they have had a number of such cases. My intuition tells me there is something else in all this, something ... I don't know how to explain it ... call it supernatural or call it sinister ...'

'Ah, now paranoia,' said Bellows, nodding his head in mock understanding.

'I can't help it, Mark. There was something very strange about the reaction of Nelson and Harris. You have to admit that Harris's reaction was totally inappropriate.'

Bellows tapped his forehead in succession with the heel of his hand. 'Susan, you've been staying up watching old horror movies. Admit it, Susan ... admit it or I'll think you're having a psychotic break. This is absurd. What do you suspect, some sort of sinister inversion layer spreading evil forces, or is it a crazed killer who hates people with minor ailments? Susan, if you hypothesize so extravagantly and with such creativity, then come up with some ideas of motive. I mean, a demented killer was OK for Hollywood and George C. Scott in *Hospital* just to create an artificial mystery ... but it's a little too far-fetched for reality. I admit Harris's performance sounds a bit weird, there's no doubt about that. But at the same time I think I could come up with some reasonable explanation for his unreasonable behaviour.'

'Try.'

'OK, I'm sure Harris is already completely uptight about this problem of coma. After all, it's his department which essentially has to shoulder the responsibility. And here comes a young medical student to drive in the painful spikes a little more. I think its understandable for an individual to overreact under that kind of stress.'

'Harris did a little more than overreact. This nut came from behind his desk with the intent of knocking me around the room.'

'Maybe you turned him on.'

'What?'

'On top of everything else maybe he was reacting to you sexually.'

'Come on, Mark.'

'I'm serious.'

'Mark, this guy's a doctor, a professor, a chief of a department.'

'That does not rule out sexuality.'

'Now you're the one being absurd.'

168

'A lot of doctors spend so much time with the nuts and bolts of their profession that they fail to ever really adequately resolve the usual social crises of life. Socially speaking, doctors are not very accomplished, to say the least.'

'Are you speaking for yourself?'

'Possibly. Susan, you have to realize you are a very seductive girl.'

'Fuck you.'

Bellows looked at Susan, stunned. Then he glanced around to see if anyone was listening to their conversation. He had not forgotten they were in the coffee shop. He took a sip of coffee and then regarded Susan for several minutes. She returned his stare.

'Why did you say that?' said Bellows with a lowered voice.

'Because you deserved it. I get a little tired of that kind of stereotyping. When you say I'm seductive you imply to me that I am actively trying to seduce. Believe me, I am not. If medicine has done anything to me, it certainly has cut into my image of myself as conventionally female.'

'All right, maybe it was a bad word. I didn't mean to imply it was your fault. You're an attractive girl ...'

'Well there's a helluva difference between saying someone's attractive and saying someone's seductive.'

'OK, I meant attractive. Sexually attractive. And there are people who may find that hard to deal with. Anyway, Susan, I didn't mean to get into an argument. Besides, I've got to go. I've got a case in fifteen minutes. If you want, we can talk about it tonight over dinner. That is, if you still want to have dinner?' Bellows started to get up, taking his tray.

'Sure, dinner's fine.'

'Meanwhile, couldn't you try to be normal for a little while?'

'Well, I have one more stone to turn over.'

'What's that?'

'Stark. If he doesn't help me, I'll have to give up. Without some support I'm doomed to failure, unless of course you want to get the computer information for me.'

Bellows let his tray drop back onto the table. 'Susan, don't ask me to do anything like that, because I can't. As for Stark, Susan, you're crazy. He'll eat you alive. Harris is a jewel in comparison to Stark.'

'That's a risk I have to take. It's probably safer than undergoing minor surgery here at the Memorial.'

'That's not fair.'

'Fair? What a word choice. Why don't you ask Berman if he thinks it's fair?'

'I can't.'

'You can't?' Susan paused, waiting for Bellows to explain himself. Susan did not want to think of the worst but it came to her automatically. Bellows started toward the tray rack without explaining himself.

'He's still alive, isn't he?' asked Susan with a tingle of desperation in her voice. She got up and walked behind Bellows.

'If you call that heart beating being alive, he's alive.'

'Is he in the recovery room?'

'No.'

'The ICU?'

'No.'

'OK, I give up, where is he?'

Bellows and Susan put their trays into the rack and walked from the coffee shop. They were immediately engulfed by the mob in the hall and forced to quicken their steps.

'He was transferred to the Jefferson Institute in South Boston.'

'What the hell is the Jefferson Institute?'

'It's an intensive care facility built as part of the area's Health Maintenance Organization design. Supposedly it's been designed to curtail costs by applying economics of scale in relation to intensive care. It's privately run but the government financed construction. The concept and plans came out of the Harvard-MIT health practices report.'

'I've never even heard about it. Have you visited it?'

'No, but I'd like to. I saw it from the outside once. It's very modern ... massive and rectilinear. The thing that caught my eye was that there were no windows on the first floor. God only knows why that caught my eye.' Bellows shook his head. Susan smiled.

'There's a tour organized for the medical community,' continued Bellows, 'to visit the place on the second Tuesday of each month. Those that have gone have been really impressed. Apparently the programme is a big success. All chronic-care ICU patients who are comatose or nearly so can be admitted. The idea is to keep the ICU beds in the acute-care hospitals available for acute cases. I think it's a good idea.'

'But Berman just became comatose. Why would they transfer him so quickly?'

'The time factor is less important than stability. Obviously he's going to be a long-term-care problem and I guess he was very stable, not like our friend Greenly. God, she's been a pain in the ass. Just about every complication known, she's had it.'

Susan thought about emotional detachment. It was difficult for her to understand how Bellows could be so out of touch emotionally with the problem Nancy Greenly represented.

'If she were stable,' continued Bellows, 'even threatened stability, I'd transfer her to the Jefferson in a flash. Her case demands an inordinate amount of time with thin rewards. Actually, I have nothing to gain by her. If I keep her alive until the services switch, then at least I've suffered no professional harm. It's like all those Presidents keeping Vietnam alive. They couldn't win, but they didn't want to lose either. They had nothing to gain but a lot to lose.'

They reached the main elevators and Bellows made sure one of the silently waiting crowd had pushed the 'up' button.

'Where was I?' Bellows scratched his head, obviously preoccupied.

'You were talking about Berman and the ICU.'

'Oh, yeah. Well, I guess he was stable.' Bellows looked at his watch, then eyed the closed doors with hatred. 'Goddamn elevators.

'Susan, I'm not one to give advice usually, but I can't help myself. See Stark if you must, but remember I've gone out on a limb for you, so act accordingly. Then after you see Stark, give this crusade up. You'll ruin your career before you begin.'

'Are you worried about my career or your own?'

'Both, I guess,' said Bellows standing aside for the disembarking elevator passengers.

'At least you're honest.'

Bellows squeezed into the elevator and waved to Susan, saying something about seven-thirty. Susan presumed he meant their dinner date. At that moment her watch said eleven forty-five.

Tuesday February 24
11:45am

Bellows looked up at the floor indicator above the door. He had to cock his head way back, as he was almost directly under it. He knew that he had to hustle in order to be on time for his case, a haemorrhoid operation on a sixty-two-year-old man. It wasn't his idea of a fascinating case but he loved to operate. Once he got going and felt the strange sense of responsibility which the knife afforded, he didn't really care where he was working, stomach or hand, mouth or asshole.

Bellows thought about seeing Susan that night, and he felt a sense of pleasurable anticipation. Everything would be fresh and unspoiled. Their conversation could range over any one of a thousand topics. And physically? Bellows had no idea what to expect. In fact he wondered how he would be able to bridge the colleague-like rapport they had already established. Within himself he sensed a very positive physical reaction toward Susan but it began to trouble him. In a lot of ways, sex meant aggression to Bellows, and he didn't feel any aggression toward Susan, not yet.

A smile crept over his face as he imagined himself kissing Susan impulsively. It made him remember those awkward adolescent moments in his early youth when he would continue some banal conversation with his pimpled date right up to her doorstep. Then without warning he would kiss the girl, hard and sloppy. Then he'd step back to see what happened, hoping for acceptance but fearing rejection. It had never ceased to amaze him when he found acceptance, because in many ways he didn't know why he was kissing the girl in the first place.

The concept of seeing Susan socially reminded Bellows of those early years of dating because he felt an inner urge for physical contact yet did not expect it. Susan was obviously palpable and luscious, yet she was going to be a doctor, as he was. Hence she would have little appreciation for the trump card Bellows always felt in a social situation – most everyone was impressed when he said he was a doctor, a surgeon! It didn't matter that Bellows himself knew that being a doctor did not assure any special attributes, contrary to popular mythology. In fact, if he used many of the attending surgeons at the Memorial as examples, the effect of admitting such an association should have been a handicap. But what really bothered Bellows was the knowledge that a penis would hold little fascination for Susan; in all probability she had dissected one.

Bellows did not reduce his own sexual urges and fantasies to anatomical and physiological realities, but what about Susan? She looked so normal with her smile, her soft skin, the hint of her breast gently rising with her breathing. But she had studied the parasympathetic reflexes, and the endocrine alterations that made sex possible, even enjoyable. Maybe she had studied too much, too much of the wrong thing. Maybe even if the occasion was auspicious, Bellows would find his penis limp, impotent. The thought made Bellows doubtful about seeing Susan. After all, once away from the hospital, Bellows wanted to escape, and mindless sex was a superb method. With Susan, if it happened at all, it wasn't going to be mindless. It couldn't be. Finally there was the sticky question about the wisdom of dating a student currently under his supervision on the surgery rotation. Bellows was undoubtedly going to be called upon to evaluate Susan's performance as a student. Dating her represented a ridiculous conflict of interest.

The elevator door opened on the OR floor and Bellows quickly crossed to the main OR desk. The clerk was preparing the OR schedule of the following day.

'What room is my case in? It's a Mr Barron, a haemorrhoid.'

The clerk looked up to see who it was, then down at the current schedule.

'You're Dr Bellows?'

'None other.'

'Well, you have been taken off the case.'

'Taken off? By whom?' Bellows was perplexed.

'By Dr Chandler, and he left word for you to meet him in his office when you appeared.'

To be taken off one of his own cases was very strange for Bellows. Certainly it was within George Chandler's prerogative since he was the chief resident. But it was highly irregular. Occasionally Bellows had been removed from a scrub on which he was to assist, usually to help on some other case, and usually for purely logistic reasons. But to be removed from one of his own cases where the patient had been assigned to Beard 5 was a totally new experience.

Bellows thanked the OR clerk without bothering to hide his surprise and irritation. He turned and headed for George Chandler's office.

The chief resident's office was a windowless cubicle on 2. From this tiny area came the tactical edicts that ran the surgical department from day to day. Chandler was in charge of all the schedules for all the residents, including the on-call and weekend duty assignments. Chandler was also in charge of the operating room schedule, assigning the staff and clinic cases as well as the assists for the attending surgeons who asked for them.

Bellows knocked on the closed door, entering after hearing a muffled 'Come in.' George Chandler was sitting at his desk, which nearly filled the tiny room. The desk faced the door, and Chandler had to squeeze past to gain access to the seat. Behind him was a file cabinet. In front of the desk was a single wooden chair. The room was bare; only a bulletin board adorned the walls. Blank but neat, the room was somewhat like Chandler himself.

The chief resident had successfully risen up the competitive pyramidal power structure of the lower world of students and residents. Now he was the liaison between the upper world, the fullfledged surgeons certified by speciality boards, and the lower world. As such he was a member of neither class. This fact was the source of his power as well as his weakness and isolation. The years of competition had taken their inexorable toll. Chandler was still young by most standards: thirty-three years old. He was not tall: about five eight. His hair was half-heartedly combed in some sort of modern Caesar look. His face had a gentle pudginess that belied his easily aroused temper. In many ways Chandler represented the young boy who has been bullied too much.

Bellows took the wooden chair opposite Chandler. At first no words were spoken. Chandler regarded a pencil he had in his fingers. His elbows were resting on the arms of his chair. He had rocked back from what he had been working on when Bellows knocked.

'Sorry about taking you off your case, Mark,' said Chandler without looking up.

'I can manage without another haemorrhoid,' said Bellows, maintaining a neutral tone.

There was another pause. Chandler tipped his chair forward to the level position and looked directly at Bellows. Bellows thought that he'd be a perfect individual to play Napoleon in a play.

'Mark, I'm going to assume you're serious about surgery, surgery here at the Memorial, to be exact.'

'I think that's a fair assumption.'

'Your record has been reasonable. In fact I've heard your name on several occasions in relation to possibly being considered for the chief residency. That leads me to one of the reasons I wanted to talk with you. Harris gave me a call not too long ago and he was completely strung out. I wasn't even sure what he was talking about for a few minutes. Apparently one of your students has been nosing around about these coma cases, and it's got Harris bullshit. Now, I have no idea what's going on, but he thinks that you might be behind getting the student interested and helping him.'

'It's a her.'

'Him, her, I don't give a damn.'

'Well, it might be significant. She happens to be a very well put together specimen. As for my role in the matter, it's a big fat zero! If anything, I have constantly tried to talk her out of the whole affair.'

'I'm not about to argue with you, Mark. All I wanted to do is warn you of the situation. I'd hate to have you gamble your chances on the chief residency because of some student's activities.'

Mark looked at Chandler and wondered what Chandler would say if he told Chandler that he was going to see Susan that night on a social basis.

'I have no idea if Harris has said anything to Stark about all this, Mark, and I can assure you that I won't unless it gets to the point where I have to cover my own tracks. But let me emphasize that Harris was livid, so you'd better tone your student down and tell him ...'

'Her!'

'OK, tell her to find something else to get interested in. After all there must be ten people who are working on the problem already. In fact most of Harris's department has been doing nothing else since the present run of anaesthetic coma catastrophes.'

'I'll try to tell her again, but it's not as easy as it may sound. This girl has a mind of her own, with a rather fertile imagination.' Bellows wondered why he chose that way to describe Susan's imagination. 'She's gotten into this thing because the first two patients she came in contact with are victims of the problem.'

'Anyway, let's just say you have been warned. What she does is going to reflect on you, especially if you aid her in any way at all. But that was only one of the reasons I wanted to talk with you. There is another problem, more serious, to be sure. Tell me, Mark, what is your locker number up in the OR?'

'Eight.'

'What about number 338?'

'That was my temporary locker. I used it for about one week before number eight became available.'

'Why didn't you stay with 338?'

'I guess it actually belonged to someone else, and I got to use it until I could get one of my own.'

'Do you know the combination of 338?'

'Maybe, if I thought long enough. Why do you ask?'

'Because of a strange finding by Dr Cowley. He claims that 338 opened by magic when he was changing his clothes and the whole Goddamn thing was filled with drugs. We checked it out and he was right. Every kind of drug that you could imagine and a few more, including narcotics. The locker list I have has you down for 338, not eight.'

'Who's down for eight?'

'Dr Eastman.'

'He hasn't done a case in years.'

'Exactly. Tell me, Mark, who gave you number eight? Walters?'

'Yup. Walters first told me to use 338, and then he gave me number eight.'

'OK, don't say anything to anybody about this, least of all to Walters. Finding a hoard of drugs like this is a pretty serious business, considering all the rigmarole you have to go through to get a narcotic in the first place. Because of my locker list, you will probably be contacted by the hospital administration. For obvious reasons they are not excited about letting this information out, especially with the recertification deal coming up. So keep it under your hat. And for God's sake, get your student interested in something else besides anaesthesia complications.'

Bellows emerged from Chandler's cubicle with a strange feeling. He wasn't surprised about hearing that he was being associated with Susan's activities. He was already afraid of that. But the news about the drugs found in a locker to which he was assigned, that was a different story. His mind conjured up an image of Walters oozing around the OR area. He questioned why anyone would hoard drugs like that. Then there was the suggestion of association. Susan had used the words *supernatural* and *sinister*. Bellows wondered exactly what kind of drugs were stored in locker 338. He also wondered if he should tell Susan about the discovery.

Tuesday February 24
2:30pm

Susan allowed her eyes to wander around the Chief of Surgery's office. It was spacious and exquisitely decorated. Large windows occupying most of two walls afforded a splendid view of Charlestown in one direction and a corner of Boston and the North End in the other. The Mystic River bridge was partially concealed by grey snow clouds. The wind had shifted from the sea and was now blowing in from the northwest with arctic air.

Stark's teak desk, with its white marble top, was situated cater-corner in the northwest section of the office. The wall behind and to the right of the desk was mirrored from floor to ceiling. The fourth wall contained the door from the reception room and carefully constructed, recessed bookshelves. A section of the shelves was hinged; partly ajar, it revealed gleaming glasses, bottles, and a small refrigerator.

In the southeast corner, where the huge expanse of windows met the bookshelves, there was a low, glass-topped table surrounded by moulded fibreglass chairs. Their leather cushions were made of bright colours ranging through the oranges and greens.

Stark himself was seated behind his massive desk. His image was recreated a hundred times in the mirror to the right thanks to the reflection from the tinted window glass to his left. The Chief of Surgery had his feet propped up on the corner of his desk so that daylight fell over his shoulder onto the paper he was reading.

He was impeccably dressed in a beige suit tailored to fit close to his lean body, accented by an orange silk scarf in his left breast pocket. His greying hair was moderately long and brushed back from his high forehead, just covering the tops of his ears. His face was aristocratic, with sharp features and a thin nose. He wore executive half-glasses framed in delicate reddish tortoiseshell. His green eyes rapidly scanned back and forth across the sheet of paper in his hand.

Susan would have been greatly intimidated by a combination of the impressive surroundings and Stark's awe-inspiring reputation as a surgical genius had it not been for his initial smile and his seemingly incongruous posture. The fact that he had his feet up on the corner of the desk made Susan feel more comfortable, as if Stark really didn't take his power position within the hospital too seriously. Susan correctly surmised that his skill as a surgeon and his ability as a medical administrator-businessman made it possible for Stark to ignore conventional executive posturing. Stark finished reading the paper and looked up at Susan sitting in front of him.

'That, young lady, is very interesting. Obviously I am totally aware of the surgical cases, but I had no idea a similar problem was occurring on the medical floors. Whether they are indeed related is uncertain but I must give you credit for coming up with the idea that they may be related. And these two recent respiratory arrests and deaths; associating them is ... well, both far-out and brilliant at the same time. It gives food for thought. You have related them because you feel that depression of respiration is the common ground for all the cases. My first reaction to that – now, this is just my first reaction – is that it does not explain the anaesthesia cases because in that circumstance, the respiratory pattern is being artificially maintained. You suggest some previous encephalitis or brain infection making people more susceptible to complications during anaesthesia ... let me see.'

Stark swung his feet from his desk and turned toward the window. Unconsciously he took his reading glasses from his nose and lightly chewed one of the earpieces. His eyes narrowed in concentration.

'Parkinsonism has now been related to previous unsuspected viral insult, so I suppose your theory is possible. But how could it be proved?'

Stark rotated around, facing Susan.

'And you must be assured that we investigated the anaesthesia complication cases ad nauseam. Everything – and I mean everything – was studied with a fine-tooth comb by a host of people, anaesthesiologists, epidemiologists, internists, surgeons ... everybody we could think of. Except, of course, a medical student.'

Stark smiled warmly and Susan found herself responding to the man's renowned charisma.

'I believe,' said Susan, her confidence rallying, 'the study should start with the central computer bank. The computer information I obtained was only for the past year and called up by an indirect method. I have no idea what data would emerge if the computer was asked directly for all cases over, say, the last five years of respiratory depression, coma, and unexplained death.

'Then with a complete list of the potentially related cases, the charts would have to be painstakingly reviewed to try to elicit any common denominators. The families of the involved patients would have to be interviewed to obtain the best possible record of previous viral illness and patterns of illnesses. The other task would be to obtain serum from all existing cases for antibody screens. '

Susan watched Stark's face, intently preparing herself for an untoward response like that she had experienced with Nelson and then more dramatically with Harris. In contrast, Stark maintained an even expression, obviously in thought over Susan's suggestions. It was apparent that he had an open, innovative mind. Finally he spoke.

'Shotgun-style antibody screening is not very productive; it is time-consuming and it is horribly expensive.'

'Counter-immunoelectrophoresis techniques have relieved some of these disadvantages,' offered Susan, encouraged by Stark's response.

'Perhaps, but it still would represent an enormous outlay of capital with a very low probability of positive results. I'd have to have some specific evidence before I could justify that type of resource commitment. But maybe you should suggest this to Dr Nelson, down in Medicine. Immunology is his special field.'

'I don't think Dr Nelson would be interested,' said Susan.

'Why is that?'

'I haven't the faintest idea. To tell the truth, I already spoke with Dr Nelson. So I already know he's not interested. And he wasn't the only one. I mentioned my ideas to another department head and I thought I was going to get swatted like some naughty child that needed chastising. Trying to incorporate that episode into the whole picture, I get a feeling that something else could be operating here.'

'And what is that?' asked Stark, glancing over the figures Susan had provided.

'Well, I don't know what word to use ... foul play ... or something sinister.'

Susan stopped talking quite suddenly, expecting either laughter or anger. But Stark merely rotated in his chair, looking out over the city again.

'Foul play. You do have an imagination, Dr Wheeler, no doubt about that.'

Stark turned back toward the room, rising up and walking around his desk.

'Foul play,' he repeated. 'I must admit I'd never even considered that.' Stark had been briefed only that morning about Cowley's discovery of the drugs in locker 338; that information had disturbed him. He leaned against his desk and looked down at Susan.

'If you think about foul play, motive becomes of paramount importance. And there just isn't any motive for such a series of heartbreaking episodes. They are too dissimilar. And coma? You'd have to implicate some very clever psychopath operating on a premise that's beyond rationality. But the biggest problem with the idea of foul play is that it would be impossible in the OR. There are too many people involved who are watching the patient too closely.

'Certainly investigative activities should be carried out with an open mind, but I don't think foul play is possible in this instance. But, I must admit, I had not thought of it.'

'Actually,' said Susan, 'I hadn't planned on suggesting foul play to you, but I'm glad that I did so that I can forget it. But back to the problem itself. If antibody screening is too expensive, the chart review and interviews would be comparatively cheap. I could take that on myself, except I'd need a little help from you.'

'What kind of help?'

'First of all, I'd need to have authorization to use the computer. That's number one. Secondly, I'd need authorization to get the charts. Thirdly, I may have run into a problem downstairs.'

'What kind of a problem?'

'Dr Harris. He's the one who blew his cool. I think he intends to have my surgical rotation here at the Memorial cut short. It seems that he is not fond of women in medicine, and perhaps I have served to underline that prejudice.'

'Dr Harris can be difficult to get along with. He's an emotional type. But at the same time he's probably the best mind in anaesthesiology in the country. So don't damn him until you see his other side. I believe he has specific personal reasons for his attitude toward women in medicine. It's not admirable, perhaps, but it is potentially understandable. Anyway, I'll see what I can do for you. At the same time I must tell you that you have picked a very touchy subject to become involved in. You have undoubtedly considered the malpractice implication, the potential bad publicity for the hospital and even the Boston medical community. Tread lightly, young lady, if you choose to tread at all. You'll make no friends on the course you are embarking on, and it's my opinion you should drop the whole affair. If you choose to go on, I'll try to help you, although I can guarantee nothing. If you do turn up any information, I will be happy to offer an opinion. Obviously the more information you have, the easier it will be for me to get you what you need.'

Stark moved toward the door from his office, opening it.

'Give me a call later this afternoon and I'll let you know if I've had any luck with your requests.'

'Thank you for your time, Dr Stark.' Susan hesitated in the doorway, looking at Stark. 'It is reassuring that you have not lived up to your reputation of being a man-, or should I say, woman-eater.'

'Perhaps you will agree with the others when you find time to come on teaching rounds,' said Stark, with a laugh.

Susan said goodbye and left. Stark returned to his desk and spoke into his intercom, talking to his secretary.

'Call Dr Chandler and see if he has talked with Dr Bellows yet. Tell him that I want to get to the bottom of those drugs in the locker room as soon as possible.'

Stark turned and looked out over the complex of buildings that made up the Memorial. His life was so closely linked to the hospital that at certain points they merged. As Bellows had told Susan, Stark had personally raised an enormous amount of the money it had taken to revitalize the hospital and build its seven new buildings. It was partly due to his fund-raising abilities that he was Chief of Surgery at the Memorial.

The more he thought about the drugs in 338 and their possible implications, the angrier he got. It was just another glaring example of how people in general could not be trusted to think in terms of the long-run effects.

'Christ,' he said out loud, his eyes mesmerized by the swirling snow clouds. Fools could undermine all his efforts at insuring the Memorial's position as the number one hospital in the country. Years of work could go down the drain. It underscored his belief that he had to attend to everything if he wanted it done right.

Tuesday February 24

7:20pm

The gloom of the winter Boston night had long since invaded the city when Susan alighted from the Harvard line train at the open-air Charles Street MBTA station. The wind, still blowing in from the Arctic, whistled in the river end of the station and traversed the length of the platform in short turbulent gusts. Susan bent over as she headed toward the stairs. The train lunged and slid out of the station, passing her on her right, its wheels screeching as it turned into the tunnel.

Susan used the pedestrian overpass to cross the intersection of Charles Street and Cambridge Street. Underneath, the traffic had dissipated to a minor dribble of cars, but the noxious odour of exhaust gases still fouled the night air. Susan descended to Charles Street. In front of the all-night drugstore there was the usual collection of wayward individuals, either drunk or stoned. Several of them reached toward Susan, asking for spare change. She responded by quickening her step. Then she collided with a seedy, bearded fellow who had deliberately stepped into her way.

'*Real Paper* or *Phoenix*, beautiful?' asked the bearded fellow with seborrheic eyelids. He held several newspapers in his right hand.

Susan recoiled, then pressed on, ignoring the lurid jibes and laughter of the night people. She passed down Charles Street and presently the surroundings changed. A few antique shop windows beckoned for her to dally, but the cold night wind urged her on. At Mount Vernon Street she turned up to the left and began to ascend Beacon Hill. From the numbers on the doors she knew she had a way to go. She passed Louisburg Square. The orange glow from the mullioned windows cast warm rays into the cold night. The houses gave a sense of peace and security behind their solid brick façades.

Bellows's apartment was in a building on the left, about a

hundred yards beyond Louisburg Square. The buildings along here sat back behind small lawns and towering elms. Susan pushed open a squeaking metal gate and went up the stone steps to the heavy panelled door. In the foyer she blew on her blue fingers while walking in place to encourage circulation in her feet. She always had cold feet and hands from November to March. While she blew and stamped she scanned the names next to the buzzer. Bellows was number five. She pushed the button hard, and was rewarded with a raucous buzz.

In a minor panic she reached for the doorknob, scraping her knuckle on the metallic guard on the door frame as the door swung open. A small amount of blood oozed from her knuckle, and she lifted her hand to her mouth. In front of her was a staircase twisting up to the left. A shining brass chandelier hovered above, and a gilded frame mirror served to make the hall seem more spacious. By reflex she checked her hair in the mirror, pressing it down at her temples. As she climbed she noticed attractively framed Brueghel prints on every landing.

Exaggerating her exhaustion, she reached the top flight and paused, gripping the banister. Down the stairwell she could see to the tiled floor of the foyer, five storeys below. Bellows opened his door before Susan knocked.

'There's an oxygen bottle in here if you need it, Grandma,' he said, smiling.

'God, the air is thin up here. Maybe I should sit here on the steps and recuperate for a few moments.'

'A glass of Bordeaux will fix you up perfectly. Give me your hand.'

Susan allowed Mark to help her into his apartment. Then she took off her coat, her eyes wandering around the room. Mark disappeared into the kitchen, returning with two glasses of ruby red wine.

Susan threw her coat over a straight-back chair near the door and pulled off her high boots. Distracted, she took the wine and sipped it. Her attention had been captured by the room she found herself in.

'Pretty tastefully decorated for a surgeon,' said Susan, walking into the centre of the room.

It was about twenty by forty feet. At each end was a large old-fashioned fireplace, and in each glowed a cheerful fire. The beamed cathedral ceiling was very high, perhaps twenty feet at the peak, slanting down toward both fireplaces. The far wall was an enormous complex of geometric shapes, some housing bookshelves, others with objets d'art and a large stereo, TV, and tape system. The near wall was of exposed brick and covered with paintings, lithographs, and mediaeval sheet music, attractively framed. An antique Howard clock ticked unobtrusively over the fireplace to the right, a ship model adorned the mantelpiece to the left. Through the windows, on either side of both fireplaces, a myriad of crooked chimneys was silhouetted against the night sky.

The furnishings were of a minimum; Bellows had relied on a collection of thick scatter rugs, dominated by a blue and cream Bukhara in the centre of the room. On it was a low onyx coffee table, surrounded by a large number of sizeable pillows covered in shocking shades of corduroy.

'This is beautiful,' said Susan twisting around in the centre of the room and then collapsing on an armful of cushions. 'I never expected anything like this.'

'What did you expect?' Mark sat down on the other side of the low table.

'An apartment. You know, tables, chairs, couch, the usual.'

They both laughed, aware that they really did not know each other very well. Conversation remained on a frivolous level as they enjoyed the wine. Susan hopefully pointed her stocking feet toward the fire, to warm her toes.

'More wine, Susan?'

'For sure. It tastes wonderful.'

Mark disappeared into the kitchen for the bottle. He poured each of them another glass.

'No one would ever believe the day I've had today, incredible,' said Susan, holding the glass of wine between her eye and the fire and appreciating its deep luscious red glow.

'If you haven't abandoned your suicidal crusade, I believe anything. Did you go and see Stark?'

'You bet your ass, and contrary to your fears, he was very

reasonable ... more than I can say about Harris or even Nelson, for that matter.'

'Be careful, that's all I can say. Stark is like an emotional chameleon. I usually get along with him extremely well. Yet today, out of the blue, I found out he's furious at me because of some nut putting half-used medicine in a locker that I had used for a while. He doesn't come to me and ask me about it the way a normal human being would. Instead he sics poor old Chandler, the chief resident, on to me, and Chandler cancels a case of mine to ask me about it. Then later he calls me out of rounds to tell me Stark wants me to get to the bottom of it. You'd think I had nothing to do.'

'What's this about drugs in a locker?' Susan remembered the doctor talking to Nelson.

'I'm not sure I have the whole story. Something about one of the surgeons coming across a whole bunch of drugs in an OR locker which old friggin' Walters still had assigned to me. Apparently there were narcotics, curare, antibiotics – a whole pharmacy.'

'And they don't know who put them there or why?'

'I guess not. It's my idea that somebody's been saving the stuff to ship off to Biafra or Bangladesh. There's always a couple of people around with some cause like that. But why they've been storing them in a locker in the lounge is beyond me.'

'Curare is a nerve blocker, isn't it, Mark?'

'Yup, a competitive nerve blocker. A great drug. Oh, in case you haven't guessed, we're dining here tonight. I got some steaks, and the hibachi is all set on the fire escape outside the kitchen window.'

'Couldn't be better, Mark. I'm exhausted. But I'm also hungry.'

'I'll put the steaks on.' Mark walked into the kitchen with his wineglass.

'Does curare depress respiration?' asked Susan.

'Nope. It just paralyses all the muscles. The person wants to breath but can't. They suffocate.'

Susan stared into the fireplace, resting the edge of her glass against her lower lip. The dancing flames hypnotized her and she thought about curare, about Greenly, about Berman. The fire crackled suddenly and angrily spat a red-hot coal against the screen. A piece of the coal richocheted off the screen, landing in the rug to the side of the fireplace. Susan jumped up, flicked it off the rug and pushed it harmlessly onto the slate hearth. She then walked over to the kitchen door, watching Mark season the steaks.

'Stark actually was interested in what I had found out and has already tried to help. I had asked him to help me get the charts of the patients on my list. When I called back later this afternoon, he said he had tried to get them for me but had been told that they were all signed out to one of the professors of neurology, a Dr Donald McLeary. Do you know him?'

'No, but that doesn't mean anything. I don't know very many of the nonsurgical types.'

'To my way of thinking, it makes McLeary look rather suspicious.'

'Oh oh, here we go again, imagination plus! Dr Donald McLeary mysteriously destroys the cerebrum of six patients ...'

'Twelve ...'

'OK, twelve, and then he signs all their charts out to eliminate any chance of suspicion. I can just picture all this in the headlines of the Boston *Globe*.'

Mark laughed as he put the steaks on the hibachi through the open window, then drew it down against the cold.

'Go ahead and laugh, but at the same time come up with an explanation for McLeary. Everyone else so far has expressed surprise at the idea of relating all these cases together. Everyone except this Dr McLeary. He has all the charts. I just think it's worth looking into. Maybe he's been investigating this thing for some time and he's far ahead of me. That would be nice to believe and if so, maybe I could help him.'

Mark didn't answer. He was wondering exactly how he was going to try to talk Susan out of the whole business. He was also concentrating on the salad dressing, his culinary speciality. When he reopened the kitchen window, the cold wind brought in the sizzling aroma of the cooking steaks. Susan leaned against the door frame, watching him. She thought about how marvellous it would be to have a wife, to be able to come home and have a wife keeping the house in order, the meals on the table. At the same time it seemed ridiculously unfair that she could never have a wife. In fact, if she married, she would be expected to be the wife. It was a mental game that Susan played with herself, always to the same impasse, at which time she would simply deny the whole problem or at least postpone it until some indeterminate future date.

'I called the Jefferson Institute today.'

'What'd they have to say?' Mark handed Susan some plates, silver and napkins, and pointed toward the onyx table.

'You were right about it being difficult to visit,' said Susan, carrying the material to the table. 'I asked if I could come out and visit the facility because I wanted to see one of the patients. They laughed. They told me that only the very immediate family can visit and only on prearranged, brief visits. They said that the mass methods of taking care of the patients is generally unacceptable, emotionally, to the families, so they have to make special arrangements for them to visit. They did tell me about the monthly tour you mentioned. My being a medical student counted about the same as a wooden nickel, so far as making them alter their routine. Actually the place sounds interesting, especially since, as you say, the concept has been successful in keeping chronic cases from taking up acute-care beds in the local hospitals.'

Susan finished setting the table, then returned to staring into the fire. 'I'd really like to visit, though, mostly to see Berman once more. I have a feeling that if I saw him again that I'd probably be able to ease up on this ... crusade, as you call it. Even I realize I've got to get back to a semblance of normality.'

Mark straightened up from his activities in the kitchen at this last sentence, entertaining a ray of hope. He turned the steaks over again and closed the window.

'Why don't you just show up there? I mean, it must be like any other hospital when it comes right down to it. It's probably as chaotic as the Memorial. If you acted like you belong, probably nobody would even question you. You could even wear a nurse's uniform. If anybody came into the Memorial dressed like a doctor or a nurse, they could go anywhere they chose.'

Susan looked back at Mark, who was standing in the kitchen door.

'That's not a bad idea ... not bad. But there's a catch.'

'What's that?'

'Simply that I wouldn't know where the hell I was going even if I were able to walk into the building. It's hard to look like you belong when you're totally lost.'

'That's not an insurmountable obstacle. All you'd have to do is visit the building department in City Hall and get a copy of the building plans or floor plans. There are plans on file of all public buildings. You'd have yourself a map.'

Mark returned to the kitchen to get the steaks and the salad.

'Mark, that's ingenious.'

'Practical, not ingenious.' He brought the food into the room and served up the steaks and a generous helping of salad. There were also asparagus with hollandaise sauce and another whole bottle of red Bordeaux.

Each thought the meal perfect. The wine tended to smooth any potential rough edges, and the conversation flowed freely as each learned bits and pieces of the other's background to fill in the gaps of the personality mosaics each was constructing of the other. Susan from Maryland, Mark from California. There was little intellectual common ground, for Mark's education had been severely skewed in the direction of Descartes and Newton, while Susan's tended toward Voltaire and Chaucer. But skiing emerged as a love of both, as well as the beach, and the outdoors in general. And they both liked Hemingway. There was an awkward silence after Susan asked about Joyce. Bellows had not read Joyce.

With the dishes cleared, they settled on a random grouping of pillows before the fireplace at the far end of the room. Bellows put on some additional oak logs, turning the smouldering embers into a crackling blaze. Grand Marnier and Fred's

Home Made vanilla ice cream made them quiet for some moments, both enjoying the peaceful and contented silence.

'Susan, getting to know you just a little better, and liking every minute of it, makes me even more motivated to urge you to forget this coma problem,' said Mark, after a while. 'You've got an enormous amount of learning to do, and believe me, there's no place better than the Memorial. In all likelihood this coma problem will be around for some time, plenty of time for you to begin again when you have a real background in clinical medicine. I'm not trying to suggest you cannot contribute; maybe you can. But the chances of making a contribution are small, just like in any research project, no matter how well conceived. And you have to consider the effect your activities will undoubtedly have, in fact already have had, on your superiors. It's a poor gamble, Susan; the odds are stacked against you.'

Susan sipped her Grand Marnier. The viscous, smooth fluid slid down her throat, and sent warm sensations down her legs. She took in a deep breath and felt a certain levitation.

'Being a female medical student must be hard enough,' continued Bellows, 'without adding a further handicap.'

Susan raised her head and looked at Bellows. He was staring into the fire. 'Exactly what do you mean by that statement?' asked Susan with a sudden slight edge to her voice. Bellows was suddenly brushing against sensitive areas.

'Just what I said.' Bellows did not look up from the fire. The dancing flames had captured his attention. 'I just think it must be particularly difficult being a female medical student. I never really thought too much about it until you forced me to come up with an alternative explanation for Harris's behaviour. Now, the more I think about it, the more I think I am right because ... well, to be truthful, I can't say I reacted to you as a medical student first. As soon as I saw you, I reacted to you as a woman, and maybe in kind of an immature way. I mean I found you immediately attractive – not seductive.' Bellows added the last comment quickly and turned to make sure Susan appreciated his reference to their previous conversation in the coffee shop.

Susan smiled. The defensive attitude, which Bellows's initial statement had rekindled, had melted.

'That was why I reacted so foolishly when you walked into the dressing room yesterday and caught me in my shorts. If I had thought of you asexually, I wouldnt have budged. But it was pretty apparent that was not the case. Anyway, I think most of your professors and instructors are going to react to you first as female and only second as a student of medicine.'

Bellows looked back into the fire; he almost had the attitude of a contrite sinner who has confessed. Susan felt a resurgence of the warmth she had begun to feel toward him. She felt again the urge to give him one of her people hugs, as she thought of them. In truth Susan was a physical person, although she did not show it often, especially since entering medicine. Even before applying to medical school, Susan had decided that the physical aspects of her personality had to be suppressed if she was going to make it in medicine. Now instead of reaching for Mark, she sipped her Grand Marnier.

'Susan, you are very apparent in any group and if you don't show up at my lecture, I'm going to have to account for you.'

'The luxury of anonymity,' said Susan, 'has not been something I could enjoy ever since I started medical school. I understand what you are saying, Mark. At the same time I feel I need just one more day. One more.' Susan held up one finger and tilted her head in a coquettish fashion. Then she laughed.

'You know, Mark, it is reassuring to hear you say that you think being a female medical student is difficult, because it is. Some of the girls in my class deny it, but they're fooling themselves. They're using one of the oldest and easiest defence mechanisms; get around a problem by saying it's not there. But it is. I remember reading a quote by Sir William Osler. He said there were three classes of human beings: men, women, and women physicians. I laughed when I read that the first time. Now I don't laugh anymore.

'Despite the feminist movement there still lingers the conventional image of wide-eyed feminine naiveté and all that bullshit. As soon as you enter a field which demands a bit of competitive and aggressive action, the men all label you as a castrating bitch. If you sit back and try to use passive, compliant behaviour, you find yourself being told that you can't respond to the competitive atmosphere. So you're forced to try to find your own compromise somewhere in the middle, which is difficult because all the while you feel like you're on trial, not as an individual but as a representative of women in general.'

There was silence for a few moments, each digesting what had been said.

'The thing that bothers me the most,' added Susan, 'is that the problem gets worse, not better, the farther into medicine one goes. I cannot imagine how these women with families do it. They have to apologize for leaving work early and then they have to apologize for getting home late, no matter what time it is. I mean, the man can work late, no problem, in fact it makes him seem that much more dedicated. But a woman physician: her role is so diffuse. Society and its conventional female mores make it very difficult.

'How did you get me on this platform?' asked Susan suddenly, realizing the vehemence with which she had been speaking.

'You were just agreeing to my statement that being a female medical student was difficult. So how about agreeing to the last part, about not taking on any more handicaps?'

'Shit, Mark, don't push me right at this moment. Obviously you can see that once I got involved in this thing, I probably need to resolve it somehow. Maybe it's related to my feeling like I'm on trial for women. God, I'd like to show that Harris where to get off. Maybe if I can see Berman again, I'll be able to give up without any loss of intellectual face or ... what should I say, self-image or self-confidence. But let's talk about something else. Would you mind if I were to give you a hug?'

'Me, mind?' Bellows sat up quickly but slightly flustered. 'Not at all.'

Susan leaned over and gave him a squeeze with a force that surprised him. Instinctively his arms went around her and he felt her narrow back. Somewhat self-consciously he patted it, as if he were comforting her. She pulled back.

'I hope you're not waiting for me to burp.'

For several moments they studied each other in the firelight. Then tentatively their lips sought each other, gently at first, then with obvious emotion, finally with abandon.

Wednesday February 25

5:45am

The alarm jangled in the darkness, making the air in the room vibrate with its piercing sound. Susan sat bolt upright from a dead sleep. At first she wondered why her eyes wouldn't open; then she realized that they were open. It was just that they could not pierce the utter blackness in the room. For several seconds she had no idea where she was. Her only thought was to try to find the alarm clock and deaden its awful nerve-shattering noise.

As suddenly as it had started, it stopped with a metallic click. At the same time Susan became conscious that she was not alone. The memory of the previous evening swept over her, and she remembered that she was still at Mark's apartment. She lay back, bringing up the covers to cover her nakedness.

'What in God's name was that noise for?' said Susan to the blackness.

'It's an alarm. I suppose you've never heard one before,' said a voice from beside her.

'An alarm. Mark, it's the middle of the night.'

'Like hell it is; it's five-thirty and time to get rolling.'

Mark threw back the covers and put his feet onto the floor. He turned on the lamp next to the bed and rubbed his eyes.

'Mark, you've got to be out of your squash. Five-thirty, Christ.' The voice was muffled; Susan had her head underneath the pillow.

'I've got to see my patients, grab a bit to eat, and be ready for rounds at six-thirty. Surgery starts at seven-thirty sharp.' Mark stood up and stretched. Disregarding his nakedness and the coldness, he started for the bathroom.

'You surgical masochists defy imagination. Why don't you start at nine or some other reasonable time? Why seven-thirty?'

'It's always been seven-thirty,' said Bellows, pausing in the doorway.

'That's a great reason. It's seven-thirty because it's always been seven-thirty – God, it's that type of reasoning that's so typical in medicine. Five-thirty in the morning. Shit, Mark, why didn't you tell me about this when you invited me to stay last night? I would have gone back to the dorm.'

Bellows walked back to the bedside, looking down at the mound of covers indicating Susan's body. The pillow was still over her head.

'If you'd take your surgical rotation a bit more seriously, I wouldn't have to tell you what is the normal modus operandi. Time to get up, beauty queen.'

Bellows grabbed the edge of the blankets and, with a forceful jerk, pulled all the covers from the bed, leaving Susan bared to the elements, except for her head, still concealed by the pillow.

'Some hospitality,' said Susan, jumping up. She grabbed a blanket and twisted herself into an instant cocoon, then collapsed back onto the bed.

'Ah, but today is the first day of your new leaf. You're going to be a normal medical student.'

A tug of war ensued with Susan's wrapping.

'I need one more full day, just one. Come on, Mark, one more. You can understand that it's important for me. If I don't get the charts today, which I think I won't, then it's all over. Besides, if I can see Berman, I'll probably give up. Then you'll have your normal medical student. But I need one more day.'

Bellows let go of the blankets. Susan fell back, one breast exposed in a fetching Amazonian way.

'All right, one more day. But if Stark is on rounds today, he'll know that you are phantomizing. I wouldn't be able to come up with any cover story. I hope you realize that.'

'Let's just play it by ear, almighty surgeon. I'm sure you'll think of something.'

'Susan, I'll just have to say that I had told you to be on rounds.'

'OK, have it your way. But I'm spending one more whole day on this thing. I've got some investment into it already.'

Susan snuggled into the warm bed. She barely heard the shower start in the bathroom. She thought she'd wait until Bellows finished before getting up.

When Susan awoke the second time, it was already quite light. Sudden gusts of wind blew rain against the window panes with a sound like rice hitting glass. With a contrariness typical of Boston weather, the wind had shifted during the night from northwest to due east. Thanks to the Gulf Stream, the temperature had risen into the high thirties, so precipitation was in the liquid rather than solid phase. The commuters were relieved, the skiers disgusted.

It was hard for Susan to believe the clock next to the bed, because it said almost nine. Bellows had showered, dressed, and exited without having reawakened her. Susan was amazed, for she was a relatively light sleeper. Just to be sure, she checked the bathroom and the living room for any sign that Bellows might still be there. She was alone.

Susan found a clean towel, then showered vigorously, remembering the previous night's passion with a pleasant sense of warmth. Bellows had turned out to be a far more sensitive and innately generous lover than Susan had surmised. She was genuinely pleased, although she had some serious reservations about the relationship going very far. Bellows's commitment to surgery seemed somehow too encompassing, as if everything else in his life would necessarily be relegated to a secondary position like a hobby.

In the refrigerator, Susan found some cheese and an orange. She helped herself to Grapenuts and toast while thumbing through the Yellow Pages. Checking to be sure that she had everything, she left Bellows's apartment, locking the door securely behind her. It was going to be a busy day.

The rain had let up significantly by the time Susan hit the street. The weather did not appear to be clearing, but now it would be more pleasant to walk about. Susan turned left up Mt Vernon toward the State House. She crossed the Boston Common at its northern tip and entered the downtown shopping area.

Of all the young girls who had come to the Boston Uniform Company retail store seeking a nurse's uniform, the salesman found Susan the easiest and fastest customer. She seemed totally uninterested in the bewildering permutations of the plain white dress. She asked for size ten and told the salesman that any size ten would do.

'We have this style here which you might like,' he said, bringing out one uniform.

Susan took the dress and held it against herself as she looked into the mirror.

'The changing rooms are in the back if you'd like to try it.'

'I'll take it.'

The salesman was stunned if gratified at the speed of the sale.

The rain started again half-heartedly as Susan walked up Washington Street toward Government Centre. As she reached the middle of the bricked mall in front of the ultrageometric City Hall, the wind brought in another moisture-laden cloud over the city. As the rain came down in earnest Susan ran for cover.

The girl at the information booth told Susan that the building department was on the eighth floor. It was easy to find. Once there, though, things were different. Susan waited for twenty-five minutes at the main counter only to be told that she was at the wrong place. This happened twice before she was directed to the rear of the vast room. There was another wait of a quarter of an hour despite the fact she was the only customer. Behind the counter were five desks, of which three were occupied. Two men and one woman. The two men looked surprisingly alike, with large red noses, plastic black-rimmed glasses, and tasteless ties. They were engaged in a heated argument about the Patriots. The woman had a ratted hairdo recalling the early sixties and shocking red lipstick that used the natural lip borders only as suggestions. She was engrossed with a pocket mirror, examining her face from every possible angle.

The smaller of the two men eventually eyed Susan and realized that she was not going to disappear despite the fact that she was being ignored. He rambled over, uninterested. When he reached the counter he took his cigarette from his mouth. A few of the ashes from the tip dusted down the front of his tie. He crushed the butt repeatedly in a cheap and already overflowing metal ashtray.

'What can I do for you?' said the bureaucrat, looking at Susan for a moment. He turned before she could answer.

'Hey, Harry, that reminds me. What are you going to do about that GRI 5 request? Remember, it was filed as urgent and it's been in your box for two months.' Looking back at Susan, 'What is it, honey? Let me guess. You want to file a complaint about your landlord. Well, this isn't the right place.'

He looked back at his colleague. 'Harry, if you're going for coffee, pick me up a regular and a Danish. I'll pay you later.' His red eyes turned to Susan. 'Now then ...'

'I'd like to look at some plans; the floor plans for the Jefferson Institute. It's a relatively new hospital in South Boston.'

'Plans. What do you want plans for? How old are you, fifteen?'

'I'm a medical student and I'm interested in hospital design and construction.'

'Kids today! With your looks you don't have to be interested in anything.' He laughed obnoxiously.

Susan closed her eyes, resisting the retort the comment deserved.

The state employee started toward a stack of oversized books on the counter. 'What ward is it in?' he asked with obvious ennui.

'I haven't the slightest idea.'

'All right then,' said the man, making an about-face. 'First we'll have to find out which ward it is in.'

A smaller book on the counter supplied the needed information.

'Ward 17.'

With calculated slowness, he returned to the large books on the counter. From his side pocket he withdrew a crumpled pack of cigarettes. He put one cigarette in his mouth, leaving it unlit. After picking several wrong volumes, he found the Ward 17 volume. The other books were pushed aside. Turning back the cover, he slobbered over his index finger. He flipped the pages forcefully, running his finger across his tobacco-stained tongue every four or five pages. Having found the reference, he copied the figures onto a piece of scrap paper. Motioning for Susan to follow, he started toward a large bank of filing cabinets.

'Harry!' called the bureaucrat, continuing his conversation with his colleague en route to the filing cabinets, the unlit cigarette bobbling up and down in his mouth. 'Before you go downstairs, call up Grosser and find out if Lester is coming in today. Somebody's goin' to have to file that stuff on his desk if he's not; that's been there longer than you GRI 5 request.'

It was a simple affair to find the correct drawer and extract a large packet of plans. 'Here you are, Goldilocks; there's a Xerox machine over in that room beyond the counter, if you want. It takes nickels.' He pointed with his unlit cigarette.

'Maybe you could show me which of these are floor plans.' Susan had withdrawn the contents from the jacket.

'You're interested in hospital construction and you don't know what floor plans look like? My God. Here, these are the floor plans ... basement, first floor, and second floor.' He lit his cigarette with a pocket lighter.

'How do you decipher these abbreviations?'

'For Christ's sake, right here in the lower corner. It says "OR," means operating room. "W (main)"; that means main ward. And "Comp. R" stands for computer room and so forth.' The man showed signs of incipient irritation.

'And the Xerox machine?'

'Over there. There's a change machine on the wall. When you finish with the plans, just put them in the metal bin on the counter.'

Susan carefully Xeroxed the floor plans and labelled the rooms on the copy with a felt-tipped pen. Then she headed for the Memorial.

Susan entered the Memorial through the main entrance. It was just after ten in the morning. Yet the inevitable daily crowds were already there. Every conceivable seat was occupied. There were people of all ages, waiting, forever waiting. These were not people seeking attention in either the clinic or the emergency room. They were people waiting for a relative to be admitted or discharged, or perhaps they were patients who had been seen and treated and were now waiting to be picked up and taken home. There was little conversation and no smiles. These people were all distinct and separate islands, united only by their healthy awe of the hospital and its shrouded mysteries.

The dense crowd impeded Susan's progress, forcing her to push her way through to the directory. The plastic letters spelled out 'Neurology Department, Beard 11.' Susan made her way to the Beard elevators and waited with the crowd. The person next to her turned and Susan recoiled in ill-concealed horror. The man's – or was it a woman's – eyes were surrounded by dark areas of haemorrhage. The nose was swollen and distorted, with nasal packs partially extruding from the nostrils. Several wires came from within the nose and were taped to either cheek. The visage was that of a monster. Susan tried to keep her eyes on the elevator indicator, unprepared for the visual surprises of the hospital.

Dr Donald McLeary was one of the younger members of the full-time neurology staff and, because of the ever-mounting pressure of space, had not been given an office on eleven.

Susan had to take the stairs up to twelve before she found the door with 'Dr Donald M. McLeary' stencilled on it in black letters. She opened the door and squeezed into a tiny outer office; the door could not be opened all the way because of a filing cabinet. The desk, of average size, appeared huge in the room. An ageing secretary looked up. She had extraordinarily thick make-up, including rouge and false eyelashes. Her totally bleached hair was glued into short, tight curls. She wore a tight pink pants-suit outfit that strained over unnatural bulges.

'Excuse me, is Dr McLeary in?'

'He's in, but he is very busy.' The secretary was annoyed at the intrusion. 'Have you an appointment?'

'No. No, I haven't, but I only want to ask him a quick question. I'm a medical student rotating here at the Memorial.'

'I'll check with the doctor.'

The secretary stood up, eyeing Susan from head to foot. Even more irritated at Susan's lissome figure, she entered the inner office to Susan's right. Susan looked around the outer office for any signs of the hospital charts she wanted.

Almost immediately, the woman returned, sat down at her desk, put a piece of stationery into the typewriter and typed several lines. Only then did she look up.

'You may go in; he says he has a moment for you.'

The secretary resumed her typing before Susan could respond. Whispering some choice epithets under her breath, Susan opened the door and entered the inner office.

Reminiscent of Dr Nelson's office, McLeary's office was equally messy, with journals and papers in innumerable haphazard stacks. Several of the stacks had tipped over at some previous time and had never been re-erected. Dr McLeary was a thin, intense-looking man with a deep crease that ran down through the middle of each cheek. His sharply angular nose and chin were separated by a small mouth that twitched as he eyed Susan over his glasses and through his bushy eyebrows.

'Susan Wheeler, I presume,' said Dr McLeary, with no friendliness in his voice.

'Yes.' Susan was surprised that he knew her name. She could not decide if that were propitious or not.

'And you have come concerning these ten charts I have here.' McLeary half-turned in his chair, waving toward a large group of hospital charts in his bookcase.

'Ten? Is that all you have?'

'Isn't ten enough?' asked McLeary somewhat sarcastically.

'Fine. I just thought that maybe you'd have more. Are those the charts of the coma victims?'

'Possibly. What do you have in mind if they are?'

'I'm not sure. Dr Stark told me you had the charts, and I thought I'd come by and ask if I could perhaps look at them or help you extract them.'

'Young lady, I'm a neurologist with considerable training. My expertise is neurology, and I am evaluating the extensive neurological evaluations that were done on these patients by our resident staff. I really don't need any help.'

'I'm not insinuating that you need help, Dr McLeary, least of all in a professional capacity. I admit that I know next to nothing about neurology. But these patients all have suffered a tragedy akin to death and there is something very strange about the whole affair. I think these cases have to be viewed in terms of some kind of association rather than as random events.'

'And of course you are going to be the one to do that.'

'Well, somebody has to do it.'

McLeary paused and Susan had the uncomfortable feeling that the conversation was rapidly deteriorating.

'Well, let me tell you this,' continued McLeary with a forceful quality to his voice. 'This kind of a problem is far broader than your current capabilities. Not only that, but your efforts so far are already responsible for a disproportionate amount of trouble in this hospital. Rather than a help you are fast becoming a definite handicap. What I want you to do now is sit down.' McLeary pointed to one of the chairs in front of his desk.

'I beg your pardon?' Susan had heard but the tone was confusing. McLeary wasn't asking; he was ordering.

'I said, sit down!' The anger in his voice now was unmistakable.

Susan sat down in the only chair without a complement of journal articles.

McLeary picked up the phone and dialled. He looked directly at Susan with unblinking, beady eyes. His mouth twitched as he waited for a connection.

'Director's office, please ... I'd like to speak to Philip Oren.'

There was a longer pause. McLeary's expression did not change.

'Mr Oren, Dr McLeary here. You were quite right. She is sitting here in front of me ... The charts? Of course not, you must be joking ... All right ... fine.'

McLeary hung up the phone, still looking directly at Susan. Susan could not detect even an iota of human warmth. She thought that he deserved the secretary he had. After an awkward silence Susan started to get up.

'I have a feeling that I should not ...'

'Sit down!' shouted McLeary even more loudly than before. Susan sat down quickly, surprised at the sudden outburst.

'What is going on here? I came in here to see if you could use some help in looking into the coma problem, not to be shouted at.'

'I really have nothing more to say to you, young lady. You have overstepped your boundaries here at the Memorial. I was told that you would probably come snooping for these charts. I was also told you obtained unauthorized information from the computer. And on top of that, you managed to alienate Dr Harris. Anyway, Mr Oren will be here in a moment and you can talk with him. This is his problem, not mine.'

'Who is Mr Oren?'

'The director of the hospital, my young friend. He is the administrator, and personnel problems are in his bailiwick.'

'I'm not personnel. I'm a medical student.'

'True enough. And that actually puts you on somewhat of a lower plane. You are a guest here ... a guest of the hospital ... and as such, your conduct should be suitable to the hospitality extended to you. Instead you have chosen to be disruptive and to ignore rules and regulations. You medical students of today somehow have gotten your sense of position in the scheme of things reversed. The hospital does not exist for your benefit. The hospital does not owe you an education.'

'This is a teaching hospital and is associated with the medical school. Teaching is supposed to be one of the major functions of this hospital.'

'Teaching, of course, but that certainly doesn't mean just medical students. It means the whole medical community.'

'Exactly. Supposedly it is a symbiotic atmosphere for everyone's benefit: student and professor alike. The hospital doesn't exist for the benefit of the medical student nor for the benefit of the professor. In fact, it's supposed to be primarily for the patient.'

'Well, it is indeed easy to understand Harris's reaction to you, Miss Wheeler. As he said, you lack respect for people as well as institutions. But it is a reflection of youth in general today. They believe their very existence alone entitles them to all the luxuries of society, education being one of them.'

'Education is more than a luxury; it is a responsibility that society owes to itself.'

'Society undoubtedly has a responsibility to itself but not to individual students, not to youth just because they are youth. Education is a luxury in that it is expensive beyond belief and the major burden, particularly in medicine, falls on the public at large, the working man. The students themselves pay a small amount of the money needed. Not only does it cost an enormous amount of money to have you here, Miss Wheeler, but your being here means that you are economically unproductive. Hence the cost to society automatically doubles. And besides, your being a woman means that your future per-hour productivity . . .'

'Oh save me,' said Susan sarcastically, standing up. 'I've heard about as much bullshit as I can stand.'

'Stay put, young lady,' shouted McLeary, furious. He too stood up.

Susan tried to look behind the face of the man trembling with anger in front of her. She thought about Bellows's suggestion relative to sexuality explaining Harris's behaviour. She was hard put to believe that was a factor in McLeary's performance. Once again she was facing very irregular behaviour, to say the least. The man was breathing rapidly, his chest heaving. She had apparently and unknowingly challenged the man. But how? In what capacity? She had no idea. Susan debated whether she should just walk out. A mixture of curiosity and respect for the apparent irrationality of McLeary's actions made her stay. She sat down, watching McLeary, who now couldn't decide what to do. He too sat down and began nervously playing with an ashtray. Susan sat motionless. She wouldn't have been surprised if the man cried.

She heard the outer office door opening. Voices drifted into the inner office. Then the inner office door opened. Without being announced or knocking, an energetic individual entered. He appeared like a businessman, in a smartly tailored blue suit. Reminding Susan of Stark's attire, a silk handkerchief peeked out of his left breast pocket. His hair was carefully combed and frozen with a ruler-straight part on the left side. There was a definite aura of authority about the man; he exuded an air of assurance at handling a wide spectrum of problems.

'Thank you for your call, Donald,' said Oren.

Then he faced Susan condescendingly.

'So this is the infamous Susan Wheeler. Miss Wheeler, you have been causing a great commotion in this hospital. Are you aware of that?'

'No, I haven't been aware of that.'

Oren leaned back on McLeary's desk, folding his arms in a professional fashion.

'Out of curiosity, Miss Wheeler, let me ask you a rather simple question. What do you think is the major goal of this institution?'

'Caring for the sick.'

'Good. At least we agree in general. But I must add a crucial phrase to your answer. We are caring for the sick of this community. That might sound redundant to you because obviously we are not caring for the sick of Westchester County, New York. Yet this is an extremely important distinction because it underlines our responsibility to the people right here in Boston. As a direct corollary, anything that could interrupt or otherwise disturb this relationship to the community would, in effect, negate our primary mission. Now this may sound very ... what should I say ... irrelevant to you. But quite the contrary. I have been receiving complaints about you over the last few days which have grown from being irritated to intolerable. Apparently you are bent on specifically disrupting our carefully maintained relationship with the community.'

Susan felt colour rising in her cheeks. Oren's condescending manner began to irritate her.

'I suppose bringing to the forefront of everyone's awareness that the chances of becoming a vegetable, of losing one's brain, is very high, intolerably high, by being a patient here would ruin the reputation of the hospital.'

'Exactly.'

'Well, it seems to me that the reputation of the hospital is nothing compared to the irreparable damage suffered by these people. I have become more and more convinced that the reputation of the hospital deserves to be ruined if that's what it takes to solve the problem.'

'Now, Miss Wheeler, you can't be serious. Where would all the people turn ... all the people who are in daily need of the facilities in this hospital? Come ... come. And by glibly drawing attention to an unfortunate but nevertheless unavoidable complication ...'

'How do you know it's unavoidable?' interrupted Susan.

'I can only believe what the chiefs of the respective departments assure me. I am not a doctor nor a scientist, Miss Wheeler, nor do I pretend to be. I am an administrator. And when I am faced with a medical student who is here to learn surgery, but instead spends her time calling attention to a problem which is already under investigation by qualified people such as Dr McLeary here – a problem whose indiscreet disclosure has the potential to cause irreparable harm to the community, I am forced to react quickly and decisively. Obviously the warnings and exhortations you have already received to assume your normal duties have gone unheeded. But this is not a debate. I'm not here to argue with you. On the contrary, with all due respect, I thought it best to give you an explanation for my decision about your surgery rotation. Now, if you'll excuse me, I will phone your dean of students.'

Oren picked up McLeary's telephone and dialled.

'Dr Chapman's office, please ... Dr Chapman, please. Phil Oren calling ... Jim, Phil Oren here. How's the family? Everyone in our house is just fine ... I suppose I told you that Ted's been accepted at the University of Pennsylvania ... I hope so ... The reason I called is about one of your third-year students rotating on surgery, a Susan Wheeler ... That's right ... Sure, I'll hold.'

Oren looked at Susan. 'You are a third-year student, Miss Wheeler?'

Susan nodded. Her nascent anger had melted into dejection.

Oren looked back at McLeary, who suddenly stood up, apparently bored. 'I'm sorry, Don, for this intrusion,' said Oren. 'I suppose we should have gone to my office. I'll be finished ...' Oren redirected his attention into the telephone. 'Yes, I'm here, Jim ... well that's nice to know she's been a good student. But nonetheless she has exhausted her welcome here at the Memorial. She is supposed to be on surgery but has decided never to attend rounds, conferences, or surgery. Instead, she has been irritating the staff, particularly our Chief of Anaesthesia, and exacting unauthorized information from our computer storage facility by some devious means. We obviously have enough trouble around here without her kind of help ... Sure, I'll tell her you want to see her ... this afternoon at four-thirty. Good enough. I'm sure the VA would be happy to have her ... right (chuckle). Thanks, Jim. Speak to you soon, and let's get together.'

Oren hung up the phone and smiled diplomatically at McLeary. Then he turned to Susan.

'Miss Wheeler, your dean, as you have plainly heard, would like to have a word with you this afternoon at four-thirty. From this moment on, your professional welcome at the Memorial has been terminated. Goodbye.'

Susan looked from Oren to McLeary and then back. McLeary's expression was unchanged. Oren sported a self-satisfied smile, as if he had just won a debate. There was an awkward silence. Susan realized that the scene was over, and she got up without a word, picked up the parcel containing the nurse's uniform, and left.

Wednesday February 25
11:15am

Finding the hospital intolerably oppressive from an emotional point of view, Susan fled. She pushed her way through the lingering crowds, out into the rainy, raw February day. Once outside and without any particular destination in mind, she just walked, aimlessly, lost in her own thoughts. She turned on New Chardon Street and then on Cambridge Street.

'Assholes,' she hissed as she kicked a stray, partially crunched Campbell's soup can. The light rain flattened her hair against her forehead. Small droplets coalesced and dripped from the tip of her nose. She wandered up Joy Street into the back side of Beacon Hill, preoccupied with her stream of consciousness. She saw but her mind did not record the clutter of life, dogs, garbage, and other debris of the decaying urban surroundings.

She could not remember ever feeling quite so rejected and isolated. She felt totally alone, and sudden fears of failure kept re-occurring in her compulsively conditioned brain. Waves of depression alternated with anger as she went over the conversations with McLeary and Oren. She yearned to talk with someone, someone whose counsel she could trust and respect. Stark, Bellows, Chapman: each was a possibility but each had a specific disadvantage. Bellows's objectivity would have to be suspect; Stark's and Chapman's overriding loyalties would be to their respective institutions.

Susan thought of the worst: being dismissed from medical school in disgrace. Not only would it be a personal failure but she felt it would be a failure for all women in medicine. Susan wished there were some woman doctor to whom she could turn, but she did not know any. There were so few on the medical school staff, and none in any positions that made them accessible for counselling.

In the middle of her tormented musing, Susan felt her right foot slide as she put her weight on it. She had to steady herself with her hand on a nearby building to keep from falling. Expecting the worst, she looked down to see that she had stepped in a large steaming pile of dog faeces.

'God damn Beacon Hill.' Susan cursed Boston and all the literal and figurative shit a city government tolerated. Using the kerb to dislodge most of the material, Susan choked on the odour. Still she couldn't help but think about the symbolic aspect of her misfortune. Perhaps she had been stepping into a pile of shit, and as she was forced to do in regard to the actual shit in the city, she should try to ignore the whole affair. Just walk around it. Her responsibility was to become a doctor; that should take precedence over everything. The Bermans and the Greenlys were not her concern.

The rain continued and rivulets ran down her cheeks. She began to walk more carefully, prudently noticing the innumerable piles of dog crap that characterized Beacon Hill as much as the gas lamps or the red brick. She watched where she put her feet and the going was easier. But she could not dismiss her sense of responsibility to the Bermans and the Greenlys so easily. She thought about the age similarity between herself and Nancy Greenly. She thought about her own periods and the several episodes when she had bled more heavily than usual; how it had frightened her and made her feel helpless and out of control. She might have had to have a D&C herself, possibly at the Memorial.

But now she was out of the Memorial, maybe out of medical school. There was little that was up to her at that point, whether she wanted to pursue the problem or not. It was finished. It embarrassed her slightly to think of the frame of mind she had when she started the affair. 'A new disease!' Susan laughed at her own vanity and deluded sense of ability.

Susan strolled down Pinckney Street, crossed Charles Street and headed for the river. As aimlessly as on her Beacon Hill wandering, Susan mounted the stairs to the Longfellow Bridge. The graffiti stood out in bold outlines and she lingered, reading some of the nonsensical phrases, the faceless names. In the centre of the span she paused, gazing up the Charles River toward Cambridge and Harvard and the BU Bridge. The river was a curious pattern of ice patches and open water, like a gigantic piece of abstract art. A flock of seagulls stood motionless on one of the floes of ice.

Susan did not know what it was that drew her attention to the left, the way she had come. She saw a man in a dark overcoat and hat who turned toward the river and stopped when Susan looked in his direction. She returned to her undirected musing and the scene in front of her without giving the man in the dark overcoat a thought. But after five to ten minutes passed, Susan noticed the man had not moved. He was smoking and gazing up the river, seemingly as oblivious to the rain as was Susan. Susan thought that it was a coincidence to have two people standing on a bridge on a rainy day in February brooding over the river when as a rule the bridge was deserted even in nice weather.

Susan crossed the bridge to the Cambridge side and walked up the river bank toward the MIT boat house. She felt a little cold as some moisture worked its way into her collar. The mild discomfort was somehow therapeutic. But presently she decided that getting back to the dorm and a hot bath were in order.

Abruptly she turned, intending to recross the Longfellow Bridge and take the MBTA home. But she stopped. The same man with the dark coat was about a hundred yards away, still staring out over the expanse of the Charles River. Susan felt an uneasiness that she couldn't characterize. She changed her plans, to avoid passing the man. She would traverse the corner of the MIT campus and take the MBTA at Kendall Station.

As she crossed Memorial Drive, she noticed that the man

began to move in her direction. Obviously it was stupid, she assured herself, to concern herself with some stranger. She had difficulty explaining to herself why she would be so apt to have ungrounded paranoia. She decided that she was more upset than she had imagined. Just to be sure, she turned another corner and walked to the end of the block, stopping in front of the Political Science Library. Trying to be natural, she adjusted the string on her parcel.

The man appeared almost immediately but did not turn into the block. Instead, he crossed the street and disappeared from sight. But Susan had not convinced herself that he was not following her. There had been the slightest suggestion that the man had reacted to her delaying tactics. Susan mounted the steps and entered the library. She used the ladies' room and relaxed for a few moments. In the mirror her face reflected a definite uneasiness. She thought about calling someone but dismissed the idea. What could she say that wouldn't sound ridiculous? Besides, she felt better and was willing to forget the episode as a construct of her imagination.

Emerging from the ladies' room, she had regained her composure enough to appreciate the architecture of the library. It was ultra-modern with a sense of serenity and space. There was none of that overbearing stuffiness one associated with old university libraries. The chairs were bright orange canvas. The shelves and the card catalogues were highly polished oak.

Then Susan saw the man again! This time at a very close range. She knew it was he although he did not look up from the magazine he appeared to be reading. He was obviously out of place in the library, dressed in a dark overcoat, white shirt, and white tie. His plastered-down hair had a shiny appearance suggesting multiple layers of Vitalis. His irregular face was pockmarked from adolescent years of acne.

Susan mounted the stairs to the mezzanine, watching the man whenever she could. He did not seem to look up from his reading. From the outside of the building Susan had noted a connection between the library and the building immediately adjacent. She found the overpass and quickly crossed. The adjacent building was a classroom-office building and a number of people were milling through it. Susan felt more comfortable as she descended to the street floor. She left the building and headed rapidly for Kendall Square.

Since the area was unfamiliar to Susan, it took her a few minutes to find the entrance to the MBTA underground. Just before she descended she hesitated, then she looked around. To her amazement and consternation, the man in the dark coat was about a block away, coming toward her. Susan felt a sinking feeling in her abdomen and a quickening pulse. She also felt undecided about what to do.

A slight breeze moving up the stairs and a low threatening rumble helped her make up her mind. A train was coming into the station. A train filled with people.

In a partially controlled panic she descended the stairs and entered the shadowy subterranean world. She fumbled for a quarter at the turnstile. She knew she had several in her pocket, but her mitten made it impossible. She tore off her mitten and pulled out her change. A few coins fell to the concrete and rolled spiralling away. No one got off the train. A few people blankly watched Susan's uncoordinated efforts at the turnstile. The quarter dropped into the slot and Susan tried to push through. With a gasp she realized she had pushed too soon; the arm of the turnstile dug into her stomach rather than giving way. She let up, and the quarter dropped into the release mechanism. On her second attempt the turnstile turned so freely that she stumbled forward, just managing to keep herself from falling. The doors to the train closed as she ran up to them.

'Please!' she shouted but the train began to pull away from the station. Susan ran alongside for a few steps. Then as the end of the train slid by her, Susan caught the image of the conductor looking at her through the glass with a blank face. The train receded rapidly into the inbound tunnel as Susan panted and looked after it.

The station was totally deserted. Even the outbound platform on the other side was empty. The sound of the departing train fell off astoundingly rapidly, to be replaced by the regular sound of dripping water. Kendall Station was not a busy station and had not been renovated. The mosaic walls which had once been fashionable were a study in decay; the place recalled some ancient archeological site. Soot covered everything, and the platform was strewn with paper debris. Stalactite forms hung from the ceiling with droplets of moisture falling from their tips, as if it were a limestone cave of the Yucatán.

Susan leaned out over the tracks as far as she could and peered into the tunnel toward Cambridge, hoping to see another train materialize. Straining her ears, she heard only the dripping water. Then there was the unmistakable sound of unhurried footsteps on the subway stairs. Susan rushed over to the heavily grated change booth. It was empty. A sign said that it was occupied only at rush hour, from 3 to 5 pm. The footsteps on the stairs grew closer and Susan backed away from the entrance. She turned and ran down the platform toward the Cambridge end of the station. At the extreme end of the platform, she once again looked into the darkness of the tunnel. There was only the steady sound of dripping water. And footsteps.

Looking back toward the entrance, Susan watched the man in the dark coat enter through the turnstile. He stopped, cupping his hands over a match to light a cigarette, casually tossing the used match onto the tracks. Obviously in no hurry, he took several puffs from his cigarette before starting toward Susan. He seemed to savour the fear he was causing. His shoes echoed metallically as he came closer and closer.

Susan wanted to scream or run but she could do neither. It occurred to her that she might be dreaming up the terrifying situation. Perhaps it was just a series of coincidences. But the appearance and the expression of the man approaching her convinced her that this was no dream.

Susan began to panic. She was cornered unless she wanted to enter the tunnel. She discarded that idea despite her panic. The other platform? She looked across the inbound and outbound tracks to the other side. Between the tracks were steel I-beam uprights with room to squeeze through between them. But next to the uprights, running along on either side of them, were the third rails, the power source for the trains with enough voltage and amperage to fry a person instantly.

About ten to twenty feet within the tunnel, the I-beam uprights terminated and the power rails switched to the outsides of the respective tracks. Susan estimated that it would be relatively easy to sprint into the tunnel just far enough to round the end of the row of uprights. That way she could avoid stepping over the third rails.

The man was within fifty feet of Susan, and he flipped his unfinished cigarette onto the tracks. He appeared to take something from his pocket. A gun? No, it wasn't a gun. A knife? Perhaps.

Susan needed no more encouragement. She switched the nurse's uniform parcel to her right hand and squatted down at the edge of the platform, placing her left palm on the edge. Then she vaulted the four feet down onto the tracks, landing on her feet but allowing herself to absorb the shock by bending her legs. In an instant she was up, running into the tunnel.

Panic flooded over her and she stumbled on the wooden ties. She fell sideways toward the third rail. Instinctively she let go of her parcel and grabbed for one of the I-beams, managing to deflect herself enough so that she missed the third rail by inches. As she landed, her left hand hit a small piece of wood, which flipped up and landed against the third rail and the ground. With a blinding flash of electricity and a popping noise the piece of wood was incinerated. The acrid smell of an electrical fire filled the air.

Scrambling to her feet despite a sharp pain in her left ankle, mindlessly clutching at her package, Susan tried to run again on the ties. Just within the mouth of the tunnel, there was a series of switches, creating a maze of tracks and a bewildering pattern of rail and ties underfoot. With no time to figure out the intricacies of the track, Susan stumbled ahead. But her dragging left boot snagged between two rails. She fell again.

Expecting her pursuer to be on her at any second, Susan struggled to one knee. Her left foot was jammed fast between the two rails. She pulled to try to extricate herself, straining forward without effect. All she managed to do was to aggravate the pain in her ankle. Bending down, she clutched at her leg with her hands and pulled in desperation. She didn't allow herself to look back.

Suddenly an agonizing screech filled the air, forcing Susan to let go of her leg and gasp for breath. She thought that something had happened to her but she was still alive. Then it happened again; a noise so loud in the underground cavern that she instinctively covered her ears with her palms. Even so, the noise caused a sharp pain deep within her middle ears. Then she knew what it was. It was the train! It was the shriek of the train whistle.

Susan looked up into the blackness of the tunnel and saw the single penetrating light. She began to feel the thundering vibration of the tons of steel bearing down at her at great speed. Then there was another sound, deeper yet even more penetrating than the whistle. It was the rasp of steel against steel as the wheels of the oncoming train locked in a vain and desperate attempt to stop. But it was useless. The momentum was too great.

Susan had no idea which track her foot was caught in, nor could she tell which track bore the train. The light seemed to be coming directly at her. With a desperate, manic jerk she pulled her foot from her boot and wrenched herself in the direction of the outbound track.

Her outstretched arms and hands cushioned the fall as she sprawled across a rail. By reflex she pulled herself into a ball and covered her head with her arms. The vibration and the rasp came to a crescendo and with a whoosh the train passed some five feet away.

Susan didn't move for a moment. She couldn't believe what had happened. Her pulse was racing and her hands were wet. But she was alive and, except for some bruises, she was all right. Her overcoat was torn and several buttons had popped off. There was a band of grease across it and part of the white lab coat she wore beneath it. Her pens and penlight were gone, scattered in the tunnel. One of the earpieces to her stethoscope was bent at right angles.

She stood up and brushed off the larger pieces of debris and reclaimed her boot. By merely depressing the heel and lifting the toe, she extricated it with ease that belied her earlier difficulties. By the time she had it on, she could see several men running toward her with lights.

When she was helped onto the platform, the whole experience already seemed like a total figment of her imagination, as if she were totally out of control. There was no man in a dark coat. There was just a large crowd of people who excitedly shouted with each other about what had happened and what should happen. Someone found her parcel on the track and brought it to her.

Susan denied injury. She thought about saying something about the man, but then again she was unsure of her own grasp of what had been real and what had been imagined. She had panicked and was still overwrought. She couldn't think and she wanted to go home more than anything else.

She had to spend fifteen minutes assuring the train crew that she had simply slipped off the platform, was now perfectly fine, and definitely didn't need an ambulance. Susan insisted that all she wanted was to get to Park Street to catch the Huntington line. Finally Susan and the others entered the train, the doors closed, and it pulled out of the station.

Susan inspected her clothes in the light. She noticed that the man across from her was staring at her. And the woman next to him was doing the same. In fact as Susan's eyes moved around the car, she realized that everyone was staring at her as if she was some sort of freak. The eyes and the faces were unbearable. She tried to look outside as the train crossed the Longfellow Bridge. Still there was no conversation. Everyone was watching her fixedly.

The train pulled into Charles Street. With great relief Susan jumped off the car and ran down the platform. In front of the Phillips Drugstore she caught a cab. Only then did she begin to calm down. Looking at her hands, she realized she was visibly trembling.

Wednesday February 25
1:30pm

By one-thirty in the afternoon, Bellows had already had a full day by most people's standards. He wasn't physically tired, because he was well accustomed to his schedule. But he was emotionally tired, on edge. The day had begun auspiciously enough when he had awakened with Susan still at his side. He had enjoyed their evening together immensely, although he was doubtful about the potential longevity of their affair. Susan was hardly the type of girl he was accustomed to escape with. She had none of that wide-eyed feminine naiveté which formed the basis of Bellows's idea of women. To his pleasant surprise, and despite his fears, sex had come naturally with Susan, although for him it was without the aggressive overtones he had learned to recognize as normal. Susan, and his own response to her, remained an absorbing enigma.

Getting up and leaving Susan sleeping in his bed had provided a certain comforting feeling for Bellows. It made his role more traditional. Had Susan gotten up and come to the hospital at the same time as he did, it would have diluted his sense of sacrifice. And a sense of sacrifice was important for Bellows since it served as a fertile source of inner satisfaction.

But then the day had deteriorated. To Bellows's horror, Stark had made a surprise appearance on early-morning rounds, and the chief was in a particularly vindictive mood. Stark had started rounds by asking Bellows what he had done to the attractive medical student assigned to him that made it so difficult for her to show up for rounds. Bellows had inwardly shuddered, realizing that Stark's off-colour implications were truer than Stark himself realized. For Bellows knew that at that very moment Susan lay sleeping in his bed.

Stark's question had caused some short laughs and a few snide remarks by the others on rounds. Bellows had felt his face tingle with blood flowing through dilated capillaries. At

217

the same time he had felt a sudden defensiveness.

Before Bellows had been given a chance to say anything, Stark had launched into a tirade about attendance and interest, performance, and reward. He had essentially told Bellows that any future absence by Susan would be debited to Bellows's own record. Bellows was to make it his personal goal to see that all the students assigned to him performed exemplarily.

During actual rounds Stark had been as nasty as ever, particularly toward Bellows. In almost every case Bellows had been asked some difficult question and his answers never satisfied the irate chief. Even some of the other residents had realized that Bellows was being raked over the coals and they had tried to interfere by answering questions even when the questions were cleary directed at Bellows.

At the end of rounds, Stark had called Bellows aside to tell him that he was not performing up to his usual level, nor to the department's expectations. Finally Stark had gotten around to what was really bothering him. After a rather lengthy pause, the Chief of Surgery had asked Bellows exactly what role he had played with respect to the drugs found in locker 338.

Bellows had denied any knowledge whatsoever of the drugs, except what Chandler had told him. Bellows had told Stark directly that he had used locker 338 for about one week before his permanent locker came available. Stark's only comment to this information had been that he wanted the affair cleaned up in short order.

For Bellows, even being remotely related to such a situation caused him a disproportionate amount of anxiety. His horribly compulsive mentality magnified the whole affair out of proportion. His tendency toward professional paranoia began to feed on itself and, as the morning passed, his anxiety had waxed rather than waned.

Bellows operated on two cases himself that morning, allowing the students to come into the OR. On the first case, Goldberg and Fairweather had scrubbed, more to wet their hands than actually to help. On the second case, Carpin and Niles had scrubbed. Bellows had been particularly careful and encouraging for Niles and it had paid off. There had been no fainting episodes. In fact, Niles had turned out to be the most dextrous of the students and had been allowed to close the skin.

During lunch Bellows found the opportunity to corner Chandler. The chief resident had reiterated what Bellows already knew – namely, that Stark was really uptight about the drugs.

'The whole Goddamned thing is ridiculous,' said Bellows. 'Has Stark talked with Walters yet to get me off the hook?'

'I haven't even talked with Walters,' said Chandler. 'I went into the OR area to talk with him but he hasn't shown up today. Nobody has seen him all day.'

'Walters?' Bellows was greatly surprised. 'He hasn't missed a day here in a quarter of a century.'

'What can I tell you? He's not here.'

Bellows responded to this information by going up to the personnel office to get Walters's home phone number. It turned out that Walters did not have a telephone. Bellows had to be satisfied with an address: 1833 Stewart Street, Roxbury.

By one-thirty Bellows was very much on edge. Another call to the OR desk confirmed the fact that Walters still had not appeared, and Bellows made a decision. He decided that he would take the time and make the effort to go and visit Walters. It was the only way that he could think of to extricate himself immediately from the drug affair. It wasn't all that difficult a decision, although it was very irregular for Bellows to leave the hospital in the middle of the day. But Bellows had the distressing feeling that over the last forty-eight hours his comfortable and promising position at the Memorial had been put in jeopardy. As he saw it, he had two problems: the first, the drug problem, was simple, because he knew that he was not involved and that all he had to do was to establish that fact; the second problem, Susan and her so-called project, was something else.

Bellows managed to foist his medical students off on Dr Larry Beard, a grandson of the Beard wing benefactor. Then, with his beeper on his belt, the operators notified, and a fellow resident by the name of Norris willing to cover for an hour, Bellows slipped out of the hospital at one-thirty-seven, and flagged a cab.

'Stewart Street, Roxbury? You sure about that?' The taxi driver's face contorted into a questioning, disdainful expression when Bellows gave his destination.

'Number 1833,' added Bellows.

'It's your money!'

With dirty steaming piles of snow pushed aside here and there, the city looked particularly depressiong. It was raining almost as hard as it had been when Bellows had walked to work in the morning. Very few people were visible along the route the driver took. The peculiar, uninhabited look of the city recalled the deserted cities of the Mayans. It was as if things had gotten so bad that everyone decided to just close their doors and leave.

As the cab penetrated Roxbury deeper and deeper, the city got worse. Their route took them down through a disintegrating warehouse area, then through decaying slums. The mid-thirties temperature, the relentless rain, and the rotting snow made it that much more depressing. Finally the cab pulled to the right and Bellows leaned forward, catching sight of the street sign for Stewart Street. At the same time the right front wheel descended into a pothole filled with rain water and the bottom of the front part of the cab crashed against the pavement. The driver swore and threw the steering wheel to the right to avoid the same hole with the rear tyre. But the rear of the car slammed down and then lurched upward with a shudder. Bellows's head hit the ceiling hard enough to hurt.

'Sorry, but you wanted Stewart Street!'

Rubbing his head, Bellows looked out at the numbers: 1831, and then 1833. After paying the fare, he stepped out and closed the door. The cab raced off, weaving its way between the potholes and turning off as soon as possible. Bellows watched it disappear from sight, wishing that he had told the driver to wait. Then he looked around, thankful that the rain had stopped. There were several gutted hulks of automobiles with everything of even questionable value removed. There were no other cars parked on the grim street, or moving, for that matter. There were no people in sight either. When Bellows looked up at the row house in front of him, he realized it was deserted, most of the windows boarded up. Then he looked at the surrounding houses. All were the same. Most were boarded up; any windows exposed were smashed.

A torn sign nailed to the front door said that the building was condemned and owned by the BHA, the Boston Housing Authority. The date on the sign was 1971. It was another Boston project that had got completely fouled up.

Bellows was perplexed. Walters had no phone, and this seemed a phoney address. Remembering Walters's appearance, it didn't seem so surprising. Curiosity made Bellows mount the stairs to read the BHA sign. There was another smaller sign saying 'No Trespassing' and that the police had the premises under surveillance.

The door had once been attractive, with a large oval stained glass window. The glass was now broken and several pieces of rough-cut lumber were haphazardly nailed across the opening. Bellows tried the door, and to his surprise it opened. One of the straps of the hasp was unattached, with the screws gone despite the fact that the hasp had a large steel padlock.

The door opened in, scratching over the broken glass. Bellows took one look up and down the deserted street, then stepped over the threshold. The door closed quickly behind him, extinguishing most of the meagre daylight. Bellows waited until his eyes adjusted to the semi-darkness.

The hall in which he found himself was in ruins. The stairs ascended directly in front of him. The banister had been pushed over and broken into pieces, presumably for firewood. The wallpaper was hanging in streamers. A small dirty drift of snow half-covered the debris on the floor and extended toward the rear of the building. Within six or seven feet it dissipated. But directly in front of him, Bellows saw several footprints. Examining them more closely, he could tell that there were at least two different sets. One set was huge, made by feet half again as large as his own. But more interesting was that the tracks did not seem very old.

Bellows heard a car coming down the street and he straightened up. Conscious of trespassing, Bellows moved over to one of the boarded-up windows in what had been the parlour, to see if the car passed. It did.

Then he climbed up the stairs and partially explored the second floor. Several crumbling mattresses were the only contents. The air had a musty, heavy odour. The ceiling in the front room had collapsed, covering the floor with chunks of plaster. Each room had a fireplace, layers of filth, and dusty cobwebs hanging from the ceiling.

Bellows glanced up the stairs to the third floor but decided not to go up. Instead he returned to the first floor and was preparing to leave when he heard a sound. It was a soft thud coming from the back of the house.

Feeling a certain quickening of his pulse, Bellows hesitated. He wanted to leave. There was something about the house that made him feel uneasy. But the sound was repeated and Bellows walked down the hall toward the rear of the building. At the end of the hall he had to turn right into what had been the dining room. The fixture for the gaslight was still in the centre of the ceiling. Walking through the dining room, Bellows found himself in the remains of the kitchen. Everything had been removed except a few naked pipes, which protruded from the floor. The rear windows were all boarded up like those in front.

Bellows took a few steps into the room and there was a sudden movement to his left. Bellows froze. His heart leaped into high gear, thumping audibly in his chest. The movement had come from the direction of several large cardboard boxes.

Having recovered from his sudden fright, Bellows gingerly approached the boxes. With his foot he nudged them. To his horror several large rats scurried from their cover and disappeared into the dining room.

Bellows's nervousness surprised him. He had always thought of himself as being the calm one, not easily shaken. His reaction to the rats had been one of paralysing fear, and it took him several minutes to recover. He kicked the cardboard boxes to reassure himself that he was in control and was about to return to the dining room when he noticed another footprint in the dust and debris by the boxes. Looking back and forth from his own footprints to the one he had just found, Bellows realized that the strange footprint must be fairly fresh. Just beyond the cardboard boxes was a door, open by a few inches. The footprint pointed in its direction.

Bellows approached the door and opened it slowly. Beyond was darkness and steps leading down into it. The steps presumably led to the cellar but were quickly swallowed in darkness. Bellows reached into the breast pocket of his white coat and pulled out his penlight. Switching it on, he found that its small beam could penetrate only five or six feet down.

Every ounce of rationality told him to leave the building. Instead he started down the cellar stairs, as much to prove to himself that he wasn't afraid as to find out what was there. But he was afraid. His imagination was working swiftly to remind him how easily horror movies affected him. He remembered the scenes in *Psycho* of the descent into the cellar.

As he advanced step by step, the penlight beam advanced until it played on a closed door. Bellows examined it, and then tried the knob. The door swung open easily.

Bellows had expected that there would be some sunken cellar windows to allow some light in but there was only darkness. He peered ahead after the pale shaft from his penlight into what seemed like a rather large room. His penlight was little help beyond six feet. By moving around the room counterclockwise, Bellows found some broken but serviceable furniture, including a bed covered with newspapers and two moth-eaten blankets. A few cockroaches fled Bellows's encroaching penlight.

There was a fireplace with a large stack of wood on the hearth. Within the fireplace were ashes that suggested a recent fire. Bellows reached down and picked up one of the newspapers to check the date. It was February 3, 1976.

Letting the newspaper drop to the floor, Bellows noticed another door, which was standing ajar about six inches. He started for the door but the penlight dimmed sharply, its miniature batteries drained by the continuous use. Bellows switched the light off for a moment to give it a chance to revive. He found himself in a blackness so dense that he literally could not see his hand in front of his face. And as long as he did not move, total silence reigned.

The sensory deprivation resulted in a building apprehension and Bellows switched on the light before he had planned to do so. The beam was significantly stronger and Bellows could make out white tile on the floor just beyond the door in front of him. A bathroom.

Bellows pushed open the door. It moved hard on its hinges as if it were made of lead. The meagre and faltering light from the penlight outlined a toilet without a seat immediately opposite the door. Once the door was half open, Bellows leaned his head into the room. The sink was on the wall to the right around the half-opened door. The light moved over the sink, then up onto the wall and over the mirrored medicine cabinet.

Bellows's scream was totally involuntary. It was not loud, but came from deep within his brain, a primeval response. The penlight dropped from his hand onto the tiled floor and shattered. Instantly Bellows was plunged into darkness. He turned and ran in the direction of the stairs, falling over the furniture. He was in a total panic, and he slammed into the wall instead of finding the stairs. Running his hand along the wall, he reached a corner and realized that he had come too far. He turned and retraced his steps. Only when he was directly facing the stairs could he see any light from above.

He stumbled up the steps and ran back through the house and out into the street. Only then did he stop, his chest heaving from exertion, his right hand bleeding from one of his falls in the darkness. He looked back at the house, allowing his mind to reconstruct the image that he had seen.

He had found Walters. In the mirror in the bathroom, Bellows had glimpsed Walters hanging by a rope around his neck from a hook on the door. Walters was terribly distorted and bloated by stagnant blood. His eyes were wide open and appeared as if they were about to extrude from his head. Bellows had seen some awful things in emergency rooms during his medical training, but never in his whole life had he seen a more gruesome spectacle than the corpse of Walters.

Wednesday February 25
4:30pm

Susan entered the dean of students' office with some trepidation, but Dr James Chapman's demeanour quickly put her at ease. He was not angry, as Susan anticipated, just concerned. A small man with dark hair, closely trimmed, he always looked the same, in his three-piece suit complete with a gold chain and a Phi Beta Kappa key. Dr Chapman paused between his sentences and smiled, not out of emotion, but more as a device to put students at ease. It was a distinctive habit and not unpleasant.

Suggesting the essence of the university, the office of the dean of students at the medical school had a more pleasant atmosphere than offices at the Memorial. A brass antique lamp stood on the desk. The chairs were all of the black academic sort, bearing a decal of the medical school's emblem on the back. An oriental rug brightened the floor. The far wall was covered with pictures of previous classes at the medical school.

After some traditional pleasantries, Susan sat down across from Dr Chapman. The dean removed his executive reading glasses and carefully placed them on his blotter.

'Susan, why didn't you come to me and discuss this affair before it got out of hand? After all, that's what I'm here for. You could have saved a lot of grief not only for yourself but also for the school. I've got to try to keep everyone as happy as possible. Obviously, keeping everybody happy is impossible, but I do a reasonable job of it. Still, I need warning when there's a special problem. I like to hear when things go poorly and when things go well.'

Susan nodded her head in agreement as Dr Chapman spoke. She was still dressed in the same clothes which she had been wearing during the MBTA mishap. There were obvious abrasions on both of her knees. The parcel containing the nurse's uniform was on her lap. It looked worse than she did.

'Dr Chapman, the whole affair began innocently enough. The first days of the clinics are difficult enough without the series of coincidences I encountered. They sent me fleeing to the library. As much to get my head together as to learn something, I started to look into anaesthetic complications. I thought I could get back to the usual routine in a day or so. But then I got involved so quickly. I turned up some information that astounded me and I thought ... maybe ... you're going to laugh when I tell you. It almost embarrasses me to think about it.'

'Try me.'

'I thought maybe I was on the track of a new disease or syndrome or drug reaction at the least.'

Dr Chapman's face lit up with a genuine smile. 'A new disease! Now that would have been a coup for someone's first days as a clinical clerk. Well, one way or the other, it's water under the bridge. I trust you feel differently now?'

'You'd better believe it. I do have a self-preservation reflex. Besides I'm starting to get delusional about the whole thing. I think I had some sort of paranoid reaction this afternoon. I was convinced a man was following me to the point that I actually panicked. Look at my knees and my clothes, as if you haven't already noticed. To make a long story short, I tried to cross from the inbound to the outbound platform at Kendall Station of the MBTA. Idiotic!' Susan tapped her head lightly with her index finger for emphasis.

'After that I realized that it behoved me to get back to normal, quickly. Like right away. But I'm still worried that there is something peculiar about these coma incidents at the

Memorial, and I would like to continue studying the problem in some capacity. Apparently there are more cases involved than I originally suspected, and maybe that is why Dr Harris and Dr MaLeary were irritated at my naive interference. One way or another, I'm sorry I've caused trouble for you at the Memorial. It goes without saying that it was not my intent.'

'Susan, the Memorial is a big place. It's probably blown over already. The only tangible legacy is that I'm going to have to switch your surgery to the VA hospital. I've already made the arrangements, and you are to report tomorrow to Dr Robert Piles's office.' Dr Chapman paused, looking at Susan intently. 'Susan, you have a long road ahead of you. There will be plenty of time to discover new diseases or syndromes, if that is what you want. But now, today, this year, your primary goal should be basic medical education. Let Harris and McLeary work on the coma incidents. I want you to get back to work because I expect nothing but good reports about you. You've done very well so far.'

Susan emerged from the medical school Administration Building with a mild sense of euphoria. It was as if Dr Chapman had powers of absolution. The ponderous problem of being ejected from medical school in disgrace had vanished. Obviously the surgery rotation at the VA was not as good as that at the Memorial, but in comparison to what could have happened, the transfer was a mild inconvenience indeed.

Although it was only a little after five, the winter night had begun in earnest. The rain had stopped as another cold front pushed the weakening warm front out over the Atlantic. The temperature had plummeted to about eighteen. The sky was speckled with bright stars, at least directly overhead. Toward the horizon the stars disappeared, their light unable to penetrate the noxious urban atmosphere. Susan crossed Longwood Avenue by running between the cars of impatient commuters in the clogging traffic.

In the lobby of the dorm she passed a few acquaintances, who were quick to notice Susan's skinned knees and the greasy stain of the rail across her coat. There were some clever jibes about how tough surgery rotation must be at the Memorial, to judge by Susan, who looked as if she had been in a bar-room brawl. Despite the fact that she thought the comments were rather funny, Susan almost stopped to snap back at the wise-cracks. Instead she passed through the lobby and crossed the quad. The tennis court in the centre had a sad, neglected winter look.

The well-trodden wooden staircase curved gracefully up, and Susan mounted the steps slowly and deliberately, looking forward to the isolation and security her room promised. She intended to take a long bath, sort out the day mentally, and, above all, relax.

As she always did, Susan entered her room and bolted the door behind her without turning on a light. The switch by the door activated the circular fluorescent bulb in the centre of the ceiling, and Susan preferred the richer glow of the incandescent lights, either the lamp by the bed or the modern floor lamp by the desk. With the help of the light coming from the parking lot she walked over to the bed to turn on the lamp. Just as her hand reached for the switch she heard a noise. It was not loud but it was nonetheless distinctive enough to make her aware that it was not part of the normal sounds of her room. It was a foreign noise. She switched on the light, listening for the noise to repeat itself, but it did not recur. She decided it must have come from a neighbouring room.

She hung up her coat and her white jacket, and unpacked the new nurse's uniform. It had survived the afternoon remarkably well. Then she unbuttoned and removed her blouse, throwing it onto the pile of dirty laundry in the easy chair. Her bra followed. Reaching behind her with her right hand, she began to struggle with the button on her skirt. At the same time she headed for the bathroom to start the bath water.

She opened the bathroom door and flipped on the fluorescent light, preparing to look in the mirror when the light came on. With a screech of plastic hooks along metal, the shower curtain was whipped back; a figure leaped into the room. Almost at the same instant the fluorescent light blinked and then filled the room with its raw light. There was a flash of a knife and a lightning blow to Susan's head. She twisted backward under

228

its impact, crashing into the wall of the bathroom. By sheer reflex her arms straightened and her hands groped to keep herself from falling. It all happened so quickly that she had no time to react. A cry had started in her throat but the blow to the head had dislodged it.

Instantly the left hand of the intruder grabbed Susan by the throat, forcing her up to her full height against the wall, her naked breasts tensing. Despite all her fantasies about what she would do if she were attacked, knees to the balls, fingernails in the eyes, Susan did nothing but breathe as best she could and gaze at her assailant in utter horror. Her eyes flung open to their very limit. The fury of the unexpected attack had been totally overwhelming. The power of the hand that held her by the throat was unmistakable. And she recognized the man. They had met on the subway platform.

'One sound and you're dead, baby,' snarled the man, bringing the knife in his right hand up beneath Susan's chin.

Just as suddenly and roughly as he had originally seized Susan's throat, the man released his hold, causing Susan to stumble forward. Her assailant backhanded her brutally, and she pitched to her hands and knees, with her lip split and numerous small capillaries broken over her left cheekbone.

Hooking his foot under Susan's shoulder, the man forced Susan to rise up on her knees. Then with a callous kick he dumped Susan backward against the wall, where she lay with one arm lewdly draped over the toilet. A trickle of blood ran down from the corner of her mouth and dropped onto a pale breast. The image of the man momentarily swam before her. When he came in focus she could see his pockmarked face crack in a fiendish grin. He was obviously relishing the thought of ravishing her. She felt numb and unable to respond.

'Too bad I'm only authorized on this visit to talk to you, or as we say in my business, to make a preliminary contact. The message is simple. There's a lot of people who are very, very unhappy with the way you have been spending your time lately. Unless you get back to your usual activities and stop getting people mad, I'll have to come back to see you again.'

The man paused to let his message sink in. Then he continued: 'And just to encourage you a little more, this boy will also get to meet me and maybe even have an unexpected, serious, and probably fatal accident.'

The man flipped a picture onto Susan's lap. In slow motion she picked it up.

'And I'm sure you don't want your brother, James, down there in Coopers, Maryland, to suffer from your hobbies. And I don't have to tell you that our little meeting here is just between us. If you go to the cops, the punishment is the same.'

Without another word, the man slipped from the bathroom. Susan heard the outside door to her room open and then close quietly. The only sound was a slight buzz from the fluorescent light over the mirror. She did not move for several minutes, uncertain whether her attacker had really left. Her arm was still draped over the toilet.

As the terror subsided, confusion and emotion mounted. Tears welled up in her eyes, forming a bulging meniscus. She lifted the picture of her younger brother with his bike, smiling in front of her parent's home. 'Christ,' said Susan, shaking her head and closing her eyes tightly. As her eyes closed, the tears overflowed from her lids, running down her cheeks in profusion. There was no doubt that the photograph was authentic.

Footsteps in the hall made Susan suddenly alert, and she pushed herself up onto her feet. The footsteps passed her room and receded down the hall. Susan staggered into her bedroom and rebolted the door. Turning, she scanned her room. Everything seemed undisturbed. Then she realized she felt wet. With her hand she felt herself and couldn't believe it. She had urinated in her panic.

The confusion began to metamorphose into analytical thought, and the thought brought the tears rapidly in check. There had been a host of unexplained episodes in the last couple of days, but one thing began to take definite form in Susan's consciousness. She was now more sure than ever that she had stumbled onto something, something big, something strange.

Looking into the mirror, Susan assayed the damage. Her left eyelids were slightly swollen and might turn into a black eye. Her left cheek sported a contused area about the size of a quarter, and her left lower lip was swollen and tender. By pulling her lip out gently and looking into the mirror Susan could see that she had a two- or three-millimetre laceration on the inside surface. It had been crushed against her lower teeth when she had been struck. The small amount of blood in the corner of her mouth came away easily, improving her appearance tremendously.

Susan decided she was not going to overreact to the latest episode. She also decided that despite Chapman's pleas she was not ready to give up completely. She had a competitive spirit and, although it was deeply buried by years of stereotypical conditioning, it was very strong. Susan had never been challenged in an equivalent capacity before. Never had the potential stakes been so high. But she was also aware of two realities: she had to be extraordinarily careful from then on, and she had to work fast.

Susan got into the shower, turning on the water as hard as it would go. She let it crash down on her head while she slowly rotated. She cupped her hands over her breasts to protect them from the needle-like jets of water. The effect was soothing and it gave her time to think. She thought about calling Bellows but decided against it. Their embryonic intimacy would make it difficult for Bellows to react to the information objectively. He'd probably respond in some idiotic male overprotective fashion. What she needed was a mind with the perspective to challenge her deductions. Then she thought about Stark. He had not been overly influenced by her lowly position as a medical student or by her sex. Besides, his astonishing grasp of medical and business matters was immediately apparent. Above all, he was maturely rational and could be counted on to be objective.

Once out of the shower, Susan wrapped her hair in a towel and donned her terrycloth bathrobe.

She sat down by the phone and dialled the Memorial. She asked for Dr Stark's office.

'I'm sorry, but Dr Stark is on another line. Can I have him call you back?'

'No, I'll wait. Just say that it is Susan Wheeler calling and that it is important.'

'I'll try, but I cannot promise anything. He's talking long distance and may be on the line for some time.'

'I'll hold just the same.' Susan was well aware that doctors often ignore returning a call.

Stark finally came onto the line.

'Dr Stark, you said that I could call you if I found out anything interesting in my little investigation.'

'Of course, Susan.'

'Well I have found out something extraordinary. This whole affair is definitely ...' She paused.

'Is definitely what, Susan?'

'Well, I'm not sure how to put it. I guess I'm now sure that there is a criminal aspect. I don't know how or why, but I'm quite certain. In fact, I have a feeling that some large organization is involved ... like the Mafia or something.'

'Sounds like a pretty wild conjecture to me, Susan. What has brought this idea to mind?'

'I've had a pretty funny afternoon with no laughs.' Susan looked closely at her abraded knees.

'And?'

'I've been threatened tonight.'

'Threatened with what?' Stark's voice changed from interest to concern.

'My life, I guess.' Susan looked at the photo of her brother.

'Susan, if that is true, then this becomes a serious affair, to say the very least. But are you sure this isn't some sort of prank by some of your classmates? Medical school pranks can get rather elaborate on occasion.'

'I must admit I hadn't thought of that.' Susan gingerly felt her lacerated lip with the tip of her tongue. 'But I think this was the real thing.'

'Conjecture is not what's needed at this point. I will personally advise the hospital executive committee of this. But, Susan, now is definitely the time for you to withdraw from further involvement. I advised you to do that before, but only because I was afraid it might hurt you academically. Now, it's apparently a different game. I think professionals should take over. Have you reported this to the police?'

'No, the threat included my younger brother, and there was a plain warning not to go to the police. That's why I've called you. Besides, if I went to the police, they'd probably dismiss it as simple attempted rape rather than a specific threat.'

'I doubt it very much.'

'Most males would.'

'But if the threat included your family, you are probably right to be careful with whom you talk. But my gut reaction suggests that you should report the incident to the police.'

'I'll give it some thought. Meanwhile, I wondered if you'd heard that I've been kicked out of my surgery rotation at the Memorial. I have to go to the VA to do my surgery.'

'No, I've not been told about that. When did this happen?'

'This afternoon. Obviously I'd much prefer to stay at the Memorial. I think that I could prove that I am a good student if given the chance. Since you are Chief of Surgery and since you are aware that I have not been merely goofing off, I thought maybe you might be willing to reverse that decision.'

'As Chief of Surgery I should have been told about your dismissal. I will get in touch with Dr Bellows immediately.'

'I don't think he knows about it, either, to tell you the truth. It was a Mr Oren.'

'Oren? Well that's interesting. Susan, I cannot promise anything, but I'll look into it. I must tell you that you have not been the most popular student here with Anaesthesia and Medicine.'

'I'd appreciate anything you can do. One other question. Would it be possible for you to arrange a visit for me to the Jefferson Institute? I'd very much like to visit the patient, Berman. I'm sort of hoping that if I can see him again that maybe I'll be able to forget this whole affair.'

'You certainly have a lot of difficult demands, young lady. But I'll call and see what I can do. The Jefferson is not university-controlled. It was built by government funds through HEW, but its operation has been turned over to a private medical management firm. So I have little voice there. But I'll check.

Give me a call after nine tomorrow, and I'll let you know.'

Susan hung up the phone. Obviously in deep thought, she bit her lower lip, as was her habit. The result was painful. She stared at one of the posters on her walls but with unseeing eyes. Her mind raced over the events of the last few days, searching for possible associations that she had missed.

Impulsively she got up and took out the nurse's uniform she had purchased. Then she began to dry her hair. Fifteen minutes later, she viewed herself in the mirror. The uniform fitted reasonably well.

She picked up the photograph of her brother for the second time. At least she felt reasonably confident that there was no immediate danger for her family. It was winter vacation for public schools and her family was skiing in Aspen for the week.

Wednesday February 25

7:15pm

Susan had no illusions about her situation. She was in danger and had to be resourceful. Whoever it was that had decided to threaten her undoubtedly expected that she would mend her ways and live in fear, at least for a while. Susan felt that she had about forty-eight hours of relative freedom of movement. After that, who knew.

The thing that encouraged her the most was that someone had decided that she was important enough to be threatened. It might mean that she was on the right track; maybe she had already found more answers than she could associate. She could be like the professor who had carefully discovered all the information necessary to break the secret of DNA. But he had not arranged it properly, and it took the ingenuity of Watson and Crick to pull it all together, to see the whole molecule as the wonderful double helix.

Susan carefully leafed through her notebook, reading all that she had written down. She reread her notes about coma and its known causes; she underlined those articles she still planned to read; she underlined the title of the new anaesthesiology text she had seen in Harris's office. Then she reread the extensive material on Nancy Greenly and the two respiratory arrest victims. Susan was sure that the answer was there but she couldn't see it. She knew that she needed more data to increase the likelihood of making correlations. The charts. She needed the charts from McLeary.

It was seven-fifteen when she was ready to leave her room. As if she were in some spy movie, she checked out the parking lot from her window, to see if she were under obvious surveillance. She looked over the cars, but saw no one. Susan pulled the curtains closed and locked her door, leaving her lights on. In the corridor, she stood for a moment, then, extrapolating from her movie experience, she rolled a small wad of paper into a ball and carefully inserted it between the door and the jamb, next to the floor.

In the basement of the dorm there was a tunnel leading over to the Anatomy and Pathology Building. It carried steam pipes and power lines, and Susan and her classmates occasionally used it during inclement weather. Susan had no idea if she would be followed but she wanted to make it difficult, hopefully impossible. From the anatomy building Susan used the passageway to the Administration Building, which she found unlocked. From there she exited by the medical library, catching a cab on Huntington Avenue. She had the cab do a U-turn after a quarter of a mile and drive back, passing the spot where she had hailed it. Nestling down in her coat to keep from being seen, Susan tried to see if anyone was following her. She saw no one at all suspicious-looking. Relaxing, she told the cab to take her to the Memorial Hospital.

Like any professional 'hit man,' Angelo D'Ambrosio felt an

inner satisfaction at having successfully completed a job. After communicating the message he had for Susan, he had walked back to Huntington Avenue and caught a cab near the corner of Longfellow. The taxi driver was delighted: finally he'd found an airport run which meant a decent fare and undoubtedly a good tip. Prior to D'Ambrosio he'd had nothing but old ladies going to the supermarket.

D'Ambrosio settled back in the cab, content with his day's work. He had no idea why he had been contracted to do what he had done in Boston that day. But D'Ambrosio rarely knew why, and in fact he did not want to know why. On the few occasions when his information and briefing had been more complete, he had had more trouble. On the current assignment, he had been merely told to fly to Boston in the evening of the twenty-fourth and stay at the Sheraton Downtown under the name of George Taranto. The following morning he was to proceed to 1833 Stewart Street and to the basement apartment of a man named Walters. He was to have Walters write a note saying, 'The drugs were mine. I cannot face the consequences.' Then he was to dispose of Walters in a fashion that would suggest suicide. Then he was to isolate a female medical student by the name of Susan Wheeler and 'scare the shit out of her,' telling her that she would be in danger if she did not return to her usual occupation. The orders had ended with the usual exhortations about being careful. There was a packet of information about Susan Wheeler, including the photo of her brother, some background, and a schedule of her current activities.

Looking at his watch, D'Ambrosio knew that he could easily make the 8:45 American flight back to Chicago. He also knew his thousand dollars would be in the usual twenty-four-hour locker, number 12 near the baggage claim for TWA. Contentedly, D'Ambrosio watched the play of lights flicker past the window. He thought about the ghoulish Walters and tried to imagine the connection he could have with the attractive Wheeler. D'Ambrosio remembered Susan's appearance, and how he had had to fight with himself not to put it to her. He began to imagine a series of sadistic delights that awakened his sleeping penis. D'Ambrosio found himself hoping that he'd be ordered back to make a second contact with Miss Wheeler. If he ever was, he decided he'd screw her in the ass.

When he reached the airline terminal D'Ambrosio entered a phone booth. There remained one small detail in a routine assignment: he had to call his central contact in Chicago and report that the job was done.

The number rang the agreed-upon seven times.

'The Sandler residence,' answered a voice on the other end.

'May I speak to Mr Sandler, please,' said D'Ambrosio, bored. He did not quite understand this manoeuvre and it took a few minutes. He always had to remember the current name. If the wrong name was used he was supposed to hang up and call an alternate number. D'Ambrosio wet his index finger with his tongue and drew circles of saliva on the phone booth glass. Finally the voice returned.

'It's clear.'

'Boston's done, no problems,' said D'Ambrosio with no inflection in his voice.

'There's an update. Miss Wheeler is to be disposed of as soon as possible. The method is up to you but it must appear to be a rape. You understand, a rape.'

D'Ambrosio couldn't believe his ears. It was like a dream come true.

'There'll be an extra charge,' said D'Ambrosio matter-of-factly, carefully concealing his anticipation of sexually assaulting Susan.

'There will be an extra five hundred dollars.'

'Seven hundred and fifty. This won't be so easy.' Easy? It was going to be a breeze. D'Ambrosio thought that he should really be paying.

'Six hundred.'

'You're on.' D'Ambrosio hung up the phone. He was immensely pleased. He checked the night flight schedule. The last departure for Chicago was 11:45 TWA. D'Ambrosio thought he could get his little kicks and still make that one. He descended to the baggage area and caught a cab. He told the driver to take him to the corner of Longwood and Huntington avenues.

By seven-thirty the ebb and flow of humanity slowed to a trickle at the Memorial. Susan entered through the main entrance. In her nurse's uniform no one even gave her a second look. She first went up to the lounge on Beard 5 and left her coat. Then she checked McLeary's office on Beard 12. The door was locked as she expected and the lights were off. She checked all the nearby offices and labs. All were empty.

Susan returned to the main entrance and walked down the corridor toward the emergency room. Unlike the rest of the hospital, as evening fell the ER became more active. There were a few gurneys with their respective patients parked in the corridor. Susan turned left just before the ER and entered the hospital security office.

The office was small and cluttered. The entire far wall was a bank of TV screens, about twenty or twenty-five of them. Displayed on each screen were images of the entryways, corridors, and key areas of the hospital, including the ER area, televised to these monitors from remote control video cameras. Some of the cameras were stationary; others repeatedly panned over an area. Two uniformed guards and one plainclothes security officer occupied the room. The plainclothesman sat behind a tiny desk, seeming even smaller next to his obese hulk. The skin on his neck overlapped his shirt collar. His breath came in audible gasps.

All three men were oblivious to the TV monitors they were paid to watch. Instead, their eyes were fixed on the screen of a small portable TV set. They were engrossed in the furious combat of a televised hockey game.

'Excuse me, but we have a problem,' said Susan, addressing the plainclothes officer. 'Dr McLeary left tonight without returning some charts to 10 West. And we cannot medicate the patients without the charts. Can you people open his office?'

The security man gave Susan a tenth of a second with his

eyes, then returned to the power play in progress. He spoke without looking up.

'Sure. Lou, go up with the nurse here and open the office she needs.'

'In a minute, in a minute.'

All three watched intently. Susan waited. A commercial came on. The guard leaped to his feet.

'OK, let's get this office open. Let me know if I miss anything, you guys.'

Susan had to run a few steps to catch up with the great determined strides taken by the guard. En route he began sorting through an immense collection of keys.

'The Bruins are down by two. If they drop this one too, I'm movin' to Philly.'

Susan didn't answer. She hurried along with the guard, hoping that no one would recognize her. She felt a slight sense of relief as they entered the office area. It was deserted.

'Goddamn, where's that key?' cursed the guard as he had to try almost every key on his ring before finding one which would open McLeary's door. The delay made Susan rather nervous, and she began to look up and down the corridor, expecting the worst at any moment. As he opened the door, the guard reached in and flicked on the light.

'Just pull the door closed when you leave. It will lock by itself. I've got to get downstairs.'

Susan found herself alone in the outer room of McLeary's office. Quickly she entered the inner room and turned on the light. Then switching off the light in the outer room, she closed herself in McLeary's inner office.

To her dismay, the charts were no longer on the shelf where she had seen them in the morning. She began to search the office. The desk was first. No sign of them. As she closed the centre drawer, the phone immediately under her arm began to ring. In the silence the noise seemed earsplitting and it startled her. She looked at her watch and wondered if McLeary often got calls in his office at a quarter of eight in the evening. The sound stopped after three rings, and Susan recommenced her search. The charts were of sufficient bulk so that they could not be hidden in many places. As she pulled out the last drawer of the file cabinet she heard the unmistakable sound of footsteps in the hall. They grew louder. Susan froze, not daring to push the drawer back into the file cabinet for fear of the sound.

To her consternation she then heard the footsteps stop, and a key go into the lock in the outer door. Susan looked around the room in a panic. There were two doors, one to the outer office, another presumably to a closet. Susan glanced at the position of the furniture, then she snapped off the light. As she did so she heard the outer door open, and the light went on in the outer office. Susan moved toward the closet door, feeling the perspiration appear on her forehead. A metallic sound came from the outer office, then another. The closet door opened easily and Susan eased herself in as quietly as possible. With difficulty she closed the closet door. Almost simultaneously the door to the inner office opened and the light went on. Susan expected the closet door to be yanked open at any second. Instead she heard footsteps going toward the desk. Then she heard the desk chair squeak, as someone sat in it. She thought it was McLeary and she wondered what he was doing in his office at this time. What if he discovered her? The thought made her weak. If he opened the door, Susan decided she would try to bolt.

Then the phone was taken off the hook and Susan heard the familiar sound of dialling. But when the person phoning spoke, the voice confused her. It was female. And the caller was speaking in Spanish. From her own meagre Spanish Susan was able to make out a part of the conversation. It was about the weather in Boston, then in Florida. All at once Susan realized that a cleaning lady was plopped down in McLeary's office using the hospital phone to make a personal call to Florida. Maybe that explained hospital overheads.

The call lasted almost a half-hour. Then the cleaning lady emptied the wastebasket, turned out the light, and departed. Susan waited for several minutes before opening the closet door. She headed in the direction of the light switch but her shin thumped painfully into the open file cabinet drawer. Susan cursed and realized what a terrible burglar she would make.

With the light on again Susan resumed her search. Out of curiosity to see where she had been hiding, she checked the closet. On the lowest shelf, stacked among boxes of stationery, she found the charts she wanted. She wondered if McLeary had actually tried to hide them. But she did not dwell on the mystery. She wanted to get out of McLeary's office.

Drawing on her basic resourcefulness, Susan piled the charts into the freshly emptied wastebasket. Then she left the office, unlocking the door. And as she had done in the dorm, she placed a minute wad of paper between the door and the jamb.

Susan carried the charts up to Beard 5 and entered the lounge. She got out her black notebook and poured herself some coffee. Then she took the first chart and began extracting it, as she had done with Nancy Greenly's.

When D'Ambrosio returned to the medical school dorm, he had no particular plan in mind. His usual method of operation was to improvise, after having observed his quarry for a period of time. He already knew quite a bit about Susan Wheeler. He knew that she rarely went out, once back in her room. He was quite sure she would be there now. What he couldn't be sure of was whether Susan had told the authorities about his initial visit. He decided there was a fifty-fifty chance. If she had told them, there was only a ten per cent chance that they would take her seriously; or at least that had been D'Ambrosio's experience. And even if they did take her seriously, there was probably only a one per cent chance that they would put her under guard. The risk factor was well within D'Ambrosio's normal range. He decided that he would return to her room.

From a telephone in the corner drugstore D'Ambrosio rang Susan's room. No answer. He knew that did not mean anything. She could be there but just not answering. D'Ambrosio could handle the lock on the door; he had determined that in the afternoon. But the bolt; she'd probably have the bolt thrown, and that would be noisy. D'Ambrosio knew he'd have to get her out of her room somehow.

He walked back to the dorm and into the parking lot. Her light was on. He then entered the quad as he had done that afternoon, by picking the padlock on the gate in the archway. It was a lock with only three tumblers. It was amazing where the university decided to save money.

He mounted the creaking wooden stairs quickly. D'Ambrosio did not look it, but he was in top physical condition. An athlete, a psychopath. Quickly, he moved over to Susan's door and listened. There were no sounds. He knocked. He was confident she would not open the door without speaking. But at this point D'Ambrosio first wanted to find out if she were there. If she answered, he intended to make it sound as if he were going back down the stairs. That usually worked.

But there was no answer.

He tried again. Still no answer.

He picked the lock in seconds. The door opened. The bolt was off. Susan had gone.

D'Ambrosio checked the closet. The wardrobe had not changed. The two suitcases he had seen on his earlier visit were still there. D'Ambrosio was always thorough and it paid off. He knew, with high probability, that Susan had not left town. That meant she would be back. D'Ambrosio decided to wait.

Wednesday February 25
10:41pm

Bellows was exhausted. It was going on eleven, and he was still at it. In fact he had not made rounds yet on Beard 5. He had to do that before he left for home. At the nurses' station he got the chart rack and wheeled it toward the lounge. A cup of coffee would help him get through the work. Opening the door, he was genuinely surprised to find Susan in the lounge; she was hard at work.

'Excuse me. I must be in the wrong hospital.' Bellows pretended to go back out through the door. Then he looked back at Susan.

'Susan, what in hell's name are you doing here? I was told in no uncertain terms that you had become persona non grata.' Without meaning to, Bellows's voice reflected some irritation. It had been a terrible day – with the low spot being his discovery of Walters.

'Who, me? You must be mistakin, sah. I'm Miss Scarlett, the new nurse on 10 West,' said Susan, feigning a higher voice with a southern accent.

'Christ, Susan, cut the bullshit.'

'You started it.'

'What are you doing here?'

'Polishing my shoes, what does it look like I'm doing?'

'OK, OK. Let's start again.' Bellows came into the room and sat on the counter top. 'Susan, this whole scene has become very serious. It's not that I'm not happy to see you, because I am. I had a fabulous time last night. God, it seems like a week ago. But if you'd been around when the shit hit the fan this afternoon, you'd understand why I'd be a little on edge. Among other things I was told that if I continued to cover and aid you in your, quote, "idiotic mission," I'd be out looking for a new residency.'

'Ah, poor boy! May have to leave Mama's warm womb.'

Bellows looked away for a moment, trying to maintain his composure. 'I can sense this conversation is going nowhere. Susan, you cannot understand that I have more to lose in this affair than you do.'

'Like hell you do!' Susan's face lit up with sudden anger. 'You're so Goddamned self-centred and worried about your residency appointment that you couldn't see a conspiracy if it involved your ... your mother.'

'Jesus Christ! The thanks I get for helping you. What the hell does my mother have to do with all this?'

'Nothing. Absolutely nothing. I just couldn't think of anything else which would come close to your residency in your warped value system. So I took a chance on your mother.'

'You're making no sense, Susan.'

'No sense, he says. Look, Mark, you're so worried about your career that you're blind. Do I look different to you?'

'Different?'

'Yeah, different. Where's that old clinical expertise, that keen sense of observation that you're supposed to have absorbed during your medical training? What do you think this is here under my eye?' Susan pointed to the bruise on her cheek. 'And what do you think this is?' Susan garbled the last few words as she held out her lower lip, exposing the laceration.

'It looks like trauma ...' Bellows extended his hand to examine Susan's lip more closely. Susan fended him off.

'Keep your cotton-pickin' mitts off. And you say that you have more to lose in this whole thing. Well, let me tell you something. I was attacked and threatened this afternoon by a man who scared the shit out of me. This man knew about me and what I've been doing these last few days. He even knew about my family. He even included my family in the threat. And you say that you have more to lose!'

'You mean somebody actually hit you?' Bellows was incredulous.

'Oh come on, Mark. Can't you say something intelligent? Do you think these are self-inflicted wounds to make people feel sorry for me? I've stumbled into something big, that I can tell you. And I have a scary feeling that it's some large organization. I just don't know how or why or who.'

Bellows looked at Susan for several minutes, his mind racing over her story, which seemed incredible, and his own experience that afternoon.

'I don't have any literal wounds to show, but I had one hell of an afternoon as well. Remember those drugs I told you about? The ones that were found in a locker in the OR doctor's lounge? They were found in a locker assigned to me, as I told you. Like it or not, I was immediately implicated. So I decided that I had to settle the whole thing once and for all by getting

Walters to explain why I was still assigned to that locker when he had given me another.

'But Walters didn't come in today. First time in I-don't-know-how-many years. So I decided to visit him.' Bellows sighed and poured himself some coffee, remembering the grisly details. 'The poor bastard committed suicide over this thing, and I had to be the guy who found him.'

'Suicide?'

'Yeah. Apparently he'd learned that the drugs had been found, and he decided to take what he considered the easy way out.'

'Are you sure it was suicide?'

'I'm not sure of anything. I didn't even see the note. I called the police and have gotten the details from Stark. But don't suggest it wasn't suicide. God, I couldn't handle that. I'd probably be considered a suspect. What on earth could make you suggest such a thing?' Bellows was intense.

'No reason. It just seems another strange coincidence to have happened at this time. Those drugs that were found may be important somehow.'

'I was afraid that your imagination would suggest that they were important. That was one of the reasons why I hesitated to tell you about the drugs in the first place. But look, all this is somewhat peripheral to the present problem, namely your presence here at the Memorial at this rather sensitive time. I mean, Susan, you are not supposed to be here. It's as simple as that.' Bellows paused and picked up one of the charts Susan had been extracting. 'What the hell are you doing anyway?'

'I finally got some of the charts of the coma patients. Not all of them, but some of them.'

'God, you really are amazing. After getting yourself kicked out of the hospital, you still manage to have the balls, so to speak, to come back here and find a way to get these charts. I don't imagine that they leave them lying around for anybody to look at who happens along. How did you manage to get them?'

Bellows looked expectantly at Susan, sipping his coffee and waiting for a response. Susan only smiled.

'Oh no!' said Bellows putting his hand to his forehead. 'The nurse's uniform.'

'Yup, worked like a charm. Great idea, I must admit.'

'Wait a minute. I don't want any credit for it, believe me! What did you do? Get security to open McLeary's or whoever-it-was's office?'

'You're getting more and more clever, Mark.'

'You do realize that you're now breaking the law.'

Susan nodded in agreement, looking down at the pile of paper filled with her tiny writing.

Bellows's eyes followed hers.

'Well, have they shed any light on this ... this crusade of yours?'

'Not much, I'm afraid. At least not yet, or at least I've not been clever enough to spot it. I wish I had all the charts. So far the ages have all been relatively young, twenty-five to forty-two. Otherwise they seem to be of random sex, racial background, social background. I can't find any relationship in their previous medical histories. Their vital signs and progress up until the onset of coma were uncomplicated in all cases. Their personal physicians were all different. Of the surgical cases, only two had the same anaesthesiologist. The anaesthetic agents were varied, as expected. There were some overlaps in the pre-operative medications. A number of the cases had Demerol and Phenergan, but others had totally different agents. Innovar was used on two cases. But all that's not surprising.

'It does seem, as far as I can tell without going up in the OR, that most if not all the surgical cases occurred in room eight. That does seem a little strange, but then again that's the room used most often for the shorter operations. And this problem is most often associated with the shorter operations. So that's probably to be expected as well. Laboratory values are all generally normal. Oh, by the way, all cases seemed to have been blood-typed and tissue-typed. Is that normal procedure?'

'They blood-type most surgical patients, especially if they anticipate much blood loss during the operation. Tissue-typing is not usual, although the lab may be doing it as part of a check on new equipment or new tissue-typing sera. See if there is an accounting number on one of the lab reports on the typing.'

Susan flipped back through the pages of the chart in front of her until she located the tissue-type report.

'No, there's no accounting number.'

'Well, that explains that, then. The lab is doing it at their expense. That's not abnormal.'

'The medical patients were all on I.V.s for one reason or another.'

'So are ninety per cent of the people in the hospital.'

'I know.'

'Sounds like you got a lot of nothing.'

'I'd have to agree at this point.' Susan paused, sucking on her lower lip. 'Mark, before the endotracheal tube is placed in a patient during anaesthesia, the anaesthesiologist paralyses the patient with succinylcholine. Isn't that right?'

'Succinylcholine or curare, but usually succinyl.'

'And when a patient is given a pharmacological dose of succinylcholine, he can't breathe.'

'That's true.'

'Could an overdose of succinylcholine be the way these patients are rendered hypoxic? If they can't breathe, then oxygen doesn't get to the brain.'

'Susan, the anaesthesiologist gives succinylcholine and then monitors the patient like a hawk; he even breathes for the patient. If there is too much succinylcholine, it just means the anaesthesiologist has to breathe the patient for a longer time until the patient metabolizes the drug. The paralysing effect is completely reversible. Besides, if something like that were being done maliciously, all the anaesthesiologists in the hospital would have to be involved, and that's hardly likely. And maybe even more important is the fact that under the combined eye of the anaesthesiologist and the surgeon, who can actually see how red the blood is and how well it is oxygenated, it would be absolutely impossible to alter the patient's physiologic state without one or both knowing it. When blood is oxygenated, it is bright red. When oxygen gets low, the blood becomes dark brownish-bluish-maroon. The anaesthesiologist meanwhile is breathing for the patient, constantly checking the pulse and blood pressure, and watching the cardiac monitor. Susan, you are hypothesizing some sort of foul play, and you don't have a why or a who or a how. You're not even sure you have a victim.'

'I'm sure I have a victim, Mark. It might not be a new disease but it's something. One more question. Where do the anaesthetic gases come from that the anaesthesiologists use?'

'It varies. Halothane comes in cans like ether. It's liquid and it's vapourized as needed in the OR. Nitrous, oxygen, and air come from central sources and are piped into the OHs. There are standby cylinders of oxygen and nitrous oxide in the OR for emergency use ... Look, Susan, I've got a little more work to do, then I'm free. How about coming over to the apartment for a drink?'

'Not tonight, Mark. I want to get a good night's sleep and I've got a few more things to do. But thanks. Also, I've got to get these charts back to their hiding place. After that I intend to look around in OR room number eight.'

'Susan, I personally think you should get your ass out of this hospital before you really get yourself in hot water.'

'You're entitled to your opinion, doctor. It's just that this patient doesn't feel like following orders.'

'I think you're carrying all of this too far.'

'You do, do you? Well, I might not have a who, but I've got a number of suspects ...'

'Sure you do ...' Bellows fidgeted. 'Are you going to make me guess or are you going to tell me?'

'Harris, Nelson, McLeary, and Oren.'

'You're out of your squash!'

'They all act as guilty as hell and want me out of here.'

'Don't confuse defensive behaviour with guilt, Susan. After all, complications are hard to live with in medicine, no matter from what cause.'

Wednesday February 25

11:25pm

Susan felt a definite sense of relief when she had returned the charts to their hiding place in McLeary's closet. At the same time, she was very disappointed. Having finally inspected them was an anticlimax of sorts. She had placed a great deal of emphasis on the importance of the charts, but after she had finished studying them, she felt no further in her mission. She had a lot more data but no correlates, no intercepts. The cases still seemed to be random and unassociated.

The elevator slowed and stopped, the door quivered, then opened. Susan stepped out into the OR area. There was still a case going on in room no.20, a ruptured abdominal aneurysm that had been admitted through the emergency room. The operation had been in progress for over eight hours; that didn't look so good. Otherwise the OR area was in its nightly repose. There were a few people busy cleaning the floor and restocking the supply room with freshly laundered linen. A girl in a scrub dress was behind the main desk, trying to fit the last few cases into the following day's master schedule.

The nurse's uniform ruse was still working well for Susan and the few people in the hall did not seem to notice her passing. She went directly to the nurses' locker rooms and changed into a scrub dress, hanging the nurse's uniform in an open locker.

Re-entering the main hall, Susan eyed the swinging doors into the area of the operating rooms. A large sign on the right door said 'Operating Rooms: Unauthorized Entry Forbidden.' The main desk was just to the side of these doors. The nurse sitting behind the desk was still hard at work. Susan had no idea if she would be challenged if she tried to enter.

In order to survey the scene in its totality, Susan walked the length of the hall several times, half-hoping the girl at the main desk would take a break and leave. But she didn't budge, nor even look up. Susan tried to think of some appropriate explanation in case the girl questioned her. But she couldn't think of any. It was almost midnight and she knew she'd have to have some reasonably convincing story to explain her presence.

Finally, with no cover story in mind except for some weak comment about wanting to check on progress in room no.20, or being sent up from the lab to do random cultures for contamination, Susan made her move. Pretending not to notice the girl at the desk, she headed for the doors. As she passed, the girl did not look up. A few more steps. When Susan reached the doors, she straight-armed the one on the right. It opened and Susan was about to enter.

'Hey, just a minute.'

Susan froze, waiting for the inevitable. She turned to face the girl.

'You forgot your conductive boots.'

Susan looked down at her shoes. As it dawned on her what the nurse was concerned about. Susan felt relieved.

'Damn, you'd think this was my second time in the OR.'

The nurse's attention went back to the master schedule. 'I forget the bastards now and then myself.'

Susan walked over to a stainless steel cabinet against the wall. The conductive booties – designed to prevent static electricity, so hazardous where inflammable gas was flowing – were kept in a large cardboard box on the lower shelf. Susan put them on the way Carpin had shown her on the first visit to the OR two days before, tucking the black tapes inside her shoes. When she opened the swinging door the second time, the nurse at the desk didn't even look up. The Memorial was large enough so that new faces were to be expected.

The operating rooms at the Memorial were grouped in a large U-shape with supply, holding area, and anaesthesia offices in the centre. The entrance to the OR area was at the bottom of the U and the recovery room was on the left arm of the U, closest to the elevators. Susan found that room no.8 was on the right arm of the U, on the outside.

No.20, where the operation continued, was in the opposite direction, and Susan found herself quite alone approaching room no.8. Pausing at the door, she looked through the glass. It looked exactly like room no.18, where Niles had passed out. The walls were tile, the floor a speckled vinyl. Although the lights were out, Susan could see the large kettledrum operating lights above, and the operating table immediately below. She opened the door and turned on the lights.

Without any specific objective in mind, Susan roamed around the room, noticing the larger objects. Then in a more systematic fashion she began to examine details. She found the gas line terminals, noticing that oxygen had a green male connector. The nitrous connector was blue and structurally different so that no mistake could be made. A third male connector was not labelled or coloured. Susan assumed it was the compressed air line. A larger female connector was labelled 'suction'; above it was a gauge with a large adjusting dial.

In the back of the room were a number of stainless steel cabinets filled with various supplies. There was a desk of sorts for the circulating nurse. The right wall had an X-ray screen. The rear wall, next to the door, had a large institutional clock. The large red second hand swept around smoothly. Another door led into an adjoining supply room, shared with OR no.10, which contained the sterilizers and other paraphernalia.

Susan spent almost an hour going over room no.8, as well as no.10 for comparison. She found nothing abnormal or even mildly curious about room no.8. It was an OR room like so many thousands. No.10 appeared no different.

Without challenge, Susan retraced her steps to the nurses' locker room and changed back into her nurse's uniform. She threw her scrubdress into a hamper and started for the door. But she paused then, looking up at the ceiling. It was a drop ceiling, made with large blocks of acoustical tile.

The wastebasket provided an intermediate step. Susan moved from the wastebasket to the sink to the top of the lockers. The ceiling was about three feet above the top of the lockers. Crouching on all fours, she tried the first ceiling block. It would not lift up because of some piping immediately above it. She tried another. Same problem. The third tile, however, lifted easily, and Susan slid it to one side. She then stood up on top of the locker, projecting half of herself into the ceiling space. Contrary to her estimate, the ceiling space was generous in its size. There was almost five feet of vertical space from the dropped acoustical ceiling to the cement of the floor slabs above. A myriad of pipes and ducts ran through this space, carrying the hospital's vital supplies and wastes. The light was very poor, with only pencil-like beams seeping up from below in scattered locations between ceiling tiles.

The dropped ceiling was composed of the cardboard tile, held in place by thin metal strips, which were in turn hung from the cement slab above. Neither the tiles nor the metal strips were strong enough to carry any weight. In order to enter the ceiling space, Susan had to pull herself up onto the pipes, which she found either ice cold or very hot. Once up in the ceiling space, she replaced the ceiling tile she had moved. It fell back into place, cutting off the direct source of light.

Susan waited until her eyes made the adjustment from the fluorescent world below to the semidarkness above. Eventually outlines took forms and Susan could move ahead along the pipes. She noticed a row of studs which continued through the ceiling space to connect with the concrete above. She guessed that they marked the wall of the corridor.

Progress was slow; it was difficult to move on the pipes, treading on one, keeping hold of another or, here and there, a stud for support. She did not want to make any noise, especially when she guessed she was over the area of the main desk. Once over the OR area itself, the going became definitely easier. The ceilings over the OR and the recovery room were fixed and made of prestressed concrete. Susan could move at will provided she avoided tripping on the piping and provided she bent over considerably, for the space here was only about three feet high.

Susan found a concrete wall which she guessed housed the elevator shafts. Then she discovered that the corridor of the OR area had a dropped ceiling. Beyond the OR corridor, over what was probably part of central supply, Susan could see that the maze of pipes and ducts running through the ceiling space converged in what seemed a tangled vortex. Susan guessed that was the location of the central chase which housed all the piping and ducts coursing vertically in the building.

Susan was interested primarily in locating room no.8. But that was not easy. There were no specific demarcations from one OR to the next. The pipes seemed to spread out and dive through the concrete to the operating rooms below in utter anarchy. The corridor ceiling led to a solution. By carefully picking up the edges of the ceiling blocks over the corridor, Susan was able to orient herself and locate the ceiling area of rooms no.8 and no.10. Susan satisfied herself that the number and configuration of the pipes to and from the two rooms were identical.

The gas lines corresponding to the painted intake connectors she had seen down below in the ORs had the same colour codes in the ceiling space. Over room no.8, Susan found the oxygen line with a splash of green paint. Susan traced the oxygen line from room no.8. It coursed back to the edge of the corridor then bent at a right angle to run parallel to it, alongside similar oxygen lines coming from other ORs. As Susan passed additional OR rooms, more lines joined the oxygen line she was trailing. In order to be sure she was still following the pipe from no.8, Susan kept her finger on it all the way to the edge of the central chase. Then her finger hit something. In the dim light she had to bend over to see what it was. She saw a stainless steel female connector. Just over the edge of the chase carrying the pipes up from the hospital depths was a high-pressure T-valve on the oxygen line leading to room no.8.

Susan stared at the valve. She looked at the other gas lines coming up the chase. There were no similar valves on any of the other lines. With her finger she examined the valve. It was obvious that the oxygen could be tapped from the line at that point. But equally as possible was that something, another gas, could be bled into the oxygen line at the same point.

Keeping to the fixed ceilings of the ORs, Susan worked her way back to the area of the main desk. Then she began the difficult part of crossing the large expanse of non-fixed ceiling. Wishing she had dropped some bread crumbs in the forest of pipes, Susan was forced to reconnoitre. She lifted a corner of a ceiling tile, but it was over the hall. She lifted another tile only to find herself over the doctors' lounge. The third tile was over the nurses' locker, but too far from the lockers she needed to step on. The fourth tile was perfect, and Susan descended with little difficulty.

Thursday February 26

1:00am

Like any major city, Boston never completely goes to sleep. But unlike many a major city, Boston becomes almost silent. As Susan settled back in the taxi speeding along Storrow Drive, only two or three cars passed, all going in the opposite direction. She was very tired, and she craved sleep. It had been an unbelievable day.

The laceration of her lip and the bruise on her cheek had grown more painful. Gingerly she touched her cheek to see if the swelling had increased. It had not. She looked out over the Esplanade and the frozen Charles River to her right. The lights of Cambridge were sparse and uninviting. The taxi banked sharply left off Storrow Drive onto Park Drive, requiring Susan to steady herself with her arm.

She tried to assess her progress. It wasn't encouraging. To keep within a reasonable limit of safety, she thought she had another thirty-six hours or so to press her search. but she was stymied. As the cab crossed the Fenway, Susan admitted to herself that she had run out of ideas on how to proceed. She felt she could not chance the Memorial by day with Nelson, Harris, McLeary, and Oren all lined up against her. She doubted the nurse's uniform would work on a direct confrontation.

But she wanted more data from the computer. She needed the other charts, too. Was there a way to do it? Would Bellows help? Susan doubted it. She now knew that he was truly anxious about his position. He really is an invertebrate, she thought.

And what about Walters's suicide? How could those drugs be tied in?

Susan paid her fare and got out of the taxi. Walking up to the door, she decided that in the morning she would try to find out as much as possible about Walters. He had to be related. But how?

Susan stood by the front door with her hand on the knob, expecting to be buzzed in by the watchman at the front desk. But he wasn't sitting there. Susan cursed as she rummaged in her coat for her keys. It was uncanny how the man at the desk seemed to disappear whenever you needed him.

The four flights up to her floor seemed longer than usual to Susan. She paused on several occasions, because of a combination of physical fatigue and mental effort.

Susan tried to remember if Bellows had said succinylcholine was among the drugs found in the locker in the doctors' dressing room. She distinctly remembered his saying curare but she could not remember succinylcholine. She got to the top of the stairs still very much lost in thought. It took another minute to find the correct key. As she had done countless times, she inserted the key in the lock. It took a bit of effort.

Despite her deep thought and exhaustion, Susan remembered about the wad of paper. Leaving the key in the door she bent down to look.

The paper was not there. The door had been opened.

Susan backed away from the door, half-expecting it to open suddenly. She remembered the horrid face of her assailant. If he was within the room, he was undoubtedly poised, expecting her to enter as usual. She thought of the knife he had not used the last time. She knew that she had very little time. The only factor in her favour was that if he were in the room, he would not know Susan suspected his presence. At least for a few moments.

If she called the authorities and the man was found, she'd be safe for some hours perhaps. But she recalled the threat about telling the police, the photograph of her brother. Did that suggest a burglar or a rapist? Not likely. Susan understood that the man who attacked her before was both professional and serious, deadly serious. She should run, perhaps even leave town. Or should she call the police anyway, as Stark had suggested? She was no professional; that was painfully apparent.

Why would they be after her already? She felt confident she had not been followed. Maybe the wad of paper had fallen out by itself. Susan advanced toward the door again.

'What the hell's the matter with this lock?' she said aloud, shaking the keys, playing for time. She remembered that the watchman was not at his desk downstairs. Should she go down and knock on someone else's door, saying that hers was stuck? Susan backed away again and moved over to the stairs. She thought that was the best idea under the circumstances. She knew Martha Fine on three well enough to knock at this hour. She didn't know what she should tell her. It was probably best for Martha if she told her nothing. All she'd say was that she couldn't get into her own room and she needed to sleep on Martha's floor.

Susan stepped slowly onto the wooden stairs. They creaked mercilessly under her weight. The sound was unmistakable and Susan knew it. If someone was poised behind her door he would have heard it. Susan ran down the stairs headlong. As she got to the third floor she heard the latch on her door snap open. She went on down, not bothering to stop. What if Martha wasn't there, or wouldn't answer? Susan knew that she could not let the man get hold of her again. The dorm seemed asleep, although it was only a little after one.

Susan heard her door fly open and hit the wall of the hall. She heard some steps and imagined that someone had run to the banister. Susan dared not look up. Her mind was made up. She'd leave the dorm. It would be easy to lose whoever was following her within the medical school complex. Susan felt she could run relatively quickly and she knew every inch of the area. She was at the ground floor when she heard her pursuer start down the stairs above.

At the bottom of the stairs Susan turned sharply to the left and ran through a small archway. Quickly she opened the door to the quad outside, but she did not exit. Instead, she let the hydraulic hinge begin to close the door. She turned and passed through the door into the adjacent wing of the dorm, shutting that door after her. She could hear feet running on the landing of the second floor.

Avoiding the noise her shoes would make if she ran normally, Susan moved down the ground-floor hall of the adjacent dorm, keeping her legs relatively stiff. She moved quickly but silently, passing the Student Health Office. At the end of the hall she opened the stairwell door quietly and allowed it to close behind her without a noise. She found herself on a stairway to the basement level and wasted no time in descending.

D'Ambrosio was tricked by the slowly closing door to the quad but not for long. D'Ambrosio was no novice at pursuit and he knew just how much time Susan was ahead of him. As he ran into the quad, he knew immediately that he had been duped. He would have been, except there were no other doors close enough for her to have got back into the building.

D'Ambrosio darted back through the door he had just opened. There were only two alternate routes. He chose the nearest door and ran forward down the hall.

Susan entered the tunnel connecting the dorm with the medical school. She was sure she must be in the clear. The tunnel proceeded straight for twenty-five or thirty yards, then twisted out of sight to the left. Susan moved ahead as quickly as she could: the tunnel was fairly well lit by bulbs in open wire cages.

At the end of the tunnel she reached for the handle on the fire door and opened it. A breeze of air hit her as she went through. A sinking feeling passed over her as she realized that could mean only one thing. The door behind her had to be open at the same time! Then she heard the unmistakable heavy footsteps of a man running in the tunnel.

'My God,' she whispered in a panic. Perhaps she had misjudged. She had left a dorm full of people, even if asleep, for the labyrinthine spaces of a dark, deserted building.

Susan rushed up the stairs ahead, feeling a sense of helplessness as she remembered the strength of D'Ambrosio. Quickly she tried to think of the layout of the building she was now in. It was the Anatomy-Pathology Building, which had four floors. There were two large lecture amphitheatres on the first floor as well as several ancillary rooms. The second floor had the anatomy hall with a number of smaller labs. The third and fourth floors were mostly offices, and Susan was not familiar with them.

She opened the door onto the first floor. Unlike the tunnel, the building was totally dark except for light from the streetlamps filtering through infrequent windows. The floor was made of marble and it echoed with her footsteps. The hall followed a circular pattern as it skirted the pit of one of the amphitheatres.

With no particular plan in mind, Susan rushed up to one of the wide but low doors leading into the first amphitheatre. It was the door through which patients were wheeled for demonstrations. As Susan closed the door she heard running footsteps on the marble hall behind her. She moved away from the low door into the centre of the amphitheatre. The banks of seats rose in regular tiers until they were lost in darkness. She mounted the steps leading up one aisle from the pit.

The footsteps got louder and Susan hurried upwards, afraid to look back. The footsteps passed and became less audible. Then they stopped altogether. Susan moved higher and higher. Behind her the pit of the amphitheatre became more and more difficult to distinguish. Susan reached the upper tier of seats and moved laterally along it. She heard the footsteps on the marble again. She had a few moments to think. She knew there was no way she could cope with this man directly; she had to lose him or hide long enough so that he would give up and leave. She thought about the tunnel to the Administration Building. But she wasn't one hundred per cent sure that it would be open. Occasionally it had been locked when she tried to take that route home from the library in the evening.

She froze as she heard the door open into the pit of the amphitheatre. The shadowy figure of a man entered. She could barely see him. But she was dressed in the white nurse's uniform and she feared that she was more easily visible. She slowly crouched down behind a row of seats, but the backs of the chairs only rose eight to twelve inches above the level she was on. The man stopped and did not move. Susan guessed that he was trying to scan the room. She carefully lay down on the floor. She could see between the backs of two of the seats. The man walked over to the podium and seemed to be searching. Of course. He was searching for the lights! Susan felt panic again take control. Ahead of her, about twenty feet away, was a door to the hall on the second floor. Susan prayed that the door would be open and not locked. If it were locked she would have to try to make it to the door on the opposite side of the amphitheatre. That would take about as long as it would take D'Ambrosio to get from thte pit up to her level. If the door ahead of her was locked, she was lost.

There was a snap of a light switch and the lamp on the podium went on. Suddenly and eerily D'Ambrosio's horrid pockmarked face was illuminated from below, casting grotesque shadows and making his eye sockets appear like burnt holes in a ghoulish mask. His hands groped along the side of the podium, and the sound of a second switch reverberated in Susan's ears. A strong ray of light sprang from the darkened ceiling, illuminating the pit in a brilliant beam. Now Susan could see D'Ambrosio clearly.

She crawled forward as rapidly as she could toward the door. Another light switch snapped and a bank of lights lit up the blackboard behind D'Ambrosio. At that point D'Ambrosio noted the switches for the room lights to the left of the blackboard. As he walked over to the switches, Susan got up and broke for the door. She turned the knob as the lights went on in the room. Locked!

Susan stared down into the pit. D'Ambrosio saw her and a smile of anticipation came to his thin, scarred lips. Then he ran for the stairs, taking them in twos and threes.

Susan shook the door in despair. Then she noted that it was bolted from within. She threw the bolt and the door opened. She flung herself through it and slammed the door behind her. She could hear D'Ambrosio's deep breaths as he neared the top row of seats.

Directly across from the second-floor amphitheatre door was a CO_2 fire extinguisher. Susan ripped it from the wall and turned it upside down. She spun around, hearing the metallic click of D'Ambrosio's shoes coming closer and closer, and got set just as the knob turned and the door swung open.

At that instant, Susan depressed the button on the fire extinguisher. The sudden phase change and expansion of the gas caused an explosive noise that shrieked and echoed in the silence of the empty building as the spray of dry ice caught D'Ambrosio full in the face. He reeled backward and tripped over the upper row of seats, his big body teetering, then crashing sideways onto the second and third rows. A seat back dug deeply into his side, snapping his left eleventh rib. His arms flew out to protect himself, grabbing at the seat backs as his feet continued over his head. He fell lengthwise facedown into the fourth row, stunned.

Susan herself was amazed at the effect and stepped into the amphitheatre, watching D'Ambrosio's fall. She stood there for an instant, thinking that D'Ambrosio must be unconscious. But the man drew his knees up and pulled himself into a kneeling position. He looked up at Susan and managed a smile despite the intense pain of his broken rib.

'I like 'em ... when they fight back,' he grunted between clenched teeth.

Susan picked up the fire extinguisher and threw it as hard as she could at the kneeling figure. D'Ambrosio tried to move, but the heavy metal cylinder struck his left shoulder, knocking him down again, and forcing the upper part of his body to fall over the backs of the seats of the next row down. The fire extinguisher bounced down four or five more rows with a terrific clatter, coming to rest in the eighth row.

Slamming the door to the amphitheatre shut on her pursuer, Susan stood panting. My God, was he superhuman? She had to find a way to detain him. She knew that she had been un-believably lucky in injuring him, but plainly he was not out of the picture. Susan thought of the large deep-freeze in the anatomy room.

The hall was dark except for the window at the far end, which provided a paltry amount of pale light. The entrance to the anatomy room was at the very end of the hall near to the window. Susan ran for the door. As she reached it, she heard the door from the amphitheatre open.

D'Ambrosio was hurt but not badly. It was painful to cough or take a deep breath, but it was bearable. His left shoulder was bruised but functioning. More than anything else, he was mad. The fact that this screwy chick had managed to get the best of him even for a few moments pissed him off. He had planned on toying with the girl, but that was over. Now he'd kill her first and fuck her later. He had his Beretta in his right hand, its silver silencer screwed in place. As he stepped from the amphitheatre, he just caught sight of Susan entering the anatomy hall. He fired without really aiming and the bullet missed Susan by several inches, slamming into the edge of the door frame and throwing splinters of wood into the air.

The sound of the gun was like that of a rug beater. Susan had no idea what it was until the noise and effect of the slug entering the woodwork made it clear to her that it was a gun, a gun with a silencer.

'All right, you bitch, the game's over,' shouted D'Ambrosio, coming down the hall at a walk. He knew he had her cornered and that it would hurt to run.

Inside the anatomy hall, Susan paused for a moment, trying to recall the layout in the faint light. Then she bolted the door behind her. The first-year class at that time of the year was in the middle of their anatomy course. The dissecting tables in the room were covered with green plastic sheets. In the dim light they appeared light grey. Susan ran between the shrouded tables to the freezer door at the far end of the room. There was a large stainless steel pin through the latch. She pulled the pin free and let it hang by its chain, releasing the latch. With some effort Susan opened the heavy insulated door and squeezed through. She pulled the door shut behind her and heard the heavy click. She groped for a light beside the door and switched it on.

The freezer was at least ten feet wide and thirty feet deep. Susan remembered all too clearly the first day she had seen it. The diener loved to show it to the students, one at a time, and he particularly liked female students for some unknown but undoubtedly perverse reason. He had charge of the cadavers stored here for dissection. After embalming, they were hung up with tongs hooked into the external ear canals. The tongs were connected to roller bearings on tracks in the ceiling, to facilitate movement. The bodies were stiff, naked, misshapen; most were the colour of pale marble. The females were mixed with the males, the Catholics with the Jews, the whites with the blacks in the equality of death. The faces were frozen into a wide variety of distorted grimaces. Most of the eyes were closed but here and there was an open one, blankly staring into infinity. The first time Susan had seen these four rows of frozen cadavers hanging up like unwanted clothes in a closet of ice, she had felt sick. She had vowed never to return. And until that night she had avoided the 'fridge,' as it was affectionately called by the diener. But now it was different.

The anatomy hall had been dark. The inside of the freezer was lit by a single hundred-watt bulb from the rear of the compartment, casting horrid shadows on the ceiling and floor. Susan tried not to look directly at the grotesque bodies. She shivered from the cold and frantically tried to think. There were only a few moments. Her pulse was racing. She knew that D'Ambrosio would be coming into the freezer within minutes. She had to have a plan but she didn't have much time.

Smiling, D'Ambrosio stepped back and kicked the locked door of the anatomy hall, but it held firm. He kicked out a pane of frosted glass, pulled out a few of the splintered pieces, and reached in, opening the door. He looked around the room, not comprehending what it was.

As a precaution against his prey bolting, he closed the door and moved a nearby table in front of it. The room was large, some sixty feet by one hundred feet, with five rows of seven shrouded tables each. D'Ambrosio went up to the nearest table and whipped off the plastic drape.

D'Ambrosio gasped, not even feeling the pain from his broken rib. He was staring at a cadaver. The head was dissected free of skin, the teeth and the eyes were bared. The hair had been undermined and folded back like a pelt. The front of the chest was gone, as was the front of the abdomen. The organs, which had been removed, were piled back into the opened body haphazardly.

D'Ambrosio walked back to the door and thought about turning on the lights. Then he decided against it because of the large windows and the fear of alerting the security police. Not that he didn't feel confident about handling a couple of inexperienced guards, but he wanted to get Susan without any interference.

Systematically D'Ambrosio removed all the shrouds from all the cadavers in the room. He tried not to look at the dissected bodies. He just wanted to make sure that Susan was not among them.

D'Ambrosio looked around the room. On the right side of the hall several skeletons hung on chains, turning slowly in the air stirred by the opening and closing of the door. Behind the skeletons was a huge cabinet containing numerous specimen jars. At the end of the room were three desks and two doors. One of the doors looked like a freezer door, the other a closet. The closet was empty. Then D'Ambrosio noted the stainless steel pin hanging from the latch on the freezer door. The slight smile returned, and he transferred the gun to his left hand. He opened the freezer door and again fell back in horror. The hanging bodies appeared like an army of ghouls.

D'Ambrosio was shaken by the appearance of the bodies and his eyes darted from one to another. Reluctantly he stepped over the threshold of the freezer, feeling the sudden chill.

'I know you're in here, cunt. Why not come out so we can have another talk?' D'Ambrosio's voice trailed off. The close quarters in the freezer and the appearance of the stiffs made him nervous, more nervous than he ever remembered being.

He looked down between the first two rows of frozen corpses. Warily he took two steps to the right and looked down the middle row. He could see the bare light bulb in the rear of the compartment. Glancing back at the door, he took several more steps to the right so he could look down the last corridor.

Susan's fingers were losing their grip around the overhead track in the back of the second row of corpses. She did not know D'Ambrosio's position, not until he called the second time.

'Come on, sweetheart. Don't make me search this place.'

Susan was sure that D'Ambrosio was at the head of the last row. She knew it was now or never. With all the force she could muster, she pushed with her legs against the back of the wizened female cadaver in front of her. By holding onto the track above, Susan had lifted her legs up and coiled them against the old woman's back. Her own back was pressed against the rock-hard chest of the last cadaver in the row, a two-hundred-pound black male.

Almost imperceptibly at first, the entire second row of frozen corpses began to move forward. Once the initial inertia was overcome, Susan was able to lunge with her feet, imparting a terrific thrust. Like a row of dominoes the entire group of bodies slid forward on their ball bearings.

D'Ambrosio's ears picked up the sound of the movement. He held himself still for a fraction of a second, trying to locate the weird sound. With the swiftness of a cat, he whirled and retreated toward the door. Not fast enough. As he stepped past the third row, he saw the movement. Instinctively he raised his gun and fired. But his attacker was already dead.

Coming at D'Ambrosio with surprising speed was a ghostly white male whose lips were frozen in a horrid half-smile. Two hundred pounds of frozen human meat slammed into the hit man, sending him crashing into the side of the freezer. In rapid succession the other corpses tumbled after the first, several falling from their hooks, creating a huddle of corpses, a tangle of frozen extremities.

Susan let go of the track, dropping to the floor. Then she ran for the open door. D'Ambrosio was trying to pull the bodies off himself. But he was in pain and had little leverage. The reek of embalming fluid was choking him. As Susan passed he tried to grab her. He struggled to free his gun and aim but it caught in the gnarled hand of a corpse.

'Fuck!' shouted D'Ambrosio as he used all of his might against oppressive weight of dead flesh.

But Susan was through the door.

D'Ambrosio was upright now. Pushing the toppled bodies right and left, he flung himself at the closing door. But outside it Susan was pushing with all her might, and the momentum of the insulated door carried it home. The latch clicked. Susan fumbled with the stainless steel pin. Inside, D'Ambrosio was grabbing for the latch release. Susan beat him by a fraction of a second as the pin dropped home.

Susan backed up, her heart pounding. She heard a muffled cry. Then there was a thud. D'Ambrosio was shooting into the door. But it was twelve inches thick. There were several more ineffectual thuds.

Susan turned and ran. She finally understood the reality of the danger she had been in. Trembling uncontrollably, she fought back tears. She had to find help, real help.

Thursday February 26

2:11am

Beacon Hill was definitely asleep. As the cab turned off Charles Street onto Mount Vernon and drove up into the residential area, there were no people, no cars, not even any dogs. The lights in the windows were few; only the gas lamps suggested that the area was populated, not deserted. Susan paid the cab driver, then looked up and down the street to see if anyone was following her.

After escaping from D'Ambrosio in the freezer, Susan was terrified and decided not to return to her room. She had no idea if D'Ambrosio was working alone or with an accomplice, but she was in no mood to find out. She had run out of the Anatomy Building, crossed in front of the Administration Building and had reached Huntington Avenue by passing the School of Public Health. At that hour it had taken fifteen minutes to find a cab.

Bellows. Susan thought that he was the only person she could turn to at two A.M. who would understand her present plight. But she was worried about being followed, and she did not want to involve Bellows in any danger. So as she entered the foyer of Bellows's building she determined to wait five minutes before ringing his apartment, to be certain she had not been followed.

The foyer was not heated and Susan ran in place for a few minutes to keep warm. Becoming rational again after the experience with D'Ambrosio, she tried to understand why D'Ambrosio had returned so quickly. As far as she knew, no one had followed her when she went back to the Memorial to get the charts and explore the ORs. No one even knew that she was there.

She stopped running and looked out at Mount Vernon Street through the glass door. Bellows! He had seen her in the lounge. He was the only one who knew that she had not given up her search. She had shown him the charts. She started running in place again, cursing her own paranoia. Then she stopped as she remembered about Bellows being involved with the drugs that were found in the locker room, about Bellows being the one who found Walters, after Walters had committed suicide.

Susan turned her head and looked through the glass of the locked inner door. The stairway rose upward, its steps covered with a red runner. Could Bellows be involved? The possibility penetrated Susan's overworked brain and fatigued body. She was beginning to suspect everyone. She shook her head and laughed; the paranoia was too obvious. Yet it started her thinking, and the thoughts troubled her.

Her watch said two-seventeen. Bellows was going to be in for a surprise, having a caller at such an hour. At least Susan thought he'd be surprised. What if he were surprised only because he expected her to be quite occupied elsewhere – that he knew all about D'Ambrosio. Susan decided impulsively that was nonsense. She pushed the buzzer with determination. She had to push it again and hold it before Bellows responded.

Susan started up the stairs. She was midway up the second flight when Bellows appeared above in his bathrobe.

'I might have known. Susan, it's after two A.M.'

'You asked me if I wanted a drink. I've changed my mind. I want one.'

'But that was at eleven.' Bellows disappeared into his apartment, leaving the door ajar.

Susan reached Bellows's floor and entered his apartment. He was nowhere to be seen. She closed the door and locked it, throwing both bolts. She found Bellows already back in bed, the covers up under his chin, his eyes closed.

'Some hospitality,' said Susan sitting on the edge of the bed. She looked at Bellows. God, she was glad to see him. She wanted to throw herself onto him, feel his arms around her. She wanted to tell him about D'Ambrosio, about the freezer. She wanted to scream; she wanted to cry. But instead she did nothing. She sat there just looking at Bellows, her mind vacillating.

Bellows didn't budge, not at first. Finally the right eye opened, then the left. Then he sat up. 'Damn, I can't sleep with you sitting here.'

'How about that drink, then? I need it!' Susan forced herself to be calm, analytical. But it was hard. Her pulse was still over one hundred fifty per minute.

Bellows eyed Susan. 'You're really too much!' He got up and put his robe back on. 'OK, what will you have?'

'Bourbon, if you have it. Bourbon and soda, light on the soda.' Susan looked forward to the fiery fluid. Her hands were still visibly trembling. She followed Bellows into the kitchen.

'I had to come over, Mark. I was attacked again.' Susan's voice reflected her forced calmness. She watched Bellows's reaction to the information. He stopped with his hands in the freezer, taking out an ice tray.

'Are you serious?'

'I've never been more serious.'

'Same person?'

'Same person.'

Bellows went back to the ice tray, chipping at it with a fork. Finally it came away. Susan felt that he was surprised at the news but not overly surprised, and not terribly concerned. Susan felt uneasy.

She tried another tack.

'I found something else out when I visited the OR. Something very interesting.' She waited for a response.

Bellows poured the bourbon, then opened a bottle of soda and poured it over the ice. The ice snapped in the glass. 'OK, I believe you. Are you going to tell me or not?' Bellows handed Susan her drink. She took a slug.

'I traced the oxygen line from room no.8 up in the ceiling space. Just before it turns down the main chase there is a valve in it.'

Bellows took a sip from his drink, motioning for them to return to the living room. The clock over the fireplace chimed. It was two-thirty.

'Gas lines have valves,' said Bellows at length.

'The others didn't have them.'

'You mean a type of valve which would allow gas to be introduced into the line?'

'I think so. I don't know much about valves and the like.'

'Did you trace the others to each room to be sure?'

'No, but room eight was the only line with a valve at the main chase.'

'Simply having a valve doesn't surprise me. Maybe they all have one someplace in their lines. I wouldn't use that valve to draw any conclusions, at least not until I had traced all the lines.'

'It's too much of a coincidence, Mark. All these cases apparently happened in room no.8, and room no.8 has an oxygen line that has a valve in it at a funny place, rather well concealed.'

'Susan, look. You're forgetting that some twenty-five per cent of your supposed victims weren't even near the OR, much less room no.8. Now, even under the best of circumstances, I find your crusade ridiculous and threatening. And when I'm exhausted, I find it numbing. Can't we talk about something soothing, like socialized medicine?'

'Mark, I'm sure about this.' Susan could sense the exasperation in Bellows's voice.

'I'm sure you're sure, but I'm also sure I'm unsure.'

'Mark, the man who attacked me this afternoon warned me, and then he returned tonight, and I don't think he wanted to talk. I think he wanted to kill me. In fact, he tried to kill me. He shot at me!'

Bellows rubbed his eyes, then the sides of his head. 'Susan, I don't know what to even think about that, much less have something intelligent to say. Why don't you go to the police if you're so sure?'

Susan did not hear Bellows's last comment; her mind was racing ahead. She started to speak out loud. 'It has to be from lack of oxygen. If they were given too much succinylcholine or curare, just enough so that the people would have a hypoxic episode ...' Susan trailed off, thinking. 'That could be why respiratory arrest occurred. The one they autopsied, Crawford.' Susan took out her notebook. Bellows took another drink. 'Here it is, Crawford. He had severe glaucoma in one eye and was on phospholine iodide. That's an anticholinesterase and that means that his ability to break down the succinylcholine would have been impaired and a sublethal dose could be lethal.'

'Susan, I've already told you that succinylcholine would not work in the OR, not with the surgeon and the anaesthesiologist right there. Besides you cannot give succinylcholine by gas ... at least, I've never heard of it. Maybe you could, but anyway, they'd just keep respiring the patient until it was gone; there wouldn't be any hypoxia.'

Susan took another slow sip from the bourbon.

'What you're saying is that the hypoxia in the OR has to

occur without the colour of the blood changing so the surgeon stays nice and happy. How could that be done? ... You'd have to block the use of oxygen by the brain somehow ... maybe at the cellular level ... or block the release of oxygen to the brain cells. It seems to me there is a drug that can block oxygen utilization, but I can't think of it offhand. If the valve on the oxygen line were significant, it would have to be a drug that comes in a gas form. But there's another way to do it. You could use a drug that blocks the uptake of oxygen on the haemoglobin and yet still keeps the colour ... Mark, I've got it!' Susan sat bolt upright, her eyes wide open, her mouth forming a half-smile.

'Sure you do, Susan; sure you do,' soothed Mark sarcastically.

'Carbon monoxide! Carefully bled-in carbon monoxide, by way of the T-valve, titrated to cause just the right amount of hypoxia. The blood colour would stay the same. In fact it would get even brighter red, cherry red. Even a very small amount would cause the oxygen to be displaced from the haemoglobin. The brain is starved of oxygen and – coma. In the OR everything has seemed absolutely normal. Then the patient's brain dies; there is not a trace of the cause.'

There was a silence as the two people looked at each other. Susan expectantly, Bellows with tired resignation.

'You want me to say something? OK, it's possible. Ridiculous but possible. I mean it's theoretically possible for the OR cases to be caused by carbon monoxide. It's an awful idea, maybe it's even ingenious, but at any rate, it's possible. The trouble is there are still twenty-five per cent of the coma victims who didn't even get close to the OR.'

'They're the easy one to explain. That was never hard. It was the OR cases that were hard. It was also hard for me to break away from the idea in the diagnosis of disease in medicine that one should search for single causes. But in this case we're not dealing with a disease. The cases on the medical floors were given sublethal doses of succinylcholine. Something like that happened in a VA hospital in the Midwest, and even in New Jersey.'

'Susan, you can hypothesize until you're blue in the face,'

said Bellows with a tinge of anger growing out of frustration. 'What you're suggesting is some fantastic organized plan – a criminal plan – with the sole purpose of making people comatose. Well, let me tell you this; you haven't given an ounce of effort to the biggest question: the question of why. Why, Susan? Why? I mean, you're spinning your mental wheels at ninety miles per hour, taking all sorts of risks with your career, and mine, I might add, to come up with a potentially plausible although fantastic explanation for what is a series of unconnected, unfortunate incidences. But at the same time, you've conveniently forgotten to ask why. Susan, there would have to be motive, for Christ's sake. It's ridiculous. I'm sorry, but it is ridiculous. And besides, I've got to go to sleep. Some of us work, you know ... And there isn't one bit of solid evidence. A valve on the oxygen line! God, Susan, that's pretty weak. I mean you've got to come to your senses. I can't take any more of this. Really. I'm finished. I'm a surgical resident, not a part-time Sherlock Holmes.'

Bellows got up and finished his bourbon in one long drink.

Susan watched him intently, her paranoia awakening once again. Bellows was no longer on her side. Why indeed? The criminal aspect of the matter was horribly apparent to her at that point.

'What makes you so sure,' continued Bellows, 'that all this has anything to do with Nancy Greenly or Berman? Susan, I think you're jumping to conclusions. There's an easier explanation for this character who seems so interested in getting hold of you.'

'I'm waiting.' Susan was angry now.

'The guy was probably looking for some action and you ...'

'Screw you, Bellows!' Susan went livid.

'Now she gets mad. God damn it, Susan, you take this whole affair as some sort of complicated game. I don't want to argue with you.'

'Every time I tell you about some aggressive behaviour from Harris to this fucker who tried to kill me, all you can come up with is some Goddamn sexist explanation.'

'Sex exists, my child. You'd better learn to face that.'

'I think it's more your problem. You male doctors never do seem to grow up. I guess it's too much fun being an adolescent.' Susan got up and put her coat back on.

'Where are you going at this hour?' said Bellows with an authoritarian air.

'I have a feeling I'm safer on the street than here in this apartment.'

'You're not going out now,' said Bellows with determination.

'Ah, now the male chauvinist is displaying his true colours. The great protector! Bull crap. The egoist says I'm not going. Just watch.'

Susan left quickly, slamming the door.

Indecision kept Bellows immobile and silent as he watched the door. He was silent because he knew that she was right in a lot of ways. He was immobile because he really wanted to be rid of the whole mess. 'Carbon monoxide, holy shit.' He walked back into his bedroom and got into bed once more. Looking at the clock, he realized morning was going to arrive very, very quickly.

D'Ambrosio began to panic. He had never liked confined spaces and the walls of the freezer began to move in on him. He began to breathe faster, gulping for air, and then he thought he might be going to suffocate. And the cold. The deathly cold wormed its way through his heavy Chicago overcoat, and despite constant motion, his feet and hands had gone numb.

But by far the most disturbing aspect of the whole miserable affair was the bodies and the acrid odour of formaldehyde. D'Ambrosio had seen a lot of grisly scenes in his life and had been through some gruesome experiences, but nothing could compare with being in the freezer with the stiffs. At first he had tried not to look at them, but involuntarily and out of mounting fear, his eyes had been drawn to the faces. After some time it had begun to look as if they were all smiling. Then they were laughing and even moving when he didn't watch them carefully. He emptied the clip in his pistol by blasting away at one particularly sneering corpse whom he imagined he recognized.

Finally D'Ambrosio retreated to the corner so he could keep

the whole group in view. Slowly he sank into a sitting position. He couldn't feel his knees any longer.

Thursday February 26

10:41am

The path dipped down to the left, through a thicket of gnarled oak trees standing in a bed of twisted briars. The branches of the trees arched over the pathway, enclosing it like a tunnel and precluding a view for more than a few feet. Susan was running and she dared not look behind her. Safety was ahead; she could make it. But the pathway narrowed and the branches clutched at her, hindering her. The briars caught in her clothing. She desperately tried to force her way through. She could see some light ahead. Safety. But the harder she pulled, the more entangled she got, as if she were in a giant spider web. With her hands, she tried to free her feet. But then her arms became hopelessly entangled. There were only minutes left. She had to get free. Then she heard a car horn and one arm came free. The horn repeated itself and she opened her eyes. She was in room 731 at the Boston Motor Lodge.

Susan sat up in the bed, looking around the room. It had been a dream, a recurrent dream which she hadn't had in years. With wakefulness came relief, and she sank back, pulling the covers up around herself. The auto horn which had awakened her sounded for the third time. There were some muffled shouts, then silence.

Susan looked around the room. Tasteless American. Two large beds with a neutral flower-print spread. The rug was a heavy shag, a shade of spring green. The near wall was papered with a repeating floral design in green. The far wall was a pale yellow. There was a picture over the bed, a tawdry reproduction, portraying an idyllic barnyard scene with a few ducks and sheep. The furniture too was cheap, but there was an impressive, twenty-eight-inch colour TV set – the indispensable solace of motel life. Aesthetics had low priority at the Boston Motor Lodge.

But the place was safe. After leaving Bellows's apartment in the wee hours of the morning, Susan had wanted only to find someplace where she could sleep in peace. She had noticed the gaudy motel sign from Cambridge Street on a number of occasions. The sign was awful, certainly not something to beckon the weary. Nonetheless, the room had provided the haven she needed. She had checked in as Laurie Simpson and had waited in the lobby for a good quarter of an hour before going up to the room. When the man at the desk looked at her strangely, she gave him an extra five dollars and told him to call her if anybody inquired about her. She said she was worried about a jealous lover. The desk clerk had winked at her, grateful both for the five dollars and the confidence she extended to him. Susan knew that he accepted the story without question; it was part of the male vanity.

Having taken those precautions, and after moving the desk in front of the door, Susan had allowed herself to fall asleep. She had not slept soundly, as her terminal dream demonstrated, but she felt reasonably refreshed.

She remembered the strong words with Bellows the night before and debated about calling him. She regretted the exchange, feeling that it had been totally unnecessary. She also remembered her feelings of paranoia and felt embarrassed. Yet she remembered her hyper state of mind and felt that her reactions were understandable. She was surprised that Bellows had not been more tolerant. But of course he wanted to be a surgeon, and she had to recognize that his career aspirations made it difficult if not impossible for him to view the situation with an open mind. Still, she regretted the split, if for no other reason than the fact that Bellows had played an effective devil's advocate to her ideas. After all, he was correct that Susan had no idea of motive, and if some large organization was involved, then there must be one.

Maybe the coma victims were the targets of some gangland vendetta? Susan dismissed the idea instantly, remembering Berman and even Nancy Greenly. No, that couldn't be. Maybe extortion was involved; perhaps the families hadn't paid off and – wham! But that seemed unlikely. It would be too hard to keep the coma business secret. It would be easier to kill people outright, outside the hospital. There had to be some reason for these comas happening in the hospital. There must be some pattern for each victim, some common denominator.

As Susan mused, she lifted the phone onto the bed. She dialled the medical school and asked for the dean's office.

'Is this Dr Chapman's secretary? ... This is Susan Wheeler ... that's right, the infamous Susan Wheeler. Look, I'd like to leave a message for Dr Chapman. There's no need to bother him. I was supposed to start a surgery rotation at the VA today, but I've spent a terrible night and I've got some abdominal cramps that won't quit. I'll be better by tomorrow morning, I'm sure, and I'll call if I'm not. Would you please see that Dr Chapman is informed of this, and the Department of Surgery at the VA? Thanks.'

Susan replaced the receiver. The time was quarter to ten. She dialled the Memorial and asked for Dr Stark's office.

'This is Miss Susan Wheeler calling. I'd like to speak to Dr Stark.'

'Oh, yes, Miss Wheeler. Dr Stark expected your call at nine. He'll be with you shortly. He was worried when you didn't call.'

Susan waited, twisting the cord to the phone between her thumb and index finger.

'Susan?' Dr Stark's voice was concerned. 'I'm very glad to hear from you. After what you described happening to you yesterday afternoon, I became concerned when you didn't call. Are you all right?'

Susan hesitated, wondering if she should use the same cover with Stark as she used for Chapman. Stark might have dealings with Chapman. She decided she'd best be consistent.

'I have some abdominal cramps which have kept me in bed. Otherwise I'm fine.'

'The rest will do you good. As for your requests: I have some good news and some bad news. What do you want first?'

'I'll take the bad.'

'I've talked with Oren, then Harris, and finally Nelson about getting you reinstated here at the Memorial, but I'm afraid they are adamant. Obviously they don't run the Surgery Department, but we do depend on cooperation around here and, to be truthful, I was not overly insistent. If they had wavered, I would have been more forceful. But they didn't. You certainly stirred the fire, young lady!'

'I see ...' Susan was not surprised.

'Besides, if you came back here, I think it would be hard for you to overcome your reputation. It would follow you. It's best to let things cool off.'

'I suppose ...'

'The VA programme is a popular affiliated programme and you'll get to do more surgery there than you would here.'

'That may be true, but as for teaching, it's far inferior to the Memorial.'

'But on your other request about the Jefferson Institute, I had some luck. I managed to speak to the director, and I told him about your special interest in intensive care. I also told him you were particularly interested in visiting his hospital. Well, he has obligingly agreed to allow you to come, if you come after the busiest part of the day, sometime after five. But there are some conditions. You must go alone, since only you will be permitted inside.'

'Of course.'

'And since I have really extended myself and have gone off channels, so to speak, I would prefer that you don't mention your visit to anyone. I must admit, Susan, that I really had to make an effort to get you invited. I'm telling you this not because I want you to feel indebted or anything, but rather as partial atonement for my not getting you reinstated here at the Memorial. The director of the institute told me categorically that he would not allow any others to visit with you. They do allow group visits when they have time to supervise them. It's a rather special place, as I believe you'll see. It would be somewhat embarrassing if you wanted to bring someone else. So you must go alone. You can understand that, I presume.'

'Of course.'

'Well, then, let me know what you think of the facility. I haven't been there myself yet.'

'Thank you very much, Dr Stark. Oh, there's one other thing . . .' Susan considered telling Stark about the second experience with D'Ambrosio. She decided against it, because he had wanted Susan to go to the police yesterday; now he'd be insistent. Susan did not want the police, not yet. If it were some large organization behind the whole affair, it was naive to think they didn't have a contingency plan to allow for police probes.

'I'm not sure,' continued Susan, 'if it's significant, but I found a valve on the oxygen line into room no.8 in the OR. It's near to the main chase.'

'Near the what?'

'The main chase where all the piping in the hospital courses from floor to floor.'

'Susan, you're pretty remarkable. How did you find out about that?'

'I went up into the ceiling space and traced the gas lines to the ORs.'

'Ceiling space!' Stark's voice rose in irritation. 'Susan, that's carrying this affair a bit too far. I cannot condone your climbing around in the ceiling spaces over the operating rooms.'

Susan waited for the axe to fall as it had with McLeary or Harris. Instead there was a pause. Stark broke it. 'Anyway, you say you found a valve in the oxygen line to room no.8.' His voice was almost back to normal.

'That's right,' said Susan cautiously.

'Well, I think I know what that's for. I'm chairman of the OR Committee, as you might have guessed. That valve is probably the bleed valve for getting rid of air bubbles when the system is charged up. But one way or another, I'll have someone check it and make certain. By the way, what is the name of the patient you wanted to see at the Jefferson Institute?'

'Sean Berman.'

'Oh yes, I remember the case. It was just the other day. One of Spallek's. A meniscus case, as I recall. Tragedy ... the man was about thirty. A real shame. Well, good luck. Tell me, are you off to the VA today?'

'No, my stomach condition will keep me in bed, at least for the morning. I'm quite sure I'll be able to get back to work tomorrow, though.'

'I hope so, Susan, for your sake.'

'Thank you for your time, Dr Stark.'

'Not at all, Susan.'

The line disconnected and Susan hung up.

The soiled gloves fell into the wastebasket beside the sponge rack. On the rack was a group of blood-stained sponges hanging like dirty clothes on a line. A nurse passed behind Bellows and undid the string at the neck of his operating gown. Bellows tossed it into the hamper by the door and left.

It had been an uncomplicated gastrectomy, a procedure Bellows usually liked to perform. But on this particular morning Bellows's mind had been somewhere else and the double-layer closure of the stomach pouch and the small bowel had been tedious rather than enjoyable. Bellows could not stop thinking about Susan. His thoughts ran the gamut from tender concern, accompanied by remorse for the words that had driven Susan away the night before, to self-righteous pleasure in the comments he had felt justified in making. He had already gone too far, gambled too much, and it was quite apparent that Susan had no intentions of easing up on her idiotic drive in the direction of career suicide.

On the other hand, the sweetness of the evening before last was still very much in Bellows's mind. He had responded to Susan in a way that had been so natural, so fresh. He had made love with her in such a manner that orgasm had been a mere part, not a goal. There had felt something so wonderfully equal, a communion of sorts. Bellows realized that he cared for Susan very much, despite the fact that he knew so little about her, and despite the fact that she was so blasted stubborn.

Bellows dictated his operative note on the gastrectomy case into a tape recorder with the usual medical monotone, ending each sentence with a vocalized 'period.' Then he went into the dressing room and began to change back to his street clothes.

Acknowledging affection for Susan put Bellows on guard. His rationality persuaded him that such feelings would diminish his objectivity and sense of perspective. He could not afford that, not now, when his career opportunities were in the balance. Since Susan had been transferred to the VA, things had already quietened down. Stark had been civil on rounds, even to the extent of semi-apologizing for his ungrounded implications concerning Bellows's association with the drugs found in locker 338.

Bellows completed dressing and walked over to the recovery room to check the post-op orders on his gastrectomy patient.

'Hey, Mark,' called a loud voice from the recovery room desk. Bellows turned to see Johnson coming toward him.

'How the hell are those students of yours? I understand that the girl's a piece of ass.'

Bellows didn't answer. He waved his hand in a questioning fashion. The last thing he wanted to do was get into some idiotic conversation with Johnson about Susan.

'Did your students tell you what happened at the med school this morning? It's one of the funniest stories I've heard in a long time. Some guy broke into the Anatomy Building last night. He must have been some kind of a nut because he discharged a fire extinguisher, unveiled all the first-year students' cadavers, shot up the place, got himself locked in the freezer, and then had a brawl with the bodies. He knocked a bunch of the corpses down and shot up some of them. Can you imagine?' Johnson erupted in gusts of laughter.

The effect was just the opposite on Bellows. He looked at Johnson but thought about Susan. She had told him that she had been chased again, that someone had tried to kill her. Could that have been the same man? The freezer? Susan was rapidly becoming a total mystery. Why hadn't she told him more?

'Did the guy freeze?' asked Bellows.

Johnson had to pull himself together in order to talk.

'No, at least not all of him. The police had been tipped off by an anonymous phone call in the middle of the night. They thought it was a med school prank so they didn't check it out until the morning shift came in. By the time they got there the guy was unconscious, sitting in the corner. His body temperature was ninety-two degrees, but the medical boys succeeded in thawing him out without any trouble with acidosis. I think that's pretty commendable for those assholes. The only trouble was that they waited for two hours before calling me on consult. Hey, you know what the nurses in the ICU call him?'

'I can't guess.' Bellows was only half-listening.

'Ice Balls.' Johnson broke down in laughter again. 'I thought that was pretty clever. It's a takeoff on Hot Lips from M*A*S*H. What a pair, Hot Lips and Ice Balls.'

'Is he going to make it?'

'Sure. I'm going to have to amputate some. At the very least he's going to lose part of his legs. How much will be determined over the next day or so. The poor bastard might even lose those ice balls.'

'Did they find out anything about him?'

'What do you mean?'

'Well, his name, where he was from, you know.'

'Nothing. It turned out he had some ID which proved to be fake. So the police are very interested. He mumbled something about Chicago. Weird!' Johnson mouthed the last word as if it were some important secret message, as he went back to the recovery room desk.

Bellows went over and checked his gastrectomy patient. Vital signs were stable. Then he checked the chart. The orders had been written by Reid, and they were fine. He thought about the man in the freezer. The story seemed so bizarre. He wondered again if it really was the man that had been chasing Susan. But how could she have locked him in the freezer? Why the hell hadn't she mentioned it? Maybe he had never given her the chance. If she had locked the man in the freezer, she was now definitely in trouble legally. Could she have been the anonymous phone caller?

Bellows examined the dressing on the patient. It was still in place and not blood-soaked. The I.V. was running well.

Then he thought about Susan again and decided that the nut in the freezer must have been the man who chased her. And if he was, then it would be important for her to know that he was hospitalized and in critical condition.

Bellows dialled the medical school and asked to be connected to the dorm. He let Susan's phone ring twelve times before giving up. Then he called back the dorm switchboard and left a message for her to call when she came back to her room.

After that, Bellows went to lunch.

Thursday February 26
4:23pm

Thirty-six dollars plus tax seemed to Susan an awfully high price for the tasteless room at the Boston Motor Lodge. But at the same time it was worth it. Susan felt refreshed and rested – and safe. She had spent the time during the day rereading her notebook. All the information she had about the OR cases fit with the idea of carbon monoxide poisoning. The information about the medical cases fit with the idea of succinylcholine poisoning. But still she had no motive, no rhyme or reason. The cases were too disparate.

Susan made a number of calls to the Memorial to try to learn Walters's home address, but she was unsuccessful. At one point she had called the Memorial and had Bellows paged, but she hung up before he could answer. Slowly but inexorably, Susan began to comprehend that she was at a dead end. She thought that it was probably time to go to the authorities, tell what she had learned, then take a vacation. She had a month's vacation coming to her as part of her third year and she was sure that she would be able to get permission to take the time immediately. She'd leave, get away, forget. She thought about Martinique. She liked things French, and she longed for the sun.

The doorman of the motel whistled a cab for her and she got in. She told the driver the address: 1800 South Weymouth Street, South Boston. Then she settled back.

It was stop and go down Cambridge Street, a little better on Storrow Drive, but worse on Berkeley. The cab driver took her through the nicer sections of the South End to avoid traffic. At Mass. Ave. he turned left and the surroundings deteriorated. Once into South Boston, Susan knew she was lost. The housing became monotonous, the streets badly littered. Soon the cab entered an area of warehouses, deserted factories, and dark streets. Nearly every streetlamp had a broken bulb.

When Susan alighted from the cab she found herself in an area that seemed isolated from life. Straight ahead, the only streetlight she could see emitted a beam of light from a modern hooded fixture which illuminated the door of a building, a sign, and the walk leading up to the door. The sign was fabricated in block letters of a deep azure. The sign read: 'The Jefferson Institute.' Below the blue letters was a brass plaque. It said: 'Constructed with the Support of the Department of Health, Education and Welfare, US Government, 1974.'

The Jefferson Institute was surrounded by an eight-foot-high hurricane fence. The building was set back about fifteen feet from the street. It was a strikingly modern structure surfaced with a white terrazzo conglomerate polished to a high gloss. The walls slanted inward at an angle of eighty degrees, rising in a first storey of some twenty-five feet. Then there was a narrow horizontal ledge before the wall soared another twenty-five feet at the same angle. Except for the front entrance, there were no windows or doors along the entire length of the façade on the ground floor. The second storey had windows but they were recessed and could not be seen from the street. Only the sharply geometric embrasures were visible and the glow of lights from within.

The building occupied a city block. In a strange way, Susan found it beautiful, though she realized that its effect was enhanced by the surrounding squalor. Susan guessed that it was the centrepiece of some urban renewal scheme. It gave the impression of a two-storey ancient Egyptian mastaba, or the base of an Aztec pyramid.

Susan walked up to the front door. Made of bronzed steel, it had no knobs, no openings of any kind. To the right of the door was a recessed microphone. As Susan stepped on to the Astroturf immediately before the door, she activated a recording which told her to give her name and the purpose of her visit. The voice was deep, reassuring, and measured.

Susan complied, although she hesitated about the purpose of the visit. She was tempted to say tourism, but she changed her mind. She wasn't feeling very jokey. So, finally, she said, 'Academic purposes.'

There was no answer. A rectangular red light beneath the microphone came on. Printed on the glass was the word *wait*. The light flashed green and the word changed to *proceed*. Without a sound the bronzed door glided to the right, and Susan stepped over the threshold.

Susan found herself in a stark white hall. There were no windows, no pictures, no decorations at all. The only illumination seemed to be from the floor, which was made of a milky opaque plastic material. Susan found the effect curious and futuristic; she walked ahead.

At the end of the hall, a second silent door glided into the wall, and Susan entered what appeared to be a large, ultramodern waiting room. Its far and near walls were mirrored from floor to ceiling. The two side walls were spotlessly white and totally devoid of any interruptions or decoration. The sameness was somewhat disorienting. As Susan looked at the walls, her eyes began to focus on her own vitreous floaters. She had to blink and make an effort to focus at a distance. Looking into the mirror at the end of the room had the opposite effect. Because of the opposing mirrors Susan saw the image of herself reflected to infinity.

The room was furnished with rows of moulded white plastic

chairs. The floor was the same as in the hall, the light from it casting strange shadows on the ceiling. Susan was about to sit down when another door slid open in the farthest mirrored wall. A tall woman entered and walked directly up to Susan. She had very short, medium brown hair. Her eyes were deeply set, and the line of her nose merged imperceptibly with her forehead. Susan was reminded of the classic features of a cameo. The woman wore a white pants suit as devoid of decoration as the walls. A pocket dosimeter peeped from her jacket. Her expression was neutral.

'Welcome to the Jefferson Institute. My name is Michelle. I will show you our facilities.' Her voice was as non-committal as her expression.

'Thank you,' said Susan, trying to see through the woman's façade. 'My name is Susan Wheeler. I believe you are expecting me.' Susan let her eyes sweep around the room once more. 'It certainly is modern. I've never seen anything quite like this.'

'We have been expecting you. But before we begin I'd like to warn you that it is very warm inside. I suggest that you leave your coat here. And please leave your bag as well.'

Susan took off her coat, a bit embarrassed by the wrinkled and soiled nurse's uniform she still had on. She took her notebook from her bag.

'Now then ... I suppose that you know that the Jefferson Institute is an intensive-care hospital. In other words, we only take care of chronic intensive-care patients. Most of our patients are in some level of coma. This particular hospital was built as a pilot project with HEW funds, although the actual running of it has been delegated to the private sector. It has been very successful in freeing up beds in the acute intensive care units of the city's hospitals. In fact, since the project has been so successful, an equivalent hospital is either being built or is in the planning stages in most of the large cities of the country. Research has shown that any city or population centre with a population of a million or more can economically support a hospital of this sort ... Excuse me, but why don't we sit down?' Michelle indicated two of the chairs.

'Thank you,' said Susan, taking one of the chairs.

'Visiting the Jefferson Institute is strictly regulated because of the methodology we use to care for the patients. We have developed very new techniques here, and if people are not prepared, some may react on an emotional level. Only immediate family may visit, and only once every two weeks on a pre-planned basis.'

Michelle paused in her monologue, then she managed a half-smile. 'I must say that your visit here is highly unusual. Normally we have a group of medical people on the second Tuesday of each month, and there is a planned programme for them. But since you have come by yourself, I guess I can improvise a bit. But we do have a short film if you would like to see it.'

'By all means.'

'Good.'

Without any sign from Michelle, the room darkened and on the wall opposite from where they were sitting, a film began to roll. Susan was intrigued. She presumed that the film was being projected through a translucent section of the wall serving as a screen.

The film itself reminded Susan of old newsreels. Its outdated technique seemed an anachronism in the modern surroundings. The first section was devoted to the concept of the intensive care hospital. The Secretary of Health, Education and Welfare was shown discussing the problem with policy planners, economists, and health care specialists. The problem of spiralling hospital costs spearheaded by the cost of long-term intensive care was illustrated by graphs and charts. The men explaining the charts were dull and uninspiring, as commonplace as the suits they wore.

'This is a terrible film,' said Susan.

'I agree. Government films are all alike. You'd think that they'd try a little creativity.'

The movie moved on to ground-breaking ceremonies, at which politicians smiled and joked idiotically. More graphs and charts followed, attesting to the enormous savings that had been accrued by the hospital. There were several more scenes showing how the Jefferson Institute's facilities freed the beds in the city's hospitals for the care of acute cases. Then followed a comparison of the number of nurses and other personnel needed at the Jefferson facility to the number needed in a conventional hospital for the same number of intensive care patients. The people used to illustrate this point were photographed milling about aimlessly in a parking lot. Finally, the film showed the heart of the new hospital: the huge computer, both digital and analog. It concluded by pointing out that all the functions of homoestasis were monitored and maintained by the computer. The film ended with a burst of inspirational marching music, like the finale of a war movie. The lights under the floor came on as the last image disappeared.

'I could have done without that,' said Susan, smiling.

'Well, at least it emphasizes the point about the economy. That's the central concept of the institute. Now, if you'll follow me, I'll show you the principal features of the hospital.'

Michelle stood up and walked toward the mirrored wall from which she had appeared. A door glided open. It shut behind them as they entered another corridor about fifty feet long. The far end of the corridor was also mirrored from floor to ceiling. As Susan passed down the hallway she noted other doors but they were all closed. None of the doors had any exposed hardware. Apparently they were automatically activated.

When they reached the far end of the corridor, a door slid open and Susan entered a familiar-looking room. It was about forty by twenty feet and looked exactly like an intensive care unit in any hospital. There were five beds and the usual assortment of gadgets, EKG screens, gas lines, etcetera. But four of the beds appeared different: each was constructed with a gap of some two feet running lengthwise. It was as if each bed were constructed of two very narrow beds with a fixed two-foot span between them. In the ceiling above the beds there were complicated tracklike mechanisms. The fifth bed, which seemed conventional, was occupied. A patient was being breathed by a small respirator. Susan was reminded of Nancy Greenly.

'This is the visiting area for the immediate families,' explained Michelle. 'When a family is scheduled to visit, the patient is transferred here automatically. When he is placed in one of these special beds and it is made up, the bed appears like a normal one. This patient was visited this afternoon.' Michelle pointed toward the patient in the fifth bed. 'We purposely did not return him to the main ward for your benefit.'

Susan was confused. 'You mean that bed the patient is in is the same as these other beds?'

'Exactly. And when family visits, these other beds are filled with other patients so that the area looks like a normal intensive care unit. Follow me, please.'

Michelle walked the length of the room, past the patient in the bed. At the end of the room was a door, which opened silently and automatically.

Susan was amazed when she passed the fifth bed with the patient. The bed appeared exactly like a regular hospital bed. There was no evidence that its central section, its basic support, was missing. But Susan had no time to examine the bed more closely as she followed Michelle into the next room.

The first thing Susan became aware of was the light; there was something strange about it. Then she felt the warmth and the humidity. Finally she saw the patients, and she stopped in utter astonishment. There were more than a hundred patients in the room, and all of them were completely suspended in mid-air about four feet from the floor. All of them were naked. Looking closely, Susan could see the wires piercing multiple points on the patients' long bones. The wires were connected to complicated metal frames and pulled taut. The patients' heads were supported by other wires from the ceiling which were attached to screw eyes in the patients' skulls. Susan had an impression of grotesque, horizontal, sleeping marionettes.

'As you can see, the patients are all suspended by wires under tension. Some visitors react strongly to this, but it has proven to be the best method of long-term care, totally preserving the skin and minimizing nursing care. Its origin was in orthopaedics, where wires are passed through bones to provide traction. Burn treatment research showed the benefits to be obtained when the skin does not rest on any kind of surface. It was a natural progression to apply the concept to the care of the comatose patient.'

'It is rather gruesome.' Susan recalled the upsetting image of the cadavers hung in the freezer. 'What is the strange lighting?'

'Oh, yes, we should put on glasses if we stay in here much longer.' Michelle fetched several pairs of goggles from a table.

'There is a low-level flux of ultra-violet light in here. It has been found useful in controlling bacteria as well as helping to maintain the integrity of the skin.' Michelle offered a set of goggles to Susan, and they both put them on.

'The temperature in here is maintained at ninety-four point five Fahrenheit, plus or minus five hundredths of a degree. The humidity is held at eighty-two per cent with a one per cent variance. That tends to reduce patient heat loss and hence reduces the patients' calorific needs. The humidity has reduced the respiratory infection problem, which you know is critical for coma patients.'

Susan was spellbound. She gingerly moved closer to one of the suspended patients. A profusion of wires perforated various long bones. The wires then passed horizontally through an aluminium frame around the patient before running up to a complicated trolley device on the ceiling. Susan looked up at the ceiling and saw that it was a maze of tracks for the trolleys. All the I.V. lines, suction tubes, and monitoring lines from the patient ascended to the trolley. Susan looked back at Michelle. 'And there are no nurses?'

'I happen to be a nurse, and there are two others on duty, plus one doctor. That's quite a reasonable ratio for one hundred and thirty-one intensive care patients, wouldn't you say? You see, everything is automated. The patient's weight, blood gases, fluid balance, blood pressure, body temperature – in fact, an enormous list of variables – are being constantly scanned and compared to standards by the computer. The computer actuates solenoid valves to rectify any abnormalities or discrepancies it finds. It is far better than conventional care. A doctor tends to concern himself with isolated variables and in a static fashion. The computer is able to sample over time, hence it treats dynamically. But more important still is that the computer correlates all the variables at any given moment. It's much more like the bodies' own regulatory mechanisms.'

'Modern medicine carried to the *n*th degree. It's incredible, really it is. It's like some science fiction setting. A machine taking care of a host of mindless people. It's almost as if these patients aren't people.'

'They aren't people.'

'I beg your pardon?' Susan looked up from the patient toward Michelle.

'They *were* people; now they're brain stem preparations. Modern medicine and medical technology have advanced to the point where these organisms can be kept alive, sometimes indefinitely. The result was a cost-effectiveness crisis. The law decided they had to be maintained. Technology had to advance to deal with the problem realistically. And it has. This hospital has the potential to handle up to a thousand such cases at a time.'

There was something about the basic philosophy Michelle elucidated that made Susan uncomfortable. She also had a feeling that her guide had herself been very carefully indoctrinated. Susan could tell that Michelle did not question what she was saying. Nevertheless Susan did not dwell on the institute's philosophical foundations. She was overwhelmed by the place's physical aspects. She wanted to see more. She looked around the room. It was more than a hundred feet long, with a fifteen- to twenty-foot ceiling. In the ceiling the maze of tracks was bewildering.

There was another door at the far end of the room. It was closed. But it was a normal door with normal hardware. Susan decided that only the doors they had so far traversed were centrally controlled. After all, most visitors, the families, never came into the main ward.

'How many operating rooms are there here in the Jefferson Institute?' asked Susan suddenly.

'We don't have operating rooms here. This is a chronic care facility. If a patient needs acute care, he is transferred back to the referring institution.'

The reply was so fast that it gave the impression of a reflex or trained response. Susan distinctly remembered seeing the ORs in the floor plans she had obtained at City Hall. They were on the second floor. Susan began to sense that Michelle was lying.

'No operating rooms?' Susan deliberately acted very surprised. 'Where do they do emergency procedures, like tracheostomies?'

'Right here on the main ward or in the ICU visiting room next door. That can be set up as a minor OR if needed. But it rarely happens. As I said, this is a chronic-care hospital.'

'I still would have thought that they would have included an OR.'

At that moment almost directly in front of Susan, one of the patients was automatically tipped back so that his head was about six inches below his feet.

'There is a good example of the computer working,' said Michelle. 'The computer probably sensed a fall in the blood pressure. It put the patient into the Trendelenburg position prior to correcting the main cause for the blood pressure fall.'

Susan was barely listening; she was trying to figure a way to do a little exploring on her own. She wanted to see those operating rooms indicated on the floor plans.

'One of the reasons I asked to come here was to see a particular patient. The name is Berman, Sean Berman. Do you have any idea where he is located?'

'No, not offhand. To tell you the truth, we don't use names here for the patients. The patients are given numbers, sample 1, sample 2, etcetera. It's infinitely easier to key into the computer. In order to find Berman's number, I'll have to match the name with the computer. It takes a minute or so, that's all.'

'Well, I would like to find out.'

'I'll use the information terminal at the control desk. Meanwhile, you could take a look here and see if you can see him. Or you can come with me and wait in the waiting room. No guests are permitted in the control room.'

'I'll wait here, thank you. There is enough of interest here to keep me occupied for a week.'

'Suit yourself, but, needless to say, don't touch any of the wires or the patients under any circumstances. The whole system is very carefully balanced. The electrical resistance of your body would be picked up by the computer and an alarm would sound.'

'No need to worry. I'm not about to touch anything.'

'Good. I'll be right back.'

Michelle removed her goggles. The door to the visiting room opened automatically and she was gone.

Michelle walked through the visitors' room and halfway down the corridor beyond it. The door to the control room opened for her. It was dimly illuminated like the control room on a nuclear submarine. A good portion of the light in the room came from the far wall, which was actually a two-way mirror permitting observation of the visitors' hall from the control room.

Two other people occupied the room when Michelle entered. Sitting in front of a large U-shaped bank of TV monitors was a guard. He was also dressed in white, and wore a wide white leather belt, a white-holstered automatic, and a two-way Sony receiver. He sat in front of a vast console with multiple switches and dials. A battery of TV monitors in front of him was scanning rooms, corridors, and doors throughout the hospital. Several screens had contrast images, such as the monitors for the front door and the entry hall. Others changed as remote control video cameras scanned their areas. The guard looked up sleepily as Michelle entered.

'You left her by herself in the ward? Do you think that was wise?'

'She'll be fine. I was told to let her see what she wanted on the first floor.'

Michelle walked toward a large computer terminal where the other occupant of the room, a nurse dressed like Michelle, sat watching the data display on the forty or more screens in front of her. Intermittently the computer's printer to her right would activate and print out information.

Michelle plopped herself down in a chair.

'Who the hell does she know to get invited here by herself?' asked the computer nurse, suppressing a yawn. 'She looks like a Goddamn LPN or something. She doesn't even have a pin or a cap. And that uniform! It looks like she's been wearing it for six months.'

'I haven't the slightest idea who she knows. I got a call from the director saying that she was coming and that we were to let her in and entertain her. I was to call Herr Direktor when she arrived. Do you think there's some hankypanky going on?'

The computer nurse laughed.

'Do me a favour,' continued Michelle, 'and punch in the name of Sean Berman. He was a Memorial referral. I need his patient number and location.'

The computer nurse began to key in the information. 'On our next shift, you can be the computer-sitter while I float. Playing with this machine is starting to drive me up the wall.'

'Gladly. The only break in the routine of floater for the past week has been this visitor. A year ago, if someone told me I would be tending a hundred intensive-care patients myself, I'd have laughed in his face.'

One of the display screens flashed: Berman, Sean. Age 33, sex male, race caucasian. Diagnosis: cerebral brain death secondary to anaesthetic complications. Sample number 323 B4. STOP.

The nurse keyed Sample number 323 B4 back into the computer.

The guard at the other end of the room sat slouched over, watching the monitors as usual, as he had been doing for two hours since his last break, as he had been doing for almost a year. The picture of the main ward appeared on screen number 15; moving as the video camera slowly panned from one end of the huge room to the other. The dangling nude patients held no interest for the guard. He was finally accustomed to the gruesome scene. Automatically screen number 15 shifted to the intensive-care visitors' ward as its camera started to scan.

The guard sat up suddenly, looking at the screen of number 15. He reached for the manual mode switch and returned the scan to the main ward. The video camera scanned the enormous room again.

'The visitor is no longer in the main ward!' said the guard.

Michelle turned from the computer display screen and squinted to see screen number 15 of the monitor. 'No? Well check the visitors' ward and the corridor. Maybe she had enough. The main ward is usually a shock for the first-time visitors.'

Michelle turned and looked out through the glass to the waiting room, but Susan was not there either.

The display screen on the computer flashed: Sample 323 B4 terminated. 0310 Feb. 26. Cause of death: cardiac arrest. STOP.

'Well if she came here for Berman, she's too late,' said Karen without feeling.

'She's not in the visitors' ward,' said the guard, activating a series of switches. 'And she's not in the corridor. It's not possible.'

Michelle got up from the chair, her eyes staying on screen 15 until she was at the door. 'Calm down. I'll locate her.' Michelle turned to the nurse at the computer. 'Maybe you should try to call the director again. I think we'd better get rid of this girl.'

Thursday February 26
5:20pm

As soon as Michelle left the main ward, Susan had removed the Xeroxed copies of the Jefferson Institute floor plans she had folded in her notebook. She oriented herself from the entrance, traced their route to the main ward, and then checked the routes for gaining access to the second floor. She saw two choices. There was a stairway from MG or an elevator from M Comp R. Susan glanced down at the key in the lower right hand corner. MG stood for morgue; M Comp R was the main computer room. Susan quickly decided that the stairs would be safer than the elevator; she thought that the computer room might well be occupied.

She walked toward the far end of the ward, where there was a conventional door, and tried the knob. It turned and Susan opened the door into the corridor beyond. It seemed to be quite dark; then she remembered the goggles. She took them off and put them in her uniform pocket. The corridor was like the others she had seen, starkly white with the illumination coming through the floor. At either end of the corridor was a large mirror, and its multiple reflections made the corridor seem infinitely long.

There were no sounds and no one in sight. Susan checked the floor plan, which indicated that the morgue and the stairs were to the right. She closed the door to the ward behind her. Moving quickly, she made her way down to a door at the end of the corridor. There were no markings on the door, but at least it too had normal hardware. Susan tried the knob; the door was unlocked.

As silently as possible, she opened the door, just a few inches at a time. She could see the tiles of the near wall. Then she began to see the upper part of a stainless steel dissecting table. A corpse lay naked on it. Susan heard some voices and a laugh, followed by the sound of a scale.

'So much for the lungs. How much should we say the heart weighed?' said one of the voices.

'Your turn to guess,' laughed the other.

Nudging the door an inch more, Susan could just glimpse the head of the corpse. She squinted, then felt weak. It was Berman.

Letting the door close without a sound, Susan stood in the doorway for a few deep breaths. She felt slightly nauseated but it passed. She realized that she had very little time. The elevator.

Susan's pause in the doorway had been perfect timing. The TV scanner behind the one-way mirror finished its five-second scan as Susan stepped back into the corridor. It would resume its scan in ten seconds.

She hurried back into the main ward and reached the doorway to the computer room. Hesitantly she tried it. It too was unlocked. She opened the door about ten inches and looked into the room. To her relief, it seemed unoccupied. As she pushed the door farther she could see a fantasy of computer consoles, input-output equipment, and tape storage systems.

A movement in the far corner near to the ceiling caught Susan's eye. She recognized it immediately. It was a TV monitor camera. As its unhurried pan brought its lens toward Susan, she ducked back and closed the door. When she guessed that the camera had panned past, she whipped open the door and began to run the length of the room, to the elevator. But her timing was off; she would be spotted by the TV camera on its return sweep. Susan dived behind a computer console only halfway to her destination.

She had to work her way down the rest of the room, from console to console, trying to avoid the roving eye of the camera. Making a dash for the elevator, she pressed the button frantically. Susan could hear the machinery start up inside the shaft. The elevator was on another floor.

The TV camera reached the end of its arc and started back. Susan pressed the elevator button several times in succession. The sound of the elevator machinery stopped, the doors quivered and then began to open. Susan glanced up at the TV

295

camera before rolling around the edge of the elevator door, groping for the 'close' button. The door closed but Susan had no idea if she had been observed or not.

The elevator was cavernous and correspondingly slow. There were only three buttons. She pressed the button for floor two and felt the machine begin to ascend. The floor plan for the second floor showed that the ORs were at the extreme opposite end of the building from the elevators. A long hall stretched from the elevators back to the OR area. Both the eighth and ninth doors to the right led into the OR complex.

When the elevator stopped and the doors opened, Susan stayed inside with her finger poised over the 'door-close' button. No one in sight. The corridor was similar to those of the first floor except that the doors were more deeply recessed. The ceilings carried tracks for the trolleys.

As the elevator doors began to close Susan plunged down the corridor, mentally checking off the number of doorways she had passed. Suddenly, in the distance, Susan saw a man driving a miniature forklift loaded with units of whole blood. He appeared to emerge from an intersecting corridor. She half-skidded, half-ran into one of the recessed doorways, crashing up against the wall, her breath coming in gasps. She listened. The sound of the machine receded. She peered into the corridor. Empty. She pushed off and reached the ninth door.

She waited until her breath returned to a semblance of normal before cracking the door and checking the room. She slipped in quickly.

She was in a dressing room. A partially smoked cigarette lay in an ashtray, its smoke curling up in the still air. An open doorway led to a bath area. Susan could hear the sound of a shower going.

Michelle re-entered the control room. Her sense of ennui had disappeared. Her mouth was set, but her eyes moved incessantly. Like the guard, she was now very nervous.

'That girl has literally evaporated. She couldn't have walked out, could she?' asked Michelle.

'Impossible. There's no way the front door, or any outside

door for that matter, can be opened without me activating the door release.' The guard was still switching from scanner to scanner.

'I think we'd better give direction another call. This affair could get serious,' said the nurse at the computer console.

'I don't understand it. We have these monitors placed in all the key areas. She's got to be in some doorway,' said the guard.

'She's not in a doorway. I went all the way through to the main ward. What about the elevator?'

'That's a thought,' said the guard. 'If she does get upstairs there could be big trouble. I'm going to secure the building and activate all the automatic locking mechanisms on all stairway doors and electrify the perimeter fence. I'll hold the general alarm until direction is reached.'

Michelle moved to a red telephone. 'This is absurd, really! Totally unnecessary. Why was she allowed in by herself without a group?'

Swinging doors opened from the dressing rooms to the OR receiving area. Susan stepped into it. Here the appearance was more traditional. The lighting came from fluorescent bulbs in the ceiling alongside the omnipresent tracks for the patient trolleys. There was a faint glow that Susan remembered from the main ward, and she guessed there was an ultra-violet component to the light. The floor was of white vinyl, the walls surfaced in white ceramic tile.

The OR reception area was not large. In the centre was an empty desk. There were apparently four operating rooms, two on each side, with ancillary rooms between. Susan's attention was attracted by muffled sounds from the first OR. Light coming through a small window suggested that an operation was in progress.

A dark window in the door of the adjacent ancillary room suggested that it was empty. Susan walked over, peered in, and stepped into the darkness.

This service room was dimly lit through a window of a door leading to the occupied OR.

Susan waited for her eyes to adjust to the darkness. Slowly

the objects in the room took form. There was a central table supporting several large objects from which emanated a low-pitched continuous noise. Counter tops ran around the room. In the left counter top there was a large sink. Immediately to her right she could see the form of a gas sterilizer.

As quietly as possible, Susan opened the cabinet beneath the sink, and with her hands she ascertained that there would be enough room to squeeze in if necessary. She then returned to the hall door and ran her fingers along its edge until she found the knob and depressed the lock. Then she paused and listened to make sure there had been no change in the pattern of noises from the OR. Susan looked at the objects on the central table, but the light was too poor to distinguish them.

Susan trod lightly to the OR door and raised herself on tip-toe. She saw two surgeons, gowned and gloved in the usual fashion, bending over a patient. But she could see no anaes-thesiologist. There was no operating table. The patient was still strung up in a frame. But he was maintained on his right side; an incision gaped across his loins. The surgeons were closing, and Susan could hear their conversation with relative ease.

'I wonder where that heart's going from that previous case?'

'San Fran,' said the second surgeon, running down a knot, pulling it tight. 'I think it's only bringing seventy-five thousand dollars. It was a poor match, only two out of four, but it was a rush order.'

'Can't win 'em all,' said the first surgeon, 'but this kidney is a four-tissue match, and I understand it's going for almost two hundred thousand. Besides, they might want the other one in a few days.'

'Well, we don't let it go until we find a market for the heart,' added the other, trying another rapid knot.

'The real problem is finding a tissue match for Dallas. The offer is a million dollars for a four-match. The kid's father is in oil.'

The second surgeon whistled. 'Any luck so far?'

'We found a three-tissue match scheduled for a T&A at the Memorial next Friday and ...'

Susan's mind was desperately trying to find some alternate explanation for what she thought she was hearing, but before she could, the door from the reception hall jiggled as someone tried to open it. Susan's first impulse was to run into the other empty OR. Instead, she raced back to the sink, as he heard someone enter the lighted operating room. She squeezed herself into the cabinet under the counter, wincing at the sound of several jars that tipped over when she pulled her feet in after her. It was tight quarters; she struggled to get her arms in. She was unable to close the door completely by the time the door to the OR opened and the room lights went on. Susan held her breath.

With her head twisted sideways, and the cabinet door slightly ajar, she could see two Plexiglas structures sitting on the table. They resembled fish tanks. Then she understood the pumping noise she had heard when she entered the room. It came from two self-contained machines, battery-driven, which perfused the two Plexiglas tanks. The first contained a human heart, suspended in a fluid. It was quivering, but not beating. The other contained a human kidney, also suspended in a fluid.

Suddenly the whole nightmare was clear to Susan. Now she had a motive, a horrible motive for making patients comatose. The Jefferson Institute was a clearing-house for black-market human organs!

Susan had little time to think. A man walked past the sink, his trousers brushing against the half-closed cabinet door. He unlocked the door to the hall, then he went over to the table. Audibly straining, he lifted the tank which contained the heart and carried it away, leaving the light on and the door ajar.

Susan's mind raced back over all the details of her investigation: the T-valve on the oxygen line, D'Ambrosio's face, the image of Nancy Greenly, and the heart in the Plexiglas container. She remembered the conversation the morgue below, and she realized that the heart must have been Berman's. She began to feel a sense of urgency, a sense of pervading panic. The concept of this lurid affair was too overwhelming. She had to get away and, for the first time, she realized how difficult that was going to be. This was no ordinary hospital. At least some of the people running it were criminals. She had to get out and get to someone who could comprehend what was going on. Stark. She had to get to Stark. He would be able to appreciate the whole business and was powerful enough to do something about it.

Carefully Susan moved her left hand out of the cabinet onto the floor, pushing open the door as she did so. She listened. There were no noises except for the quiet whir of the pump perfusing the kidney on the table. With great effort she began to pull her right leg from the far corner of the cabinet. Then she heard footsteps in the hall. There was only a second. Her foot went back where it had been. She pulled in her arm, pushing herself into the cabinet as far as possible. The elbow of the drain from the sink above dug into her back.

The man came back into the room at a fast walk. He came between the sink and the table and kicked the cabinet door shut. The sound and compression made Susan's ears ring. She heard him strain with the second tank. Then his footsteps left the room and receded down the corridor.

Susan stayed still for another two or three minutes before she dared to move, listening. There were no footsteps, only a muffled laugh from the first OR. Susan extracted her cramped body from beneath the sink. A spray can fell out onto the floor and rolled a short distance. Susan froze. Nothing. Then she ran for the door into the unlit operating room.

She had to pause once again to allow her eyes to adjust to the darkness. Here the forms of the overhead operating lights were visible. Carefully Susan moved to the common wall with the corridor, feeling for the door handle. Once she found it, she cracked the door and looked into the scrub area immediately beyond.

At that instant a piercing alarm shattered the stillness and all the lights went on in the previously darkened room. In a panic Susan let go of the door and turning threw herself against the wall expecting an assailant.

The room was empty.

A red light was blinking on and off next to a small loudspeaker. The loudspeaker crackled: 'There is an unauthorized intruder in the building. Female. She must be detained immediately. I repeat ... there is an unauthorized individual in the building ... detain immediately.' The loudspeaker went dead. Susan sighed in relief. She left the OR and peered around the wall of the scrub area. The corridor was clear.

Two white-uniformed guards strode briskly through the main ward, oblivious to the hundred-odd human beings strung up around them. Each had a pistol in his hand. The larger of the two was listening to his Sony two-way radio. He replaced it on his belt. 'I'm to take the elevator in the computer room up to two. You're to head through the morgue and down to the machinery spaces.'

The two men entered the corridor beyond the ward.

'And remember, our orders are clear. If you find her and she comes along willingly, fine; if not then shoot her. But shoot her in the head. They may want the kidneys or the heart, depending on her tissue type.'

The two men split. The larger man walked down the corridor and entered the computer room. Methodically he checked the room, then he summoned the elevator.

Susan dashed down the OR reception area, past the first operating room. She opened the door to the dressing area but heard voices within. Without hesitation she changed her plan and turned for a door she knew must open into the main corridor. Then she spotted a large pair of scissors on the reception desk. She picked them up; they were a weapon of sorts. Then she let herself into the main corridor.

The corridor was still empty, to Susan's intense relief. She could see all the way down to the closed elevator doors at the far end. Taking a deep breath, she sped toward the elevator.

She was about halfway down the hundred-and-fifty-foot hall when the elevator arrived. Susan slowed as the doors quivered and opened. The guard stepped out and Susan stopped. Each was startled to see the other.

'All right, young lady, we'd like to talk to you downstairs.' The guard's voice was not threatening. He began to advance slowly toward Susan, keeping his pistol behind his back.

Susan took a few indecisive steps backward, then she spun and raced toward the OR area. The guard pelted after her. In desperation Susan tried several doors. The first was locked; so was the second. The guard was almost on her. The handle of the third door turned and the door opened.

She rolled around the door, trying to slam it shut. But the guard gripped the edge of the door with his left hand and wedged his left foot between the door and the casing.

Susan pushed with every ounce of strength she could muster but it was hardly an even match. The guard was over two hundred pounds, and his weight and strength prevailed despite Susan's efforts. The door began to open.

Keeping her shoulder and left hand against the door, Susan gripped the scissors like a dagger. With a quick overhand stroke, she plunged the scissors into the guard's hand.

The point of the scissors struck between the knuckles of the second and third fingers. The force of the blow carried the blades between the metacarpal bones, shredding the lumbrical muscles and exiting through the back of the hand. The guard screamed in agony, letting go of the door. He staggered back into the corridor with the scissors still embedded in his hand. Holding his breath and grinding his teeth, he pulled them out. A small arterial pumper squirted blood in short pulsating arcs onto the opaque plastic floor, forming a pattern of red polka-dots.

Susan slammed the door shut and locked it. She whirled to survey the room. It was a small laboratory, with a laboratory bench in the centre. To the left were two desks back to back. Against the wall were several filing cabinets. At the far end was a window.

The guard in the hall recovered enough to wrap a handkerchief about his left hand and curb the spurting blood. He passed the cloth between his index and middle fingers and tied it around his wrist. He was furiously angry, as he fumbled with his passkeys. The first key would not turn in the lock. The second key he selected would not fit it. The third key also would not turn. Finally, the fourth key turned, and the lock mechanism sprang back, releasing the door. With his foot, the guard kicked the door open with such force that the knob went through the plaster wall to the right. With his pistol cocked, the guard sprang into the room, spinning around. Susan was gone. The window was open and frigid February air was streaming into the warm room. The guard ran to the window and leaned out enough to see the ledge. He returned to the room and took out his two-way radio.

'OK, I found the girl, floor two, the tissue lab. She's something. She stabbed me, but I'm OK. She went out the window onto the ledge ... No, I can't see her. The ledge goes around the corner ... No, I don't think that she would jump. Did the Dobermans get released? ... Good. The only worry is that she might attract some attention if she gets to the front of the building ... OK ... I'll check the ledge on the other side.'

The guard put his radio back on his belt, closed the window and locked it. Then he ran out of the room, clutching his wounded hand.

Thursday February 26

5:47pm

The heavy industrial-weight vinyl ceiling tile was slowly slipping from Susan's grip, and she clenched her teeth. Her hands were numb from holding it with just the tips of her fingers, forcing the tile against its metal supports on the opposite side of its six-foot expanse. She could hear the guard below talking on his two-way radio. If the tile fell, he'd find her. She closed her eyes as tightly as she could to take her mind off her fingers and her aching forearms. It was slipping. It was going to fall.

The guard switched off. Then the window closed. Susan held on somehow. She didn't hear the guard exit, but the tile fell with a dull thud that jarred the whole suspended ceiling. Susan listened intently as blood rushed into her tingling fingers, painfully. There was no sound below. She let herself take a deep breath.

Susan was up in the ceiling space above the tissue lab. It was ironic that before her search of the ORs at the Memorial, Susan never knew of the existence of ceiling spaces. Now clambering up there had saved her life. Thank God for the filing cabinet on which she had stood to lift the tile.

Susan took out her floor plans and tried to examine them in the spare light filtering up through the edges of the ceiling tiles. She found it impossible even after her eyes had adjusted. Looking around in the gloom, she noticed a rather concentrated beam of light coming from some larger fissure in the ceiling about twenty feet from her position. With the help of the upright studding marking the wall of the tissue lab and a neighbouring office, Susan managed to work her way over to the light source and position herself so that she could see the plans. What she wanted to find was the main chase like the one she had seen at the Memorial. She thought that if it were big enough it would be a possible way out. But the chase was not listed in the key. However she did find a rectangular enclosure drawn next to the elevator shaft. Susan decided that it probably represented the chase she was after.

She moved along the top of the wall of the tissue lab, holding onto the upright studs until she reached the step up to the fixed ceiling of the corridor. It was made of concrete, to support the tracks for the trolleys. Once on it, the going was much easier. She moved toward the elevator shaft.

The closer she got to the elevator shaft the more difficult was her progress both because it got significantly darker and because more and more pipes, wires, and ducts converged in the direction she was heading. She had to move by feel, advancing a foot forward slowly, blindly. Several times she touched a steam pipe and it burned her. The smell of burnt flesh drifted into her nose.

In utter darkness she reached the elevator shaft and felt the vertical concrete. Rounding its corner, she followed a pipe with her hands and felt it turn down at a ninety-degree angle. Other pipes did the same. Leaning over them, she looked down into the darkness. A faint light filtered up from far below.

With her hands Susan determined the size of the chase. It was about four feet square. The wall common to the elevator shaft was concrete. She selected a pipe about two inches in diameter. Lowering herself into the chase, she put her back against the concrete wall and grabbed the pipe with both hands. Then she put her feet against other pipes and pushed back firmly against the concrete wall. In this fashion she inched herself down the chase, like a mountaineer in a chimney.

The going was not easy. Moving only inches at a time, she tried, although not always successfully, to avoid the steam pipes, which were blistering hot. After a while she was able to distinguish the pipes in front of her. Looking into the darkness, she could see vague forms, and she realized that she had reached the ceiling space of the first floor. She was making progress and she felt a certain elation. But it was tempered by the thought that if she could use the chase to go down, someone could use it to go up. And she realized then how relatively easy it was for someone to gain access to the T-valve in the oxygen line at the Memorial.

Susan continued inching downward. Below her there was a bit more light filtering upward. There was also the progressively louder sound of electrical machinery. As she approached the basement level, Susan realized that there was no suspended ceiling below her in the basement. There would be no way to conceal herself and move laterally. She worked herself down until her eyes cleared the structural floor on the first level then stopped her movement, wedging herself securely against the concrete to survey the scene.

The machinery room and its power plant were lit by a few work lights. The pipe Susan was using for her descent, apparently a water pipe from its feel, continued to the floor. But several other pipes, larger than the one she was holding, angled off horizontally, hanging by metal straps about four feet below the concrete slab of the building's first floor. They ran high above the machinery area.

Susan stepped onto one of these pipes. She was no acrobat, but perhaps her natural ability as a dancer helped. With her right hand and her head pressed against the solid concrete, she moved crouching along the pipe, trying not to look down.

She teetered a bit but gained confidence. Ahead she saw a wall and beyond, another ceiling space. By maintaining pressure on the ceiling above she did a tightrope walk along the pipe. Susan passed directly over the power plant and was within four feet of her goal when there was a startling flash of light very close to her, almost causing her to lose her balance. The lights had come on in the machinery room.

Susan shut her eyes, pressing her hands against the ceiling and hooking the groove of her shoes against the pipe. Beneath her a guard moved slowly around the machinery, a big flashlight in one hand, a pistol in the other.

The next fifteen minutes were probably the longest single period of time in Susan's life. She felt so exposed, with a white dress against the dark pipes and ceiling, that she could not fathom why she was not seen. The guard searched carefully, even the cabinets under the workbench. But he never looked up. Susan's arms began to tremble from the tension necessary to keep her balance secure. Then her legs followed, so that she was afraid her shoes would soon be tapping a message against the pipe. Finally the guard was satisfied and left, turning out the main lights.

Susan did not move immediately. She tried to relax, conquering her tension and incipient vertigo. She longed for the fixed ceiling about four feet away. It was so close yet so far. She moved her right foot forward about six inches, then put weight on it. Then she moved the left up to the right. Both her arms and legs pained her tremendously. She thought about just letting herself fall forward onto the ceiling but she was afraid of the noise being heard. Instead she continued in her painful caterpillar way. When she reached the ceiling, she collapsed onto her back, breathing hard and letting the blood flow back into her deprived muscles.

But she knew she could not rest for long. She had to find a way out of the building. Lying on her back, she again consulted the floor plans. There were two possible exits. One was the supply room very close to where she now was. Another was at the far end of the building, beyond a room labelled 'Dp.' Susan checked the key. Dp stood for dispatch.

Thinking about the man carrying the heart and the kidney from the auxiliary room between the ORs made Susan opt for the dispatch room despite the proximity of the supply room. She thought that perhaps they were planning on transporting the organs. She knew that transplant organs should be used as soon as possible.

Replacing the floor plans, Susan pulled herself to her feet. Her dress was now badly soiled and torn. She kept to the fixed ceiling over the basement corridor as she made her way in the direction of the dispatch room. The going was comparatively easy because it was not totally dark. Like the machinery space, large sections of the basement had no ceiling at all, and enough light was transmitted along Susan's path that she could move at a regular pace, avoiding the pipes and ducts with ease.

She arrived at the extreme corner of the building and guessed from another glance at the floor plans that she had reached her goal. She lay supine on the fixed corridor ceiling with her head over the dropped ceiling of the dispatch room. As carefully as she could, she lifted a tile until she could just get her fingers under its edge. With effort she pulled it up until she could just see below. The room was occupied!

Not daring to let the ceiling tile go for fear of noise, Susan watched the man below, bent over a desk, filling out a form. He was dressed in an unzipped leather coat. On the floor were two insulated cardboard boxes. They were boldly labelled: 'Human Transplant Organ – This side up – Fragile – Rush.'

A door which she could not see opened below. A second man appeared. It was one of the guards.

'Let's go, Mac. Let's get these things loaded and out of here. We've got work to do.'

'I'm not taking nothing until the proper papers are done.'

The guard left by a swinging door on the far side of the

room. Susan got a glimpse of another area before the door closed. It looked like a garage.

The driver finished his forms and tossed a copy into a basket on the counter. The other copy he put into his pocket. He loaded the cartons onto a dolly and backed through the swinging doors.

Susan let the ceiling tile fall back into place. Quickly she moved over to the wall at the far end of the corridor. She could hear the noise of a truck door being shut and latched.

It was darker near the wall, and Susan ran her hand along the wall expecting to feel concrete. Instead she felt vinyl tile, oriented vertically. Susan could plainly hear a truck engine turning over. She pushed against the tile but it seemed to be securely held in place by a metal flange. The truck engine caught, coughed, and quit. The starter began to whine again.

Desperately Susan pushed against the metal flange, feeling it bend up. She repeated the manoeuvre in several locations. The truck engine caught again, rattled and coughed and then roared, finally sinking back to a controlled idle. Susan then heard the distinctive rumble of a massive and heavy garage door being elevated. Her fingers clawed for the top of the vinyl tile. She pulled it toward herself but it stayed firm. She raised more of the flange and pulled again. The tile came in suddenly, causing Susan to fall backward. She recovered quickly and stared through the vertical opening into an underground garage area. Directly below was a relatively large truck belching exhaust. By the entrance stood the guard, activating the overhead door switch. He was watching the door ascend.

Susan leaped into space and hit the top of the truck with her feet and hands at the same time. The noise of the impact was lost within the echo of the truck engine and the rumble of the garage door. She flattened herself spread-eagled as the truck lurched forward. She felt the inertia of her body cause her to slide backward. She tried to grip something, anything, but the top of the truck was smooth metal and her hands groped in vain. She managed to clear the garage door, but as the truck mounted the incline to the street, Susan's backward slide became more uncontrollable. Her feet actually slipped over the rear of the truck as she tried to press her hands flat against the smooth surface.

The truck reached the street and the driver braked before turning left. Susan's body then slid forward, careening counter-clockwise. The frigid cold struck her. The driver picked up speed, and Susan felt a sense of helpless terror. She inched toward the cab and clamped her numb fingers over a low ventilator. Then there was a bump and Susan's body flew up, only to slam down on the metal roof a moment later. Her chin and nose hit the surface so hard that it dazed her. She was only vaguely conscious of what happened after that.

Susan became lucid rather suddenly. She lifted her head and recognized that her nose and lip were bleeding. She watched the buildings and recognized the area. It was the Haymarket. Of course, she thought, the truck was heading for Logan Airport.

The truck halted for a traffic light. Traffic was still rather heavy. Susan worked her way right up to the cab. She pulled her feet around and stood up on the roof of the cab. Then she sat down and let her feet onto the hood. At that point she lowered her head and looked through the windshield at the driver. The man was shocked and immobile, his eyes staring without believing, his hands rigidly gripping the steering wheel.

Susan slid from the hood to the fender, then leaped for the ground. She scrambled to her feet and ran between the cars toward Government Centre. The driver recovered somewhat, opened his door, and shouted after her. Other angry yells and blaring horns drove him back into his cab. The light had changed. As he put the truck into gear and pulled forward, he told himself that no one would believe this story.

Thursday February 26
8:10pm

The tattered and flimsy nurse's uniform was little protection against the razor-sharp cold. It was seventeen degrees with a twenty-five-knot north wind, making the wind chill factor somewhere around twenty below zero. Susan ran along the deserted Haymarket vegetable stalls, trying to avoid the empty cardboard boxes that were being blown across her path. The debris made her progress slow, and it reminded her of the nightmare that had started the day.

At the corner she turned left and braved the full power of the wind. She was shivering now, and her upper and lower jaws clattered against each other as if they were beating out some urgent message in Morse code. On the City Hall mall it got worse. The particular design of the Government Centre area, with its curved façades and expansive mall, functioned as a wind tunnel, pushing the north wind to greater effort. Susan had to bend herself into the wind to make progress up the wide steps. To her left the remarkable modern architecture of the City Hall loomed eerily in the darkness; its stark geometric protrusions formed dark, intervening shadows, giving the whole scene an ominous air.

Susan needed a telephone. When she got to Cambridge Street there were a few other humans, bent over, faceless in the wind and the cold. Susan stopped the first pedestrian; it was a woman. The stranger's head came up, the eyes looked at Susan first with disbelief, then fright.

'I need a dime and a telephone,' said Susan through her chattering teeth.

The woman pushed Susan's arm away and hurried on without looking back and without saying a single word.

Susan looked down at her nurse's uniform. It was torn, soiled, and bloodstained. Her hands were totally black. Her hair was irretrievably tangled and matted. She realized she looked like a psychotic, or at best a derelict.

Susan stopped a man and asked her question. The man backed up from Susan's appearance. He reached into his pocket and extended some change toward Susan, his eyes also revealing a mixture of incredulousness and consternation. He dropped the coins into Susan's hand as if he were afraid to touch her.

Susan took the change. It was more than the single dime she had asked for.

'I think there's a phone in the diner down on the left,' said the man, looking at Susan. 'Are you all right?'

'I'll be all right if I get to a phone. Thank you very much.'

Susan's cold fingers had trouble wrapping around the change. Her hands were so numb that she could not even feel the coins in her palms. She ran across Cambridge Street toward the diner.

The steamy, greasy warmth of the place was a welcome relief as Susan entered. A few faces looked up from their food, and noted her strange look. But in deference to the anonymity guaranteed by a large American city, the diners returned to their fare, to keep from becoming involved.

Susan was gripped by an irrational paranoia, and her eyes went from person to person, trying to detect an enemy. The warmth brought even greater shivering. She hurried to the pay phone near the restrooms.

Her hands had great difficulty manipulating the coins, and most of them dropped to the floor before she got a dime into the slot. No one got up to help her retrieve her money. The grease-smeared tattooed counterman watched her blankly, inured to the curiosities of Boston street life.

The operator answered at the Memorial.

'I'm Dr Wheeler and I must speak with Dr Stark immediately. It is an emergency. Do you have his home number?'

'I'm sorry, but we cannot give out the doctor's number.'

'But this is an emergency.' Susan glanced around the diner, half-expecting someone to challenge her.

'I'm sorry, but we have our orders. If you want to leave your number, I'll have the doctor call.'

Susan's eyes roamed around for the number.

'523–8787.'

There was a click. Susan replaced the disconnected receiver. She had one dime left in her hand. She thought perhaps hot tea would help. She searched around for more change on the floor. She found a nickel. She looked in a wider area. She knew that she had had a quarter.

One of the patrons got up from the counter and sleepily walked around to use the phone. He was reaching for the receiver when Susan spotted him.

'Please. I'm expecting a call. Please don't use the phone for just a few moments.' Susan stood up, beseeching the stubbly-faced man.

'Sorry, sister, got to use the phone.' The man picked up the receiver and reached up to drop in his dime.

For the first time in her life, Susan lost all semblance of control or rationality.

'No!' she screamed at the top of her lungs, causing every head in the diner to snap around in her direction. To emphasize her determination, Susan clasped her two hands together, the fingers interlocking, and brought them up swiftly, hitting the man's forearms. The surprisingly fast blow knocked both the receiver and the dime from his grasp. With her hands still clasped, Susan brought them down so that the heels of her hands hit the man on the forehead and the bridge of his nose. It sent the surprised individual stumbling backward into the edge of a booth. Almost in slow motion, he sank to a sitting position, his feet outstretched. The suddenness and the fury of the attack had left him momentarily dumbfounded, and he didn't move.

Susan quickly replaced the receiver on the phone, holding onto it, closing her eyes tightly, hoping it would ring. It did. It was Stark. Susan tried to contain herself in the surroundings, but the words bubbled out of her.

'Dr Stark, this is Susan Wheeler. I have the answers ... all of them. It's unbelievable, really it is.'

'Calm down, Susan. What do you mean you have all the answers?' Stark's voice was reassuring and calm.

'I have a motive; I have both the method and a motive.'

'Susan, you're talking in riddles.'

'The coma patients. They're not accidental complications. They're planned. When I was doing the chart extractions, I found out that all the victims had been tissue-typed.'

Susan paused, remembering how Bellows had talked her out of attaching any significance to the tissue-typing.

'Go on, Susan,' said Dr Stark.

'Well, I didn't give it any significance. But I do now. Now that I've been to the Jefferson Institute.'

Saying the name made Susan look around the diner suspiciously. Now most of the eyes in the place were directed at her. But no one moved. Susan withdrew into the alcove by the restrooms, cupping her hand over the receiver.

'I know it will sound incredible, but the Jefferson Institute is a clearinghouse for black-market transplant organs. Somehow these people get orders for organs with a specific tissue type. Then whoever runs the show searches around in the hospitals here in Boston till they find patients with the proper type. If it's a surgical patient, they merely add a little carbon monoxide to his anaesthesia. If it's a medical patient he – or she – gets a shot of succinycholine in his I.V. The victim's upper brain is destroyed. He's a living corpse, but his organs are alive and warm and happy until they can be taken out by the butchers at the Institute.'

'Susan, that's an incredible story,' said Stark. He sounded stunned. 'Do you think you can prove this?'

'That's one of the problems. If there is a big fuss – say the police were brought to the Jefferson Institute for a look-see – they probably have a contingency plan to cover up. The place masquerades as an intensive-care hospital. Besides, both carbon monoxide and the succinylcholine are metabolized quickly in the victims' bodies, leaving no trace whatsoever. The only way to break up the organization behind these crimes is for someone like yourself to convince the authorities to make a real surprise raid on the place.'

'That might be an idea, Susan,' said Stark. 'But I'd have to hear the particulars that brought you to your fantastic conclusions. Are you in any danger now? I can come and pick you up.'

'No, I'm all right,' said Susan, glancing into the diner. 'It would be easier if I met you somewhere. I can catch a cab.'

'Fine. Meet me at my office in the Memorial. I'll leave immediately.'

'I'll be there.' Susan was about to hang up.

'Susan, one more thing. If what you say is true, then secrecy is tremendously important. Don't say anything to anybody until we've talked.'

'Agreed. See you in a few minutes.'

Replacing the receiver, Susan looked up a cab company. She used her last dime to order a cab. She gave the name Shirley Walton. They said it would take ten minutes.

Dr Harold Stark lived in Weston, along with nine-tenths of Boston's other doctors. He had a sprawling Tudor house which also boasted a Victorian library. After speaking with Susan, he replaced the receiver on the phone on top of his desk. Then he pulled open the right-hand drawer and extracted a second phone, a phone carefully maintained and checked electronically for any additional resistance or interference. It could not be tapped without Stark's knowledge. He dialled quickly, watching the tiny oscilloscope in the drawer. It functioned normally.

In the control room of the Jefferson Institute a manicured man, slight of build, reached for the ringing red telephone.

'Wilton,' yelled Stark, only partially concealing his anger, 'for a whiz kid with figures and an aptitude for business, you're pretty impotent when it comes to catching young, unarmed girls in a building built like a castle. I cannot understand how you could allow this matter to get so far out of hand. I warned you about her days ago.'

'Don't worry, Stark. We'll find her. She got out on the ledge but obviously has to return to the building. All the doors are sealed, and I've got ten men here now. Don't worry.'

'Don't worry,' snarled Stark. 'Well, let me tell you something. She just called me on the phone and outlined the entire core of our programme. She's already out, you ass.'

'Out! Impossible!'

'Impossible. What kind of statement is that? I said she just called me. What do you think, she's using one of your phones? Christ, Wilton. Why didn't you take care of her?'

'We tried. Apparently she's eluded a very reliable hit man. The same man who took care of Walters.'

'God, that was another thing. Why didn't you just dispose of him rather than stage that suicide?'

'For your benefit. You're the one that was so uptight when the drugs that old codger was hoarding were found. I mean you were the one who was so worried that it might drag in the authorities for some sort of grand investigation. We not only had to get rid of Walters but we had to associate him with his goddamn drugs.'

'Well, this whole affair has made up my mind for me. I think it's time we wind down this operation. Do you understand, Wilton?'

'So the great doctor wants out, does he? At the first ripple of trouble in almost three years, you want out. You got all the money to rebuild that whole hospital of yours. You got yourself appointed Chief of Surgery. And now you want to leave us dry. Well let me *you* something, Stark, something that you're going to find hard to take. You are not giving orders anymore. You're going to follow them. And the first order is to get rid of this girl.'

Stark found himself holding a dead connection. He slammed the phone down and replaced it in the drawer. He was trembling with rage. He had to hold back from smashing his own belongings. Instead he gripped the edge of the desk until his fingers turned milky white. Then his fury began to abate. Anger per se had never solved anything, Stark knew. He had to rely on his analytical powers. Wilton was right. Susan represented the first ripple of trouble in his progress in almost three years. The progress that had been made was beyond Stark's wildest dreams. It had to go on. Medical science demanded it. Susan had to be eliminated. That was certain. But it had to be done in a way so as not to cause suspicion or alarm, especially from some narrow-minded people like Harris or Nelson, who lacked the vision Stark knew he had.

Stark got up from behind his massive desk and walked along the ranks of bookshelves. He was deep in thought and he let his hand carelessly caress the gilded edges of a first-edition Dickens. Suddenly it came to him in a moment of inspiration that brought a smile to his face.

'Beautiful ... so appropriate,' he said out loud. He laughed, his anger already forgotten.

Thursday February 26
8:47pm

Susan dashed from the cab without paying and made a bee-line for the Memorial entrance. She had no money and did not intend to get into an argument. The driver jumped out of the cab, too, shouting angrily. He caught the attention of one of the guards, but Susan was already through the entrance.

Susan had to slow to a walk in the main hall. Ahead of her she was dismayed to see Bellows, headed in the same direction. Susan worked her way up to a position directly behind him and debated with herself about catching his attention. She thought again about how he had caused her to disregard the tissue typing done on the coma patients. There was a chance that Bellows was involved. Besides, she remembered Stark's admonition to speak to no one. So when they reached the corner of the corridor, Susan let Bellows continue down toward the ER. She turned toward the Beard elevators. One was waiting, and she got on and pushed 10.

Susan's view of the hall became progressively occluded by the closing door. But at the very last minute a hand wrapped around the edge of the door, halting it. Susan stared blankly at it before the face of a guard came into view.

'I would like to have a word with you, Miss,' he said, still holding the door open despite its continued attempts to close, as Susan pressed on the 'door close' button.

'Please come off the elevator.'

'But I'm in a terrible hurry. It's an emergency.'

'The emergency room is on this floor, Miss.'

Susan reluctantly complied with the guard's demand and got off the elevator. The doors closed behind her, and the car began its ascent to the tenth floor without any occupants.

'It's not that kind of emergency,' pleaded Susan.

'So much of an emergency you couldn't pay your cab?' The guard's voice was a mixture of admonition and concern. Susan's appearance lent a definite credence to her plea that it was an emergency.

'Take his name and company, and I'll settle it later. Look, I'm a third-year medical student. My name is Susan Wheeler. I have no time at this moment.'

"Where are you going at this hour?' The guard's tone had become almost solicitous.

'Beard 10. I'm meeting one of the doctors there. I've got to go.' Susan depressed the up button.

'Who?'

'Howard Stark. You can call him.'

The guard was confused, dubious. 'All right. But stop by the security office on your way down.'

'Of course,' agreed Susan as the guard turned to go.

Just then the next elevator arrived and Susan boarded it, pushing past a few departing passengers, who looked at her dishevelled appearance curiously. On the slow ride up to 10 she leaned against the car's wall gratefully.

The corridor presented a totally different environment from

the one she remembered from her previous daytime visit. The typewriters were quiet. The patients gone. The floor was as still as a morgue. The thick carpet absorbed the sound of her own hesitant footsteps as she moved toward her goal and safety. The only light came from a lonely table lamp in the middle of the hall. The *New Yorker* magazine stacks which could be seen were carefully straightened. The faces on the portraits of the former Memorial surgeons were smudges of violet shadow.

Susan approached Stark's office and hesitated for a moment, composing herself. She was about to knock, but tried the door. It opened. The anteroom of Stark's secretary was dark, but the door to his private office was slightly ajar, light slanting through it. Susan pushed open the door and stepped in.

The door shut behind her that instant. Susan's overwrought psyche caused a tremendous panic reaction as she whirled to face an assailant. She had to fight to keep from screaming.

Stark was locking the door. He must have been behind her.

'Sorry for the dramatics, but I don't think we want anyone interrupting this conversation.' He smiled suddenly. 'Susan, you'll never know how glad I am to see you. After these experiences you told me about, I should have insisted on picking you up from where you called. But no matter, you got here safely. Do you think you were followed?'

Susan's fright reaction tapered, her heart rate reached an apogee and began to slow. She swallowed. 'I don't think so, but I can't be sure.'

'Come and sit down. You look like you've been through World War I.' Stark touched Susan's arm, guiding her to a chair in front of his desk. 'Looks like you could use a little Scotch, at the very least.'

Susan felt a terrible exhaustion; mental, physical, and emotional, descend over her. She didn't respond audibly. She simply followed, her chest heaving. She sank into the chair, barely comprehending what she had been through.

'You're an amazing girl,' said Stark, walking over to the small bar cabinet across the room.

'I don't think so,' returned Susan, her voice reflecting her exhaustion. 'I just happened to walk blindly into an amazing horror.'

Stark got a bottle of Chivas Regal. He carefully poured out two drinks and brought them over to the desk. He handed one to Susan. 'I think you're being too modest.' Stark rounded his desk and sat down, his gaze fixed on Susan. 'You're not hurt, are you?'

Susan shook her head, her hand inadvertently shaking her drink so that the ice clinked against the side of the glass. She tried to steady herself by using both hands. She took a mouthful of the comforting, fiery liquid, letting it slide down her throat between deep breaths.

'Now then, Susan. I want to make sure where we stand. Have you spoken to anyone since we talked?'

'No,' said Susan taking another drink.

'Good, that's very good.' Stark paused, watching Susan sip her drink. 'Does anyone besides yourself have any idea about all this?'

'No. No one.' The Scotch felt delightfully warm inside Susan, and she began to feel a calmness settle over her. Her breathing began to slow to normal. She looked at Stark over her glass.

'OK, Susan, now why do you think the Jefferson Institute is a clearing house for transplant organs?'

'I heard them talking. I even saw the shipping cartons for the organs myself.'

'But Susan, it isn't surprising to me that a hospital filled with chronic-care, comatose patients would be a source of transplant organs as the patients succumb to their disease processes.'

'That might be true. But the problem is that the people behind this were the ones making at least some of those patients comatose in the first place. Besides, they were getting paid for these organs. Paid a lot of money.' Susan felt her upper eyelids droop, and she raised them forcefully. She felt a torpor stealing over her. She knew she was exhausted but dragged herself straighter in the chair. She took another mouthful of the Scotch and tried not to think about D'Ambrosio. At least she felt warm.

'Susan, you are amazing. I mean, you were only in the place for a short time. How did you learn so much so quickly?'

'I had floor plans from City Hall. They showed operating rooms, and the girl who was showing me around said there were no operating rooms. So I checked them out myself. Then it was clear. Frightfully clear.'

'I see. Very clever.' Stark nodded his head, marvelling at Susan. 'And they let you leave. I would have imagined that they would have preferred that you stay.' He smiled again.

'I was lucky. Extremely lucky. I left with a heart and a kidney on their way to Logan.' Susan suppressed a yawn, trying to hide it from Stark. She felt tired, very tired.

'That's all very interesting, Susan and that's probably all the information I really need. But ... you are to be commended. Your activities over the last few days are a study in clairvoyance and perseverance. But let me ask you a few more questions. Tell me ...' Stark put his hands together and rotated in his chair so that he could see out over the black waters of the harbour. 'Tell me if you can think of any other reasons for this fantastic operation you have so cleverly exposed.'

'You mean, other than money?'

'Yes, other than money.'

'Well, it is a good way to get rid of someone you don't want around.'

Stark laughed inappropriately, or so it seemed to Susan.

'No, I mean a real benefit. Can you think of any benefits other than financial?'

'I guess the recipients of the organs get a certain benefit, if they don't have to know how the donor organ was obtained.'

'I mean a more general benefit. A benefit for society.'

Susan again tried to think, but her eyes wanted to close. She straightened up again. Benefit? She looked at Stark. The meaning of the conversation was becoming diffuse, strange.

'Dr Stark, I hardly think this is the time ...'

'Come on, Susan. Try. You've done such a remarkable job

at uncovering this thing. Try to think. It's important.'

'I can't. It's such a horror that I have difficulty even considering the word *benefit*.' Susan's arms began to feel heavy. She shook her head. For a second she thought she had actually fallen asleep.

'Well, then I'm surprised at you, Susan. From the intelligence that you have so amply displayed over the last couple of days, I thought that you would have been one of the few to see the other side.'

'Other side?' Susan closed her eyes tightly, then opened them, hoping they could stay open.

'Exactly.' Stark rotated back toward Susan, leaning forward, arms on the desk. 'Sometimes there are situations where ... what should I say ... the common folk, if you will, cannot be depended upon to make decisions which will provide long-term benefits. The common man thinks only of his short-run needs and selfish requirements.'

Stark got up and wandered over to the corner where the expansive walls of glass joined. He looked out over the great medical complex he had helped to build. Susan felt herself unable to move. She even had difficulty turning her head. She knew she was tired but she never felt so heavy, so languorous. Besides, Stark kept going in and out of focus.

'Susan,' Stark said suddenly, turning around to face her again, 'you must realize that medicine is on the brink of probably the biggest breakthrough in all of its long history. The discovery of anaesthesia, the discovery of antibiotics ... any of those epochal achievements will pale before the next giant step. We are about to crack the mystery of the immunological mechanisms. Soon we'll be able to transplant all human organs at will. The fear of most cancer will become a thing of the past. Degenerative disease, trauma ... the scope is infinite.

'But such breakthroughs do not come easy, not without hard work and sacrifice. Not without a price. We need first-rate institutions, like the Memorial and its facilities. Next we need people like myself, indeed like Leonardo Da Vinci, willing to step beyond restrictive laws in order to insure progress. What if Leonardo Da Vinci had not dug up his bodies for dissection? What if Copernicus had knuckled under to the laws and dogma of the church? Where would we be today? What we need for the breakthrough to actually happen is data, hard data. Susan, you have the mind to appreciate that.'

Despite the darkening cloud she felt settling over her brain, Susan began to realize what Stark was saying. She tried to get up, but she found she could not lift her arms. She strained but only succeeded in knocking the remains of her drink to the floor. The ice cubes scattered.

'You do understand what I am saying, Susan? I think you do. Our legal system is not geared to handle our needs. My God, they cannot make a decision to terminate a patient even after it is certain that his brain has turned to lifeless Jell-O. How can science proceed under a public policy handicap of that proportion?

'Now, Susan, I want you to think carefully. I know it is a little hard for you to think at this moment, but try. I want to say something to you and I want your response. You are a bright, very bright, girl. You're obviously one of the ... what should I say? ... *elite* sounds too much like a cliché, but you know what I mean. We need you, people like you. What I want to say is that the people who run the Jefferson Institute are on our side. Do you understand, our side?'

Stark paused, looking at Susan. She struggled to keep her eyelids above her pupils. It took all her strength.

'What do you say to that, Susan? Are you willing to dedicate that brain of yours to the good of society, science, and medicine?'

Susan's mouth formed words but they came out in a whisper. Her face was expressionless. Stark leaned forward to hear. He had to bring his head up to inches of Susan's lips.

'Say it again, Susan. I'll be able to hear if you say it again.'

Susan's mouth struggled to bring her lower lip against her upper teeth to form the first consonant. It spilled out in a whisper.

'Fuck you, you cra—' Susan's head slumped back, her mouth gaping and her respirations coming in regular deep-sounding breaths.

Stark looked at Susan's drugged body for a few moments. Susan's defiance angered him. But after a few moments of silence his emotion faded into disappointment. 'Susan, we could have used that brain of yours.' Stark shook his head slowly. 'Well, maybe you can still be useful.'

Stark turned to his phone and called the emergency room. He asked for the admitting resident.

Thursday February 26
11:51pm

The surgical residents' on-call room at the Memorial was rather minimal in its amenities. It had a bed, a hospital bed, which could be cranked into a number of interesting positions, a small desk; a TV which got two stations provided you didn't mind a double image; and a collection of torn, stained old *Penthouse* magazines. Bellows was sitting at his desk, trying to read an article in the *American Journal of Surgery*, but he couldn't concentrate. His mind, particularly his conscience, was functioning in an abnormally irritating manner. It kept reminding him of Susan's appearance a few hours earlier. Bellows had seen her when she entered the Memorial. He knew she had come up behind him, and he had expected her to stop him. It had been a surprise when she didn't.

Bellows had not looked at Susan directly, but enough to see her matted hair, her bloodied and torn dress. He had felt immediate concern, but at the same time felt a definite inclination to leave well enough alone. His job at the Memorial was on the line. If Susan needed medical help, she had come to the right place. If she needed psychological support, it would have been better to call and meet him outside the hospital. But Susan had not stopped him and had not called.

Now Bellows had learned that Susan had been admitted as a patient, that Stark himself was handling her case. As the senior surgical resident on call, Bellows knew that Susan was scheduled for an appendectomy. It seemed quite a coincidence, but there it was. Stark was going to operate. At first Bellows thought he'd scrub. Then prudence told him he was far from objective about Susan and that could become a handicap in the OR. So he decided to send a junior resident and wait it out.

Bellows looked at his watch. It was almost midnight. He knew that they'd be starting Susan's appy in ten minutes or so. He tried to go back to the *Journal* article but something else bothered him. Bellows stared out of the grimy window and brooded. Then he picked up the phone and asked in which room the appy was scheduled.

'Number eight, Dr Bellows,' said the OR duty nurse.

Bellows put the phone down. Funny. Susan had told him about finding the T-valve in the oxygen line to that room, the room in which so much had gone wrong.

Bellows looked at his watch again. Suddenly he got up. He'd forgotten about getting his mid rats in the cafeteria. He was hungry. Bellows pulled on his shoes and set off for the cafeteria. But he thought about the T-valve.

He got on the elevator and pushed 1 for the cafeteria. In the middle of the descent he changed his mind and pushed 2. What the hell, he could take a look for that T-valve on the oxygen line himself, while Susan was having her surgery. It was stupid, but he decided to do it anyway. At least it would satisfy his conscience.

A phantasmagoria of geometric images, colour and motion emerged from the darkness, gradually expanding. The geometric images collided, split, and recombined into forms and shapes without meaning. Out of the confusion the image of a hand being stabbed by scissors preceded a sequence of chase. The autopsy room at the Memorial appeared with a realism that included auditory and olfactory aspects. A spiral staircase took dominance; then a corridor filled with the face of D'Ambrosio grinning in sadistic delight seemed to move closer and closer. But D'Ambrosio's face disintegrated and he fell spinning into the abyss. The corridor twisted and turned kaleidoscopically.

Susan regained her consciousness in fluctuating stages. Finally she realized that she was looking at a ceiling, the ceiling of a corridor that was moving. No, she was moving. Susan tried to move her head but it seemed to weigh a thousand pounds. She tried to move her hands. They too were unbelievably heavy, and it took all her concentration just to lift her hands up from her elbows. Susan was lying on her back, moving down a corridor. Sounds started to appear. Voices ... but they were unintelligible. She felt someone grip her hands and push them down to her side. But she wanted to get up. She wanted to know where she was. She wanted to know what happened to her. Was she asleep? No, she'd been drugged. Suddenly Susan knew that. She fought with the effects of the drug, to try to lift herself from its grasp. Her mind began to clear. She could understand the voices.

'She's an emergency appendectomy. Apparently a hot one, too. And she's a medical student. You'd think she would have had enough sense to be seen sooner.'

Another voice, deeper than the first. 'I understand she had called in sick this morning to the dean's office, so obviously she knew something was wrong. Maybe she was worried about being pregnant.'

'Maybe you're right. But she tested negative.'

Susan's mouth tried to form words but no sounds issued from her larynx. She found that her head could move from side to side. The drug was beginning to wear off. Then the movement stopped. Susan recognized the area. She was in the scrub room. By turning her head to the right she could see the scrub sink. A surgeon was scrubbing.

'You want one or two assistants, sir?' said one of the voices behind Susan.

The man at the scrub sink turned. He was wearing a hood

and a mask. But Susan recognized him. It was Stark.

'One's enough for a simple apply. I'll have it out in twenty minutes.'

'No, no,' cried Susan, voicelessly. Only a bit af air hissed between her lips. Then she began to move toward the operating room. She could see the door open. She saw the number over it. Room No. 8.

The drug was wearing off. Susan could lift her head and her left arm. She saw the huge operating room lights. The glare dazzled her. She knew she had to get up ... to run.

Strong arms gripped her waist, her ankles and head. She felt hands thrust under her, and she was lifted effortlessly onto the operating table. Susan lifted her left hand to grasp at anything. She grabbed an arm.

'Please ... don't ... I am ...' the words came slowly, almost inaudibly from Susan's throat. She was trying to sit up despite the weight of her head.

A strong arm was laid across her forehead. Her head was pressed back.

'Don't worry, everything will be all right. Just take some deep breaths.'

'No, no,' said Susan, her voice gaining slightly in power.

But an anaesthesia mask dropped over her face. She felt a sudden pain in her right arm ... an I.V. The liquid started into her vein. No. No. She tried to shake her head from side to side but strong arms held her. She looked up and saw a masked face. The eyes looked into hers. She saw an I.V. bottle with bubbles dancing up through the fluid. She saw someone thrust a syringe into the I.V. line. The Pentothal!

'Everything will be all right. Just relax. Take a deep breath. Everything will be all right. Just relax. Take a deep breath ...'

The atmosphere in room eight at 12:36am that February 27 was extremely tense. The junior resident had found himself all thumbs during the case, even dropping clamps and fumbling ties. Stark's presence and reputation had been too much for the fledgling surgeon, especially after the initial rapport had evaporated.

The anaesthesiologist's handwriting was even more erratic than usual as he put the finishing touches on his anaesthesia record. He wanted the case to be over. The patient's sudden cardiac irregularities in the middle of the case had totally unnerved him. But even worse had been the sudden closure of the non-return valve on the wall oxygen line. In his eight years as an anaesthesiologist, it was the first time that piped-in oxygen had actually failed. He had made the transition to the green emergency cylinders smoothly, and he was fairly confident there had been no change in the amount of oxygen he had been delivering. But the experience had been frightening; he knew he could have lost the patient.

'How much longer?' the anaesthesiologist asked over the ether screen, putting his pen down.

Stark's eyes were wildly dancing from the clock to the door, then back to the operative field. He had taken over tying the skin sutures from the bumbling resident.

'Five minutes, tops,' said Stark as he ran a knot down with his deft fingers. Stark too was nervous. That was obvious to the resident, who thought he himself must be the cause. But Stark was nervous because he knew that something was not right.

The oxygen non-return valve should not have failed. That meant that the oxygen pressure had fallen to zero in the main oxygen line. Of the operating team, only Stark knew that the patient's cardiac irregularities meant that she had received carbon monoxide with the mainline oxygen. But when that oxygen source failed, he couldn't be sure whether Susan had received enough of the deadly gas for his purposes.

And then there had been the muffled shouts which had caused the circulating nurses to check the corridor. But Stark knew that the noises came from above, from the ceiling space.

But that wasn't all. As Stark was making the next to last skin stuture, his eyes caught a surge of movement in the corridor through the window of the OR door. The corridor seemed to be filled with people, and at 12:35am that was inappropriate, to say the least.

Stark placed the last skin suture and dropped the needle

holder onto the instrument tray. As he picked up the ends to tie the knot, the OR door swung open, and Stark saw at least four people advance into the room. Mark Bellows was among them.

The sudden visitors wore surgical gowns, and Stark's pulse began to race as he realized that most of them had thrown their gowns over blue uniforms. A deadly silence hung in the OR. But as Stark straightened up from the operating table, he knew now that something was wrong. Something was very wrong.

Author's Note

This novel was conceived as an entertainment, but it is not science fiction. Its implications are scary because they are possible, perhaps even probable. Consider a classified advertisement that appeared in the San Gabriel (California) *Tribune*, May 9, 1968, col. 4:

NEED A TRANSPLANT?
Man will sell any portion of body for financial remuneration to person needing an operation. Write Box 1211-630, Covina.

The advertiser did not specify what organ or organs, or even whose body they were to come from.

And there have been other advertisements, many others, in various newspapers across the country. Even specific offers of the hearts from living people!

As gruesome as these ads sound, they should come as no great surprise. There are plenty of precedents for the market economy in medicine. Blood – which may be considered as an organ – is routinely bought and sold. There is a commerce in semen, which, while not an organ, is the product of an organ.

Other organs have been bought and sold. In the 1930s, a rich Italian man bought a testis from a young Neapolitan and had it transplanted into himself. (He not only wanted the product but he wanted to be a distributor as well.) In the last few years there have been episodes where families have declined to give their own kidneys to dying relatives and have sought out and paid volunteer donors. Such cases have not been common, but they have occurred.

The larger problem, the danger, arises from the simple matter of scarcity. There are thousands of people waiting for kidneys and corneas today. The reason that these two organs are particularly coveted is because they have most frequently been transplanted – successfully. Thanks to dialysis machines, potential kidney recipients (some of them ... others are left to die because of shortages of dialysis machines, personnel, and funds) can be kept alive, but their lives are far from normal. In many situations they border on the desperate, so much so that kidney dialysis centres have reported a so-called 'Holiday Syndrome.' What that means is that when a holiday weekend approaches, the patients' spirits rise as they anticipate the rush of auto accidents and the victims who may supply the eagerly awaited and desperately needed organs.

The tragedy in this situation is that the solution to the problem is already within our grasp. Medical technology has advanced to the point where approximately seven per cent of all cadaver kidneys are suitable for transplant (and the figure is much higher for corneas), if they are taken from the donor body within an hour of death. But instead of being put to this noble use, these organs are regularly delivered to the worms or to the fires of the crematorium because of legal mumbo jumbo whose origins lie in the dark ages of English law. For back in those times corpses came under the jurisdiction of the ecclesiastical rather than civil law. It seems inconceivable that such a legacy should limit our lives today. But it does.

However, most, if not all, states have now passed the Uniform Anatomical Gift Act. This law has helped to provide cadavers for medical schools (whose supply was already adequate), but it has not helped in rectifying the sad need for useful 'live' organs for transplant purposes. An alternate approach, by which all cadaver organs would be immediately available for salvage unless the deceased or the next of kin had made prior refusal, has been proposed. But alas, the wheels of change turn agonizingly slowly, and potential recipients are allowed to die while organs are wasted in the ground. Hard questions remain to be answered: such as an acceptable definition of death, and the legal rights of an individual after death. But such difficulties should not preclude a solution to the egregiously wasteful practice of discarding valuable human resources.

The problem of organ scarcity for transplantation represents only one flagrant example of the failure of society in general and medicine in particular to anticipate the social, legal, and ethical ramifications of a technological innovation. For some inexplicable reason, society waits to the very end before creating appropriate policy to pick up the pieces and make sense out of chaos. And in the instance of transplantation, failure to recognize mounting problems and enact appropriate solutions will certainly open Pandora's box, with its countless unconscionable possibilities: the Stark *et al.* of my fiction suggest only possible, execrable aberrations.

For those readers who are interested in delving into the complex problems of organs for transplantation, I recommend two excellent articles which are delightfully illuminating, despite the fact that they appeared in law journals. This is not to cast aspersions on law journals, but rather to emphasize that the lay individual will find these articles very readable: J. Dukeminier, 'Supplying Organs for Transplantation,' *Michigan Law Review*, vol. 68 (April 1970), pp811–66; D. Sanders and J. Dukeminier, 'Medical Advance and Legal Lag: Hemodialysis and Kidney Transplantation,' *UCLA Law Review*, vol. 15 (1968), pp357–413.

For those who are interested in medical policy and its phlegmatic character, combined with some positive suggestions for future change, I recommend: J. Katz and M. Capron, *Catastrophic Diseases: Who Decides What?* Russell Sage Foundation, 1975. This is an excellent, thought-provoking book, probably years ahead of its time. Its only drawback is that not enough people in positions of power in medicine will read it.

A final word about women in medicine: I must admit that the research I did on the subject (there is not much available) caused me to alter my opinions. I now have a heightened regard for female physicians and female medical students. I recognize that their training experiences are much more difficult and stressful than those of their male counterparts. Things are getting better in this respect, but at a snail's pace. The article I found the most illuminating is: M. Notman and C.

Nadelson, 'Medicine: Career Conflict for Women,' *American Journal of Psychiatry*, vol. 130 (October 1973) pp1123–26.

Robin Cook MD, August 1976.

ABDUCTION

CHAPTER ONE

An odd vibration roused Perry Bergman from a restless sleep, and he was instantly filled with a strange foreboding. The unpleasant murmur put him in mind of fingernails scraping down a blackboard. He shuddered and threw off his thin blanket. As he stood up, the vibration continued. With his bare feet on the steel deck it now reminded him of a dentist's drill. Just beneath it he could detect the normal hum of the ship's generators and the whir of its air conditioning fans.

"What the hell?" he said aloud, even though there was no one within earshot to provide an answer. He'd helicoptered out to the ship, the *Benthic Explorer*, the previous evening after a long flight from Los Angeles to New York to Ponta Delgada on the Azorean island of San Miguel. Between time zone changes and a long briefing about the technical problems his crew was experiencing, he was understandably exhausted. He didn't like being awakened after only four hours of sleep, especially by such a jarring vibration.

Snatching the ship's phone from its cradle he punched in the number for the bridge. While he waited for the connection to go through he peered out the porthole of his V.I.P. compartment on his tiptoes. At five foot seven Perry didn't think of himself as short, just not tall.

Outside, the sun had barely cleared the horizon. The ship cast a long shadow across the Atlantic. Perry was looking west over a misty, calm sea whose surface resembled a vast expanse of beaten pewter. The water undulated sinuously with low, widely separated swells. The serenity of the scene belied the goings-on below the surface. The *Benthic Explorer* was being held in a fixed position by computer driven commands to her propellers as well as to her bow and stern thrusters over a portion of the volcanically and seismically active Mid-Atlantic Ridge, a twelve-thousand-mile-long, jagged range of mountains that bisects the ocean. With the constant extrusion of enormous quantities of lava, submarine explosions of steam, and frequent mini earthquakes, the submerged cordillera was the antithesis of the ocean surface's summer tranquillity.

"Bridge," a bored voice responded in Perry's ear.

"Where's Captain Jameson?" Perry snapped.

"In his bunk as far as I know," the voice said casually.

"What the hell is that vibration?" Perry demanded.

"Beats me, but it's not coming from the ship's power plant if that's what you're asking. Otherwise I would have heard from the engine room. It's probably just the drilling rig. Want me to call the drilling van?"

Perry didn't answer; he just slammed the phone down. He couldn't believe whoever was on the bridge wasn't moved to investigate the vibration on his own. Didn't he care? It irked Perry to no end that his ship was being operated so unprofessionally, but he decided to deal with that issue later. Instead he tried to focus on getting into his jeans and heavy wool turtleneck. He didn't need someone to tell him the vibration might be coming from the drilling rig. That was pretty obvious. After all, it was difficulty with the drilling operation that had brought Perry here from Los Angeles.

Perry knew that he had gambled the future of Benthic Marine on the current project: drilling into a magma chamber within a seamount west of the Azores. It was a project that was not under contract, meaning the company was spending instead of being paid, and the cash hemorrhage was horrendous. Perry's motivation for the undertaking rested on his belief that the feat would capture the public's imagination, focus interest on undersea exploration, and rocket Benthic Marine to the forefront of oceanographic research. Unfortunately, the endeavor was not going as planned.

Once he was dressed, Perry glanced in the mirror over the sink in the cubbyhole bathroom. A few years ago he wouldn't have taken the time. But things had changed. Now that he was in his forties, he found that the tousled look that used to work for him made him look old, or at best tired. His hair was thinning and he required glasses to read, but he still had a winning smile. Perry was proud of his straight, white teeth, especially since they emphasized the tan he worked hard to maintain. Satisfied by his reflection, he dashed out of his compartment and ran down the passageway. As he passed the doors to the captain's and first mate's quarters, Perry was tempted to pound on them to vent his irritation. He knew the metal surfaces would reverberate like kettledrums, yanking the sleeping occupants from their slumbers. As the founder, president, and largest shareholder of Benthic Marine, he expected people to be more on their toes while he was on board. Could he be the only one concerned enough to check this vibration out?

Emerging onto the deck, Perry tried to locate the

source of the strange hum, which was now merged with the sound of the operating drill rig. The *Benthic Explorer* was a four-hundred-fifty-foot vessel with a twenty-story drilling derrick amidship that bridged a central bay. In addition to the drilling rig, the ship boasted a saturation diving complex, a deep-sea submersible, and several remote-controlled mobile camera sleds, each mounted with an impressive array of still cameras and television camcorders. Combining this equipment and an extensive lab, the *Benthic Explorer* gave its parent company, Benthic Marine, the ability to carry out a wide range of oceanographic studies and operations.

Perry saw the door to the drilling van open. A giant of a man appeared. He yawned and stretched before hoisting the straps of his coveralls over his shoulders and donning his yellow hard hat, which had SHIFT SUPERVISOR written in block letters over the visor. Still stiff with sleep, he headed in the direction of the rotary table. He was obviously in no hurry despite the vibration coursing through the ship.

Quickening his pace Perry caught up to the man just as two other deckhands joined him.

"It's been doing this for about twenty minutes, chief," one of the roustabouts yelled over the noise of the drilling rig. All three men ignored Perry.

The shift foreman grunted as he pulled on a pair of heavy work gloves and blithely walked out across the narrow metal grate spanning the central well. His sangfroid impressed Perry. The catwalk seemed flimsy and there was only a low, thin handrail to block the fifty-foot drop to the ocean surface below. Reaching the rotary table, the supervisor leaned out and placed both gloved hands about the rotating shaft. He didn't try to grip it tightly but rather let it rotate across his palms. He cocked his head to the side while he tried to interpret the tremor transmitted up the pipe. It took only a moment.

"Stop the rig!" the giant shouted.

One of the roustabouts dashed back to the exterior control panel. Within a moment the rotary table came to a clanking halt and the grating vibration ceased. The supervisor walked back and stepped onto the deck.

"Chrissake! The bit's busted again," he said with an expression of disgust. "This is fast becoming a god-damned joke."

"The joke is that we've only drilled for two or three feet in the last four or five days," the remaining roust-about said.

"Shut up!" the giant intoned. "Get the hell over there and raise the drill string to the well head!"

The second roustabout joined the first. Almost immediately there was a new sound of powerful machinery as the winches were engaged to do the fore-man's bidding. The ship shuddered.

"How can you be sure the bit's broken?" Perry yelled over the new noise.

The foreman looked down at him. "Experience," he yelled then turned and strode off toward the ship's stern.

Perry had to run to catch up. Each of the foreman's strides was double his. Perry tried to ask another question but the foreman either didn't hear or was ignoring him. They reached the companionway and the foreman started up, taking the stairs three at a time. Two decks above he entered a passageway and then stopped outside a compartment door. The name on the door was MARK DAVIDSON, OPERATIONS COMMANDER. The foreman knocked loudly. At first the only response was a fit of coughing but then a voice called out to come in.

Perry pressed into the small compartment behind the foreman.

"Bad news, chief," the foreman said. "I'm afraid the drill bit's busted again."

"What the hell time is it?" Mark asked. He ran his fingers through his messy hair. He was sitting on the side of his bunk dressed in skivvies. His facial features had a puffy look, and his voice was thick with sleep. Without waiting for a reply he reached for a pack of cigarettes. The air in the room was imbued with stale smoke.

"It's around oh-six-hundred," the foreman said.

"Jesus," Mark said. His eyes then focused on Perry. Surprise registered. He blinked. "Perry? What are you doing up?"

"There's no way I could have slept through that vibration," Perry said.

"What vibration?" Mark asked. He looked back at the foreman, who was staring at Perry.

"Are you Perry Bergman?" the foreman asked.

"Last time I checked," Perry said. Sensing the foreman's unease gave him a modicum of satisfaction.

"Sorry," the foreman said.

"Forget it," Perry said magnanimously.

"Was the drill train rattling?" Mark asked.

The foreman nodded. "Just like the last four times, maybe a little worse."

"We only have one more diamond-stubbed tungsten carbide bit left," Mark lamented.

"You don't have to tell me," the foreman said.

"What's the depth?" Mark asked.

"Not much change from yesterday," the foreman said.

"We've got out thirteen hundred thirty-three feet of pipe. Since the bottom is just shy of a thousand feet and there's no sediment, we're down into the rock about three hundred and forty feet, give or take a few inches."

"This is what I was explaining to you last night," Mark said to Perry. "We were doing fine until four days ago. Since then we've gone nowhere, maybe two or three feet tops, despite using up four drill bits."

"So you think you've hit up against a hard layer?" Perry said, thinking he had to say something.

Mark laughed sarcastically. "Hard ain't the word. We're using diamond-studded bits with the straightest flutes made! Worse yet is we got another hundred feet of the same stuff, whatever it is, before we get to the magma chamber, at least according to our ground-penetrating radar. At this rate we'll be here for ten years."

"Did the lab analyze the rock caught in the last broken bit?" the foreman asked.

"Yeah, they did," Mark said. "It's a type of rock they'd never seen before. At least according to Tad Messenger. It's composed of a type of crystalline olivine that he thinks might have a microscopic matrix of diamond. I wish we could get a bigger sample. One of the biggest problems of drilling in open sea is not getting a return of circulated drilling fluids. It's like drilling in the dark."

"Could we get a corer down there?" Perry asked.

"A lot of good that would do if we can't make any headway with a diamond-studded bit."

"How about piggybacking it with the diamond bit. If we could get a real sample of this stuff we're trying to drill through, maybe we could figure out a reasonable game plan. We got too much invested in this operation to give up without a real fight."

Mark looked at the foreman, who shrugged. Then he looked back at Perry. "Hey, you're the boss."

"At least for now," Perry said. He wasn't joking. He wondered how long he was going to be the boss if the project came to naught.

"All right," Mark said. He put his cigarette down on the edge of an overflowing ashtray. "Pull the drill bit up to the well head."

"The boys are already doing that," the foreman said.

"Get the last diamond drill bit from supply," Mark said. He reached for his phone. "I'll have Larry Nelson get the saturation dive system up and running and the submersible in the water. We'll replace the bit and see if we can get a better sample of what it is we're drilling into."

"Aye, aye," the foreman said. He turned and left while Mark lifted his phone to his ear to call the diving commander.

Perry started to leave himself when Mark held up his hand to motion for him to stay. After finishing his call to Larry Nelson, Mark looked up at Perry.

"There's something I didn't bring up last night at the briefing," he said. "But I think you ought to know about it."

Perry swallowed. His mouth had gone dry. He didn't like Mark's tone of voice. It sounded like more bad news.

"This might be nothing," Mark continued, "but when we used the ground-penetrating radar to study this layer we're trying to drill through like I mentioned before, there was an unexpected incidental finding. I got the data here on my desk. Do you want to see it?"

"Just tell me," Perry said. "I can look at the data later."

"The radar suggested that the contents of the magma chamber might not be what we thought from the original seismic studies. It might not be liquid."

"You're joking!" This new information added to Perry's misgivings. It was by accident the previous summer that the *Benthic Explorer* had discovered the seamount they were presently drilling. What was so amazing about the find was that as part of the Mid-Atlantic ridge, the area had been extensively studied by Geosat, the U.S. Navy's gravity measuring satellite used to create contour maps of the ocean bottom. Yet somehow this particular undersea mountain had evaded Geosat's radar.

Although the *Benthic Explorer* crew had been eager to get home they'd paused long enough to make several passes over the mysterious mount. With the ship's sophisticated sonar they did a cursory study of the guyot's internal structure. To everyone's surprise the results were as unexpected as the mountain's presence. The seamount appeared to be a particularly thin-skinned, quiescent volcano whose liquid core was a mere four hundred feet beneath the ocean floor. Even more astounding was that the substance within the magma chamber had sound propagation characteristics identical to those of the Mohorovičić discontinuity, or Moho, the mysterious boundary between the earth's crust and the earth's mantle. Since no one had ever been able to get magma from the Moho, although both Americans and Russians had tried during the Cold War, Perry decided to go back and drill into the mountain in hopes that Benthic Marine might be the first organization to sample the molten material. He reasoned that the material's analysis would shed light on the structure and perhaps even the origin of the earth. But now his *Benthic Explorer*'s operations commander was telling him that the original seismic data might be wrong!

"The magma chamber may be empty," Mark said.

"Empty?" Perry blurted.

"Well, not empty," Mark corrected himself. "Filled with some kind of compressed gas, or maybe steam. I know extrapolating data at this depth is pushing ground-penetrating radar technology beyond its limits. In fact a lot of people would say the results I'm talking about are just artifact, sort'a off the graph so to speak. But the fact that the radar data doesn't jibe with the seismic worries me just the same. I mean, I'd just hate to make this huge effort only to get nothing but a bunch of superheated steam. Nobody's going to be happy with that, least of all your investors."

Perry chewed the inside of his cheek while he mulled over Mark's concern. He began to wish he'd never heard about Sea Mount Olympus, which was the name the crew had given the flat-topped, underwater mountain that they were trying to poke a hole into.

"Have you mentioned this to Dr. Newell?" Perry asked. Dr. Suzanne Newell was the senior oceanographer on the *Benthic Explorer*. "Has she seen this radar data you're talking about?"

"Nobody's seen it," Mark said. "I just happened to notice the shadow on my computer screen yesterday when I was preparing for your arrival. I was thinking about bringing it up at your briefing last night but decided to wait to talk to you in private. In case you haven't noticed, there's a bit of a morale problem out here with certain members of the crew. A lot of people have begun to think that drilling into this guyot's a bit like tilting at windmills. People are starting to talk about calling it quits and getting home to their families before the summer's out. I didn't want to add fuel to the fire."

Perry felt weak-kneed. He pulled Mark's chair out from his desk and sat down heavily. He rubbed his eyes. He was tired, hungry, and discouraged. He could kick himself for betting so much of his company's future based on so little reliable data, but the discovery had seemed so fortuitous. He'd felt compelled to act.

"Hey, I don't like to be the bearer of bad news," Mark said. "We'll do what you suggested. We'll try to get a better idea of the rock we're drilling. Let's not get overly discouraged."

"It's kind of hard not to," Perry said, "considering how much it is costing Benthic Marine to keep the ship out here. Maybe we should just cut our losses."

"Why don't you get yourself something to eat?" Mark suggested. "No sense making any snap decisions on an empty stomach. In fact, I'll join you if you can wait for me to shower. Hell! Before you know it we'll have some more information about this crap we've hit up against. Maybe then it will be clear what we ought to do."

"How long will it take to change the bit?" Perry asked.

"The submersible can be in the water in an hour," Mark said. "They'll take the bit and the tools down to the well head. Getting the divers down there takes longer because they have to be compressed before we lower the bell. That'll take a couple of hours, more if they get any compression pains. Changing the bit is not hard. The whole operation should take three or four hours, maybe less."

Perry got to his feet with effort. "Give me a call in my compartment when you're ready to eat." He reached for the door.

"Hey, wait a sec!" Mark said with sudden enthusiasm. "I got an idea that might give you a boost. Why don't you go down with the submersible? It's reputed to be beautiful down there on the guyot at least according to Suzanne. Even the submersible pilot, Donald Fuller, the ex-naval line officer, who's usually a tight-lipped, straight-arrow kind of guy, says the scenery is outstanding."

"What can be so great about a flat-topped, submerged mountain?" Perry asked.

"I haven't gone down myself," Mark admitted. "But it has something to do with the geology of the area. You know, being part of the Mid-Atlantic Ridge and all. But ask Newell or Fuller! I tell you, they're going to be ecstatic about being asked to go back down. With the halogen lights on the submersible and the clarity of the deep sea water, they said the visibility is between two and three hundred feet."

Perry nodded. Taking a dive wasn't a bad idea since it would undoubtedly take his mind off the current situation and make him feel like he was doing something. Besides, he'd only been in the submersible once, off Santa Catalina Island when Benthic Marine took delivery of the sub, and that had been a memorable experience. At least he'd get a chance to see this mountain that was causing him so much aggravation.

"Who should I tell I'll be part of the crew?" Perry asked.

"I'll take care of it," Mark said. He stood up and pulled off his T-shirt. "I'll just let Larry Nelson know."

CHAPTER TWO

Richard Adams pulled a pair of baggy long johns from his ship's locker and kicked the door closed. Once he had the underwear on he donned his black knit watch stander's hat. Thus attired he left his compartment and banged on Louis Mazzola's and Michael Donaghue's doors. Both responded with a slurry of expletives. The curses had lost their sting since they constituted such a large percentage of these crew members' vocabularies. Richard, Louis, and Michael, professional divers, were the hard drinking, hard living sort who regularly risked their lives by welding underwater if that were required, or blowing things up like reefs, or changing bits during submarine drilling operations. They were underwater hard-laborers and proud of it.

The three had trained together in the U.S. Navy, becoming fast friends as well as accomplished members of the Navy's UDT force. All had aspired to become Navy Seals, but that turned out not to be in the cards. Their predilection for beer and fistfights far exceeded that of their fellows. That the three had grown up with alcoholic, brutish, abusive, bigoted, blue-collar, wife-beating fathers was an explanation for their behavior, but not an excuse. Far from being embarrassed by their patriarchal examples, the three looked upon their harsh childhoods as a natural progression to true manhood. None of them ever gave even a passing thought to the old adage Like father like son.

Manliness was a critical virtue for all three men. They were ruthless in punishing anyone they perceived as being less manly than they who had the nerve to enter a bar in which they were drinking. Their judgment fell heavily on "shyster" lawyers and fat-assed Army personnel, they also condemned anyone they deemed a dork, a nerd, or a queer. Homosexuality bothered them the most, and as far as they were concerned the military's "don't ask don't tell" policy was ridiculous and a personal affront.

Although the Navy tended to be lenient with divers and tolerant behavior it wouldn't brook with other personnel, Richard Adams and his buddies pushed the envelope too far. One hot August afternoon the men retreated to their favorite hole-in-the-wall diver's bar on San Diego's Point Loma. It had been an exhausting day of difficult diving. After numerous rounds of boiler makers and an equal number of arguments about the current baseball season, they were shocked and dismayed to see a couple of Army guys jauntily walk in. According to the divers at their court-martial, these men proceeded to "love it up" in one of the back booths.

The fact that the soldiers were officers only made the divers' outrage all the more impassioned. They never asked themselves why a couple of Army officers might be in San Diego, a known Navy and Marine town. Richard, their perennial ringleader, was the first to approach the booth. He asked—sarcastically—if he could join the orgy. The Army men, mistaking Richard's meaning which was for them to get the hell out, laughed, denied any orgy of any sort, and offered to buy him and his friends a round of celebratory drinks. The result was a one-sided brawl that put both Army officers into Balboa Naval Hospital. It also put Richard and his friends into the brig and eventually out of the Navy. The Army men happened to have been members of JAG, the Army's Judge Advocate General corps.

"Come on, you assholes!" Richard yelled when the others still hadn't appeared. He glanced at his diving watch. He knew Nelson would be pissed. His orders on the phone had been to get the diving command center ASAP.

The first to appear was Louis Mazzola. He was almost a head shorter than Richard, who stood six feet. Richard thought of Louis as a bowling ball kind of guy. He had meaty features, an omnipresent five o'clock shadow, and short dark hair that lay flat on his round head. He appeared to have no neck; his trapezius angled out from his skull without any indentation.

"What's the hurry?" Louis whined.

"We're going on a dive!" Richard said.

"So what else is new?" Louis complained.

Michael's door opened. He was somewhere between Richard's rawboned silhouette and Louis's stockiness. Like his friends he was well muscled and in obviously good shape. He was also equivalently slovenly, dressed in the same baggy long johns. But in contrast to the others he had on a Red Sox baseball hat with the visor angled off sideways. Michael hailed from Chelsea, Massachusetts, and was an avid Sox and Bruins fan.

Michael opened his mouth to complain about being awakened, but Richard ignored him and set out for the main deck. Louis did likewise. Michael shrugged and then followed. As they descended the main companionway,

Louis called ahead to Richard: "Hey, Adams, you got the cards?"

"Of course I got the cards," Richard shot back over his shoulder. "Have you got your checkbook?"

"Screw you," Louis said. "You haven't beat me in the last four dives."

"It's been a plan, man," Richard returned. "I've been setting you up."

"Screw the cards," Michael said. "Have you got your porno mags, Mazzola?"

"You think I'd go on a dive without them?" Louis questioned. "Hell! I'd rather forget my fins."

"I hope you checked to make sure you've got the mags with the chicks and not the dudes," Michael teased.

Louis stopped abruptly. Michael bumped into him.

"What the hell are you saying?" Louis growled.

"I'm just checking to make sure you brought the right ones," Michael said with a wry smile. "I might want to borrow them, and I don't want to find myself looking at any shlongs."

Louis's hand shot out and he grabbed a handful of Michael's long john top. Michael responded by grabbing Louis's forearm with his left hand and balling his right hand into a fist. Before it could go farther, Richard intervened.

"Come on, you dorks!" Richard yelled, inserting himself between his two friends. With an upward blow he knocked Louis's arm aside. There was a tearing sound, and Louis's hand came away with a torn swatch of Michael's undershirt clutched in his fingers. Like a bull seeing red, Louis tried to push past Richard. When that didn't work he tried to grab Michael's top over Richard's shoulder. Michael howled with laughter and ducked away.

"Mazzola, you meathead!" Richard yelled. "He's just trying to pull your chain. Chill out, for chrissake!"

"Bastard!" Louis hissed. He threw the swatch of torn fabric he'd yanked out of Michael's undershirt at his tormentor. Michael laughed again.

"Come on!" Richard said with disgust as he continued down the passageway. Michael reached down and picked up the piece of fabric. When he pretended to stick it back onto his chest, Louis laughed in spite of himself. Then they ran to catch up to Richard.

When the divers emerged onto the deck they could see that the derrick was raising the pipe.

"They must have broken the bit again," Michael said. Both Richard and Louis nodded. "At least we know what we'll be doing."

They entered the diving van and draped themselves over three folding chairs near the door. This was where Larry Nelson, the man who ran all the diving operations, had his desk. Behind him, on the right-hand side of the van and extending all the way down to the far end, was the diving console. Here were all the readouts, gauges, and controls for operating the diving system. On the left side of the van's dash were the controls and monitors for the camera sleds. Also on the left side was a window that looked out on the central well of the ship. It was down this central well that the diving bell was lowered.

The diving system on the *Benthic Explorer* was a saturation system, meaning the divers were expected to absorb the maximum amount of inert gas during any given dive. That meant that the decompression time required to rid themselves of the inert gas would be the same no matter how long they stayed at pressure. The system was composed of three cylindrical deck decompression chambers (DDC), each twelve feet wide and twenty feet long. The DDCs were hooked together like enormous sausages with double pressure hatches separating them. Within each were four bunks, several fold-down tables, a toilet, a sink, and a shower.

Each DDC also had an entrance port on the side and a pressure hatch on the top where the diving bell, or personal transfer capsule (PTC), could mate. Compression and decompression of the divers took place in the DDC. Once they had reached the equivalent pressure of the depth where they were to work, they climbed up into the PTC, which was then detached and lowered into water. When the PTC reached the appropriate depth the divers opened the hatch through which they'd entered the bell and swam to the designated workstation. While in the water the divers were tethered with an umbilical cord containing hoses for their breathing gas, for hot water to heat their neoprene dry suits, for sensing wires, and for communication cables. Since the divers on the *Benthic Explorer* used full face masks, communication was possible although difficult due to voice distortion in the helium-oxygen mixture they breathed. The sensing wires carried information about each diver's heart rate, breathing rate, and breathing gas oxygen pressure. All three levels were monitored continuously on a real-time basis.

Larry looked up from his desk and regarded his second team of divers with disdain. He couldn't believe how slovenly, brazen, and unprofessional they invariably appeared. He noted Michael's jaunty baseball hat and ripped shirt, but he didn't say anything. Similar to the Navy, he tolerated behavior in the divers that he would not tolerate with other members of his team. Three other divers who were equally aggravating and obstreperous were still in one of the DDCs, decompressing from the last dive on the well head. When diving to almost a thousand feet, decompression time is measured in days not hours.

"I'm sorry to have awakened you clowns from your beauty sleep," Larry said. "It took you long enough to get down here."

"I had to floss my teeth," Richard said.

"And I had to do my nails," Louis said. He flapped his hand in a swishy, loose wrist fashion.

Michael rolled his eyes with mock disgust.

"Hey, don't start!" Louis growled while eyeing Michael. He pointed one of his meaty fingers in his friend's face. Michael batted it away.

"All right, listen up, you animals!" Larry yelled. "Try to control yourselves. This is going to be a nine-hundred-and-eighty-foot dive to inspect and change the drill bit."

"Oh, something new, eh, chief?" Richard said in a high, squeaky voice. "This is the fifth time this dive's been done and the third time for us. Let's get on with it."

"Shut up and listen," Larry commanded. "There's something new involved. You're going to be piggy-backing a corer on the diamond bit so that we can see if we can get a decent sample of whatever the hell we're trying to drill into."

"Sounds good," Richard said.

"We're going to speed up compression time," Larry said. "There's some brass aboard who's in a hurry for results. We're going to see if we can get you down to depth in a couple of hours. Now I want to hear immediately if there's any joint pain. I don't want anybody playing macho diver. Understand?"

All three divers nodded.

"We'll lock in chow as soon as it comes up from the galley," Larry continued. "But I want you guys in your bunks for the compression, and that means no screwing around and no fights."

"We're going to play cards," Louis said.

"If you play cards do it from your bunks," Larry said. "And I repeat: no fights. If there are any, the cards are coming out. Do I make myself clear?"

Larry eyed each man in turn, who averted his gaze. No one contested the terms of the arrangement.

"I'm going to take this rare silence as acquiescence," Larry said. "Now, Adams, you'll be red diver. Donaghue, you'll be green diver. Mazzola, you'll be bell diver."

Richard and Michael cheered and then leaned across to one another and high-fived. Louis blew out disgustedly through pursed lips. The bell diver's job during the dive was to remain inside the PTC to play out the tethers for the red and green divers and watch the gauges; he did not enter the water except in an emergency. Although this position was safer, it was looked down upon by divers. The designations of red and green diver were used to avoid any confusion in communications with topside that might occur if given or surnames were used. On the *Benthic Explorer* red diver was recognized to be the on-site leader.

Larry reached down on his desk and picked up a clipboard. He handed it over to Richard. "Here's the predive checklist, red diver. Now get your asses in DDC1. I want to start compression in fifteen minutes."

Richard took the clipboard and led the way out of the van. Once outside, Louis began a long lament about being bell diver, complaining that he'd been bell diver on the last dive.

"I guess the chief thinks you're the best at it," Richard said while giving Donaghue a wink. He knew he was goading Louis. But he couldn't help it. He felt relieved that he'd not been selected, since it was his turn.

As the group passed the occupied DDC3 each man took the time to glance through the tiny viewing port and give a thumbs-up sign to the three occupants, who still had several more days of decompression ahead of them. Divers might fight with each other at times, but they also shared a close camaraderie. They respected each other because of the inherent risks. The isolation and danger of being on a saturation dive was ironically similar in certain respects with being in a satellite circling the globe. If a problem occurred it could be hairy, and it was difficult to get you back home.

At DDC1 Richard was first through the narrow round entrance port on the cylinder's side. It required him to grasp a horizontal metal bar, lift his legs, and enter feet first by wiggling through the aperture.

The interior was utilitarian, with the bunks at one end and emergency breathing apparatuses hanging from the walls. All the diving gear, including the neoprene suits, weight belts, gloves, and hoods, and other paraphernalia, was in a pile between the bunks. The diving masks were up in the diving bell with all the hoses and communication lines. At the other end of the DDC was the exposed shower, toilet, and sink. Saturation diving was a communal affair of the first order. There was no privacy whatsoever.

Louis and Michael entered right after Richard. Louis climbed directly up inside the diving bell while Michael started sorting through the material on the floor. As Richard called out the names of individual pieces of equipment, either Louis or Michael would yell out whether it was present or not, and Richard would check it off on his list. Anything not present was immediately handed through the open port by one of the watch standers.

When the four pages of checklist were completed, Richard gave a thumbs-up to the dive supervisor via the camcorder mounted on the ceiling.

"O.K., red diver," the supervisor said over the intercom, "close and dog the entrance hatch and prepare to start compression."

Richard did as he was told. Almost immediately there was the hiss of the compressed gas, and the needle on the analog pressure gauge began to rise. The divers happily took to their bunks. Richard pulled the worn deck of playing cards from his long john pocket.

CHAPTER THREE

Perry emerged from the interior of the ship and stepped out onto the grate that formed the deck of the fantail. He was dressed in a maroon jogging suit over sweats—Mark's suggestion. He told Perry it was what he'd worn the last time he'd been in the submersible. The quarters were tight, so the more comfortable the clothes, the better, and layers were good because it could be cool. The outside water temperature was only around forty degrees, and it was foolish to expend too much battery power on heat.

At first Perry found walking on the metal grate disconcerting since he could see down into the ocean surface some fifty feet below. The water had a cold, gray-green look. Perry shivered despite the pleasant ambient temperature, and he wondered if he should go on the dive after all. The strange foreboding that he'd awakened with returned, raising the hackles on the back of his neck. Although he wasn't claustrophobic per se, he'd never been comfortable when he found himself in a tight space like the interior of the submersible. In fact one of Perry's most horrid memories as a child was having been caught hiding under the covers by his older brother. His brother pounced on him instead of pulling the covers back and, for a time that seemed like an eternity, wouldn't let him out. Occasionally Perry still had nightmares that he was back in that cloth prison with the desperate sensation he was about to smother.

Perry stopped and stared at the little submarine, which was sitting on chocks at the very stern of the ship. Angled over it was a large derrick capable of swinging the vessel out over the water and lowering it to the surface. Workers were swarming around the craft like bees hovering around a hive. Perry knew enough to recognize they were involved in a predive check before launch.

Perry was relieved that the vessel looked considerably larger than it had when it was in the water, a fact that appeased his recently awakened claustrophobia. The submersible was not as tiny as many were. It was fifty feet long with a twelve-foot beam, and bulbous in shape, like a bloated, HY-140 steel sausage with a fiberglass superstructure. There were four view ports made of eight-inch-thick, conical sections of Plexiglas: two forward and one to either side. Hydraulic manipulator arms, folded up under the bow, made it look like an enormous crustacean. The hull was painted scarlet with white lettering along the sides of the sail. Its name was *Oceanus*, after the Greek god of the outer sea.

"Handsome little devil, isn't she?" a voice said.

Perry turned. Mark had come up behind him.

"Maybe it'd be better if I didn't go on the dive after all," Perry said, trying to sound casual.

"And why is that?" Mark asked.

"I don't want to be a bother," Perry said. "I came out here to be a help, not a hindrance. I'm sure the pilot would prefer not to have the equivalent of a tourist tagging along."

"Poppycock!" Mark said without hesitation. "Both Donald and Suzanne are thrilled you're coming. I spoke with them not twenty minutes ago, and they said as much. In fact that's Donald on that scaffolding, supervising the connection to the launching crane. I understand you've never met him."

Perry followed Mark's pointing finger. Donald Fuller was an African American with a shaved head, a neat pencil-line mustache, and an impressively muscled frame. He was dressed in crisply ironed dark blue coveralls with epaulets and shiny name tag. Even from a distance Perry could appreciate the man's martial bearing, especially when he heard his deep, baritone voice and his clipped, no-nonsense manner as he called out commands. During the current operation there was no doubt who was in charge.

"Come on," Mark urged before Perry could respond. "Let me introduce you."

Reluctantly, Perry allowed himself to be led over to the submersible. It was painfully obvious that he would not be able to get out of diving on the *Oceanus* without a significant loss of face. He'd have to admit to his fears, and he hardly thought that would be appropriate. Besides, he had enjoyed his first ride on the sub even though that had been done in only a hundred feet of water just outside of the harbor on Santa Catalina, a far cry from the middle of the Atlantic Ocean.

Once Donald was satisfied with the submersible's connection to the hoisting cable, he swung down from the scaffolding and began walking around the boat. Although the topside dive team had responsibility for the predive check, Donald wanted to make his own visual check on all the penetrations through the pressure hull. Mark and Perry caught up to him at the bow. Mark introduced Perry as the president of Benthic Marine.

Donald responded by clicking his heels and saluting. Before Perry knew what he was doing, he saluted back. Only Perry didn't know how to salute; he'd never executed the gesture in his life. He felt as pathetic as he probably looked.

"Honored to meet you, sir," Donald said. He was standing ramrod straight with his lips pressed together and his nares flared. To Perry he appeared like a warrior about to do battle.

"Pleased to meet you," Perry said. He gestured toward the *Oceanus*. "I don't want to interrupt you."

"No problem, sir," Donald snapped back.

"I also don't have to go on this dive," Perry said. "I don't want to be in the way. In fact . . ."

"You won't be in the way, sir," Donald said.

"I know this is an operational dive," Perry persisted. "I wouldn't want to take your attention away from your job."

"When I am piloting the *Oceanus*, no one takes my attention away from my job, sir!"

"I appreciate that," Perry said. "But I won't be at all offended if you feel I should stay topside. I mean, I'll understand."

"I'm looking forward to showing you the capability of this craft, sir."

"Well, thank you," Perry said, recognizing the futility of trying to excuse himself graciously.

"My pleasure, sir," Donald snapped.

"You don't have to call me sir," Perry said.

"Yes, sir!" Donald responded. Then his mouth formed into a thin smile when he realized what he'd said. "I mean, yes, Mr. Bergman."

"Call me Perry."

"Yes, sir," Donald said. Then he allowed himself a second smile when he realized he'd slipped again in so many seconds. "It's hard for me to change my ways."

"I can see that," Perry said. "I guess it's not a wild guess that you got your experience for this type of work in the armed forces."

"That's affirmative," Donald said. "Twenty-five years in the submarine service."

"Were you an officer?" Perry asked.

"Indeed. I retired as a commander."

Perry's eyes wandered to the submersible. Now that he'd reconciled himself to the upcoming dive, he wanted reassurance. "How's the *Oceanus* been performing?"

"Flawlessly," Donald answered.

"So it's a good little ship?" Perry asked. He patted the cold steel pressure hull.

"The best," Donald said. "Better than anything I've ever piloted, and I've been in quite a few."

"Are you just being patriotic?" Perry asked.

"Not at all," Donald said. "First of all, it can go deeper than any other manned craft I've piloted. As I'm sure you know, it's got a certified operating depth of twenty thousand feet and a crush depth not until thirty-five thousand. But even that's deceiving. With the built-in safety margin, we could probably dive to the bottom of the Mariana Trench without a hitch."

Perry swallowed. Hearing the term *crush depth* brought back the shiver he'd experienced a few minutes before.

"Why don't you give Perry a quick rundown on the rest of the *Oceanus*'s statistics," Mark said. "Just to refresh his memory."

"Sure," Donald said. "But stand by for a second." He

cupped his hands around his mouth and yelled out to one of the workmen completing the predive check: "Have the TV camcorders been checked out on the inside?"

"That's an affirmative!" the worker responded.

Donald directed his attention back to Perry. "The craft's sixty-eight tons with room for two pilots, two observers, and six other passengers. We have lockout capability for divers, and we can be mated to the DDCs if the need arises. We've got life support for a maximum of two hundred sixteen hours. Power comes from silver zinc batteries. Propulsion is from a varivec propeller, but maneuverability is also enhanced with vertical and horizontal thrusters directed by twin joysticks with top-mounted thumb balls. There's short-range, narrow-beam, and side-scan sonar, ground-penetrating radar, proton magnetometer, and thermistors. Recording equipment includes silicon-intensified target video cam-corders. Communications are with FM surface radio and UQC underwater telephone. Navigation is inertial."

Donald paused while he let his eyes roam around the submersible. "I think that covers the basics. Any questions?"

"Not for the moment," Perry said quickly. He was afraid Donald might ask him a question. The only thing Perry retained out of the entire monologue was the thirty-five-thousand-foot crush depth figure.

"Ready to launch the *Oceanus*!" a voice crackled over a loudspeaker.

Donald herded Perry and Mark away from the sub. The hoisting wire became taut. With a creak the submers-ible lifted from the deck. It was kept from swinging by multiple launching lines attached at key points along the hull. A high-pitched squeak heralded the movement of the davit as it swung the boat out off the stern of the ship and started lowering it toward the water.

"Ah, here comes the good doctor," Mark said.

Perry turned briefly to look behind him. A figure was emerging through the main door into the ship's interior. Perry did a rapid doubletake. He'd only seen Suzanne Newell once before and that was when she'd presented the original seismic studies on Sea Mount Olympus. But that had been in L.A., where there was no dearth of beautiful people. Out in the middle of the ocean on the utilitarian *Benthic Explorer* with its nearly hundred percent frowzy male crew, she stood out like a lily in a patch of weeds. In her late twenties, she was vibrant and athletic looking. Dressed in coveralls similar to those worn by Donald, she gave off a stunning gender message which was the absolute antithesis of Donald's. A dark blue baseball hat, with a gold braid embroidered on the visor and BENTHIC EXPLORER sewn across the crown, was perched on top of her head. Out of the back of the hat just above the adjustment band protruded a ponytail of thick, shiny chestnut hair.

Suzanne saw the group and waved, then headed in their direction. As she approached, Perry's mouth slowly dropped open, a response that was not lost on Mark. "Not bad, huh?" Mark said.

"She's rather attractive," Perry admitted.

"Yeah, well, wait a few days," Mark said. "She gets better the longer we're out here. Quite a shape for a geophysical oceanographer, wouldn't you say?"

"I haven't met too many geophysical oceanographers," Perry said. Suddenly he thought that maybe the dive wouldn't be so bad after all.

"Too bad she isn't a medical doctor," Mark said under

his breath. "I wouldn't mind her doing a hernia check on me."

"If you'll permit me, I'll continue getting the *Oceanus* ready for the dive," Donald said.

"Of course," Mark said. "The new bit and the corer will be up shortly, and I'll have them loaded directly into the tray."

"Aye, aye, sir!" Donald said with a salute. He walked back to the edge of the fantail and looked down at the descending submersible.

"He's a bit stiff," Mark said, "but one hell of a reliable worker."

Perry wasn't listening. He couldn't take his eyes off Suzanne. She had an unmistakable spring to her step; her smile was friendly and welcoming. With her left hand she was pressing two large books against her chest.

"Mr. Perry Bergman!" Suzanne exclaimed, reaching out with her right hand. "I was delighted to hear you'd come out to the ship and am thrilled that you're going to dive with us. How are you? You must be recovering from a long flight."

"I'm just fine, thank you," Perry said while shaking hands with the oceanographer. Then he unconsciously reached up to make sure his hair was appropriately arranged over the thinning spot on the top of his head. He noted that Suzanne's teeth were as white as his own.

"After our meeting in Los Angeles I never got to tell you how pleased I was that you decided to bring *Benthic Explorer* back to Sea Mount Olympus."

"I'm glad," Perry said, forcing a smile. He was bewitched by Suzanne's eyes. He couldn't tell if they were blue or green. "I only wish the drilling were proceeding more successfully."

"I'm sorry about that," Suzanne said. "But I have to admit, from my personal, selfish perspective I'm a happy camper. The seamount is a fascinating environment, as you're about to see, and the drilling problems are getting me down there. So you won't hear any complaints from me."

"I'm glad it's making somebody happy," Perry said. "What's so fascinating about this particular seamount?"

"It's the geology," Suzanne said. "Do you know what basaltic dikes are?"

"I can't say that I do," Perry admitted. "Other than I suppose they're made out of basalt." He laughed self-consciously and decided that her eyes were a light blue tinted green by the surrounding ocean. He also realized that he liked the sparing way she used makeup. She seemed to be sporting only the slightest bit of lipstick. Cosmetics were a sore subject for Perry and his wife. She worked as a makeup artist for a movie studio and wore a significant amount herself, to Perry's chagrin. Now their eleven- and thirteen-year-old daughters were following their mother's example. The issue had become a full-blown feud that Perry had little chance of winning.

Suzanne's smile broadened. "Basalt dikes are indeed made of basalt. They are formed when molten basalt is forced up through fissures in the earth's crust. What makes some of them so intriguing is that they're geometric enough to look manmade. Wait till you see them."

"Sorry to interrupt," Donald said. "The *Oceanus* is ready to dive and we should be on board. Even in a calm sea it's dangerous to have her moored too long next to the ship."

"Yes, sir!" Suzanne said smartly. She saluted crisply but

with a lingering, mildly mocking smile. Donald was not amused. He knew she was teasing him.

Suzanne gestured for Perry to precede her down the companionway that led to a combination dive platform and launching dock. Perry started but hesitated as another involuntary shudder rippled down his spine. Despite his efforts to reassure himself about the safety of the submersible and despite his anticipation of Suzanne's pleasant company, the foreboding he'd experienced earlier came back like a cold draft through an underground crypt which is what he thought the interior of the *Oceanus* was going to feel like. A voice in the back of his mind was telling him he was crazy to lock himself up inside a boat in the middle of the Atlantic Ocean that was already sunk.

"Just a second!" Perry said. "How long is this dive going to take?"

"It can be as short as a couple of hours," Donald said, "or as long as you'd like. We usually stay down as long as the divers are in the water."

"Why do you ask?" Suzanne asked.

"Because . . ." Perry sought for an explanation. "Because I have to call back to the office."

"On Sunday?" Suzanne questioned. "Who's at the office on Sunday?"

Perry felt himself blush anew. Between the night flights from New York to the Azores he'd gotten his days mixed up. He laughed hollowly and tapped the side of his head. "I forgot it was Sunday. It must be early Alzheimer's."

"Let's move out!" Donald announced before descending to the dive platform below.

Perry followed, one step at a time, feeling like a ridiculous coward. Then, despite his better judgment, he inched across the swaying gangplank. It was shocking how much motion was involved in what appeared to be a calm sea.

The gangplank led directly to the top of the *Oceanus*'s sail. The deck of the submersible was already awash since it was close to being neutrally buoyant. With some difficulty Perry got himself through the hatch. As he worked his way down into the sub he had to press tight against the steel ladder's icy cold rungs.

The interior was as tight a space as Mark had warned. Perry began to doubt the claims that there was room for ten people. They'd have to be packed like sardines. Contributing to the cramped atmosphere the walls of the front of the sub were lined with gauges, LCD readouts, and toggle switches. There wasn't a square inch without a dial or knob. The four viewing ports seemed tiny within the profusion of electronic equipment. The only positive was that the air smelled clean. In the background Perry could make out the hum of a ventilation fan.

Donald directed Perry to a low-slung chair directly behind his on the port side. In front of the pilot's seat were several large CRT monitors whose computers could construct virtual images of the sea floor to help in navigation. Donald was using the FM radio to talk with Larry Nelson in the dive control van as he continued the predive check of the equipment and electrical systems.

Perry heard the hatch close above with a thud followed by a distinctive click. A few moments later Suzanne dropped down from the sail with a good deal more agility than Perry had exhibited. She'd even managed to do it with the two large books in hand. She proceeded to hand them to Perry.

"I brought these for you," she said. "The thick one is

on oceanic marine life and the other is on marine geology.
I thought it might be fun for you to look up some of the
things we'll be seeing. We don't want you to get bored."

"That was thoughtful," Perry commented. Little did
Suzanne realize, he was far too anxious to be bored. He
felt the way he did when he was about to take off in an
airplane: there was always the chance that the next few
minutes would be his last.

Suzanne sat down in the starboard pilot's seat. Soon
she began flipping toggle switches and calling out the
results to Donald. It was apparent the two worked as a
team. Once Suzanne joined in the predive check,
haunting pinging sounds began reverberating through
the confined space. It was a unique sound that Perry
associated with old World War II submarine movies.

Perry shivered again. He closed his eyes for a moment
and tried not to think about his childhood trauma of
being pinned under the covers by his brother. But the
ploy didn't work. He looked out the view port to his left
and struggled to comprehend why he felt he was making
the worst decision in his life by taking this short, routine
dive. He knew it wasn't a rational feeling since he recognized he was with professionals for whom this dive was
routine. He knew the submersible was reliable and that
he'd recently paid for an overhaul.

All at once Perry started. A masked face had materialized literally before his eyes. An involuntary, pitiful squeak
escaped from Perry's lips before he realized he was
looking into the face of one of the submersible's handlers
who'd entered the water with scuba equipment. A
moment later Perry saw other divers. In a slow motion
underwater ballet the divers quickly detached the hand-

ling lines. There was a knock on the outside of the hull. The *Oceanus* was on its own.

"All-clear signal received," Donald said into the radio mike. He was talking to the launch team supervisor on the fantail. "Request permission to power away from the ship."

"Permission granted," a disembodied voice responded.

Perry felt a new linear motion add to the passive roll, yaw, and pitch of the sub. He pressed his nose against the view port and saw the *Benthic Explorer* move out of his field of vision. With his face still pressed against the Plexiglas he looked down into the oceanic depths where he was about to descend. The sunlight did strange visual tricks as it refracted off the undulating water surface above, making him imagine he was staring into the maw of infinity.

With another shiver Perry acknowledged he was as vulnerable as an infant. A combination of vanity and stupidity had drawn him into this alien environment in which he had no control of his destiny. Although he was not religious, he found himself praying that the little underwater cruise would be short, sweet, and safe.

CHAPTER FOUR

"No contact," Suzanne said in response to Donald's question whether the sonar echo sounder showed any unexpected obstacles beneath the *Oceanus*. Even though they were bobbing around in open ocean, part of the predive check was to make sure no other submarine craft had surreptitiously moved under them.

Donald took the VHF radio mike and established contact with Larry Nelson in the diving van. "We're clear of the ship. Oxygen is on, scrubbers are on, hatch is closed, underwater phone is on, grounds are normal, and the echo sounder is clear. Request permission to dive."

"Is your tracking beacon activated?" Larry's voice questioned over the radio.

"That's affirmative," Donald said.

"You have permission to dive," Larry said with a small amount of static. "Depth to the well head is nine hundred ninety-four feet. Have a nice dive."

"Roger!" Donald said.

Donald was about to hang up the mike when Larry added, "The DDC is nearing depth so the bell will be starting down ASAP. I'd estimate the divers will be at the site in half an hour."

"We'll be waiting," Donald said. "Over and out." He

hung up the mike. Then to his fellow submariners he added, "Dive! Dive! Vent the main ballast tanks!"

Suzanne leaned forward and threw a switch. "Venting the ballast tanks," she repeated so there was no chance for misunderstanding. Donald made an entry on his clipboard.

There was a sound like a shower in a neighboring room as the cold Atlantic water rushed into the *Oceanus*'s ballast tanks. Within moments the craft's buoyancy plummeted, and once negative she silently slipped beneath the surface.

For the next few minutes both Donald and Suzanne were totally occupied, making sure all systems were still operating normally. Their conversation was restricted to operational jargon. In a rapid fashion they went through most of the predive checklist for the second time while the submersible's descent accelerated to a terminal velocity of a hundred feet per minute.

Perry occupied his time by looking out the view port. The color went from its initial greenish blue to rapidly advancing indigo. In five minutes all he could see was a blue glow when he looked upward. Downward it was dark purple fading into blackness. In stark contrast, the interior of the *Oceanus* was bathed in a cool electronic luminosity from the myriad monitors and readout devices.

"I believe we're a little front heavy," Suzanne said once all the electronic equipment had been checked.

"I agree," Donald said. "Go ahead and compensate for Mr. Bergman!"

Suzanne threw another switch. A whirring noise could be heard.

Perry leaned forward between the two pilots. "What

do you mean, 'compensate' *for me?*" His voice sounded funny even to himself. He swallowed to relieve a dry throat.

"We have a variable ballast system," Suzanne explained. "It's filled with oil, and I'm pumping some of it aft to make up for your weight forward of the center of gravity."

"Oh!" Perry said simply. He leaned back. As an engineer he understood the physics. He was also relieved they weren't referring to his timidity, which his self-consciousness had irrationally suggested.

Suzanne turned the variable ballast pump off when she was satisfied with the boat's trim. Then she turned around to face Perry. She was eager to make his dive to the seamount as positive as possible. Once they were back on ship, she hoped to present him with a case for conducting purely exploratory dives on the guyot. At the moment, the only time she got down there was to change the drill bit. She'd had no luck persuading Mark Davidson of the value of research-inspired dives.

Adding to Suzanne's anxiety was the widespread rumor that the drilling operation would be scrapped because of technical problems. Sea Mount Olympus would be abandoned before she could get a closer look. That was the last thing she wanted, and not only because of her professional interests. Just before leaving on the current project, she had what she hoped was the final breakup of an unhealthy, volatile relationship with an aspiring actor. At the moment returning to L.A. was the last thing she wanted to do. Perry Bergman's sudden appearance on-site was serendipitous. She could take her case right to the top.

"Comfortable?" Suzanne asked.

"I've never been more comfortable in my life," Perry averred.

Suzanne smiled despite the obvious sarcasm in Perry's response. The situation was not looking good. The Benthic Marine president was still tense as evidenced by his gripping the arms of his seat as if he were about to leap out of it. The books that she'd made the effort to bring were lying unopened on the floor grate.

For a moment Suzanne studied the taut president whose eyes looked everywhere but into hers. What she could not tell was whether Perry's anxiety was from apprehension of being in the submersible or just a reflection of his basic personality. Even on her first meeting with the man six months ago, she had found him a mildly eccentric, vain, and nervous guy. He was obviously not her type in addition to being short enough for her to look directly in the eye in her tennis shoes. Yet despite having little in common with him especially since he was an engineer-cum-entrepreneur and she a scientist, she trusted that he'd be receptive to her arguments. After all, he'd already responded positively to her request to bring the Benthic Explorer back to Sea Mount Olympus even if it was only to drill into the supposed magma chamber.

Sea Mount Olympus had been Suzanne's main pre-occupation for almost a year, since she'd stumbled on its existence by switching on the side-scan sonar on the *Benthic Explorer* out of boredom when the ship was heading back to port. Initially, her curiosity only involved her inability to explain why such a massive, apparently extinct volcano had not been detected by Geosat. But now, after making four dives in the submersible, she was equally fascinated by the geological formations on its flat crown, especially since she'd only been afforded the opportunity to explore in the immediate vicinity of the well head. But then the most intriguing fact emerged when she took it on herself to date the rock that had been brought up with the broken drill bit.

To Suzanne the results were startling and a lot more intriguing than the rock's apparent hardness. From the seamount's position near the Mid-Atlantic Ridge, she expected the rock sample's age to register in the seven-hundred-thousand-year range. Instead it had tested to be around four billion years old!

Knowing that the oldest rocks ever found on earth's surface or on the ocean floor were significantly less than this figure, Suzanne had thought that either the dating instrument was out of whack, or she'd made some stupid procedural error. Unwilling to risk ridicule, she decided to keep the results to herself.

With painstaking care she spent hours recalibrating the equipment, and then running additional samples over and over. To her disbelief, the results were all within three or four hundred million years of each other. Still believing there had to be a dating instrument malfunction involved, Suzanne had Tad Messenger, the head lab tech, recalibrate it. When she ran the sample again, the result was within a few million years of the previous one. Still in doubt, Suzanne reconciled herself to waiting until she got back to L.A. so she could use the university lab's equipment. Meanwhile the results were hidden away in her ship's locker. She tried to reserve judgment, but her interest in Sea Mount Olympus soared.

"We have hot coffee in a thermos aft if you'd like some," Suzanne said. "I'd be happy to get it for you."

"I think I'd be happier if you stay at the controls," Perry said.

"Donald, how about turning on the outside lights for a moment," Suzanne suggested.

"We're only passing through five hundred feet," Donald said. "There's nothing to see."

"It's Mr. Bergman's first open ocean dive," Suzanne said. "He should see the plankton."

"Call me Perry," Perry said. "I mean, why be formal while we're packed in here together like so many sardines in a can?"

Suzanne acknowledged Perry's offer of informality with a smile. She was only sorry he so clearly was not enjoying the trip.

"Donald, as a favor to me, turn on the lights," Suzanne said.

Donald complied without further comment. He reached forward and snapped on the external halogen lamps on the port side. Perry turned his head and glanced out.

"Looks like snow," he said.

"It's trillions of individual plankton organisms," Suzanne explained. "Since we're still in an epipelagic zone, it's probably mostly phytoplankton, or plant plankton that can carry on photosynthesis. Along with the blue-green algae, those are the guys who are at the bottom of the entire oceanic food chain."

"I'm glad," Perry said.

Donald switched the light off. "No sense in using up valuable battery power with that type of reaction," he explained to Suzanne sotto voce.

In the ensuing darkness, Perry witnessed twinkling bursts of muted neon green and yellow sparkles. He asked Suzanne what it was.

"That's bioluminescence," Suzanne said.

"Is it the plankton?" Perry asked.

"It could be," Suzanne said. "If so, it would probably be dinoflagellates. Of course, it could also be tiny crustaceans or even fish. I've put a yellow bookmark in the marine life book marking the bioluminescence section."

Perry nodded but made no attempt to pick up the text.

Nice try, Suzanne thought glumly. Her optimism about ensuring Perry's enjoyment sagged appreciably.

"*Oceanus*, this is *Benthic Explorer*," Larry's voice sounded in the acoustic phone speaker. "Suggest a course two hundred and seventy degrees at fifty amps for two minutes."

"Roger," Donald said. He quickly made the course adjustment with the joysticks and changed the power output to the propeller to the suggested fifty amps. He then noted the changes on his clipboard.

"Larry has plotted our position by tracking our pinger and relating it to the bottom hydrophones," Suzanne explained. "By powering forward while descending we'll reach bottom directly at the well head. It's like we're gliding to the target."

"What will we do until the divers arrive?" Perry asked. "Just sit and twiddle our thumbs?"

"Hardly," Suzanne said. She forced another smile along with a shallow laugh. "We'll unload the drill bit from the tray along with the tools we're carrying. Then we'll back off. At that point we'll have about twenty to thirty minutes to explore around the site. That's the part I think you are going to truly enjoy."

"I can't wait," Perry said with the kind of sarcasm Suzanne was beginning to dread. "But I don't want you doing anything out of the ordinary on my behalf. I mean, don't try to impress me. I'm already impressed enough."

Suddenly the monotonous pinging of the sonar changed. The sub was nearing the bottom, and the forward short-range sonar had a solid contact. The tiny screen showed the well head and the pipe snaking down from above. Donald jettisoned several of the descent weights and the craft's gliding plunge slowed. He then began a careful adjustment of the variable ballast system to achieve neutral buoyancy.

While Donald was busy pumping oil, Suzanne reached behind her and turned on a small CD player. It was part of her master plan. All at once the sound of Igor Stravinsky's *Rite of Spring* filled the sub's interior. Taking the music as a cue, Donald leaned forward and switched on the outside lights.

Perry's eyes widened as he glanced out the view port. The planktonic snow had all but disappeared, and the clarity of the icy water was more than he imagined. He was able to see for several hundred feet, and what he saw left him flabbergasted. He'd expected a flat, featureless plain similar to what the bottom looked like on his dive off Santa Catalina Island. At most he thought he might see a few sea cucumbers. Instead he was gazing at a misty tableau the likes of which he'd never imagined: huge dark gray, columnar forms with flat tops dotted the landscape, jutting up in a stepwise fashion like the frozen pistons of an enormous engine. The haunting shapes extended out as far as Perry could see. A few long-tailed, big-eyed fish lazily darted in and around them. On some of the rock ledges sea fans and sea whips waved sinuously in the current.

"Good God!" Perry exclaimed. He was mesmerized, especially with the dramatic music in the background.

"Rather exceptional, eh?" Suzanne said. She was

encouraged. Perry's reaction to the scenery was his first auspicious response.

"It looks like some ancient temple area," Perry exclaimed.

"Like Atlantis," Suzanne suggested. She was intent on milking the situation for all it was worth.

"Yeah!" Perry blurted. "Like Atlantis! Jeez! Can you imagine bringing tourists down here and telling them that it was Atlantis? What a freaking gold mine this could be."

Suzanne cleared her throat. Bringing tourists down to her precious seamount was the last thing she wanted to see happen, but she appreciated Perry's enthusiasm. At least he was engaged.

"Current is less than an eighth of a knot," Donald said. "Coming up on the well head. Prepare to off-load the drill bit."

Suzanne swung around to attend to her duties as copilot. She powered up the servos for the manipulator arms. Meanwhile Donald set the *Oceanus* down expertly on the rock floor. While Suzanne prepared to lift the drill bit and tools from the submersible's tray, Donald used the UQC phone.

"On the bottom," Donald said. "Off-loading the payload."

"Roger," Larry said in reply over the speaker. "I guessed as much when I heard Suzanne's music. Is that the only freaking CD she has?"

"It's the best one for the scenery down here," Suzanne interjected.

"If we make any more dives I'll loan you some new age CDs," Larry answered. "I can't stand that classical stuff."

"Am I looking at basaltic dikes out here?" Perry questioned.

"That's my guess," Suzanne said. "Have you ever heard of the Giant's Causeway?"

"Can't say that I have," Perry said.

"It's a natural rock formation on the northern coast of Ireland," Suzanne said. "It looks something like what you're seeing here."

"How big is the top of this seamount?" Perry questioned.

"I'd estimate about four football fields," Suzanne said. "But, unfortunately, that's nothing but a guess. The problem is we haven't had enough bottom time to explore the whole thing."

"Well, I think we ought to," Perry said.

Right on! Suzanne said to herself. She had to resist the temptation to yell out to ask if Larry and Mark had heard Perry's comment over the UQC.

"Does the whole top of the mountain look just the same as it does here?" Perry asked.

"No, not entirely," Suzanne said. "On the limited amount we've seen there are some areas of more typical undersea lava formations. On the last dive, though, we caught a glimpse of what might be a transverse fault, but we were called back before we could check it out. The mount remains largely unexplored."

"Where was the fault in relation to the well head?" Perry asked.

"Due west from here," Suzanne said. "Just about in the direction you're looking right now. Can you see a particularly high row of columns?"

"I think so," Perry said. He pushed his face against the Plexiglas to try to look slightly behind the sub. There was a row of columns at the edge of his visibility. "Would finding a transverse fault be significant?" he asked.

"It would be astounding," Suzanne responded. "They occur up and down the Mid-Atlantic Ridge system, but finding one at such a distance from the ridge, and through the middle of what we assume is an old volcano, would be quite unique."

"Let's go take a look," Perry suggested. "This place is fascinating."

Suzanne grinned in triumph. She glanced at Donald. Even he couldn't suppress a smile. He'd been sympathetic to Suzanne's plan but had not been optimistic.

It took Suzanne only a few minutes to unload everything that Mark had stowed in the submersible's tray. Once the material was lined up next to the well head, she folded the manipulating arms into their retracted position.

"So much for that job," Suzanne said. She turned off the power to the servo links.

"*Oceanus* to surface control," Donald said into the UQC mike. "The payload has been off-loaded. What's the status of the divers?"

"Compression is nearing depth," Larry's voice reported over the speaker. "The bell should be starting its descent shortly. ETA on the bottom, thirty minutes give or take five."

"Roger!" Donald said. "Keep us informed. We are going to move due west to investigate a scarp we caught sight of on the last dive."

"Ten-four," Larry said. "We'll let you know when the bell is lifted off the DDC. We'll also let you know when it is passing through five hundred feet so you can take up an appropriate position."

"Roger!" Donald repeated. He hung up the UQC mike. With his hands resting gently on the joysticks he jacked up the power to the propulsion system to fifty amps. He expertly guided the submersible away from the well head, careful to avoid the vertical run of pipe. A few moments later the *Oceanus* was slowly flying over the strange topography of the guyot's top.

"What I believe we're looking at here is a pristine section of the mantle's crust," Suzanne said. "But how and why the lava cooled to form these polygonal shapes is beyond me. It's almost like they're gigantic crystals."

"I like the idea of it being Atlantis," Perry said. His face remained glued to the view port.

"We're coming up to the place where we glimpsed that fault," Donald said.

"It should be just over that ridge of columns coming up," Suzanne said for Perry's benefit.

Donald cut back on the power. The submersible slowed as they cleared the ridge.

"Wow!" Perry commented. "It certainly drops off quickly."

"Well, it's not a transverse fault," Suzanne said as she got a full view of the formation. "In fact, if it were a fault at all it would have to be a graben. The other side is just as steep."

"What the hell is a graben?" Perry asked.

"It's when a fault block falls in relation to the rock on either side," Suzanne explained. "But something like that doesn't happen on the top of a seamount."

"It looks like a huge rectangular hole to me," Perry said. "What would you say? About a hundred and fifty feet long and fifty wide?"

"I'd say that's about right," Suzanne said.

"It's incredible!" Perry commented. "It's like some

giant took a knife and cut out a chunk of rick just the way you'd take a plug out of a watermelon."

Donald powered the *Oceanus* out over the hole, and they all looked down.

"I can't see the bottom," Perry said.

"Neither can I," Suzanne said.

"Neither can our sonar," Donald said. He pointed to the echo sounder monitor. It wasn't getting a return signal. It was as if the *Oceanus* were poised over a bottomless pit.

"My word!" Suzanne said. She was dumbfounded.

Donald gave the monitor a tap, but there was still no readout.

"That's very strange," Suzanne said. "Do you think it's malfunctioning?"

"I can't tell," Donald reported. He tried changing the adjustments.

"Wait a sec," Perry voiced tensely. "Are you two pulling my leg?"

"Try the side-scan sonar," Suzanne suggested, ignoring Perry for the moment.

"It's just as weird," Donald said. "The signal is aberrant unless we want to accept the pit's only six or seven feet deep. That's what the side-scan monitor is suggesting."

"Clearly the hole is a lot deeper than six or seven feet," Suzanne said.

"Obviously," Donald agreed.

"Hey, come on, you guys," Perry said. "You're starting to scare me."

Suzanne turned briefly to face Perry. "We're not trying to scare you," she said. "We're just mystified by our instruments."

"My guess is there's one hell of a thermocline just within the rim of this formation," Donald said. "The sonar has to be bouncing off something."

"Would you mind translating that?" Perry said.

"Sound waves bounce off sharp temperature gradients," Suzanne said. "We think that's what we have here."

"In order to get a depth readout we have to descend ten or fifteen feet into the pit," Donald said. "I'll do that by decreasing our buoyancy, but first I want to change our orientation."

With short bursts Donald used the starboard front thruster to turn the submersible until it became parallel with the long axis of the hole. Then he manipulated the variable ballast system to make the sub negatively buoyant. Gradually the submersible started down.

"Maybe this isn't such a good idea," Perry said. He was nervously looking back and forth between the side-scan sonar monitor and his view port.

The UQC speaker cracked to life: "Surface control to *Oceanus*. The bell is lifting off the DDC as I'm speaking. The divers will be passing through five hundred feet in about ten minutes."

"Roger, surface control," Donald said into the mike. "We're about one hundred feet west of the well head. We're going to check out an apparent marked thermocline in a rock formation. Communications might be interrupted momentarily, but we'll be on station for the divers."

"Ten-four," Larry's voice said.

"Look at the luster of the walls," Suzanne remarked as the submersible sank below the tip of the huge hole.

"They're perfectly smooth. It almost looks like obsidian!"

"Let's head back to the well head," Perry suggested.

"Could this be an opening into an extinct volcano?" Donald asked. A slight smile flitted across his otherwise rigid face.

"That's a thought," Suzanne said with a laugh. "Although I have to say I've never heard of a perfectly rectilinear caldera." She laughed again. "Our dropping down in here like this reminds me of Jules Verne's *Journey to the Center of the Earth*."

"How so?" Donald asked.

"Have you read it?"

"I don't read novels," Donald said.

"That's right, I forgot," Suzanne said. "Anyway, in the story the protagonists entered a kind of pristine netherworld via an extinct volcano."

Donald shook his head. His eyes stayed glued to the thermistor readout. "What a waste of time," he said. "That's why I don't read novels. Not with all the technical journals I can't get to."

Suzanne started to respond but changed her mind. She'd never be able to make a dent in Donald's rigid opinions about fiction in particular and art in general.

"I don't mean to be a pest," Perry said, "but I—"

Perry never got out the last part of his sentence. All at once the submersible's descent accelerated markedly and Donald cried out, "Christ almighty!"

Perry gripped the sides of his seat with white-knuckle intensity. The rapid increase in downward motion scared him, but not as much as Donald's uncharacteristic outburst. If the imperturbable Donald Fuller was upset, the situation must be critical.

"Jettisoning weights!" Donald called out. The descent immediately slowed, then stopped. Donald released more weight and the sub began to rise. Then he used the port-side thruster to maintain orientation with the long axis of the pit. The last thing he wanted was to hit up against the walls.

"What the hell happened?" Perry demanded when he could find his voice.

"We lost buoyancy," Suzanne reported.

"We suddenly got heavier or the water got lighter," Donald said as he scanned the instrumentation.

"What does that mean?" Perry demanded.

"Since we obviously didn't get heavier, the water indeed got lighter," Donald said. He pointed to the temperature gauge. "We passed through the temperature gradient we suspected, and it was a lot more than we bargained for—in the opposite direction. The outside temperature rose almost a hundred degrees Fahrenheit!"

"Let's get the hell out of here!" Perry cried.

"We're on our way," Donald said tersely. He snapped the UQC mike from its housing and tried to raise the *Benthic Explorer*. When he had no luck, he returned the mike to its cradle. "Sound waves don't come in here and they don't go out either."

"What is this, some sort of sonar black hole?" Perry asked irritably.

"The echo sounder is giving us a reading now," Suzanne said. "But it can't be true! It says this pit is over thirty thousand feet deep!"

"Now why would that be malfunctioning?" Donald asked himself. He gave the instrument an even harder rap with his knuckles. The digital readout stayed at 30,418.

"Let's forget the echo sounder," Perry said. "Can't we

get out of here faster?" The *Oceanus* was rising, but very slowly.

"I've never had trouble with this echo sounder before," Donald said.

"Maybe this pit could have been some kind of magma pipe," Suzanne said. "It's obviously deep, even though we don't know how deep, and the water is hot. That suggests contact with lava." She bent forward to look out the view port.

"Could we at least turn off the music?" Perry said. It was reaching a crescendo that only added to his anxiety.

"Well, I'll be damned!" Suzanne exclaimed. "Look at the walls at this level! The basalt is oriented transversely. I've never heard of a transverse dike. And look! It has a greenish cast to it. Maybe it's gabbro, not basalt."

"I'm afraid I'm going to have to pull rank here," Perry snapped with uncamouflaged exasperation. He'd had it with being ignored. "I want to be taken up to the surface, *pronto*!"

Suzanne swung around to respond but only managed to open her mouth. Before she could form any words a powerful, low-frequency vibration shook the submersible. She had to grab the side of her seat to keep from falling. The sudden quake sent loose objects flying to the floor. A coffee mug hit and shattered; the shards skittered across the floor along with pens that had fallen. At the same time, there was a low-pitched rumbling that sounded like distant thunder.

The rattling lasted for almost a minute. No one spoke although an involuntary squeak escaped from Perry's lips as the blood drained from his face.

"What on earth was that?" Donald demanded. He rapidly scanned the instruments.

"I'm not sure," Suzanne said, "but if I had to guess, I'd say it was an earthquake. There's a lot of them up and down the Mid-Atlantic Ridge."

"An earthquake!" Perry blurted.

"Maybe this old volcano is awakening," Suzanne said. "Wouldn't that be a trip if we got to witness it!"

"Uh-oh!" Donald said. "Something is wrong!"

"What's the problem?" Suzanne asked. Like Donald her eyes made a quick circuit of the dials, gauges, and screens in her direct line of sight. These were the important instruments for operating the submersible. Nothing seemed amiss.

"The echo sounder!" Donald said with uncharacteristic urgency.

Suzanne's eyes darted down to the digital readout located close to the floor between the two pilot seats. It was decreasing at an alarming rate.

"What's happening?" she asked. "Do you think lava is rising in the shaft?"

"No!" Donald cried. "It's us. We're sinking, and I've jettisoned all the descent weights. We've lost our buoyancy!"

"But the pressure gauge!" Suzanne yelled. "It's not rising. How can we be sinking?"

"It mustn't be working," Donald said frantically. "There's no doubt we're sinking. Just look out the damn view port!"

Suzanne's eyes darted to the window. It was true. They were sinking. The smooth rock face was moving rapidly upward.

"I'm blowing the ballast tanks," Donald barked. "At this depth there won't be much effect, but there's no choice."

The sound of compressed air being released drowned out Stravinsky's *Rite of Spring* but only for twenty seconds. At such a pressure the compressed air tanks were quickly exhausted. The descent was not affected.

"Do something!" Perry yelled when he could find his voice.

"I can't," Donald yelled. "There's no response to the controls. There's nothing left to try."

CHAPTER FIVE

Mark Davidson was dying for a cigarette. His addiction was absolute, although he found giving them up was easy since he did it once a week. His craving was maximum when he was relaxing, working, or anxious, and at the moment, he was very anxious indeed. For him, deep diving operations were always a walk on the wild side; from experience he knew how quickly things could go horribly wrong.

He looked up at the large institutional clock on the wall of the diving van, with its monstrous sweep second hand. Its intimidating presence made the passage of time hard to disregard. It had now been twelve minutes since there had been any contact with the *Oceanus*. Although Donald had specifically warned that there might be a short communication break, this seemed longer than reasonable, especially since the submersible had not responded to Larry Nelson's last message. That was when Larry had tried to tell them that the divers were passing through five hundred feet.

Mark's eyes darted down to the pack of Marlboros he'd casually tossed onto the diving van's countertop. It was an agony not to reach over, take one out, and light up. Unfortunately, there was a newly instituted prohibition about smoking in the ship's common areas, and

Captain Jameson was a stickler about rules and regulations.

With some difficulty Mark pulled his eyes away from the cigarettes and scanned the van's interior. Everyone else present seemed calm, which only made Mark feel more tense. Larry Nelson was sitting perfectly still at the diving operations monitoring station along with the sonar operator, Peter Rosenthal. Just beyond them were the two watch standers, who were in front of the diving system's operating console. Although their eyes were constantly scanning the pressure gauges of the two pressurized DDCs and the diving bell, the rest of their bodies were motionless.

Across the watch standers was the winch operator. He was perched on a high stool in front of the window looking out on the central well. His hand rested on the gear shift for the winch. Outside, the cable attached to the shackle on top of the diving bell was being played out at the maximum permitted velocity. From a neighboring drum came a second, passive cable that contained the compressed gas line, hot water hose, and communications wires.

At the far end of the van was Captain Jameson, absently sucking on a toothpick. In front of him were the controls that formed an extension of the bridge. Even though the ship's propellers and thrusters were being controlled by computer to keep it stationary over the well head, Captain Jameson could override the system if the need arose during diving operations.

"God damn it!" Mark spat. He slammed a pencil he'd been unconsciously torturing to the countertop and stood up. "What's the divers' depth?"

"Passing through six hundred ten feet, sir," the winch operator reported.

"Try the *Oceanus* again!" Mark barked to Larry. He started to pace back and forth. He had a bad feeling in the pit of his stomach, and it was getting worse. He began to lambaste himself for encouraging Perry Bergman to go on the dive. Being personally aware of Dr. Newell's interest in the seamount and her desire to make purely exploratory dives, he worried that she might try to impress the president to get her way. That might mean she'd pressure Donald to do things he might not normally do, and Mark was aware that Dr. Newell was the only person on the ship who potentially had that kind of influence over the normally strictly-by-the-book ex-naval line officer.

Mark shuddered. It would be a disaster of the first order if the submersible got wedged in a fissure or a crevice where it may have descended to examine a particular geological feature up close. That had almost happened to the submersible *Alvin*, out of Woods Hole, and the near tragedy had been on the Mid-Atlantic Ridge, not that far away from their present location.

"Still no response," Larry said after several unsuccessful tries to raise the *Oceanus* on the UQC.

"Any sign of the submersible on side-scan sonar?" Mark demanded from the sonar operator.

"That's a negative," Peter said. "And bottom hydrophones have no contact with their tracking beacon. The thermocline they found must be impressive. It's like they dropped down into the ocean floor."

Mark stopped his pacing and looked back at the clock. "How long has it been since that tremor?" he asked.

"That was more than a tremor," Larry said. "Tad Messenger measured it four point four on the Richter scale."

"I'm not surprised—it knocked over that pile of pipe on the deck," Mark said. "And as much as we felt it up here, it would have been a hell of a lot worse on the bottom. How long ago was it?"

Larry looked down at his log. "It's been almost four minutes. You don't think that has anything to do with our not hearing from the *Oceanus*, do you?"

Mark was reluctant to answer. He was not superstitious, yet he hated to voice his worries, as if articulating them made them that much more possible. But he was concerned that the 4.4 earthquake may have caused a rock slide that trapped the *Oceanus*. Such a catastrophe surely wasn't out of the question if Donald had indeed descended into a narrow depression at Suzanne's insistence.

"Let me talk to the divers," Mark said. He walked over to Larry and took the mike. While he pondered what he wanted to say, he glanced up at the monitor where he could see the tops of the heads and the foreshortened bodies of the three men.

"Shit, man!" Michael moaned. "You just kicked me in the balls!" His voice came out as a series of squeaks and squeals that would have been mostly unintelligible to normal humans. The distortion was a function of the helium he was breathing in place of nitrogen.

At the equivalent pressure of 980 feet of seawater, nitrogen acted as an anesthetic. Replacing the nitrogen with helium solved the problem but caused marked changes in voice. The divers were used to it. Although they sounded like Walt Disney's Donald Duck, they could understand each other perfectly.

"Then get your balls out of my way," Richard said. "I'm having trouble getting these freaking fins on."

All three divers were wedged up inside the diving bell, whose pressure hull was a sphere a mere eight feet in diameter. Crammed in with them were all their diving equipment, many hundreds of feet of looped hose, and all the necessary instrumentation.

"Get out of the way, he says," Michael jeered. "What do you want me to do, step outside?"

A speaker crackled to life. It was mounted at the very apex of the sphere next to a tiny camcorder fitted with a fish-eye lens. Although the divers knew they were being constantly observed, they were totally indifferent to the surveillance.

"Let me have your attention, men!" Mark commanded. In contrast to the divers', his voice sounded relatively normal. "This is the operations commander."

"Holy crap!" Richard complained as he eyed the swim fin that was giving him the problem. "No wonder I can't get this freaking thing on. It ain't mine. It's yours, Donaghue." Without warning Richard clobbered Michael over the head with the flipper. Michael was troubled by the blow only because it knocked off his prized Red Sox hat. The cap tumbled down into the trunk, coming to a rest on the sealed hatch.

"Hey, nobody move!" Michael said. "Mazzola, get my hat for me! I don't want it to get wet." Michael was already fully outfitted for the dive in his neoprene dry suit complete with the buoyancy control vest and weights. The ability to bend over, as would be required to retrieve the hat, was out of the question.

"Gentlemen!" Mark's voice was louder and more insistent.

"Screw you," Louis said. "I might be bell diver, but I'm not your slave."

"Hey, listen up, you animals!" Larry's voice yelled from the tiny speaker. The sound reverberated around the cramped sphere at a level just shy of pain. "Mr. Davidson wants a word with you, so shut up!"

Richard shoved the flipper and its mate into Michael's hands, then looked up at the camera. "All right already," he said. "We're listening."

"Stand by for a moment," Larry's voice said. "We didn't realize the helium unscrambler wasn't on line."

"So let me have my fins," Richard said to Michael in the interim.

"You mean the ones I have on aren't mine?"

"Duh!" Richard voiced mockingly. "Since you're holding yours in your hands they can't be on your feet, birdbrain!"

Michael squatted awkwardly, clutching his fins under his arm, and stripped those from his feet. Richard snatched them away disdainfully. Then the two divers clumsily bumped into each other as they struggled to slip on their respective flippers at the same time.

"Okay, men," Larry's voice said. "We're on line with the scrambler so stop screwing around and listen up! Here's Mr. Davidson."

The divers didn't bother to look up. They slouched against the sides of the PTC and assumed bored expressions.

"We haven't been able to raise the *Oceanus* on the UQC or track it on sonar," Mark's voice said. "We're anxious for you to make visual contact. If you don't see them when you arrive at the well head, let us know and we'll give you further instructions. Understand?"

"That's affirmative," Richard said. "Now can we get back to getting ready to dive?"

"That's affirmative," Mark said.

Richard and Michael stirred, and by giving each other an iota of leeway they managed to get their flippers on their feet. Michael even tried to reach his hat while Richard proceeded to don his buoyancy vest and weight belt, but it was beyond his grasp, as he'd feared.

Five minutes later the winch operator's voice told them they were passing through nine hundred feet. With that announcement the descent slowed appreciably. While Richard and Michael tried to stay out of the way, Louis readied the hoses. As the bell diver it fell to him to handle the lines.

"Powering the exterior lights," Larry announced.

Richard and Michael twisted themselves enough to glance out the two tiny view ports opposite each other. Louis was too busy to look out either of the two remaining windows.

"I see bottom," Richard said.

"Me, too," Michael said.

With a single main hoisting cable the diving bell was rotating slowly, although its rotation was restricted by the life-support lines. The bell would rotate in one direction for several revolutions and then turn and go the other way. As the bell settled down to the 980-foot mark and stopped, the rotation slowed to a stop as well, but not before each diver had been afforded a 360-degree view.

Since the bell was suspended fourteen feet above the rock face at one of the higher sections of the seamount's summit, the divers could see a relatively wide area bounded by the illumination of the exterior halogen lights. Their view was somewhat restricted only to the west, where it was blocked by a ridge of rock. To Richard and Michael the ridge appeared like a series of connected columns whose crest was slightly higher than their line of sight. But even that formation was at the periphery of the sphere of light.

"Do you see the sub?" Richard asked Michael.

"Nope," Michael said. "But I can see the bits and the tools by the well head. They're all stacked up nice and neat."

Richard leaned away from the view port and tilted his face up toward the camcorder.

"That's a negative on the *Oceanus*," he said. "But she's been here."

"That means there will be a change in the dive plan," Larry's voice answered. "Mr. Davidson wants red and green divers to proceed due west. Can you make out a scarp in that direction?"

"What the hell is a scarp?" Richard asked.

"It's a wall or cliff," Mark's voice cut in.

"Yeah, I guess," Richard said. He looked back out at the columnar ridge.

"Mr. Davidson wants you to proceed over the ridge," Larry said. "How high is the ridge in relation to the bell?"

"About even," Richard said.

"All right, swim over the ridge and see if you can make visual contact with the submersible. Mr. Davidson thinks there might be a crevice. And watch the temperature. Apparently there's quite a gradient in the area."

"Got it," Richard said.

"Remember," Larry added, "you're limited to a one-fifty deep excursion dive. Don't rise more than ten feet above the bell. We don't want any bends to muck things up. Understood?"

"Got it," Richard repeated. Larry's admonitions were the standard for a saturation dive.

"Bell diver," Larry said, "the breathing mixture is to stay at one and a half percent oxygen and ninety-eight and a half percent helium. Do you copy?"

"I copy," Louis said.

"One last thing," Larry said. "Red and green divers, I don't want any of you macho bums taking any chances, so be careful!"

"Check!" Richard said. He gave a thumbs-up sign for the camcorder's benefit while making a scornful face at Michael and saying: "Telling us to be careful down here is like telling your kid to be careful before sending him out to play in the middle of the interstate."

Michael nodded but he wasn't listening. This part of the dive was serious. He was all business while attaching his umbilical and other paraphernalia. When he was ready Louis handed him his full face mask cradled in a bright orange fiberglass helmet. Michael held it under his arm to wait for Richard. Despite his extensive experience he always got butterflies just before entering the water.

Richard quickly followed suit with his equipment. Then he took two underwater lights, tested both, and handed one to Michael. When he was ready he nodded to Michael, and they both put on their helmets at the same time.

The first thing they checked after Louis opened the manifold was the gas flow. Next was the hot water, a necessary adjunct since the outside water temperature was only thirty-six degrees; it was difficult for a diver to work if he was cold. Finally they tested the communications and their sensor lines. When all was in order, Louis informed topside and asked for permission for the divers to enter the water.

"Permission granted," Larry's voice responded. "Open the hatch!"

With some difficulty and a lot of grunts Louis squeezed his bulky frame down into the trunk of the bell.

"My hat!" Michael yelled, although his voice was muffled by the sound of his escaping breathing gas.

Louis grasped the baseball hat and handed it up to Michael. Michael gingerly hung it on one of the many protuberances in the bell. He treated it as his most valuable possession. What he didn't admit was that he considered it his lucky charm.

Louis undogged the pressure hatch and, with some difficulty, raised it. He secured it against the wall. Below, the luminous aquamarine seawater rose menacingly up through the trunk. All three divers breathed a silent sigh of relief when it predictably stopped just shy of the lip of the hatch. They all knew it would, but they also knew that if it did not there was no place to go.

Richard gave Michael a thumbs-up sign. Michael returned the gesture. Richard then carefully climbed down through the trunk. Once he was free he dropped out the bottom of the bell.

For Richard, getting out of the cramped bell was a relief he likened to being born. The sudden freedom was exhilarating. The only part of him that could sense the coolness of the water was his gloved hands. He scanned the area while adjusting his buoyancy. It took him only a moment to see the dark shape cruising just at the periphery of light. It wasn't the submersible. It was a shark with luminous eyes. The length of the huge fish was more than twice the diameter of the diving bell.

"We got company," Richard said calmly. "Toss down my rebar just in case and have Michael bring his." Of all the fancy antishark paraphernalia on the market, Richard preferred a simple, three-and-a-half-foot metal rod. It had been his experience that sharks avoided the rod like the plague if it was just pointed in their direction. During a feeding frenzy he wasn't as confident it would work, but in that situation, nothing worked one hundred percent.

Seconds later the rebar came down and clanked mutely against the rock. A moment later Michael's legs appeared as he struggled out of the trunk. Once he was free the two divers made eye contact. Richard gestured in the direction of the shark, which now wandered into the light.

"Ah, it's only a Greenland shark," Richard said to Louis, who made sure Michael had heard it as well. Now Richard was even less concerned. It was a big shark, but not dangerous. He knew that another name for the monster was sleeper shark because of its sluggish habits.

After Michael made his adjustments Richard pointed toward the ridge. Michael nodded and the two started off. Both held their lights in their left hands and the rebars in their right. As accomplished swimmers they covered the distance in a short time without rushing. At a pressure of almost thirty atmospheres the sheer work of breathing the viscous, compressed gas sapped their energy.

Inside the diving bell Louis was frantically playing out both sets of tethers. He didn't want to restrict the divers or give them too much slack lest they get tangled up. Until the divers got down to work the bell diver was a busy man. The job required concentration and quick reflexes. At the same time Louis was handling the lines, he had to keep his eye on the pressure gauges and the digital oxygen percentage readout. On top of that he was in constant communication with each diver and with diving control up in the diving van. To keep his hands free, a headset kept a tiny speaker in his ear and a microphone positioned over his mouth.

Out in the water the two divers swam to the top of the ridge and paused. At that distance from the diving bell the amount of illumination fell off sharply. Richard motioned to his flashlight and both turned them on.

Behind them, the diving bell glowed eerily like an orbiter nesting in a rocky, alien landscape. A stream of bubbles issued from the bell and dribbled toward the far-off surface. Ahead, the divers faced darkness fading to indelible blackness with only a faint hint of a glow when they looked up toward the surface almost a thousand feet above. In the back of their minds they knew the huge shark was somewhere just beyond their vision. Shining their lights forward provided meager cones of light that penetrated the icy darkness only forty to fifty feet ahead.

"There's a drop-off beyond the ridge," Richard reported. "This must be the scarp."

Louis relayed the information up to the dive station. Although the dive control could listen to the divers and talk to them, Larry preferred to use the bell diver as an intermediary. The combination of the helium voice distortion and the noise of the divers' breathing gas flow made comprehension by those up in the diving van extremely difficult even with the helium unscrambler on-line. It was much more efficient to use the bell diver since he was more accustomed to the speech distortions.

"Red diver," Louis called out. "Control wants to know if you see any sign of the *Oceanus*."

"That's negative," Richard said.

"How about a crevice or a hole?" Louis relayed.

"Not at the moment," Richard reported, "but we're about to start down this rock wall."

Richard and Michael swam over the edge and down the face of the cliff.

"The rock is as smooth as glass," Richard commented. Michael nodded. He'd run his hand along it briefly.

"You're coming up on your last one hundred feet of hose," Louis said. He quickly took the last two loops down from their storage hooks, already cursing under his breath. Soon he'd be coiling it all up again. Divers rarely wandered this far from the diving bell, and it was just his luck to be assigned as the bell diver when they did.

Richard stopped his descent. He grabbed Michael to stop him as well. Richard pointed to his wrist thermometer. Michael looked at his and did a double take.

"The water temperature just changed," Richard reported. "It just went up almost one hundred degrees. Shut off our hot water!"

"Red diver, are you shitting me?" Louis asked.

"Michael's reads the same," Richard said. "It's like we've climbed into a hot tub."

Richard had been shining his light down as they descended, searching for the base of the scarp. Now he shined it around. At the very periphery of illumination he could just make out a wall opposite the one they were descending.

"Hey! Apparently we are in some kind of huge crevice," he said. "I can just barely see the other side. It must be about fifty feet wide."

Michael tapped Richard on the shoulder and pointed off to their left. "There's an end to it as well," he said.

"Michael's right," Richard said when he'd looked. Then he swung around and pointed the light in the opposite direction. "I guess it's like a box canyon 'cause I can't see a fourth side, at least not from where we are."

"Hey," Michael said. "We're sinking!"

Richard looked at the wall behind him. It was true they were sinking—more quickly than he would have thought possible. There was little sensation of resistance against the water.

Richard and Michael gave a few powerful kicks upward. To their astonishment there was little effect. They were still sinking. With a mixture of confusion and alarm, both responded by reflex and inflated their buoyancy vests. When that seemed to have little effect, they released their weight belts. Still significantly negatively buoyant, they jettisoned their rebars. Finally with some continued kicking their descent slowed and stopped.

Richard pointed upward and the two started swimming. Despite the heavy work of breathing they were swimming hard. The strange sinking episode had unnerved them, and to make matters worse, they were beginning to feel the heat through their suits.

The two were even with the top of the cliff when a sudden sustained vibration swept up from the depths like a shock wave. For a few seconds both men were mildly disoriented. They had trouble breathing and swimming at the same time. The shaking was similar to what they had experienced in the diving bell on the descent, only much worse. They realized this was an underwater earthquake, and both of them intuitively sensed they were at or near the epicenter.

For Louis, the quake was even more violent. At the moment of impact he'd been frantically hauling in the tethers, which had gone suddenly slack. He'd been forced to let go of the lines to keep himself from being impaled on one of the many wall-mounted protrusions.

Richard recovered enough to take a breath although doing so was painful. The pressure wave had bruised his chest. As an experienced diver, his first response was to check on his buddy, and he frantically searched by spinning around. For a heart-stopping second he could not find Michael. Then he looked down. Michael appeared to be clawing his way up through the water. Richard reached down to lend a hand. When he did, he realized that they were both sinking—and sinking fast.

With no other way to decrease his weight Richard joined Michael in an attempt to swim upward. In desperation they even discarded their lights to free their hands. But they made no progress. If anything, they seemed to be going down. Then they plummeted, caroming off the rock wall until they were inexorably sucked into the abyss.

Inside the bell Louis had recovered his balance enough to grab the tethers, which were still slack. Quickly he pulled in a loop, but before he could get it over the rack, there was a sudden tug in the opposite direction. At first he tried to hold the lines from going out, but it was impossible. Had he held on, they would have pulled him from the bell.

Louis cursed as he frantically got out of the way of the hoses, which were now being yanked out of the bell at a furious rate. It was as if Richard and Michael were lures that had been taken by a gigantic fish.

"Bell diver, are you all right?" Larry's voice asked.

"Yeah, I'm all right!" Louis yelled. "But something crazy is going on! The hoses are going out at a hundred miles an hour!"

"We can see that on the monitor," Larry said urgently. "Can't you stop it?"

"How?" Louis pleaded through tears. He glanced at the remaining hose. There wasn't much left. He froze. He had no idea what to expect. The last loops whipped out of the bell and for a brief moment the lines went taut. Then to Louis's utter horror they were torn from their housings and disappeared down into the trunk and out into the unforgiving sea.

"Oh, my God!" Louis cried as he struggled to turn off the gas supply manifold.

"What's happening down there?" Larry demanded.

"I don't know," Louis cried. Then to add to his terror the vibration and rumbling started again. Frantically he reached out to grab whatever he could as the diving bell shook as though it were a salt shaker in the hand of a giant. He screamed, and as if in answer to a prayer, the shaking lessened to a mere trembling. At the same time he became aware of a sizzling sound and a red glow that penetrated through the view ports.

Letting go of the death grip he'd had on the high-pressure piping, Louis twisted to glance out one of the view ports. What he saw made him freeze anew. Over the nearby ridge, which the divers had so recently scaled, came a surreal cascade of glowing, red hot lava. The leading edge sputtered and popped and smoked as it turned the icy water into steam.

When Louis recovered enough to find his voice, he threw his head back to look up into the camcorder lens.

"Get me out of here!" he shrieked. "I'm in the middle of a goddamn erupting volcano!"

*

The van's interior had become quiet. A sense of shock hung over the room. The only noise came from the deck-mounted motors driving the winches that were hauling up the diving bell and the life-support lines. Moments before, utter pandemonium had prevailed as it became apparent they'd lost two divers in some kind of pyroclastic catastrophe. The only consolation was that the third diver was okay, and he was on his way up.

Mark took a long, nervous drag on his Marlboro. Oblivious to the new rules, he'd reached for his cigarettes by reflex at the first rumblings of trouble, and now that the extent of the tragedy had rapidly unfolded, he was chain-smoking out of pure anxiety. Not only had he managed to lose a hundred-million-dollar submersible with two trained operators plus two experienced saturation divers; he'd also lost the president of Benthic Marine. If only he hadn't encouraged Perry Bergman to make the dive. For that he was solely responsible.

"What the hell are we going to do?" Larry asked in stunned bewilderment. Even he was smoking although he was supposed to have given it up six months before. As the diving supervisor he, too, felt responsible for the disastrous outcome.

Mark sighed heavily. He felt weak. He'd never had a single loss of life on his watch in his entire career, and that included hairy diving operations in some dicey locations like in the Persian Gulf during Desert Storm. Now he'd lost five people. It was too much to think about.

"The bell is passing through five hundred feet," the winch operator called out to no one in particular.

"What about the drilling operation?" Larry wondered aloud.

Mark took another long drag on his cigarette and almost burned his fingers. Angrily he stubbed it out, then lit another.

"Get ready to launch the camera sled," Mark said. "We got to look at what's going on down there."

"Mazzola was pretty clear," Larry quavered. "As we were pulling him up he said the whole top of the seamount as far as he could see was molten lava, bubbling up from behind the ridge. And we're recording almost continuous tremors. Hell, we're sitting on a live volcano. Are you sure you want the sled down in that kind of an inferno?"

"I want to see it," Mark said slowly, "and I want to record it. I'm sure there's going to be one hell of an inquiry about this whole mess. And I want to look at the area where the canyon or hole was that the *Oceanus* disappeared into. I've got to be sure there's no chance . . ." Mark did not finish his sentence. He knew in his gut it was hopeless; Donald Fuller had dropped the submersible down into a volcanic vent just prior to its erupting.

"Fair enough," Larry conceded. "I'll have the crew get the sled ready to go. But what about the drilling? I hope you're not thinking of sending down another dive team if and when this volcano quiets down."

"Hell no!" Mark said with emotion. "I've lost interest in drilling into this freaking mountain, especially now that Perry Bergman is no longer with us. It was his foolhardy obsession, not mine. If the camera sled confirms that the vent hole or whatever it was is filled with fresh lava, and we can't find any trace of the *Oceanus*, we're getting the hell out of here."

"That sounds good to me!" Larry said. He stood up. "I'll get the sled ready and in the water ASAP."

"Thanks," Mark said. He leaned forward and buried his head in his hands. He'd never felt worse in his life.

CHAPTER SIX

Suzanne was the first to recover enough from the terror of the precipitous descent to find her voice. Hesitantly she said, "I think we've stopped! Thank God!"

For a time that had seemed an eternity to its three terrified occupants, the submersible had fallen like a stone down the mysterious shaft. It was as if they had been sucked down an enormous drain in the bottom of the ocean. During the plummet the *Oceanus* had been totally unresponsive to the controls no matter which Donald Fuller manipulated.

Although initially the plunge had been straight down, the boat had eventually begun to spiral and even carom off the walls. One of the first such collisions destroyed the outside halogen lights. Another stripped off the starboard manipulator with a grinding crunch.

Perry had been the only one to scream during the ordeal. But even he fell silent once the helplessness of their situation had sunk in. He could only watch helplessly as the digital depth recorder whirred into the thousands. The numbers had flashed by so quickly, they'd become a blur. And when twenty thousand feet approached, all he'd been able to think about was the chilling statistic he'd heard earlier: the *crush depth!*

"In fact, I don't think we're moving at all," Suzanne

added. She was whispering. "What could have happened? Could we be on the bottom? I didn't feel an impact."

No one moved a muscle, as if doing so might disturb the sudden but welcome tranquillity. They were breathing shallowly in short gasps, and beads of perspiration dotted their foreheads. All three were still holding on to their seats for fear the plunge would recommence.

"It feels like we stopped, but look at the depth gauge," Donald managed. His voice was raspy from dryness.

All eyes returned to the readout that only moments earlier had inexorably held their gaze. It was moving again, slowly at first but then rapidly gathering speed. The difference was that it was moving in the opposite direction.

"But I don't feel any movement," Suzanne said. She exhaled deeply and tried to relax her muscles. The others did likewise.

"Nor do I," Donald admitted. "But look at the gauge! It's going crazy."

The readout device had returned to its previous furious whirring.

Suzanne leaned forward slowly as if she thought the submersible was precariously balanced and her movement might tip it over an edge. She peered out the view port, but all she could see was her own image. With the outside lights sheared off from collisions with the rock, the window was as opaque as a mirror, reflecting the interior light.

"What's happening now?" Perry croaked.

"Your guess is as good as ours," Suzanne answered. She took a deep breath. She was beginning to recover.

"The depth gauge says we're rising," Donald said. He glanced at the other instruments, including the sonar monitors. Their erratic signals suggested there was a lot of interference in the water, particularly affecting the short-range sonar. The side-scan was a bit better, with less electronic noise, but it was difficult to interpret. The hazy image hinted that the sub was sitting stationary on a vast, perfectly flat plain. Donald's eyes went back to the depth gauge. He was mystified; in contrast to what the sonar was suggesting, it was still rising, and faster than it had been moments before. Quickly he reopened the ballast tanks, but there was no effect. Then he put the dive planes down and added more power to the propulsion system. There was no response to the controls. But they continued to rise nonetheless.

"We're accelerating," Suzanne warned. "Rising like this we'll be on the surface in just a couple of minutes!"

"I can't wait," Perry said with obvious relief.

"I hope we're not coming up under the *Benthic Explorer*," Suzanne said. "That would be a major problem."

Everyone's eyes were riveted to the depth gauge. It passed through one thousand feet and showed no sign of slowing. Five hundred feet shot by. As it passed one hundred feet Donald said urgently: "Hold on! We're going to broach badly."

"What does broach mean?" Perry yelled. He heard the desperation in Donald's voice, and it sent a new chill through him.

"It means we're going to leap out of the water!" Suzanne shouted. Then she repeated Donald's warning. "Hold on!"

As the frantic whirring of the depth gauge reached a crescendo, Perry, Donald, and Suzanne once again grabbed their seats and held tight. Holding their breath they braced themselves for the impact. The depth gauge reached zero and stopped.

Immediately following that final click of the gauge, a loud sucking noise emanated from somewhere outside the craft. After that, comparative silence reigned within the sub. Now the only sound was a combination of the ventilation fan and an augmented but still muffled electronic whir of the propulsion system.

Almost a minute passed without the slightest sensation of movement.

Finally Perry breathed out. "Well," he said. "What happened?"

"We can't be airborne for this long," Suzanne admitted.

Everyone relaxed their death grips and looked out their respective view ports. It was still as dark as pitch.

"What the hell?" Donald questioned. He looked back at his instruments. The sonar monitors were now filled with meaningless electronic noise. He turned them off. He also dialed down the power to the propulsion system, and its whirring stopped. He looked at Suzanne.

"Don't ask me," Suzanne said when their eyes met. "I haven't the slightest idea what's going on."

"How come it's dark outside if we're on the surface?" Perry asked.

"This doesn't make any sense," Donald said. He looked back at his instruments. Reaching forward, he put power back to the propulsion system. The whirring noise reappeared but there was no motion. The craft stood absolutely still.

"Somebody tell me what's going on," Perry demanded. The euphoria he'd felt a few moments earlier had dissipated. They obviously were not on the surface.

"We don't know what is happening," Suzanne admitted.

"There's no resistance to the propeller," Donald reported. He turned the propulsion system off. The whirring died away for a second time. Now the only sound was the ventilation fan. "I think we are in air."

"How can we be in air?" Suzanne said. "It's totally dark and there is no wave action."

"But it's the only explanation for the sonar not working and the lack of resistance to the propeller," Donald said. "And look. The outside temperature has risen to seventy degrees. We've got to be in air."

"If this is the next life, I'm not ready for it," Perry said.

"You mean we're out of the water entirely?" Suzanne still had trouble believing it.

"I know it sounds crazy," Donald admitted. "But it's the only way I can explain everything, including the fact that the underwater phone doesn't work." Donald next tried the radio and had no luck with that either.

"If we're sitting on dry land," Suzanne said, "how come we haven't tipped over? I mean, this hull is a cylinder. If we were on dry land, we'd surely roll over on our side."

"You're right!" Donald admitted. "That I can't explain."

Suzanne opened an emergency locker between the two pilot seats and pulled out a flashlight. Turning it on, she directed it out her view port. Pressed up against it on the outside was cream-colored, coarse-grained muck.

"At least we know why we didn't tip over," Suzanne said. "We're sitting in a layer of globigerina ooze."

"Explain!" Perry said. He'd leaned forward to see for himself.

"Globigerina ooze is the most common sediment on the ocean floor," Suzanne said. "It's composed mainly of the carcasses of a type of plankton called foraminifera."

"How can we be sitting in ocean sediment and be in air?" Perry asked.

"That's the question," Donald agreed. "We can't, at least not in any way that I know of."

"It's also impossible for globigerina ooze to be this close to the Mid-Atlantic Ridge," Suzanne said. "That sediment is found in the middle of the abyssal plains. Nothing makes sense."

"This is absurd!" Donald snapped. "And I don't like it at all. Wherever we are, we're stuck!"

"Could we be completely buried in the ooze?" Perry asked hesitantly. If he was right, he did not want to hear the answer.

"No! Not a chance," Donald said. "If that were the case there would be more resistance to the propeller, not less."

For a few minutes no one spoke.

"Is there any chance we could be inside the seamount?" Perry asked, finally breaking the silence.

Donald and Suzanne turned to face him.

"How could we be inside a mountain?" Donald asked angrily.

"Hey, I'm only making a suggestion," Perry said. "Mark told me this morning he had some radar data that suggested the mountain might contain gas, not molten lava."

"He never mentioned that to me," Suzanne said.

"He didn't mention it to anyone," Perry said. "He wasn't sure of the data since it was coming from a shallow study of the hard layer we were trying to drill through. It was an extrapolation, and he only mentioned it to me in passing."

"What kind of gas?" Suzanne asked while her mind tried to imagine how a submerged volcano could become void of water. Geophysically speaking it seemed impossible, although she knew that on land some volcanoes did collapse in on themselves to form calderas.

"He had no idea," Perry said. "I guess he thought the most promising candidate was steam held in by the extra-hard layer that was giving us so much trouble."

"Well, it can't be steam," Donald said. "Not at a temperature of almost seventy degrees."

"What about natural gas?" Perry suggested.

"I can't imagine," Suzanne said. "This close to the Mid-Atlantic Ridge, it's a geologically young area. There can't be anything like petroleum or natural gas around here."

"Then maybe it is air," Perry said.

"How could it get here?" Suzanne asked.

"You tell me," Perry said. "You're the geophysical oceanographer. Not me."

"If it is air, there is not a natural explanation that I know of," Suzanne said. "It's as simple as that."

The three people stared at each other for a beat.

"I guess we'll have to crack the hatch and see," Suzanne said.

"Open the hatch?" Donald questioned. "What if the gas is not breathable or it's even toxic?"

"Seems to me we have little choice," Suzanne said. "We have no communications. We're a fish out of water. We've got ten days of life support but what happens after that?"

"Let's not ask that question," Perry said nervously. "I say we crack the hatch."

"All right!" Donald said with resignation. "As captain I'll do it." He stood up from his pilot's seat and took a giant step over the central console. Perry leaned out of the way so that Donald could pass.

Donald climbed up inside the sail. He paused while Suzanne and Perry positioned themselves just underneath him.

"Why don't you just undo it but not open it," Suzanne offered. "Then see if you smell anything."

"Good idea," Donald said. He took Suzanne's suggestion, grabbing the central wheel and turning it. The sealing bolts retracted into the hatch's body.

"Well?" Suzanne called up after a few moments. "Smell anything?"

"Just some dampness," Donald said. "I guess I'll go for it."

Donald cracked the hatch for a brief moment and sniffed.

"What do you think?" Suzanne asked.

"Seems okay," Donald said with relief. He opened the hatch about an inch and smelled the damp air that flowed in. When he was satisfied it was as safe as he could determine, he pushed the hatch all the way up and poked his head out the top. The air had the salty dampness of a beach at low tide.

Donald slowly rotated his head through 360 degrees, straining his eyes in the darkness. He saw absolutely nothing but intuitively he knew that it was a big space. He was staring into a silent, alien blackness as frightening as it was vast.

Poking his head back inside the submersible, he asked for the flashlight.

Suzanne got it for him, and as she handed it up she asked what he'd seen.

"A whole lot of nothing," he replied.

Reemerging from the hatch, Donald shined the flashlight in the distance. The mud stretched away in all directions as far as the light could penetrate. A few isolated mirrorlike puddles of water reflected back at him.

"Hello!" Donald called after cupping his hands around his mouth. He waited. A slight echo seemed to come from the direction of the *Oceanus*'s bow. Donald yelled again; a distinct echo came back in what he estimated to be around three or four seconds.

Donald climbed back down into the submersible after lowering the hatch. The others looked at him expectantly.

"This is the damnedest thing I've ever seen," he said. "We're in some kind of cavern that apparently was recently filled with water."

"But now it's filled with air," Suzanne said.

"It's definitely air," Donald said. "Beyond that, I don't know what to think. Maybe Mr. Bergman is right. Maybe we've somehow been pulled inside the seamount."

"The name is Perry, for chrissake," Perry said. "Give me the light! I'm going to take a look." He took the flashlight from Donald and clumsily climbed the ladder up through the sub's sail. He had to hook one elbow around the top rung and jam the flashlight into his pocket to raise the heavy, wedged-shaped hatch.

"My God!" Perry exclaimed after he had imitated Donald's actions, including testing for echoes. He climbed back down but left the hatch ajar. He handed the flashlight to Suzanne, who took her turn.

When Suzanne returned the three looked at each other and shook their heads. None of them had an explanation although each hoped one of the others might.

"I suppose it goes without saying," Donald began, breaking an uncomfortable silence, "we're in a difficult situation to say the least. We cannot expect any help from the *Benthic Explorer*. With the series of earthquakes, they'll naturally assume we suffered some kind of disaster. They might send down one of the camera sleds, but it's not going to find us in here, wherever the hell we are. In short, we're on our own with no communication and little food and water. So . . ." Donald paused as if thinking.

"So, what do you suggest?" Suzanne asked.

"I suggest we go out and reconnoiter," Donald said.

"What if this cavern or whatever it is floods again?" Perry questioned.

"It seems to me we have to take the chance," Donald said. "I'll be willing to go on my own. It's up to you if you want to join me."

"I'll go," Suzanne said. "It's better than just sitting here and doing nothing."

"I'm not staying here by myself," Perry announced.

"Okay," Donald said. "We have two more flashlights. Let's take them but only use one to conserve the batteries."

"I'll get them," Suzanne said.

Donald was the first one out. He used the ladder rungs mounted on the side of the sail and the hull to climb down. The rungs were there to provide access to the submersible when it was in its chocks on the afterdeck of the *Benthic Explorer.*

Standing on the final rung, Donald shined the light down at the ground. Gauging how deep the *Oceanus* had sunk, he estimated the mud was twenty to twenty-four inches deep.

"Is something the matter?" Suzanne asked. She was the second one out and could see that Donald was hesitating.

"I'm trying to guess how deep the muck is," he said. Still holding onto a rung, he lowered his right foot. It disappeared into the ooze. It wasn't until the mud reached the lower edge of his kneecap that he felt solid ground.

"This is not going to be pleasant," he reported. "The mud is knee-deep."

"Let's hope that's our only problem," Suzanne said.

A few minutes later the three were standing in the mud. Save for a slight glow emanating from the open submersible hatch, the only light came from Donald's flashlight. It cast a meager cone of light in the utter blackness. Suzanne and Perry carried flashlights, too, but as Donald had suggested, they were not turned on. There was no sound in the vast dark space. To conserve the submersible's batteries, Donald had turned off most everything in the sub, even the ventilation fan. He'd left on one light to serve as a beacon to help them find the sub again if they wandered too far afield.

"This is intimidating," Suzanne said with a shudder.

"I think I'd use a stronger word," Perry said. "What's our game plan?"

"That's open to discussion," Donald said. "My suggestion is we head in the direction the *Oceanus* is pointing. That seems to be the closest wall, at least according to my echo." He looked at his compass. "It's pretty much due west."

"Seems like a reasonable plan to me," Suzanne said.

"Let's go," Perry said.

The group set out with Donald in the lead followed by Suzanne. Perry brought up the rear. It was difficult walking in the deep mud and the smell was mildly offensive.

There was no talk. Each was acutely aware of the precariousness of the situation, especially the farther they got from the submersible. After ten minutes Perry insisted they pause. They had not come to any wall, and his courage had waned.

"Walking in this muck is not easy," Perry said, avoiding the real issue. "And it also stinks."

"How far do you think we've gone?" Suzanne asked. Like the others she was out of breath from exertion.

Donald turned and looked back at the submersible, which was no more than a smudge of light in the inky blackness. "Not that far," he said. "Maybe a hundred yards."

"I would have said a mile, the way my legs feel," Suzanne remarked.

"How much farther to this supposed wall?" Perry asked.

Donald yelled again in the direction they were going. The echo came back in a couple of seconds. "I'd guess somewhere in the neighborhood of three hundred yards."

Sudden movement and a series of slapping sounds in the darkness to their immediate left made them all jump. Donald whipped the light around and shined it in the direction of the noise. A stranded fish made a few more agonal flip-flops against the wet mud.

"Oh, my gosh, that scared the bejesus out of me," Suzanne admitted. Her hand was pressed against her chest. Her heart was racing.

"You and me both," Perry confessed.

"We're all understandably on edge," Donald said. "If you two want to go back, I'll continue the reconnoiter myself."

"No, I'll stick it out," Suzanne said.

"Me too," Perry said. The idea of returning to the submersible by himself was worse than forging ahead through the mire.

"Then, let's move out," Donald said. He started off again and the others fell in behind him.

The group slogged ahead in silence. Each step into the unknown blackness ratcheted up their fears and anxiety. The submersible behind them was being swallowed up in the darkness. After another ten minutes they were all as tense as a piano wire about to snap, and that was when the alarm sounded.

The short burst of sound crashed out of the stillness like cannon fire. At first the group froze in their tracks, frantically attempting to determine from which direction the alarm had come. But with the multiple echoes it was impossible to tell. In the next instant they were all slogging their way back toward the submersible.

It was flight in full panic; a mad dash for supposed safety. Unfortunately, the mud did not cooperate. All three tripped almost immediately and fell headfirst into the odious ooze. Regaining their feet, they tried to run again, with the same result.

Without a word to establish consensus, they resigned

themselves to a slower gait. After a few minutes, their lack of significant headway made the futility of their flight apparent. Since there had been no surge of water refilling the cavern, all three stopped within steps of each other, their chests heaving.

The multiple echoes from the horrendous alarm died out and in their wake the preternatural stillness returned. Once again it settled back over the inky darkness like the smothering blanket in Perry's nightmare.

Suzanne raised her hands. The muck, which she knew was a combination of planktonic carcasses and feces of innumerable worms, dripped from her fingers. She wanted desperately to wipe her eyes, but she didn't dare. Donald, who was slightly ahead, turned to face Suzanne and Perry. Mud was streaked across the glass of his flashlight, reducing its effect so that he was lost in shadow to the others. They could just make out the whites of his eyes.

"What in God's name was that alarm?" Suzanne managed. She spit some grainy debris from her mouth. She didn't want to think of what it might have been.

"I was afraid it meant the water was returning," Perry admitted.

"Regardless of what its actual meaning is," Donald said, "for us it has an overarching significance."

"What are you talking about?" Perry questioned.

"I know what he means," Suzanne said. "He means that this is no natural geological formation."

"Exactly!" Donald said. "It's got to be a remnant of the Cold War. And since I had top-secret clearance in the United States submarine service, I can tell you it's not our installation. It has to be Russian!"

"You mean like some kind of secret base?" Perry asked.

He glanced around the black void, now more awestruck than frightened.

"That's the only thing I can imagine," Donald said. "Some kind of nuclear submarine facility."

"I suppose it's possible," Suzanne said. "And if it is, our future is suddenly significantly brighter."

"Maybe yes, maybe no," Donald said. "First, it's going to make a difference only if somebody is still manning the facility. If there is, then our next worry has to be how much they want to keep it a secret."

"I hadn't thought of that," Suzanne admitted.

"But the Cold War is over," Perry said. "Surely we don't have to worry about that old cloak-and-dagger stuff."

"There are people in the Russian military who feel differently," Donald said. "I know because I have met them."

"So what do you think we should do at this point?" Suzanne asked.

"I think that question has just been answered for us," Donald said. He raised his free hand and pointed over the shoulders of the others. "Look over there, in the direction we were going before the alarm sounded!"

Suzanne and Perry spun around. About a quarter of a mile away a single door was slowly opening inward into the blackness. Bright artificial light spilled from the room beyond into the dark cavern, forming a line of reflection that extended to their feet. The trio was too far away to see any interior details, but they could tell the light was intense.

"So much for the question whether the facility is manned or not," Donald said. "Obviously, we are not alone. Now the question becomes how happy they are to see us."

"Do you think we should walk over there?" Perry asked.

"We don't have much choice," Donald said. "We'll have to go at some point."

"Why didn't they just come in here and meet us in person?" Suzanne asked.

"A good question," Donald said. "Maybe it has something to do with the welcome they are planning for us."

"I'm getting scared again," Suzanne said. "This is very bizarre."

"I've never stopped being scared," Perry admitted.

"Let's go meet our captors," Donald said. "And let's hope they don't consider us spies—and that they are familiar with the terms of the Geneva Convention."

Straightening himself, Donald started forward, seemingly oblivious to the mud sucking at his feet. He passed his two companions, who had to admire his courage and leadership.

Perry and Suzanne hesitated for a moment before falling in behind the retired naval commander. Neither spoke as they resignedly trudged in his footsteps toward the beckoning door. They had no idea whether it would provide deliverance or further trials, but as Donald had said, they did not have any choice.

CHAPTER SEVEN

It was slow going. At one point, Perry slipped and fell back into the mire. He was covered with the ooze.

"The first thing I'm going to do is demand a shower," Perry sputtered trying to lighten the mood. He was not successful. No one responded.

As they approached the open door they hoped that their misgivings would be allayed. But no welcoming figures appeared at the threshold, and the light spilling out into the darkness was so bright they were unable to see inside. It was even difficult to look at the opening without shielding their eyes.

When they got close enough they could appreciate that the door was almost two feet thick with a ring of huge throw bolts countersunk into its periphery. It looked like a door to a vault. The edges of the massive portal were angled in. It was obviously constructed to withstand the enormous pressure of seawater flooding the cavern.

At about twenty-five feet from the wall Suzanne and Perry stopped. They were reluctant to proceed without a clearer idea of what they were getting into. They studied the door for clues. From what they could tell, it appeared as if the walls, floor, and ceiling within were constructed of stainless steel that gleamed like mirrors.

Donald had proceeded ahead on his own, and

although he did not step over the threshold, he leaned in. With his forearm acting as a shield against the reflected light, he surveyed the room.

"Well?" Suzanne called. "What do you see?"

"It's a large, square room made out of metal," Donald yelled back over his shoulder. "There's a couple of huge shiny balls in it but nothing else. There also doesn't appear to be any door except this entrance. And I can't tell where the light is coming from."

"Any sign of people?" Perry asked.

"That's a negative," Donald said. "Hey, I think the balls are made of glass. And they must be four to five feet in diameter. Come and take a look!"

Perry glanced at Suzanne. He shrugged. "Why put off the inevitable?"

Suzanne was gripping her arms. She shuddered. "I was hoping by the time we got over here I'd have a better feeling about all this, but I don't. This can't be a submarine base. We're talking about an engineering feat that would make building the Great Pyramid seem like a walk in the park."

"Then what do you think it is?" Perry questioned.

Suzanne turned to look back toward the submersible. The light from the open door was illuminating it despite the distance. Beyond it was blackness. "I truly have no clue."

When Donald saw that Suzanne and Perry were looking back at the submersible, he went ahead and stepped over the threshold into the room. Immediately he put his hands out to balance himself to keep from falling. A combination of the wet mud on his shoes and the polished metal made the floor as slippery as ice.

Once he had his equilibrium Donald again scanned the

room. Now that his eyes had partially adjusted he could
see much better, including hundreds of reflections of
himself in all directions. The walls, floor, and ceiling were
seamless. The only apparent door was the one he'd
entered through. He specifically searched for a source of
the dazzling light but mysteriously could not find any.
When his line of sight took in the huge glass balls, he did a
double take. He was now able to appreciate that the glass
was not entirely opaque. They were clear enough to just
make out what was inside.

"Suzanne, Perry!" Donald yelled. "There are a couple
of people in here after all. But they're sealed inside glass
spheres. Get in here!"

A moment later Suzanne and Perry appeared at the
door.

"Careful about the floor!" Donald warned. "It's as
slick as ice."

Sliding their feet in short movements as if skating
without skates, Suzanne and Perry staggered over to
Donald's side, eager for a better look at the glass spheres.

"My word!" Suzanne exclaimed. "They're floating
around in some kind of fluid."

"Do you recognize them?" Donald asked.

"Should I?" Suzanne responded.

"I think I do," Donald said. "I think it's two of our
divers."

Suzanne stared at Donald in disbelief. Then, to get a
better look, she cupped her hands around her eyes and
leaned against one of the spheres, the surface so opal-
escent it reflected the room's bright illumination.

"I think you're right," Suzanne said. "I can just make
out the *Benthic Explorer* logo on the neoprene suit and
the side of the helmet."

Perry mimicked Suzanne by shielding his eyes with his hands and pressing them against the same sphere Suzanne was gazing into. Donald did likewise from another angle.

"He's breathing!" Perry said. "He must be alive."

"There's something like an umbilical cord coming from some kind of device pressed up against his abdomen," Suzanne said. "Can anybody see where it goes?"

"It goes under him," Donald said. "To the base of the container."

Suzanne moved away enough to allow her to bend down. The sphere had a flat area on which it sat. She did not see any penetrations, and if there were any they would have come directly through the floor.

"This is as astounding as the cavern," Suzanne said while regaining her feet. She reached out and touched the sphere with the tip of her index finger. The material looked like glass but she was not sure.

The others straightened up.

"How on earth did they get here?" Perry asked.

"A lot of questions," Donald said, "and very few answers."

"Are you still thinking this is some kind of military installation?" Suzanne asked Donald.

"What else could it be?" Donald demanded defensively.

"If these divers are alive in these spheres, I can't even guess what the technology is," Suzanne said. "They look like a couple of giant embryos. Not that I can explain the cavern either. Even this room is a step beyond."

"Beyond what?" Donald asked.

"The door!" Perry cried.

All eyes shot to the entrance. The massive door was silently closing.

Frantically the three tried to rush back to it to keep it from sealing them in, but the slippery floor hindered their progress. By the time they arrived the door was almost closed. Collectively they leaned against it to force it back open, but with its mass and the slick floor it was a useless endeavor. With a resounding thud the door closed. Then they heard the muffled mechanical sound of the numerous throw bolts sliding into place.

With renewed sense of terror the three moved away from the door.

"Somebody is controlling all this," Suzanne said gravely. Her worried eyes swept around the seamless room. "And now we are trapped."

"It's got to be Russians," Donald said.

"Enough about the Russians!" Suzanne shouted. "You were in the military too long. You see everything in terms of yesterday's hostilities. This isn't about Russians."

"How do you know?" Donald yelled back. "And don't you dare denigrate my service to my country."

"Oh, please!" Suzanne intoned. "I'm not disparaging your naval service. But look around, Donald! This isn't anything earthly. Look at the light, for goodness' sake." Suzanne held out her hand. "There's no light source, but the illumination is totally even. And there's no shadow."

Perry held out his hands and tried to form shadows, but it was impossible. Donald watched but did not try it himself.

"It's a uniform photon flux that must be penetrating these walls somehow," Suzanne said. "And if I had to guess I'd say there was a significant ultraviolet component."

"How can you tell?" Perry said.

"I can't," Suzanne admitted. "Not for sure since the human eye doesn't pick up ultraviolet, but to my mind there's a definite distortion of the blue of our coveralls and the maroon of your jogging suit."

Perry looked down at his clothing. To him the color was the same as it always had been.

"The spheres!" Donald yelled.

All eyes shifted to the glass balls. Their opalescence had suddenly and dramatically increased so that they were glowing. A moment later there was a cracking sound, and beginning at both apices the spheres opened like enormous flowers losing their petals. With a gush of fluid the divers spilled out onto the floor.

Donald was the first to overcome his shock. As quickly as he could, he rushed to Richard's side. Realizing the unconscious diver was trying to breathe, Donald pulled off the man's helmet and tossed it aside. Richard coughed violently.

Perry rushed to Michael. While he removed his helmet he could hear Richard begin to cough. Michael, however, was not even breathing. Calling upon his CPR training, Perry knew what to do. First he hauled Michael from the debris of the collapsed sphere, pulling his still attached umbilical with him. After a quick check to make sure the diver's mouth was clear, he pinched his nostrils closed, took a breath, and gave Michael a lungful of air. Turning his head to the side, Perry took another breath. He was about to repeat the cycle when he noticed that Michael's eyes were open.

"What the hell are you doing, man!" Michael questioned. He pushed Perry's face away, which was inches from his own.

"I was doing mouth-to-mouth," Perry said. He got to his feet. "I didn't think you were breathing."

"I'm breathing!" Michael insisted. He made a face of disgust and wiped his mouth with the back of his hand. "Believe me, I'm breathing."

Richard's coughing jag came to an abrupt end, and he blinked away the tears it had brought on. His first concern was Michael. When he saw that his buddy was alive and well, he glanced around the room before looking up at the others.

"What's going on?" he asked. "What happened?"

"That's the million-dollar question," Perry answered.

"Where the hell are we?" Richard asked. His eyes took a second quick dash around the room. A questioning expression clouded his face.

"An equally interesting question," Perry said.

"Were you looking for us on your dive?" Donald asked Richard.

For a moment Richard merely looked confused. Then Donald's question helped restore his memory. "Oh, my God!" he cried. "We were on a nearly thousand-foot sat dive! We didn't decompress!" Richard struggled to his feet. His legs were wobbly, especially on the slippery floor. "Michael, we've got to get into the DDC!"

"Take it easy!" Donald said. He grabbed Richard around the upper arm to calm him and keep him from falling. "There's no DDC here. Besides, you're all right. Obviously you don't have the bends."

Richard's confusion deepened. He extended his legs and his arms to check his joints. Blinking repeatedly, he looked around the room again, and while doing so noticed the umbilical connecting him to the base of the collapsed sphere. "What the hell is this?" he demanded.

He grasped the composite group of hoses and wires and immediately let go. His lips curled in revulsion. "Jeez, it feels soft, like I'm holding someone's intestines."

"It has to be some kind of life support," Suzanne said, speaking up for the first time since the divers had emerged from their shells. "Considering the shape you're in without decompressing, I guess it had something to do with that as well."

Richard gingerly touched the device attached to his stomach. It was the size and shape of the head of a toilet plunger. As soon as he touched it, it detached. Catching it in his hand, he looked at its business end. To his horror a series of wormlike appendages protruded from it, their wriggling heads soaked in blood—his blood.

"Ah!" Richard cried. He dropped the device, which quickly retracted into the base of the flattened sphere like a disappearing vacuum cleaner cord. In a panic Richard unzipped the front of his neoprene suit down to his pubis. When he looked at his stomach he cried out again. There were six puncture wounds in a circular pattern around his navel.

After watching Richard, Michael struggled to his feet and hesitantly looked down at his own stomach. He was dismayed to see a similar apparatus. With an expression mirroring Richard's, he reluctantly touched it with his index finger. To his relief it immediately detached and retracted. Opening his dive suit he found the same peculiar pattern of oozing stab wounds around his umbilicus.

"Holy crap!" Michael voiced. "It looks like we were stabbed a bunch of times with an ice pick." He shivered. "I can't stand blood."

Richard zipped his suit back up and then tried to take a few steps on shaky legs. He reached out and supported himself against the wall. "Man, I feel like I've been drugged."

"I feel like I was run over with a goddamn truck," Michael said.

"Where's Mazzola?" Richard asked.

"We wouldn't have any idea," Donald said. "What happened during your dive?"

Richard scratched the back of his head. At first all he could remember was getting into the DDC for the compression, but then, with Michael's participation, they both were able to remember sketchy details of the descent in the bell and entering the water.

"Is that it?" Donald asked. "Nothing after you left the bell?"

Richard nodded. Michael did the same.

"How come you guys all look like you've been in a pigpen?" Richard asked. He didn't wait for an answer. Instead, he looked more closely at the walls. "What is this, some kind of hospital or something?"

"It's no hospital," Donald said. "We can't tell you much else other than how we got here, but that includes how we got dirty."

"That's a start," Richard said. "Fire away!"

Donald explained while the two divers slouched against the wall. It was a hard story to swallow, and their eyes narrowed in disbelief.

"Oh, come on!" Richard scoffed. "What is this? Some kind of a put-on?" He regarded the trio with suspicion. This had to be a prank. Michael nodded in agreement.

"This is no put-on," Donald assured him.

"Just look around this room," Suzanne said.

"Listen!" Donald said, trying to be patient. "Can't

either of you remember anything about how you got here? Didn't you see anybody?"

Richard shook his head. With his foot he pushed around the deflated segments of the sphere. The material was now limp instead of rigid and brittle. "Are you serious about us being inside this stuff? You said it looked like glass. It sure doesn't now."

"It did just a short time ago," Suzanne assured him.

"What we think is that this is a Russian submarine base," Donald continued.

"Correction!" Suzanne interrupted. "That's what *you* think."

"Russians?" Richard echoed. "No shit!" He visibly straightened up. He looked around the room with renewed interest, as did Michael. Both put their hands against the highly polished walls. Richard rapped on the glossy surface with his knuckle. "What is this stuff anyway, titanium?"

Suzanne started to answer but was interrupted by a hissing noise. Everyone looked back to the locations where the spheres had stood. A vapor billowed out of the exposed holes. Quickly an acrid smell pervaded the sealed chamber, and everyone's eyes began to tear.

"We're being gassed!" Suzanne cried before she was overcome by violent coughs.

The group shrank back in terror, pressing themselves against the cold metal walls in a vain attempt to get away from the gas. But before long everyone was coughing and squeezing their eyes shut against the burning sensation.

"Get on the floor!" Donald cried.

Everyone except Perry flattened themselves on the floor while trying ineffectually to cover their mouths and noses with their hands. Perry stumbled back to the door to the cavern and began pounding on it, while screaming for it to be opened.

The door did not budge, but Perry had the presence of mind to notice something despite his panic and physical torment. He was not blacking out nor was he even feeling the slightest bit dizzy. The gas seemed not to have the lethal effect he most feared.

With strength of will Perry held his coughing in check and managed to crack his eyes for an instant despite the discomfort. The room was thick with the foglike vapor. Perry couldn't see far, but he noticed that his arms were suddenly bare.

Curious as to what could have happened to the sleeves of his jogging suit, Perry squinted. He saw that his sleeves had fallen into tatters. They were hanging in shreds as if he'd dipped his arms into acid.

Aware that his whole body now felt cool, Perry patted his hands along his chest. His jogging suit—indeed, all his clothes—were suffering the same fate as his sleeves. The fabric of the clothing itself was progressively losing its structural integrity.

Perry had had nightmares in the past when he was under stress that he was naked in public. Suddenly it was coming to pass as he felt his clothes peel from his body in strips. He clutched at them and felt them disintegrate in his hands.

"It's our clothes!" Perry shouted to the others. "The gas is dissolving our clothes!"

At first fear kept everyone else from responding. Perry yelled his message again and stumbled forward in the fog, almost tripping over Donald. "The gas is dissolving our clothes," he repeated. "And I don't feel any mental effect whatsoever."

Donald pushed himself up to a sitting position. His coveralls experienced the same fate as Perry's jogging suit. Quickly he patted himself to verify that he was indeed becoming naked. But he couldn't open his eyes; the gas stung too much. Even without the visual confirmation, he was convinced. He called out to the others: "Perry's right!"

Suzanne, like Perry, was able to get her eyes open intermittently. She saw that it was true about her clothes. Her coveralls literally fell apart. She also noticed that there was no effect on her mental state despite the discomfort she felt in her throat and chest. Relieved, she got to her feet.

Richard and Michael pushed themselves up into sitting positions. With the drugged feeling they were still experiencing, they could not tell if the gas was affecting their consciousness, but both were coughing heavily. For them, the respiratory effect was more difficult than it was for the others.

"My dive suit's fine," Richard managed between coughs. But then he made the mistake of running his hand over his shoulder. When he did, the neoprene completely depolymerized. At his touch it fell into tiny spheres.

Through blinks, Michael had glimpsed the fate of Richard's suit. He glanced intermittently at his own suit, reluctant to touch it or even move, but Richard reached out and gave his shoulder a sharp slap. The effect was instantaneous. One minute the dive suit looked normal, the next it was running off Michael like so many drops of water.

Suddenly, an alarm sounded and a red light on the wall opposite the door to the cavern began to flash—moments before, that same wall had appeared seamless. Through the caustic vapor, the five began to discern the outline of an open doorway below the light.

The alarm ceased after a few minutes but the light continued to blink. Then they noticed the sound of a high-pitched whistle. Air was being forced through a narrow vent.

Perry advanced slowly toward the flashing light. When he reached the wall, he saw that the outline of the door was more distinct. He felt around its edges. When he did he could feel a steady current of air pushing in. That explained the whistling. He tested with his foot to make sure the floor was level across the threshold. Then he stepped through.

Perry was immediately relieved. The curtain of fast-moving air kept the acrid gas from the hallway he'd entered. The walls, floor, and ceiling were constructed of the same polished metal as the gas-filled room, but the level of illumination was significantly less. Twenty feet ahead Perry could see that the corridor opened up into another chamber.

Perry poked his head back through the air curtain.

"There's another room," he shouted. "And it's clear. Quick!"

The other four struggled to their feet and moved toward the blinking light. Suzanne had to guide Donald; he couldn't stand to open his eyes. In a minute, the entire party made it into the new room.

The gas wore off swiftly. They were so relieved, they weren't troubled by the complete disintegration of their clothes. All five were stark naked, but other concerns were more pressing. Ahead the second room beckoned.

"Let's move," Donald said. He gestured for Perry to precede them since he was already in the lead.

Perry flattened himself against the wall and motioned for Donald to pass. "I think you should be first. You're still the captain of the ship."

Donald nodded and pushed past. Perry fell in behind him followed by Suzanne. The two divers brought up the rear.

"It's pretty obvious what's going on now," Donald said.

"I'm glad it's obvious to you," Perry said.

"What do you mean?" Suzanne asked.

"We're being prepared for interrogation," Donald said. "It's a recognized technique to strip away a person's sense of identity as a way to break down resistance. Our clothes are certainly part of our identity."

"I don't have any resistance," Perry said. "I'll tell whoever it is whatever they want to know."

"Donald, does that mean you know what that gas was?" Suzanne asked.

"That's a negative," Donald said.

Donald halted at the second room's threshold and peered in. It was considerably smaller than the first chamber although it, too, was lined with the same mysterious, metallic material. From where he was standing, he could make out a glass-doored exit as well as a white hall with what appeared to be framed pictures on the walls. Within the chamber he noticed that the floor sloped toward the center, where there was a grate, and the ceiling peaked to a central point with a second grate.

"Well?" Suzanne questioned. From where she was she couldn't see what lay ahead.

"It looks encouraging," Donald said. "There's a relatively normal looking corridor beyond a glass door."

"Then let's move," Richard called impatiently from behind Suzanne.

With both hands on the doorjamb for support, Donald moved first one foot onto the sloped floor and then brought the other to it. As he'd anticipated he began to slide once he let go. He slid for about three feet with his hands flailing to keep from falling. At that point the floor angled out to be almost level. He turned and warned the others.

Everyone was careful except Michael. Having grown up in Chelsea, Massachusetts, where he'd played hockey since age five, he wasn't concerned about the slick floor. But its angle took him by surprise. His feet went out from under him on his first step, and he careened into the others like a bowling ball. In a flash the entire group was a pile of entwined naked limbs.

"For chrissake!" Donald snapped. He extricated himself and helped Suzanne to her feet. The others struggled up by themselves. Michael was hardly remoreful. Now that his eyes were open, he was much more interested in appreciating Suzanne's body. Richard swore and cuffed Michael on the top of his head. Michael shoved Richard in return, effectively sending them both to the ground again.

"Knock it off!" Donald shouted. Being careful not to fall, he separated the two divers. Richard and Michael obeyed, but continued to glare at each other.

"My God!" Suzanne voiced. "Look!" She pointed back at the doorway they'd just come through. Everyone gaped in astonishment. The doorway was silently sealing over, as if the metal wall were fusing together. Within moments the opening was gone without a trace. The wall was seamless once again.

"If I'd not seen that with my own eyes, I'd never believe it," Perry said. "It's supernatural, like a movie special effect."

"I can't begin to understand the technology," Suzanne said. "I think it lets the Russians off the hook."

A deep gurgling sound then issued from the central grate. All eyes turned in its direction.

"Oh no!" Suzanne said. "What's coming now?"

Before anyone could respond, a clear fluid that looked like water bubbled up through the central floor grate. The group shrank back, then scrambled toward the glass door. The angle and slippery surface of the floor forced them to their hands and knees. The first to the door began to bang on the glass, desperate for a way to open it. Behind them the inrushing water had become a geyser; the water level was rising rapidly.

Within minutes they were waist-deep in water. Moments later they were all treading water watching with horror as the ceiling approached. Even if they could keep treading indefinitely, there soon would be no room to breathe. Rapidly the group was faced together while struggling for the last remnants of air in the very peak of the ceiling. As the strongest swimmers Richard and Michael were at the center directly below the grate, and in a desperate attempt to find more air they stuck their fingers through the holes and tried to pull the grate from its housing.

But their efforts were fruitless. The grate would not budge, and the water level continued to rise until the room was filled to the ceiling. No sooner had everyone gone under, than the room began to drain, and at an extraordinary rate. Within seconds there was headroom again; within minutes Donald and Richard, the tallest of the five, felt their feet brush the floor.

Soon there was a loud, rude sucking noise as the last of the water disappeared down the drain, and the group was left in a wet, naked heap in the central basin of the floor. For some time no one moved. A combination of utter terror, panic driven exertion, and having inadvertently swallowed sizable gulps of the fluid left them physically and emotionally exhausted.

Donald finally pushed himself up to a sitting position. He felt light-headed. He had an odd feeling that more time had passed than he could account for. It occurred to him that they might have been drugged by the water that had filled the room. He closed his eyes for a moment and rubbed his temples. When he reopened his eyes he looked at the others. They all appeared to be sleeping. He looked toward the glass door when his gaze shot back to Suzanne.

"Good Lord!" Donald muttered. He couldn't believe his eyes. Suzanne was bald! Donald ran a hand over the top of his head, but he'd kept it shaved for several years. He felt for his mustache. It was gone! Raising his forearm he saw that, too, was totally devoid of hair. He glanced down at his chest; there wasn't a hair there.

Donald shook Perry, then nudged Suzanne. When both of them were awake enough to understand what he was saying, he filled them in.

"Oh, no!" Perry cried. He sat bolt upright. Using both hands he reached up and gingerly touched his scalp. There was no hair, only smooth skin. He pulled his hands away as if he'd touched something hot. He was horrified.

Suzanne was more curious than dismayed. Something

had rendered them completely hairless. How had it happened—and why?

"What's happening?" Richard asked. His words were slurred. He sat up, then had to steady himself. "Ooo . . . I feel like I tied one on."

"I'm a bit dizzy myself," Perry admitted. "Maybe there was something in the water. I know I swallowed some."

"I think we were drugged," Donald said.

"We all swallowed a lot of the water," Richard said. "It's hard not to in that kind of ordeal. That was worse than submarine escape training."

"I think I know what is going on," Suzanne said.

"Yeah, me, too," Perry said. "We're being tortured and humiliated."

"All techniques of interrogation," Donald added.

"I don't think it has anything to do with interrogation," Suzanne said. "The strange intense light, the acrid gas, and now the depilation suggests something else."

"What's depilation?" Richard asked.

"It's what happened to your head," Perry said.

Richard blinked. He stared at Perry, then touched the top of his head. "My God, I'm bald." He looked over at Michael, who was still slumbering. Then he reached over and gave him a shove. "Hey, you hairless wonder. Wake up!"

Michael had trouble opening his eyes.

"I think we're being decontaminated," Suzanne said. "I think that's what all this is about: getting rid of microorganisms like bacteria and viruses. We've effectively been sterilized."

No one spoke. Perry nodded as he considered what Suzanne had said. He thought it was possible.

"I still think all this is to prepare us for interrogation," Donald said. "Sterilizing us doesn't make sense to me. I don't know if it is Russians who are behind this or not, but somebody wants something from us."

"Maybe we're going to know pretty soon," Perry said. He nodded toward the glass door, which was now ajar. "I think the next stage is ready."

Donald unstably struggled to his feet. "There was definitely some kind of drug in the water," he said. He waited until a fresh episode of dizziness passed, then headed toward the open door. Where the slippery floor angled up he had to go on all fours. Once he reached the doorway, he stood up and looked down a white, fifty-foot corridor.

"I feel drugged but I also feel strangely hungry," Suzanne said.

"I was just thinking the same thing," Perry admitted.

"Listen, you guys," Donald called. "Things are looking up. There's living quarters down the end of this hallway. Let's mobilize!"

Suzanne and Perry got their feet under them and stood up, battling the same fleeting dizziness Donald had experienced.

"I guess living quarters means beds," Suzanne said. "And that sounds good to me. Besides, I want out of this room in case that water comes back."

"My feelings exactly," Perry said.

Richard and Michael had fallen back asleep. Suzanne gave them both a poke but neither stirred. Perry lent a hand.

"Whatever was in that water affected them more than us," Suzanne said as she shook Richard to get him to open his eyes.

"They felt drugged from being in the spheres, even before the dousing," Perry said. He pulled Michael, who groaned to be let alone, up to a sitting position.

"Let's move it!" Donald called. "I don't want this door to close before you're all out of here."

Despite their groggy state, the warning about the door penetrated Richard and Michael's stupor, and they got to their feet. As they moved their mental state rapidly improved. By the time the group joined Donald, the divers were even talking.

"This isn't half bad," Richard said as he inspected the corridor with lidded eyes. Instead of mirrorlike metal, the walls and ceiling were a high-gloss white laminate. Framed, three dimensional pictures lined the walls. The floor was covered with a tight-weave white carpet.

"These pictures are something else," Michael commented. "They're so realistic. It looks like I can see into them for twenty miles."

"They're holographs," Suzanne said. "But I've never seen a holograph with such vivid, natural color. They are startling, especially in this otherwise white environment."

"They all look like scenes from ancient Greece," Perry said. "Whoever our tormentors are, at least they're civilized."

"Let's go, men!" Donald called. He was standing impatiently just over the next threshold. "We've got some tactical decisions to make."

"Tactical decisions," Perry mimicked in a whisper to Suzanne. "Doesn't he ever relax this military posturing?"

"Not often," Suzanne admitted.

The group walked the length of the hallway and paused, taken aback by the scene in front of them. After the series of stark, industrial chambers, they were unprepared for the room's sumptuousness. The decor was futuristic, with lots of mirrors and white marble, yet it had a calm, cool, inviting ambiance. A dozen, canopied, couchlike beds with white cashmere blankets lined both walls. Five of the beds were invitingly turned down with folded clean clothes lying atop each pillow. In the background, soft instrumental music completed the mood.

Down the center of the room stretched a large, low table with chaiselike, deeply cushioned chairs. The table was laid for a meal with covered servers and pitchers of iced drinks. The dishes were white, the tablecloth was white, and the flatware was gold.

"If this is heaven, I'm not ready," Perry said when he had recovered enough to speak.

"I don't think chow smells this good in heaven," Richard said. "And I just realized I'm more hungry than tired." He started forward with Michael at his heels.

"Hold up!" Donald said. "I'm not sure we should eat anything. The food's probably drugged or even worse."

"You really think so?" Richard said with obvious disappointment. He wavered, looking back and forth between Donald and the laden table.

"And those mirrors," Donald said, pointing to the huge sheets that formed the far end of the room. "I'd assume they are two-way, which would mean we're being watched."

"Who the hell cares if they treat us like this," Michael said. "My vote is we eat."

Suzanne's eyes fell on the folded garments on each bed. She had not noticed them sooner because they were white like most everything else and blended perfectly with the white linen. She went over to the nearest bed. She lifted the garments and shook them out. There were two simple pieces: a long-sleeved tunic that opened at the front and a pair of boxer shorts. Both were made of a silky white satin, and both were curiously seamless.

"My word! Pajamas!" Suzanne commented. "Now this is downright thoughtful." Without a moment's hesitation, Suzanne pulled on the shorts. The tunic was generously proportioned and came to knee length, covering the boxers. It tied with a gold braided rope. Along the sides were several pockets.

Suzanne's dressing reawakened everyone's self-consciousness. The four men grabbed clothing sets from the beds and donned them.

Michael eyed himself in the mirrors at the end of the room. "Not much to these things," he said. "But they're comfortable."

Richard laughed at him. "You look like a faggot."

"As if you don't, asshole," Michael shot back hotly.

"That's enough!" Donald barked. "There's to be no fighting among ourselves. Save it for whoever it is we'll be facing. Which brings me to the issue of setting up watches to stand guard."

"What the hell are you talking about?" Richard asked. "This isn't some kind of military exercise. I'm going to eat and then I'm racking out. I'm not standing any watch."

"We're all tired," Donald said. "But there is a door to consider that we don't have any control over."

All eyes swung around to gaze at the door at the end of the room opposite the mirrors. It was white like everything else and was without a knob, latch, or hinges.

"We have to stay vigilant," Donald added. "I don't want these Russians or whoever these people are sneaking in here and doing whatever they want to us."

"Judging by the pains they have taken with these accommodations, I don't think your paranoia is justified," Suzanne said. "And I thought we decided we're not dealing with Russians here."

"Well, you people argue about all that," Richard said. He walked over to the table and lifted the cover of one of the chafing dishes. The savory aroma filled the room.

"What is it?" Michael asked. He leaned over to look.

"I don't have a clue," Richard said. He lifted the spoon. The steaming food was cream colored and had a pasty consistency, like hot cereal's. "It looks like Cream of Wheat, and it smells mighty good." He brought the spoon to his mouth and tasted it. "Well, I'll be damned! How'd they know? It tastes like my favorite food: steak."

Michael took a taste. "Steak? What, are you crazy? It tastes like sweet potatoes."

"Get outta here!" Richard complained. "You and your sweet potatoes." He sat down on one of the chaises and helped himself to a sizable ladle of the food. "You're always talking about sweet potatoes."

Michael sat opposite and took a portion for himself. "Hey, I'm sorry," he said sarcastically. "I happen to like sweet potatoes."

Suzanne and Perry stepped to the table, their curiosity piqued by this exchange. They were experiencing almost irresistible hunger. Suzanne was the first to try the food.

"That's incredible," she remarked. "It tastes like mango."

"That's hard to believe," Perry said. "Because to me it tastes exactly like fresh corn right off the cob."

Suzanne took another taste. "To me it's mango, without a doubt. Maybe there's some way it tricks our brains to interpret the taste according to our own predilections."

Even Donald was intrigued. He came over to the table and tried a minute amount. He shook his head in disbelief. "It tastes like biscuits to me: fresh buttermilk biscuits." He took one of the chairs. "I guess I'm as hungry as everybody else."

Everyone helped themselves to varying amounts of the curious food. They found it difficult to resist going back for seconds. They also discovered that the iced drink had a similar variable effect. It tasted different to each person, according to his or her preference.

As soon as the group's ravenous hunger had been slaked, the exhaustion and sleepiness that they'd experienced earlier returned, and with a vengeance. Fighting against sagging eyelids they pushed back from the table and sought their separate beds. No sooner had they drawn up the covers than everyone but Donald fell into a deep, hibernating sleep. Donald struggled vainly in hopes of maintaining a vigil, but it was impossible. Within minutes he, too, was slumbering.

The moment Donald's eyes closed, tiny red lights appeared on the canopy of each bed. At the same time, a glow emanated from the canopy and enveloped the sleeping individual below in a violet halo.

CHAPTER EIGHT

The tiny red lights above the beds in the living quarters switched momentarily to green and the violet glow faded. A moment later the green lights blinked off.

Perry was the first to wake up. It was not a gradual transition but rather a sudden change from deep sleep to full consciousness. For a few seconds he stared at the canopy above him, attempting to put the strange structure in context and orient himself. But he couldn't. He'd awakened to nothing like what he expected: namely, the blank ceiling of the supposed V.I.P. suite on the *Benthic Explorer*.

Perry was confused, but as soon as he turned his head, it all came back to him. It hadn't been a dream. The *Oceanus*'s horrifying plunge to unfathomable depths had been a reality.

There was a simple clothes tree standing within reach of his bed. A set of white satin drawers and tunic similar to those he'd put on were hanging on it. Perry realized he felt quite naked under the coverlet. He lifted the edge of the cashmere blanked and looked at himself. Not only was he naked, he detected the same peculiar ring of puncture wounds around his navel as he'd seen on Richard and Michael when they'd emerged from the spheres.

Perry let out a low-pitched cry, then leaped from the

bed to examine his wounds more carefully. He spread the soft skin of his abdomen. The puncture wounds were not deep and they weren't painful, much to Perry's relief. Most important of all, they seemed healed.

As Perry absorbed this discovery, he had another shock. His legs and groin were hairy again! He inspected his forearm and discovered that the hair had returned there, too. He put a hand to his scalp, and smiled.

Perry grabbed the clothes from the ebony rack and pulled them on as he transversed the length of the room.

His reflection in the mirror practically made him swoon. His scalp was covered with a full head of hair. It was only about an inch long, but it was as thick and dark as it had been when he was in junior high school. He felt like he'd discovered the fountain of youth.

Perry heard the others stirring. He turned in time to see Donald and Suzanne slipping back into their clothes. Richard and Michael were sitting on the edges of their beds, gawking at the surroundings. Their clothes were neatly piled in their laps.

"Just as I thought," Donald said to no one in particular. "I knew those bastards would be in here screwing around with us when we were sleeping. That's why I wanted to set up watches."

"It isn't all bad," Perry said as he sauntered over. "We've got hair! Can you imagine? Mine is thicker than it was when I lost it."

"I noticed my hair," Suzanne said with less enthusiasm.

"Aren't you thrilled?" Perry said.

"I preferred the length I had yesterday," Suzanne said. "Or actually the length I had three days ago."

"What do you mean, three days ago?" Perry questioned.

"Yesterday was July twenty-first," Suzanne said. "Right?"

"I guess," Perry said. He wasn't sure thanks to the overnight flight to the Azores.

"Well, my watch, which someone took off my wrist but was nice enough to leave behind, says it's now the twenty-fourth."

Suzanne's watch had been the only one to last through the gassing. Her gold bracelet band remained undissolved.

"Maybe whoever removed it advanced the date," Perry suggested. The idea of being asleep for three days was disturbing, to say the least.

"It's possible," Suzanne said. "But I doubt it. I mean, to grow as much hair as we have, it would have taken more than three days. Maybe we've been asleep for a month and three days."

Perry shivered. "A month?" he gulped. "I can't imagine. Besides, the hair growth we've had has to have come from some kind of amazing treatment. My hair's back to the way it was when I was fourteen. I'll tell you something: as a businessman, I'd kill to find out the secret. Can you imagine? What a product."

"They didn't do me any favors," Donald said. "I didn't want hair on my head."

"Did you notice the puncture wounds on your stomachs?" Suzanne asked Perry and Donald.

They both nodded.

"I think that means we were on life support of some kind," Suzanne said. "Maybe the same kind our divers had been on in those spheres."

"That was my thought," Perry said. "I suppose they had to keep us on something if we were out so long."

"Hey, are you guys okay?" Suzanne called over to Richard and Michael, who were finishing dressing.

"I'm all right," Richard said. "Except for the fact that I was wishing this was all a bad dream."

"Drugging us is in violation of the Geneva Convention," Donald growled. "We're civilians! Who knows what these puncture wounds mean. They could have given us anything—AIDS, or truth drugs."

"Actually, I feel really good," Perry admitted. He flexed his arms and stretched his legs. It was as if his body as well as his hair had been rejuvenated.

"Me, too," Michael said. He touched his toes and then ran in place for several strides. "I feel as if I could swim for twenty miles."

"I got my hair back but now my beard's gone," Richard said. "Explain that!"

The other men reflexively stroked their chins. It was true. They had no stubble.

"This is getting more and more interesting," Perry said.

"I'd say it's getting more and more surreal," Suzanne said. She looked closely at Perry's cheeks. Previously he'd had a definite five o'clock shadow. Now his complexion was perfectly clear.

"Hang on, guys!" Richard exclaimed. He pointed at the door on the wall opposite the mirrors. "Looks like we're being let out of the cage."

All eyes turned to see the door silently open. Beyond was another long white corridor with framed holographs. The light coming from the other end of it was bright and natural.

"That looks like daylight," Suzanne said.

"It can't be daylight," Donald said. "Unless we got moved somehow."

Perry felt a chill go down his spine. Intuitively he knew that everything that had happened so far was a preamble of what was going to happen in the next few minutes. The problem was he had no idea what it was going to be.

Richard walked to the doorway to get a better look. He shielded his eyes against the brightness reflecting off the glossy white walls.

"Can you see anything?" Suzanne asked.

"Not much," Richard admitted. "It opens up at the end and there's a wall opposite. It must be open to the sky. Let's go!"

"Hold up a minute," Suzanne said. Then she looked at Donald. "What do you say? Should we go? Obviously our hosts expect us to."

"I think we should go but as a group," Donald said. "We should stick together as much as we can, but maybe we should pick one person to speak for us if we encounter our captors."

"Fine," Suzanne said. "I nominate Perry."

"Me?" Perry squeaked. He cleared his throat. "Why me? Donald's still the captain."

"True," Suzanne said. "But you are the president of Benthic Marine. Whoever is holding us might appreciate the fact that you speak with some authority, especially about the drilling operation."

"You think the reason we're down here is because of the drilling?"

"It has crossed my mind," Suzanne said.

"Still, Donald's been in the military," Perry whined. "I haven't. What if this is a Russian military base?"

"I think it is safe to say it is not a Russian base," Suzanne replied.

"It's not completely out of the question," Donald said. "But I think Perry is a good choice regardless. It will give me a better chance to assess the situation, especially if things get hostile."

"Richard and Michael!" Suzanne called. "Do either of you have an opinion about who speaks for us?"

"I think the prez should be the one," Michael said.

Richard merely nodded. He was impatient to go.

"Then it's decided," Suzanne said. She gestured for Perry to lead them down the corridor.

"Okay!" Perry said with more alacrity than he felt. He tightened the golden braid around his tunic, squared his shoulders, and headed toward the corridor. Richard gave him a supercilious glance as he passed and then fell in behind him. The others followed in single file with Michael in the rear.

Perry slowed as he approached the end of the hallway. He was even more certain the light streaming in was sunlight since he could feel its radiant warmth. He gauged the space ahead to be an open sky enclosure approximately twenty feet square.

About six feet away Perry stopped and Richard bumped up against him.

"What's the matter?" Suzanne asked. She pushed past Richard.

Perry didn't answer since he didn't know exactly why he'd stopped. Slowly he leaned forward so that he could see progressively more of the opposite wall. He was looking for the top, but he couldn't yet see it. After a step forward he tried again. This time he could see the top of the wall which he estimated to be about fifteen feet high.

Above that he could see feet, ankles, bare calves, and the hems of outfits like the one he had on.

Perry straightened up and turned to the others. "There are people on top of the opposite wall," he whispered. "They're dressed the way we are."

"Really?" Suzanne questioned. She leaned forward to try to see for herself, but she was too far back.

"I can't be positive," Perry said. "But I think they're wearing these same flimsy satin clothes we are." He and everyone else had assumed the flimsy, weird, lingerie-like outfits were prisoners' garb.

"Come on!" Richard said, even more impatient now. "This I gotta see. Let's go!"

"Why would they be dressed like ancient Greeks?" Suzanne asked Donald.

Donald shrugged. "You've got me. Let's just move out and see for ourselves."

Perry led the way. With his hand over his eyes to shield against the glare of a square of bright sky, he looked up. What he saw astounded him to the point that he stopped dead in his tracks and his mouth gaped in wonderment. Suzanne bumped into him and the rest of the group nudged against her all equally dumbfounded.

They were standing in a penlike enclosure. Fifteen feet above was a glass-enclosed loggia ringed by a marble balustrade and supported by fluted columns whose capitals were encrusted with gilded sea creatures. Fronting the enclosure the entire loggia was packed with people pressed against the glass and staring down in unmoving, silent, intense curiosity. As Perry had surmised from his limited earlier view, they were all dressed in identical, lingerie-like, loose-fitting satin tunics and shorts.

Perry had had no specific mental image of what the

people were going to look like, but what he was confronted with hadn't even been part of his imagination which leaned toward expecting fiercer-looking captors. Before he'd caught the glimpse of the satin outfits he'd anticipated uniforms, and he'd expected stern if not openly aggressive expressions. Instead he found himself staring at the most beautiful collection of people he'd ever seen, whose faces reflected an almost divine serenity. Although the ages varied from tiny children to vigorous elders, the vast majority were in their early to mid twenties. Everyone radiated good health with lithe bodies, sparkling eyes, lustrous hair, and teeth so white they made Perry think of his own yellow by comparison.

"I don't believe this!" Richard gushed as he took in the spectacle.

"Who are these people?" Suzanne asked, her voice an awed whisper.

"I've never seen such a gorgeous group of people," Perry managed. "Every one of them. There's not even an average-looking one in the bunch."

"I feel like we're rats in a huge experiment," Donald said under his breath. "Look at them gawk at us! And remember, appearances can be deceptive! Keep in mind these people have been toying with us for their own amusement. All this show might be some kind of trap."

"But they're stunningly beautiful," Suzanne commented as she slowly turned to take in more, "particularly the children and even the aged. How could this be a trap? I can tell you one thing for sure, seeing these people certainly puts to bed the idea of this being a secret Russian submarine base."

"Well, they're not American either," Perry said.

"There's not one overweight person in the entire crowd."

"This must be heaven," Michael said in a dazed whisper.

"I think it is more like a zoo," Donald spat. "The difference is that here we're the animals."

"Try to think of something positive," Suzanne suggested. "I have to say I'm relieved."

"Well, there is one thing," Donald commented. "At least I don't see any weapons."

"You're right!" Perry said. "That's definitely encouraging."

"Of course they don't need any weapons, with us imprisoned down here and them up there," Donald added.

"I suppose that's true," Perry said. "What do you think, Suzanne?"

"I can't think," Suzanne said. "This whole experience continues to be too surreal. Are we looking at a patch of sky up there?"

"It certainly looks like it," Perry said.

"Do you think there is a chance we could have been transported eastward when the *Oceanus* fell down the shaft?" Suzanne asked. "I mean, could we be on one of the Azores Islands?"

"The only way we're going to find out is if they decide to tell us," Donald said.

"Who cares where we are," Michael said. "Check out the women! What bodies! Can they be real or are we just imagining this?"

"That's an interesting thought," Suzanne said. "Last night—or whenever it was that we ate—the food tasted as we wished. Could that be happening now with our vision?

I mean, it's another sense. Maybe we're seeing what we want to see."

"That's too far out for me to even contemplate," Perry said. "I've never been a big believer in the supernatural."

"Hey, who the hell cares," Richard said. "Look at that chick with the long brown hair. What a figure! Hey, she's looking at me."

Richard smiled broadly, raised his hand, and waved enthusiastically. The woman smiled back and held up her hand, pressing her palm against the glass.

"Hey!" Richard crooned. "She likes me!" Richard blew kisses, which made the woman smile more broadly.

Encouraged by Richard's success, Michael made eye contact with a woman with shiny, jet black hair. She acknowledged him by putting her palm against the glass just as Richard's acquaintance had done. Michael went crazy jumping up and down and waving frantically with both hands. The woman responded by laughing heartily, although there was no sound because of the glass.

Suzanne lowered her gaze and got Donald's attention. "I don't see any suggestion of hostility," she said. "They all look so peaceful."

"It's probably just a ruse," Donald said. "A way of putting us off guard."

Perry reluctantly took his eyes off the beautiful people to consult with Suzanne and Donald. Richard and Michael continued their antics for the benefit of the two women. They were both trying to improvise a sign language.

"What are we going to do?" Perry asked.

"I personally don't like standing here making a spectacle of myself," Donald said. "I suggest we go back to the living quarters and wait to see what happens. Obviously the ball's in their court. Let them come to us in our office, so to speak.''

"But who are these people?" Suzanne questioned. "This is bizarre, like a science fiction movie."

Perry was about to respond but the words stuck in his throat. He pointed over Suzanne and Donald's shoulders. One of the enclosure's walls was mysteriously opening. Behind it was a staircase leading up to the loggia.

"Well," Suzanne exclaimed. "Like you said, Donald, the ball is in their court, and I think we're being invited to a face-to-face meeting."

"What should we do?" Perry questioned nervously.

"I think we should go up," Donald said. "But let's go slowly and stay together, and, Perry, you do the talking like we decided."

Richard and Michael had not seen the silent appearance of the stairway thanks to their communication gestures which had competitively progressed to pure silliness. Above, the crowd was responding gleefully to their antics which only encouraged them to new heights. But when they caught sight of the stairs, they bolted for them. They were both eager to make more intimate contact with their newfound female friends.

"Hold it!" Donald barked. He'd stepped sideways to block the divers' mad dash. "Fall in! We're going as a group and Mr. Bergman is doing the talking."

"I gotta meet this brunette," Richard said eagerly.

"I got a date with the raven-haired honey," Michael added out of breath.

Both divers tried to step around Donald, but he reached out and grasped their upper arms in a viselike grip. They both started to protest but changed their minds when they saw Donald's face. The ex-naval officer's nostrils were flared and his mouth pressed into a grim line of determination.

"I suppose it can wait a few minutes," Richard managed.

"Yeah, sure," Michael said. "There'll be time."

Donald let go of the divers' arms, then gestured for Perry to lead the way.

Perry had a good deal more self-assurance as he started up the stairs than he'd had earlier in the corridor. Confronting a mixed group of handsome individuals in matching lingerie seemed less intimidating than what his imagination had previously conjured up. Yet the uniqueness of the circumstances undermined his confidence as he progressed. He found himself wondering if Michael could be right about the whole scene being a collective hallucination and thereby be an elaborate trap as Donald suggested. But then Perry's normally optimistic nature had trouble thinking up a rationale for a trap, especially since whoever these people were, they didn't have to spring any trap since they were already completely in charge of the situation.

The beautiful people, as Perry called them to himself in his confused musings, had initially surged forward to crowd around the head of the stairs like a group of teenagers anticipating the appearance of a rock star. But as Perry and the others neared the top they shrank back. Even this confused Perry since they retreated as if in fear or at least in attentive respect like people would do around a trained but potentially ferocious animal.

Perry mounted the top step and stopped. Ten feet away the throng of beautiful people were arranged in a semicircle. No one moved. No one spoke. No one smiled.

Perry had assumed their captors would be the first to

speak. He hadn't planned to go first but eventually decided to break the ensuing uncomfortable silence with a tentative, "Hi."

His greeting brought on a few giggles from the beautiful people but not much else. Perry turned to glance back at his colleagues for suggestions. Suzanne shrugged. Donald had nothing to volunteer. He still seemed far more mistrustful than Perry felt.

Perry turned back to the crowd. "Does anyone speak any English?" he called out in desperation. "Any English at all or maybe some Spanish?" Perry could speak a little.

A couple stepped forward. Both appeared to be in their mid twenties, and like everyone else, they were shockingly handsome. They had archetypally perfect features which reminded Perry of images he'd seen on ancient cameos. The man had blond hair of medium length. His eyes were an intense sky blue. The woman had fiery red hair with a prominent widow's peak. Her green eyes were as bright as emeralds. Both had rosily radiant, flawless skin. Back in L.A., there would be no question: these two were movie star material.

"Hello, friends, how are you?" the man said with a perfect American accent. "Please don't be afraid. You'll not be harmed. My name is Arak and this is Sufa." The man gestured toward the woman next to him.

"I'd like to say hi, too," Sufa said. "What would each of you like to be called?"

Perry was stunned to hear such regular English come out of their mouths. It was oddly reassuring to hear something so familiar, given the alien quality of everything they'd encountered since the *Oceanus* sunk.

"Who are you people?" Perry managed.

"We are inhabitants of Interterra," Arak said. His resonant baritone was not dissimilar to Donald's.

"And where the hell is Interterra?" Perry demanded. Without meaning to, his voice had a harsh edge. It had suddenly occurred to him that perhaps this whole setup was some kind of elaborate joke, rather than the kind of trap Donald feared.

"Please!" Arak said solicitously. "I know you are confused and exhausted, and you certainly have a right to be after what you've been through. We are well aware how taxing the decontamination sequence can be, so please try to relax. There's a lot of excitement in store for you."

"Are you expatriate Americans?" Perry asked.

Both Arak and Sufa slapped their hands over their mouths in a vain effort to contain their laughter. All the beautiful people close enough to hear Perry's question did the same.

"Please excuse our laughter," Arak said. "We don't mean to be rude. No, we are not Americans. We Interterrans happen to be quite accomplished in your languages. English in all its varieties happens to be Sufa's and my specialty."

Suzanne leaned next to Perry's ear and whispered: "Ask them again where Interterra is."

Perry complied.

"Interterra is beneath the oceans," Arak said in response. "It resides in a gap between what you people call the earth's crust and the earth's mantle. It's an area your seismic scientists call the Mohorovičić discontinuity."

"This is an underground world?" Suzanne blurted. She looked up at what appeared to be a patch of sky filled with sunlight. She was stupefied.

"Undersea is more correct," Sufa interjected. "But please . . . we know you will have many questions. They will all be answered in due time. For now we graciously beg for your forbearance."

"What's forbearance?" Richard asked.

"It means patience," Sufa said. She smiled graciously.

"But we do need to know how we should address each of you," Arak said.

"I'm Perry, president of Benthic Marine," Perry said while patting his chest. He then identified the others with their given names.

Arak stepped forward and presented himself directly to Suzanne. He was a good head taller than she. He held his right arm outstretched with his palm facing her. He gestured toward it with his other hand. "Perhaps you will do me the honor of an Interterran greeting," he said. "Press your palm against mine."

Suzanne hesitated and furtively glanced at Perry and Donald before complying. Her hand was a good deal smaller than Arak's.

"Welcome Dr. Newell," Arak said once their hands had met. "We are particularly pleased that you have come to visit us." He bowed and took his hand away.

"Well, thank you," Suzanne said. She was confused yet flattered that she'd been singled out for an individual welcome.

Arak backed away. "Now, my honored guests," he said. "You will be taken to your quarters, which I'm sure you will find agreeable."

"Wait a sec, Arak!" Richard called. He raised himself up on his tiptoes. "There's a gorgeous brunette somewhere around here who's dying to meet me."

"And there's a raven-haired beauty that I want to meet," Michael said.

The two divers had been scanning the crowd for the women since they'd come up the stairs. To their chagrin they'd not been able to spot either one.

"There will be plenty of time for socializing," Arak said, "but for now it is important to get you to your rooms since you've yet to eat and properly wash. There will be a gala celebration for your arrival later, which we hope you will all attend. So, please follow me."

"This will only take a couple of minutes," Richard said. He started forward, intending to walk around Arak and Sufa and mingle in the crowd. But Donald grabbed him as hard as he had when they were downstairs.

"Knock it off, sailor!" Donald snarled under his breath. "We stay together! Remember!"

Richard glared back for a moment, fighting the urge to tell Donald to drop dead. He was so close to connecting with that beautiful woman, it was hard to deny himself. Self-restraint had never been his strong point. But once the intensity of Donald's gaze gave him pause, he relented.

"I guess some chow's not a bad idea," he said to save face.

"You'd better stay in line, bro," Donald snapped. "Otherwise you and I are going to be banging heads."

"Just for the record," Richard said. "I ain't afraid of you."

CHAPTER NINE

Suzanne put one foot ahead of the other as she followed Arak and Sufa but she felt disconnected, as if her feet were not solidly on the ground. It wasn't dizziness that she was feeling, but it was close. She'd heard the psychiatric term *depersonalization* and wondered if she was suffering some variation of it. Everything she was experiencing felt so surreal. It was as if she were in a dream, although her senses seemed very tangibly engaged. She could see, smell, and hear just like normal. But nothing else was making sense. How could they be under the ocean!

As a geophysical oceanographer Suzanne was well aware that the Mohorovičić discontinuity was the name given to a specific layer within the earth that marked an abrupt change in the velocity of sound or seismic waves. It was located approximately two and a half to seven miles beneath the ocean floor and about twenty-four miles beneath the continents. She also knew that its eponymous name came from the Serbian seismologist who'd discovered it. But despite having a name, no one had any idea what the layer represented. As far as she knew, neither she nor any other geologist or seismologist had ever considered the possibility it was an enormous, air-filled cavern. The idea was too preposterous to have been seriously entertained.

"Please give our secondary humans the courtesy they deserve," Arak called out to his fellow Interterrans as he moved forward into their midst. "Back up and give us room!" He motioned for the people to give way, and they silently complied.

"Please!" Arak said gently to Suzanne and the others as he gestured toward an open lane leading out from under the roof of the loggia. He moved ahead and waved for them to follow. "As soon as we depart the foreign arrival hall, it will only be a short journey to your accommodations."

As if watching herself in a movie Suzanne walked between the crowds of Interterrans. She sensed that Perry was directly behind her and imagined that Donald and the divers were close as well. The situation was no longer scary. The beautiful people were full of smiles and gave furtive, almost shy gestures of greeting. Suzanne found herself unable to keep from smiling in response.

Can this truly be happening? she kept asking herself as she followed. *Is this a dream?* Everything was certainly surreal enough, yet there was no doubt she could feel the marble on her bare feet and the caress of a gentle breeze on her cheeks. Never had she felt such subtle sensory details in a dream no matter how realistic it had been.

Sufa turned to Suzanne. "You'll notice that you people are true celebrities. Second-generation humans are very, very popular. You are all so refreshingly stimulating. I better warn you that you will be in great demand."

"What do you mean, 'second-generation humans'?" Suzanne questioned.

"Now, Sufa," Arak chided gently. "Remember what we decided! These guests are going to be introduced more slowly to our world than we've done with others in the past."

"I remember," Sufa replied. Then to Suzanne she added: "We'll be discussing everything in due time, and all your questions will be answered, I promise you."

The group soon emerged on a spacious verandah that opened up into a stupendously colossal underground cavern so immense, it gave the impression of being outdoors. The illumination was like daylight although there was no sun. The domed ceiling was a pale blue like the color of the sky on a hazy summer day. A few thin clouds floated lazily with the breeze.

The verandah was at the side of a building located on the outer edge of a city. Stretching out from the balustrade was a bucolic vista of rolling hills, lush vegetation, and lakes with a few towns in the near distance. The buildings were constructed of black basalt, highly polished and fashioned into a mixture of curves, domes, towers, and classically columned porticos. In the far distance a series of conical mountains rose up from wide bases to merge with the fan out against the dome above to form gargantuan supporting columns.

"If you'll all wait for just a moment," Arak said. He then spoke softly into a tiny microphone on an instrument attached to his wrist.

The five "second-generation humans" were spellbound by the unexpected beauty and breathtaking dimensions of the subterranean paradise. It was beyond anything that their imaginations could have possibly conjured. Even the divers were speechless.

"We're waiting for a hovercraft," Sufa explained.

"Is this Atlantis?" Perry asked, his mouth agape.

"No!" Sufa said, mildly offended. "This is not Atlantis.

This city is Saranta. Atlantis is due east from here. But you can't see it. It's behind those columns that support the surface protuberances you people call the Azores."

"So Atlantis does exist?" Perry said.

"Well, of course," Sufa said. "But personally I don't find it nearly as agreeable as Saranta. It's a young, upstart city with rather brazen people if you ask me. But you'll have to judge for yourselves."

"Ah, here we go," Arak exclaimed as a domed, saucer-like craft silently materialized at the base of the steps. It arrived so quietly, only those who happened to be looking in the proper direction saw its arrival.

"Sorry it took so long," Arak said. "There must be a particularly high demand at the moment for some reason. But please, after you." He gestured down the steps toward an open entrance port that had miraculously appeared on the side of the saucer.

The group descended the steps and boarded the craft, which was hovering motionlessly several feet off the ground. It was about thirty feet in diameter with a clear, domed top similar to the kind of purported UFOs seen on the covers of tabloids at grocery checkout lines. Inside was a circular banquette cushioned in white with a black, round central table. There were no controls.

Arak was the last to board, and as soon as he did the entrance port disappeared as silently and as mysteriously as it had appeared.

"Ah, it's always the way," Arak complained after glancing around at the interior. "Just when we're trying to impress you we get one of the old hovercrafts. This one is on its last legs."

"Stop complaining," Sufa said. "This vehicle is perfectly serviceable."

Suzanne glanced at Donald, who raised his eyebrows ever so slightly. Suzanne looked around the hovercraft. She was so full of questions she didn't know where to begin.

Arak placed his hand, palm down, in the center of the black table and leaned forward. "Visitors' palace," he said. He then leaned back and smiled. A moment later the scenery outside began to move.

Suzanne reflexively reached out to grasp the edge of the table to steady herself, but it wasn't necessary. There was no sensation of motion nor was there any sound. It was as if the craft were staying still and the city moving as they rose some hundred feet before accelerating horizontally.

"You'll be instructed how to call and use these air taxis very soon," Arak said. "You'll have plenty of time to explore."

Several heads nodded. The *Benthic Explorer* team was overwhelmed by everything they were seeing. They seemed to be cruising through the center of a bustling metropolis with countless people going about their business and thousands of other air taxis zipping in every direction.

For Suzanne, this world seemed full of strange contradictions. The city and the advanced technology seemed so futuristic yet the trees and vegetation had a hauntingly prehistoric aspect. The flora reminded her of what had flourished during the Carboniferous period three hundred million years ago.

Soon the shiny black basalt multistoried buildings gave way to a less dense, apparently residential area with grass, trees, and pools of water. The crowds of people disappeared as did the swarms of air taxis. Now there were only individual people or small groups walking among the parks. Many were accompanied by curious-looking pets that Suzanne thought were a chimeric combination of dog, cat, and monkey.

The scenery began to slow as they approached a magnificent walled palace compound. It was dominated by a large central domed structure supported by fluted black Doric columns. Sprinkled around the enclosure were numerous other smaller buildings oval in shape and constructed of the familiar polished black basalt. Walkways snaked through crystal pools, expanses of lawn, and patches of luxurious ferns.

The air taxi stopped its horizontal movement and rapidly descended. A moment later the port opened as silently and as mysteriously as it had before.

"Dr. Newell," Sufa said. "This will be your cottage. If you wouldn't mind, please disembark. I will accompany you to be sure you are comfortable." She gestured toward the exit.

A flustered Suzanne glanced from Sufa to Donald. She had not expected to be separated from the group, and she was well aware Donald felt they should remain together.

"What about the others?" Suzanne asked. She tried to read Donald's expression, but couldn't tell what he wanted her to do.

"Arak will see to their accommodation," Sufa said. "Each will have his own bungalow."

"We were hoping to stay together," Suzanne said.

"But you will," Arak said. "This palace and its grounds are just for you visitors. You'll take your meals together and if you want to double up in the lodges for your sleeping arrangements, that is up to you."

Suzanne's and Donald's eyes met. Donald shrugged.

Assuming that left the decision up to her, she climbed out of the hovercraft. Sufa followed. A moment later the saucer silently moved across the lawn to stop at a neighboring cottage.

"Come on!" Sufa encouraged. She'd started up the walkway but had turned back when she was aware that Suzanne wasn't behind her.

Suzanne took her eyes off the hovercraft and hurried to catch up with her host.

"You will be meeting up with your friends for a meal shortly," Sufa said. "I just want to be certain your accommodations are acceptable. Besides, I thought you'd like to take a quick refreshing swim before eating. That was my first wish when I emerged from the decon experience."

"You experienced what we went through?" Suzanne questioned.

"I did," Sufa said. "But it was a long, long time ago. Several lifetimes, actually."

"Excuse me?" Suzanne said. She assumed she'd not heard correctly. The phrase *several lifetimes* didn't make any sense.

"Come!" Sufa said. "We have to get you settled. The questions must wait." She took Suzanne's arm. Together they climbed the few steps from the walkway and entered the cottage.

Suzanne stopped just beyond the door, awestruck by the decor. In sharp contrast to the black exterior, the interior was almost exclusively white: white marble, white cashmere, and multiple mirrored surfaces. It reminded Suzanne of the living quarters where she had so recently slept but on a much more lavish scale. An added feature was an azure pool that stretched from inside the room to the outdoors. The pool was fed by a waterfall that cascaded out of the wall.

"The room doesn't please you?" Sufa questioned with concern. She'd been watching Suzanne's face and mistook her wonderment for dissatisfaction.

"Whether I like it or not is hardly the question," Suzanne said. "It's unbelievable."

"But we want you to be comfortable," Sufa said.

"What about the others?" Suzanne asked. "Are their quarters anything like this?"

"They are identical," Sufa said. "All the visitors' cottages are the same. But if there is something else you might need, please tell me. I'm sure we can provide it."

Suzanne's eyes moved to the enormous circular bed, which was on a raised marble dais at the center of her quarters. A large canopy was draped above it. From its circumference hung gathered bundles of sheer white fabric.

"Perhaps you could tell me what you feel is lacking," Sufa said.

"Nothing is lacking," Suzanne said. "The room is breathtaking."

"Then you do like it," Sufa said with relief.

"It's stunning," Suzanne said. She reached out and touched the marble wall. Its surface was polished to a mirrorlike perfection, and it felt warm as if heated by inner radiation.

Sufa stepped over to a cabinet that lined the wall to the right. She gestured down its length. "Inside here you have media consoles, extra clothing, reading material in your language, a large refrigerator with a selection of refreshments, personal toilet articles that you'll recognize, and just about anything else you might need."

"How do I open it?" Suzanne asked.

"Just use a voice command," Sufa said simply. She pointed at one of two doors on the wall opposite the cabinetry. "Personal facilities are through there."

Suzanne walked over to stand next to Sufa and faced the cabinet. "What exactly do I say?"

"Whatever it is you're looking for," Sufa explained. "Followed by an exclamatory word like 'please' or 'now'."

"Food, please!" Suzanne said self-consciously.

No sooner had she uttered the words when one of the cabinet doors opened to reveal a sizable refrigerator well stocked with containers of liquid refreshment and solid food of varying consistency and color.

Sufa bent over and glanced inside. She shuffled through some of the contents. "I might have known," she said, standing back up. "I'm afraid you have just the standard selection, even though I requested some specialty items. But it doesn't matter. A worker clone will get you anything you might desire."

"What do you mean, 'worker clone'?" Suzanne asked. The term sounded ominous.

"Worker clones are the workers," Sufa said. "They do all the manual work in Interterra."

"Have I seen a worker clone?" Suzanne asked.

"Not yet," Sufa said. "They prefer not to be seen until they are called. They favor their own company and their own facilities."

Suzanne nodded as if she understood, but it was not in the way Sufa surmised. Suzanne nodded because she knew that in most situations of bigotry, the dominant group always attributed attitudes to the oppressed which made the oppressors feel better about the oppression.

"Are these worker clones true clones?" Suzanne asked.

"Absolutely," Sufa said. "They've been cloned for ages. Their primary origin was from primitive hominids, something akin to what you people call Neanderthals."

"What do you mean, we people?" Suzanne said. "What makes us different from you besides the fact that you are all so gorgeous?"

"Please . . ." Sufa begged.

"I know, I know," Suzanne repeated with frustration. "I'm not supposed to ask any questions, but your answers to even simple questions always demand some explanation."

Sufa laughed. "It's confusing you, I'm sure," she said. "But we're just asking you to be patient. As we've intimated, we've learned from experience that it is best to go slowly with the introduction to our world."

"Which means you have had visitors like us in the past," Suzanne said.

"For sure," Suzanne said. "We've had many over the last ten thousand years or so."

Suzanne's mouth slowly dropped open. "Did you say ten thousand years?"

"I did," Sufa said. "Prior to that we had no interest in your culture."

"Are you suggesting—"

"Please," Sufa interrupted. She took a deep breath. "No more questions unless they are about your accommodations. I have to insist."

"All right," Suzanne said. "Let's get back to the worker clones. How do I call one?"

"A voice command," Sufa said. "It's the same for most everything in Interterra."

"I just say 'worker clone'?" Suzanne asked.

" 'Worker clone' or just 'worker,' " Sufa said. "Then, of course, it has to be followed by an exclamatory word that you feel comfortable with. But the phrase has to be said as a true exclamation."

"I could do it right now?" Suzanne asked.

"Of course," Sufa said.

"Worker, please," Suzanne said. She maintained eye contact with Sufa. Nothing happened.

"That wasn't enough of an exclamation," Sufa explained. "Try it again."

"Worker, please!" Suzanne cried.

"Much better," Sufa said. "But it doesn't have to be so loud. It's not the volume that counts. It's the intended meaning. Humanoids have to know without equivocation that you want them to appear. Their default mode is not to come, so as to be less bothersome."

"Did you mean to use the term *humanoid?*" Suzanne asked.

"Of course," Sufa said. "Worker clones look very humanlike although they are a fusion of android elements, engineered biomechanical parts, and hominid sections. They are half-machine, half-living organisms who conveniently take care of themselves and even reproduce."

Suzanne stared at Sufa with an expression that was a combination of dismay and disbelief. Sufa interpreted it as fear.

"Now, don't worry," Sufa said. "They are very easy to deal with and are inordinately helpful. In fact, they are truly wonderful creatures as you will undoubtedly discover. Their only minor drawback is that, like their particular hominid forebears, they are unable to speak— but they will understand you perfectly."

Suzanne continued to stare. Before she could ask another question, one of the doors opposite the cabinets opened and in walked a statuesque woman. Suzanne realized she'd been expecting a grotesque automaton, but the woman before her was hauntingly beautiful with classical features and blonde hair, alabaster skin, and dark, penetrating eyes. She was wearing black satin coveralls with long sleeves.

"Here is a fine example of a female worker clone," Sufa said. "You'll notice she is wearing a hoop earring. They all wear them for some reason I've never understood, although I believe it has something to do with pride or lineage. You'll also notice that she is rather comely, as are the male versions. But most importantly, you'll find her amenable to your wishes. Whatever you want, just tell her and she will try to do it, short of injuring herself."

Suzanne stared into the woman's eyes; they were like dark pools. Her facial features were as sculptured and attractive as Sufa's yet they bore no expression.

"Does she have a name?" Suzanne questioned.

"Heavens no," Sufa said with a chuckle. "That certainly would complicate things. We wouldn't want to personalize our relationship with workers. That's part of the reason they have never been engineered to speak."

"But she will do what I ask?"

"Absolutely," Sufa said. "Anything at all. She can pick up your clothes, wash them, draw your bath, restock your refrigerator, give you a massage, even change the temperature of the water in your pool. Whatever you want or need."

"At the moment I think it would be best if she left," Suzanne said. She shuddered imperceptibly. The idea of someone being half alive and half machine was disquieting.

"Go, please!" Sufa said. The woman turned and left as quietly as she'd appeared. Sufa looked back at Suzanne. "Of course, next time you call for a worker clone it will most likely be a different one. Whoever is available comes."

Suzanne nodded as if she understood, but she didn't. "Where do they come from?"

"Underground," Sufa said.

"Like in caves?" Suzanne asked.

"I suppose," Sufa said vaguely. "I've never been down there nor do I know anyone else who has. But, enough about worker clones! We have to get you over to the dining hall for your meal. Would you like to swim or bathe? It's entirely up to you, but there isn't an overabundance of time."

Suzanne swallowed. Her throat was dry. Given everything she'd been presented with, she found it difficult to make even a simple decision. She looked over at the pool. Its color, now more aquamarine than azure, was as inviting as was its gently flickering surface.

"Maybe a swim would be a good idea," Suzanne said.

"Excellent," Sufa answered. "There are fresh clothes in the cabinet. And shoes, too, I might add."

Suzanne nodded.

"I'll wait for you outside," Sufa said. "I have a feeling it would be good for you to be alone for a few minutes to catch your breath."

"I think you are right," Suzanne said.

CHAPTER TEN

The dining room was situated in a building similar in size and shape to the cottages but without a pool. It was also open to the exterior but faced the dramatic central pavilion rather than the expansive lawns and fern thickets. Its long central table was like the one in the decon area's living quarters. The deeply cushioned chaises looked the same, too.

The group had arrived from their separate lodgings at about the same time, in distinctly different moods about their circumstances. Richard and Michael pointedly refused to acknowledge any misgivings. They were completely exhilarated, like two children let loose in the theme park of their dreams and intent on taking advantage of every available perquisite. Perry was also excited about the possibilities inherent in this new world, but he remained outwardly cooler than the giddy divers. Suzanne was still more confused than excited. She continued to toy with the notion that they were experiencing a kind of collective hallucination according to their own predilections. In contrast to everyone else, Donald was sullen, convinced as he was that the whole construct was an elaborate, purposeful delusion toward some nefarious end.

The conversation centered on the saucer ride and the

marvels of their accommodations. Richard and Michael were the most animated, particularly after they learned that Suzanne's worker clone had been female. Richard hinted at the desires that might be sated by such a pliant creature.

Suzanne was appalled, and let him know in no uncertain terms. "Try to act like you're from a civilized race!"

The food was similar to the fare they had had in the decon quarters, with the same curious variation in perceived taste although it was presented in elaborate, self-serve courses. It was brought out by two extremely handsome men in black satin, long-sleeved overalls that zipped up the front. Each was wearing a hoop earring.

Suddenly Donald threw his gold fork with some force onto his gold platter. The clatter was surprisingly loud in the marbled room as it reverberated off the stone walls. Richard was caught in mid sentence, describing the plunge he took in his pool, with his mouth stuffed with what he insisted was a dollop of hot fudge sundae. Suzanne jumped from fright and dropped her own fork with somewhat less of a clatter, emphasizing to herself how tense she was. Michael choked on what he was experiencing as sweet potato pie.

"How can you people eat under these circumstances!" Donald shouted.

"What circumstances?" Richard asked, his mouth still brimming with food. His eyes darted rapidly around the room, fearful that the place had been invaded.

Donald leaned toward Richard. "What circumstances?" he repeated with accentuated derision while shaking his head in scornful wonderment. "The thing I've never been able to understand about saturation divers is whether they have to be stupid in order to be willing to do it, or whether it's the pressure and inert gas that destroys the handful of brain cells they may have had when they started."

"What the hell are you talking about?" Michael asked, taking immediate offense.

"I'll tell you what I'm talking about," Donald snapped. "Look around you! Where the hell are we? What are we doing here? Who are these people dressed up like they're going to a college toga party?"

For a few minutes there was silence. Everyone avoided Donald's glare. They had been scrupulously avoiding such questions.

"I know where we are," Richard said finally. "We're in Interterra."

"Oh, jeez," Donald exclaimed, throwing up his hands in frustration. "We're in Interterra," he repeated. "That explains everything. Well, let me tell you, it tells us nothing. It doesn't tell us where we are or what we're doing here or who these people are. And they now have us conveniently isolated in separate living quarters."

"They said they would tell us all we want to know," Suzanne said. "They asked us to be patient."

"Patient!" Donald mocked. "I'll tell you what we're doing here . . . We're prisoners!"

"So what!" Richard said.

Silence reigned again. Michael put down his fork, chastened by Donald's outburst. Richard resumed enjoying his dessert, brazenly staring Donald down. Suzanne and Perry just watched, as did the mute worker clones.

Richard took another large bite of his dessert. With his mouth still full, he said, "If we're prisoners, I want to see how these people treat their friends. I mean, just look at this place. It's fantastic. If you don't want to eat, Fuller, don't! Me, I like this stuff, so screw you!"

Donald leaped to his feet with the intention of lunging across the table at Richard. Perry intervened before punches could be thrown.

"All right, you two," Perry yelled. "Stop baiting each other! Let's not fight amongst ourselves. Besides, you're both right. We don't know squat about the what, where, and why we're here, yet we're being treated well. Maybe even too well."

Perry let go of Donald's arm when he felt the man relax and glanced over at the immobile worker clones, wondering if this mild outburst bothered them. But it didn't. Their faces were as immobile and blank as they had been throughout the meal.

Donald followed Perry's line of sight while straightening his tunic. "You see what I mean," he growled. "They even have jailors keeping tabs on us while we eat."

"I don't think that's the case," Suzanne said. Then in a louder voice, she added, "Workers, go, please!"

Without any acknowledgment of Suzanne's command the two worker clones disappeared through one of the three doors leading from the dining lodge.

"So much for the watchful eyes of the attendants," Suzanne said.

"Ah, that doesn't mean a thing," Donald said. His eyes roamed the chamber. "There's probably hidden mikes and camcorders all over this room."

"Hey," Michael said. "Looking at this dish and fork, I've been wondering. Is this stuff real gold or what?"

Suzanne picked up her own fork to gauge its weight. "I was thinking about that earlier," she said. "Surprisingly enough, I believe it is."

"No shit!" Michael said. He picked up the plate and hefted the two items. "We got a small fortune here."

"We're being treated okay for the moment," Donald said, returning to the main topic.

"You think it is going to change?" Perry asked.

"It could change in a second," Donald said with a snap of his fingers. "As soon as they've gotten whatever it is they want, who knows what will happen. We're completely vulnerable."

"It could change, but I don't think it will," Suzanne said.

"How can you be so sure?" Donald demanded.

"I can't be sure," Suzanne admitted. "But it stands to reason. Look around. These people, whoever they are, are so advanced. They don't need anything from us. In fact I think we stand to learn extraordinary things from them."

"I know we've been avoiding this issue," Perry said. "But when you say they are so advanced, are you suggesting that these people are aliens?"

Perry's question brought on another period of silence. No one knew quite what to think, much less say.

"You mean like people from another planet?" Michael said finally.

"I don't know what I'm suggesting," Suzanne said. "But we all experienced the astounding ride in the saucer. It must represent some kind of maglev technology that none of us has ever heard of. And we're supposed to be under the ocean, which I still have trouble accepting. But I have to tell all of you. The Mohorovičić discontinuity definitely exists, and no one ever has been able to explain it."

Richard waved a dismissive hand. "These people are no aliens. Christ, did you see those girls! Hell, I've seen a lot of movies about aliens, and they sure didn't look like these people."

"They could be altering their appearance to our liking," Suzanne said.

"Yeah," Michael said. "That's what I thought at first. We're dreaming they look so good."

"That's why I don't give a god damn," Richard said. "It's what's in my mind that counts. If I think they're gorgeous, they're gorgeous."

"The real issue is their motives," Donald said. "It was no accident that brought us here. It's even more apparent that we were literally sucked down that shaft. They want something from us or we'd already be dead."

"I think you are right that we were specifically brought here," Suzanne said. "Sufa admitted several things to me. First, she confirmed that what we'd gone through was a decontamination."

"But why were we decontaminated?" Perry asked.

"She didn't say," Suzanne said. "But she admitted that they have had visitors like us in the past."

"Now that is interesting," Donald said. "Did she say what happened to them?"

"No, she didn't," Suzanne said.

"Well, you guys can worry yourselves sick," Richard commented. Then he put his head back and yelled. "Worker clones, come!"

Instantly two humanoids appeared, one male and one female. Richard took one look at the female and glanced at Michael conspiratorially. "Pay dirt!" he whispered with unbridled excitement.

"Richard," Suzanne called. "I want you to promise that you will not do anything that will embarrass us or put us in jeopardy as a group."

"What are you, my mother?" he asked. Then he glanced up at the female worker clone and said: "How about some more of that dessert, honey."

"Me too," Michael said. He clanked his golden fork on his golden dish.

Donald started to rise but Perry restrained him again. "No fighting," Perry said. "It's no use."

Richard smiled provocatively at Donald, relishing the man's frustration and anger.

A soft chime interrupted the muted background music and echoed about the room. A moment later Arak energetically swept into view. He was attired in the standard fashion with a small addition. Around his neck was a plain blue velvet ribbon that perfectly matched the particular blue hue of his eyes. It was tied in a simple bow.

"Hello, my friends," he called exuberantly. "I trust that your meal was to your liking."

"It was great," Richard answered. "But what is it made out of? I mean, it doesn't look anything like what it tastes like."

"It's mostly planktonic proteins and vegetable carbohydrates," Arak said. He rubbed his hands enthusiastically. "Now then! What about the celebration I mentioned to you earlier? You have no idea how many people here in Saranta are extremely pleased about your arrival to our city. We've had to turn people away. You see, we're not a city that gets many visitors from your world: certainly not like Atlantis to the east or Barsama to the west. Everyone is anxious to meet you. So that brings us to the pivotal question: are you willing to come over to the pavilion or are you too tired from the decon?"

"Where's the pavilion?" Michael asked.

"Right there," Arak said, pointing out the open end of

the dining hall. "The celebration is to be held in the pavilion here on the visitors' palace grounds. It's very convenient. In fact it's only a little more than a hundred yards, so we can walk. What do you all say?"

"Count me in," Richard said. "I never pass up a party."

"Likewise," Michael said.

"Splendid!" Arak said. "What about the rest of you?"

There was an awkward silence. Perry eventually cleared his throat. "Arak, to be truthful, we're a little nervous."

"I'd use a stronger word," Donald said. "Frankly, before we do anything, we'd like to have some idea who you people are and why we are here. We know our presence is not an accident. To put it bluntly, we know we were abducted."

"I empathize with your concerns and your curiosity," Arak said. He spread his hands palms up in a conciliatory gesture. "But, please, for tonight allow my experience to prevail. I've dealt with visitors to our world before, not terribly many, it is true, and not in as large a group, but still enough to know what is best. Tomorrow I will answer all your questions."

"Why wait?" Donald demanded. "Why not tell us now?"

"You don't realize how stressful the decon procedure was," Arak said.

"Can you at least tell us how long the procedure lasted?" Suzanne asked.

"A little more than one of your months," Arak said.

"We were asleep for over a month?" Michael questioned in disbelief.

"Essentially, yes," Arak said. "And it's stressful on the brain as well as the body. Tomorrow you will have to deal with more startling information. We've learned that it is easier to absorb when our visitors are rested. Even one night makes a big difference. So please, tonight relax, either here together or alone in your lodges or, best of all, with us at our celebration of your arrival."

Perry searched Arak's face. The man's blue eyes held his gaze and exuded a sincerity he could not deny. "Okay," he said. "At this point I don't think I can sleep anyway. So, I'll come, but tomorrow I'm going to hold you to your word."

"Fair enough," Arak said. He looked at Suzanne. "And Dr. Newell, what is your pleasure?"

"I'll come," Suzanne said.

"Marvelous," Arak said. "And you, Mr. Fuller? What is your decision?"

"No," Donald said. "Under the circumstances I would find celebrating rather difficult."

"Very well," Arak said, rubbing his hands again in obvious delight. "This is wonderful indeed. I'm glad most of you are willing to come. There would have been a lot of disappointed people if I had returned alone. Mr. Fuller, I understand your feelings and respect them. Please enjoy your rest. The worker clones will do your bidding."

Donald nodded morosely.

"Now, let's get on our way," Arak said to the others. He motioned toward the open end of the dining hall.

"Will there be eats at this party?" Richard asked.

"Absolutely," Arak said. "The finest Saranta can muster."

"Then I'll skip seconds on my dessert," Richard said. He tossed his spoon onto the table, stood up, stretched, and belched loudly.

Suzanne glared at him. "Richard, have some respect for the rest of us even if you don't have it for yourself."

"But I do," Richard said with a sly smile. "I restrained myself from farting in this mixed company."

Arak laughed. "Richard, you are going to be a big hit. You're delightfully primitive."

"Are you yanking my chain?" Richard asked.

"Not at all," Arak said. "You'll be in great demand, I assure you. Come on! Let's show you off!" With a wave, Arak started toward the open end of the room.

"All right!" Richard said, giving Michael an enthusiastic thumbs-up sign. Michael returned it with equal exuberance.

"Let's party!" Michael cried. The two divers eagerly followed Arak.

Suzanne looked at Perry, who shrugged and said, "This is crazy, going to a celebration under these circumstances, but we might as well take it all in stride."

Then she glanced at Donald. "Are you sure you don't want to come?"

"Yeah, I'm sure," Donald said gloomily. "But if you two want to fraternize, be my guests."

"I'm going because I might learn some more," Suzanne said. "Not to fraternize, as you put it."

"Come on!" Perry called from the far end of the room.

"We'll see you later," Suzanne said. She hurried after Perry and the others, who were already on their way across the lawn.

Donald mulled over what Arak had said. All he knew for sure was that he didn't trust him. From Donald's point of view the man was too ingratiating. All this fantastic hospitality had to be some kind of trap. Yet Donald had no idea for what purpose other than to get them off their guard.

Donald turned and looked out the end of the room. The group was halfway to the columned pavilion and silhouetted its illuminated exterior. Redirecting his eyes, Donald stared at the two worker clones, who were standing motionless to the side against the wall. They appeared so human it was hard for Donald to believe they were part machine as Arak had said. Maybe it was just another lie, Donald thought.

"Worker, I want some more drink," Donald said.

The female worker clone immediately picked up the pitcher on the sideboard and stepped over to the table. Her shoulder-length hair was sorrel colored. She had pale, translucent skin. Leaning over she began to fill Donald's cup.

Donald suddenly grabbed her wrist without warning. Her skin felt cold beneath his fingers. She did not jump or even appreciably respond. Instead she kept on pouring.

Donald tightened his grip to get a reaction, but it was to no avail. The woman finished filling the glass then righted the pitcher despite Donald's grasp. Donald was taken aback. The woman was shockingly strong.

Tilting his head back Donald looked up into the woman's frozen face. She did not try to detach herself from his grasp but rather blankly returned his stare. Donald let go of the woman's arm.

"What is your name?" he asked.

She did not respond verbally or in any other fashion. Other than rhythmical breathing there was no other movement. She didn't even blink.

"Worker clone, speak!" Donald ordered.

Silence persisted. Donald looked over at the male worker clone, but there was no response from him either.

"How come you people work and the others don't?" Donald said.

There was no response from either clone.

"All right," Donald said. "Workers, leave!"

Instantly the two workers went to the door from which they'd come and disappeared. Donald got up and opened the door. Beyond it, a stairway descended into darkness.

Closing the door, Donald walked over to the open end of the room. He looked out at the scene. The light, which had been so bright earlier, had faded, as if the nonexistent sun had nearly set. Donald could just make out Arak and the others approaching the pavilion. He shook his head. He wondered again if he was dreaming. Everything seemed so bizarre yet disturbingly real. He felt his arms and his face. He felt normal to his touch.

Donald took a deep breath. Intuitively he knew that he was facing the most demanding mission of his career. He hoped that his training wouldn't fail him, particularly his training about being a prisoner of war.

CHAPTER ELEVEN

In their own scatological vernacular Richard and Michael were "scared shitless," but their unspoken credo was to deny it. Just like their reaction to the perils of saturation diving they responded with a distorted macho bravado designed to conceal their true feelings.

"Do you think those girls we saw earlier will be here at the party?" Richard asked Michael. They had lagged a few steps behind the others en route to the celebration in the pavilion.

"We can always hope," Michael responded.

They walked in silence for a few steps. They could hear Arak talking with Suzanne and Perry, but they didn't care to listen.

"Do you really think we were asleep for over a month?" Michael asked.

Richard stopped short. "You're not going soft on me, are you?"

"No!" Michael insisted. "I was just asking." Sleep had never been the solace for Michael that it was for others. As a child he used to be plagued with nightmares. After he'd gone to sleep, his father would come home drunk and beat up his mother. When he woke up, he tried to intervene, but the result was always the same: he, too, was beaten. Unfortunately, the process of sleep got inextricably associated with these episodes, so for Michael the idea of being asleep for a month was a source of enormous anxiety.

"Hello!" Richard said while giving Michael a series of slaps on the face. "Anybody home?"

Michael deflected Richard's irritating jabs. "Cut it out!"

"Remember, we're not worrying about all this horseshit," Richard said. "There's something screwy going on here sure as shooting, but who cares. We're going to enjoy ourselves, not like that jerk, Fuller. God! Just listening to him talk makes me glad we were tossed out of the freakin' navy. Otherwise we'd be taking orders from guys like him."

"Of course we're going to enjoy ourselves," Michael insisted. "But I was just thinking, like, you know, it's a long time to be zonked."

"Well, don't think!" Richard said. "You'll get yourself all screwed up."

"All right!" Michael said.

Suzanne called out for them to catch up; she and the others were waiting.

"And to top it all off, we got to deal with old mother hen," Richard added.

The two divers caught up to the rest of the group, who'd stopped at the base of the steps leading up to the pavilion entrance.

"Is everything okay?" Suzanne asked them.

"Peachy," Richard said, forcing a smile.

"Arak just told us something you two might find interesting," Suzanne said. "I assume you've noticed how it is getting dark as if the sun had set."

"We noticed," Richard said testily.

"They have night and day down here," Suzanne said. "And we learned the light comes from bioluminescence."

The two divers tilted their heads back to look straight up.

"I see stars," Michael said.

"Those are relatively small pinpoints of blue-white bioluminescence," Arak said. "It was our intent to recreate the world as we knew it, which certainly included the circadian cycle. The difference from your world is that our days and nights are longer, and they are the same length year-round. Of course our years are longer as well."

"So you lived in the external world before you moved down here," Suzanne said.

"Absolutely," Arak answered.

"When did you make the move?" Suzanne asked.

Arak held up his hands defensively. He laughed. "We are getting ahead of ourselves. I'm not supposed to be encouraging you to ask questions this evening. Remember, that's to be tomorrow."

"Just one more," Perry pleaded. "It's an easy one, I'm sure. Where do you get all your energy down here?"

Arak sighed with exasperation.

"It's the last question, I promise," Perry said. "At least for tonight."

"And you are a man of your word?" Arak questioned.

"For sure," Perry said.

"Our energy comes from two main sources," Arak said. "First is geothermal by tapping the earth's core. But that creates the problem of getting rid of excess heat, which we do in two ways. One by allowing magma to well up along what you people call the mid-oceanic ridge, and two by cooling with circulated seawater. The seawater heat exchange requires a large volume, which does provide us an opportunity to filter out plankton. The downside is that the process creates oceanic currents, but you people have learned to live with them, particularly the one you call the Gulf Stream.

"The second source of energy is from fusion. We split water into oxygen, which we breathe, and hydrogen, which we fuse. But this is the kind of discussion we'll be having tomorrow. Tonight I want you to experience and enjoy, mostly enjoy."

"And we aim to do just that," Richard said. "But tell me, is this going to be a wet or dry party?"

"I'm afraid that is a term I'm not familiar with," Arak said.

"It refers generally to alcohol," Richard said. "Do you people have any on hand?"

"But of course," Arak said. "Wine, beer, and a particularly pure spirit we call crystal. The wine and the beer are similar to what you are used to. But the crystal is different, and I advise you to go easy until you are accustomed to it."

"No need to worry, bro," Richard said. "Michael and I are professionals."

"Let's party!" Michael said enthusiastically.

Perry and Suzanne had to be nudged forward. Both had been bowled over by Arak's explanations, particularly Suzanne. All at once she had answers to two of the mysteries of oceanography, namely, why magma wells up at the mid-oceanic ridges and why there are oceanic currents, particularly the Gulf Stream. The answers to both questions had completely eluded scientists.

The group climbed the stairs with Arak in the lead. As they passed between two of the massive columns supporting the domed roof, Suzanne caught sight of

Richard's overeager expression. Worried his conduct might be under the influence, she leaned toward him and whispered, "Remember to behave yourself."

Richard glanced at her. His expression was one of scornful disbelief.

"I'm serious, Richard," Suzanne added. "We have no idea what we are up against, and we don't want to put ourselves in any more jeopardy than we already are. If you have to drink, do it sparingly."

"Drop dead!" Richard said. He quickened his pace and caught up to Arak just as two oversized bronze doors swung open.

The first thing that greeted the visitors was the murmur of thousands of excited voices as they reverberated around the pavilion's vast, white marbled interior. The level they'd entered formed a ballustraded balcony that ran around the circular hall. Together the group moved to the top of a grand staircase and looked down.

"Talk about a party!" Richard cried. "My God! There must be a thousand people here."

"We could have had ten thousand if we'd had the room," Arak told them.

In the center of the huge domed ballroom was a round pool illuminated in such a way as to make it appear like an enormous aquamarine cabochon jewel. Surrounding the pool was a foot-high, ten-foot-wide lip. Numerous stairways connected the balcony to the level below.

The floor of the pavilion was packed with people. Everyone was dressed in the same simple white satin outfits except for an occasional worker clone in their usual black. The worker clones were carrying large trays loaded with golden goblets and food. Each guest sported a velvet ribbon tied around his or her neck just like the one Arak had on. Only the color varied, not the size, the shape, or the way it was tied. And as before, everyone was strikingly beautiful or handsome.

Word that the visitors had arrived spread like wildfire through the crowd. Conversations stopped and faces tilted up. It was a dramatic sight to look down on so many silently expectant people.

Arak raised his hands over his head with his palms toward the audience. "Greetings to everyone! I am pleased to announce that all our visitors, save one, have graciously deigned to come to our celebration of their arrival to Saranta."

A general cheer erupted from the audience as everyone lifted their arms, mirroring Arak's gesture.

"Come!" Arak said. He motioned for the group to follow him as he started down the broad flight of stairs.

Richard and Michael scampered forward eagerly, followed by a more hesitant Suzanne and Perry.

"This is too much!" Richard whispered in excitement. "Look at the women! It looks like a Victoria's Secret slumber party."

"Every one of them could be a centerfold," Michael responded.

"It's hard to keep this all in perspective," Suzanne whispered to Perry. "I feel like we're in a Cecil B. De Mille movie spectacular."

"I know what you mean," Perry answered. "It also gives me an idea what it's like to be a rock star. These people are really happy to see us. And look how young everybody is. Most of these people appear as if they're in their early twenties."

"True, but there's a significant number of children,"

Suzanne said. "I can see a few that can't be any more than three or four."

"Not very many senior citizens," Perry commented.

At the base of the stairs the people shrank back as the group descended, but as soon as they reached the floor, the crowd surged forward with their hands held up, palms forward.

Suzanne and Perry instinctively retreated a few steps back despite the obvious warmth of the crowd. In contrast Richard and Michael allowed themselves to be engulfed. The two divers soon realized that the crowd wanted physical contact with their hands, and the divers happily reached out to touch the palms that sought theirs. It was a greeting similar to the one Arak had employed when he'd first welcomed Suzanne earlier.

"I love you all," Richard cried out, to the pleasure of the Interterrans in his immediate vicinity, but he selectively chose the palms of young, beautiful women as he worked his way through the crowd. In his enthusiasm he even grabbed a few and kissed them—which brought the festivity to a sudden, screeching halt.

Richard eyed the women he'd kissed and wondered for a fleeting moment if he should retreat up the stairs. The stunned women proceeded to touch their lips, then examine their fingers as if they expected to see blood. Clearly kissing was not part of the Interterrans' normal salutational repertoire. Richard glanced guiltily at Michael, who was equally tense at the precipitous change in the mood of the crowd. "I couldn't help myself," Richard explained.

Three women he'd kissed looked at each other and burst out laughing. Then all three launched themselves simultaneously at Richard to return the gesture. The crowd cheered with delight and pressed in around the two divers even more. After several fumbled attempts at kissing, the three women graciously moved away to make room for others.

A sly smile spread across Richard's face. "Looks like we're going to be teaching these chicks a thing or two," he said beaming. He felt encouraged enough to be even more demonstrative. Michael, seeing Richard's successes, quickly followed suit. But soon their activities were interrupted by a worker clone who had responded to a suggestion of Arak's to give their guests something to drink. The clones arrived and pressed golden goblets into their hands.

Even Suzanne and Perry's reserve began to erode in the face of the infectious conviviality. They were surrounded by friendly, beautiful people eager to press palms with them. Some of the welcomes were the very young children Suzanne had seen when they'd first arrived. Suzanne asked one of them her age after being impressed by her flawless English and apparent intelligence.

"How old are you?" the child asked without answering Suzanne's question.

Suzanne was about to respond when a man who could have played a Greek god in the Cecil B. De Mille movie asked her if she lived with a mate. Before Suzanne could answer this curious question an older man, no less attractive, asked her if she knew her parents.

"Just a moment here," Arak said, coming between Suzanne and her admirers. "As you all know, we have specifically told our guests that their questions must wait until tomorrow. It is only fair that ours wait as well. Tonight is to celebrate this wonderful event for Saranta and to enjoy."

"Hey, Arak!" Richard yelled from the center of a group of fans. He was holding up his golden goblet. "Is this the crystal liquor you were talking about?"

"It is indeed," Arak called out.

"It's fantastic!" Richard yelled back. "I really dig it."

"I'm glad," Arak said.

"One other thing," Richard yelled. "Don't you guys have any music? I mean, what's a party without music?"

"Right on," Michael yelled.

"Workers, music!" Arak shouted over the din. Within moments background music miraculously could be heard over the babble. It was as soothing as the music in the decon living quarters.

Michael let out a contemptuous laugh.

"I'm not talking about elevator music," Richard shouted back at Arak. "I mean something with some base and a beat. Something we can dance to."

Arak barked another order to the worker clones and soon the music changed.

Richard and Michael exchanged bewildered glances. The music had more base and a beat, but with its strange syncopation it was not like any music they had ever heard.

"What the hell is this?" Michael asked. He cocked his head to the side to listen better.

"Beats me," Richard said. He closed his eyes and moved his head in an undulating fashion. At the same time he took a few unsteady steps and swiveled his hips. His movements brought some giggles from the girls he'd amassed around him.

"You like that, huh?" Richard questioned.

The women nodded.

Richard brought his tankard to his lips and tossed off the entire drink, to the surprise of the people around him.

Putting the vessel on the floor he grabbed the hand of the nearest woman and charged toward the raised platform surrounding the pool in the center of the arena. With lots of laughter the crowd gave way and shouted encouragement to the couple. Reaching his goal, Richard leaped up and dragged the woman with him. He turned to face her and was momentarily taken aback by her beauty. Having seen so many beautiful people he'd already had begun to take it for granted, but he was particularly struck by this one's looks.

"You're gorgeous!" he whispered, his words slightly slurred.

"Thank you," she said. "You're attractive as well."

"You think so?" Richard asked.

"You're very entertaining," the woman said.

"I'm glad," Richard said. He then had to take a lateral step to regain his balance. For a second the image of the woman went out of focus. He was feeling light-headed.

"Are you all right?" the woman asked.

"Yeah, I'm fine," Richard assured her. He could feel the ends of his fingers tingling. "That crystal stuff packs a wallop."

"It's my favorite," the woman said.

"Then it's mine, too," Richard said. "Hey, do you want to learn to dance?"

"What does that mean exactly?" the woman asked.

"Like I was doing before," Richard said. "Only we do it together."

Richard closed his eyes and repeated his earlier gyrations. It only lasted for a second since he had to open his eyes to catch his balance a second time. The crowd responded with cheers and applause. They shouted for more.

Richard faced out into the audience and did an exaggerated bow. There were more cheers. Turning back to the woman, Richard began to strut, twist, and shake as best as he could to the music. The woman watched him with great interest and amusement but had trouble imitating him. The only thing she was able to do with any degree of accomplishment was raise her hands in the air and move them as Richard was doing.

"Let me show you," Richard said. He reached out and grasped the woman about the hips and tried to get her to shake rhythmically. She couldn't get the idea but found her awkward attempts hilarious. So did the crowd.

Suzanne and Perry watched with understandable misgivings. Suzanne told Perry she was worried that Richard was drunk, and Perry agreed. But they couldn't help but notice how much the crowd was enjoying his antics.

"Your friend is very amusing," a voice said behind Perry. He turned to face a darling young woman whom he guessed to be around eighteen. She had lively light blue eyes that reminded him of Suzanne's and an infectious smile. She reached out with her palm. Perry pressed his against hers self-consciously; he could feel his face flush. The woman was disarmingly attractive and several inches taller than him.

"My name is Luna," the woman said in a voice that made Perry's knees feel weak.

"I'm Perry."

"I know," Luna said. "You are very appealing. I see you have whiter teeth than Richard."

Perry blushed even more. He nodded. "Thank you," he managed to say.

Luna's eyes drifted out toward the center of the arena. "Can you dance like Richard?"

Perry glanced back at the diver. He was now doing his own interpretation of break dancing and at that moment was on his back spinning around with his legs thrust up in the air.

"I can, I suppose," Perry said noncommittally. "Maybe not quite as well as Richard. He's a bit more extroverted than I. But to tell you the truth, I haven't tried dancing for a few years."

"I think Richard is as good as an entertainment clone," Luna said. She seemed to be mesmerized by Richard, who was now moon walking to the enjoyment of the crowd.

"That's a compliment I bet Richard has never gotten before," Perry said.

Forever the follower, Michael took the hand of one of the women surrounding him and joined Richard on the pool's raised border. No sooner had he started to dance than a dozen other women stepped up on the platform to join in.

There was now a bevy of beautiful women surrounding Richard and Michael. They tried to move their arms and swivel their hips in imitation of the two tipsy divers with modest results, even the divers were having trouble coordinating their movements to the peculiar beat of the music.

Several of the more adventuresome young Interterran men climbed onto the platform to attempt the strange dance. Richard was not amused. Without interrupting his gyrations, he worked his way over to each of the men. With sudden, exaggerated movements of his hips, he knocked each man in turn off the platform. The crowd and even the men themselves loved it, thinking it was all part of the exercise.

After a half hour of uninterrupted dancing, the limits of endurance were reached. Forever the leader, Richard swept his arms out and grabbed as many women as he could before collapsing in giggles to the floor. Michael aped Richard's maneuver, adding to the pile to create a tangle of legs, arms, and lightly clad, perspiring torsos. The recumbent divers didn't mind keeping up with the palm pressing, and the women were happy to return the favor with kisses. At Arak's suggestion, worker clones rushed up with more drinks.

"This place is a dream come true," Michael cried after taking a swig from his freshly filled goblet.

"Poor Mazzola," Richard said. "Good old bell diver misses all the fun."

"What do you think this crystal liquor is made from?" Michael asked. He peered into his glass. The fluid was completely transparent.

"Who cares?" Richard squealed as he reached out and gave an exuberant one-armed hug to one of the women pressed up against his chest, spilling his drink in the process on his chest to the merriment of all who noticed.

"Michael, I have something for you," a blue-eyed, dark brunette said.

"What, gorgeous?" Michael asked. He was on his back, looking upside down at the woman who was standing next to the raised platform. She smiled and held up a small jar.

"I want you to try some caldorphin," she said as she unscrewed the jar's top. She extended the jar toward Michael, who used his free hand to scoop out a glob of the creamy contents. "That's a bit more than you need," she said, "but it's okay."

"Sorry," Michael said. "What do I do with it?" He brought it to his nose and sniffed. It was odorless.

"Rub it on your hand," she said. "I'll do the same and then we touch palms."

"Hey, Richie," Michael said as he rolled over and sat up. "Here's something new." Richard didn't respond. He was busy getting another refill of crystal.

Michael rubbed the cream on his palm and then looked up at the attractive woman who'd given it to him. She had a dreamy look about her, her eyes were half closed. Slowly she raised her hand, and Michael pressed his palm against hers.

The reaction for Michael was swift and overpowering. His eyes shot open, then closed in utter pleasure. For a few minutes of rapturous ecstasy he couldn't move. When he was finally able to, he snatched the jar away from the woman. He reached over and yanked on Richard's arm.

"Richie!" Michael yelled. "You got to try this stuff."

Richard tried to detach himself from Michael's grasp, but Michael hung on. "Hey, can't you see I'm occupied," Richard said. He was trying to kiss two women at the same time.

"Richie, you got to try this stuff," Michael repeated. He held out the jar.

"What the hell is it?" Richard said. He pushed himself up on one elbow.

"It's hand cream," Michael said.

"You're interrupting me to try some hand cream?" Richard couldn't believe it. "What's the matter with you?"

"Try it," Michael said. "It's like no hand cream you've ever tried. It's better than coke. I tell you it's dynamite!"

Sighing, Richard reached out and took a small amount

of the cream and rubbed it on his hands. He looked up at Michael. "So, now what's supposed to happen?"

"Press your palm against one of the girls'," Michael said.

Richard beckoned one of the two he'd just been kissing, but she motioned for him to wait. She took a bit of the cream for herself, rubbed it into her palm, and then pressed hers against Richard's. The result was the same as it had been for Michael. It took Richard a full minute to pull out of the blissful delirium that enveloped him.

"Oh, my God," Richard cried. "That was like an orgasm. Gimme some more!"

Michael snatched the jar away from his groping hand.

"Find your own," he said.

Richard made another lunge for the jar, but Michael batted his hand away.

Perry was in the middle of explaining to Luna what it meant to be the president of Benthic Marine when he felt someone tap him on the shoulder. It was Suzanne. She looked concerned.

"Richard and Michael are starting to quarrel," Suzanne said. "I'm worried. Arak is seeing to it that their glasses are never empty, and they're already very drunk."

"Uh-oh!" Perry said. "That could spell trouble." He glanced in the divers' direction and saw them pushing and shoving each other.

"I think we'd better walk out there and try to control them," Suzanne said.

"I guess you're right," Perry said. He hated to leave Luna.

"Let them have their fun," a voice said behind Suzanne. "Everyone is enjoying them. They're quite lively." She turned to find the same man who'd asked her if she lived with a mate.

"We're afraid their behavior could become disruptive," Suzanne said. "We don't want to take advantage of your hospitality."

"Let Arak worry about their behavior," the man said. "As you can see, he is encouraging their drinking."

"I noticed that," Suzanne said. "It's not a good idea."

"Leave it up to Arak," the man said. "It's his job to take care of them, not yours. Besides, I'd like to talk with you in private for a moment."

"You would?" Suzanne responded. She was nonplussed by the request. She glanced back at the divers and was relieved to see they'd stopped their squabbling and had settled back down into their bevy of reclining women. Suzanne looked at Perry, wondering if he'd heard the man's request. He had. Perry smiled mischievously and gave Suzanne an encouraging nudge.

"Why not?" Perry whispered leaning toward her. "We're supposed to be enjoying ourselves, and the diver emergency has passed for the time being."

"It will be just for a moment," the man said.

"What do you mean, 'in private'?" Suzanne asked. She took in the stranger's chiseled features and liquid eyes and felt her heart skip a beat. She'd never seen a man quite so classically handsome, much less spoken with one.

"Well, not really in private," the man said with a disarming smile. "I thought we could just withdraw a few steps or perhaps climb the stairs to the balcony. I only wish to be able to speak to you alone for a moment."

"Well, I suppose," Suzanne said. She looked back at Perry.

"I'll be right here," Perry said, "with Luna."

Suzanne let herself be led up the stairs.

"My name is Garona," the man said as they climbed.

"Mine is Suzanne Newell," Suzanne responded.

"That I know," Garona said. "Dr. Suzanne Newell, to be precise."

They reached the top of the stairs and leaned against the balustrade. Below, it was apparent the gala was a great success: laughter and lively conversation drifted up from the throng. Most people were milling around the central pool area where the divers and their harem were the focus of attention. The crowd was orderly, gracious, and respectful. Those closest to the dancing were constantly giving way so that those on the periphery could move up to get a close-up view.

"Thank you for giving me this moment," Garona said. "It's unfair for me to monopolize your time."

"It's quite all right," Suzanne said. "It's a relief of sorts to step back and get this overview."

"I had to talk with you to tell you I find you irresistible," Garona said.

Suzanne peered into Garona's handsome face. She expected to see at least a faint vestige of a sly smile. Instead he was regarding her with a warm, smiling intensity that suggested utter sincerity.

"Run that by me again," Suzanne said.

"I find you absolutely irresistible," Garona repeated.

"You do?" Suzanne asked. She chuckled nervously.

"Truly," Garona said.

Suzanne's eyes wandered back to the crowd to give her a chance to process this unexpected encounter. She hesitated before turning back to him. "You're very flattering, Garona," she said. "At least I think you are. So I'm sorry if I seem skeptical, but with all these absolutely gorgeous and flawless females, I find it a bit hard to believe you'd be interested in me. I mean, I know my limitations. In the irresistible arena, I'm no competition for any of these women here."

Garona's smile never faltered. "Perhaps it is hard for you to believe," he said. "But nonetheless it is true."

"Well, then I am sincerely flattered," Suzanne said. "But perhaps you could tell me why you find me so irresistible."

"It's hard to put into words," Garona said.

"At least give it a try," Suzanne said.

"I suppose I'd have to say it involves your freshness or your innocence. Or perhaps it's your alluring primitiveness."

"Primitiveness?" Suzanne echoed. "That's how Arak characterized Richard."

"Well, he definitely has it, too," Garona said.

"And that's supposed to be a compliment?" Suzanne asked.

"Here in Interterra it is," Garona said.

"What exactly is Interterra?" Suzanne asked. "And how long has it been in existence?"

Garona smiled patronizingly and shook his head. "I've been warned against answering any questions other than purely personal ones about myself."

Suzanne rolled her eyes. "Sorry," she said with a touch or sarcasm. "I guess it just slipped out."

"It's quite all right."

"So, I have to think up some personal questions?"

"If you'd like," Garona said.

"Well . . ." Suzanne said as she tried to think up one. "Have you always lived down here?"

Garona roared with laughter, loudly enough to attract

the attention of two men on the floor below. They looked up, waved when they recognized Garona, and began making their way toward the stairs.

"I'm sorry I laughed," he said, "but your question underlines how wonderfully innocent you are. It's so refreshing. I'd love to get better acquainted. When you have had enough of the festivities and you want to leave, let me know. I'd love to take you to your room. We can spend some intimate time together pressing palms, just you and I. What do you say?"

Suzanne's mouth slowly dropped open as the true meaning of Garona's proposal dawned on her. She again laughed mockingly. "Garona, I don't believe this," she said. "Only a short time ago I thought I was going to die. Now I'm in a fantasyland with a great-looking guy making a pass at me and wanting to come to my room. How am I supposed to respond?"

"Just say yes," Garona said.

"I'm afraid I'm a little too stunned to reply so smoothly."

"I can appreciate that," Garona said. "But I can comfort you and make you relax."

Suzanne shook her head. "I don't think you understand. I'm having trouble just thinking straight."

"You excite me," Garona said. "You enthrall me. I want to be with you."

"I have to give you high marks for persistence," Suzanne said.

"We will talk more later," Garona said. "here come two of my friends."

Suzanne turned to see the two men who'd been roused by Garona's outburst of laughter mount the top step of the main stairway and approach. She couldn't help but notice that both were as attractive as Garona. They walked arm in arm, like two lovers.

"Greetings, Tarla and Reesta," Garona said. "Have you met our honored guest, Dr Suzanne Newell?"

"Not yet," the two men said in unison. "We were hoping to have the honor." They both bowed elegantly.

Suzanne forced a smile. This was all so enchantingly odd. She felt it all had to be a dream.

Richard knew he was drunk, but he'd certainly been drunker in the past. His inebriation didn't seem to deter any of the women who were still flocking around him. He was aware the faces of the women changed as he danced, meaning there was a rotation of sorts, but it didn't matter since they were all so beautiful.

Without meaning to, he bumped up against Michael hard enough to knock both of them off balance. They collapsed to the floor, too limp to hurt themselves. When they realized what had happened, they laughed so hard, they brought tears to their eyes.

"What a party!" Michael cried when he'd recovered enough to speak. He wiped his eyes with the back of his hand.

"Nobody's going to believe us when we get home," Richard said. "Especially when we tell them that every single chick is available. I mean, it's like a turkey shoot. It's unreal."

"The men down here just don't care," Michael said. "Hey, look at that girl over there."

"Which one?" Richard asked. He rolled over and tried to follow Michael's line of sight through the milling crowd. His eyes finally came to rest on a statuesque redhead walking arm in arm with a young boy.

"Wow," he said.

"I saw her first," said Michael.

"Yeah, but I'm going to get her first."

"No way."

"Screw you," Richard said as he scrambled to his feet.

Michael reached out and grabbed one of Richard's legs and tripped him. He fell head first and skidded off the edge of the platform, striking his forehead on the floor. He wasn't hurt, but he was angry, especially when Michael tried to run past him toward the girl.

Richard managed to put a foot out in time to trip Michael. As he tried to get up, Richard threw himself on top of him. Then he grabbed the front of his tunic and punched him in the nose.

The sudden violence caused the party-goers to shrink back in alarm. A collective gasp was uttered as Michael's nose began to bleed.

Michael bucked Richard off his body and got his legs under him. Richard tried to do the same, but Michael caught him on the side of the head with a blow that sent him sprawling back to the floor.

"Come on, you bastard," Michael taunted. "Get up and fight." Blood trickled down the front of his chin and dripped onto the floor. He swayed on his feet.

Richard got to his hands and knees. He looked up at Michael. "You're a dead man," he growled.

"Come on, you twerp!" Michael responded.

Richard pushed himself up to a standing position, but he, too, was unsteady on his feet.

Arak, who'd been at some distance from the divers when their melee started, pushed through the stunned and silent crowd. He stepped between the two drunken divers.

"Please," he said. "Whatever is the problem we can resolve it."

"Outta my way," Richard spat. He shoved Arak to the side and launched a roundhouse blow to Michael's head. Michael ducked but lost his balance in the process and fell to the floor. Richard lost his balance when the blow failed to connect.

"Worker clones, restrain the guests!" Arak yelled.

Richard and Michael both managed to get themselves upright and throw several more ineffectual punches before two large male worker clones intervened. Each grabbed a diver in a bear hug. Richard and Michael continued trying to hit each other until they were moved a body length apart. At that moment Perry pushed through the crowd.

"Have you idiots forgotten where you are?" Perry shouted. "For chrissake, no fighting! What's the matter with you two?"

"He started it," Richard said.

"He started it," Michael said.

"No, he did."

"No, it was him."

Before Perry could respond to this juvenile tit-for-tat, the divers suddenly broke out laughing. Every time they tried to look at each other they laughed harder. Soon everyone but Perry and the worker clones were laughing as well. At Arak's command the worker clones let go of the divers, who immediately exchanged high fives.

"What was the fighting about?" Arak asked Perry.

"Too much of your crystal," Perry said.

"Perhaps we should switch them to a less potent drink," Arak said.

"Either that or cut them off completely," Perry said.

"But I don't want to ruin the party," Arak said. "Everyone is enjoying them immensely."

"It's your party," Perry said.

Richard and Michael started back toward the platform.

"I tell you what," Richard whispered to Michael. "We'll make it fair. I'll shoot you for the redhead."

"Okay," Michael said.

"You call," Richard said. "Odds or evens."

"Evens," Michael said.

On the count of three, they both threw out a single finger. Michael smiled with satisfaction. "Justice!" he exclaimed.

"Crap!" Richard said.

"Now where the hell is she?" Michael questioned. The two divers scanned the crowd.

"There she is," Richard said. He pointed. "And she's still with the little squirt."

"I'll be back in a flash," Michael said. He made a beeline for the woman whom he noticed was watching his approach with great interest.

"Hi, baby," Michael said, avoiding making eye contact with the preteen beside her. "My name is Michael."

"My name is Mura. Are you hurt?"

"Hell, no," Michael said. "A little tap on the nose doesn't hurt old Michael. No way."

"We are not accustomed to seeing blood," Mura said.

"Listen!" Michael said. "How would you like to come over and rub palms with me? We got our own little party going on over by the pool."

"I'd love to touch palms with you," Mura said. "But first, may I introduce Sart."

"Yeah, hi, Sart," Michael said offhandedly. "You've got a great looking mother here, but why don't you go off and play with some friends."

Both Mura and Sart giggled. Michael wasn't amused.

"Pretty funny, huh?" he questioned irritably.

"Unexpected is a better word," Mura managed.

Michael reached out and took Mura's arm. "Come on, honey." To the youngster he said, "See you later, Sart."

With Mura in tow, Michael strutted with a few unplanned wobbles back to Richard and the rest of the group. Richard had singled out two women who were particularly demonstrative in their affection for him. He introduced them as Meeta and Palenque. One was blonde and the other brunette, and both were incredibly voluptuous.

"Richie, meet Mura," Michael said proudly.

Richard pretended not to notice the striking redhead. Instead he pointed over Michael's shoulder and asked about the preteen. Michael looked behind and was irritated to see the boy had tagged along.

"Beat it, kid," Michael snapped.

Mura ignored Michael and encouraged Sart to step forward. She introduced him to Richard.

"Hey, nice to meet you, Sart," Richard said. "You, too, Mura. Why don't you two take a load off and sit down?"

"We'd enjoy that," Mura said.

"Indeed," Sart added.

Michael rolled his eyes in frustrated irritation as Richard managed to preempt his triumph. For a moment he considered cold-cocking Richard on the spot.

"Hey, you, too, Mikey," Richard goaded. "Come on, buddy, take a seat and relax! It'll do you good. After all, we're all one big, happy family."

That comment brought giggles from all the Interterrans within earshot, only adding to Michael's embarrassment. He swallowed his pride and sat down.

"Listen, Mikey," Richard continued. "My little blonde bombshell, Meeta, just told me something interesting. Everybody loves to swim in Interterra."

"No kidding," Michael said, lightening up. "Did you mention that we were professionals?"

"Of course," Richard said. "But I'm not convinced they quite got what I was talking about. Seems that the idea of work is not something they can relate to."

"If you swim for work, does that mean you like to swim?" Meeta asked.

"Sure we like to swim," Michael said.

"Well, why don't we all take a dip?" Meeta suggested.

"Why not," Mura agreed. "You people need to cool down."

"I think it is a wonderful idea," Sart said.

Richard looked at the inviting aquamarine pool. "Are you talking about swimming right now?" he asked.

"What time could be better?" Palenque said. "We're all so warm and sweaty."

"But our clothes," Richard said. "We'll be sopping."

"We don't wear clothes when we swim," Meeta said.

Richard looked at Michael. "This place just keeps getting better and better," he said.

"Well?" Meeta questioned. "What do the professional swimmers say?"

Richard swallowed. He was afraid to say anything lest he wake up.

"I say we go for it," Michael cried.

"Wonderful!" Meeta said. She leaped to her feet and helped Palenque to hers. Sart got up and gave Mura a hand. In the blink of an eye the Interterrans unabashedly threw off their tunics and stepped out of their shorts. In their naked nubile splendor, they all dove cleanly into the water and swam out toward the center of the pool with strong, practiced strokes.

Richard and Michael were momentarily too stunned to follow. Instead they glanced around at the people in the immediate vicinity. To their added surprise, no one had taken much notice other than Perry. Then Richard and Michael's eyes met.

"What the hell are we waiting for?" Richard asked as he smiled drunkenly.

In a rush, the two divers clumsily struggled to get out of their clothes. At the same time they made a dash to the pool. Michael had trouble with his shorts and ended up tripping. Richard was more successful and was soon racing toward the shallow area at the center of the pool.

On his arrival Richard was literally set upon by Meeta and Palenque who playfully and repeatedly dunked him. Richard took the harassment from the naked beauties gleefully but was soon out of breath. By the time Michael arrived and engaged in similar activities with Mura since Sart and Palenque had swum to the far end of the pool, Richard was content to languish in a place where he and Meeta could sit with their heads above the surface.

"Richard, Richard, Richard," Meeta cried happily as she repeatedly pressed her palm against his and stroked his head. "You are the most primitively attractive visitor we've ever had in Saranta. Maybe in all of Interterra for at least several thousand years."

"I thought only my mother appreciated me," Richard said jokingly.

"You knew your mother?" Meeta questioned. "How quaint."

"Of course I knew my mother," Richard said. "Don't you know yours?"

"No," Meeta said with a laugh. "No one in Interterra knows his mother. But let's not get into that. Instead, why don't you take me to your room?"

"Now there's an idea," Richard said. "But what about your friend, Palenque? What will we say to her?"

"Anything you like," Meeta said unconcernedly. "But it's easiest to just ask her. I'm sure she'll want to come. And Karena. I know she wants to come, too."

Richard tried to act nonchalant, but he was afraid his surprise at this unexpected good fortune was all too apparent. At the same time with this auspicious turn of events, he wished he hadn't drunk quite so much.

It was a boisterous group that set out from the pavilion to the dining hall. Suzanne, Perry, and the divers were singing old Beatles songs at the top of their lungs, to the delight of their companions who, surprisingly, knew the words. Suzanne was walking with Garona, Perry with Luna, Richard with Meeta, Palenque, and Karena, and Michael with Mura and Sart.

Although Suzanne and Perry had resisted drinking very much, what they had drunk had gone to their heads. They were not nearly as drunk as Richard and Michael, but both recognized they were tipsy. They were also enjoying themselves immensely.

Arak had bid them farewell as the gala wound down

and promised to meet with them in the morning. He had wished them a pleasant rest and had thanked them for coming to the celebration.

"Hey," Richard called out when they'd finished a rendition of "Come Together." "Don't you guys know any songs of your own?"

"Of course," Meeta said. Immediately the Interterrans burst into song, and although the words were in English, the beat was as irregular as the music at the gala had been.

"Cut!" Richard cried out. "That sounds too weird. Let's go back to the Beatles."

"Richard, let's be fair," Suzanne said.

"It's all right," Meeta said. "We'd rather sing your songs."

"Michael? What the hell are you doing with the glasses?" Richard asked when he saw that his partner was carrying several empty goblets.

"I asked Arak," Michael said. "He told me I could take them. They're gold. I bet I have enough money here for a down payment on a new pickup truck."

Richard leaned over and snatched one of the goblets.

"Hey, gimme that back," Michael demanded.

Richard laughed. "Go out for a pass. I'll hit you long!"

Michael handed the rest of the goblets to Mura. Then he staggered ahead for the pass. Richard tossed the goblet like a football, and it spiraled into Michael's hands. Everyone clapped. Michael took a bow, lost his balance, and fell. Everyone giggled and clapped harder.

"We have pets that play that game," Mura said.

"I saw some pets when we were flying in," Suzanne said. "They looked like composite creatures."

"They are," Mura said.

"Do you have sports games down here?" Richard asked.

Michael came back and collected the rest of his goblets.

"No, we don't have sports," Meeta said. "Unless you mean mind games, things like that."

"Hell no!" Richard said. "I mean like hockey or football."

"No," Meeta said. "We don't have physical competition."

"Why not?" Richard asked.

"It's not necessary," Meeta said. "And it is unhealthy."

Richard glanced at Michael. "No wonder the men are all such wimps," he said. Michael nodded.

"How about 'Lucy in the Sky with Diamonds,' " Suzanne suggested. "It seems so apropos."

A few moments later, still singing the refrain, the group stumbled into the dining hall. It was dark, but the Interterrans somehow brought up the illumination. Perry was about to ask how it was done when he noticed Donald. The former naval officer was sitting silently in the dark. His face was as grim as it had been when they'd left for the celebration.

"My gosh," Richard said. "Mr. Straight Arrow is right where we left him."

Michael proudly deposited his cache of golden goblets on the table with fanfare.

Richard lurched over to a position across the table from Donald. He dragged the three women with him like trophies. "Well, Admiral Fuller," he said in a mocking tone while comically saluting. "I guess you can tell by our present company and booty that you really missed out."

"I'm sure I did," Donald said sarcastically.

"You can't imagine how great it was, smart ass," Richard said.

"You're drunk, sailor," Donald said scornfully. "Luckily, some of us have enough self-control to keep our wits about us."

"Yeah, well, let me tell you what's wrong with you," Richard said, pointing a wavering finger at Donald's face. "You still think you are in the goddamned Navy. Well, let me tell you something. You ain't."

"You're not only stupid," Donald hissed. "You're disgusting."

Something snapped in Richard's brain. He shoved the women away and launched himself across the marble table, catching Donald by surprise. Despite his inebriation, he was able to straddle the man and land a few ineffectual punches on the side of his head.

Donald responded by enveloping Richard in a bear hug. Locked in a violent embrace, both men rolled off the chaise Donald had been sitting on. Neither man could do much damage to the other, but pummeled each other with short punches nonetheless. They did succeed in crashing into the table which caused Michael's goblet collection to fall to the floor with a great clatter.

The Interterrans shrank back in dismay. While Suzanne and Perry intervened. It wasn't easy, but they finally managed to separate the two men. This time it was Richard's turn to have a bloody nose.

"You bastard," Richard sputtered as he touched his nose and looked at the blood.

"You're lucky your friends are here," Donald told him. "I might have killed you."

"That's enough," Perry said. "No more baiting and

no more fighting. This is ridiculous. You're both acting like children."

"Idiot!" Donald added. He shook off Perry's restraining arms and straightened his satin tunic.

"Jerk!" Richard retorted. He moved away from Suzanne and turned to his three women friends. "Come on, girls!" he said. "Let's go to my room, where I won't have to look at this guy's ugly mug."

Richard took a few unsteady steps toward the women, but they shrank back. Then, without another word, they fled out the open end of the room into the night. Richard hurried after them but stopped at the edge of the lawn. The women were already halfway back to the pavilion.

"Hey!" Richard yelled through cupped hands. "Come back! Meeta . . ."

"I think it's time you went to bed," Suzanne said. "You've caused enough trouble for one night."

Richard turned back into the room disappointed and angry. He slammed his open palm down on the table top hard enough to make everyone in the room jump. "Shit!" he shouted to no one in particular.

Perry punched open the door of his cottage with a trembling hand he did his best to hide and let Luna enter before him. It had been a long time since he'd been alone with a woman like this. He had no idea whether his anxiety was from marital guilt or from recognizing Luna's inappropriate youth. On top of that he was tipsy with drink, but even more intoxicating than the crystal was the fact that an absolutely gorgeous young woman found him attractive.

As Perry struggled to conceal his nervousness he was sensitive enough to notice that Luna was agitated herself.

"Can I get you something?" Perry asked. "I'm supposed to have food and drink available." He watched as the girl went over to the pool and bent down to test its temperature.

"No, thank you," Luna said. She began to wander aimlessly around the room.

"You seem upset," Perry said. For lack of anything better to do, he went over and sat on the bed.

"I am," Luna admitted. "I've never seen a person act the way Richard did."

"He's not our best ambassador," Perry said.

"Are there many people like him where you come from?" Luna asked.

"Unfortunately, his type is not uncommon," Perry said. "Usually there's a history of abuse that gets handed down from generation to generation."

Luna shook her head. "Where does the stimulus for the abuse come from?"

Perry scratched the top of his head. He'd not meant to get into a sociological discussion nor did he feel capable at the moment. At the same time he felt he had to say something. Luna was looking at him intently. "Well, let's see," he said. "I haven't really thought about this too much, but there's a lot of discontentment in our society from heightened expectation and a sense of entitlement. Nobody's ever really satisfied."

"I don't understand," Luna said.

"Let me give you an example," Perry said. "If somebody gets a Ford Explorer the next thing they see is an ad for a Lincoln Navigator, that makes the Explorer seem unappealing."

"I don't know what those are," Luna said.

"It's just stuff," Perry said. "And we're conditioned through relentless advertising to feel it's never the right stuff."

"I don't understand that kind of covetousness," Luna said. "We don't have anything like that here in Interterra."

"Well, then it's hard to explain," Perry said. "But anyway there's a lot of discontentment which especially comes to a head in poor families which have even less stuff than everyone else, and within families people tend to take it out on each other."

"It's sad," Luna said. "And frightening."

"It can be," Perry agreed. "But we're kind'a conditioned not to think about it since it all drives our economy."

"It seems strange to have a society that encourages violence," Luna said. "Violence is shocking for us since we have none in Interterra."

"None?" Perry asked.

"No, never," Luna said. "I've never seen a person hit another. It makes me feel weak."

"Then why don't you sit down?" Perry said. He patted the bed next to him, feeling self-consciously transparent. Nonetheless Luna came to the bed and sat down beside him.

"You don't feel dizzy, do you?" Perry asked, struggling to make conversation now that she was so close. "I mean, you're not going to faint or anything?"

"No, I'll be all right."

Perry looked into Luna's pale blue eyes. For a moment he couldn't speak. When he could he said, "You know, you are very young."

"Young? What does that have to do with anything?"

"Well . . ." Perry said, searching for words. He wasn't sure himself whether he was referring to her reaction to Richard's behavior or his reaction to her. "When you're young you haven't had as much experience as when you are older. Maybe you haven't had time to see violence."

"Listen, there's no violence here," Luna said. "It's been selected against. Besides, I'm not as young as you probably imagine. How old do you think I am?"

"I don't know," Perry stammered. "About twenty."

"Now you seem to be upset."

"I guess I am a little," Perry admitted. "You could be my daughter."

Luna smiled. "I can assure you I'm over twenty. Does that make you feel better?"

"Some," Perry admitted. "Actually, I don't know why I feel so nervous. Everything is so nice here, but it's still quite unnerving."

"I understand," Luna said. She smiled again and raised her palms toward his. Self-consciously Perry put his against hers. "What is this with our hands?" he asked.

"It's just the way we show love and respect. You don't like it?"

"When it comes to showing love I'm partial to kissing," Perry said.

"Like Richard was doing this evening?"

"A bit more intimately than Richard's technique," Perry said.

"Show me," Luna said.

Perry took a breath, leaned over, and lightly kissed Luna on the lips. When he pulled back, Luna responded by touching her lips gently with the very tips of her fingers as if amazed by the sensation.

"Do you dislike it?" Perry asked.

Luna shook her head. "No, but my fingers and palms are more sensitive than my lips. But show me more."

Perry swallowed nervously. "Are you serious?"

"I'm sure," Luna said. She moved closer to him and looked at him with those dreamy eyes. "I find you very alluring, Mr. President of Benthic Marine."

Perry wrapped his arms around her and pulled her down onto the white cashmere coverlet.

Michael was in seventh heaven. Mura was the woman of his dreams. It couldn't get better than this. He didn't even mind Sart's continued presence. The boy was in the pool, leaving him to enjoy Mura by himself.

Just when Michael was about to pass out from sheer delight, his rapture was interrupted by a knock at his door. He tried to ignore it, but finally staggered to the door, stark naked. He felt even drunker on his feet. "Who the hell is it?" he demanded.

"It's me, your buddy Richard."

Michael opened the door. "What's the problem?"

"No problem," Richard said. He tried to look around Michael. "I just thought maybe you might need some help, if you know what I mean."

It took Michael's drugged brain a few seconds to catch Richard's drift. He glanced back at Mura on the circular bed, then back to Richard.

"Are you kidding?" Michael asked.

"No," Richard said. He smiled crookedly.

"Mura," Michael called out. "Do you mind if Richard comes in and joins us?"

"Only if he promises to behave," Mura called back.

Michael looked back at Richard with an exaggerated expression of surprise. "You heard the lady," he said with a sly smile. He opened the door wider and let Richard into the room. As the two men approached the bed Mura held up both hands.

"Come on, you two primitives!" she said. "I'd love to press palms with you both."

The two divers exchanged a glance of appreciative disbelief before Michael climbed back onto the bed, and Richard struggled out of his satin garments. As Richard settled next to Mura, he said, "You people are pretty free with love."

"It's true," Mura said. "We have lots of love. It's our wealth."

A short time later the two drunken divers were swooning with pleasure in Mura's arms. It wasn't sex per se, since in their drugged state neither was capable of consummation, but nonetheless they couldn't have been more content.

Sart had observed Richard's arrival from the far end of the pool. He was both attracted and repelled by Richard. Mainly, he was curious. After tiring of swimming he got out of the water. He dried himself off, then walked over to the blissful threesome. Mura smiled up at him. She had her arms around both divers, who had fallen fast asleep.

Mura motioned for Sart to sit down on the bed. She'd been gently stroking both divers' backs but was happy to let Sart take over with Richard. That freed her to concentrate on Michael.

Sart initially just stroked Richard's back as Mura had been doing, but tiring of this, he began to improvise. First he rubbed Richard's exposed arm and shoulder. Richard's skin felt intriguingly strange to Sart. It wasn't as firm as

Interterran skin and had many curious, tiny imperfections. Sart transferred his attentions to Richard's head, where he'd noticed a small, poorly defined, bluish red discoloration within the hairline above his ear. As Sart bent over to examine this flat blemish more closely, touching it gently with the tip of his finger, Richard's eyes popped open.

Sart smiled at him dreamily and went back to his tender stroking.

"What the hell?" Richard cried. He knocked Sart's hand to the side. With drunken clumsiness he leaped from the bed.

Sart stood up as well. He wondered if the mark above Richard's ear was inordinately sensitive. Maybe he should not have touched it.

Richard's sudden movement was enough to awaken Michael. Sleepy and dazed, he sat up despite Mura's restraining arm. He saw Richard swaying by the bedside and glaring at Sart, who looked somewhat guilty.

"What's the matter, Richie?" Michael asked with a slurred, gravelly voice.

Richard didn't answer. Instead he wiped his hand over his head while continuing to glower at Sart.

"What happened, Sart?" Mura asked.

"I touched Richard's blemish," Sart explained. "The one above his ear. I'm sorry."

"Michael, come here!" Richard snapped. He waved Michael away from the bed while walking unsteadily in the direction of the pool.

Michael got to his feet feeling giddy from the short snooze. He followed Richard. The two men staggered out of earshot. Michael could tell that Richard was major-league perturbed.

"What's going on?" Michael asked in a whisper.

Richard wiped his mouth with the back of his hand. He was still glaring back at Sart.

"I think I figured out why all these guys don't care if we make it with their women," Richard whispered back.

"Why?" Michael asked.

"I think they're all a bunch of queers."

"Really?" Michael looked back at Sart. The possibility had crossed his mind at the gala when he'd seen so many men walking around arm in arm, but then he'd forgotten about it in the general excitement.

"Yeah, and I'll tell you something else," Richard said.

"That little nerdy squirt over there has been rubbing my back and head. The whole time I thought it was the girl."

Michael laughed despite Richard's evident rancor.

"It's not funny," Richard snapped.

"I bet Mazzola would think it was funny," Michael said.

"If you tell Mazzola, I'll kill you," Richard hissed.

"You and ten other people," Michael scoffed. "But, in the meantime, what do you want to do?"

"I think we should show this little twerp what we think of his kind," Richard said. "The guy had his hands all over me, for chrissake. I'm not about to let that pass without a reaction. I don't think we should let any of these people get the wrong idea of our persuasion."

"All right," Michael said. "I'm with you. What do you have in mind?"

"First, get rid of the girl!" Richard said.

"Oh, no! Do we have to?" Michael questioned.

"Absolutely," Richard said impatiently. "And ditch the long face. You can tell her to come back tomorrow. It's important to teach this guy a lesson, and we don't want an audience. She'd yell bloody murder and the next thing you'd know we would be dealing with a couple of those worker clones."

"Okay," Michael said. He took a breath to fortify himself and walked back to the bed.

"Is Richard all right?" Mura inquired.

"He's fine," Michael said. "But he's tired. In fact, we're both tired. Maybe exhausted is a better word. Plus we're drunk, as I'm sure you've noticed."

"It hasn't bothered me," Mura said. "I've been enjoying myself."

"I'm glad," Michael said. "But now we're wondering if we could put off any more palm pressing until tomorrow. What I mean is, maybe you should leave."

"Certainly," Mura said without hesitation. She immediately slid off the bed and began dressing. Sart did the same.

"I don't want you to get the wrong impression," Michael said. "I'd like to see you tomorrow."

"I understand you are tired," Mura said graciously. "Don't worry. You are our guests, and I will return tomorrow if it is your wish."

Sart cinched his braided rope around his waist and looked back at Richard, who'd not moved from where he was standing halfway to the pool's edge.

"Sart," Michael said, following the boy's line of sight. "Why don't you hang around? Richard wants to apologize for scaring you when he leaped off the bed."

Sart looked at Mura. Mura shrugged. "It's up to you, my friend."

Sart looked back at Michael, who smiled and winked at him.

"If the guests wish me to stay, I will stay," Sart said. He stepped back to the bed with a bit of swagger and sat down.

"That's wonderful," Michael said.

Mura finished dressing and went first to Michael and then to Richard to press her palm against each of theirs one last time. She told them both that they had given her great pleasure to be with them, and said she was eager to see them the following day. Before closing the door behind herself she bid them good night.

After the sound of the door closing drifted away, there was a brief, uncomfortable silence. Richard and Michael eyed Sart while Sart looked back and forth between the two men. Sart began to fidget. He stood up.

"Perhaps I should call for more drink," Sart said, to make conversation.

Richard forced a smile and shook his head. Then he approached Sart with a gait that suggested he didn't quite know where his feet were.

"How about more food?" Sart said.

Richard shook his head again. He was in an arm's distance of the boy. Sart took a step back.

"Me and my buddy here have something important we want to say to you," Richard told him.

"This is true," Michael said. He walked equally as unsteadily around the end of the bed to join Richard, effectively boxing Sart in a corner between the bed and the wall.

"To put it bluntly, so there is no misunderstanding," Richard continued, "we can't stand queers like you."

"In fact they make us a little crazy," Michael said.

Sart's eyes darted from one drunken, sneering face to the other.

"Perhaps it would be best if I go," Sart said nervously.

"Not before we're absolutely certain you know what we're talking about," Richard said.

"I don't know what you mean by 'queer,'" Sart admitted.

"Homo, gay, fag, fairy," Richard said derisively. "The term doesn't matter. The point is we don't like guys who like men. And we have a sneaking suspicion you fall into that category."

"Of course I like men," Sart said. "I like all people."

Richard looked at Michael then back at Sart. "We don't like bisexuals either."

Sart made a dash for the door, but he didn't make it. Richard grabbed one arm while Michael grabbed a handful of hair.

Richard quickly got Sart's other arm as well and with a triumphant laugh pinned both behind the boy. Sart struggled, but it was no use, especially with Michael still clutching a shock of his hair. Once the boy was immobilized, Michael punched him in the stomach, doubling him over.

Both divers let go of the boy and then laughed while they watched him take a few staggering steps. Sart was desperately trying to catch his breath. His face was purple.

"Okay, pansy," Richard slurred. "Here's one for putting your filthy paws on me."

Richard lifted Sart's face with his left hand and hit him with his right. It was not a jab but rather a wild, roundhouse uppercut that he put his entire weight behind. This second blow caught the boy full in the face, crushing his nose, sending him hurling backward off his feet. Sart's head smashed into the sharp corner of the marble nightstand, which penetrated several inches into his skull.

Richard was initially unaware of the fateful consequences of his powerful punch. He was too preoccupied
by the intense pain of his bruised knuckles. Wincing, he
cradled his throbbing hand with his other and cursed
loudly.

Michael watched in horror as Sart's flaccid body came
to a rest. Bits of brain tissue oozed from the ugly wound.
Suddenly sober, Michael bent down over the stricken boy,
who was making gurgling sounds.

"Richard!" Michael called out in a loud whisper. "We
got a problem!"

Richard refused to respond. He was still in pain, pacing
the room and shaking his hand in the air with his fingers
widely spread.

Michael stood up. "Richard! Christ! The guy's dead."

"Dead?" Richard echoed. The finality of the word
penetrated Richard's self-absorption.

"Well, almost. His head's caved in. He hit the goddamned table."

Richard staggered back to where Michael was standing
and looked down at Sart's motionless form. "Holy shit!"
he said.

"What the hell are we going to do?" Michael
demanded. "Why'd you hit him so freakin' hard?"

"I didn't mean to, okay!" Richard shouted.

"Well, what are we going to do?" Michael repeated.

"I don't know," Richard said.

At that moment Sart's battered body let out a final sigh
and the gurgling stopped.

"That's it," Michael said with a shudder. "He's dead!
We got to do something and fast."

"Maybe we should get outta here," Richard said.

"We can't get out of here," Michael complained.

"Where are we going to go? Hell, we don't even know where we are."

"All right, let me think," Richard said. "Shit, I didn't mean to hurt him."

"Oh, sure," Michael said sarcastically.

"Well, not that much," Richard said.

"What if someone comes in here?" Michael questioned.

"You're right," Richard said. "We've got to hide the body."

"Where?" Michael demanded urgently.

"I don't know!" Richard yelled. He looked around the room frantically. Then he looked back at Michael. "I just got an idea that might work."

"Good," Michael said. "Where?"

"First help me pick him up," Richard said. He stepped over the body, rolled it over, and then got his hands under Sart's arms.

Michael got Sart's feet, and together they hoisted the boy off the floor.

CHAPTER TWELVE

The new day arrived gradually just as it would on the earth's surface. The light slowly increased in intensity, causing the darkened, vaulted ceiling to lose its stars. Its color went in stages from deep indigo to a rosy pink and finally to a pure sky blue. Saranta began to stir.

Suzanne was the first of the earth surface visitors to awaken as the artificial dawn broke. As she scanned her room, taking in the white marble, the mirrors, and the pool, she realized that the surreal Interterran experience had not been a dream.

Slowly she turned her head to the side and gazed at Garona's sleeping form. He was on his side, facing her. She was amazed at herself for having allowed the man to stay the night. This was not her norm. The only way she'd shown some restraint had been by staunchly refusing to remove her silken tunic and shorts. She had spent the night with her clothes on, such as they were.

Suzanne wasn't sure she could blame her decision to allow him to stay on the small amount of crystal she'd drunk or whether it was simply Garona's handsome looks and winning flattery. As much as she hated to admit it, when it came to men, physical attractiveness was important to her. In fact, it had been part of the reason she'd remained mired in a volatile relationship with an actor back in L.A. long after it had ceased to be healthy.

As if sensing her gaze, Garona opened his dark, liquid eyes and smiled dreamily. It was difficult for Suzanne to feel much regret.

"I'm sorry if I woke you," Suzanne managed. He was as handsome in the first light of day as he'd been the night before.

"Please, don't be sorry," Garona said. "I appreciate being awakened to see that I am still with you."

"How is it you always say the right thing?" Suzanne said. She was being sincere, not sarcastic.

"I say what I would like to be told," Garona said.

Suzanne nodded. It was a sensible variation of the Golden Rule.

Garona rolled toward her and tried to envelop Suzanne in an embrace. Suzanne ducked under his arm and slid off the bed.

"Please, Garona," Suzanne said. "Lt's not replay last night. Not now."

Garona flopped back onto the bed and stared up at Suzanne.

"I don't understand your reluctance," he said. "Could it be that you don't care for me?"

Suzanne groaned audibly. "Oh, Garona, for all your sophistication and sensitivity, I can't imagine why this is so hard for you to grasp. As I told you last night, it takes me a little time to get to know someone."

"What do you need to know?" Garona questioned. "You can ask me any personal question you like."

"Look," Suzanne said. "I certainly care for you. Just letting you stay here is a testament to that. It's not usual for me when I've known someone for such a short time.

But I did let you stay, and I'm glad I did. But you can't expect too much from me. Think of everything I'm trying to take in."

"But it's unnatural," Garona said. "Your emotions should not be so contingent."

"I disagree!" Suzanne remarked. "It's called self-protection. I can't go around allowing spur-of-the-moment desires to dictate my behavior. And it should be the same for you. After all, you don't know anything about me. Maybe I have a husband or a lover."

"I assume you do," Garona said. "In fact, I would be surprised if you didn't. Anyway, it doesn't matter."

"That's nice." Suzanne put her hands defiantly on her hips. "It doesn't matter to you, but what about me?" Suzanne stopped herself. She reached up and rubbed her sleep filled eyes. She was getting herself all worked up, and she'd only been awake for a few minutes.

"Let's not discuss any of this right now," Suzanne said. "This day is going to be challenging enough. Arak has promised to answer our questions, and believe me, I have a lot." She walked over to one of the many mirrors and cautiously moved into the line of sight of her image. She grimaced at the reflection. Her mind might have been in a turmoil, but there was one thing she knew for certain: she did not look her best in inch-long hair.

Putting his legs over the edge of the bed, Garona sat up and stretched. "You second-generation humans are so serious."

"I don't know what you mean by second generation," Suzanne said. "But I think I have reason to be serious. After all, I didn't come here on my own accord. As Donald said, we've been abducted. And I don't have to remind you that means being carried off by force."

As he had promised, Arak showed up just after the group had eaten breakfast and asked if everyone was ready for the didactic session. Perry and Suzanne were demonstrably eager, Donald less so, and Richard and Michael completely uninterested. In fact, they acted tense and subdued, hardly their normal brazen selves. Perry assumed they were suffering from hangovers and suggested as much to Suzanne.

"I wouldn't doubt it," Suzanne responded. "As drunk as they were it stands to reason. How do you feel?"

"Great," Perry said. "All things considered. It was an interesting evening. How about your friend, Garona. Did he stay long?"

"For a while," Suzanne said evasively. "How about Luna?"

"The same," Perry said. Neither one looked the other in the eye.

As soon as the group was ready, Arak led them across the lawn toward a hemispherical structure similar to the pavilion although on a much smaller scale. Perry and Suzanne kept up with Arak. Donald lagged a few steps behind and Richard and Michael even more so.

"I still think you should tell Donald," Michael insisted in a whisper. "He might have an idea about what to do."

"What the hell is that bastard going to do?" Richard responded. "The kid's dead. Fuller's not going to bring him back to life."

"Maybe he'll have a better idea where to put the body," Michael said. "I'm worried about the kid being found. I mean, I don't want you to find out what they do down here to murderers."

Richard stopped short. "What do you mean, me?"

"Hey, you killed him," Michael said.

"You hit him, too," Richard said.

"But I didn't kill him," Michael said. "And the whole thing was your idea."

Richard glowered at his friend. "We're in this together, dirtbag. It's your room. Whatever happens to me is going to happen to you. Plain as day."

"Come on, you two," Arak called. He was holding open a door to the small hemispherical, windowless structure. The other members of the group were standing to the side and looking back in the divers' direction.

"Regardless," Michael whispered nervously, "the point is that the body is hardly hidden. You got to ask Donald if he can think of a better place for it. He might be an ex-officer asshole, but he's smart."

"Okay," Richard said reluctantly.

The two divers quickened their pace and caught up to the others. Arak smiled congenially and then entered the building followed by Suzanne and Perry. As Donald crossed the threshold Richard gave his sleeve a tug. Donald snatched his arm away and glared back at Richard, but kept walking.

"Hey, Commander Fuller!" Richard whispered. "Hold up a second."

Donald glanced briefly over his shoulder, treated Richard to a contemptuous look, and continued walking Arak was leading them along a curved, windowless corridor.

"I wanted to apologize about last night," Richard said, catching up to Donald so that he was walking right behind him.

"For what?" Donald asked scornfully. "Being stupid, being drunk, or allowing yourself to be duped by these people?"

Richard bit his lower lip before responding. "Maybe all three. We were bombed out of our gourds. But that's not the reason I want to talk to you."

Donald stopped short. Richard all but collided with him. Michael did bump into Richard.

"What is it, sailor?" Donald demanded in a no-nonsense voice. "Make it on the double. We've got an interesting talk ahead of us that I don't want to miss."

"Well, it's just that . . ." Richard began, but then he stumbled over his words, unsure of how to begin. Contrary to his early braggadocio, he was intimidated by Donald.

"Come on, sailor," Donald snapped. "Out with it."

"Michael and I think we better get the hell out of Interterra," Richard said.

"Oh, that's very intelligent of you boneheads," Donald said. "I suppose this sudden epiphany just occurred to you this morning. Well, perhaps I should remind you that we don't know where the hell we are until Arak decides to tell us. So once we've learned that, maybe we can talk again." Donald made a motion to leave. Richard grabbed his arm out of desperation. Donald glared down at Richard's hand. "Let go of me before I lose complete control."

"But—" Richard said.

"Can it, sailor!" Donald snapped, cutting off the conversation and yanking his arm away from Richard. He walked briskly ahead and ducked through a door at the end of the corridor in pursuit of the others.

"Why the hell didn't you tell him?" Michael demanded in an irritated whisper.

"You didn't tell him either," Richard pointed out.

"Yeah, because you said you'd do the talking,"

Michael said. He threw up his hands in frustration. "Some talking! My grandmother could have done a better job. Now we're back where we started. And you've got to admit, that body's not in the world's best hiding place. What if they find it?"

Richard shuddered. "I hate to think. But it was the best we could do under the circumstances."

"Maybe we should just stay in the room," Michael suggested.

"That's not going to solve anything," Richard said. "Come on! Let's at least find out where we are so we can figure out how to get the hell out."

The two men followed Donald and found themselves in a futuristic, circular room thirty feet in diameter with a domed ceiling. There were no windows. A single row of a dozen molded seats surrounded a dark, slightly curved central area.

Arak and Sufa were sitting directly opposite the entrance, in seats with consoles built into their arms. To Arak and Sufa's immediate right were two people the divers had never seen before. Although this couple was dressed in the usual white, they were not as attractive as the other Interterrans. Suzanne and Perry were seated to Arak and Sufa's left. Donald was to the far right, sitting by himself with lots of empty seats between him and the others.

"Please, Richard, Michael," Arak called out. "Take your seats. Anyplace you'd like. And then we'll begin."

Richard made it a point to pass several empty seats to take one next to Donald. Richard nodded to him, but Donald responded by shifting his weight away from the diver. Michael took the seat next to Richard.

"Welcome again to Interterra," Arak said. "Today we

are going to challenge your intellects in a very positive way. And in the process you will soon learn how very lucky you all are."

"How about starting by telling us when we'll be heading home?" Richard said.

"Shut the hell up!" Donald growled.

Arak laughed. "Richard, I do appreciate your spontaneity and impulsiveness, but be patient."

"First we'd like to introduce everyone to two of our distinguished citizens," Sufa said. "I'm certain you will find talking with them extremely helpful since they, like yourselves, have come from the surface world. May I present Ismael and Mary Black."

The couple stood for a moment and bowed. Michael clapped from habit but immediately stopped when he realized he was the only one doing so. Suzanne and Perry regarded the couple with wide-eyed curiosity.

"Mary and I would like to extend our welcome as well," Ismael said. He was a rather tall man with gaunt, hatchetlike features and deeply set eyes. "We are here because we have experienced what you are about to experience, and because of that we may be able to help. As for a general suggestion, I would encourage you at this point not to try to absorb too much too quickly."

Michael leaned over to Richard and whispered, "Do you think he's referring to that fabulous hand cream stuff we used last night?"

"Shut up!" Donald snapped, emphasizing each word. "If you men keep interrupting, I want you to move away from me."

"All right already," Michael said.

"Thank you, Ismael," Arak said. Then looking at each of the visitors in turn he added, "I hope you will all take advantage of the Blacks' offer. We feel that a division of labor will be helpful. Sufa and I will be available for informational issues whereas adjustment issues will be best handled by Ismael and Mary."

Suzanne leaned over to Perry. There was a new look of concern on her face. "What does he mean, adjustment issues? How long do you think they intend to keep us here?"

"I don't know," Perry whispered back. He'd been struck by the same implication.

"Before we begin I would like to present each of you with a telecommunicator and an eyepiece," Sufa said. She opened a box that she'd brought to the meeting and lifted out five small parcels, each with a name printed in bold letters across the top. Carrying them in her arms she walked around the room and handed them out to the designated recipients. Richard and Michael tore theirs open like kids attacking Christmas presents. Suzanne and Perry opened theirs with care. Donald let his sit unopened on his lap.

"It's like a pair of glasses and a wristwatch without a face," Michael said. He was disappointed. He tried on the glasses. They were aerodynamically shaped with clear lenses.

"It's a telecommunicator system," Sufa said. "They are voice activated, and each is mated to your individual voices, so they are not interchangeable. We'll be showing how to use them later."

"What do they do?" Richard asked. He tried the glasses on as well.

"Just about everything," Sufa said. "They connect with central sources whose information will be displayed virtually through the glasses. They also provide communication with anyone else in Interterra by sight and sound. They even do such mundane things as call air taxis, but more about them later."

"Let's get started," Arak said. He touched the pad on the console in front of him and the darkened curtain area turned a phosphorescent blue.

"The first thing we must talk about is the concept of time," Arak said. "This is perhaps the most difficult subject for people like yourselves to grasp because here in Interterra time is not the immutable construct it appears to be on the earth's surface. Your scientist, Mr. Einstein, recognized the relativity of time in the sense that it depends on one's position of observation. Here in Interterra you will confront many examples of such relativity. The simplest, for example, is the age of our civilization. From the perspective of earth surface references, our civilization is incredibly ancient, whereas from our reference point and those of the rest of the solar system, it is not. Your civilization is measured in terms of millennia, ours in millions, and the solar system in billions."

"Oh, for chrissake," Richard complained. "Do we have to sit through all this? I thought you were going to tell us where the hell we are."

"Unless you comprehend the basics," Arak said, "what I'm going to be telling you will be unbelievable, even meaningless."

"Why not work backwards," Richard said. "Tell us where we are and then the other stuff."

"Richard!" Suzanne snapped. "Be still!"

Richard rolled his eyes for Michael's benefit. Michael showed his impatience by uncrossing and recrossing his legs.

"Time is not a constant," Arak continued. "As I said,

your clever scientist Mr. Einstein recognized this, but where he made his mistake was thinking that the speed of light was the upper boundary of motion. It is not the case, although it takes huge quanta of focused energy to break the boundary. A good analogy from everyday life is the extra amount of energy necessary for a phase change that takes a solid to a liquid or a liquid to a gas. Pushing an object beyond the speed of light is like a phase change into a dimension where time is plastic and related only to space."

"Good grief," Richard blurted. "Is this a joke?"

Donald stood up and took a seat far from the two divers.

"Try to be patient," Arak said. "And concentrate on time not being a constant. Think about it! If time is truly relative then it can be controlled, manipulated, and changed. Which brings us to the concept of death. Listen carefully! On the earth's surface death has been a necessary adjunct of evolution, and evolution the only justification of death. But once a sensate, cognitive being has evolved, death is not only not needed, it is a waste."

At the mention of death Richard and Michael sank lower into their seats. Perry raised his hand. Arak immediately acknowledged him.

"Are we permitted to ask questions?" Perry asked.

"Absolutely," Arak said agreeably "This is to be more of a seminar than a lecture. But I ask you only to question what I have already said and not question what you believe I am about to say."

"You talked about measuring time," Perry said. "Did you mean to imply that your civilization, as you put it, predates our civilization on the earth's surface?"

"Indeed," Arak said. "And by a quantum of time

almost incomprehensible to your experience. Our Interterran recorded history goes back almost six hundred
million years."

"Get out of here!" Richard scoffed. "That's impossible. This is all a bunch of bull crap. That's older than the
dinosaurs."

"Much older than your dinosaurs," Arak agreed. "And
your disbelief is entirely understandable. That is why we
go slowly with this introduction to Interterra. I don't
mean to belabor the point, but it is far easier to adapt to
your present reality in stages."

"That's all well and good," Richard announced. "But
how about some proof for all this baloney. I'm starting to
think this whole setup is an elaborate put-on, and frankly,
I'm not interested in sitting here wasting time."

Neither Donald nor Suzanne complained about
Richard's current interruption. Both were harboring
similar thoughts although Suzanne certainly would not
have worded her skepticism so rudely. Arak, however, was
unfazed.

"All right," Arak said patiently. "We will provide some
proof that you can relate to your civilization's history.
Our civilization has been observing and recording the
progress of your second-generation human civilization
since the time of your evolution."

"What do you mean exactly by second-generation
human?" Suzanne asked.

"That will be apparent shortly," Arak said. "First, let's
show you some interesting images. As I said, we have
been observing your civilization's progress, and until
about fifty years ago we could do so at will. Since then
your increasing technological sophistication has limited
our surveillance to avoid detection. In fact, we have

stopped using most of our old-fashioned exit ports, like the one used to admit you to interterra or the one at Barsama, our sister city to the west. Both were ordered to be sealed with magma, but worker clone bureaucratic ineptitude has stalled the execution of the decree."

"My God, you're one long-winded dude," Richard said. "Where's the proof?"

"The cavern our submersible ended up in?" Suzanne questioned. "Was that what you call an exit port?"

"Exactly," Arak said.

"Is it normally filled with seawater?" Suzanne asked.

"Correct again," Arak said.

Suzanne turned to Perry. "No wonder Sea Mount Olympus was never picked up by Geosat. The seamount doesn't have the mass to be sensed on a gravimeter."

"Come on!" Richard complained. "Enough stalling. Let's see the proof!"

"Okay, Richard," Arak said patiently. "Why don't you suggest some period in your history that you would care to observe from our reference files. The more ancient the better in order to make my point."

Richard looked at Michael for help.

"How about gladiators," Michael said. "Let's see some Roman gladiators."

"Gladiatorial combat could be seen," Arak said reluctantly. "But such violent recordings are under strict censorship. To view them would require special dispensation by the Council of Elders. Perhaps another era would be more suitable."

"This is goddamn ridiculous!" Richard voiced.

"Try to control yourself, sailor," Donald snapped.

"Let me understand what you mean," Suzanne said. "Are you suggesting that you have recordings of all of human history, and you want us to suggest some historical time so we can see some images of it?"

"Precisely," Arak answered.

"How about the Middle Ages?" Suzanne said.

"That's a rather large era," Arak said. "Can you be more specific?"

"Okay," Suzanne said. "How about fourteenth-century France."

"That's during the Hundred Years' War," Arak said without enthusiasm. "It's curious even you, Dr. Newell, request images from such a violent time. But then again, you second-generation humans have had a violent record."

"Show people at play, not war," Suzanne said.

Arak touched the keypad on his console and then leaned forward to speak into a small microphone at its center. Almost immediately the room's illumination dimmed, and the floor screen came alive with blurred images flashing by at an incredible speed. Captivated, everyone leaned over the low wall and watched.

Presently the images slowed, then stopped. The projected scene was crystal clear with natural coloring and perfect holographic three dimension. It was of a small wheat field in the late summer from an altitude of about four or five hundred feet. A group of people had paused in their harvest activities. Their scythes were haphazardly strewn around several blankets on which a modest meal was spread. The audio was of summer cicadas buzzing intermittently.

"This is not interesting," Arak said after a quick glance. "It's not going to be proof of anything. Other than the people's crude garments, there is no indication of the time frame. Let's let the search recommence."

Before anyone could respond the screen again blurred as thousands of images flashed by. It was dizzying to watch the rapid flickering, but soon it again slowed and then stopped.

"Ah, this is much better," Arak exclaimed. Now the view was of a castle erected on a rocky prominence that was hosting a tournament of some kind. The vantage point was significantly higher than the previous scene. The coloration of the vegetation around the castle walls suggested mid autumn. The courtyard was packed with boisterous people whose voices formed a muted murmur. Everyone was dressed in colorful medieval attire. Heraldic pennants snapped in the breeze. At either end of a long, low log fence running down the center of the courtyard, two knights were in the final preparations for a joust. Their colorfully caparisoned horses were facing each other, pawing with excitement.

"How are these pictures taken?" Perry asked. He was transfixed by the image.

"It's a standard recording device," Arak said.

"I mean from what vantage point?" Perry asked. "Some kind of helicopter?"

Arak and Sufa laughed. "Excuse our giggles," Arak said. "A helicopter is your technology. Not ours. Besides, such a vehicle would be too intrusive. These images were taken by a small, silent, unmanned antigravity ship hovering at about twenty thousand feet."

"Hey, Hollywood does this stuff all the time," Richard said. "Big deal! This is not proof."

"If this is a set it's the most realistic one I've ever seen," Suzanne said. She leaned closer. As far as she was concerned the detail was far more than Hollywood was capable of.

As they watched, the attendant pages of the armored knights stepped back, and the men-at-arms lowered their lances. With a crisp fanfare sounding, the two horses charged forward on opposite sides of the log fence. As they bore down on each other the cheering of the crowd mushroomed. Then, just before the horsemen made contact, the screen went blank. A moment later it reverted back to its initial phosphorescent blue. A message window popped up and said: "Scene censored. Apply to Council of Elders."

"Damn!" Michael voiced. "I was getting into it. Who the hell won: the guy in green or the guy in red."

"Richard's right," Donald said suddenly, ignoring Michael. "These scenes can be staged too easily."

"Perhaps," Arak said without taking the slightest offense. "But I can show you whatever you want. We wouldn't be able to stage the full complement of first-generation history subject to your on-the-spot whim."

"How about something more ancient?" Perry suggested. "How about Neolithic times in the same location where the castle was."

"Clever idea!" Arak said. "I'll plug in the coordinates without a specific time other than, say, prior to ten thousand years ago, and let the search engine see if there is an image in storage."

The screen again came to life. Once again images flashed by. This time the flashing continued much longer.

Suzanne touched Perry's arm. She leaned toward him when he turned to her. "I think we're looking at real images," she said.

"I do, too," Perry said. "Can you imagine the technology involved!"

"I'm thinking less about the technology than the fact

that this place is real," Suzanne whispered. "We're not dreaming all this."

"Ah!" Arak commented. "I can tell the search has found something. And the time frame will be in the twenty-five-thousand-year range." As he spoke, the images slowed and again stopped.

The scene was the same rocky prominence although there was no castle. Instead the crown of the hill was dominated by a short escarpment undercut in the center to form a shallow cave. Grouped around the entrance to the cave was an assemblage of Neanderthals clothed in fur and working on crude implements.

"It does look like the same place," Perry commented.

As everyone watched, the image telescoped in on the domestic scene.

"And the pictures are clearer," Perry added.

"At that time we didn't worry about our ships being seen," Arak explained, "so we felt comfortable dropping down to a mere hundred feet or so to study behavior."

As they watched, one of the Neanderthal men straightened up from scraping a hide. In the process of stretching he happened to look straight up. When he did, his brutish face suddenly went blank, and his mouth dropped open in a mixture of surprise and terror. The image on the screen was close enough and clear enough to reveal his large square teeth.

"Well," Arak commented, "here's an example of our antigravity drone being seen. The poor devil probably thinks he's being visited by the gods."

"My gosh," Suzanne said. "He's trying to get the others to look up!"

"Their language was very limited," Arak said. "But I know that there was another subspecies in this same time frame and in the same general area that you called the Cro-Magnon. Their language skills were far better."

The Neanderthal grunted and leaped up and down while pointing toward the camera. Soon the entire group was looking skyward. Several of the women with young children immediately scooped their babies into their arms and disappeared into the cave while others dashed out.

One enterprising man bent down, picked up an egg-sized stone, and hurled it skyward. The missile approached, then went out of sight to the side.

"Not a bad arm," Michael said. "The Red Sox could use him out in center field."

Arak touched his console and the image faded. At the same time the lights went up in the room. Everyone moved back in their seats. Arak and Sufa looked around the room. The visitors were all quiet for the moment, even Richard.

"What was the supposed date of that recording?" Perry asked finally.

Arak consulted his console. "In your calendar it would have been July fourteenth, 23342 B.C."

"Didn't it bother you people that your camera platform was seen?" Suzanne asked. The image of the Neanderthal's face was haunting her.

"We were starting to be concerned about detection," Arak agreed. "There was even some talk among our conservative wing at the time to eliminate cognitive beings from the surface of the earth."

"Why would you be concerned about such primitive people?" Perry asked.

"Purely to avoid detection," Arak said. "Obviously twenty-five thousand years ago, due to the primitivism of your civilization, it didn't matter. But we knew it would, eventually. We know that our ships have been sighted occasionally even in your modern times, and it does concern us. Thankfully the sightings have mostly been greeted with disbelief, or if not with disbelief then with the idea that our interplanetary ships have come from someplace else in the universe, not from within the earth itself."

"Wait a second," Donald said suddenly. "I don't like to rain on anyone's parade, but I don't think this little show you're putting on here proves anything at all. It would be too easy to pull this off with computer-generated images. Why don't you cut all this gibberish, and just tell us who you represent and what you want from us."

For a moment no one spoke. Arak and Sufa leaned over and consulted with one another sotto voce. Then they conferred with Ismael and Mary. After a short, hushed conference, the hosts repositioned themselves back in their chairs. Arak looked directly at Donald.

"Mr Fuller, your skepticism is fully understandable," Arak said. "We're not sure everyone else shares your suspicions. Perhaps later they can influence your opinion. Of course there will be more proof as your introduction proceeds, and I'm confident that you will be won over. Meanwhile, we'd like to beg for your patience for a while longer."

Donald did not respond. He merely glared back at Arak.

"Let's move on," Arak said. "And allow me to give you a capsule history of Interterra. To do that we must begin in your domain, the earth's surface. Life there began about five hundred million years after the earth formed and took several billion years to evolve. Your earth scientists are well aware of this. What they are not aware of is that we, the first-generation humans, evolved about five hundred and fifty million years ago during evolution's first phase. The reason your scientists are unaware of this first phase is because almost the entire fossilized record of it disappeared during a time we call the Dark Period. More about that later. First we have some images of these early times of our civilization, but the quality is not good."

The light dimmed progressively. In the gathering darkness Suzanne and Perry exchanged glances, but didn't speak. Their attention was soon directed at the floor screen. After another flickering interval a scene appeared taken at eye level, depicting an environment similar to the one the visitors had seen in Interterra. The main difference was that the buildings were white instead of black although the shapes were similar. And the people appeared like normal human beings—they weren't all gorgeous and they were engaged in a variety of everyday tasks.

"Watching these scenes makes us smile at our own primitiveness," Sufa said.

"Indeed," Arak agreed. "We didn't have worker clones at that ancient time."

Suzanne cleared her throat. She was trying to sort through everything Arak was saying. As an earth scientist, his lecture collided with everything she knew about evolution in general and human evolution in particular. "Are you suggesting that these images we're seeing are from five hundred and fifty million years ago?"

"That's correct," Arak answered. He suppressed a laugh. He and Sufa were apparently amused by the antics of an individual trying to lift a block of stone. "Excuse us from finding this so funny," he said. "We haven't seen any of these sequences for a very long time. It was back when we had something akin to your nationalities, although they disappeared after the first fifty thousand years of our history. Wars disappeared at the same time, as you might imagine. As you can see, the surface of the earth was very different from how it is now, and it is that appearance that we have re-created here in Interterra. Back then there was just one supercontinent and one superocean."

"What happened?" Suzanne asked. "Why did your civilization choose to go underground?"

"Because of the Dark Period," Arak said. "Our civilization had almost a million years of peaceful progress until we became aware of ominous developments in a galaxy close to ours. Within a relatively short time a series of cataclysmic supernova explosions occurred, effectively showering earth with enough radiation to dissipate the ozone layer. We could have dealt with that, but our scientists also recognized that these galactic events also upset the delicate balance of the solar system's asteroid population. It became evident the earth was to be showered with planetesimal collisions, just as had happened when it was in its primordial state."

"For crying out loud!" Richard moaned. "I can't take much more of this."

"Quiet, Richard!" Suzanne snapped without taking her eyes off Arak. "So Interterra was driven underground."

"Exactly," Arak said. "We knew the surface of the earth would become uninhabitable. It was a desperate time. We searched the solar system for a new home without success, and had not yet developed the time technology to search other galaxies. Then it was suggested that our only chance for survival was to move underground, or actually under the ocean. We had the technology so we did it in a miraculously short time. And very soon after we moved, the world as we knew it was consumed in deadly radiation, asteroidal bombardment, and geological upheaval. It was a close call even under the protective layer of the ocean, because at one point the ocean came close to boiling away from the intense heat. All life forms on earth were destroyed except for some primitive bacteria, some viruses, and a bit of blue-green algae."

Suddenly the screen went blank and the illumination in the room returned.

Everyone was quiet.

"Well, there you have it," Arak said. "A concentrated capsule of Interterran history and scientific fact. Now, I'm sure you'll have questions."

"How long did the Dark Period last?" Suzanne asked.

"A little more than twenty-five thousand years," Arak answered.

Suzanne shook her head in amazement and disbelief, yet it all made a certain amount of scientific sense. And most important, it explained the reality she presently found herself in.

"But you stayed under the ocean," Perry said. "Why didn't your people return to the earth's surface?"

"For two main reasons," Arak said. "First, we had everything we needed and we'd become accustomed to our environment. And second, when surface life evolved anew, the bacteria and viruses that developed were organisms to which we had never been exposed. In other words, by the time the climate would have permitted our reemergence, the biosphere was antigenically inimical to us. Perhaps deadly is a better word, unless we were willing to go through a strenuous adaptation. And so here we remain, very happy and content especially since here under the ocean we are not at the whim of nature. Of all the universe we have visited thus far, this small planet is the best suited to the human organism."

"Now I understand why we had to go through such a strenuous decontamination," Suzanne said. "We had to be microorganism-free."

"Exactly," Arak said. "And at the same time you had to be adapted to our organisms."

"In other words," Suzanne continued, "evolution occurred twice on earth with essentially the same outcome."

"Almost the same outcome," Arak said. "There were some differences in certain species. At first we were surprised about this, but then it made sense in that the original DNA is the same. Multicellular life evolved from the same blue-green algae in both instances and with approximately the same climatic conditions."

"Which is why you refer to yourselves as first-generation humans," Suzanne said, "and to us as second-generation humans."

Arak smiled with satisfaction. "We counted on your understanding all this as rapidly as you have, Dr. Newell," he said.

Suzanne turned to Perry and Donald. "Scientific studies confirm some of this," she said. "Both geological and oceanographic evidence suggest there was an ancient single continent on earth, called Pangaea."

"Excuse me," Arak said. "I don't mean to interrupt, but that's not the same as our original continent. Pangaea formed de novo during the latter part of the Dark Period geological upheavals. Our continent suffered complete subduction into the asthenosphere prior to that."

Suzanne nodded. "Very interesting," she said. "And that must be the reason the fossil record of the first evolution is not available."

Arak smiled contentedly again. "Your grasp of these basic fundamentals is heartening indeed, Dr. Newell. But we had anticipated as much even before your arrival."

"Before I arrived?" Suzanne questioned. "What is that supposed to mean?"

"Nothing," Arak added quickly. "Nothing at all. Perhaps we should remind your colleagues that it was the breakup of Pangaea that formed the present continental configuration."

"That's true," Suzanne agreed while she eyed Arak searchingly. She had the uncomfortable sense that there was something Arak was not telling her. She looked over at Donald and Perry and wondered how much even they were taking in. Arak's presentation was clearly beyond Richard and Michael. They looked like bored schoolkids.

"Well, then," Arak said, marshaling some enthusiasm by rubbing his hands together. "I can only imagine how all this information affects you people. Having one's preconceived and accepted notions dashed is a daunting experience. That's why we have been insisting on going slowly with your introduction to our world. I'd venture to guess that you've already had enough talk, too much perhaps. At this point I think it would be better to show you some of the ways we live, firsthand."

"You mean go out into the city?" Richard asked.

"If that will be agreeable to everyone?" Arak said.

"Count me in," Richard said eagerly.

"Me, too," Michael echoed.

"What about the rest of you?" Arak asked.

"I'll go," Suzanne said.

"Of course I'll go," Perry said when Arak looked at him.

When it was Donald's turn he merely nodded.

"Wonderful," Arak said. He stood. "Now if you'll give Sufa and me a few minutes by remaining in your seats, we'll make the arrangements." He extended a hand toward Sufa, and she rose as well. Together they exited the small conference room.

Perry shook his head. "I feel shell-shocked. This whole situation keeps getting more and more unbelievable."

"I'm not sure I believe anything," Donald said.

"Ironically enough, it seems to me to be too fantastic not to be true," Suzanne said. "And it all makes a certain amount of scientific sense." She looked over at Ismael and Mary Black, who had been sitting patiently. "Please, folks, tell us your story. Is it true you are from the surface world?"

"Yes, it is," Ismael said.

"From where?" Perry asked.

"From Gloucester, Massachusetts," Mary said.

"No kidding," Michael said. He sat up. "Hey, I'm from Massachusetts, too: Chelsea. Ever been there?"

"I've heard of it," Ismael said. "But I've never been there."

"Everybody from the North Shore has been to Chelsea," Michael said with a snicker. "Because one end of the Tobin Bridge sits on it."

"I've never heard of the Tobin Bridge," Ismael said. Michael's eyes narrowed in disbelief.

"How'd you two end up down here in Interterra?" Richard questioned.

"We were very lucky," Mary said. "Very lucky indeed. Just like you people."

"Were you diving?" Perry asked.

"No," Ismael said. "We ran into a terrible storm en route from the Azores to America. We should have drowned like the others on our ship. But, as Mary said, we were lucky, and we were inadvertently rescued by an Interterran interplanetary vehicle. We literally got sucked into the same exit port you people did and were then revived by the Interterrans."

"What was the name of your ship?" Donald asked.

"It was called the *Tempest*," Ismael said, "which turned out to be rather appropriate considering the fate. It was a schooner out of Gloucester."

"A schooner?" Donald questioned suspiciously. "What year did this happen?"

"Let's see," Mary said, "I was sixteen. That makes it eighteen hundred and one."

"Oh, for chrissake," Donald muttered. He closed his eyes and ran a hand over his bald head. He'd shaved that morning. "And you people wonder why I'm skeptical?"

"Mary, that's just about two hundred years ago," Suzanne said.

"I know," Mary said. "It's hard to believe, but isn't it wonderful? Look how young we look."

"You expect us to believe that you are over two hundred years old?" Perry questioned.

"It's going to take time for you to comprehend the world that you are now in," Mary said. "All I can say is that you should try to avoid making any hardened opinions until you've seen and heard more. We can remember how we felt when we were being subjected to the same information. And remember, for us it was even more astounding since your technology has come a long way in the last two hundred years."

"I second Mary's advice," Ismael said. "Try to keep in mind what Arak said at the beginning of the session. Time has a different meaning here in Interterra. In fact, Interterrans don't die the way they do on the surface."

"My ass they don't die," Michael whispered.

"Shut up," Richard whispered back through clenched teeth.

CHAPTER THIRTEEN

To Perry and the others the air taxi looked the same as the one they'd been in the day before, but Arak said it was a newer model and far superior. Regardless, it whisked the group in a similarly effortless and silent fashion from the visitors' palace grounds into the bustling city.

"Immigrants usually spend an entire week in the conference room before venturing out like this," Sufa said. "It can be taxing to the intellect as well as the emotions. We hope we're not pushing you too fast."

"Do you have any thoughts about this?" Arak asked. "We're certainly open to suggestions."

The group eyed each other, each hoping another would respond. As Sufa intimated, the situation was stupefying, especially with the cloud of other air taxis zipping by in every conceivable direction. The fact that there were no collisions was astounding in and of itself.

"Doesn't anybody have an opinion?" Arak persisted.

"Everything is overwhelming," Perry admitted. "So it's hard to have an opinion. But I believe from my perspective, the more I see, the better. Merely experiencing your technology like this air taxi makes everything you've said more credible."

"What are you going to show us?" Suzanne asked.

"That was a difficult decision," Arak said. "It's why

Sufa and I took so long arranging things. It was hard to decide where to start."

Before Arak could finish, the hovercraft came to a sudden stop then rapidly descended. A moment later the exit port appeared where previously there had not even been a seam.

"How does the door open like that?" Perry asked.

"It's a molecular transformation in the composite material," Arak said. He gestured for everyone to disembark.

Perry leaned over to Suzanne as he got up. "As if that's an explanation," he complained.

The air taxi had deposited the group in front of a relatively low, windowless structure sheathed in the same black basalt as all the other buildings. Its sides were about a hundred feet long and twenty feet high, and they slanted in at sixty degrees to create a squat, truncated pyramid. There was little pedestrian traffic. Even so, the moment the secondary humans appeared, a crowd began to form.

"I hope you people don't mind being celebrities," Arak said. "As I'm sure you realized from last night, all of Saranta is thrilled about your arrival."

The gathering crowd was boisterous but polite. Those closest to the visitors eagerly put out their hands in an effort to press palms with them. Richard and Michael were happy to oblige, especially with the women. Arak had to act like a border collie to get the group through the door, particularly the two divers. The crowd respectfully stayed outside.

"I'm liking this place more and more," Richard said.

"I'm glad," Arak said.

"Everyone is remarkably friendly," Suzanne said.

"Of course," Sufa said. "It is our nature. Besides, you people are extraordinarily entertaining."

Suzanne glanced at Donald to see his reaction. All he did was give an almost imperceptible nod, as if his suspicions were confirmed.

Inside the group found themselves in a large square room with a black interior instead of the usual white. It was quite plain, with no decoration, furniture, or even doors save for the entrance. A number of Interterrans were standing in the room facing blank walls. When they saw who had arrived, they became animated.

Arak hustled the five through the well-wishers to an empty section of wall and murmured into his wrist communicator. To the group's astonishment, the wall before them opened the same way the air taxis had. Arak shepherded them into a small cubicle beyond.

"Sometime you've got to explain to me how this opening and closing works," Perry said to Arak. Perry put his hand on the wall once he'd stepped into the smaller but equally blank room. The material's texture and heat conductivity suggested to him something akin to fiberglass.

"Certainly," Arak said, but he was distracted by talking into his communicator. A moment later the wall sealed over and the room plunged.

Everyone instinctively grabbed onto whomever was next to them as they became practically weightless.

"My God!" Michael blurted. "The room is falling."

"It's only an elevator," Arak said.

All the second-generation humans laughed self-consciously.

"Hey, how was I supposed to know?" Michael complained. He thought people were laughing at him.

"Getting back to the decision of what to show you first," Arak said. "Sufa and I decided to do the opposite of what you might do on the surface. Instead of showing you life from the cradle to the grave, we thought we'd show you life from the grave to the cradle." Arak smirked at this apparent illogical inversion and Sufa joined.

"We must be going rather deep," Suzanne said. She was too preoccupied by the surroundings to respond to Arak's comment. Although there was no noise or perceived movement, the comparative weightlessness gave a clue as to the speed of the descent.

"We are going deep indeed," Arak said. "As a consequence, it will be a bit warm down here."

Eventually the descent slowed, and everyone braced themselves instinctively. Perry put his hand back on the wall and felt a pulse of heat prior to its opening up. Arak and Sufa led the way out.

Brightly illuminated corridors stretched out in three directions: straight ahead and to either side. Each was a study in perspective. Multiple other corridors could be seen oriented at right angles.

Waiting at the elevator was a small, open vehicle. It suggested the same technology as the air taxi since it was silently suspended several feet off the floor. Arak motioned for everyone to board. Perry and Suzanne climbed on along with Sufa, but Donald hesitated, effectively blocking Richard and Michael. He looked up and down the apparently endless hallways. As Arak had warned, the air was warm. The top of his head glistened with sweat.

"Please," Arak said, gesturing again toward a seat on the small antigravity bus.

"This looks like some kind of prison," Donald said suspiciously.

"It is not a prison," Arak assured him. "There are no prisons in Interterra."

Michael glanced at Richard and gave a thumbs-up sign.

"If it's not a prison, what is it?" Donald asked.

"It's a catacomb," Arak said. "There's no need to be concerned. It is entirely safe, and we'll only be here for a short, instructive visit."

Reluctantly, Donald stepped up into the bus. It was apparent he wasn't much more thrilled about being in a burial vault than he had been about being in a prison. Richard and Michael followed. Once Arak was seated, he spoke into the microphone on the console. Within seconds they were shooting along the corridor like a silent express train save for the sound of the wind.

The reason for the vehicle was apparent after they had been underway for a few minutes. Traveling as quickly as they were at a speed magnified by the proximity of the walls, they covered a great distance in what turned out to be an enormous, subterranean labyrinthine grid. After a quarter hour and a half dozen dizzying right-angle turns, the vehicle slowed and stopped.

Small rooms budded off each corridor, and into one of these Arak directed the group. Donald made it plain he was not happy to be so isolated and stayed by the entrance.

The walls of the small room were filled with niches. Arak went to a particular niche chest-high and pulled out a box and a book. "I haven't been here for a long time," he said. He brushed off dust from both objects. "This box is my tomb." He held it up. It was black and about the size of a shoebox. "And this book contains a list of the dates of all my previous deaths."

"Bull!" Richard blurted. "Now you want us to believe you've risen from the dead! And not once but rather a bunch of times. Come on, man!"

Suzanne found herself nodding as Richard put words to her own reaction. Just when she was beginning to believe everything she'd been told, Arak had to come out with a statement that totally defied credulity. She glanced at Perry to see if he had the same response. But Perry was transfixed by the book, which Arak had placed in his hands.

Arak carefully opened the lid of the box, looked in, and then passed it around for the others to examine. Suzanne glanced in reluctantly, unsure of what she was going to see. It turned out to be only a mat of hair.

Arak and Sufa both smiled. It was as if they were deriving enjoyment out of their guests' confusion.

"Let me explain," Arak said. "In the box is a lock of hair from each of my former bodies. The bodies themselves have been returned to the molten asthenosphere, which is not far from where we are standing. As you might expect, everything is recycled in Interterra."

"I don't understand this book," Perry said. He flipped through some of the pages, glancing at the columns of handwritten figures, which made no sense as dates in the Gregorian calendar. As an added complication there were hundreds of them.

"You're not supposed to," Arak said with a playful smile. "Not yet. Or at least not until we go up to the main processing hall." He took the book from Perry and replaced it along with the box in the niche.

Confused the group followed Arak out of the small

room and reboarded the antigravity vehicle. The inbound trip seemed to take less time than the outbound and soon they were back to the elevator.

"If we're supposed to get something out of this little visit, it didn't work," Suzanne said as they entered the lift.

"It will," Arak assured her. "Have a little patience."

They exited the elevator onto a busy floor thronged with primary humans and a few worker clones. It was so crowded it was difficult for the group to stay together, especially when a number of individuals recognized the secondary humans from the gala the night before and mobbed them in hopes of pressing palms. Richard and Michael were particularly sought after.

Despite this congestion, Arak and Sufa were eventually able to herd their charges over to a large screen. On the screen were hundreds of names of individuals followed by room numbers and times. Arak scanned it for a few moments before finding a name he recognized.

"Well, well," Arak said to Sufa. He pointed to one of the names. "Reesta has decided to pass on. How wonderfully convenient. And he has reserved room thirty-seven. That couldn't be better. It's one of the newer rooms with the download apparatus in full view."

"It's about time he passed on," Sufa commented. "He's been full of complaints with that body for years."

"It will be perfect for our purposes," Arak said.

"Perhaps, with that decided, I'll run over to the spawning center," Sufa said. "It will give me a chance to prepare things and let the clones know the group will be over shortly."

"Wonderful idea," Arak said. "We should be there within the hour. See if you can manage to have an emergence about that time."

"I'll try," Sufa said. "And what about taking the group to our quarters afterward?"

"That was the idea," Arak said. "I just hope we have time."

"See you shortly," Sufa said as she touched palms lightly with Arak. Then she was gone.

"All right, everybody," Arak called to the group. "Let's try to stick together. If anybody gets separated, just ask for room thirty-seven." Arak set out by easing himself through the cluster of people viewing the screen.

Suzanne made it a point to stay abreast of him as best she could. "Is 'passed on' the same euphemism it is in our world?" Suzanne asked.

"Similar is a better word," Arak said. He was distracted by the divers who were busy pressing every female palm they encountered. "Richard and Michael," he called. "Please keep up! There will be plenty of time for palm pressing this evening. You'll be at your leisure."

"Are we going to witness some kind of euthanasia?" Suzanne asked with misgiving.

"Heavens no!" Arak said.

"Ismael and Mary said that you people don't die the way we do," Suzanne said.

"That's for certain," Arak said. Then he had to stop and walk back to where Richard and Michael had been surrounded. As he was busy freeing the two divers Suzanne leaned toward Perry.

"I'm not prepared to witness any morbid scene," she said.

"Me neither," Perry agreed.

"Maybe we should have opted for more seminar time before this field trip," Suzanne said, trying to indulge in a little humor.

Perry laughed hollowly.

Arak got Richard and Michael moving and stayed with them to ward off enthusiastic fans. Suzanne and Perry followed in their wake with Donald close behind. In that configuration they managed to arrive outside room thirty-seven.

Perry looked at the relief on the large bronze door. He recognized it as the three-headed dog, Cerberus, who guarded the underworld in Greek mythology. Surprised, he mentioned it to Arak.

"We didn't get it from your Greeks," Arak said with a smile. "No, it was the other way around."

"You mean the Greeks got it from Interterra?" Perry asked.

"Exactly," Arak said.

"How?" Perry asked.

"From a failed experiment," Arak said. "A number of thousands of years ago, a contingent of liberal-minded individuals from Atlantis endured the surface adaptation with grandiose plans of modifying earth surface socio-logical development. Unfortunately it turned out to be a bust. After several hundred years of fruitless endeavor, it became painfully apparent there was no way to alter the second-generation humans' penchant for violence. So the whole experiment was abandoned. Yet a number of Interterran legacies remained after the island they'd raised was sunk, like our architectural forms, the concept of democracy, and a smattering of our own primitive myth-ology including Cerberus."

"So there was a factual basis for the Atlantis legend," Suzanne interjected.

"Absolutely," Arak said. "Atlantis pushed up one of its

seamount exit ports to form an island just outside the entrance to the Mediterranean Sea."

"Hey, come on!" Richard complained. "Let's cut the jawboning! Either we're going in here or Mike and I are going back to the main hall where all the action is."

"All right, I'm sorry," Arak replied. Then to Suzanne he added, "We can talk more about the Atlantean experiment at another time if you'd like."

"I'd very much like to do that," Suzanne said. Then as Arak was opening the door she leaned toward Perry. "Plato did put the island of Atlantis outside the Strait of Gibraltar in his dialogues."

"Really?" Perry questioned. But he was distracted by the sights and sounds of the scene beyond the bronze door. It was hardly morbid as Suzanne had feared. Instead it was a joyous gala reminiscent of the one the group had attended the evening before, although on a smaller scale. The room was only the size of a large living room. The hundred or so people assembled were dressed in the usual garb save for one individual who stood out sharply. He was dressed in red instead of white. In the back of the room built into the wall opposite the door was a large donut-shaped apparatus that reminded Perry of an MRI machine. Next to it was a table with a box and a book similar to the ones Arak had shown the group in the vault below.

"Arak!" the man in red called out as he caught sight of the new visitors. "What a pleasant surprise!" He immediately excused himself from the people he was chatting with and headed over toward the door. "And you have brought your wards! Welcome!"

"My gosh," Suzanne whispered to Perry as the man in red neared. "I met him last night." Suzanne distinctly remembered him as one of the two men who'd joined her and Garona. "He hardly looks like he is about to pass on." To her he appeared to be the picture of health and the archetype of masculine attractiveness with thick dark hair, flawless skin, and sparkling eyes. She guessed he was in his late thirties.

"This is hardly a mournful wake," Perry commented.

"Thank you, Reesta," Arak said. "I didn't think you would mind if our visitors looked in on your party. Did you meet them at the celebration last night?"

"I had the honor of meeting Dr. Newell," Reesta said. He bowed to Suzanne and then extended his upright palm.

Self-consciously, Suzanne touched her own palm with his. He beamed.

"Let me present Perry, Donald, Richard, and Michael," Arak said. He pointed toward the men as he spoke. Reesta responded by bowing to each in turn. Richard and Michael were not paying much attention. They were more interested in the female guests, several of whom they'd seen the previous night.

"Sufa and I have decided to show our visitors some of our culture," Arak continued. "We're doing it before much explanation. We thought it might reduce the disbelief usually encountered in orientation."

"A wonderful plan," Reesta commented. "Come in! Please." He stepped out of the way and graciously gestured for them to enter.

"So they have no idea what this celebration is for?" Reesta asked as the second-generation humans filed into the room.

"Not really," Arak said.

"Ah, such wonderful innocence," Reesta commented. "It's so refreshing."

"But we did just come from a visit to my niche," Arak added. "Yet I purposefully did not give them a full explanation."

"A masterful approach," Reesta commented while winking and giving Arak a nudge with his elbow. Then he looked at the group, before locking eyes with Suzanne. "Today is an important day for me. Today this body of mine dies."

Suzanne could not help but recoil at this news. Not only did the man appear perfectly hale, but he acted it as well. The announcement even got Richard and Michael's attention.

"Ah, but do not despair," Reesta said, smiling at Suzanne's unease. "Here in Interterra it is a reasonably happy time, more in the realm of an inconvenience or nuisance. And for me it is none too soon. This body was somewhat of a lemon from the beginning. I've had to replace many of the organs and the knees twice. Every day it seems that there is another problem. It's been an endless struggle. And I've just heard this morning that the downtime has dropped to only four years due to lack of current demand. For some reason, no one is dying these days."

"Only four years!" Arak exclaimed. "That's wonderful! I was wondering why you decided so abruptly. Only last week you'd said you were thinking about doing something over the next couple of years."

"It's one of those things that never seems to be convenient," Reesta said. "I had been putting it off, I have to admit. But now I can't pass up this current, short downtime offer."

"Excuse me," Perry said. "I'm confused, but how long do you people generally live in Interterra?"

"It depends on what you're talking about," Reesta said with a twinkle in his eye. "There's a big difference between the body and the essence in terms of life span."

"Each body generally lasts two to three hundred years," Arak said. "But there can be exceptions."

"As I've had to learn the hard way," Reesta added. "I've only gotten one hundred and eighty out of this one. It's been the worst one I've had."

"Are you suggesting that mind-body dualism is a fact in Interterra?" Suzanne said.

"We are indeed," Arak said. He smiled like a proud parent. Then to Reesta he added: "Dr. Newell is a quick study."

"That's apparent," Reesta said.

"What the hell are you people talking about?" Richard asked.

"If you'd listen instead of gawk you might have a better idea," Suzanne said.

"Pardon me!" Richard said, faking an English accent.

"What do you mean by essence?" Perry questioned.

"I mean your mind, your personality, the full complement of your spiritual and mental being," Arak said. "Everything that makes you you. And here in Interterra essences live forever. They are transferred intact from an old body to a new one."

Both Suzanne and Perry erupted with a slew of questions, then Perry tried to defer to Suzanne. But Arak raised his hands to quiet them both.

"Remember we are intruders here," he said. "I'm sure you have many questions. That's the purpose of this visit. But it is rude to interrupt this private time, and I will

explain more of the details later." Then he turned to
Reesta. "Thank you, my friend. We won't bother you any
longer. Congratulations, and have a good rest."   ·

"There is no need to thank me," Reesta said. "It is an
honor for me that you have brought these guests. Their
presence makes this occasion that much more special."

"We'll communicate later," Arak said. "When are you
going to die?" He began to herd the group back through
the door.

"Sometime later," Reesta said casually. "We have the
room for several more hours. But wait!"

Arak stopped and turned back to his friend.

"I just got an idea," Reesta said with excitement.
"Perhaps our second-generation guests would like to see
me die."

"That's a very generous offer," Arak said. "We certainly do not want to impose, but it would be
instructive."

"It's no imposition," Reesta said, warming to the idea.
"I've had enough of this party, and they can surely keep
going without my physical presence."

"Then we accept," Arak said. He waved for Richard
and Michael to come back since the bored divers had
moved out into the hall.

"I hope this isn't gruesome," Suzanne whispered to
Arak.

"Certainly not in comparison to what you people
watch for entertainment in your surface world," Arak
said.

Reesta used his wrist communicator before making a
circuit around the room to press palms with everyone
present. This caused a building sense of excitement. Then
he approached the table with the box and the book. As he

did so the crowd began to cheer. First he cut a lock of his hair and put it inside the box. Next he entered a date in the book and the cheering reached a crescendo.

A door appeared next to the MRI-like machine and two worker clones stepped into the room. Both carried golden goblets which they gave to Reesta. Reesta held the goblets aloft and the crowd went silent. Then Reesta drained both vessels, one after the other.

Applause followed the drinking. Reesta bowed to his guests and even to the secondary humans. Then the two clones helped him climb into the three-foot-wide opening of the MRI-like machine. He entered feet first and slid in until his head was well within the lip. At that point a mirror dropped down so that Reesta could look back at his guests and his guests could see his face. After a final wave, Reesta closed his eyes and appeared to settle down as if in sleep.

One of the worker clones stepped to the side of the apparatus and placed his hand palm down on a white square. Almost immediately a hum could be heard followed by a reddish glow that filled the apparatus's aperture. A moment later Reesta's body went rigid and his eyes flew open. This tentaic state was maintained for several minutes, after which Reesta's body went flaccid, his eyes sank in their sockets, and his mouth sagged in death.

The murmuring crowd fell silent. The red glow within the opening of the machine faded and the hum dissipated. Next, a powerful sucking sound could be heard, followed by the thump of a large valve closing, and Reesta's body disappeared from sight. One minute it was in plain view, the next minute it was gone.

The crowd remained still and mute. Seconds ticked

away. Suzanne was confused emotionally as well as intellectually. Death in any form disturbed her. She hazarded a glance at Perry. He shrugged his shoulders in equivalent bewilderment.

"So, is that it?" Richard queried.

Arak gestured for him to be silent and to wait.

Michael shifted his weight and yawned.

All at once there was a simultaneous activation of everyone's wrist communicators, including those of the secondary humans. Although Ismael and Mary Black had given them the simple instructions to use the units—which involved merely speaking into them in an exclamatory fashion—no one had actually tried them yet. So when Reesta's voice issued forth, the five were taken aback.

"Hello, my friends," Reesta's voice said. "All is well. Death was successful and without complication. See you all in four years, but don't forget to communicate."

A general cheer arose from the primary humans, and they enthusiastically touched palms with each other in obvious celebration.

"Death's no big deal down here," Michael whispered to Richard.

"Yeah, but I think it's got to be done in this special way," Richard whispered back.

"This is a good time for us to leave," Arak said. As unobtrusively as possible, he shepherded the secondary humans out into the hallway and then directed them back toward the elevators. Suzanne and Perry were full of questions, but Arak put them off. He was too busy keeping Richard and Michael moving. Donald was his usual stony self.

It wasn't until they were back in an air taxi that conversation was possible. Even before the craft's entrance sealed over Perry said, "I'm afraid this visit has posed more questions than it has answered."

Arak nodded. "Then it was successful," he said. He put his palm onto the central, circular black table and said, "Spawning center, please!" Almost immediately the saucer scaled, rose, then shot off horizontally.

"What actually did we witness back there?" Suzanne asked.

"The death of Reesta's current body," Arak said. He sat back and began to relax. He was unaccustomed to the stress of being out in public with such a large, uninitiated, group of secondary humans.

"Where did the body go?" Richard asked.

"Back into the molten asthenosphere," Arak said.

"And what about his essence?" Perry asked.

Arak paused as if he were searching for words. "It's difficult to explain these things, but I suppose you'll get the idea if I say his memory and personality imprint was downloaded into our integrated informational center."

"Holy shit," Michael exclaimed. "Look down there in front of that building! It's a goddamned 'Vette!"

Despite everyone's intense interest in Arak's explanation, they couldn't help but respond to Michael's outburst and follow his pointing finger. What they saw was a barnacle-encrusted vintage Chevrolet Corvette on a basalt dais in front of a building that appeared like a haphazard pile of children's blocks.

"What's a 'Vette doing down here?" Michael asked as they zipped past. "It's a sixty-two," he continued. "I had one just like it but in green."

"That building is our Earth Surface Museum," Arak

explained. "The automobile is the one object we feel that currently symbolizes your culture."

"It's in sorry shape," Michael said. He sat back down.

"Obviously," Arak said. "It had spent a good deal of time underwater before we salvaged it. But getting back to Perry's question. When the worker clone started the death sequence, Reesta's entire mind in terms of memory, personality, emotions, self-awareness, and even his unique way of thinking was extracted and stored en masse available for total recall."

The secondary humans stared at Arak in stunned silence.

"Not only can Reesta's essence be recalled," Arak continued. "He can be consulted and even chatted with through your wrist communicator prior to his recall. Or better yet, he can be not only communicated with but viewed in his last body configuration via the media center in each of your quarters. Central Information creates a virtual image in conjunction with whatever conversation you are having."

"What if someone dies before they get to that download machine?" Richard asked.

"It doesn't happen," Arak said. "Death is a planned exercise in Interterra."

"This is all too much," Perry said. "What you are telling us is so far from believability that for the moment I don't even know what to ask."

"I'm not surprised," Arak said. "That's exactly why Sufa and I decided to start showing you things rather than just telling you about them."

"I have a hard time believing the mind can be downloaded," Suzanne said. "Intelligence, memory, and personality are associated with dendritic connections in the human brain. The number is staggering. We're talking about billions of neurons with up to a thousand connections each."

"It's a lot of information," Arak agreed. "But hardly overpowering by cosmic standards. And you are right that dendritic arrays are important. What our Central Information does is reproduce the dendritic arrays on a molecular level using isomeric, double-bonded carbon atoms. It's like a fingerprint, we call it a mindprint."

"I'm lost," Perry said.

"Don't despair," Arak encouraged. "Remember, this is just the beginning. There will be time for you to put all of this into context. Besides, our upcoming visit to the spawning center will show you what we do with the mindprint."

"What's in that Earth Surface Museum we passed?" Donald asked.

Arak hesitated. Donald's question had interrupted his train of thought.

"I mean, what's specifically on display?" Donald said. "Other than the water-soaked Corvette."

"Many different objects," Arak said vaguely. "A cross-section of things representing secondary human history and culture."

"Where have they come from?" Donald asked.

"Mostly from the ocean floor," Arak said. "Besides maritime tragedies and war, you people have been progressively and foolishly using the ocean as your garbage dump. You'd be surprised what refuse says about a culture."

"I'd like to visit there," Donald said.

Arak shrugged. "As you wish," he said. "You're the first visitor to voice such a request. Considering the wonders of Interterra that are now available to you, I'm surprised you are interested. Certainly there's nothing in there that you are not already entirely familiar with."

"Everybody's different," Donald said laconically.

A few minutes later the air taxi deposited the group at the front steps of the spawning center. It was housed in a building that resembled the Parthenon—only it was black. When Perry mentioned the resemblance, Arak told him it was again the other way around, similar to the Greek adaptation of Cerberus, since the Interterran spawning center was many millions of years old.

Like the death center, the structure was sited in a less congested section of the city. Regardless, once the secondary humans appeared, they again attracted a crowd, forcing Arak to be put to the task of maneuvering Richard and Michael inside the door and out of reach of the primary humans' eagerly outstretched hands.

This interior was the antithesis of the death center's. It was bright and white like the buildings at the visitors' palace. The other difference was many more worker clones were in evidence here, busily scurrying from place to place.

Arak hustled the group into a side room with a vast number of small stainless steel tanks that looked like miniature bioreactors to Suzanne. They were attached to each other by a complicated tangle of piping in what looked like a high-tech assembly line. The air was warm and moist. A number of worker clones were monitoring various gauges and dials.

"This is not the most interesting part," Arak said. "But we might as well start at the beginning. These tanks hold our ovarian and testicular tissue cultures. Eggs and sperms are randomly selected and their chromosomes are scanned for molecular imperfections and then microsomally shuffled. The re-formed germ cells are then checked before allowing them to fertilize. If anyone would care to take a peak, there's a view port available." Arak pointed toward a binocular eyepiece along the assembly line apparatus.

Suzanne was the only one who took him up on the offer. She bent over and peered within. Inside a tiny chamber below the microscope objective she could see an oocyte being penetrated by an active sperm. The process happened rapidly. A moment later the zygote was gone, and two new gametes were injected into the chamber.

"Anybody else?" Arak asked after Suzanne straightened up.

No one moved.

"Okay," Arak said. "Let's move along to the gestation room and a more interesting phase." He led the way down the length of the gamete room to a room the size of several football fields placed end to end. Within the room were numerous rows of shelves supporting countless numbers of clear spheres. Between the rows walked hundreds of worker clones checking each sphere in turn.

"My word!" Suzanne murmured as it dawned on her what she was seeing.

"The replicating zygotes coming from the fertilization process are checked again for chromosomal molecular abnormalities," Arak explained. "Once they are determined to be free of any imperfection whatsoever, and they have reached the requisite number of cells, they are implanted into a sphere and allowed to develop."

"Can we walk along the spheres?" Suzanne asked.

"Of course," Arak said. "That's why we are here, so you can see for yourselves."

Slowly the group walked down an aisle several hundred

yards long with lines of spheres on either side. Suzanne was fascinated and appalled at the same time. Each sphere contained a floating embryo of varying size and age. Plastered to the base of each sphere was an amorphous, dark purple placenta.

"This is all so artificial," Suzanne said.

"Indeed," Arak said.

"Is all reproduction in Interterra done by ectogenesis?" Suzanne asked.

"Absolutely," Arak said. "Something as important as reproduction we're not about to leave to chance."

Suzanne stopped and looked in at an embryo no more than six inches in length. She shook her head. Its tiny arms and legs were moving as if swimming.

"Does the process trouble you?" Arak asked.

Suzanne nodded. "It's mechanizing a process I think that's best left to nature."

"Nature is uncaring," Arak said. "We can do so much better, and we care."

Suzanne shrugged. She wasn't about to get into an argument. She started walking again.

"These are like the spheres you guys were in," Perry said to Richard and Michael.

"No shit!" Richard said.

"Please!" Suzanne barked irritably at Richard. "I'm getting tired of the language you fellows seem compelled to use."

"Sorry to offend your majesty," Richard shot back.

"These containers are similar but not the same," Arak said quickly. The last thing he wanted was any kind of an altercation in the spawning center.

Suzanne stopped abruptly and peered into one of the spheres. She was aghast at what she saw. Inside, was a child who looked at least two years old. "Why is this child still in the sphere?" she questioned.

"It's perfectly normal," Arak assured her.

"Normal?" Suzanne questioned. "At what age are they . . ." she struggled for the right word, "decanted?"

"We still say born," Arak said. "Or, as a more technical term, we say emerge."

"Whatever," Suzanne said. Seeing the child imprisoned in the fluid-filled sphere made her shiver with nausea. It seemed so cold, calculating, and cruel. "At what age are the children freed?"

"Preferably not until four," Arak said. "We wait until the brain is mature enough to receive the mindprint. We also don't want the brain cluttered with unorganized natural input any more than necessary."

Suzanne exchanged a look with Perry.

"Come!" Sufa called out. She beckoned them over. "There's an emergence imminent. I've tried to delay it as much as possible; you'll have to hurry." Sufa turned and darted back in the direction she'd come.

Arak urged the group to follow with the intent of passing quickly through a room he called the imprinting room in order to get to the emergence room beyond. But Suzanne faltered on the imprinting room threshold taken aback by the spectacle.

The room was a quarter the size of the gestation room. Instead of sealed spheres with embryos the space was filled with transparent tanks containing angelic-looking four-year-olds. Each child was suspended in fluid but in a fixed position. Umbilical cords and placentas were still present despite the children's relatively advanced ages.

"I'm not sure I want to see this," Suzanne said as Arak gently prodded her.

The others silently gathered around the first tank with mouths agape. The child's head was immobilized as if prepared for stereo tactic brain surgery. His eyes were held open with lid retractors, and the eyes themselves were fixated with limbal sutures. From a gunlike apparatus, beams of light were directed through the side of the transparent tank and into each of the child's pupils. The beams flickered with a rapid, alternating frequency.

"What's happening here?" Perry asked. It looked like torture.

"It's perfectly safe and painless," Arak said. He joined the group and motioned for Suzanne to do likewise.

"The kid looks like he's being shot with an arcade gun," Michael said.

"From your violent culture I can understand why that would be your assumption," Arak said. "But it couldn't be further from the truth. To extend the previous analogy about downloading that I used at the death center, this child is merely receiving the download of a mindprint from an individual whose essence had been stored in Central Information. What you are seeing here is the recall procedure."

Suzanne advanced slowly with a hand over her mouth. She felt like a child at a scary movie: afraid to watch but unable to take her eyes away. Gazing at the immobilized toddler she shuddered. For her, the image was the embodiment of biotechnology gone amuck.

"As you saw at the death center," Arak continued, "it only takes seconds to extract the mindprint. But implanting it is another matter. We have to rely on a primitive technique using low-energy laser since no one has ever come up with a better access route than the retina. Of course, the retinal route makes sense since the retina is embryonically an out-pocketing of the brain. The process works, but it's not fast. In fact, it can take up to thirty days."

"Jeez!" Richard commented. "The poor kid has to be strung up like that for a month?"

"Believe me, there is no suffering involved," Arak said.

"What about the child's own essence?" Suzanne asked.

"We're giving him his essence as we speak," Arak said, "along with an extraordinary fund of knowledge and experience." He smiled proudly.

Suzanne nodded, but not in agreement. She saw the process as pure exploitation. For her it was a kind of parasitism, attaching an old soul to an innocent newborn. The mindprint was abducting the infant's body.

"Arak! Hurry!" Sufa called insistently from a doorway at the opposite end of the room. "You're missing the event!"

"Come on!" Arak urged to the group. "This is important for you to see. It's the finished product."

Suzanne was happy to break off from the disquieting image of the fixated child. She hurried after Arak, purposefully avoiding looking into any of the other tanks. Donald, Richard, and Michael lingered, mesmerized by the sight. Michael lifted his finger and reached out with the intention of interrupting the laser beam. Donald batted his hand away.

"Don't screw around, sailor!" Donald growled.

"Yeah," Richard said, "the kid might miss his piano lessons." He laughed.

"This is freakin' weird," Michael said. He walked around the tank to see if he could see into the barrel of the laser gun.

"Well, look on the bright side," Richard said. "It's a

lot easier than going to school. If it doesn't hurt nothing, like Arak says, I would have gone for it. Hell, I hated school."

Donald looked at Richard scornfully. "As if I couldn't have guessed."

"Come on!" Arak called back to the three men from the distant doorway. "You need to see this."

The three men hurried after their hosts. In the next room they found Arak, Sufa, Suzanne, and Perry standing around a satin-upholstered area at the base of a stainless steel slide. The slide came out of the wall, its upper end was closed off by double swinging doors. Sitting in the center of the cushioned depression was a darling four-year-old girl already dressed in the typical Interterran manner. It was apparent she'd recently arrived by sliding down the slide. A number of worker clones were in attendance.

"Welcome, gentlemen," Arak said to Donald and the divers. He pointed to the little girl. "Meet Barlot."

"Hey, sugarplum," Richard said in squeaky, babylike voice. He reached out to pinch the girl's cheek.

"Please," Barlot said as she ducked Richard's hand. "It's better not to touch me for fifteen or twenty minutes since I've just come out of the dryer. The nerves in my integument need a chance to adapt to the gaseous environment."

Richard recoiled.

"These three men are also newly arrived earth surface visitors," Arak said as he gestured toward Donald, Richard, and Michael.

"My word," Barlot said. "Isn't this an occasion! Five surface visitors at the same time. I'm happy to be so honored on my emergence day."

"We were just welcoming Barlot back to the physical world," Arak explained.

Barlot nodded. "And it's wonderful to be back." She examined her tiny hands, turning them over and then stretching them out. She then glanced at her legs and her feet. She wiggled her toes. "Looks like a good body," she added. "At least so far." She giggled.

"I think it looks like a superb body," Sufa said. "And such beautiful blue eyes. Did you have blue eyes last body?"

"No, but I did the body before that," Barlot said. "I like variation. Sometimes I allow the eye color to be selected randomly."

"How do you feel?" Suzanne asked. She knew it was a stupid question, but under the circumstances she couldn't think of anything else to ask. She was distracted by the marked contrast between the puerile voice and the adult syntax.

"Mainly, I'm hungry," Barlot said. "And impatient. I'm looking forward to getting home."

"How long have you been in storage?" Perry asked. "If that's the right word."

"We call it being in memory," Barlot said. "And I'm assuming it was about six years. That was the advertised waiting time when I was extracted. But to me, it seems like it was overnight. When we're in memory our essences are not programmed to record time."

"Do your eyes hurt?" Suzanne asked.

"Not in the slightest," Barlot said. "I suppose you're referring to the flamelike scleral hemorrhages I undoubtedly have."

"I am," Suzanne admitted. The whites of both Barlot's eyes were fire engine red.

"That's from the limbal fixation sutures," Barlot said. "They were probably just removed."

"Do you remember being in the fish tank?" Michael asked.

Barlot laughed. "I've never heard the implant tank referred to as a fish tank. But to answer your question, no! My first conscious memory in this body, and in all previous bodies for that matter, was waking up on the conveyor belt in the dryer."

"Is the experience of extraction, memory, and recall at all stressful?" Suzanne asked.

Barlot thought for a moment before responding. "No," she said finally. "The only stressful part is that now I have to wait until puberty to have any real fun." She laughed, as did Arak, Sufa, Richard, and Michael.

"This is our home," Sufa said from a hovering air taxi as the exit door materialized. She pointed to a structure similar to the cottages at the visitors' palace minus the large lawns. It was clustered Levittown-style with hundreds of others just like it. "Arak and I thought it would be instructive for you to experience how we live and perhaps have a bite to eat. Are you all too tired or would you like to come inside for a visit?"

"I could eat," Richard said eagerly.

"I would love to see your home," Suzanne said. "It's very hospitable of you."

"I'm honored," Perry said.

Donald merely nodded.

"I'm starved," Michael said.

"Then it's decided," Sufa said. She and Arak climbed

from the hovercraft and motioned for the others to follow.

Similar to the quarters at the visitors' center, the interior was uniformly white—white marble with white fabric and lots of mirrors. Also the main room opened to the outdoors with a pool extending from the inside to the outside. The place was sparsely furnished. Several large holographic displays like those the group had seen in the decon quarters were the only decoration.

"Please come in," Sufa said.

The group filed in, taking in the surroundings.

"It looks like my apartment in Ocean Beach," Michael said.

"Get outta here!" Richard scoffed while he playfully cuffed him on the top of his head.

"Are all Interterran homes open to the exterior?" Perry questioned.

"Indeed," Arak said. "As ironic as it may seem we who dwell inside the earth prefer to be outdoors."

"Makes it kind of hard to lock up," Richard said.

"Nothing is locked in Interterra," Sufa said.

"Nobody steals anything?" Michael questioned.

Both Arak and Sufa giggled. They then self-consciously excused themselves.

"We don't mean to laugh," Arak said. "But you people are so entertaining. We can never anticipate what you are going to say. It's very endearing."

"I suppose it's our charming primitiveness," Donald said.

"Exactly," Arak agreed.

"There's no thievery in Interterra," Sufa said. "There is no need because there is plenty for everyone. Besides, no one owns anything. Private ownership disappeared early in our history. We Interterrans merely use what we need."

The group sat down. Sufa called for worker clones, who appeared instantly. Along with them came one of the pets the secondary humans had seen from the air taxis. Up close it was even more bizarre looking, with its curious mixture of dog, cat, and monkey traits. The animal loped into the room and made a beeline for the visitors.

"Sark!" Arak bellowed. "Behave!"

The animal obediently stopped in its tracks and, using catlike eyes, it regarded the secondary humans with great curiosity. When it stood up on its hind feet, which were monkeylike with five distinct toes, it was about three feet tall. Its doglike nose twitched as it sniffed.

"This is one weird-looking animal," Richard said.

"It's a homid," Sufa said. "A particularly fine homid, actually. Isn't he adorable?"

"Get over here, Sark!" Arak cried. "I don't want you bothering our guests."

Sark immediately darted behind Arak and, standing on its hind legs, began scratching Arak's head.

"Good boy," Arak said contentedly.

"Food for the guests," Sufa commanded the worker clones, who quickly disappeared.

"Sark looks like a bunch of animals rolled into one," Michael said.

"That's one way to put it," Arak said. "Sark is a chimera developed eons ago and cloned ever since. He's a remarkable pet. Would anyone care to see one of his best tricks?"

"Sure," Richard said. To him the animal looked like a biology experiment that went haywire.

"Me too," Michael echoed.

Arak stood and motioned for Sark to head outside. As he followed the animal he asked Richard and Michael to join him out in the yard. The divers dutifully got up and trooped into the garden, where they found Arak busily searching for something in the depths of a fern thicket.

"Okay, here's one," Arak said. He straightened up, clutching a short stick in his hand. He stepped out onto the grass. "Now you men are not going to believe this. It's very entertaining."

"Try us!" Richard said dubiously.

Arak bent down and extended the stick to Sark. Sark took the stick with great excitement, chattering like a monkey. Then after a windup he threw the stick to the far corner of the yard.

Arak watched the piece of wood until it came to a complete halt. Then he turned back to the divers. "Quite a throw, wouldn't you say?"

"Not bad," Michael agreed. "At least for a homid."

The corners of Richard's mouth curled into a wry smile.

"Wait until you see the rest," Arak said. "Just a second." Arak ran out to where the stick had fallen, picked it up, and carried it back. He then returned it to Sark. The animal wound up and threw the stick back to approximately the same spot. Dutifully Arak trotted out and retrieved it for the second time. When he returned he was slightly out of breath. "Can you believe it?" he asked. "This cute little devil will keep this up all day. As long as I get the stick, he'll throw it."

The two divers looked at each other. Michael rolled his eyes while Richard swallowed a laugh.

"The food is here!" Sufa called from inside.

Arak extended the stick toward Richard. "Would you like to give it a try?"

"I think I'll pass," Richard said. "Besides, I'm starved."

"Then let's eat," Arak said agreeably. He tossed the stick back into the fern thicket and headed back inside. Sark followed.

"This place is getting weirder by the minute," Richard mumbled to Michael as they skirted the pool.

"You can say that again," Michael said. "No wonder they didn't care when I took the gold goblets last night. Nothing belongs to nobody. I'm telling you, we could make a fortune down here, and they wouldn't care."

Along with food, the worker clones had brought a folding table, which they'd placed in the center of a ring of seven contour chairs. Arak and the divers joined the others. Sark climbed the back of Arak's chair and began scratching behind his ears. Everyone helped themselves to the food and started eating.

"Well, here's where we spend most of our time," Arak said after a short awkward silence. He sensed the secondary humans were a bit confounded by the day's events. "Does anyone have any questions for us?"

"What do you do here?" Suzanne asked to make conversation. She was happier to stick to small talk rather than tackle the larger issues swimming in her head.

"We enjoy our bodies and our minds," Arak explained. "We read a lot and watch a lot of holographic entertainment."

"Don't people work in Interterra?" Perry asked.

"Some people do," Arak said. "But it is not necessary, and those who do, only do what they want to do. All menial work, which most work is, is done by worker clones. All monitory and regulatory work is done by Central Information. Thus, people are free to pursue their own interests."

"Don't the worker clones mind?" Donald asked. "Don't they ever strike or revolt?"

"Heavens no," Arak said with a smile. "Clones are like . . . well, like your domestic pets. They were made to look like humans for esthetic reasons, but their brains are much smaller. They have limited forebrain function so their needs and interests are different. They love to work and serve."

"Sounds like exploitation," Perry said.

"I suppose," Arak said. "But that is what machines are for, like automobiles in your culture, which I don't believe you feel you exploit. The analogy would be better if your automobiles had living parts as well as machine parts. I'm sure you have to use your cars or they'd deteriorate. Same with worker clones, only it's leisure they cannot tolerate. They become despondent and regress without work and direction."

"It is uncomfortable for us," Suzanne said. "Since they appear so human."

"You have to remind yourself that they are not," Sufa said.

"Are there different types of clones?" Perry asked.

"They all look essentially the same," Arak said. "But there are servant, worker, and entertainment clones, male and female. It's in the programming."

"With your technology, why not use robots?" Donald asked.

"A good question," Arak said. "We had androids ages ago; a whole line of them, in fact. But pure machines tend to break down and have to be fixed. We had to have androids to fix androids ad infinitum. It was inconvenient, even ridiculous. It wasn't until we learned to wed the biological with the mechanical that we solved the problem. The ultimate result of this research and development was worker clones, and they are far superior to any android. They take care of themselves completely, even to the point of repairing themselves and reproducing to keep their population in a steady state."

"Amazing," Perry said simply. Suzanne nodded.

The group fell silent. When they were through with their food Sufa said, "I think perhaps it's time to take you all back to your quarters at the visitors' palace. You need some time to process what you've seen and heard. Also, we don't want to overburden you on your first day. There is always tomorrow." She smiled benignly as she stood up.

"You're right about needing some time," Suzanne said, getting to her feet as well. "I think I've been a bit overburdened already. Without an ounce of doubt, this has been the most startling, staggering, and stunning day of my life."

Michael hesitated at the door to his cottage. Richard was standing directly behind him. They just had been dropped off by Arak and Sufa.

"What do you think we're going to find?" Michael asked.

"For chrissake!" Richard complained. "How am I supposed to know until you open the goddamn door?"

Michael grasped the handle and pulled. The two divers stepped over the threshold and glanced around the room.

"Do you think anybody was here?" Michael questioned nervously.

Richard rolled his eyes. "What do you think, bird-brain?" he said. "The bed's made and the place has been picked up. Look, somebody even stacked all the dishes and the goblets you lugged back from the gala and the dining hall."

"Maybe it was just the clones," Michael said.

"It's possible," Richard said.

"Do you think the body is still there where we put it?"

"Well, we sure as shootin' ain't going to know until we look," Richard said.

"All right, I'll see."

"Hold on!" Richard said, grabbing Michael's arm. "Let me make sure the coast is clear."

Richard looked around and was quickly satisfied. No one was near. "Okay, check the body."

Michael walked over to the cabinets on the right. "Drinks, please!" he commanded. The refrigerator door swung open. It was crammed full of various containers of beverage and food.

"It looks like the way we left it," Michael said.

"That's encouraging," Richard said.

Michael bent down and removed several containers exposing Sart's pale face. The lifeless eyes stared back at Michael accusingly. Michael quickly jammed the containers back to hide the horrid image. Sart's was the first dead body Michael had seen other than his grandfather's corpse. But his grandfather had been laid out in a casket in a tuxedo. Besides, the old man had been ninety-four.

"Well, that's a relief," Richard said.

"For now," Michael said. "But it doesn't mean they might not find him tonight or tomorrow. Maybe we should take him out and bury him in one of those clumps of fern."

"What are we going to dig with, teaspoons?" Richard asked.

"Then maybe we should carry him over to your cottage and put him in your refrigerator. It gives me the creeps having him here."

"We're not going to take the chance carrying him around," Richard said. "He stays where he is."

"Then let's swap rooms," Michael suggested. "Remember, you killed him, not me."

Richard's eyes narrowed threateningly. "We already had this conversation," he said slowly. "And it was decided: we're in this together. Now shut the hell up about the body."

"What about telling Fuller?" Michael said.

"Nah," Richard said. "I changed my mind about that."

"How come?"

"Because that straight arrow nerd's not going to have any better idea of what to do with the body. Besides, I don't think we have to be so worried. Hell, nobody has even asked about the twerp all day today. Besides, Arak said they don't have any prisons."

"That's because they don't have any thievery," Michael snapped. "Arak didn't say anything about murder, and with all that stuff they showed us about mind extraction, I have a bad feeling they'll be pretty upset about it. We might get ourselves recycled, like Reesta."

"Hey, calm down!" Richard said.

"How can I calm down with a dead body in my refrigerator?" Michael yelled.

"Shut the hell up," Richard yelled back. Then in a lower voice he added, "Jeez, everybody in the neighborhood is going to hear you. Get control of yourself. The main thing is to get our asses out of here ASAP. Meanwhile Sart's in the cooler, which is going to keep him from stinking up the joint. We'll think about moving him if someone starts nosing around and asking about him. Okay?"

"I suppose," Michael said but without much enthusiasm.

CHAPTER FOURTEEN

The ceiling of the subterranean cavern darkened gradually, mimicking a normal evening just as it had the previous night. Suzanne and Perry, marveling how much the vaulted roof looked like sky, watched in awe as the pseudo stars began to blink on in the purple twilight. The ever glum Donald in contrast was staring pensively at the darkening shadows beneath the fern thickets. All three were standing on the lawn about forty feet away from the open end of the dining room. Inside, worker clones were busily laying out the dinner. Richard and Michael were already in their chairs eager for food.

"This is absolutely amazing," Suzanne said. She was craning her neck to look straight up.

"The bioluminescent stars?" Perry questioned.

"Everything," Suzanne said. "Including the stars." She'd just joined the others from her quarters, where she'd taken a swim, bathed, and had even tried to take a nap. But sleep had been impossible. She had too much on her mind.

"There are some astounding aspects," Donald admitted.

"I can't think of anything that's not," Suzanne said. She looked across the lawn at the dark hall of the pavilion where the gala had been held the previous evening.

"Starting with the fact that this spacious paradise is buried in the earth under the ocean. How strange that I mentioned Jules Verne's *Voyage to the Center of the Earth* back when we were starting our dive, since now we're actually here."

Perry chuckled. "Pretty apropos."

"One way or the other it's all mind boggling," Suzanne added. "Especially now that it appears everything Arak and Sufa have been telling us is true, no matter how fantastic it all seems."

"It is hard to deny the technology we're seeing," Perry said animatedly. "I can hardly wait to learn more of the details—like the biomechanics of the worker clones or the secrets of the air taxis. Patents on any of this could make us all billionaires. And what about tourism? Can you imagine what the demand for coming down here will be? It's going to be off the charts." Perry chuckled again. "One way or the other, Benthic Marine is going to become the Microsoft of the new century."

"Arak's revelations are extraordinary," Donald agreed grudgingly. "But there are a couple of important gaps that you bedazzled people seem to be forgetting."

"What are you talking about?" Perry questioned.

"Take off the rose-colored glasses," Donald said. "As far as I'm concerned, the overarching question hasn't even come up: What are we doing here? We weren't saved from drowning from a wrecked schooner like the Blacks. We were purposefully and deliberately sucked into their so-called exit port, and I'd like to know why."

"Donald's right," Suzanne said, suddenly thoughtful. "In the excitement, I keep forgetting we are, after all, victims of an abduction. That certainly does beg the question of what we are doing here."

"They are certainly treating us well," Perry said.

"For the moment," Donald said. "But as I said before it could change in the blink of an eye. I don't think you people realize how vulnerable we are."

"I know how vulnerable we are," Perry said with a touch of irritation. "Hell, as advanced as these people are, they could snuff us out in an instant. Arak talked about interplanetary travel, even galactic travel and time technology. But they like us. It's apparent to me even if it isn't to you. I think we should be more appreciative and not so paranoid."

"Like us, my foot," Donald spat. "We're entertaining to them. How many times have they told us that? They find our primitiveness funny or cute, sort of like a house pet. Well, I'm tired of being laughed at."

"They wouldn't be treating us this well unless they liked us," Perry persisted.

"You are so naive," Donald said. "You refuse to remember that we're prisoners, for all intents and purposes, who have been forcibly kidnapped and manipulated in that decon center. We were brought here for a reason that has yet to be revealed."

Suzanne nodded. Donald's remarks reminded her of an offhand comment of Arak's that had given her the impression he'd been anticipating her arrival. She'd found the comment unsettling at the time, but then it had gotten buried by other more astonishing disclosures.

"Maybe they're recruiting us," Perry said suddenly.

"For what?" Donald asked dubiously.

"Maybe they're making such an effort to show us everything to prepare us to be their representatives," Perry said, warming to the idea as he spoke. "Maybe they have finally decided it's time to relate to our world, and they want us to be ambassadors. Frankly, I think we could do a damn good job, especially if we handled it through Benthic Marine."

"Ambassadors!" Suzanne repeated. "That's an interesting idea! They are not fond of going through the adaptation to our atmosphere because of their lack of immunity to our bacteria and viruses, and they don't like the decon process necessary to return to Interterra either."

"Exactly," Perry said. "If we were their representatives they wouldn't have to do any of that."

"Ambassadors? Good God!" Donald mumbled. He threw up his hands and shook his head in frustration.

"What's the matter now?" Perry asked, his irritation returning. Donald was beginning to get on his nerves.

"I knew you two were optimists," Donald grunted, "but this ambassador idea takes the cake."

"I think it is a perfectly reasonable possibility," Perry said.

"Listen, Mr. President of Benthic Marine!" Donald spat as if the appellation were derogatory. "These Inter-terrans don't plan to let us go. If you weren't such a hopeless optimist you'd understand that."

Suzanne and Perry were silent as they mulled over Donald's comment. The issue was something neither had wanted to think about much less discuss.

"You feel that they plan to keep us here forever?" Suzanne asked finally. She had to admit that nothing either Arak or Sufa had said had indicated a plan to return the five visitors to their ship back upon the ocean's surface.

"I believe that's what it means if they never let us go," Donald said sarcastically.

"But why?" Perry pleaded. The anger had gone out of his voice.

"It stands to reason," Donald said. "These people have been avoiding detection of Interterra for thousands of years. How could they feel good about letting us return to the surface knowing what we know?"

"Oh dear!" Suzanne whispered.

"Do you think Donald's right?" Perry asked.

"I'm afraid he has a point," Suzanne said. "There's no reason they would be less worried about contamination now than in the past. And with our advancing technology there's reason they should be more worried. They might be entertained by our primitiveness but I'd suspect they're terrified of our culture's violence."

"But they keep referring to us as visitors," Perry interjected. "This place we're staying is called the visitors' palace. Visitors don't stay forever." Then, irrationally, he added, "Besides, I can't stay here forever. I've got a family. I mean, I'm already worried that I haven't been able to let them know I'm okay."

"That's another point," Donald said. "They know a lot about us. They know about our families. With all their technology they could have offered us an opportunity to let our loved ones know we're not dead. The fact that they haven't, I believe, is more proof they intend to keep us here."

"Good point," Suzanne said. She sighed. "Just a half hour ago in my room I was wishing there was an old-fashioned phone so I could call my brother. He's the only relative I have who'll miss me."

"No family?" Donald asked.

"I'm afraid not," Suzanne said. "That part of my life

just hasn't come together, and I lost both parents years ago."

"I've got a wife and three kids," Donald said. "Of course, that doesn't mean much to the Interterrans. To them the whole concept of parenthood seems quaintly out of date."

"My God!" Perry said. "What are we going to do? We have to get out of here. There has to be a way."

"Hey, everybody!" Michael called out from the dining room. "Soup's on. Come and get it!"

"Unfortunately they're holding all the cards," Donald said, ignoring Michael who disappeared back into the dining room. "There's nothing we can do at this point except keep our eyes open."

"Which means taking advantage of their hospitality," Suzanne said.

"To a point," Donald said. "I'm never one to condone fraternizing with the enemy."

"That's the confusing part," Suzanne said. "They don't act like enemies. They're so gracious and peaceful. It's hard to imagine them doing anything unkind to anybody."

"Keeping me away from my family is about as mean as I can imagine," Perry said.

"Not if you consider it from their perspective," Suzanne said. "With reproduction carried out mechanically and four-year-old newborns imbued with the mind and personality of adults, there are no families in Interterra. It's possible they cannot understand the bond."

"What the hell are you people doing out there in the dark?" Michael shouted. He'd returned to the juncture between the dining room and the lawn. "The worker clones are waiting for you. Aren't you going to eat?"

"I guess we might as well," Suzanne said. "I am hungry."

"I'm not sure I am, after this discussion," Perry said.

They started walking toward the light spilling out onto the dark grass.

"There has to be something we can do," Perry said.

"We can avoid offending them," Donald said. "That could be critical."

"What could we do to offend them?" Perry asked.

"It's not us that I'm worried about," Donald said. "It's the numbskull divers."

"What about being direct about all this?" Perry suggested. "Why not ask Arak when we meet him tomorrow whether we're going to be able to leave? Then we'd know for sure."

"That might be risky," Donald said. "I don't think we should let on that we are interested in leaving. If we do, they might curtail our freedoms. As it is now, theoretically we can call air taxis with our wrist communicators. I believe we can come and go as we want. I don't want to lose that privilege. We may need it if there's any chance of our breaking out of here."

"That's another good point," Suzanne agreed. "But I don't see any reason we couldn't ask why we are here. Maybe the answer to that question will tell us whether they expect us to stay forever."

"Not a bad idea," Donald said. "I could go for that provided we don't make a big deal asking. In fact, why don't I ask tomorrow morning at the session Arak mentioned we'd be having."

"Sounds good to me," Suzanne said. "What do you think, Perry?"

"I don't know what to think at this point," Perry said.

"Come on, hurry up!" Michael said as the others entered the room. "This asshole worker clone won't let us touch the serving dishes until everybody's here, and he's stronger than an ox."

A worker clone was standing next to the center table with his hands resting on the corners of the chafing dishes.

"How did you know he was waiting for us?" Suzanne asked as she took one of the chairs.

"Well, we didn't know for sure, since the bozo doesn't talk," Michael admitted. "But we're hoping it's the case. We're starved."

Perry and Donald sat down. Almost immediately the worker clone lifted the covers from the food.

"Bingo!" Richard said.

Within minutes the food was served. For a time, there was no conversation. Richard and Michael were too busy eating; the others were absorbed in thoughts of their recent conversation on the lawn.

"What were you people doing out there in the dark?" Richard asked, then burped loudly. "Talking about a funeral? You're all so gloomy."

No one responded.

"Lively group," Richard muttered.

"At least we have table manners," Donald snapped.

"Screw you," Richard answered.

"You know, I suddenly find this strangely ironic," Suzanne said.

"What, Richard's table manners?" Michael questioned with a loud guffaw.

"No, our response to Interterra," Suzanne said.

"What do you mean?" Perry asked.

"Think about what we have here," Suzanne said. "It's

like heaven even though it's not up in the sky like our traditional image. Nonetheless, it has everything that we consciously and unconsciously yearn for: youth, beauty, immortality, and plenty. It's a true paradise."

"We can attest to the beauty, eh, Mikey?" Richard said.

"Why do you find it ironic?" Perry asked, ignoring Richard.

"Because we're worried about being forced to stay," Suzanne said. "Everyone else dreams about getting to heaven, and we're worried we're not going to be able to leave."

"What do you mean, forced to stay?" Richard demanded.

"I don't find it ironic," Donald said. "If my family were here with me, maybe I would. But not now. Besides, I don't like to be forced to do anything. It may sound corny, but I value my freedom."

"We're getting out of here, aren't we?" Richard asked insistently.

"Not according to Donald," Perry said.

"But we have to," Richard blurted.

"And why is that, sailor?" Donald asked. "What makes you so eager to get out of Suzanne's heaven?"

"I was speaking in general terms, not personal," Suzanne interjected. "Frankly, finding out how they manage their immortality made me a little sick today."

"I don't know what you people are talking about," Richard said. "But I want to get out of here ASAP."

"Me, too," Michael seconded.

A soft chime sounded that no one had heard before. Everyone looked at each other quizzically, but before anyone could speak, the door opened and in walked Mura, Meeta, Palenque, and Karena. The bevy of beautiful women were in high spirits. Mura went directly to Michael and extended her palm in the usual Interterran greeting. After a quick palm press, she sat down on the edge of Michael's chair. Meeta, Palenque, and Karena approached Richard, who leaped to his feet.

"Oh, babies, you came back!" Richard cried. He touched palms with all three and then hugged them enthusiastically. They briefly acknowledged Suzanne, Perry, and Donald but lavished their attention on Richard, who swooned with utter delight. As he tried to collapse back onto his chaise, they restrained him. They told him they were eager to get him back to his room to go for a swim.

"Well, yeah, sure," Richard stammered. He saluted Donald before exiting with his mini harem.

"Come on! Let us go as well," Mura urged Michael. "I've brought you a present."

"What is it?" Michael asked. He allowed himself to be pulled toward the door.

"A jar of caldorphin!" Mura said. "I heard you liked it."

"Loved it is more accurate," Michael cried. With that, the two of them skipped out of the room.

Before the remaining diners could comment, the soft chime sounded again. This time it heralded the arrival of Luna and Garona. The Interterrans seemed to be rounding up their previous evening's partners.

"Oh, Suzanne!" Garona cooed as he pressed palms with her. "I have been longing for the night so that I could come and once again spend it with you."

"Perry, my love," Luna gushed. "It's been too long a day. I hope it was not too stressful for you."

Neither Suzanne nor Perry could decide if they were

mortified or delighted, especially being greeted with such mushily amorous protestations. Both stammered unintelligible responses while allowing themselves to be lifted to their feet.

"I guess we're leaving," Suzanne said to Donald as Garona playfully towed her toward the open end of the room.

"And we must be going to the same place they are," Perry said to him as Luna dragged him.

"I don't know where we are going," Perry called over after Suzanne and Garona.

Donald gave a halfhearted wave but didn't say anything. The next instant, he found himself alone with the two silent worker clones.

Michael could not remember ever being so excited. Never had a woman this gorgeous and desirable seemed so interested in him. At her insistence they began to spin around as they cavorted across the dark lawn toward his room. With her long hair floating in the wind, the image was intoxicating for Michael, and he would have gone on for hours had his inner ear not intervened.

Feeling dizzy, Michael stopped revolving but his surroundings didn't. He staggered to his right, vainly trying to maintain his balance. Unable to keep his legs under him, he collapsed in a heap. Mura collapsed with him. Together they laughed uncontrollably. They got to their feet unsteadily, then ran on to his cottage. Once they got inside, they were both out of breath.

"Well," Michael said. He took a couple of deep breaths but still felt light-headed. Just looking at Mura in the slinky outfit made his heart race. "What would you like to do first? Take a swim?"

Mura gazed at Michael provocatively. She shook her head. "No, I don't want to swim now," she said, her voice husky. "Last night you were too tired for intimacy. You sent me away before I could make you happy."

"But that's not true," Michael protested. "I was happy."

"You mean, Sart made you happy?"

"Hell, no!" Michael barked. "What the hell kind of question is that?"

"Don't get upset," Mura soothed. "I'm not suggesting anything. Besides, it's perfectly all right to have pleasure from either sex."

"Hey, it's not okay with me," Michael told her. "No way!"

"Michael, please calm yourself," Luna pleaded. "What's making you so agitated?"

"I'm not agitated!" Michael snapped.

"Did Sart do something to make you angry?"

"No, he was fine," Michael said nervously.

"Something made you angry," Mura said. "Did Sart stay all night? I didn't see him all day."

"No! No!" Michael stammered. "He left right after you did. Richard just apologized for getting mad at him and that was it. He was out of here. Nice kid, though."

"Why did Richard get mad at him?"

"I don't know," Michael said irritably. "Do we have to talk about Sart all night? I thought you came here to see me."

"I did indeed," Mura said. She sidled up to Michael and stroked his chest. Beneath her fingers she could feel that his heart was racing. "I think you must have had a difficult day. We should get you to calm down, and I know just the thing."

"What's that?"

"You lie down on the bed," Mura instructed. "I will rub your body and massage your muscles."

"Now you're talking."

"And once you are serene we will press palms with the caldorphin."

"Sounds great, baby," Michael said. "Let's do it."

"All right, I'll be there in a moment," Mura said. She gave Michael a gentle nudge toward the bed. Dutifully Michael sauntered over and lay down on the soft coverlet.

Mura went to the refrigerator to get something cold to drink. She gave the command directly to the receptor so she could do it as softly as possible so as to avoid disturbing Michael. After his minor outburst, she sensed he was tense and needful of every consideration. She knew from experience how easily agitated secondary humans could become over the strangest things.

Mura was surprised to discover the compartment so full. "My word," she said. "What do you have in here?"

In response to Mura's nagging about Sart, Michael's ardor with her had significantly waned. Instead of fantasizing as he lay down on the bed waiting for her ministrations, he found himself fretting over the dinner table discussion that he and Richard were stuck in Interterra. Consequently her comment about his refrigerator being full didn't even penetrate his consciousness until he heard beverage and food containers crash to the floor followed by a gasp. It was only then that he remembered Sart's body, and by then it was too late . . .

"Oh shit!" Michael whispered as he leaped off the bed. Just as he'd feared, Mura was standing in front of the open refrigerator with a hand clasped over her mouth. Her expression was one of pure horror.

Inside the refrigerator, Sart's frozen, pale face was framed haphazardly by stacked containers.

Michael rushed to Mura's side and enveloped her with his arms. She sagged against him and would have collapsed had he not been supporting her.

"Listen! Listen!" Michael urged in a forced whisper. "I can explain."

Mura regained her balance and pulled herself from Michael's embrace. With a trembling hand she reached into the refrigerator and felt Sart's cheek. It was as firm as wood and as cold as ice. "Oh, no!" she moaned. Cradling her own drained cheeks with her hands, she shivered as if a cold wind had suddenly wafted through the room. When Michael tried again to put his arms around her, she shoved him to the side to keep Sart's face in view. As frightful as the image was, she could not turn away.

Frantically Michael bent down, retrieved the fallen objects and crammed them back into the refrigerator to block her view of the dead boy. "You have to calm down," he said nervously.

"What happened to his essence?" Mura demanded. Blood surged back into her face turning her cheeks crimson. Shock and dismay were turning to anger.

"It was an accident," Michael said. "He fell and hit his head." Michael reached for her again, but she backed up to keep him at arm's length.

"But his essence?" Mura repeated, although she had to appreciate the horrid truth.

"Look, he's dead, for chrissake," Michael snapped.

"His essence is lost!" Mura managed. Her fleeting

anger was already giving way to grief. Tears welled up in her emerald green eyes.

"Look, baby," Michael said in a tone halfway between solicitude and irritation. "Regrettably, the kid is dead. It was an accident. You have to pull yourself together."

Tears turned to sobs as the reality of the tragedy struck the core of Mura's own essence. "I must go and tell the elders," she said. She turned and started toward the door.

"No, wait!" Michael said. He was frantic. He rushed around to head her off. "Listen to me!" He grabbed her with both hands.

"Let me go!" Mura cried. She tried to break from his grasp. "I must announce the calamity."

"No, we must talk," Michael insisted. He grappled with her as she tried to free herself.

"Let go!" Mura yelled, her voice rising through her sobs. She got one arm free.

"Shut up!" Michael shouted back. He slapped her across the face with an open palm, hoping to snap her out of her hysteria. Instead, she opened her mouth and let loose an earsplitting scream. Fearful of the consequences, Michael clapped a hand over her mouth. But it was not enough. Mura was a tall, strong woman, and she twisted from his grasp, letting out another cry.

With some difficulty Michael got his hand over her mouth again, but no matter what he tried, he could not keep her quiet. Impulsively he dragged her over to the deep end of the pool and launched them both into the water. But even the sudden dunking did not contain her screams until he forced her head beneath the water's surface.

Still she struggled, and when he brought her up for a breath, she let out a cry as loud as any previous. Again

Michael pushed her under the water, and this time he held her until her violent flailing slowed, then ceased.

Slowly he eased up on the grip he had around her head, afraid she'd suddenly rear up and yell once more. Instead her limp body slowly bobbed to the surface, her face submerged.

He pulled her body to the edge and lifted her onto the pool's marble lip. A foamy mixture of mucus and saliva issued from her nose and slack mouth. As he looked at her and realized she was dead, a shudder passed down his spine. His teeth began to chatter uncontrollably. He had killed someone—someone he cared for.

For a moment he stood perfectly still. He wondered if anyone could have heard Mura's screeches. Thankfully, the night was still. In a panic, he dragged her over to the bed, laid her alongside, and pulled the coverlet over her. Then he ran past the pool and out into the night.

Richard's cottage was no more than fifty yards away, and Michael covered the distance in seconds. He pounded on the door.

"Whoever it is, go away!" Richard's voice commanded from within.

"Richard, it's me!" Michael shouted back.

"I don't care who it is!" Richard yelled back. "We're busy in here."

"It can't wait, Richie," Michael insisted. "I got to see you."

A string of expletives preceded a short silence. Finally the door was pulled open. "This better be good," Richard growled. He was buck naked.

"We got a problem," Michael announced.

"You're about to have another one," Richard warned.

Then he noticed that Michael was sopping wet. "Why'd you go swimming with your clothes on?" he asked.

"You gotta come with me back to my cottage," Michael stammered.

Richard noted the degree of his friend's anxiety. Richard glanced over his shoulder to make sure none of the women were close enough to hear. "Does this have something to do with Sart's body?" he asked in a whisper.

"Yeah, unfortunately," Michael said.

"Where's Mura?"

"She's the problem," Michael said. "She saw the body."

"Oh, Christ!" Richard moaned. "Is she upset?"

"She went ballistic on me," Michael said. "You gotta come!"

"All right! Calm down. So she really got psycho?"

"I'm telling you, she went completely crazy. You gotta get your ass over there."

"Okay already," Richard soothed. "Don't shout! I'll be over in a few minutes. I'll have to get rid of my friends."

Michael nodded as Richard closed the door in his face. Turning around, he sprinted back to his quarters. After checking to make sure Mura's body was where he'd left it, he changed clothes to a dry set. Then he paced up and down the room, waiting for Richard.

True to his word, Richard arrived in less than five minutes. He scanned the room the moment he stepped over the threshold. Everything looked peaceful enough. He half expected to see Mura sobbing uncontrollably on the bed, but she was nowhere to be seen. "Well, where is she?" he demanded. "In the bathroom?"

Michael didn't answer. He motioned for Richard to

follow him and walked around the end of the bed. Reaching down with a shaky hand, he grasped the corner of the coverlet and whipped it aside to expose the corpse. Mura's previously translucent alabaster skin had become a mottled blue and the foam oozing from her mouth and nose was tinged with red.

"What the hell?" Richard gasped. He knelt down and felt for a carotid pulse. He stood back up. His face was slack with shock. "She's dead!"

"She opened the refrigerator," Michael explained. "She saw Sart's body."

"All right, I understood that," Richard said. He stared at his friend. "But why did you kill her?"

"I told you, she went crazy," Michael said. "She was screaming bloody murder. I was afraid she was going to wake up the entire goddamn city."

"Why the hell did you let her open the refrigerator?" Richard demanded angrily.

"I wasn't watching for two seconds," Michael said.

"Yeah, well, you should have been more careful," Richard complained.

"That's easy for you to say," Michael snapped. "I told you I didn't want the body over here. He should have been in your refrigerator, not mine."

"Okay, calm down," Richard said. "We got to think what to do."

"There's no more room in my refrigerator," Michael said. "She's got to go in yours."

Richard wasn't wild about dragging the body over to his place, but he couldn't come up with an alternate idea, and he knew they had to do something quickly. If Mura were found, then Sart would be, too. One way or the other he'd be involved.

"All right," Richard said reluctantly. "Let's get it over with."

With dispatch they rolled Mura up inside the coverlet. Then with Richard at the head and Michael at the foot, they carried her across the lawn to Richard's cottage. They had a little trouble navigating her in through the door since it was relatively narrow.

"Jeez," Michael complained. "Carrying a body is a little like carrying a mattress. It's harder than you'd think."

"That's because it's so much dead weight," Richard said, smirking at the double meaning.

They dumped the body in the middle of the floor. While Michael unraveled the blanket, Richard went to the refrigerator and emptied it. Since this was his second time through the body-in-the-refrigerator routine, he knew exactly what to do, meaning to get Mura inside required a complete rearrangement of the contents.

"All right," Richard said. "Give me a hand."

Together they got Mura wedged into place. She was taller and heavier than Sart, so she was a tighter fit. In the end, they had to leave a few containers out.

Richard straightened up after finally managing to get the door to shut. "This has got to stop," he said.

"What?" Michael asked.

"Knocking off these Interterrans," Richard said. "We're out of refrigerators."

"Very funny," Michael said. "How come I'm not laughing?"

"Don't make me answer that, birdbrain," Richard said.

"I'll tell you what it really means," Michael said. "We gotta get our asses out of Interterra! With two bodies, the chances of someone stumbling across one has just doubled."

"You should have thought of that before you knocked her off," Richard said.

"I'm telling you, I didn't have any choice!" Michael yelled. "I didn't want to ice her, but she wouldn't shut up."

"Don't shout!" Richard said. "You're right. We got to get the hell out of here. The only good news is that it seems the straightlaced admiral is thinking the same way we are."

Suzanne couldn't remember the last time she'd swum in the nude, and she was pleasantly shocked by the sensation as she struck out across the pool. And although she was mildly self-conscious about being naked, especially given Garona's perfect form, she wasn't as uptight as she had imagined she'd be. It was probably because Garona made her feel so accepted the way she was despite her physical imperfections.

Reaching the far end of the pool, Suzanne flipped over and, with a burst of speed, swam back to where Garona was contentedly sitting at the edge with just his feet in the water. She grasped one of his ankles and succeeded in pulling him into the water. They ducked under the water and embraced.

Eventually tiring of their underwater play, they swam to the side, and hauled themselves out of the water. With the slight breeze wafting in from the open end of the room, Suzanne felt goose flesh pop out along the backs of her arms and the sides of her thighs. "I'm glad you came back tonight," she said. She was genuinely glad to see him.

"I'm glad, too," Garona said. "I was anticipating it all day."

"I wasn't sure if you would come back," Suzanne said. "To be honest, I was worried you wouldn't. I'm afraid I acted immaturely last night."

"What do you mean?"

"I should have made a clearer choice," Suzanne said. "Either I should not have allowed you to stay or, having done so, I should have acted more appropriately. What I did was somewhere in between."

"I enjoyed every minute," Garona said. "Our interaction was not goal-oriented. The idea was just to spend time together, which we did."

Suzanne gazed at Garona appreciatively, silently lamenting that it required a trip to a surreal, mythic world to find such a sensitive, giving, and handsome man. As her mind naturally drifted to the idea of taking him back with her, the thought yanked her back to the reality of whether she was ever going to be able to go back herself. It also brought up the other, major unanswered question. "Garona, can you tell me why we've been brought to Interterra?" Suzanne asked suddenly.

Garona sighed. "I am sorry," he said. "I cannot interfere with Arak. You and your group are his charges."

"Just telling me why we're here would be interfering?"

"Yes," Garona said without hesitation. "Please don't put me in that position. I want so much to be open and honest with you, but in that sphere I cannot, and it distresses me to have to deny you anything."

Suzanne stared into her new friend's face and could see his sincerity. "I'm sorry for asking," she said. She lifted her hand and he lifted his. They slowly pressed palms. Suzanne smiled with contentment; she was becoming pleasantly acclimated to the Interterran embrace.

"Perhaps I should ask how Arak is doing with his orientation?" Garona said.

"I'd say very well," Suzanne commented. "He and Sufa are such gracious hosts."

"But of course," Garona said. "They were lucky to get such an interesting group. I heard that they have already taken you out into the city. Did you enjoy that?"

"It was fascinating," Suzanne said. "We visited the death center and the spawning center as well as Arak and Sufa's home."

"Such rapid progress," Garona commented. "I'm impressed indeed. I've never heard of second-generation humans progressing so quickly. What is your reaction to what you have seen and heard? I can hardly imagine how extraordinary it must be for you."

"The expression *beyond belief* has never been so apropos."

"Have you found anything disturbing?"

Suzanne tried to figure out if Garona wanted the truth or platitudes.

"There was one thing that bothered me," Suzanne began, deciding to give Garona honesty. She went on to explain her negative reaction to the implant process.

Garona nodded. "I can appreciate your point of view," he said. "It is a natural consequence of your Judeo-Christian roots, which puts such high value on the individual. But I assure you we do as well. The child's essence is not ignored but rather added to the implanted essence. It is a mutually beneficial process, a true symbiosis."

"But how can an unborn's essence compete with that of a learned adult?"

"It is not a competition," Garona said. "Both benefit, although obviously the child benefits the most. I can tell you, as someone who has gone through the process countless times, I have been strongly influenced by each essence from each body. It is definitely an additive process."

"It seems like a rationalization," Suzanne said. "But I'll try to keep an open mind."

"I hope you do," Garona said. "I'm sure Arak plans to return to this issue in the didactic sessions. Remember, today's outing was not to explain things thoroughly but rather to help overcome the usual disbelief with which our visitors initially struggle."

"I'm aware of that," Suzanne said. "But it is true I tend to forget. So thank you for reminding me."

"My pleasure," Garona said.

"You're a sensitive, beautiful man, Garona," Suzanne said with all sincerity. "It is a delight to be with you." She found herself wondering what it would be like to walk with him on the beach at Malibu or driving on Route 1 around Big Sur. One thing that Interterra lacked was an ocean, and as an oceanographer, the ocean was central to Suzanne's universe.

"You are a beautiful woman. You're extraordinarily entertaining."

"Thanks to my alluring primitiveness," Suzanne said. She guessed Garona imagined he was complimenting her, but she would have preferred a word other than *entertaining*, especially after Donald's complaint.

"Your primitiveness is endearing," Garona agreed.

Briefly Suzanne entertained the idea of letting Garona

know her response to being called primitive, but she resisted. At this stage of their relationship she wanted to be positive. Instead she said, "Garona, there's something I want you to know about me."

Garona pricked his ears.

"I want you to know I don't have another lover. I did, but that ended."

"It doesn't matter," Garona said. "The only thing that matters is that you are here this moment."

"It matters to me," Suzanne said, mildly hurt. "It matters to me a lot."

CHAPTER FIFTEEN

The morning of the secondary humans' second full day in Interterra began as the first day had. Suzanne and Perry were offhand with each other about their previous evening's experiences and eager for what the day was to bring. Donald was less enthusiastic and even a touch morose. Richard and Michael were tense and silent, and when they did talk, it was only about leaving. Donald had to shut them up when Arak made his entrance.

After bringing the group back to the same conference room they used the day before, Arak and Sufa launched into an educational session that dragged on for hours. This was mainly a scientific discussion that included the way Interterra tapped the earth's geothermal energy; how the Interterran climate was maintained, including the mechanism used to generate the nightly rain; how bioluminescent technology was used to provide even lighting both indoors and out; how water, oxygen, and carbon dioxide were handled; and how photosynthetic and chemosynthetic food plants were grown hydroponically.

As the image on the floor screen faded and the general illumination began to return, the only two secondary humans paying attention were Suzanne and Perry. Donald was staring off, obviously absorbed in his own thoughts. Richard and Michael were fast asleep. As the lighting reached its apogee both divers revived, they and Donald tried to make it appear as if they had been listening all along.

"In conclusion for this morning's session," Arak said, seemingly mindless of certain parties' inattention, "I'm sure you have a clearer idea of why we have remained here in our subterranean world, that is, in addition to the microbial issue. In contrast to what transpires on the earth's surface, we have been able to construct a perfectly stable environment with no climatic fluctuations such as ice ages or other weather-related disasters; essentially limitless, pollution-free energy; and a completely adequate and replenishable food source."

"Is plankton your exclusive source of protein?" Suzanne asked. She and Perry remained fascinated by all the scientific revelations.

"The major source," Arak said. "The other source is vegetable protein. We used to use some fish species, but we stopped when we became concerned about the ability of sea animals to be able to replenish themselves. Unfortunately, this is a lesson secondary humans seem unwilling to accept."

"Particularly with whales and cod," Suzanne said.

"Exactly," Arak said. He looked around the room at the others. "Any more questions before we go back out into the field?"

"Arak, I have a question," Donald said.

"Of course," Arak said. He was pleased. Donald had thus far shown very little interest in participating.

"I'd like to know why we were brought here," Donald said.

"I was hoping you had a question about what we have been discussing," Arak said.

"It's hard for me to concentrate on technical matters when I don't know why I'm here."

"I see," Arak said. He bent over and conferred in a hushed whisper with Sufa and the Blacks. Then, leaning back, he added, "Unfortunately, I cannot answer your question completely since we have been specifically proscribed from telling you the main reason why you are here. But I can say this: one of the reasons was to stop the attempted drilling into the Saranta exit port, which I can happily say was accomplished. I can also assure you that today you will learn the main reason. Will that suffice for the moment?"

"I suppose," Donald said. "But if we're going to learn, I don't see why you can't tell us now."

"Because of protocol," Arak said.

Donald nodded reluctantly. "As a retired naval officer, I suppose I can accept that."

"Any other questions about today's presentation?" Arak asked.

"I'm a bit overwhelmed at the moment," Perry admitted. "But I'm sure I'll have questions as the day progresses."

"Well, then," Arak said. "Let's begin our excursion. With what you have heard this morning, where would you like to visit first?"

"How about the Earth Surface Museum?" Donald suggested before anyone else could respond.

"Yeah!" Michael blurted enthusiastically. "The place with the 'Vette out front."

"You'd like to see the Earth Surface Museum?" Arak questioned with obvious bewilderment. He glanced at Sufa. Her reaction was the same.

"I think it would be interesting," Donald said.

"Me, too," Michael said.

"But why?" Arak questioned. "Pardon our surprise, but with all the things we have been telling you, we're mystified that you would rather look back than forward."

Donald shrugged. "Maybe it's just a touch of nostalgia."

"Seeing what you have chosen to display might give us a feeling for your response to our world," Suzanne offered. She wasn't as interested in seeing the museum as the other sites Arak had been describing, but was happy to support Donald's request.

"Very well," Arak said agreeably. "The Earth Surface Museum shall be our next stop."

Everyone got to their feet. For the first time Donald acted eager, especially when they got outside. He asked Arak to show them how to call an air taxi, and Arak was happy to oblige. Arak went a step further and had Donald place his palm on the taxi's center black table and give the destination command.

"That was easy," Donald said as the craft silently and effortlessly rose, then shot off in the corresponding direction.

"Of course," Arak said. "It's meant to be easy."

All of the visitors found the air taxi rides a high point of the day. They never tired of the vista of the city and the surrounding area. With craning necks they tried to take in everything, but it was difficult; there was so much to see and because they were traveling so fast. Within a few minutes they were left standing before the entrance to the museum, a few steps from the barnacle-encrusted Chevrolet Corvette.

"God, I loved that car," Michael said with a wistful sigh as he climbed from the hovercraft. He paused and gazed longingly at the monument. "I was dating Dorothy Drexler at the time. I don't know which had the better body."

"Did they both need an ignition key to get them started?" Richard asked with a smirk.

Michael took a swipe at his buddy with an open palm, but Richard evaded it with ease. Then he danced briefly on his toes like a professional boxer before taking a swing of his own.

"No fighting," Donald snapped, insinuating himself between the two divers.

"Your Corvette might have been fine for you and Dorothy," Suzanne said, "but I feel rather embarrassed the Interterrans feel that this symbolizes our culture."

"It does suggest we're rather superficial," Perry agreed. "Besides being rusty and in sorry shape."

"Superficial and materialistic," Suzanne said, "which, I suppose, is probably the case when you think about it."

"You're reading too much into the symbolism," Arak said. "The reason we have put it here at the front of the museum is much simpler. Since we are now relegated to observing you from afar to keep from being detected by your advancing technology, the automobile is what we notice most. From a great distance it almost appears that the cars are the dominant life form on the surface of the earth, with secondary humans acting like robots to take care of them."

Suzanne had trouble suppressing a laugh at such an absurd suggestion, but when she thought about it, she could understand how it might seem from a distance.

"What is more symbolic is the design of the structure," Arak said.

All eyes turned to the museum itself. Up close, the

structure possessed an overpowering sepulchral aura. Four and five stories tall, it was composed of rectilinear segments either stacked or at right angles to create a complicated, sharply geometric form. Most segments were covered with square windows.

"The building symbolizes secondary human urban architecture," Arak commented.

"It's rather ugly in its boxiness," Suzanne said.

"It isn't pleasing to the eye," Arak admitted. "Nor are most of your cities, which are essentially so many box-like skyscrapers built on grids."

"There are some exceptions," Suzanne said.

"A few," Arak agreed. "But unfortunately, most of the architectural lessons the Atlanteans bestowed on your ancient forebears have been lost or disregarded."

"It's an enormous building," Perry commented. It covered the equivalent of a modern city block.

"It needs to be," Arak said. "We have an extensive earth surface collection. Remember, we're talking about a time span of millions upon millions of years."

"So the museum is not just of secondary human culture?" Suzanne asked.

"Not at all," Arak said. "It is also the whole panoply of current earth surface evolution. Of course, we have been mostly interested in the last ten thousand years or so for obvious reasons. Although that segment of time represents a mere eyeblink in comparison to the period as a whole, we have concentrated our collections on it."

"What about dinosaurs?" Perry questioned.

"We have a small but representative exhibit of preserved specimens," Arak said. Then he added as an aside:

"Such frightfully violent creatures!" He shook his head as if experiencing a passing wave of nausea.

"I want to see that exhibit," Perry said eagerly. "I've been dying to know what color dinosaurs were."

"For the most part they were a rather nondescript gray-green," Arak said. "Rather ugly if you must know."

"Let's go inside," Sufa suggested.

The group trooped into the entrance hall. It was an enormous room sheathed in the same black basalt as the exterior. Shafts of bright light came from apertures in the high ceiling. They crisscrossed in the general dimness like miniature searchlights to illuminate displayed objects in a dramatic fashion. Multiple corridors emanated from this central hub.

"Why are there no people?" Suzanne asked. In every direction she looked, all she saw was empty, marbled hallways. Her voice echoed repeatedly in the sepulchral silence.

"It's always like this," Arak explained. "As important as this museum is, it is not particularly popular. Most people would rather not be reminded of the threat your world poses for us."

"You mean threat of detection," Suzanne added.

"Precisely," Sufa said.

"This looks like a place where it would be easy to get lost," Perry said. He peered down some of the lengthy, dimly lit, and silent corridors.

"Not really," Arak said. He pointed to the left. "Starting here, with blue-green algae, the evolutionary exhibits are chronological." Then he pointed to the right. "And on this side we have secondary human culture starting with the earliest African hominids and extending up to the present. At any given location in the museum one could determine how to find the way back here to the entrance hall by following the direction of progressively older specimens."

"I'd like to see the exhibits depicting our modern times," Donald said.

"Certainly," Arak said. "Follow me. We'll take a shortcut through the first five or six million years."

The group followed Arak and Sufa like schoolchildren on a day trip to the museum. Suzanne and Perry found it difficult not to stop and view every display, especially when they reached the halls devoted to Egyptian, Greek, and Roman artifacts. Neither Suzanne nor Perry had seen anything quite like them. It was as if someone had stepped back in time with free rein to pick the choicest objects. Suzanne was particularly enthralled with the period clothing tastefully displayed on life-sized mannequins.

"You'll notice there is a marked quantity difference in our collections," Arak explained. He had remained with Suzanne and Perry as the others wandered on. "We have comparatively little modern material. The farther back in your history, the more extensive the exhibits are. A very long time ago we used to make actual trips in isolation suits to collect for the museum. Of course, we eventually had to stop that practice for fear of exposure once your forebears developed writing."

"Arak!" Sufa called from several galleries ahead. "Donald, Richard, and Michael are moving quickly, so I'll go ahead with them!"

"That's fine," Arak called back. "We'll all meet up in the entrance hall in about one hour."

Sufa nodded and waved good-bye.

"Why were you worried about exposure to ancient peoples?" Suzanne asked. "They certainly did not have the technology to cause you any trouble."

"Very true," Arak admitted. "But we knew you second-generation humans would have it someday, and we didn't want any record of our visits. It was enough to worry about the failed Atlantean experiment, although that was less of a concern since the primary humans involved had been posing as second-generation humans."

Suzanne nodded, but her attention had drifted to an elaborate, ancient Minoan dress which would leave the breasts completely exposed.

"There is one period in your modern history that we have a lot of artifacts from," Arak said. "Would you care to see?"

Suzanne looked at Perry, who shrugged. "Certainly," Suzanne said.

Arak turned left and strode off through a side gallery filled with exquisite Greek pottery. With Suzanne and Perry at his heels he turned another corner and climbed a nondescript flight of stairs. On the floor above they emerged at a huge gallery filled with World War II materiel. The artifacts ranged from items as small as dog tags and uniform insignia to those as large as a Sherman tank, a B-24 Liberator aircraft, and an intact U-boat, with all sorts of objects in between. It was apparent that everything in the gallery was at one time submerged in the ocean.

"My word," Perry commented as he strolled between the displays. "This is more like a junkyard than a museum exhibit."

"It appears that our last world war contributed substantially to your museum's collection," Suzanne said. She and Arak remained at the head of the stairs. This was not an exhibit Suzanne was at all interested in.

"A big contribution," Arak agreed. "Objects such as

you see here rained down to the ocean floor for over five years. For the last few hundred years of your history, scavenging the ocean floor has been our only source of curios."

Suzanne glanced at the U-boat. "Did the explosive growth of submarine technology and operations concern you?"

"Only in regard to sonar capability," Arak said. "Especially when the sonar technology was combined with making bathypelagic contour maps. Such technology was one of the reasons we'd elected to close the entrance ports like the one you came through."

While Suzanne and Arak continued to discuss sonar and its threat to Interterran security, Perry wandered the full width of the World War II gallery. Some of the paraphernalia seemed in pristine condition, other objects were barnacle-encrusted like the Corvette outside the museum. At the end of the aisle, he poked his head out a window facing east and caught a glimpse of the immense spires that served as supports for the Azores.

Perry glanced down at the courtyard below and did a doubletake. The *Oceanus*, the Benthic Marine submersible, was sitting on what appeared to be a flatbed attached to a large air taxi.

"Hey, Suzanne!" Perry cried out. "Come look!"

Suzanne hurried over to join him. Arak followed. Both leaned out the window and followed Perry's pointing finger.

"My gosh!" Suzanne said. "It's our submersible! What is it doing here?"

"Oh, yes," Arak said. "I forgot to mention how much interest your ship has generated with the curators of the museum. I believe, with your permission, they intend to make it one of the exhibits."

"Was it damaged?" Perry asked.

"Only minimally," Arak said. "Skilled worker clones have repaired the outside lights and manipulator arm. It's also been decontaminated, but is otherwise intact. Are you familiar with the boat's components?"

"Somewhat," Perry said. "But not from an operational perspective. Suzanne knows more than I. I've only been in it twice."

"Donald is the real expert," Suzanne said. "He knows the craft like the back of his hand."

"Excellent," Arak said. "We do have some questions about the sonar, which we have found to be even more sophisticated than we'd imagined."

"He's the one to ask," Suzanne said.

"What's the submersible sitting on?" Perry asked.

"That's an air taxi freighter," Arak said.

Michael made it a point to keep up with Donald, who was cruising through the museum as if he were out for exercise rather than studying the exhibits. Every few steps Michael had to run a couple of strides. Donald had long since left Sufa and Richard far behind.

"Why the hell are you going so fast?" Michael panted. "What is this, a race?"

"You don't have to stay with me," Donald shot back. He turned another corner and continued on. They were moving through a gallery containing Renaissance sculptures and paintings.

"Richard and I think we should get out of Interterra ASAP," Michael managed. He was short of breath.

"You both made that clear over breakfast," Donald said jeeringly. He turned another corner and entered a room hung with carpets.

"We're getting a little worried," Michael continued, trying to stay alongside the fast-moving ex-naval officer.

"About what, sailor?" Donald asked.

"Because . . . well . . . we have a problem," Michael said hesitantly. "It involves a couple of these Interterrans."

"I'm not interested in your personal problems," Donald snapped.

"But there was an accident," Michael said. "Or actually, two accidents."

Donald stopped short and Michael did the same. Donald stabbed the air in front of Michael's face. Donald's lips were pulled back in a sneer. "Listen, bonehead! You two decided to fraternize with these Interterrans. I don't want to hear about your difficulties getting along with them. Understand?"

"But—"

"No buts, sailor!" Donald spat. "I'm trying to get us out of here, and I don't want to be distracted by either you or your half-wit buddy."

"Okay, okay," Michael said, raising his hand defensively. "I'm glad you're working on it. Getting out of here as soon as we can is all I'm concerned about. I mean, I'll help any way I can."

"I'll keep that in mind," Donald said scornfully.

"Do you have any ideas about how we're going to be able to do it?"

"It'll be difficult," Donald admitted. "We're going to have to find someone besides Arak to get some real answers. Information is the key. The best thing, of course, would be to find someone who's not happy here, yet who's been around long enough to be knowledgeable about how to get out."

"Nobody seems unhappy," Michael commented. "It's like they're living one big party."

"I'm not talking about Interterrans," Donald said. "Arak has implied that a number of people from our world have ended up down here. Some of them must be homesick and not quite as chummy with the Interterrans as Ismael and Mary Black seem to be. It's human nature, or at least secondary-human nature, to resist constraint. That's the kind of person I'd like to find."

"How do you propose to do it?"

"I don't know," Donald admitted. "We've got to keep our eyes open for when opportunity knocks. I can tell you I like being out in the city. We're surely not going to find such a person while we're sitting in that damn conference room."

"But this place is deserted," Michael complained. His eyes took a momentary detour up and down the empty corridors.

"I didn't come here to meet anyone," Donald said. "I came to this damned museum with the hope of coming across some weapons. I thought there'd be some, but I haven't seen a single one. Having a museum about human history without weapons is ridiculous. The pacifism of these Interterrans is driving me up the wall."

"Weapons!" Michael commented. He nodded. The idea hadn't dawned on him, but he immediately was intrigued. "Cool idea! To tell you the truth, I was wondering why you wanted to come here."

"Well, now you know, sailor," Donald said. "And

maybe you can even help, since this place is so enormous. If we spread out we can cover a lot more ground."

No sooner had Donald uttered this suggestion than his eye caught something he'd not seen in any other exhibition hall: a closed door with the words RESTRICTED ENTRY written over its upper panel. Curious as to what it might conceal, he approached it, with Michael at his heels. As Donald got closer he could see that there were several other words in smaller letters: FOR ENTRY, APPLY TO COUNCIL OF ELDERS.

"What the hell is the Council of Elders?" Michael asked over Donald's shoulder.

"Some sort of governing body, I imagine," Donald said. He put his hand on the door and pushed. It was unlocked, like all doors in Interterra.

"Eureka!" Donald said as he caught a glimpse of some of the objects displayed in the room beyond. He pushed the door all the way open and stepped over the threshold. Michael entered behind him and whistled.

"No wonder we haven't seen any weapons," Donald said. "It looks like they got their own hidden gallery." The room was comparatively narrow but extremely long. On both sides were display shelves cluttered with arms.

The two men had entered the gallery approximately halfway along its length. On the shelf directly opposite the entrance was a medieval crossbow with a quiver of needle-sharp quarrels. Michael leaned over and lifted the crossbow from its resting place. He whistled again. He'd never handled such a weapon. "Jeez!" he commented. "What a fierce-looking contraption." He knocked the stock with his knuckle. The sound was a solid thunk. He twanged the bowstring. It was still sound. He held it up in the air and sighted along its shaft. "I bet this thing still works."

Donald had started off to the right, but soon recognized he was going in the wrong chronological direction. The weapons were becoming older. Ahead he could see a collection of Greek and Roman short swords, bows, and spears. He turned and passed Michael, who was busy trying to bend the crossbow with a hand crank to slip the string into its locking device.

"There's still a lot of strength in the bow," Michael said as he succeeded finally. He placed one of the bolts into the guide and held the loaded weapon up for Donald to see. "What do you think?"

"It's got possibilities," Donald said vaguely while heading down the other way. He was encouraged when he saw the first examples of early harquebuses. "But I was hoping for something a bit more definitive than an arbalest."

"I thought this thing was called a crossbow," Michael said.

"Same thing," Donald said without turning back.

Michael put his finger on the release lever and, without meaning to, discharged the weapon. The bolt hissed from its position in the guide, ricocheted off the basalt wall with a high-pitched scraping sound, shot past Donald's right ear, and buried itself into one of the wooden shelves. Donald had felt the wind from the missile as it sailed by.

"Jesus H. Christ!" Donald roared. "You almost nailed me with that goddamn thing!"

"Sorry," Michael said. "I hardly touched the trigger."

"Put it down before one of us gets hurt," Donald yelled.

"At least we know it works," Michael said.

Donald shook his head with disgust while he reached up with his hand to check his ear. Thankfully there was no blood. The bolt had come that close. Mumbling expletives about the clowns he'd gotten stranded with, he continued down the gallery. Soon he was looking at a collection of World War II rifles and handguns. To his chagrin, they were in sorry shape, having suffered the ill effects of salt water. He became progressively discouraged until he came across a German Luger near the room's end. At first sight it appeared to be in excellent condition.

Unaware he was holding his breath, Donald reached for the pistol and hefted it. To his delight, the gun appeared pristine even under close scrutiny. With great anticipation he released the magazine. A smile spread across his face. The clip was full!

"Did you find something good?" Michael asked. He'd come up behind Donald.

Donald pushed the magazine home in the pistol's hand grip. It made a definitive, reassuringly solid mechanical sound. He held the gun aloft. "This is what I've been looking for."

"Cool!" Michael said.

Lovingly Donald put the Luger back where he'd found it.

"What are you doing?" Michael questioned. "Aren't you going to take it?"

"Not now," Donald said. "Not until I know what I'm going to do with it."

Richard stopped dead in his tracks. He could not believe what he was seeing. It was a room chock full of treasure, mostly from ancient times. There were innumerable cups, bowls, and even whole statues made of solid gold, all dramatically lit with concentrated beams of light. In one corner was a series of chests filled with doubloons. The display was dazzling.

What made the sight even more astounding for Richard was that the entire collection of inestimable value was all within easy grasp since the objects were out in the open and not behind protective glass barriers like he was accustomed to in all the museums he'd ever visited. And this was on top of the fact that the museum's front door had no guards.

"This is unbelievable," Richard managed. "God, this is fantastic. What I would do for a wheelbarrow of this stuff!"

"You like these objects?" Sufa questioned.

"Like them? I love them," Richard stammered. "I've never seen anything like this. I doubt there's this much gold in Fort Knox."

"We have storerooms filled with these things," Sufa said. "Ships have been sinking with gold for years. I can arrange to have a quantity of similar objects sent to your room for your own enjoyment if you'd like."

"You mean stuff like we're seeing here?"

"Certainly," Sufa said. "Do you prefer the large statues or the smaller objects?"

"I'm not picky," Richard said. "But what about jewels? Does the museum have jewels too?"

"Certainly," Sufa said. "But most of it comes from your ancient times. Would you care to view it?"

"Why not?" Richard answered.

On the way to the gallery of ancient jewelry, Richard caught sight of an artifact in a display of twentieth-century curios that brought a smile to his face. On a chest-high pedestal a Frisbee was carefully illuminated with a pencil of light, as if it, too, were as priceless as gold.

"Well, I'll be!" Richard said as he stopped in front of the chartreuse disk. He noticed a few canine indentations along the Frisbee's edge. "What on earth is this here for?" he called ahead to Sufa.

Sufa came back to where Richard was standing to see what he was referring to. "We don't know exactly what that is," she admitted. "But some have suggested it might be a model of one of our antigravity vehicles like our air taxis or like our interplanetary cruisers. We were afraid for a time that there had been a direct sighting."

Richard threw his head back and laughed. "You got to be kidding," he said.

"No, I'm not joking," Sufa said. "Its shape is very suggestive, and it can be spun to capture a cushion of air that mimics an antigravity ship."

"It's not a model of anything," Richard said. "It's nothing but a Frisbee."

"What is it used for?" Sufa asked.

"It's to play with," Richard said. "You spin it like you said and then someone else catches it. Let me show you." Richard picked up the Frisbee and gently flipped it up into the air on an angle. The toy reached an apogee then returned. He caught it in his palm between his thumb and fingers. "That's all there is to it," he said. "It's easy, don't you think?"

"I suppose," Sufa said.

"Let me throw it to you and you catch it just like I did," Richard said. He trotted down the gallery about fifty feet. He turned and tossed the Frisbee toward Sufa. She went through the motions as if she were going to catch it, but she was too clumsy. Although it grazed her hand, she failed to grab it; it clattered to the floor. After rolling his eyes at her ineptness, Richard trotted back and showed her again how to do it. But his efforts were in vain. On the next toss she was even more awkward than on the first.

"You people aren't into physical activity, are you?" Richard said scornfully. "I've never met anyone who couldn't catch a Frisbee."

"What's the purpose?"

"There's no purpose," Richard snapped. "It's just fun. It's a sport. Tossing this thing back and forth gives you a chance to run around."

"It seems pointless to me," Sufa said.

"Don't you people get any exercise down here in Interterra?"

"Certainly," Sufa said. "We enjoy swimming particularly but also walking and playing with our homids. Of course there's always sex, as I'm sure Meeta, Palenque, and Karena have shown you."

"I'm talking about a sport!" Richard complained. "Sex is not a sport."

"It is for us," Sufa said. "And it's certainly a lot of exercise."

"What about a sport in which you try to win?" Richard asked.

"Win?" Sufa questioned.

"You know, competition!" Richard said with annoyance. "Don't you have any competitive games?"

"Heavens no!" Sufa said. "We stopped that kind of nonsense eons ago when we eliminated wars and violence."

"Oh, for chrissake," Richard blurted. "No sports!

That means no ice hockey, no football, not even golf! Jeez! And to think Suzanne thinks this place is heaven!"

"Please calm down," Sufa urged. "Why are you so agitated?"

"Do I seem agitated?" Richard questioned innocently.

"Indeed you do," Sufa said.

"I guess I need some exercise," Richard offered. With the Frisbee under his arm, he nervously cracked his knuckles. He knew he was strung out, and he knew why: in his mind's eye he kept picturing a worker clone stumbling onto Mura's corpse scrunched up inside his refrigerator.

"Why don't you take the Frisbee?" Sufa suggested. "Perhaps Michael or one of the others will participate with you."

"Why not," Richard said, but without much enthusiasm.

"All right, everybody!" Arak called out. The group had reunited out on the terrace in front of the museum after spending more than an hour inside. They were all discussing what they had seen during the visit, except for Richard, who remained on the periphery, repeatedly tossing the Frisbee into the air and catching it. At the base of the steps three air taxis were waiting.

"Let's talk about the arrangements for the rest of the morning," Arak said. "Sufa will accompany Perry to the air taxi construction and repair facility. Perry, I believe that is what you had wanted to see."

"Very much so," Perry agreed.

"Ismael and Mary will accompany Donald and Michael to Central Information," Arak continued.

Donald nodded.

"What about you, Richard?" Arak asked. "Which of those two destinations appeals to you?"

"I don't really care," Richard said, continuing to flip the Frisbee into the air.

"You have to choose one or the other," Arak said.

"Okay, then, the air taxi factory," Richard said impassively.

"What about Suzanne?" Perry questioned.

"Dr Newell will go with me for a meeting with the Council of Elders," Arak said.

"By herself?" Feeling protective, Perry glanced at Suzanne.

"It's okay," Suzanne said reassuringly. "While you climbed into the U-boat in the World War II hall, Arak explained the elders wanted to talk with me professionally, as an oceanographer."

"But why alone?" Perry asked. "And why not me? After all, I run an oceanographic company."

"I don't think it's the business side they're interested in," Suzanne said. "Don't worry."

"Are you sure?" Perry persisted.

"Quite sure," Suzanne said. She patted Perry's shoulder.

"Then let us go," Arak called out. "We'll all meet back at the visitors' palace later in the day." Beckoning for the others to follow, he skirted the old Corvette's dais and started down the wide steps toward the hovering air taxis.

It did seem strange to Suzanne to be alone with Arak as the air taxi swept them off to their destination. It was the first time Suzanne had been away from the others except to sleep in her cottage. She looked over at Arak, and he smiled back at her. Being in such quiet proximity made her again aware of how handsome he was.

"Are you enjoying your orientation?" Arak questioned. "Or are you finding it frustratingly fast or slow?"

"Overwhelming is the best way to describe how I'm finding it," Suzanne said. "Speed is not the issue, and I certainly don't feel frustrated in the slightest."

"Your group is quite a challenge for designing and tailoring the best orientation protocol. You are all so different, a fact that we Interterrans find fascinating but also daunting. You see, because of selection and adaptation, we are all very much alike, which I'm sure is something you've recognized."

"You are all very nice," Suzanne said with a nod. She realized that until Arak mentioned it, she hadn't given it much thought. Now that she had, she realized it was true. Not only were they all similarly attractive in a classical sense, but they all were equally gracious, intelligent, and easygoing. There was little if any variation in their temperaments.

"*Nice* is a rather sanitized word to choose," Arak said. "I hope you are not bored with us."

Suzanne gave a little laugh. "It's hard to be bored when you are overwhelmed," she said. "I can assure you, I am not bored." Her eyes wandered to the incredible vista out over the city with the swarms of air taxis whizzing by. Being bored was the furthest thing from her mind, yet she suddenly understood what Arak was alluding to. After a while, Interterra might become tiresome because of its homogeneity. Some of the very aspects that made it such a paradise also rendered it bland.

Suzanne focused on a striking structure that loomed

out of the tapestry of the city and pulled her from her musing as the air taxi quickly approached. It was an enormous black pyramid with a bright gold top. As the air taxis stopped and then descended to a causeway that led up to the pyramid's entrance, she was struck by its resemblance to the Great Pyramid of Egypt at Giza. Having been to Giza, she could tell that the Interterran version was even approximately the same size. When she mentioned this similarity to Arak, he smiled patronizingly.

"The design was one of our gifts to that culture," Arak said. "We had great hopes for them since they were, initially, a rather peaceful civilization. We sent a delegation to live among them early in their history with the idea of promoting them over the other extremely warlike peoples who had evolved. The experiment wasn't as big an undertaking as the Atlantean movement, and we did try, but it all came to naught."

"Did you show them how to build it as well as provide the design?" Suzanne asked. For her the riddle of the Great Pyramid was one of the most fascinating of the ancient world.

"Of course," Arak said. "We had to. We also showed them the concept of the arch, but they steadfastly refused to believe it would work and never tried it on a single structure."

The air taxi came to a stop and the side opened.

"After you," Arak said graciously.

Once they gained entry, Suzanne realized that any similarity between the two structures vanished. The Interterran pyramid interior was gleaming white marble, and the interior spaces were grand instead of claustrophobic.

As Suzanne and Arak walked down a corridor heading toward the center of the building, Suzanne was met by another surprise. Garona stepped out of a side passageway directly in front of her and enveloped her in a warm embrace.

"Garona!" Suzanne murmured with obvious delight. She hugged him back. "What a nice surprise! I didn't expect to see you until tonight. Or at least I was hoping I'd see you tonight."

"Of course you would have," Garona said. "But I could not wait." He looked into her eyes. "I knew you were coming to the Council of Elders today so I came over to wait for you."

"I'm pleased," Suzanne said.

"We'd better move," Arak said. "The council is waiting."

"Certainly," Garona said. He took his arms from Suzanne and grasped her hand instead. The three began walking.

"How was your morning?" Garona inquired.

"Enlightening," Suzanne said. "Your technology is astounding."

"We had a scientific session," Arak explained.

"Any site visits?" Garona asked.

"We went to the Earth Surface Museum," Suzanne said.

"Really?" Garona seemed surprised.

"It was a specific request of Mr. Donald Fuller," Arak explained.

"Did you find it instructive?" Garona asked.

"It was interesting," Suzanne said. "But it wouldn't have been my choice, not with what we had learned during the didactic session."

They approached an impressive set of bronze doors. Within each panel was an embossed figure Suzanne recognized as an ankh, or ancient Egyptian symbol of life. It was another reminder for her of the apparent exchange of information from the Interterrans to ancient secondary human civilization. It made her wonder what else had come from this advanced culture.

The moment they arrived at them, the doors swung inward on silent hinges. Beyond was a circular room with a domed ceiling supported by a colonnade. Like the rest of the pyramid's interior it was constructed of white marble, although the capitals of the columns were gold.

At Arak's urging, Suzanne stepped over the marble threshold. She took a few hesitant steps before stopping. She scanned the stately chamber. Twelve imperial-looking chairs ringed the periphery. Each was situated between a pair of columns. All the chairs were occupied—presumably by council members—who ranged in age from about five to twenty-five. The unexpectedness of such a mixed age group had Suzanne mildly flustered. Some of the people were so young, their feet didn't reach the ground when they sat.

"Come in, Dr. Suzanne Newell," one of the elders said in a clear preadolescent voice. To Suzanne she looked like a ten-year-old girl. "My name is Ala, and it is my rotation as speaker of the council. So, please, don't be afraid! I know these surroundings are imposing and intimidating, but we only desire to speak with you, and if you will come to the center of the room we will all be able to hear you clearly."

"I'm more surprised than fearful," Suzanne said as she advanced to a point directly beneath the high point of the dome. "I was told I was coming to the Council of Elders."

"And indeed you have," Ala said. "The determining

factor for sitting on the council is the number of body lives you've passed, not the age of the current body."

"I see," Suzanne said, although she still found it unsettling to be standing before a governmental body partially composed of children.

"The Council of Elders formally welcomes you," Ala said.

"Thank you," Suzanne replied, not knowing what else to say.

"You were brought to Interterra with the hope that you could provide us with information we have not been able to glean from monitoring your earth surface communications."

"What kind of information?" Suzanne asked. She felt her guard go up. In the back of her mind she heard Donald's voice saying that the Interterrans wanted something from them, and once they got it, they might treat them very differently.

"Don't be alarmed," Ala said soothingly.

"It is hard not to be," Suzanne said. "Especially when you help remind me that I and my colleagues have been abducted into your world which, I have to say, was a terrifying experience."

"For that we extend our apologies," Ala said. "And you should understand that we intend to reward your sacrifice. But it is we who are alarmed. You see, the integrity and safety of Interterra are our responsibility. We know that you are a learned oceanographer in your world."

"That's being overly generous," Suzanne said. "The reality is that I am a relative newcomer to the field."

"Excuse me," one of the other elders said. He was a teenager at the very beginning of his growth spurt. "My name is Ponu, and I am currently the vice-speaker. Dr. Newell, we are aware of the esteem in which you are held by your professional colleagues. It is our belief that such respect is reliable testament to an individual's abilities."

"As you will," Suzanne said. It wasn't a point she wanted to argue under the circumstances. "What is it you want to ask me?"

"First," Ala said, "I'd like to make sure you have been informed that our environment is devoid of your common bacteria and viruses."

"Arak has made that clear," Suzanne said.

"And I assume you understand that detection of our civilization by a civilization like yours would be disastrous."

"I can understand the worry about contamination," Suzanne said. "But I'm not convinced it would necessarily be disastrous, especially if the proper safeguards were put in place."

"Dr. Newell, this is not meant to be a debate," Ala said. "But surely you must be cognizant of the fact that your civilization is still in a very early stage of social development. Naked self-interest is the prime motivational force, and violence is an everyday occurrence. In fact your particular country is so primitive that it allows anyone and everyone to own a gun."

"Let me paraphrase," Ponu offered. "What my esteemed fellow elder is saying is that your world's hunger and greed for our technology would be so great that our special needs would be forgotten."

"Exactly," Ala said. "And we cannot accept such a risk. Not for at least another fifty thousand years or so, to give secondary humans a chance to become more civilized.

Provided, of course, they don't destroy themselves in the process."

"Okay," Suzanne said. "As you say, this is not a debate, and you have convinced me that you believe my culture is a risk to yours. Assuming that as a given, what do you want from me?"

There was a pause. Suzanne looked from Ala to Ponu. When neither responded she glanced at the other faces. No one spoke. No one moved. Suzanne looked back at Arak and Garona. Garona smiled reassuringly. Suzanne turned back to Ala. "Well . . .?" she asked.

Ala sighed. "I would like to ask you a direct question," she said. "A question whose answer we are afraid to hear. You see, your world has started several deep-ocean drilling operations over the last few years, on a seemingly random basis. We have watched these episodes with growing concern since we are uncertain what the goals are. We know the drilling is not for petroleum or natural gas since there is none in the areas where this drilling is being undertaken. We've been monitoring communi-cations as we have always done, but without success of learning why this drilling is occurring."

"Are you interested in knowing why the *Benthic Explorer* has been drilling into the seamount?" Suzanne asked.

"I am very interested," Ala said. "You were drilling directly over one of our old-style exit ports. The prob-ability of that occurring purely by chance is extremely small."

"It wasn't by chance," Suzanne admitted. As soon as she spoke these words a general murmur erupted among the elders. "Let me finish," Suzanne called out. "We were drilling into the seamount to see if we could tap directly into the asthenosphere. Our echo sounder suggested the seamount was a quiescent volcano with a magma chamber filled with low-density lava."

"Was any part of the decision to drill at that particular site motivated by a suspicion of the existence of Interterra?" Ala asked.

"No!" Suzanne said. "Absolutely not!"

"There was no thought of an undersea civilization in the decision-making process?" Ala questioned.

"As I said, we were drilling purely for geological reasons," Suzanne said.

The elders again conferred loudly with one another. Suzanne turned and glanced back at Arak and Garona. Both smiled encouragement.

"Dr. Newell," Ala said to redirect Suzanne's attention to herself, "have you, in your professional capacity, ever heard of anything from any source that would suggest someone suspected the existence of Interterra?"

"No, not in any scientific circles," Suzanne said. "But there have been a few novels written about a world within the earth."

"We are aware of the work of Mr. Verne and Mr. Doyle," Ala said. "But that was purely entertainment fiction."

"That's correct," Suzanne said. "It was pure fantasy. No one thought their story lines were based in any way on fact, although they probably got the theme from a man by the name of John Cleves Symmes, who did believe the center of the earth was hollow."

The elders erupted in another loud, anxious murmuring.

"Did Mr. Symmes's beliefs influence scientific opinion?" Ala asked.

"To some degree," Suzanne said. "But I wouldn't give it much concern since we're talking about the early part of the nineteenth century. In eighteen thirty-eight his theory did launch one of the first United States scientific expeditions. It was under the command of Lt. Charles Wilkes, and its initial purpose was to find the entrance to the earth's hollow interior, which Symmes believed to be beneath the South Pole."

Additional excited murmuring echoed throughout the room.

"And the result of this expedition?" Ala questioned.

"Nothing that would concern Interterra," Suzanne said. "In fact, the goal of the expedition changed even before it began. Instead of looking for the entrance to the interior of the earth, by the time they got underway they were tasked to find new sealing and whaling grounds."

"So Mr. Symmes's theory was ignored?" Ala questioned.

"Completely," Suzanne said. "And the idea has never resurfaced."

"We are indeed thankful," Ala said, "especially considering Mr. Symmes was correct in some respects. The South Pole was and still is our major interplanetary and intergalactic port."

"Isn't that curious," Suzanne said. "Unfortunately it's a bit late for Mr. Symmes to be vindicated. Be that as it may, I gather from your questions that you are asking me if your secret is safe, and I have to say it is, as far as I know. But while we're on the subject, perhaps I should mention that although no one currently believes in a hollow earth, there have always been fringe groups who talk about aliens from advanced cultures that have visited us or are among us. There has even been a hit TV show with that as its theme. But these ideas of alien visitations refer to aliens coming from outer space, not from within the earth."

"We are aware of what you are describing," Ala said. "And we have been pleased with that association. It has been particularly useful on the few occasions that one of our interplanetary craft have been observed by secondary humans."

"The only other thing I should mention," Suzanne said, "is that our culture has had enduring myths about Atlantis that have come down to us from the ancient Greeks. But I assure you the scientific community considers them to be pure myths or possibly the result of the destruction of an ancient secondary human culture by a violent volcanic eruption. There has never been a theory that a primary human culture lives beneath the ocean."

The elders noisily conferred again. Suzanne shifted uncomfortably as they deliberated.

Ala concluded the private discourse with a nod to her colleagues and then redirected her attention to Suzanne. "We would like to inquire about the episodes of random deep-ocean drilling that have been occurring over the last number of years in the general area of Saranta. None of these have been on the crest of a seamount."

"I imagine you are referring to the drilling that has been done to confirm the latest theories of sea-floor spreading," Suzanne said. "It's been done merely to provide rock cores for dating purposes."

The elders again erupted in a short burst of excited chatter. At its conclusion Ala asked, "Was there ever any suggestion the supposed magma chamber into which you were drilling was filled with air instead of low-density lava?"

"Not that I was aware of," Suzanne said. "And I was the senior scientist on the project."

"Those exit ports should have been sealed ages ago," one of the other elders said with some vehemence.

"This is not a time for recrimination," Ala advised diplomatically. "We are dealing with the present." Then, looking back at Suzanne, she said, "To summarize, in your professional life you have never heard any suggestion that a civilization exists under the ocean or any theories to that effect?"

"Only as myths, as I've mentioned," Suzanne said.

"And now for the last question we would like to direct to you," Ala said. "We have become increasingly apprehensive about your civilization's progressive lack of respect for the ocean environment. Although we have heard some mention of this problem in your media, the rate of pollution and overfishing has increased. Since we are dependent to some degree on the integrity of the ocean, we wonder if your civilization's talk of this issue is mere lip service or a real concern?"

Suzanne sighed. This issue was close to her heart. She knew all too well that the truth was discouraging at best.

"Some people are trying to change the situation," Suzanne said.

"That response suggests it is not considered an important issue by the majority," Ala said.

"Perhaps not, but those who do care, care passionately."

"But perhaps the general public is not aware of the crucial role the ocean plays in the grand scheme of earth surface environment, for example, the fact that plankton modulates both oxygen and carbon dioxide on the earth's surface?"

Suzanne felt her face flush, as if somehow she were to blame for the way secondary humans treated the world's oceans. "I'm afraid that most people and most countries view the ocean as an inexhaustible food supply and a bottomless pit for refuse and waste."

"That is sad indeed," Ala said. "And worrisome."

"It is self-interested shortsightedness," Ponu said.

"I have to agree," Suzanne admitted. "It's something I and my colleagues are working on. It's a battle."

"Well, then," Ala said. She pushed herself off her chair. Once she got her feet on the ground she walked directly over to Suzanne with her hand outstretched, palm forward.

Suzanne raised her own hand and pressed palms with Ala. Ala's head only came to Suzanne's chin.

"Thank you for your helpful counsel," Ala said with sincerity. "At least in relation to the security of Interterra, you have allayed our fears. As a reward we offer to you the full panoply of the fruits of our civilization. You have much to see and experience. With your background you are uniquely qualified, far better than any of our other earth surface visitors. Go and enjoy!"

Sudden applause by the other elders left Suzanne momentarily flustered. She self-consciously acknowledged the acclaim by nodding before speaking above the persisting applause. "Thank you all for providing me this opportunity to visit Interterra. I'm honored."

"It is we who are honored," Ala said. She gestured toward Arak and Garona, directing Suzanne to follow.

Later as the three exited the great pyramid, Suzanne paused to glance back at the imposing structure. She wondered if she should have posed the question to the Council whether she and the others were temporary visitors to Interterra or permanent, captive residents. Part of the reason she hadn't was her fear of what the answer would be. But now she found herself wishing she had.

"Are you okay?" Garona asked, interrupting her thoughts.

"I'm fine," Suzanne replied. She resumed walking, still engrossed in her thoughts. The one thing the visit did clear up was the reason she and the others had been brought to Interterra. The elders had wanted to quiz a professional oceanographer about suspicions of Interterra's existence. She didn't think that the treatment she and her crewmates would receive was about to change now that the Interterrans had achieved their goal. On the other hand she now felt solely responsible for their plight. If it hadn't been for her, they would not have been abducted.

"Are you sure you are all right?" Garona asked. "You seem so pensive."

Suzanne forced herself to smile. "It's hard not to be," she said. "There's so much to take in."

"You have provided a great service to Interterra," Arak remarked. "As Ala said, we all are grateful."

"I'm glad," Suzanne said as she tried to maintain her grin. But it was difficult. Sensing that Donald was right and that they were in Interterra to stay, her intuition was telling her that a confrontation was inevitable, and given the personalities of some of her colleagues, the situation could soon turn violent and ugly.

CHAPTER SIXTEEN

"This place gives me the creeps," Michael said.

"It is weird that it is so deserted," Donald said. "It's also weird that they let us roam around in here by ourselves."

"They are trusting," Michael said. "You got to give them that."

"I'd call it foolish," Donald said.

The two second-generation humans were wandering around inside Central Information. Ismael and Mary Black had accompanied them to the entrance of the vast building but had chosen to remain outside while Donald and Michael paid their visit. Inside the two men found themselves in an enormous labyrinth of intersecting corridors and passageways. The place was a hive of rows filled floor to ceiling with what appeared to be the hard drives of a colossal computer array. Except for two worker clones they'd come across in one room near the entrance, they had not seen another living thing.

"You don't think we're going to get lost in here, do you?" Michael asked uneasily. He looked back the way they'd come. Every corridor looked the same.

"I've been keeping track of our movements," Donald said.

"Are you sure?" Michael said. "We've made a lot of turns."

Donald stopped. "Listen, bonehead," he said. "If you're worried why don't you just go the hell back to the entrance and wait?"

"That's okay," Michael said. "I'm cool."

"Cool, my ass," Donald said. He started walking again.

"What did you want to come here for anyway?" Michael asked a few minutes later.

"Let's just say I was curious," Donald replied.

"It's like a nightmare," Michael said. "Or like a horror movie about technology gone wild." He shuddered.

"For once, I agree with you, sailor," Donald said. "It's like technology has taken over."

"What do you think all this equipment does?"

"Arak suggested it runs the place," Donald said. "Apparently it monitors everything. And it stores people's essences. God knows how many people are locked up inside this thing right now."

Michael shuddered again. "Do you think they know we're here?"

"You got me there, sailor," Donald said.

They walked for a few minutes in silence.

"Haven't you seen enough?" Michael questioned.

"I suppose," Donald said. "But I'm going to press on for a while yet."

"I wonder if this thing repairs itself."

"If it does," Donald said, "then we'd have to question who was more alive, this machine or these people who seem to have so little to do."

Suddenly Donald put out a hand, stopping Michael in his tracks.

"What is it?" Michael cried.

Donald pressed a finger to his lips for Michael to be quiet. "Don't you hear that?" Donald whispered.

Michael cocked his head and listened intently. He did hear faint sounds in the far distance: soft bursts piercing the otherwise heavy silence.

"Do you hear it?" Donald asked.

Michael nodded. "It sounds like laughter."

Donald nodded as well. "A curious kind of laughter," he said. "It comes at such regular intervals."

"If I didn't know better I'd say it was canned laughter, like what you hear on a TV sitcom."

Donald snapped his fingers. "You're right! I knew it sounded familiar."

"But that's crazy," Michael said.

"Let's check it out!" Donald said. "Let's follow our ears!"

With mounting curiosity the two men proceeded, hoping to find the source. At the junctures of each corridor they had to stop and listen to choose a direction. Gradually the sounds became louder, and with it, their choices became clear. As they rounded a final bend, they could tell the noise was coming from the first room on the left. At that point they were convinced they really were hearing a TV sitcom; they could even hear the dialogue.

"It sounds like a *Seinfeld* rerun," Michael whispered.

"Shut up!" Donald mouthed. He flattened himself against the wall to the side of the room's entrance and motioned for Michael to move beside him. Slowly Donald eased himself forward. To his surprise, it looked like the screening room of a TV station. The far wall was covered with more than a hundred monitors. All were turned on, most tuned to various programs although a few aired only test patterns.

Leaning forward a bit more Donald noticed a man sitting in a white contour chair in the center of the room facing the monitors. The guy was a far cry from the typical Interterran; he was balding with scruffy gray hair. Sure enough, on the screen directly in front of him were Elaine, George, Kramer, and Jerry.

Donald flattened himself back against the corridor wall, away from the open door. He looked at Michael and whispered, "You were right! It's an old episode of *Seinfeld*."

"I'd recognize those voices anyplace," Michael said.

Donald raised his finger to his lips again. "There's a geezer in there watching it," he whispered. "And he surely doesn't look like an Interterran."

"No shit?" Michael questioned in a whisper.

"This is unexpected," Donald said. He rolled his lower lip into his mouth while he gave the situation some thought.

"That's for sure," Michael said. "What should we do?"

"We're going to walk in and meet this guy," Donald said. "We might have lucked out here. But listen! Let me do the talking, okay?"

"Be my guest," Michael said.

"All right, let's go," Donald said. He pushed off the wall and stepped into the room. Michael followed. They moved quietly although the TV was so loud, the man could never have heard their approach.

Unsure of how to avoid startling the man and yet get his attention, Donald merely stepped into what he thought was the man's field of vision but off to the side.

The ploy didn't work. The man was mesmerized by the show; his face was frozen into a slack, comatose expression with lidded, unblinking eyes glued to the screen.

"Excuse me," Donald said, but his voice was lost in another burst of canned laughter.

Gently Donald reached out and nudged the man's arm. The man leaped from his seat. Seeing the two intruders in the process, he shrank back. But his recovery was almost as rapid.

"Wait a minute! I recognize you two!" he said. "You are two of the surface people who've just joined us."

"*Join* is not the right word," Donald said. "We had no choice in the matter. We were abducted." He eyed the man, who was no more than five-two with a stooped, bony frame. He had deeply set, rheumy eyes, coarse features, and a heavily lined face. He was the oldest-looking man Donald had seen in Interterra.

"You weren't shipwrecked?" the man asked.

"Hardly," Donald said. He introduced himself and Michael.

"Glad to meet you," the man said cheerfully. "I was hoping I would." He came forward to shake their hands. "And that's the way people should greet each other," he added. "I've had it with that foolish palm-pressing nonsense."

"What's your name?" Donald asked.

"Harvey Goldfarb! But you can call me Harv."

"Are you here by yourself?"

"Sure as shootin'. I'm always here by myself."

"What are you doing?"

"Not much," Harvey said. He glanced briefly at the

bank of monitors. "Watching TV shows, particularly the ones that take place in New York."

"Is this a job?"

"Sorta, I suppose, but it's more like I'm a volunteer. It's mostly that I like to see bits and pieces of New York. I like *All in the Family* quite a bit but it's hard to catch reruns nowadays. It's too bad. *Seinfeld*'s all right but I don't get much of the humor."

"What is this room for?" Donald asked. "Just entertainment?"

Harvey laughed derisively while shaking his head. "The Interterrans are not interested in TV, and they don't watch it much. It's Central Information that's interested. Saranta Central Information is one of the main media reception sites for Interterra. It monitors the surface media to make certain there is no reference to Interterra's existence." Harvey made a sweep toward the monitors with his hands. "This stuff plays twenty-four hours a day, seven days a week.

"Hey, that reminds me. You guys got a lot of coverage up there on CNN and the networks. You're all in the news for having gotten consumed in an undersea volcano."

"So there were no suspicions about anything abnormal?" Donald asked.

"Not a peep," Harvey said. "Just a lot of geological jabber. Anyway, to get back to me, I volunteered to come down here and monitor TV shows for the files and to censor out any violence."

"That doesn't leave much TV," Donald said with a cynical laugh. "Why bother?"

"I know, it doesn't make much sense," Harvey agreed. "But if they do watch it, it can't have any violence. I don't know if you know it or not, but these people, the real Interterrans, cannot stand violence. It makes them sick. Literally!"

"So you're not a real Interterran."

Harvey gave another short laugh. "Me? Harvey Gold-farb an Interterran? Do I look like an Interterran? With this face?"

"You do look a bit older than everyone else."

"Older and uglier," Harvey snorted. "But that's me. They've been trying to get me to agree to let them do all sorts of stuff to me, even grow me hair, but I've refused. Yet, I have to say they have kept me healthy. No question about that. Their hospitals are like taking your car to a garage. They just put in a new part and out you go. Anyway, I'm not an Interterran. I'm a New Yorker. I have a wonderful house in the best section of Harlem."

"Harlem has gone through some changes," Donald said. "How long has it been since you've been home?"

"It was nineteen twelve when I came to Interterra."

"How'd you get here?"

"A bit of luck and the intervention of the Interterrans. I was saved from drowning along with a few hundred others after our ship ran into an iceberg."

"The *Titanic?*" Donald questioned.

"None other," Harvey said. "I was on my way home to New York."

"So there are quite a few *Titanic* passengers in Inter-terra?" Donald asked.

"Several hundred at least," Harvey said. "But they're not all in Saranta. A lot of them moved over to Atlantis and on to other cities. They were in demand. You see, the Interterrans find us entertaining."

"I've gotten that impression," Donald said.

"Take advantage of it while you can," Harvey advised. "Once you become acclimated here, you won't be considered so entertaining anymore. Trust me."

"You must have had a horrible experience," Donald said.

"No, I've been pretty happy here," Harvey said defensively. "It's got its ups and downs."

"I meant the night of the *Titanic* sinking."

"Oh, yeah! It's true. That night was awful. Awful!"

"Do you miss New York?"

"In a way," Harvey said. He got a faraway look in his eye. "Actually, it's funny what I really miss, and that's the stock exchange. I know it sounds strange, but I was a self-made man . . . a broker actually, and I loved trading. I worked hard, but how I thrived in the excitement." Harvey took a deep breath and then let it out all at once with a sigh. He refocused on Donald. "Well, so much for my story. What about you? Were you people really abducted to Interterra? If you were, you're the first in my experience. I was under the impression you'd been saved from the undersea volcano CNN reported."

"There was some sort of an eruption at the time," Donald said. "But I think it was a cover for our being sucked into one of the Interterran exit ports. One way or the other, our arrival in Interterra wasn't an act of nature. We were hijacked here for a purpose, which we've not yet been told."

Harvey looked from Donald to Michael and then back to Donald. "You sound less than enchanted with Interterra."

"I'm impressed," Donald said. "It would be hard not to be, but I'm not enchanted."

"Hmmm," Harvey said. "That puts you in a unique

category. Everybody else who's been brought here becomes an overnight advocate. What about your friend here?"

"Michael feels the way I do," Donald said. Michael nodded. "You see," Donald continued, "we don't like to be forced into anything, no matter how good it may seem. But what about you, Harv?"

Harvey studied Donald's face and even took another quick glance at Michael, who at the moment was laughing in sync with the sitcom laughter. "You're serious, you're not enthralled with this place even with all the beautiful people and their parties?"

"I'm telling you, we don't appreciate being coerced."

"And you're actually interested in my opinion?"

Donald nodded.

"Okay," Harvey said. He leaned closer and lowered his voice. "Let me put it to you this way: if I could leave for New York City tonight it wouldn't be soon enough. It's so damn peaceful and perfect here it's enough to drive a normal person crazy."

Donald couldn't help but smile. The old codger was a man after his own heart.

"I'm telling you, nothing ever happens down here," Harvey continued. "Everything's the same day in and day out. Nothing goes wrong. I can't tell you what I'd do for one day on the New York exchange. I mean, I need a little stress to make me feel alive, or at the very least, some bad news or trouble once in a blue moon to make me appreciate how good life is."

Michael flashed Donald a thumbs-up. But Donald ignored him. Instead he asked Harvey if anyone had ever left Interterra.

"Are you kidding? We're under the goddamn ocean! I

mean, really. What do you think, you can just walk out of here? If that were the case you wouldn't see Harvey Gold-farb sitting in here trying to catch a glimpse of the Big Apple. I'd be there, kicking up my heels."

"But the Interterrans go out," Donald said.

"Sure they go out. But the exits and entrances are all controlled by Central Information. And when the Inter-terrans go out, they're sealed in their spacecraft. Besides, they usually just send their worker clones. You see, the Interterrans are very careful about any connection between this world and ours. Remember, one wayward streptococcus would cause havoc down here."

"It sounds like you've given this some thought."

"Absolutely," Harvey said. "But only in my dreams."

Donald directed his attention to the bank of TV moni-tors. "At least you can feel connected to the surface world in this room."

"That's why I'm here," Harvey said proprietarily. "It's a fantastic setup. I hang out here all the time. I can watch just about every major TV channel in the surface world."

"Can you transmit as well as receive?" Donald asked.

"No, it's a passive system," Harvey said. "I mean, there's unlimited power and antennae in just about every mountain range on the surface of the globe, but there's no camera. Interterra's own telecommunication is totally different and a lot more sophisticated, as I'm sure you've gathered."

"If we gave you a standard TV analog camcorder, do you think you could connect it with the equipment you've got here without anybody knowing about it and be able to transmit?"

Harvey stroked his chin as he pondered Donald's ques-tion. "Maybe if I got one of the electronic worker clones to help, it could be done," he said. "But where are you going to get a TV camera?"

"I know what you're thinking," Michael said as a conspiratorial smile spread across his face. "You're thinking about the cameras on the submersible." When the group had gathered out in the front of the museum after their visit, Perry and Suzanne told them about spotting the *Oceanus* in the museum's courtyard.

Donald treated Michael to another glare. Michael took the hint and closed his mouth.

"But I don't understand," Harvey said. "Why would you want to do that?"

"Look, Harv," Donald said, regaining his composure. "My colleagues and I are not enthused about being compelled to stay here to serve as entertainment for these Interterrans. We'd like to go home."

"Wait a minute," Harvey said. "I must be missing something. You think setting up a TV camera can get you out of Interterra?"

"It's possible," Donald said. "At this stage it's just an idea: one piece of a puzzle I haven't figured out yet, but whatever it might be, we won't be able to do it alone. We'd need your help since you've been here long enough to know the ropes. The question is: would you be willing?"

"Sorry!" Harvey said with a shake of his head. "You have to understand that the Interterrans would not take kindly to this at all. If I were to help, I'd be one of the most unpopular guys in town. They'd turn me over to the worker clones. The Interterrans don't like to do anything nasty, but the clones don't mind. They just do what they're told."

"But why would you care what the Interterrans

thought?" Donald asked. "You'd be with us. In return for your help, we'd give you New York."

"Really?" Harvey asked. His eyes lit up. "Are you serious? You'd get me to New York?"

"It would be the least we could do," Donald said.

The fluorescent Frisbee sailed across the lawn. Richard had made an excellent toss, and the Frisbee slowed and began to settle just within the grasp of the worker clone that Richard had ordered to play with him. But instead of grabbing the Frisbee, the worker clone allowed it to float past his outstretched hand. It hit him in the forehead with a resounding thud. Richard slapped a hand to his own forehead in total frustration. He swore like the sailor he'd been.

"Nice toss, Richard," Perry called out, suppressing a giggle. Perry was sitting by the dining room pool with Luna, Meeta, Palenque, and Karena. Sufa had ferried the two men back to the visitors' palace after their stopover at the air taxi works before any of the others had returned from their respective excursions. Initially Richard had been cheered by the near simultaneous arrival of his three girlfriends and Luna, but that euphoria had worn off when none of them could master the Frisbee.

"This is freakin' ridiculous," Richard complained as he walked over to retrieve the Frisbee from the worker clone's feet. "Nobody down here can catch a goddamned Frisbee, much less throw one."

"Richard seems so high-strung again today," Luna said.

Perry agreed. "He's been this way all day as near as I can tell."

"He was strange last night, too," Meeta said. "He sent us away early."

"Now *that*, I'd have to guess, is really out of character," Perry said.

"Can't you do anything?" Luna asked.

"I doubt it," Perry said. "Unless I go out there and toss that stupid piece of plastic around some more."

"I wish he'd calm down," Luna said.

Perry cupped his hands around his mouth. "Richard!" he called. "Why don't you just come over here and relax. You're working yourself up for no reason."

Richard flipped Perry the finger.

Perry shrugged at Luna. "Obviously he's not in a very amenable mood."

"Why don't you at least walk out there and talk to him?" Luna suggested.

With a groan Perry heaved himself to his feet.

"We have a surprise for him when we get him back to his cottage," Meeta said. "Try to convince him to go."

"Did you ask him yourselves?" Perry questioned.

"We did, but he said he wanted to play Frisbee."

"Cripes!" Perry said, shaking his head. "Well, I'll give it a whirl."

"Don't mention the surprise," Meeta said. "Otherwise it won't be as much fun. We don't want him guessing what it might be."

"Yeah, sure," Perry grumbled. Irritated to be pulled away from Luna, he strode out to Richard, who was impatiently instructing the worker clone.

"You're wasting your time," Perry said. "They don't play our games here, Richard. They don't have the mindset. Physical prowess is not something they're interested in."

Richard straightened up. "That's pretty damn obvious." He sighed and cursed anew. "It's frustrating because they've got great bodies. The trouble is, they have zero sense of competition, and I need it. Hell, even the girls are too easy. There's no chase or hot pursuit. The whole freakin' place seems dead to me. What I'd give for a good hard game of hoops or in-line hockey."

"I tell you what," Perry said. "I'll race you across the big pool over at the pavilion. What do you say?"

Richard eyed Perry for a moment before giving the Frisbee a good toss off into the distance. Then he told the worker clone to go and get it. Dutifully the worker clone took off at a jog. Richard watched him for a moment before turning back to Perry.

"Thanks but no thanks," Richard said. "Beating you at swimming is not going to make my day. In fact, what would make my day is getting the hell out of here. I'm a nervous wreck."

"I think we are all concerned about the *leaving* issue," Perry said, lowering his voice. "So we're all a little nervous."

"Well, I'm more than a little nervous," Richard said. "What do you think they do down here to people who commit a major crime?"

"I haven't the faintest idea," Perry said. "I don't think they have major crime. Arak said they have no prisons. Why do you ask?"

Richard fidgeted with his toe against the grass and then looked off into the distance. He started to speak and then stopped.

"Are you worried what they'll do if we try to leave and they catch us?"

"Yeah, that's it," Richard said, jumping on the suggestion.

"Well, that's something we'll have to consider," Perry said. "But until then, worrying about it's not going to accomplish anything."

"I guess you're right," Richard said.

"Why don't you just enjoy yourself with those three gorgeous ladies?" Perry said. He indicated Meeta, Palenque, and Karena with a nod of his head. "Why not channel some of that wild energy of yours by taking them back to your cottage? I can't quite understand it, but they seem crazy about you."

"I'm not sure I ought to take them back to my room," Richard said.

"And why not?" Perry asked. "Isn't it a dream come true? I mean, look at those three girls. They're like lingerie models."

"It's too complicated to explain," Richard said.

"Whatever it is, I can't imagine it being more important than satisfying three eager sirens."

"Yeah, well, maybe you're right," Richard said without much enthusiasm. He snatched the Frisbee away from the worker clone, who had brought it back again. He returned to the dining room with Perry. Meeta, Palenque, and Karena got to their feet and greeted him with outstretched palms. Richard reacted perfunctorily.

"Are you ready to retire to your cottage?" Meeta asked.

"Let's go," Richard said. "But there's one condition. There's going to be no eating or drinking the stuff from my refrigerator. Agreed?"

"Sure," Meeta said. "We won't even be tempted. We've got something in mind other than food." She and the other girls giggled conspiratorially as they draped themselves over Richard's shoulders.

The group started off across the lawn. "I'm serious," Richard said.

"So are we," Meeta answered.

Perry watched them for a beat before turning back to Luna. "Is Richard so aggressive because of his young age?" she inquired.

Perry sat down next to her. "No. That's just the way he is. He'll be the same in ten years, even twenty years."

"And that's because of the dysfunctional family that you surmise he had," Luna said.

"I suppose," Perry said vaguely. He didn't want to encourage another sociological discussion. He felt ill equipped in such an arena as evidenced by their last discussion.

"It's hard for me to understand since we don't have families," Luna said. "But what about friends, acquaintances, and the schooling secondary humans attend? Can't they overcome negative familial influence?"

Perry stared off into the distance and tried to organize his thoughts. "Schooling and friends can help," he said, "but friends can be a negative influence as well. Within some communities social pressure keeps kids from taking much advantage of the education that is afforded them, and often it's the lack of education that breeds bigoted narrow-mindedness."

"So, for someone as young as Richard there is a chance he'll improve."

"I already told you, Richard's not going to change!" Perry said with a tone that bordered on irritation. "Look, I'm no sociologist so maybe we should talk about something else. Besides, he's not that young. He's almost thirty."

"Well, that's young," Luna contended.

"You should talk," Perry snapped.

Luna laughed and batted her pale blue eyes. "Perry, my dear, how old do you think I am?"

"You said you were over twenty," Perry said nervously. "What are you? Twenty-one?"

Luna smiled and shook her head. "No, I'm ninety-four and that's just this body."

Perry's mouth slowly fell open as he made one of his characteristic high-pitched squeaks.

After issuing several more admonitions against going in his refrigerator, Richard allowed the three women to lie him out on his bed with his arms outstretched. As soon as they had positioned him, they began massaging him with an oil that made his skin tingle and his tense muscles relax.

"Whow!" Richard closed his eyes and purred with delight. "You girls are good! I feel like a piece of wet spaghetti."

"And this is just the beginning," Meeta cooed. The three women looked at each other over Richard's reclining body and tried to suppress their laughter. If Richard had been more aware he would have known they were up to something.

After a quarter hour of intense massaging, Palenque detached herself from the 'group, unbeknownst to Richard, and silently made her way around the pool to the edge of the lawn. There she waved silently for others to join them.

Within minutes two men appeared and, suppressing

their own laughter, they tiptoed over to the bed. Smoothly they took over massaging Richard from Karena, so that it was now Meeta and the two men who were providing the ministrations to Richard's body. Palenque and Karena directed their attention to the bodies of the two men. The goal was an orgy on an ancient Roman scale.

"You know," Richard mumbled, his voice muffled from the coverlet, "if it weren't for you girls this place would drive me certifiably crazy. And to think, I've never even had a massage before. I never knew what I was missing!"

The men and women exchanged fervid glances. They were building each other up to a fever pitch.

"I just can't help being an active person," Richard continued, totally unaware of what was happening around him. "I need competition. It's that simple."

One of the men allowed his bulky, masculine hands to run down Richard's forearms and massage his hands. Something didn't feel quite right. Richard opened his eyes. The hands massaging his were as large as his own.

"What the hell?" Richard snapped. With a suddenness that took everyone by surprise, Richard flipped over and found himself looking up into five flushed faces instead of three, and, worst of all, two of them were male.

"What the hell is this?" Richard bellowed. He leaped from the bed, inadvertently knocking Palenque to the floor. The others quickly stood up from their kneeling positions.

"It's all right, Richard," Meeta said urgently, seeing the sudden rage reflected in Richard's face. "It is a surprise orgy for your pleasure."

"Pleasure?" Richard shouted. "Who the hell are these men? How'd they get here?"

"They are our friends," Meeta said. "Cuseh and Uruh. We invited them."

"What the hell do you think I am?" Richard bellowed.

"We've come to make you happy," the man closest to Richard said. He stepped forward and extended his palm.

Richard reacted with a vicious blow to the man's jaw, sending him hurling back against the wall. Everyone gasped at the unexpected violence.

"Get out of here!" Richard shouted. To make his point he swept the night table clear of the golden goblets he'd been collecting. They clattered to the floor with a tremendous racket. As his guests fled out the open end of the room, he looked around the room in a frenzy for something to smash to smithereens.

Suzanne let out a whoop of joy as she and Garona ran hand in hand down a frond-canopied path through a fern forest. Reaching the edge of a crystal clear lake, they came to a sudden stop. Mesmerized by the sublime vista, and out of breath from their run, Suzanne gazed out at the scene.

"This is gorgeous!" she cried.

Garona, who was even more out of breath than Suzanne, had to rest before he could speak. "It's my favorite spot," he gasped. "I come here often. I've always thought it to be very romantic."

"I should say," Suzanne commented. Several other lakes could be seen in the middle distance, nestled among the luxuriant vegetation. In the far distance, jagged mountains rose and merged with the vaulted ceiling. "Which direction are we facing?"

"West," Garona said between breaths. "Those mountains are the bases of what you people call the Mid-Atlantic Ridge."

Suzanne shook her head in amazement. "It is so beautiful. Thank you for sharing it with me."

"It is my pleasure," Garona said. "It is nice to see you more relaxed."

"I suppose I am," Suzanne said. "At least now I know why we were brought to Interterra."

"You have been a great help to us."

"I really didn't do much."

"But you did! You have relieved our anxieties about deep-sea drilling."

"But there's been drilling for many years," Suzanne said. "Why the anxiety now?"

"That was drilling for oil," Garona said. "We don't mind that. In fact, it helps us because oil is a bother. It can seep into our deepest buildings and cause havoc. It was the random drilling that had us concerned."

"Well, I am glad to have been of assistance."

"It calls for a celebration," Garona said. "How about coming to my home for a few hours? We are very close. We'll absorb caldorphin for our mutual pleasure, and then we'll dine."

"In the middle of the day?" Suzanne questioned. As a motivated, hard worker, who as a student had had little time for personal pleasure, the idea of an afternoon tryst seemed unusually decadent. Yet enticingly erotic.

"Why not?" Garona questioned seductively. "Your essence will ring with ecstasy."

"You make it sound so deliciously libidinous," Suzanne joked.

"And it will be," Garona said. "Come." He grabbed her hand and led her back the way they'd come.

Garona's home was a mere five-minute air taxi ride away. As they disembarked Suzanne mentioned his home was similar to Arak and Sufa's although his neighborhood seemed slightly less congested.

"The structure is exactly the same," Garona said. "But we have more space since we are farther away from the town center." He again took her hand, and the two ran up the causeway and into the cottage together.

Once inside, the pair acted like impatient adolescents in their haste to shed their satin robes and slip into the pool. Suzanne exuberantly struck out for the opposite end. She swam with strong strokes, excited to have Garona right behind her. They came face-to-face after Suzanne executed a racing turn against the pool's far end. They embraced in the water. Garona touched his palm with hers and beamed with pleasure. Suzanne laughed with joy.

"This is paradise," Suzanne proclaimed. She dipped her head beneath the water to smooth her short hair back. "It goes beyond my wildest imagination."

"I have so much to show you," Garona told her. "Millions of years of progress. I shall take you to the stars . . . to other galaxies."

"You have already," Suzanne said playfully.

"Come," Garona said. "Let us share some cal-dorphin."

They swam back across the pool. Garona helped her out of the water. She was again taken by how comfortable she felt in his presence despite her nakedness.

"Please!" Garona said, gesturing toward a satin divan.

"I'm soaked," Suzanne said.

"It doesn't matter," Garona said. He bent down and picked up a small jar and removed the top.

"Are you sure?" Suzanne questioned. The upholstered couch was immaculate.

"Absolutely," Garona said. He held the jar out for Suzanne to put some onto her palm. He did the same, and as they both reclined they pushed their hands together.

Suzanne swooned with pleasure to the very core of her being. Over the next half hour she and Garona made love in a sensitive, giving way that reached a crescendo of passion before melding into sublime, intimate relaxation.

Suzanne had never felt so close to another person. Never in her life had she acted with such abandon, and yet she did not feel guilty. In this utopian netherworld, the usual constraints just didn't apply.

Time seemed to stand still as Suzanne luxuriated in the afterglow of an intimacy the likes of which she'd never experienced. But then, suddenly, it all changed. A soft feminine voice coming from close range shattered her mental and physical repose: "If you two have finished your beautifully tender lovemaking, which I have to say I've enjoyed vicariously, I've arranged a lovely lunch."

Suzanne opened her eyes. To her shock, she found herself looking into the smiling face of an exquisitely attractive woman with stunning features, ice blue eyes, and flaxen hair. The woman's expression was like a proud parent gazing down at her adorable children.

Suzanne sat bolt upright and pulled the coverlet up. Her sudden movement disturbed Garona, who rolled over and opened his eyes. "What did you say, Alita?" he asked.

"Time for you two to eat," she said. She pointed to a table by the pool, which was being set by a worker clone.

"Thank you, my dear," Garona said. He sat up. "I think we're both quite hungry."

"The food will be out momentarily," Alita said. She turned and walked back to the worker clone to help with the preparations by arranging three chaiselike chairs around the table.

Garona stretched, yawned, and then reached for his clothing.

Suzanne made a beeline for her own clothes. Although she hadn't been self-conscious earlier, she was now. She put on the tunic and pulled on the shorts.

"Who is this woman?" she whispered.

"Alita," Garona said. "Come, let us eat."

Still confused, Suzanne let herself be led over to the table. She took the chair Garona indicated and allowed the worker clone to serve her some food. While Garona and Alita attacked theirs with relish, Suzanne toyed with hers. Having been caught flagrante delicto she felt acutely embarrassed and emotionally fragile.

"Suzanne met with the Council of Elders today," Garona said to Alita between mouthfuls of food. "She was very helpful and gave us good news."

"Wonderful," Alita said.

Garona leaned over and gave Suzanne's shoulder an affectionate squeeze. "She's assured us that the secret of Interterra is still secure."

"What a relief," Alita said sincerely. "We sorely needed the reassurance."

Suzanne could only nod.

Garona and Alita launched into a discussion of Interterra's security needs vis-à-vis the surface world. Suzanne didn't listen; instead she watched Alita, who was directing her full attention to Garona. Suzanne was amazed at how calm the woman seemed. Suzanne was still feeling too awkward to eat or speak.

Gradually Suzanne's emotions calmed and she began to collect her thoughts. What began to bother her acutely was the apparently familiarity with which Garona and Alita treated each other. Eventually, Suzanne's curiosity got the better of her. "Excuse me, Alita," she said during a break in her fellow diners' conversation. "Have you and Garona known each other for long?"

Both Garona and Alita laughed heartily.

"I'm sorry," Alita said, struggling to contain herself. "It's a perfectly reasonable question, but so very unexpected here in Interterra. You see, Garona and I have known each other for a long, long time."

"Years then," Suzanne suggested curtly. Despite Alita's apology, she found the laughter rude.

Garona burst out laughing again. He had to cover his face with his hand.

"Certainly years," Alita said. "Years and years."

"Alita and I have spent many lives together," Garona explained as he wiped tears from his eyes.

"Oh, I see," Suzanne said, struggling to keep calm. "Isn't that wonderful."

"It is indeed," Garona said. "Alita is . . . well, I guess you'd call her my permanent woman."

"Or we can say Garona is my permanent man," Alita said.

"Either way," Garona agreed.

"It's nice that it is mutual," Suzanne commented

sarcastically. "Now, perhaps you can tell me what 'perma-nent' means socially in Interterra."

"It's something like your institution of marriage," Alita said. "Only it transcends one body life to another."

Suzanne rolled her lower lip into her mouth and bit down on to it to keep from allowing her rekindled emotions to bubble over into tears. After her uncon-ditional surrender to her feelings toward Garona in response to his persistence and flattery, she felt violated now that she knew he was already in a type of long term commitment that she could not even fathom. She also felt stupid and appalled that her intuition had let her down so dramatically and that she hadn't even asked about his social status.

"Well, that's all very interesting," Suzanne managed. She put down her flatware and napkin and stood up. "Thank you for the meal and a most enlightening after-noon. I think it's time I got back to the visitors' palace."

Garona got to his feet. "Are you sure you want to leave so quickly?"

"Quite sure," Suzanne said. Then to Alita she added. "It's been a pleasure."

"For me as well," Alita said. "Garona has spoken so highly of you."

"Has he now?" Suzanne said. "That's very nice."

"I trust we'll be seeing a lot of you," Alita said.

"Perhaps," Suzanne said vaguely. She nodded goodbye to Garona and started for the door. Garona was immediately at her side.

"I'll see you to an air taxi," Garona said. "Unless you'd prefer that I accompany you back to the visitors' palace."

"That's quite all right," Suzanne said as she passed out

of the house. "I'm sure you and Alita have things you need to discuss."

"Suzanne, you are acting strangely," Garona said. He took a few running steps to keep up with her while he used his wrist communicator to summon an air taxi.

"You think?" Suzanne asked. "How sensitive of you to notice."

"What is the matter, Suzanne?" Garona reached for her arm, but she pulled away from his grasp and kept walking.

"It's just a minor cultural thing," she said over her shoulder.

"Come now," Garona said. Catching up with her, he grabbed her arm again and this time succeeded in bringing her to a stop. "Be open with me. Don't make me guess."

"It would be interesting to have you guess. But from my perspective it wouldn't be much of a challenge."

"I suppose this has something to do with Alita."

"Very clever," Suzanne said. "Now, if you let go of me, I'm going back to the visitors' palace."

"Suzanne, you are in Interterra. We have different customs. You must adjust."

Suzanne stared into Garona's dark eyes. One part of her wanted him to leave her alone; the other side of her wanted to give him the benefit of the doubt. After all, this was Interterra, not L.A. "My background is so different . . ." she said.

"I know," Garona insisted. "But I ask you not to judge by your earth surface standards. Try not to be selfish. You don't have to feel you own things to enjoy them. We share ourselves with those we love, and love is an endless font."

"I'm happy for you," Suzanne said. "I'm glad you

have all this love. Unfortunately, I'm used to sharing love with only one person."

"Can't you look at it from the Interterran perspective?"

"At this point, I doubt it."

"Remember, a lot of your earth surface morality tends to be self-indulgent, selfish, and ultimately destructive."

"From your perspective," Suzanne said. "From ours it's good for raising children."

"Perhaps," Garona said. "But that's not important here."

"Garona, look," Suzanne said. She put a hand on his shoulder. "You're probably a wonderful Interterran man. Since we are in Interterra, I admit this is my problem not yours. I'll try to deal with it."

The air taxi suddenly loomed out of nowhere, and its side opened up.

"Do you need me to command the air taxi?" Garona asked.

"I prefer to do it myself," Suzanne said.

"Then I will come over tonight," Garona said. "Is that all right?"

"As we secondary humans say, I believe I need a little space," Suzanne said. "Let's just let things slide for a day or so." She climbed in and took a seat.

"I will come anyway," Garona insisted.

"It's up to you," Suzanne said. She was too emotional to get into any kind of argument. Instead she put her palm onto the center table and said, "Visitors' palace." She waved to Garona as the craft's skin sealed over.

CHAPTER SEVENTEEN

"I'm sure you are all a bit overwhelmed," Arak said. "I can see it in your faces."

Arak and Sufa had brought the group back to the circular conference room for a debriefing late in the afternoon. The Interterrans were standing in the central area, looking up at their charges whose moods differed drastically and not from what Arak assumed.

Perry was irritated with Richard. Just when he had gotten cozy with Luna, Meeta and the others had appeared in a panic, saying that Richard had gone berserk. Worried that Richard's violent behavior might ruin it for all of them, Perry had run back and spent an hour trying to calm the diver down—with little success.

Richard sat sullen and silent. He glowered at Arak and Sufa as if his problems were their personal fault.

Suzanne was sitting next to Perry, reviewing her own emotional wounds. She was also feeling responsible for their predicament. As soon as she'd gotten back, she'd explained how she was the reason behind their abduction. She'd apologized, and everyone had assured her that they didn't hold her responsible, but still she felt bad.

Only Donald and Michael seemed unphased. Arak interpreted this as a reflection of their particularly successful visit to Central Information. Engaging Donald with direct eye contact, Arak addressed him directly: "Before we close for the day, are there any questions or comments about what you have seen during your excursions? Perhaps it might be helpful for each to share with the others your experiences."

"I have a question that I'm sure all of us are interested in," Donald said.

"Then by all means ask it," Arak said.

"Are we prisoners here for life?"

Everyone was taken aback, especially Suzanne and Perry who were jolted from their inward preoccupation. The question surprised them because it was just the previous night that Donald had urged the issue not be broached for fear of having their freedoms curtailed.

Arak was more disappointed than shocked. It took a moment for him to gather his thoughts. "*Prisoners* is not the right word," he said finally. "We'd rather emphasize that you will not be forced to leave Interterra. Instead, we welcome you to our world with full rights to enjoy the panoply of advances to which you have just begun to be exposed."

"But we weren't asked—" Perry began.

"Hold up!" Donald ordered, interrupting Perry. "Let me finish! Arak, just to make this crystal clear, you're saying that we will not be able to leave Interterra, even if we want to."

Arak squirmed uncomfortably.

Sufa interceded. "Generally, we eschew discussing such an emotional subject so early in your introduction to Interterra. It's our experience that visitors are better equipped to deal with this topic after they have been acclimated to the benefits of life here."

"Please, just answer the question," Donald said bluntly.

"A simple yes or no will do," Michael added.

Arak and Sufa conferred in whispered tones. Donald leaned back and haughtily crossed his arms while the other visitors watched in stunned, nervous silence. Their fate hung in the balance.

Finally Arak nodded. He and Sufa had come to an agreement. He looked up at the group and eventually fixed his gaze on Donald. "All right," he said. "We shall be honest. The answer to your question is, no. You will not be able to leave Interterra."

"Never?" Perry gasped.

"What about communicating with our families?" Suzanne asked. "We need to let them know we are alive."

"To what end?" Arak questioned. "Such a message would be cruel to people destined never to see you again and who are already adapting to your loss."

"But we have children," Perry cried. "How do you expect us not to contact them?"

"It's out of the question," Arak said firmly. "I'm sorry, but the security of Interterra supersedes personal interests."

"But we didn't ask to come here," Perry exclaimed, close to tears. "You brought us here to help you, and Suzanne did. I've got a family!"

"We can't stay here," Richard sputtered.

"No way," Michael seconded.

"We all have emotional ties to our world," Suzanne added. "As sensitive fellow humans you can't think that we can just forget them."

"We understand it is difficult," Arak said. "We empathize with you, but remember the rewards are infinite.

Frankly I'm surprised none of you is tempted at this early juncture. But it will change. It always does. Remember we have had thousands of years of experience with earth surface visitors."

"Temptation is not the point," Donald said haughtily. "In our ethical value system, ends do not justify means. The problem is, we're being forced, and particularly because of our heritage as Americans, we find that a difficult cross to bear."

"Oh please!" Perry shouted angrily at Donald. "Cut the patriot nonsense. This is not about being American, or French, or Chinese. This is about being human."

"Calm down!" Arak ordered. He took a breath then added: "It is true you are in a sense being forced due to the security needs of Interterra, but a better term would be *directed* because in this instance the analogy of parent to child is apropos. Due to your primitive innocence you are confusing short term interests with long term benefit. We who have lived for lifetime after lifetime know better and are more capable of making a more rational decision. Try to keep in mind what we are directing you to: namely the goal of all your religions. You have been brought into a very real heaven."

"Heaven or no heaven," Richard sputtered, "we ain't staying here."

"I'm sorry," Arak said quite sincerely. "You are here and here you will stay."

Suzanne, Perry, Richard, and Michael looked at each other with varying mixtures of agitation, dismay, and resentment. Donald, on the other hand, still had his arms folded in an attitude of priggish self-satisfaction.

"Well," Arak said with a sigh, "this has not gone as planned. I regret that you have insisted on talking about this so early in your orientation. But please trust me; you will all change your minds as time goes on."

"What is the general plan for us?" Suzanne asked.

"The orientation period usually lasts one month," Arak said, "depending on each visitor's individual needs. During that time you will have the opportunity to travel to other cities. After the completion of orientation, you will be relocated to a city of your choice."

"Can you tell us where these cities are located?" Donald asked.

"Of course," Arak said. He was glad to move the conversation away from the emotional issue of their custody. Swinging up into his seat with the console, Arak dimmed the lights and turned on the floor screen. A moment later an enormous map of the Atlantic portion of Interterra appeared, including overlying oceans and continental margins. The cities were either orange, blue, or green. Sufa stepped to the side to avoid blocking anyone's view.

"I'm sure you all recognize Saranta," Arak said. He touched his console and its name blinked in orange. Then the entire image switched to the Pacific part of Interterra. "Here you see the older cities beneath the Pacific Ocean. You'll be visiting many of them. All have their own, individual characters, and you will be able to live in any one you choose."

"Does the orange type signify anything?" Donald asked.

"They are cities with the interplanetary exit ports," Arak said. "Like the port you entered through. But most of these have become obsolete and are not used. Here you see Calistral in the southern Indian Ocean. That's probably the only one still in operation, although it's used rarely. Nowadays we rely almost exclusively on the intergalactic ports under the south pole."

"Could we see the other map again?" Donald asked. He leaned forward.

"Certainly," Arak said. The image of the Atlantic portion of Interterra reappeared.

"So the city of Barsama due east of Boston has an interplanetary port?" Donald said.

"It does," Arak said. "But it has not been used for hundreds of years. The city of Barsama is very pleasant, however, although it is quite small."

"When you say unused," Donald continued, "does that mean it has been sealed like the port here in Saranta?"

"Not yet," Arak said. "But it will be soon. The shafts of those outmoded ports were all supposed to have been sealed ages ago, as I said yesterday. Just today the Council of Elders issued a new decree to speed up the process."

Donald nodded. He eased back in his chair and recrossed his arms.

"Any other questions?" Arak asked.

No one moved.

"I think we are too stunned for more questions," Perry said.

"You need to spend time together to help each other adapt," Sufa said. "And we encourage you to seek the counsel of Ismael and Mary. I'm sure you can benefit from their wisdom and experience."

No one responded.

"Well then," Arak said. "We'll resume your orientation in the morning after you've had a deserved rest. Remember, in addition to everything else, you are all still recovering from the decon process. We know that the stress of that ordeal heightens emotional volatility."

A quarter hour later the group found themselves walking back toward the dining hall after Arak and Sufa's departure. Evening was beginning to fall. Trudging through the thick grass no one spoke. Each was absorbed in his own thoughts.

"We have to talk," Donald said, suddenly breaking the silence.

"I agree," Perry said. "Where?"

"I think it best if we do it outside," Donald said. "But let's wait until we get to the dining hall so we can leave our wrist communicators inside. I wouldn't be surprised if they serve as a surveillance device along with their other functions."

"Good idea," Perry said. He had recovered enough to be angry.

"I want to apologize again to everyone," Suzanne said. "I just feel terrible that I'm responsible for everyone being here."

"You're not responsible," Perry said irritably.

"We don't blame you," Michael said. "It's these goddamn Interterrans."

"Let's keep the talk to a minimum until we get rid of our communicators," Donald suggested.

The group walked the rest of the way in silence. Inside the dining hall they stripped off the wrist units, then filed back outside.

"How far do you think we should go?" Perry asked. He glanced over his shoulder. They were already about a hundred feet from the tip of the dining room pool. Light from the interior spilled out into a puddle on the lawn.

"This is fine," Donald said. He stopped and the others huddled around him.

"So now we know," Donald said. "I don't like to say that I told you so."

"Then don't say it," Perry grumbled.

"At least we know where we stand," Donald said.

"That's a lot of comfort," Perry said sarcastically.

"I was surprised you posed the question," Suzanne said. "Why did you change your mind about not being direct?"

"Because we needed to know sooner rather than later," Donald said. "If we've got to break out of here, which we now know is the case, then we've got to do it soon."

"Do you think there is a way?" Suzanne asked.

"I think it is possible," Donald said. "The most promising piece of news is your having seen the *Oceanus* and it being intact. If we could get it to that exit port in Barsama and figure out how to flood the chamber and open the shaft, we'd have enough power and life support to get us to Boston."

"That's not going to work," Suzanne said. "As paranoid as the Interterrans are, the exit ports have to be heavily guarded and monitored. Even if we knew how it worked, we wouldn't be able to get away with it."

"Suzanne's right," Richard said. "They'd have a bunch of those worker clones hanging around for sure."

"I agree," Donald said. "We can't sneak out or even break out. We have to be let out."

"Cripes!" Perry complained. "They're not going to let us out. Arak made that perfectly clear."

"Not willingly," Donald said. "We have to force them."

"And how do you propose to do that?" Suzanne asked. "We're talking about an extremely advanced civilization here, with powers and technology that we can't even anticipate."

"Blackmail," Donald said. "We have to convince them it would be safer to let us out than detain us."

"Keep talking," Perry said dubiously.

"They are terrified of exposure," Donald said. "My idea is to threaten to transmit to surface TV and expose this place."

"Do you think people on the surface would believe it?" Suzanne asked.

"All that matters is that the Interterrans believe it," Donald said.

"Do they have facilities to transmit TV signals?" Perry asked.

"No, but they receive. Michael and I found a man who will help us."

"It's true," Michael said. "He's an old bird from New York City named Harvey Goldfarb. He's been here for years but spends his days hidden in Central Information watching TV reruns. He wants out too, big time."

"The important thing is that he's familiar with their TV equipment," Donald said. "We've got two camcorders on the *Oceanus* that could be jury-rigged to transmit. Goldfarb says there's plenty of power."

"Hmmm. You know," Perry said, "it sounds promising."

"Not to me," Suzanne said with a shake of her head. "I don't see how it is going to work. I get the threat idea, but how do we use it to pressure the Interterrans into doing something they obviously do not want to do?"

"I don't know exactly," Donald admitted. "We've got

to put our heads together and work it out. I envisioned having Goldfarb with his finger on the switch ready to transmit."

"Is that all?" Perry questioned with dismay. "If that's all you've got, then Suzanne's right. It wouldn't work. I mean, they could just send a worker clone in to clobber Goldfarb or, simpler still, they could just shut the power off. If blackmail is going to work, it's got to be more involved to be a credible threat."

"It's a start," Donald said. "Like I said, we've got to brainstorm on this."

Suzanne looked at Perry. "What do you mean, 'more involved'?" she asked.

"Something like having two coexisting threats," Perry said. "That way if they block one, the other does the job. You know what I mean? In order to neutralize the threat they'd have to address both flanks."

"That's not a bad idea," Donald said. "Can anybody think of another threat?"

No one volunteered anything.

"I can't think of anything on the spur of the moment," Perry said.

"Nor can I," Suzanne said.

"We'll start off with the camcorder idea," Donald said. "While we're getting that set up, something else will occur to us."

"What about the weapons in the museum?" Michael asked.

"You found some weapons?" Perry asked.

"A whole room full," Donald said. "But unfortunately they're mostly old, outdated, damaged ordnance scavenged off the ocean floor from ancient Grecian times to

World War II. The most promising piece we saw was a German Luger."

"Do you think it would fire?" Perry asked.

"It might," Donald said. "The clip is full. Mechanically it seemed clean."

"Well, that's something," Perry said. "Especially if it works."

"One thing we know for sure," Donald said, "we're not going to be able to pull this off once we get separated into different cities."

"That's right," Perry said. "So we've got less than a month."

"We might have a lot less time than a month," Richard said.

"Why do you say that?" Suzanne asked.

"Michael and I had a little problem," Richard said. "And I imagine all hell is going to break loose around here one of these days when it's discovered."

"Richard, no, don't say anything!" Michael cried.

"What is it?" Perry questioned. "What have you done now?"

"There was an accident," Richard said.

"What kind of accident?" Donald demanded.

"Maybe it would be better if I showed you," Richard said. "You might have an idea of what to do in the interim."

"Where?" Donald barked.

"My room or Mikey's room," Richard said. "It's the same difference."

"Lead the way, sailor," Donald growled.

No one spoke as the group hiked across the expanse of lawn to the open end of Richard's cottage. They filed in around the edge of the pool. Richard went to the cabinet containing the refrigerator and commanded it to open. Once it had, he bent down and yanked on several of the tightly packed containers, which then tumbled out onto the marble floor. Framed by the remaining haphazardly stacked containers was the frozen, pallid face of Mura. Her hair was matted against her forehead, and the bloody froth had collapsed onto her cheek in a brownish smudge.

Suzanne immediately covered her eyes.

"Now, you got to understand, it was an accident," Richard explained. "Michael didn't really mean to kill her. He was just trying to get her to shut up from screaming by holding her head under water."

"She went crazy," Michael blurted. "She saw the body of the guy Richard killed."

"What guy?" Perry demanded.

"It was a little squirt from the gala," Michael said. "The one who hung around Mura."

"Where's his body?" Donald demanded.

"He's jammed into my refrigerator," Michael said.

"You idiots!" Perry snapped. "How did the boy die?"

"It doesn't matter," Donald muttered. "What's done is done, and Richard is right: the moment these bodies are discovered all hell could break loose."

"Of course it matters," Suzanne snapped as she took her hands away from her face to glare at the divers. "I cannot believe this! You men killed two of these peace loving, gentle people and for what?"

"He made a pass at me," Richard explained. "I punched him and he fell and hit his head. I was stoned. I didn't mean to kill him."

"You narrow-minded, bigoted bastards," Suzanne sneered.

"Okay, okay," Perry intoned. "Let's ratchet it down a

notch. We've still got to work together if there's any hope of getting out of here."

"Perry's right," Donald said. "If we're going to make a break it has to be soon. In fact, we'd better start tonight."

"I'm with you," Richard said as he squatted down to jam the packages back into the refrigerator to re-cover Mura's lifeless face.

"What can we do tonight?" Perry asked.

"A lot, I'd suspect," Donald said.

"Well, you're the military man," Perry said. "Why don't you take command?"

"How does that set with everyone else?" Donald asked.

Richard stood up and managed to get the refrigerator door closed with the help of his hip. "Fine by me," he said. "The sooner we're out of here the better."

"Me, too," Michael said.

"What about you, Suzanne?" Donald asked.

"I can't believe this has happened," Suzanne muttered. She was staring into the middle distance. "They spent a month decontaminating us but we managed to bring disease in anyway."

"What the hell are you mumbling about?" Perry asked.

Suzanne sighed sadly. "It's like we're Satan's minions invading heaven."

"Suzanne, are you all right?" Perry asked. He grasped her shoulders and looked into her eyes. They were brimming with tears.

"I'm just sick at heart," she said.

"I'll take three out of four to be a reasonable mandate," Donald said, ignoring Suzanne. "Here's what

I propose. We'll get our wrist communicators, call an air taxi, and get ourselves over to the Earth Surface Museum. Richard and I will visit the submersible to check it out. He'll help me salvage one of the TV cameras. Perry, you and Michael will go into the museum and get weapons. Michael can show you where they are. Take anything you think might be appropriate but be sure you get the Luger."

"Sounds good," Perry said. "What about you, Suzanne? Do you want to come along?"

Suzanne didn't answer. Instead, she lifted her hands back to her face and massaged her watery eyes. She could not get over the fact that they were responsible for the death of two Interterrans. She wondered what kind of grief such a crime was likely to evoke in Saranta. Two essences who'd survived for eons had been lost forever.

"Okay," Perry said soothingly. "You stay here. We shouldn't be long."

Suzanne nodded but didn't even watch as the group filed out of the room through the open end of the cottage. Instead, she looked at the cabinetry that hid the refrigerator and allowed herself to cry. The violent and ugly confrontation she feared was already coming to pass.

CHAPTER EIGHTEEN

Donald treated the operation like a military exercise, as did Richard and Michael, who'd had even more covert operational experience than he. Getting into the spirit of the affair, the two divers blackened their faces and garments with soil. Perry wasn't as gung ho, but he was relieved to be taking his fate in his own hands.

"Is that necessary?" Perry asked when he saw what Richard and Michael had done with the mud.

"It's what we did for any night operation in the Navy," Richard replied.

The ride in the air taxi was in some respects even more exhilarating at night than it had been during the day. There was significantly less traffic but what traffic there was lurched unexpectedly out of the shadows.

"This is like a goddamned amusement park ride," Richard said after a particularly close pass.

"I wish I could find out how these things work," Perry commented. "There were only worker clones at the factory Richard and I visited this morning."

"That was one colossal waste of time," Richard commented.

"What do you think about Suzanne?" Donald asked Perry.

"What do you mean?" Perry responded.

"Do you think we have to worry about her?" Donald asked. "She could mess up this whole operation."

"You mean alert the Interterrans?" Perry asked.

"Something like that," Donald said. "She seemed pretty upset back there about the two casualties."

"She was upset, but it wasn't just about the deaths," Perry said. "She confided to me that Garona disappointed her somehow. And she feels responsible about us being here, as she said. Anyway, I don't think we have to worry about her. She'll be okay."

"I hope so," Donald said.

The craft decelerated, hovered for a moment, then rapidly descended.

"Stand by, troops," Donald said.

As Donald had directed, the air taxi was settling down in the museum's courtyard. Over the edge of the craft the dim outline of the *Oceanus* could be seen, silhouetted against the black basalt of the museum.

"There's the target," Donald said. "Once the side of the taxi opens I want everyone flat against the museum wall. Understood?"

"That's affirmative," Richard said.

The moment the exit appeared the group piled out, ran to the wall, and flattened themselves against it. All eyes swept the immediate area. It was dark, particularly in the shadows, and perfectly still without any signs of life. Behind them the sharply geometric form of the museum soared up into the blackness. The only light on the scene came from the thousands of faux, bioluminescent stars above and a low-level glow emanating from the museum's windows. The dark hulk of the submersible was about fifty feet away, sitting on chocks on the flatbed of an antigravity freighter.

The air taxi's side seamlessly sealed over and the craft silently rose before disappearing in the darkness.

"I don't see a soul," Richard whispered.

"I guess the museum's not much of a night spot," Michael whispered back.

"Keep the conversation to a minimum," Donald ordered.

"The place is deserted," Perry said. He let himself relax. "That's going to make this a whole lot easier."

"Let's hope it stays that way," Donald said. He pointed to a window to their left. "Perry, you and Michael climb through and come back out through the same one. We'll either be working on the *Oceanus* or we'll be waiting here in the shadows."

"Do you think there's an alarm system in the museum?" Perry questioned.

"Nah!" Richard said. "There's no locks or alarms or any of that kind of stuff. Apparently nobody ever steals anything down here."

"All right," Perry said. "We're off."

"Good hunting," Donald said. He waved as Perry and Michael ran hunched over to just below the window. Grunting and groaning. Perry boosted Michael up so he could get a grip on the sill. Once he was inside, he leaned back out and pulled Perry up. A moment later the two disappeared inside the building.

Donald redirected his attention to the submersible.

"Well, are we going over there or not?" Richard questioned.

"Let's do it!" Donald said.

They kept low to the ground as they sprinted over to the mini submarine. Donald lovingly patted its HY-140 steel hull. In the darkness its scarlet color was a dull gray although the white lettering on the sail stood out sharply. Donald made a slow inspection of the craft with Richard close on his heels. He was impressed with the Interterran repairs; the outside lights and the manipulator arm that had been destroyed in the plunge down the vent shaft looked completely normal.

"It looks perfect," Donald said. "All we have to do is get it into the ocean and we're home free."

"None too soon for me," Richard said.

Donald went to an outside toolbox, opened it, and took out several wrenches. He handed them to Richard.

"Start with the starboard side camcorder," he said. "Just detach it from its housing. I'm going below to check out the battery level. If we don't have power, we're not going anywhere."

"Roger," Richard said.

Donald climbed the familiar rungs, rapidly ascending to the ship's hatch. He was mildly surprised to find it undogged and slightly ajar. Grabbing it with two hands he raised it all the way. After one last visual sweep around the area, he lowered himself into the opening and clambered down into absolute darkness.

Once Donald had reached the deck, he moved forward by feel. He was so familiar with the craft, he could literally move around inside with his eyes closed, or so he thought until he tripped over the two books Suzanne had brought along to impress Perry. Donald cursed less for the tripping than for striking his hand against the back of one of the passenger seats while trying to maintain his balance. At least he didn't fall which could have been lethal in the tight quarters.

After rubbing his hand to dispel the pain, he inched forward. As he neared the dive station a bit of light filtered in through the four view ports, making his progress easier. Careful not to hit his head on any of the protruding instrumentation, Donald lowered himself into the pilot seat. Outside he could hear Richard clanking against the hull with the wrench.

The first thing Donald did was switch on the instrument lights. Then, with trepidation, he allowed his eyes to move over to the battery level indicator. He sighed with relief. There was plenty of power. Then, as he was about to check gas pressures, he froze. A noise coming from behind him told him that he was not alone. Someone besides himself was inside the submersible.

At first Donald held his breath, straining to listen. Cold sweat appeared along his hairline. Seconds passed, though it seemed like hours, but the noise did not repeat itself. Just when Donald began to wonder if his imagination had misinterpreted the sounds of Richard removing the camcorder, a voice came out of the darkness. "Is that you, Mr. Fuller?"

Donald swung around. His eyes vainly tried to penetrate the darkness. "Yes," he said with a voice that cracked. "Who's here?"

"Harv Goldfarb. Remember me from Central Information?"

Donald relaxed and took a breath. "Of course," he said irritably. "What the devil are you doing in here?"

Harvey inched forward. The lights from the instruments illuminated his deeply creased face. "You got me thinking today," Harvey said. "You're the first hope I've ever had for getting back. I was afraid you might forget me, so I thought I'd sleep in here."

"Mr. Goldfarb, we can't forget you," Donald said.

"We need you. Did you check out the TV cameras on the outside?"

"I did," Harvey said. "I don't think they'll be a problem. What is it you are planning on transmitting?"

"We're not sure at this stage," Donald said. "Maybe you or us or even all of us."

"Me?" Harvey questioned.

"Actually we only want the capability to transmit," Donald said. "It's the threat that's important."

"I'm getting the picture," Harvey said. "They let you out because they're afraid that I'll expose Interterra over the airwaves."

"Something like that," Donald said.

"It won't work," Harvey said flatly.

"Why not?"

"Two reasons," Harvey said. "First, they'd cut my power before they'd let you out. And second, I won't do it."

"But you said you'd help."

"Yeah, and you said you'd take me to New York."

"That's true," Donald admitted. "Actually we haven't worked out any of the details."

"Details, ha!" Harvey scoffed. "But listen. I live here. I can tell you how to get out. Many a night I've dreamed about escaping the monotony of all these interminably pleasant days."

"We're open to suggestions," Donald said.

"I gotta be sure you'll take me along," Harvey said.

"We'll be happy to include you," Donald said. "What's your idea?"

"Will this submarine work?" Harvey asked.

"That's what I'm checking," Donald said. "We've got

plenty of power, so if we can get it out into the water, it will work."

"Okay, now listen," Harvey said. "Has your orientation gotten around to telling you that the Interterrans live forever? Not in the same body but in multiple bodies?"

"Yes," Donald said. "We've already visited the death center and witnessed an extraction."

"I'm impressed," Harvey said. "They are moving you right along. So you understand that the process works only if they are extracted before death. In other words, it all has to be planned. You get what I'm saying?"

"I'm not sure," Donald admitted.

"They have to be alive when the memory is extracted," Harvey said. "Or more properly, their brains have to be functioning normally. If they die by violent means, the story's over. That's why they are so terrified of violence, and that's why there hasn't been any violence in Interterra for millions upon millions of years. They are incapable of it except by proxy."

"So we threaten violence," Donald said. "We already thought of that."

"I'm talking about something more specific than just violence," Harvey said. "You threaten death specifically. Death without any of their extraction nonsense unless they do what you want."

"Aha!" Donald exclaimed. "Now I get you. You're talking about taking hostages."

"Correct!" Harvey said. "Two, four, as many as you can get, and not clones, because they don't count. And a word of caution: the clones don't mind violence. They do whatever they are told."

"Slick!" Donald commented. "It's a multiple threat built into one."

"Correct," Harvey said proudly. "And you don't have to monkey around with this TV camera nonsense."

"I like it," Donald said. "How about you going out and telling Richard to hold up on removing the camcorder. I just want to check the gas pressures, and I'll be right out."

"You promise you'll be taking me," Harvey said.

"You're going," Donald said. "Stop worrying."

"All right, hold up!" Perry ordered. "Either you know where you are going or you don't. We've been wandering around in here like a couple of dopes for twenty minutes. Where are the goddamn weapons?"

Michael shook his head. "I'm sorry, but I get lost in museums even in the daytime."

"Try to remember something about the gallery," Perry said.

"I remember it was long and narrow," Michael said.

"What was it near? Can you remember anything like that?"

"Wait a second," Michael said. "Now I remember. It was behind a door that said we were supposed to get permission from the Council of Elders to enter."

"I haven't seen many doors," Perry said as his eyes scanned the immediate area. "And there are none here so obviously we're not in the right place."

"I also remember we'd stopped in a gallery filled with Persian carpets," Michael said. "It's coming back to me now. The carpets were beyond the room with all the Renaissance stuff."

"That's a start," Perry said. "I know where that gallery is. Come on! Follow me for a change!"

A few minutes later the two men were standing outside the door with the restricted entry admonition. It was located near the window they'd climbed in.

"Is this it?" Perry asked. "If it is, we've come full circle."

"I think so." He reached around Perry, pushed the door open, and glanced inside. "Pay dirt!" he exclaimed.

"It's about time," Perry grumbled as he entered. "The others are going to start thinking we got lost, so we'd better make this snappy."

"What should we take?" Michael asked.

The two men stopped just inside the door while Perry looked up and down the dimly lit room. He was impressed with the room's length and the subsequent square footage the shelving afforded. "This is more than I expected!" he commented. "We've got quite a selection in here."

"The older stuff is to the right, newer to the left," Michael said.

"I guess it doesn't matter what we take as long as it functions," Perry said, "and as long as I find the Luger."

"I know one thing I want," Michael said. He reached over and picked up the crossbow and its quiver. As he did so he nicked his finger. "Jeez, these arrow points are razor sharp."

"Those are quarrels, or bolts, not arrows," Perry said.

"Whatever," Michael said. "They're damn sharp."

"Do you remember which way the Luger was?"

"To the left, Bozo," Michael said.

"Don't call me Bozo," Perry warned.

"Well, I just got finished telling you the modern stuff was to the left."

Perry set out without responding to Michael's last comment. It irritated him that he had to put up with the divers. He had never been forced to spend time with two more juvenile idiots in his life.

Michael turned and went the other way. As long as everything was water-damaged and barnacle-encrusted, he thought the ancient armaments would be better since, in their simplicity, there were fewer working parts for the salt water to foul up. Soon he was in an area with a superb collection of ancient Greek weapons. He gathered an armful of short swords, daggers, and shields along with several helmets, greaves, and a brace of breastplates. What impressed him was the worked gold and the encrusted jewels he could see despite the darkness. Thus encumbered he clanked his way back to the door they'd entered.

"Any luck yet?" Michael called out to Perry.

"Not yet," Perry called back. "Just a bunch of rusted rifles."

"I'm going to take this stuff I got back to the window."

"All right, I'll be here as soon as I find the pistol."

Michael added the crossbow to his burden and then struggled with the door. No sooner had he taken a step into the hall than he collided with Richard.

Michael whimpered and dropped everything he was carrying. The heavy gold and bronze implements made a tremendous clatter against the marble floor.

"Shut up, you ass!" Richard hissed. The racket exploding in the silence of the dark, deserted museum had scared him as much as the unexpected encounter had scared Michael.

"What do you mean sneaking in here and scaring me shitless?" Michael spat.

"What the hell's been taking you so long?" Richard demanded.

"We couldn't find the room, okay?"

Perry appeared in the doorway. "Good God, what on earth are you guys doing? Trying to wake up the entire city?"

"It wasn't my fault," Michael said as he bent down to retrieve his booty.

"Did you guys find the Luger?" Richard asked.

"Not yet," Perry said. "Where's Donald?"

"He's already on his way back to the visitors' palace," Richard said. "There's been a change in plans. The old fart Harvey Goldfarb was hiding in the submersible, and he's come up with a new and better escape plan for us."

"Really?" Perry questioned. "What is it?"

"We're going to take hostages," Richard said. "He says the Interterrans are so afraid of violent death that they'd do anything, including letting us out into the ocean with the submersible, if we got a couple of their people and threaten to do them in."

"I like it," Perry said. "But why did Donald go back before us?"

"He's worried about Suzanne, especially now that things look so promising. But he told me to tell you to get a move on it; as soon as you're ready I'll call an air taxi to get us back."

"All right," Perry said. "Both of you come on in here. With all of us looking for the damn pistol we should be able to find it a lot faster."

*

The air taxi came to a halt and opened. It was hovering directly in front of the visitors' palace dining room. Richard and Michael disembarked with some difficulty, both weighed down with an array of ancient armament. All Perry was carrying was the Luger, which he'd finally found.

The three made their way up the ramp to the door. Both divers had donned the breastplates, helmets, and greaves rather than carry them in their arms. It was enough to be holding the shields, swords, daggers and crossbow. Perry had tried to talk them out of taking the armor, but they were determined, and he gave up trying to reason with them. Michael and Richard were convinced in their words that the stuff was going to be worth a fortune topside.

To their surprise the dining room was empty.

"That's odd," Richard said. "He told me to meet him here."

"You don't suppose he's planning on bugging out of here without us, do you?" Michael questioned.

"I don't know," Richard responded. "The idea never occurred to me."

"He's not going without us," Perry assured the two divers. "We just saw the *Oceanus* still parked where it's always been, and he's not going anyplace without that."

"How about Suzanne's room?" Michael suggested.

"I'd say that's a good possibility," Perry said. The long walk across the lawn was significantly noisy thanks to the continual clatter of the ancient armor.

"You guys sound ridiculous," Perry commented.

"We didn't ask for your opinion," Richard said.

As they rounded the open end of Suzanne's cottage they saw Donald, Suzanne, and Harvey sitting in contour chairs near the pool's edge. It was obvious the atmosphere was tense.

"What's wrong?" Perry questioned.

"We've got a problem," Donald said. "Suzanne's not sure we're doing the right thing."

"Why not, Suzanne?" Perry asked.

"Because murder is wrong," Suzanne said. "If we take hostages to the surface world without adaptation, they will die, plain and simple. We brought violence and death here and now we want to escape by it. I say it's ethically despicable."

"Yeah, but I didn't ask to come here," Perry said hotly. "I don't like to sound like a broken record, but we're being held against our will. I think that justifies violence."

"But that's confusing ends with means," Suzanne said. "That's exactly what we're supposed to be against."

"All I know is that I have a family that I miss," Perry said. "I'm going to see them again come hell or high water!"

"I empathize with you," Suzanne said. "Truly! And I feel responsible about the whole situation. And it is true we were abducted. But I don't want to see any more deaths, nor do I want to see Interterra unwittingly destroyed. We're ethically obligated to negotiate. These people are so peaceful."

"Peaceful?" Richard questioned. "I'd say boring!"

"I can vouch for that," Harvey said.

"Perry, this is Harvey Goldfarb," Donald said.

Perry and Harvey shook hands.

"I don't know what we're supposed to negotiate," Donald said. "Arak made it clear we're here for good, not buts, ifs, or maybes. A statement like that precludes negotiation."

"I think we should let a little more time pass," Suzanne said. "What's wrong with that? Maybe we will change our minds, or maybe we'll be able to convince them to alter theirs. We've got to remember that we've all brought down here our personalities and psychological baggage geared to the world above, plus we're so accustomed to seeing ourselves as the 'good guys' that it's difficult to realize when we are the monsters."

"I don't feel like a monster," Perry said. "I don't belong here."

"Me neither," Michael said.

"Let me make another point," Suzanne said. "For the sake of argument, let's say we manage to get out of here. What happens then? Do we reveal Interterra's existence?"

"It will be hard not to," Donald said. "Where would we say we've been for the last month or however long it's been?"

"And what about me?" Harvey said. "I've been here for almost ninety years."

"That's even harder to explain," Donald agreed.

"We'd also have to have some explanation where we got all the gold and armor," Richard said. " 'Cause this stuff's going with me."

"And what about the economic possibilities of our serving as intermediaries?" Perry said. "We could help both sides and end up millionaires many times over. Just the wrist communicators alone will cause a technological sensation."

"I rest my case," Suzanne said. "One way or the other we'd be exposing Interterra. Stop and think about our civilization and its exploitive greed. We don't like to think of ourselves in that light, but it's true. We are selfish, both as individuals and as nations. There'd be a confrontation

without doubt, and as advanced as the Interterran civilization is, with power and weapons we cannot even
imagine, it will be a disaster, maybe even the end of the
world as far as secondary humans are concerned."

For several minutes no one spoke.

"I don't care about all that crap," Richard said suddenly, breaking the silence. "I want out of here."

"No question," Michael chimed in.

"Me, too," Perry said.

"Ditto," Donald said. "Once we're out, we can negotiate with these Interterrans. At least at that point it will
be a real negotiation without them dictating to us."

"What about you, Harvey?" Perry asked.

"I've been dreaming about getting out for years,"
Harvey said.

"It's decided, then," Donald said. "We're going!"

"Not me," Suzanne said. "I don't want any more
deaths on my conscience. Maybe it's because I don't have
any immediate family, but I'm willing to give Interterra a
chance. I know I've got a lot of adjusting to do, but I like
paradise. It's worth a bit of self-examination."

"I'm sorry, Suzanne," Donald said, staring her in the
eye. "If we go, you go. Your high moral standards are not
going to screw up our plan."

"What are you going to do, force me to go?" Suzanne
demanded irritably.

"Absolutely," Donald said. "Let me remind you, field
commanders have been known to shoot their own men
if the men's behavior threatens to compromise an
operation."

Suzanne didn't respond. Instead she slowly looked
around at the others in the room. Her expression was
blank. No one made a motion in her defense.

"Let's get back to business," Donald said finally. "Did you get the Luger?"

"We did," Perry reported. "It was hard to find, but we managed."

"Let me see it," Donald said.

As Perry took the pistol out of his tunic pocket, Suzanne bolted from the room. Richard was the first to respond. Dropping what he had in his hands, and disregarding the armor he was wearing, he raced out into the night after her. Thanks to his superb physical shape he was able to close the gap quickly and managed to get hold of Suzanne's wrist. He pulled her to a stop. Both were panting.

"You're playing into Donald's hands," Richard managed to say between breaths.

"As if I care," Suzanne replied. "Let me go!"

"He'll shoot you," Richard said. "He loves playing this military crap. I'm warning you."

Suzanne struggled for a moment in an attempt to free herself, but it was soon clear that Richard was not about to let her go. The others arrived and gathered round. Donald was holding the Luger.

"You're forcing me to act," Donald said menacingly. "I hope you realize that."

"Who is forcing whom?" Suzanne asked scornfully.

"Bring her back inside!" Donald said. "We have to resolve this once and for all." He started back toward the cottage. The others followed with Richard maintaining an iron grip on Suzanne's wrist. She tried briefly to struggle but quickly became resigned to be dragged back toward her room.

"Bring her in and sit her down," Donald called over his shoulder as the group rounded the pool.

Coming into the light Richard noticed how blue Suzanne's hand had become. Concerned about her circulation, he loosened his hold. The instant he did, she yanked herself free and straight-armed him with a resounding thump in the center of his chest. Caught off guard, Richard toppled into the deep end of the pool. Suzanne bolted back out into the night.

With the heavy armor dragging him under the surface, Richard floundered despite his being a powerful and accomplished swimmer. Donald tossed the pistol into one of the contour chairs and dove into the water. Perry and Michael did what they could from the pool's edge until they realized that Suzanne had escaped yet again.

"Get her!" Perry cried. "I'll help here."

Michael took off and the effort expended gave him unqualified respect for the famed hoplites of old, and he wondered how those ancient warriors had managed. He found the breastplate particularly difficult to run in although the heavy helmet and greaves did not help either. Once clear of the cone of light emanating from the interior, he clanked to a halt. Without being dark adapted he was blinded by the darkness. Suzanne was nowhere to be seen although she'd had only a minute or so head start.

As the minutes ticked by and his eyes adjusted, details of the scene emerged from the gloom but still no Suzanne. Then, sudden movement and a startling patch of bright light off to his right got his attention. When he looked his heart leaped. It was an air taxi that had arrived and opened some fifty yards away in the vicinity of the dining hall.

Michael took off running again with his strong legs pumping. As he rapidly closed on the craft, he knew it was going to be close. Ahead he could see Suzanne clamber aboard and throw herself onto the banquette with her right hand palm down on the central table.

"No!" Michael yelled as he launched himself at the taxi's port. But he was too late. What had been an opening only moments earlier was now the seamless cowling of the air taxi. Michael collided against it and ricocheted off with the clang of metal against metal. The collision knocked him to the ground and the helmet from his head. In the next instant the air taxi ascended with a whoosh, leaving Michael momentarily weightless in its wake. Like a helium balloon he floated free from the ground for almost a foot before falling back like a dead weight.

The second collision knocked the wind out of him. He writhed on the ground. When he managed to catch his breath, he scrambled to his feet and made his way back to the cottage. By then, the others had gotten the sodden Richard into one of the contour chairs, where he was coughing deeply.

Donald looked up as Michael charged in. "Where the hell is she?"

"She got away in an air taxi!" Michael gasped.

"You let her get away?" Donald cried. He stood up from where he was squatting next to Richard. He was incensed.

"I couldn't stop her," Michael said. "She must have called the damn taxi the second she left here."

"Christ!" Donald said. He put a hand to his forehead and shook his head. "Such incompetence! I can't believe it!"

"Hey, I did what I could," Michael complained.

"Let's not argue," Perry chimed in.

"Shit!" Donald shouted as he stormed around in a circle.

"I should have decked her," Richard choked.

Donald stopped his angry pacing. "We've hardly started this operation, and we've already got a crisis. There's no telling what she'll do. We've got to move and move fast! Michael, you get your ass back to the *Oceanus* and don't let anyone near it!"

"Roger!" Michael said. He grabbed his crossbow and quiver and darted back out into the night.

"We need hostages and we need them fast," Donald said.

"What about Arak and Sufa?" Perry said.

"They'd be perfect," Donald said. "Let's call them over here and hope Suzanne hasn't talked to them first. We'll have them come to the dining hall."

"What about Ismael and Mary Black?" Perry suggested.

"The more the better," Harvey said.

"Fine," Donald said. "We'll call them, too. But that's all the room we have in the *Oceanus*."

Suzanne's pulse was racing. She'd never felt such anxiety. She knew she was lucky to have gotten away from the group and couldn't help wondering what would have happened had she not been able to. She shuddered. They seemed to have become strangers, even enemies in their single-mindedness to escape and their concomitant willingness to murder.

Despite what she'd said on the spur of the moment back in her cottage, she wasn't sure how she felt about anything other than her abhorrence at the idea of being a party to more death. Yet despite her confusion, in order to flee by air taxi she'd had to come up with a destination quickly to get the craft to seal. The first place that had come to her mind was the black pyramid and the Council of Elders.

By the time the air taxi deposited Suzanne at her destination, she was more composed. The transit time had given her an opportunity to think more rationally. She reasoned that the Council of Elders more than anyone should know how to handle the crisis quickly and without injury to anyone.

As she mounted the causeway leading to the pyramid she noticed the entire area was deserted. As a major Interterran governmental center, she'd assumed there would be people available twenty-four hours a day. But this hardly seemed to be the case even after she'd entered the gigantic structure.

Suzanne walked down the gleaming white marble corridor. She saw no one. Approaching the huge, paneled bronze doors, she began to wonder what she should do. Knocking seemed ridiculous given the scale of the surroundings. But she need not have been concerned. The doors opened automatically just as they had that morning.

Walking into the circular colonnaded room beyond, Suzanne advanced to the center and stopped in the same place she'd stood that morning. She looked around at the empty chamber, wondering what to do next.

The silence was complete.

"Hello!" Suzanne called. When there was no answer she called again louder. Then she called out again, this time at the top of her lungs. Thanks to the dome, she heard her voice echo clearly.

"Can I be of assistance?" a young girl's voice asked calmly.

Suzanne turned. Behind her, framed in the huge portal, was Ala. Her fine blonde hair was in disarray, as if she'd just been pulled from her bed.

"I'm sorry to bother you," Suzanne said. "I've come because of an emergency. You must stop my fellow secondary humans. They are about to attempt an escape, and if they do, the secret of Interterra will be lost."

"Escape is difficult from Interterra," Ala said. She rubbed her eyes with the back of her hand. It was a gesture so childlike that Suzanne had to remind herself she was dealing with an individual of extraordinary intelligence and experience.

"They plan to use the submersible we arrived in," Suzanne said. "It is at the Earth Surface Museum."

"I see," Ala said. "It would still be difficult, but perhaps it would be best if I send some worker clones to incapacitate the vessel. I will also call the Council for an emergency session. I trust you will be willing to stay and confer with us."

"Of course," Suzanne said. "I want very much to help." She thought about bringing up the tragic deaths that had already occurred but decided there would be time for that later.

"This is an unexpected and disturbing development," Ala said. "Why have your friends decided to try to escape?"

"They say because of their families and because they have not been given a choice. But they are a very varied group, and there are other issues as well."

"It sounds as if they don't yet realize how very lucky they are."

"I think that's fair to say," Suzanne agreed.

An air taxi settled down and opened in the dark and deeply shadowed museum courtyard. Two heavily muscled worker clones disembarked. Both carried sledge-hammers, but only one set out for the Benthic Marine submersible. The other kept the air taxi from leaving by maintaining a grip on the edge of the taxi's opening port.

The first worker clone wasted no time. Reaching the submersible he went directly to the housing for the main battery pack. With practiced hands he opened the fiber-glass access panel to expose the main power connector. Then, stepping back, he raised the sledge over his head in preparation of rendering the unit inoperable.

But the heavy hammer did not come down in its normal arc. Instead it slipped from the clone's hands and fell to the ground with a thud the moment a crossbow bolt pierced the clone's throat. With a gasping sound he staggered back, clawing at the imbedded missile. A mixture of blood and a clear fluid like mineral oil gushed forth, drenching his black coveralls. After a few awkward steps, the clone toppled over onto his back. Several twitches later, he was still.

Michael cranked the crossbow drawstring back and positioned another bolt. Thus armed he stood up from his hiding place alongside the museum wall and cautiously approached the downed clone. Michael had neither seen nor heard the air taxi: it had landed just out of sight. He felt lucky he'd looked back at the submersible the moment he did, for he had been dozing on and off despite his efforts to stay alert.

Keeping the crossbow trained on the clone, Michael reached out with his right foot and gave the body a kick. The clone didn't respond although there was another small surge of blood and fluid from the through-and-through neck wound.

Taking one hand away from the crossbow to give himself better balance, Michael gave the body one last, good kick to make sure there was no question about its status. To his shock, the crossbow was ripped out of his hand.

Startled, Michael whirled around to find himself facing a second clone, who'd tossed the crossbow aside and was raising a sledgehammer over his head. Michael instinctively put his hands up although he knew it would be no defense against the coming blow. Back peddling he tripped over the fallen clone and fell across the downed worker, losing his helmet in the process.

Michael desperately rolled to the side as the hammer came down with jarring force, crunching the already incapacitated clone. As the second clone regained his balance and retracted his weapon for another blow, Michael pushed himself up on one knee and drew his Greek short sword. As the clone again lifted the sledge over his head, exposing his abdomen, Michael lunged forward. With Michael's full weight behind the thrust the sword buried itself to its hilt. A mixture of blood and clear oil gushed onto Michael's chest.

The startled clone dropped the sledge and grabbed Michael's head with his two hands. Michael felt himself being lifted off the ground. But it didn't last. The inordinate strength of the clone ebbed, and he toppled over, dragging Michael with him.

It took almost five minutes for the worker clone's grip around Michael's head to relax enough for Michael to extract himself. As he got to his feet he shuddered through a wave of nausea at the smell of the fluid leaking out of the two downed clones. It was like a combination of a slaughter house and an auto repair shop.

Michael retrieved the crossbow. He had new respect for the danger the clones represented. He'd been surprised the second clone had attacked him, and he reasoned that they must have been given some blanket order. The episode also underlined the fact that the clones had no trouble with violence, just as Harv had warned.

CHAPTER NINETEEN

"Maybe we should have pulled this off after dinner," Richard said. "I'm starved."

"This is no time for humor," Perry said.

"Who's making a joke?" Richard said.

"This must be them," Harvey called from the door, where Donald had ordered him to stay as a lookout. "An air taxi has just dropped down outside."

The group were in the dining room waiting for Arak, Sufa, and the Blacks.

"All right, troops," Donald said. "This is it. Let's be prepared."

Richard picked up one of the Greek swords. After his dunk in the pool he'd dispensed with the armor. Donald removed the clip from the Luger for the twentieth time, checked it, and replaced it. He made sure a cartridge was in the firing chamber.

Arak, Sufa, the Blacks, and four large worker clones swept into the room.

"Okay," Arak said, slightly out of breath. "Everything is going to be fine, so please just relax."

According to plan, Harvey pushed the door closed with a resounding thud. Arak ignored the noise. Harvey walked around the periphery of the room. Along with Perry and Richard he stood behind Donald.

"First," Arak said, "you must understand that you cannot escape. We cannot permit it."

"Word travels fast," Donald said. "So Suzanne has already gotten to you."

"We were informed by the Council of Elders," Arak said. "We heard from them just after you requested our presence. Now that we are here, we'd like to request that you return to your individual cottages. I repeat: you cannot escape."

"We shall see," Donald said. "For the time being, *we* are going to be giving the orders."

"That is out of the question," Arak remarked. Then, turning to the clones, he said, "Restrain them without hurting them, please!"

Obediently the clones surged forward.

Donald brandished the pistol and took several steps back. His coconspirators did the same.

"Don't come any closer!" Donald commanded.

"I don't think they know what a gun is," Perry said nervously.

"They are going to learn quickly," Donald said: While continuing to back up he raised the gun and aimed at the face of the clone coming directly at him.

"Arak!" Ismael cried. "He's got a gun. Arak—"

"Stop, please!" Donald ordered the clones.

Having been commanded by an Interterran, the clones ignored Donald and continued closing in on the retreating secondary humans. Donald pulled the Luger's trigger and it fired with a roar. The slug hit the lead clone in the forehead. He wobbled and then collapsed backward to the floor. A clear viscous fluid flowed out of the wound onto the marble. Curiously his legs continued to move as if he were still advancing.

Arak and Sufa gasped.

Undaunted, the other clones continued to approach. Donald swung the gun around to the one closing on Perry and fired again. The bullet struck the second clone in the temple. He collapsed as well, though his legs, too, continued moving.

"Halt, please," Arak shouted with a quavering voice to the two remaining clones. The clones obeyed instantly. Arak's face had gone pale and he was shaking. Meanwhile, the scissoring motion of the legs of the two on the ground slowed, then stopped.

Donald was now holding the pistol with two hands. He swung it around and pointed it at Arak. "That's better," he told the terrified Interterran. "Just so we understand one another, you are next."

"Please," Sufa cried. "No more violence. Please!"

"We're happy to oblige," Donald said without lowering the gun. "Just do as we say, and everything will be cool. Arak, I want you to make a few contacts with your wrist unit, then we'll be leaving here."

Suzanne was impressed with the equanimity the elders displayed despite the grave crisis. She, on the other hand, was growing progressively more anxious; the dispatches coming back to the council suggested that her former colleagues were succeeding.

While the council had been convened, Suzanne had been offered food and then returned to the colonnaded hall. Like that morning she was again asked to be in the center although on this occasion she'd been supplied with a chair similar in style although smaller than those occupied by the elders. She was facing Ala with the bronze doors at her back.

"The problem seems to be getting worse," Ala said after listening for a moment to her wrist communicator. Her clear, high-pitched voice was not hurried or harried. "The wayward group along with four human hostages are now approaching Barsama with their intact submersible. Arak is awaiting our orders."

"I've never dealt with such a situation as this in all my lifetimes," Ponu said. "Four worker clones have been prematurely dispatched. That is disturbing, indeed."

"You can stop them, can't you?" Suzanne blurted. She was beginning to find the calmness of the council unnerving. "And you can do it without injuring them, can't you?"

Ala leaned forward toward Suzanne, ignoring her questions. "There is one issue we must be absolutely sure of," she said calmly. "We have witnessed that your colleagues have surprisingly little compunction about damaging worker clones. What about humans? Would they really be capable of hurting a human?"

"Yes, I'm afraid so," Suzanne said. "They are desperate."

"It is hard to believe they would do such a thing after they have had an opportunity to experience our culture," Ponu said. "All our other visitors have unerringly adapted to our peaceful ways."

"Perhaps they would, too, given more of a chance," Suzanne said. "But at this point they are dangerous to anyone who would thwart them."

"I'm not sure I believe that," another elder said. "It's contrary to our experience, as Ponu mentioned."

Suzanne felt frustrated to the point of anger. "I can

prove the iniquity they are capable of," she snapped. "They've left ample evidence in two of the cottages."

"And what might that be?" Ala asked as serenely as if she were discussing gardening.

"They have already caused the deaths of two primary humans."

Suzanne's words clearly stunned the council. They sat dumbfounded. "Are you sure of this?" Ala asked. For the first time her voice reflected distress.

"I saw the bodies a few hours ago," Suzanne said. "One was bludgeoned and the other drowned."

"I'm afraid this tragic news puts the current situation on a different plain," Ala said.

I should hope so, Suzanne thought to herself.

"I recommend we seal the Barsama vent immediately," Ponu said.

A murmur of assent filled the chamber.

Ala raised her wrist communicator and spoke briefly then lowered her arm. "It will be done," she said.

"How long will it take to connect the vent to the earth's core?" Ponu asked.

"A few hours," Ala said.

The doors were enormous, about two stories high and nine feet thick. They began to open inward on silent hinges. Arak was directing the activity with his wrist unit. He was in direct contact with Central Information. Donald was standing behind him with the pistol pressed into his back.

Perry, Richard, and Michael were off to the side, keeping Sufa, Ismael, and Mary under close guard. Michael was still in his Greek armor, refusing steadfastly to give it up. Harvey was in the passenger portion of the antigravity freighter, which was carrying the *Oceanus* as its payload. He was ready to direct the craft into the decon chamber behind the great doors.

"That looks familiar," Donald said as he caught sight of the stainless steel interior. "It reminds me of the room where we had our unsolicited bath on our way into Interterra."

A sudden rumble shook the ground, causing everyone to struggle with their balance. It lasted four or five seconds.

"What the hell was that?" Perry demanded.

Harvey poked his head out of the freighter. "We'd better hurry," he called. "They must be opening a geo-thermal shaft."

"What would that do?" Donald yelled back.

"Seal the exit vent," Harvey shouted.

"Come on, Arak!" Donald growled. "Speed this process up."

"I can't do any more than I'm doing," Arak said. "Besides, Harvey is right, there won't be enough time. The port is going to be disabled."

"We're not giving up after coming this far," Donald warned. "In fifteen minutes Sufa's going to be shot if we're not out of here."

Another short vibration rumbled through the ground, signifying that the monstrous pressure doors were fully open.

"Now it's up to you," Arak said. He waved to Harvey to bring in the freighter. "When the inner door opens, power into the launch/retrieval chamber. When that floods and the launch doors are open you're free to ascend the vent."

"That's not the way it is going to happen," Donald said. "You're going all the way, Arak. You and Sufa."

"No!" Arak cried. "No, please! We can't. I've done what you've asked, and we cannot be exposed to the atmosphere without adaptation. We'll die."

"I'm not asking," Donald said. "I'm ordering."

Arak started to protest. Donald responded by pistol-whipping him across the face. Arak screamed and slapped his hands to his face. Blood oozed out between his fingers. Donald pushed him into the stainless steel room.

The freighter responded to Harvey's commands, effortlessly gliding into the decon chamber.

"Come on, you guys," Donald called to Perry and Richard. "Bring Sufa but leave the others."

As soon as everyone was inside, Donald pulled Arak away from Sufa, who was trying to comfort him. The man's right eye was deeply purple and swollen.

"Get this outer door closed and the inner one open, Arak," Donald ordered.

Arak mumbled into his wrist communicator and the big doors began to close. Another rumble, signaling a second earthquake, echoed through the room; it lasted slightly longer than the first.

"Come on, Arak," Donald warned. "Speed this up!"

"I told you I can't," Arak cried.

"Richard," Donald called. "Get over here with one of your knives and cut off one of Sufa's fingers."

"No, wait!" Arak sobbed. "I'll do what I can."

Arak spoke into his wrist unit and the swing of the great doors quickened.

"That's much better," Donald said. "Much better indeed."

The whole room shook for a moment with the concussion of the doors sealing. Almost simultaneously, inner doors of equal size began to swing open. Beyond was a huge black cavern similar to the one in which the secondary humans had found themselves on their way into Interterra. It had the same briny odor, no doubt from having been filled with salt water long ago.

As soon as the inner door was fully open, Harvey directed the freighter to carry the submersible within. The others ran after it but were impeded by the mud.

"Damn," Perry said. "I forgot about this part."

"Get those inner doors closed!" Donald yelled to Arak as they caught up to the freighter. His voice echoed. He handed the gun to Perry. "We need lights. I'm going inside the submersible."

"Okay," Perry said. He slipped his index finger around the trigger. It gave him a strange feeling. He'd never held a handgun, much less shot one.

As Donald ascended the submersible's rungs another earthquake hit. He had to hold on to keep from being flung off. In the distance a sputtering sound heralded a geyser of lava.

"Shit!" Richard exclaimed. "We're in a goddamn volcano."

As soon as the latest tremor stopped, Donald scampered the rest of the way up the ladder and disappeared inside the *Oceanus*. A moment later the exterior lights came on. It was none too soon; the inner doors were nearing their jambs. Once they were shut the only light sources would be the submersible and the fountain of lava in the distance. It was growing by the second.

Donald's head popped out of the submersible. "Let's go, everybody," he said. "Power's up and life support's on. We're ready to button up."

Arak and Sufa were ordered to climb into the submersible followed by Harvey, Perry, and Michael. Michael finally had to take off the breastplate in order to get down the hatch. Richard was the last in. As he closed the hatch, he saw a surge of water begin to fill the cavern. He also heard popping noises as the water collided with lava to form steam.

When Richard climbed down the ladder into the submersible, Donald told him to take a seat: he didn't have any idea how much buffeting they would experience as the cavern filled. A few minutes later the *Oceanus* was bouncing around like a cork. Everyone held on for dear life.

"What are we supposed to do at this point?" Donald yelled to Arak.

"Nothing," Arak said. "The water will carry the ship up the vent."

"So does this mean that we've made it?" Donald asked.

"I guess you made it," Arak responded sullenly. He reached over and gripped Sufa's hand.

Ala slowly lowered her arm. She'd had an ear to her wrist communicator. Although she'd been visibly upset at the word of Sart and Mura's murders, her expression was again tranquil. In a calm voice she announced, "The Barsama vent was not sealed in time. The submersible has left the lock and is now in open ocean heading due west."

"And the hostages?" Ponu queried.

"Only two are on board," Ala said. "Arak and Sufa are still with the secondary humans. Ismael and Mary were left behind and are safe."

"Excuse me," Suzanne said, trying to get her attention. What she was hearing seemed impossible. With all the powers and technology she'd imagined the Interterrans to have at their disposal, her erstwhile colleagues had apparently gotten away!

"I believe we must now deal directly with these people," Ala said, continuing to ignore Suzanne. "Too much is at stake."

"I think we should send them back and be over with this problem," one of the elders to Suzanne's left said. Suzanne swung around to face the women. In contrast to the speaker of the council, this elder appeared to be in her mid twenties.

"You have the power to send them back?" Suzanne asked incredulously. She felt that, with such a simple solution possible, it was no wonder none of the elders appeared particularly distraught by the developments.

"I agree we must send them back," an elder on the opposite side of the room said, disregarding Suzanne. Suzanne turned to look at the speaker, a boy of five or six.

"Do we have general agreement?" Ala asked.

A murmur of assent rose up from all the elders.

"So be it," Ala said. "We'll send out a clone in a small intergalactic ship."

"Tell them to use the lowest power possible on the grid," Ponu said as Ala spoke briefly into her wrist communicator.

"Such an unfortunate episode," one of the other elders said. "It is a tragedy, indeed."

"They aren't going to be hurt, are they?" Suzanne asked. She refused to give up and, to her surprise, Ala finally responded to this question.

"Are you asking about your friends?" Ala asked.

"Yes!" Suzanne said with vexation.

"No, they will not be hurt," Ala said. "Just very surprised."

"I think Arak and Sufa's sacrifice should be publicly acknowledged," Ponu said.

"With full honors," the boy child said. There was another general murmur of assent.

"Won't Arak and Sufa be sent back too?" Suzanne questioned.

"Of course," Ala said. "They will all be sent back."

Suzanne looked from one elder to another. She was totally confused.

"I see light out the view port!" Perry said excitedly. They had been running for several hours with no conversation and with the instrument lights providing the only illumination. Everyone was exhausted.

"Me, too," Richard said from the opposite side of the *Oceanus.*

"There better be light," Donald said. "According to the gauge we're at a depth of a hundred feet, and it's dawn up there on the surface."

"Sounds reassuring," Perry said. "How much longer do you think?"

Donald glanced down at his sonar display. "I've been watching the bottom contours. I'd say in a couple of hours at most we'll be within sight of the harbor islands off Boston."

"All right!" Richard and Michael cried simultaneously. They high-fived across the narrow aisle.

"How much battery time do we have left?" Perry asked.

"That's the only problem," Donald said. "It's going to be close. We may have to swim the last hundred yards."

"That's fine by me," Harvey said. "I'd swim all the way to New York if I had to."

"What about my armor?" Michael said, suddenly concerned about his booty.

"That's your problem, sailor," Donald said. "You're the one who insisted on bringing it all."

"I'll give you a hand if you share it with me," Richard offered.

"Screw you," Michael said.

"No arguments!" Perry said emphatically.

They traveled in silence for several minutes until Arak spoke up. "You have your freedom from Interterra. Why did you take us, knowing what would happen to us?"

"Insurance," Donald said. "I wanted to be certain there would be no interference by your Council of Elders once we'd left Barsama port."

"You guys will also come in handy if anyone is foolish enough to doubt our story," Richard said.

Michael let out a guffaw.

"But we shall perish," Arak said.

"We'll take you to Massachusetts General Hospital," Donald said. He smiled wryly. "I happen to know they like challenges."

"It would be to no avail," Arak said glumly. "Your medicine is too primitive to help."

"Well, it's the best we can do," Donald said. He started to say something else, but then stopped. His smile faded.

"What's the matter?" Perry demanded. As tense as Perry was he was particularly sensitive to Donald's expression.

"We've got something weird here," Donald said. He reached out to adjust the sonar display.

"What is it?" Perry demanded.

"Check the sonar," Donald said. "It looks as if something is pursuing us, and it is coming very rapidly."

"How rapidly?" Perry asked.

"This can't be true," Donald said with growing urgency. "The instruments are telling me it's going over a hundred knots underwater!" He whirled about to face Arak. "Is this thing for real, and if so, what the hell is it?"

"Probably an Interterran interplanetary ship," Arak said, leaning forward to see the display.

"They still know you are aboard, don't they?" Donald demanded.

"Certainly," Arak said.

Donald swung back around to the controls. "I don't like this," he snapped. "I'm going to surface."

"I don't think we can," Perry said. "It just got dark outside. It must be hovering directly over us."

The submersible began to shake with a low-frequency vibration.

"Arak, what the hell are they doing?"

"I don't know," Arak said. "Maybe they are about to draw us up into their air lock."

"Harvey, do you have any idea what's going on?" Donald demanded.

"Not the slightest idea," Harvey said. Like the others he was holding on to the sides of his seat with white-knuckle intensity. The vibration was increasing.

Donald snatched the Luger and pointed it at Arak. "Contact these bastards and get them to stop whatever they are doing! If not, you are history."

"Look," Perry called out, pointing to the side-scan

sonar display. "You can see an image of the craft. It looks like a double-layered saucer."

"Oh, no!" Arak exclaimed when he saw the new image. "It's not an interplanetary ship! It's an intergalactic cruiser!"

"What difference does that make?" Donald yelled.

The vibration had increased to the point that it was difficult to stay in their seats. The heavy steel hull of the submersible creaked and groaned under the stress.

"They are going to take us back!" Arak cried. "Sufa, they are going to take us back!"

"It is all they could do," Sufa sobbed. "It's all they could do."

The vibration stopped with a jarring suddenness, but before anyone could respond, there was a tremendous upward acceleration. All the occupants were pressed into their seats with such force, for a moment they could not move or even breathe. They were brought to the brink of unconsciousness. The inertial force was accompanied by a strange light that enveloped the submersible's interior. In the next instant, everything reverted to normal except for a yaw, suggesting a wave action that wasn't present earlier.

"My God!" Donald groaned. "What the hell happened?" He moved, but his limbs felt heavy and sluggish, as if the air had become viscous. But the effect lasted only until he'd flexed his joints several times. Then he felt normal. Instinctively, his eyes scanned the instruments. He was surprised to see they were reading normally. But then he glanced at the battery level. To his dismay, the gauge showed the batteries had been drained of what charge they had had, indicating the submersible was on the brink of losing power. Then he saw something else astonishing: they were in only fifty feet of water! No wonder they were being buffeted by waves.

Donald's eyes shot over to the sonar display. The Interterran vessel, or whatever it was, had disappeared. Instead Donald could see that the ocean floor sloped upward. It appeared that dry land was a mere hundred fifty feet ahead.

The other occupants of the submersible were reviving themselves after the bizarre ordeal.

"I wonder if that's what astronauts feel when they blast off into space?" Perry moaned.

"If it is, I'm not interested in going," Richard said.

"It's similar," Arak said. "But not the same. Of course, you are too unsophisticated to recognize the difference."

"Shut up, Arak," Donald said. "I've had enough of you."

"Indeed you have," Arak said. "And you deserve your fate."

"Prepare to surface," Donald said. "We're running out of power."

"Oh, no!" Perry cried.

"It's going to be okay," Donald assured everyone as he used compressed gas to blow ballast. "We've got dry land dead ahead."

The surge of the submersible increased dramatically as they came up and broached. While there was still a bit of power left, Donald frantically tried to get a LORAN fix. When that didn't work he tried the Geosat. That didn't work either. "I can't understand this," he said. He scratched his head. It didn't make sense. "Somebody go up into the sail, crack the hatch, and see if they recognize where we are. We should be somewhere in Boston Harbor."

"I'll go," Michael said. "This area's my old stomping ground."

"Be careful with this wave action," Donald warned.

"As if I haven't been in boats much," Michael scoffed.

While Michael climbed the ladder up into the hatchway, Donald rapidly took everything nonessential off-line to conserve what little power remained in the batteries. But it was no use. The batteries were drained, and a moment later the lights went out, and they lost all headway.

Up in the sail they heard Michael crack the hatch. Pale morning light shined down into the darkened submersible. They could feel the humid sea air and hear the harsh but welcome cry of seagulls.

"That's music to my ears," Richard said.

"We're just off one of the harbor islands," Michael called out from above. "I don't know which one."

At that moment the submersible struck the sandy bottom with a jolt and began to turn sideways in the surf.

"We've got to get out of here!" Donald cried. "This thing is going to founder."

As the secondary humans scrambled out of their seats, Arak and Sufa raised their hands and pressed palms lovingly. "For Interterra," Arak said.

"For Interterra," Sufa repeated.

"Come on, you two," Donald yelled to the two primary humans. "This sub's about to tip over, and when it does it's going to flood."

Arak and Sufa ignored him but instead continued to press palms dreamily.

"Suit yourselves," Donald said.

"Someone bring up my armor," Michael yelled down the hatch.

There was a mad scramble up the ladder, especially after the sub careened and a slosh of water came crashing down the hatchway. Topside everyone except Michael jumped into the surf and struck out for nearby shore. Michael tried to go back down the ladder but changed his mind when the boat heeled over completely. It was with some difficulty that he managed to swim free.

Harvey had to be helped in the wild surf, but everyone except the Interterrans made it to the steeply pitched beach, where they flopped down in the warm sand. Michael was the last to pull himself from the undertow. Richard teased him mercilessly about his sunken Greek armor.

The weather was superb. It was a mild, hazy summer morning. Warm sunlight sparkled across the water, giving an inkling of what its midday power would be. After the effort in the surf, the group was content to rest, suck in the fresh air, watch the gulls soar, and allow the sun to dry the flimsy satin garments clinging to their bodies.

"Now I feel sad about Arak and Sufa," Perry said wistfully. The *Oceanus* had tipped over on its side and was filled with water. It was already farther off the shore than when they'd disembarked. The wave action was dragging it back out to sea.

"Not me," Richard said. "Good riddance as far as I'm concerned."

"It's too bad about the submersible, though," Donald said. "It's not going to last long out there. It will probably end up on the bottom off the continental shelf. Damn! I was hoping to power it right into Boston Harbor."

Just after Donald spoke a particularly big set of waves

reared up. After they broke and the foam receded, the submersible was gone from sight.

"Well, there it goes," Perry said.

"After our story is told I'm sure there will be a lot of pressure to salvage it," Michael said. "It'll probably end up in the Smithsonian."

"Where are we?" Harvey asked. He pushed himself up on one elbow and looked back at the low, windswept island. It seemed to be only rock, sand, seashells, and saw grass.

"We told you," Donald said. "It's one of the many Boston Harbor islands."

"How are we going to get to town?" Perry asked.

"A couple hours from now there'll be pleasure boats all around here," Michael said. "Once people hear our story they're going to be fighting over the honor of giving us a ride."

"I'm looking forward to a nice dinner where I know what I'm eating," Perry said. "And a telephone! I want to call my wife and daughters. Then I want to sleep for about forty-eight hours."

"I'll second that," Donald said. "Come on! Let's walk around to the windward side. Even from a distance a gander at old Beantown will do my heart good."

"I'm with you," Perry said.

The group got to their feet, stretched, and started hiking along the beach in the hard-packed sand at the water's edge. Despite their exhaustion, they began to sing. Even Donald was drawn into the merriment.

Rounding a point forming the side of a small inlet, the group stopped in their tracks and fell silent. Not more than a couple of hundred feet upwind from them was an old gray-haired man clamming in the shadows. He had beached a moderate-sized skiff. Its lateen sail was luffing in the steady breeze.

"Isn't this a happy coincidence?" Perry said.

"I can taste the coffee and feel those clean sheets already," Michael said. "Come on, let's make this old guy a hero. They'll probably put him on CNN."

With a whoop, the group broke into a run. The fisherman panicked at the sight of the pack of bellowing men charging toward him across the dunes. Dashing to his boat, he tossed in his pail and net and tried to flee.

Richard was the first on the scene, and he raced out into waist-deep water to grasp the boat's transom and slow its progress.

"Hey, old man, what's the rush?" Richard questioned.

The fisherman responded by releasing his sail. With an oar he tried to fend Richard off. Richard grabbed the oar, yanked it out of the man's grip, and tossed it aside. The others ran out into the water and latched onto the boat.

"Not a very friendly chap," Richard remarked. The fisherman was standing amidships, glaring at the group.

Harvey retrieved the oar and brought it back.

"No wonder," Perry said. He looked down at himself and then at the others. "Look at us! What would *you* think if four guys dressed in lingerie came running out of the morning mist?"

The entire group broke down into giddy laughter fueled by exhaustion and stress. It took them several minutes to regain a semblance of control.

"Sorry, old man," Perry said between chokes of laughter. "Pardon our appearance and our behavior. But we've had one hell of a night."

"Too much grog, I suspect," the fisherman said.

The fisherman's response sent them off on another

laughing jag. But eventually they recovered enough to convince the man that they were not dangerous and that he would be generously compensated if he gave them a ride into Boston proper. With that decided, the men climbed into the boat.

It was a pleasant ride especially in comparison with the tense hours in the tight, claustrophobic submersible. Between the warm sun, the soft whisper of the wind in the sail, and the gentle roll of the boat, all but the fisherman were fast asleep before the skiff rounded the island.

With a steady breeze the fisherman expertly brought the boat into the harbor in good time. Unsure of where his passengers wanted to be dropped off, he gave the nearest person's shoulder a shake. Perry responded groggily to the prodding and for a moment had trouble opening his eyes. When he did, the fisherman posed his question.

"I guess it doesn't matter where," Perry said. With supreme effort he sat up. His mouth was dry and cottony. Blinking in the bright sunlight, he glanced around the harbor. Then he rubbed his eyes, blinked again, and stared at the surroundings.

"Where the hell are we?" he demanded. He was confused. "I thought we were supposed to be in Boston."

"'Tis Boston," the fisherman said. He pointed to the right. "Them there is Long Wharf."

Perry rubbed his eyes again. For a moment he wondered if he were hallucinating. He was looking at a harbor scene of square-rigged sailing ships, schooners, and horse drays along a granite quay. The tallest buildings were wood frame and a mere four or five stories.

Fighting off a wave of disbelief that bordered on terror, Perry shook Donald awake in a panic, crying that something was terribly wrong. The commotion awoke the others as well. When they took in the scene, they were equally dumbfounded.

Perry turned back to the fisherman, who was lowering the sail. "What year is this?" he asked hesitantly.

"Year of our Lord seventeen hundred ninety-one," the fisherman said.

Perry's mouth dropped open. He looked back at the square-rigged sailing ships. "Good God! They put us back in time."

"Come on!" Richard complained. "This has got to be some kind of joke."

"Maybe they're making a movie," Michael suggested.

"I don't think so," Donald said slowly. "That's what Arak meant when he said they were going to take us back. He meant back in time not back to Interterra."

"The intergalactic ships must involve time technology," Perry said. "I guess that's the only way travel to another galaxy is possible."

"My God," Donald muttered. "We're marooned. Nobody is going to believe our story about Interterra, and the technology doesn't exist to prove it or for us to get back there."

Perry nodded as he stared ahead with unseeing eyes. "People are going to think we're mad."

"What about the submersible?" Richard cried. "Let's go back!"

"And do what?" Donald asked. "We'd never find it, much less salvage it."

"I'm not going to see my family after all," Perry cried. "We gave up paradise for colonial America? I don't believe it."

"You know, I've finally figured out where you lubbers are from," the fisherman said as he readied the oars.

"Really," Perry said, without interest.

"There's not a doubt in my mind," the fisherman continued. "You've got to be from that college up the Charles River. You Harvard fellows are always making fools of yourselves."

GLOSSARY

Asthenosphere A zone within the earth ranging in depth from 50 to 200 km; it is the upper part of the mantle (see below), situated directly below the lithosphere (see below). This area is theorized to be molten and yielding to plastic flow.

basalt A dark, almost black rock formed from the cooling and solidification of molten silicate minerals. It forms a large part of the oceanic crust.

bathypelagic An adjective relating to moderately deep ocean depths (2,000–12,000 ft).

caldera A crater formed by the collapse of a volcano's summit.

circadian An adjective relating to a twenty-four-hour cycle.

dike A tabular rock formation arising from molten rock forced up a cleft or fissure and then solidifying.

dinoflagellates A type of plankton (see below) that includes many bioluminescent varieties. Dinoflagellates also cause red tide.

ectogenesis Embryonic development outside the womb.

epipelagic An adjective relating to the part of the surface ocean in which enough light penetrates to support photosynthesis.

foraminifera Tiny marine protozoans whose calcerous shells form chalk and the most widely distributed limestone.

gabbro A dark, sometimes green rock that makes up a significant part of the lowest part of the oceanic crust.

gamete A male or female germ cell.

globigerina ooze A cream-colored muck that covers a good portion of the deep ocean floor and is composed mainly of the minute skeletons of foraminifera (see above).

graben A fault block that has dropped below the height of the surrounding rock.

guyot A seamount (see below) with a flat top.

lithosphere The rigid crust of the earth; it includes the sea floor as well as the continents.

mantle An inner layer of the earth, between the lithosphere (see above) and the central core.

microsome Any of the various minute subcellular structures.

Mohorovičić discontinuity An area within the earth where there is a large change in the transmission of seismic waves. It is between 5 and 10 km below the ocean floor and about 35 km below the continents.

Pangaea   A single continent that began breaking up in the Mesozoic era by the action of plate tectonics to form the present-day continents.

peridotite   A dark rock deep within the mantle.

plankton   Microscopic plants (phytoplankton) and animals (zooplankton) that exist in such prodigious numbers that they form the base of the oceanic food chain.

Richter scale   A method of expressing the magnitude of earthquakes.

seamount   An underwater mountain usually formed by volcanic activity.

thermocline   A relatively stable, abrupt temperature change in a body of water.

zygote   A cell formed by the union of two gametes (see above) which has the potential to form a new individual.

SELECTED BIBLIOGRAPHY

1. Ballard, Robert, *Explorations: A Life of Underwater Adventure*. New York: Hyperion, 1995.
2. Ellis, Richard, *Deep Atlantic: Life, Death, and Exploration in the Abyss*. New York: Knopf, 1996. The illustrations alone make this a joy!
3. Ellis, Richard, *Imaging Atlantis*. New York: Knopf, 1998.
4. Kunzig, Robert, *The Restless Sea*. New York: Norton, 1999. An extremely well-written, enjoyable book that gives one a sense of the importance and breadth of oceanography.
5. Verne, Jules, *Voyage au Centre de la Terre*. Paris: 1864. (English translation: *Voyage to the Center of the Earth*. New York: Kensington, 1999.)
6. Verne, Jules, *Vingt Mille Lieues Sous les Mers*. Paris: 1870. (English translation: *Twenty Thousand Leagues Under the Sea*. Annapolis, MD: United States Naval Institute, 1993.)